OXFORD ENGLISH NOVELS

General Editor: JAMES KINSLEY

ADVENTURES OF
A YOUNGER SON

EDWARD JOHN TRELAWNY

———

ADVENTURES OF
A YOUNGER SON

———

Edited with an Introduction by
WILLIAM ST. CLAIR

LONDON
OXFORD UNIVERSITY PRESS
NEW YORK   TORONTO
1974

Oxford University Press, Ely House, London W. 1

GLASGOW NEW YORK TORONTO MELBOURNE WELLINGTON
CAPE TOWN IBADAN NAIROBI DAR ES SALAAM LUSAKA ADDIS ABABA
DELHI BOMBAY CALCUTTA MADRAS KARACHI LAHORE DACCA
KUALA LUMPUR SINGAPORE HONG KONG TOKYO

ISBN 0 19 255361 5

© *Oxford University Press 1974*

*Printed in Great Britain
at the University Press, Oxford
by Vivian Ridler
Printer to the University*

CONTENTS

―――

INTRODUCTION

———

EDWARD JOHN TRELAWNY (or John Edward as he sometimes called himself) would probably have objected to seeing his work reproduced in the *Oxford English Novels* series. His book was not a novel, he insisted, although it was first published and promoted as such, but the true story of his early life. He never wavered from this and most people came to believe him. Until recently critics and biographers too have tended to take Trelawny at his own word —with some discounting for exaggeration, no doubt. Nothing would have pleased him more. He understood the persuasive power of a well-placed rumour or amusing apocryphal story, and long before the book was published, he had won himself a reputation as a mysterious sailor with a dark, romantic, and violent past. To Byron and Shelley he was 'The Pirate' and half a century later, in his eighties, he was still spinning tale on tale. As a piece of effrontery it was magnificent.

Actually the *Adventures* is a curious mixture of fact and fiction. The first dozen or so chapters which describe his boyhood and service in the Navy contain numerous points which can be corroborated from other sources, such as family letters and Admiralty records. But the rest of the book is largely fantasy. Trelawny never deserted from the Navy and certainly did not become a privateer in the French service or fight the British in the Eastern seas. For some incidents in which he claimed to be personally involved, it can be shown that he drew on the experiences of friends or took over stories from books. This is not to say that he did not incorporate many of his own experiences in the imaginary framework, but essentially the *Adventures* is a work of imagination, a sailor's yarn in which adventure follows adventure with only the lightest thread of plot to give some unity or cohesion to the story.

The curious thing to most readers is that Trelawny should have wished to be identified with the hero of the book, for even by the standards of the age he is a repulsive character. He claims to be a liberal always on the side of the poor oppressed peoples of the

East against the imperialist Europeans, yet he himself was surely one of the worst. He swaggers about fighting, robbing, and killing on the slightest excuse. In the course of the book, he casually kills a man on at least six occasions, to say nothing of 'a leash or two' others, as he might say (p. 281), in sundry skirmishes. In many of these incidents he is decidedly in the wrong on any reasonable judgement of the circumstances. Very occasionally he acknowledges this to himself. At Penang, in a drunken state, he picks a quarrel with a jeweller in a bazaar, stabs the man's brother, totally destroys his property, almost strangles a policeman, and finally causes the death of the jeweller himself. This incident causes 'a pang of remorse' (p. 256). On the whole, however, justifications are on his lips for any savagery, and his pride in the ferocity of his own anger is scarcely concealed. Violence is in the essence of his character and he glories in it, whether he is killing tigers or Arabs. His first instinct on encountering any animal is to kill it, and his numerous hunting expeditions usually entail the incidental deaths of a few anonymous servants or followers.

He has an enormous contempt for the conventional values and morals of his time. He is an atheist and a republican. But the new concepts of liberty and internationalism which he proclaims are slogans and little more. His racialist hatred of the French and the Scots is paraded at every opportunity, and his much-vaunted sympathy with the peoples of the East is never permitted to interfere with casual plundering and destruction. The weak, the poor, and the old arouse his disgust as often as his sympathy unless, as in the case of the Mauritius slaves, they provide an excuse for violent condemnation of some other group. The hero of the story carries a rag-bag of political prejudices, incoherent and inconsistent. When it suits his purpose the old values will do well enough. On the strength of the technicality of a *lettre de marque* he is ready to sink ships and kill men (even his fellow countrymen and former comrades) on behalf of the despised French. Loyalty to one's country is an outmoded concept, but for this liberal, the sanctity of the *lettre de marque* lives on. And who but a younger son could indulge such a sense of outrage at the convention of primogeniture? The precise regulation of the division of inherited wealth among heirs is not usually a matter of burning concern to those who demand a radical reform of society.

At the same time the hero is forever congratulating himself on his honesty and sense of honour. He is hasty and prone to anger, he admits, but magnificent and noble. And, we can be sure, no artistic antithesis or irony is intended. For if ever a man existed who admired these qualities and cultivated them in his own life, it was Trelawny himself.

'I have met today the personification of my Corsair', Lord Byron told his mistress on his first encounter with Trelawny. 'He sleeps with the poem under his pillow and all his past adventures and present manners aim at his personification.' When Joseph Severn met him for the first time, the impression was the same: 'There is a mad chap come here whose name is Trelawny. . . . They talk of him as a camelion who went mad on reading Lord Byron's Corsair.' Trelawny attempted to live out in reality the character of a Byronic hero, silent, mysterious, violent, contemptuous of convention, ambitious, magnificent. During the long years of Queen Victoria, when romantic Byronism was as outmoded as the dandyism of Beau Brummel and the free love of Shelley, Trelawny stuck to his part, until at last, towards the end of his life, when the cycle of fashion had begun to turn, he was re-discovered and enjoyed a brief celebrity as a living relic of the past, a survival from the age of giants. The hero of the *Adventures* and the author are the same man, romantics caught in the fashion of the days when Byron's eastern tales were devoured with shock and excitement by the ladies of London.

But it would be wrong to judge the *Adventures* by the standards of a political tract or as an attempt at autobiographical justifica-tion. It is, first and foremost, a story of adventure, and as such it is marvellous, surpassing the works of the more famous Captain Marryat (whose first work incidentally was published by Colburn in 1831 at the same time as the *Adventures*) in interest and momen-tum. It gives the undiluted flavour of life at sea and life in the Eastern settlements before the curtain of Victorian respectability, reticence, and hypocrisy descended. Life was harsh and cruel and unfair. The men who sailed the privateers, like their col-leagues in the official navies, had a small but not negligible chance of winning a fortune from prize money or plunder. To keep their ticket in the lottery they dared enormous odds against death, mutilation, and disease, to say nothing of the crushing boredom of interminable sea voyages. The log books record with dry pre-cision the incessant floggings by which drunkenness and disorder were combated, but give little else except information about the weather. The *Adventures* gives a glimpse of the attractions of such a life without concealing the barbarity. We sail with the hero over the Indian Ocean and into the China seas. We visit strange peoples and unknown lands. We laze in the shade on the deck of the grab or enjoy the luxuriance of Mauritius. But danger is always near. Storms, wild beasts, enemies. Every sail sighted on the horizon is a new excitement. Will this opportunity at last bring the riches for which every sailor craves? At least there will be fighting and a break from the deadening routine.

Just as adventure follows adventure with virtually no connecting link, so the characters of the *Adventures* come and go without regard for the needs of plot or structure. Many of the people who appear early in the book are drawn from life, seen through the eyes of a frightened but very recalcitrant adolescent put unwillingly under their authority. Time did not mellow Trelawny's boyhood memories. No mercy is shown to his childhood oppressors, family, schoolmasters, naval officers, many of whom can be individually identified from the records. Later in the book Trelawny elaborates, with the same malicious humour, the characters of two of his pirate crew, the fat gluttonous cook Louis who would betray his dearest friends for a mouthful of turtle fat, and the cruel surgeon, van Scopveld, thrilling with delight at the pain his probes inflict on his unwilling patients.

With the major characters Trelawny is less successful, perhaps because they are not sketched from real people. No trace of de Ruyter, alias de Witt, has been found in the records. There is evidence that he is based on the French privateer Robert Surcouf who was well known in the Indian Ocean at the time of Trelawny's voyages, but, if so, the correspondence is far from exact. De Ruyter is noble and clever, a good sailor, a good fighter, the hero of a thousand schoolboy stories and just as unconvincing. The unrestrained adulation by the young hero of the story (said to be seventeen at the time although originally written in as fifteen) cannot fail to suggest sexual overtones to the modern reader.

Zela, his Arab child wife, is also a conventional figure. She is beautiful, kind, and dutiful, totally selfless, and an incarnation of all the feminine virtues. She may be modelled on Trelawny's own Greek child wife, Tersitsa, with whom he lived for a few months in 1825 without their having any language in common (a daughter born of that marriage was called Zella). The description of Zela's funeral pyre on the beach probably owes something to Trelawny's own experience at the burning of Shelley's exhumated body at Viareggio in 1822. Zela too is Byronic. If the hero is Conrad of *The Corsair*, she is Gulnare. But neither Trelawny nor Byron, for all their experience of women, ever met anyone as colourless as she.

As he was writing the book Trelawny took a few friends into his confidence, and Walter Savage Landor was among those who were allowed to read the draft. Trelawny was conscious of his lack of formal education, his poor spelling and punctuation, and the *Adventures* was his first book. Writing it, he says, was 'a painful and arduous undertaking' and Landor gave a measure of editorial assistance. A good deal of polishing was also done by Charles Armitage Brown, the friend of Keats, who undertook the labour of writing out the finished text. But these influences should not be exaggerated. The book is Trelawny's through and through. From a notebook which has recently come to light we can see how Trelawny worked into the story scraps of knowledge about the history and customs of the peoples of the East that he had noted down from his own experience or taken from books. He had the habit too—like many good authors—of jotting down memorable phrases that he had heard or invented and copying out striking passages from books he admired, for possible use in his own writings. He took especial pleasure in drafting his vigorous insults on priests, bluestockings, Scotsmen, and other favourite targets, not all of which were included in the final version.

In the plot as originally outlined by Trelawny in his notebook, there are some differences from the version eventually adopted. For example, the hero and de Ruyter attack and capture an island and liberate the slaves from their Malay masters. They like the island and decide to stay. They build a fort and the island becomes their base of operations and the centre of the story. They 'retain 3 girls' one of whom later bears the hero an heir on board. Instead of killing the Javanese prince (pp. 356 ff.) the hero helps him to put down a rebellion. And it was originally intended that, as a climax to the story, the hero should convey secret intelligence of the imminent British invasion to the French in Mauritius. (Presumably Trelawny, who was himself present at the capture of Mauritius on board a British warship, thought better of this point when he recalled how feeble and unprepared the French had actually been.) But on the whole Trelawny carried through his plan as he had intended. He had his list of adventures to be included and juggled the order to find the best balance.

The fair-copy manuscript prepared by Brown is now in the Houghton Library of Harvard University. Trelawny says in one of his letters that no other manuscript existed, and it is clear that it was from this document that the first edition was set up.

Since Trelawny was in Italy, he needed someone in London to find a publisher and see the work through the press. He persuaded Mary Shelley to undertake this task and from the fascinating correspondence between them on the subject, it is possible to follow the development of the work in some detail. The time was unpropitious—with the agitation over the Reform Bill, many thought that Britain was on the verge of a violent revolution, and publishers were reluctant to invest in untried works and authors. Trelawny was eager that his work should be published anonymously, and he hinted at unspeakable catastrophes that would occur if his secret came out (although in the event he was named as the author in the first reviews, and no one took any notice).

Mary Shelley herself, although the authoress of the best-selling *Frankenstein*, was having difficulty in finding a market for her own latest novel in which, incidentally, there is a minor character modelled on Trelawny. She willingly agreed (not without a touch of literary condescension) to do her best for her old friend although she firmly declined his other proposal that she should marry him.

How far Trelawny's friends were themselves taken in by his pretensions and how far they simply played along with his bravado is difficult to judge. He was certainly less than honest with Mary Shelley about the nature of the work. Yet, despite his continuing claims that it was autobiographical and that it would be followed by subsequent works on his later years, including his association with Byron and Shelley, there was never any question but that it should be published as a novel in three volumes. Mary Shelley, after some difficult negotiation, obtained from Colburn, the publisher, an offer of £300 for the manuscript plus a promise of a further £100 if there was a second edition.

The question of the title caused difficulty. Trelawny at first intended to call the work *Treloen* which was to be the name of the hero. But with such a transparent device there could be no hope of maintaining the anonymity of the author, and it appears that another less revealing name was thought of, perhaps Hafleton or Hansford—the name cannot now be deciphered from the manuscript. In the end, however, it was decided to leave the hero of the story without any name at all, and every reference in the text was carefully excised. At this point, Trelawny decided that the book should be called *A Man's Life*, but owing to a misunderstanding (the publishers thought his suggestion was for the far weaker *History of a Man*) his wishes were overruled. The title *Adventures of a Younger Son* was chosen by Mary Shelley and the publishers, and Trelawny disliked it as much as their earlier suggestion, *The Discarded Son*, which he had rejected as 'too much like romance or a common novel'.

Mary was delighted when she first read the manuscript. 'It is full of passion, energy and novelty . . .', she wrote; 'I should imagine that it must command success.' But from the first she was adamant that excisions would have to be made. Otherwise, she declared, the book 'would be interdicted to women'. The coarseness of some of the book shocked her. 'Certain words and phrases, pardoned in the days of Fielding', she wrote, 'are now justly interdicted, and any gross piece of ill taste will make your booksellers draw back.' In a later letter she confirmed that the publishers agreed with her judgement and 'insist on certain parts being expunged—parts of which I alone had the courage to speak to you, but which had been remarked upon as inadmissible'.

Trelawny defended himself vigorously against Mary's protests. 'My life', he wrote,

though I have sent it to you, as the dearest friend I have, is not written for the amusement of women; it is not a novel. If you begin clipping the wings of my true story, if you begin erasing words, you must then omit sentences, then chapters; it will be pruning an Indian jungle down to a clipped French garden. I shall be so appalled at my MS. in its printed form that I shall have no heart to go on with it. Dear Mary, I love women, and you know it, but my life is not dedicated to them; it is to men I write, and my first three volumes are principally adapted to sailors. England is a nautical nation and, if they like it, the book will amply repay the publisher.

Nevertheless he did consent to allow changes to be made, taking the best care he could to minimize Mary's own influence. 'Let Hogg or Horace Smith', he wrote, 'read it, and without your *giving any* opinion, hear theirs; then let the booksellers, Colburn or others, see it, and then if it is their general opinion that there are *words* which are better omitted, why I must submit to their being omitted; but do not prompt them by prematurely giving your opinion.' To judge from the Harvard manuscript this procedure appears to have been followed, and numerous important excisions were made from Trelawny's text. It is impossible to assign individual responsibility for all these editorial changes, since none of the amending hands in the manuscript is Mary Shelley's, or T. J. Hogg's, or Horace Smith's. It is clear, however, that most of the excisions were made after the text left Trelawny's hands; for often the manuscript itself has not been amended, the printer simply printing his own version. In addition, the printer introduced numerous mistakes and misreadings in transcribing the manuscript into print.

The deleted passages are printed for the first time in this new edition. They are interesting in themselves but they also throw a revealing light on the taste of the time. Only a few examples can be mentioned here. A few changes were made apparently to reinforce Trelawny's anonymity. The question of the title and of the name of the hero has already been remarked upon; the editors also carefully deleted other names which might help towards identification, such as some of the author's shipmates and captains of his ships. Even the fact that his boyhood was spent near the sea was concealed by changing 'cliffs' to 'hills' and 'sea' to 'rivers' (p. 4). The bitterness towards his family to which he gives vent at various places in the book is occasionally toned down (e.g. pp. 1, 171), but unfortunately one deleted passage of a few sentences which apparently concerned his family cannot now be recovered in full. However, with this chief exception, almost all of the deletions made by the editors can be read and have been restored. Few modern readers of either sex in this liberated age are likely to be offended by these passages even if they do not add to Trelawny's reputation.

The longest and most important of these are the description of the run ashore with the Master's Mate at Portsmouth (pp. 19 ff.); the visit to the brothel in India (pp. 63 ff.); and the invasion of the ship by the naked Malay women (pp. 413 ff.). But there are innumerable other smaller amendments. Most of the 'By Gods', 'damns', and 'hells' were excised and a good deal of sailorly dialogue bowdlerized. Playful and disrespectful references to Christianity were omitted (e.g. pp. 93, 170, 174, 203) or rendered

innocuous according to the standards of the time, by amending
them so as to refer to Roman Catholicism only (e.g. p. 189). References to 'sons of bitches' were cut out (p. 22); 'trulls' became 'female
companions' (p. 23); 'stews' are 'most degraded places' (p. 231);
and even 'thefts' is altered to 'delinquencies' (p. 15). Remarks on
the body odour of the Dutch merchant (p. 394) and of the fat
Chinese (p. 280) were judged too coarse, as was the fact that the
boys 'unbreeched' their hated schoolmaster before flogging him
(p. 11). Trelawny was not permitted to apply his pike to the
brothel keeper's 'nether parts' (p. 69). The callous story of the
Arab woman giving birth on board was deleted (p. 334) and also
the occasional cynical remark about marriage (e.g. p. 36). The
fact that the Master's Mate ordered a 'woman' as well as a bed,
a warming pan, a red herring, and a bowl of punch from the
tavern, was omitted (p. 23), and when the hero himself sends a
coolie to bring him a hooka (p. 73), the original text adds 'and a
girl from the village'. For some reason the word 'virgin' applied
to 'the barren sect of mouldy blues' (i.e. bluestockings) (p. 87)
was thought objectionable, although apparently no offence was
foreseen in substituting 'soddened'. Occasional political remarks
(particularly about monarchy) were toned down. For example,
Trelawny was not permitted to say that the crown above the
tavern door was the only place he ever wished to see it (p. 20),
or after the horrible tiger hunt, to say he wished tigers had the
hearts of kings (p. 315). And the editors carefully cut out several
vigorous racialist insults directed principally at the Scots and the
French (e.g. pp. 213, 265, 301, 395).

A suitable verse motto was inserted at the head of each chapter,
all quotations from the works of Byron, Shelley, and Keats, the
three poets of liberty as Trelawny called them. Most were suggested by Trelawny himself but the gaps were filled by Mary
Shelley and the other editors. Some of the Keats quotations were
taken from manuscripts, at that time unpublished, in the possession of Charles Armitage Brown. The *Adventures* thus constitutes
the first printed version of some lines of Keats. A study of these
quotations is being undertaken by Mr. Rodney G. Dennis, the
Curator of Manuscripts at the Houghton Library, Harvard.

ACKNOWLEDGEMENTS

I SHOULD like to record my thanks to Mr. Rodney G. Dennis, the Curator of Manuscripts at the Houghton Library, for permission to make use of the manuscript of *Adventures of a Younger Son*, and for other kindnesses and assistance. My thanks are also due to Lady Anne Hill, who first separated fantasy from reality in Trelawny's life, for many helpful suggestions and for generously putting at my disposal the results of her own researches.

NOTE ON THE TEXT

THE present text is much fuller and closer to the author's wishes than any hitherto published. Unlike earlier versions, it follows the text as finalized by Trelawny himself in so far as this can be established. The multifarious printer's errors have been corrected and the deleted passages have been restored.

The book was first published in three volumes in 1831. French and German translations appeared soon after. Further English editions are noted in the Select Bibliography. These all followed the early printed editions except the version edited by Edward Garnett, which is said to have included corrections made by Trelawny himself to his copy of the first edition. The present whereabouts of Trelawny's copy is unknown, but the only changes which Garnett made to the text were to correct a few (mostly obvious) spelling mistakes and misreadings: many errors deriving from the first edition remained and none of the material excised from the manuscript was restored.

The heavy punctuation of the first edition has been retained, unattractive though it is. The punctuation of the manuscript is minimal and Trelawny himself cared nothing for such matters. The division into chapters made by the first editors has also been retained (except for the restoration of correct numbering from Chapter XXXV of Volume III) although it differs from the original division of the manuscript.

SELECT BIBLIOGRAPHY

EDITIONS. *Adventures of a Younger Son*, 3 volumes (anonymous), 1831; reprinted (anonymous) Bentley's Standard Novels, 1835, and Hodgson's Parlour Library (author named) about 1856; Edward Garnett's edition, 1890, in T. Fisher Unwin's *Adventure* series; Bohn edition with introduction by H. N. Brailsford, 1914; Oxford University Press World's Classics Series, with introduction by Ethel Colburn Mayne, 1925.

OTHER WORKS BY TRELAWNY. *Letters of Edward John Trelawny*, ed. by H. Buxton Forman, Oxford University Press, 1910; *Recollections of the Last Days of Shelley and Byron*, first published 1858; *Records of Shelley, Byron, and the Author*, first published 1878. This enlarges and modifies the previous work.

BIOGRAPHY ETC. The biographies are useful for Trelawny's middle and later life only, since they all appeared before the publication of the discoveries of Lady Anne Hill in the *Keats-Shelley Journal* of 1956. Margaret Armstrong, *Trelawny, A Man's Life* (1941); R. Glynn Grylls, *Trelawny* (1950); Lady Anne Hill, *Trelawny's Family Background and Naval Career*, in *Keats-Shelley Journal*, v (1956); Lady Anne Hill, *Trelawny's Strange Relations* (privately printed, 1956); H. J. Massingham, *The Friend of Shelley, A Memoir of Edward John Trelawny* (1930); *The Letters of Mary W. Shelley*, collected and edited by Frederick L. Jones (Norman, Oklahoma, 1944).

A CHRONOLOGY OF
EDWARD JOHN TRELAWNY

═══

Age

1792   (13 November) Born in London, younger son of Lieutenant-Colonel Charles Trelawny, who later took the surname Trelawny-Brereton. At boarding school kept by Revd. Samuel Seyer at Bristol

1805   (October) Enters Navy as midshipman   12

Serves in H.M.S. *Téméraire* and *Colossus*

1806   (January) Sent to Dr. Burney's Navigation School, Gosport, for a short time   13

(January) Joins H.M.S. *Woolwich*, commanded by Captain Francis Beaufort. Sails to India via Cape of Good Hope, and on another voyage to South America

1808   (February) Returns to England   15

(April) Joins H.M.S. *Resistance*, commanded by Captain Charles Adam. Cruises off Havre and Lisbon

(December) Joins H.M.S. *Cornelia*, a 32-gun frigate and sails for the East   16

1809   (May) Reaches Bombay. Then to Madras, Penang, Colombo, and back to Bombay. Takes part in operations against native pirates and French ships in Indian Ocean

1810   (August) Joins H.M.S. *Cornwallis*, soon renamed *Akbar*, which joins the British fleet assembled for an attack on Mauritius   17

(November) Present at capture of Mauritius   18

1811   (February) Returns to Madras. Joins fleet assembled for attack on Java

(August) Present at capture of Java

(November) Returns to Bombay. Transferred to H.M.S. *Piedmontaise*   19

1812   (August) Returns to England. Discharged from the Navy

1813   (May) Marries Caroline Julia Addison, aged 19   20

1816   T. discovers his wife in an illicit affair. Starts divorce proceedings   23

1819   After long court proceedings, the Act of Parliament granting divorce is passed   26

1822   (January) Introduced to Shelley and Byron and their circle at Pisa   29

(July) Shelley drowned. T. arranges cremation and burial

VOLUME I

CHAPTER I

Love or lust makes man sick, and wine much sicker,
    Ambition rends, and gaming gains a loss;
But making money, slowly first, then quicker,
    And adding still a little through each cross
(Which will come over things) beats love and liquor.

BYRON

My birth was unpropitious. I came into the world, branded and denounced as a vagrant, not littered by a drab in a ditch but still worse; for I was a younger son of a family, so proud of their antiquity, that even gout and mortgaged estates were traced, many generations back, on the genealogical tree, as ancient heir-looms of aristocratic origin, and therefore reverenced. In such a house a younger son was like the cub of a felon-wolf in good King Edgar's days, when a price was set upon his head. There have been laws compelling parents to destroy their puny offspring; and a Spartan mother might have exclaimed with Othello, while extinguishing the life of her yet unconscious infant,

'I that am cruel, am yet merciful,
    I would not have thee linger in thy pain;'

which was just and merciful, in comparison with the atrocious law of primogeniture. My grandfather was a general,[1] and had little to give my father,[2] his only son, but patronage in his profession. Nature, in some sort, made him amends by bestowing that which leads to fortune oftener than genius, virtue, or such discarded claimants—a handsome exterior set off by courtly manners. His youth was not distinguished by any marked peculiarity, running the course of the gallants of the day. Women, wine, the court, the camp, formed the theatre of his ambition, and there he was accounted to play his part well. In his twenty-fourth year he became enamoured of a lovely and gentle girl. His thoughts took a new turn. He discovered (for in that he was learned) that the passion was mutual; and the only barrier to the completion of their wishes was fortune. Their families, but not their expectations, were equal. Youth and love are generally proof against the admonitions of parents and guardians. As to money, settlements, and deeds, first love is of too sincere and passionate a character to be controlled by worldly calculating selfishness; in after life it is mingled up more or less in all our dealings with women, and theirs with us. The noble and generous passions, animated by first love, often impress on the unsettled and fluctuating character of youth a fixedness, which time cannot wholly destroy. Would to Heaven my father had united his fate with her's, for her worth has stood proof against time and change! While he was labouring to overcome the impediments to his marriage, he was ordered with a party to recruit in the west. Thinking their separation temporary, they parted, as all those, under such circumstances, have parted, with protestations of eternal fidelity; but, what is not so general, considering his heedless age and moreover his being a gay soldier, he did continue true to his oaths for three months.

At a ball, given by the county sheriff on his nomination, his daughter, an heiress, when desired by her father to give her hand, for the first dance, to the man of highest rank in the room, who happened to be the oldest, declared she would give it to the handsomest. She selected my father, and with him she danced. This preference flattered him, and its being a subject of conversation gave birth to ideas which, otherwise, might not have entered his head. She was a dark, masculine woman of three-and-twenty; but she was the richest, and that was enough to make her seem at least the most interesting. My father was naturally, or by the example of the world, of a selfish turn of mind. Rich and beautiful soon became synonymous terms with him. He received marked encouragement from the heiress. He saw those he had envied, envying him. Gold was his god, for he had daily experienced those mortifications to which the want of it subjected him; he determined to offer up his heart to the temple of Fortune alone, and waited but an opportunity of displaying his apostacy to love. The struggle with his better feelings was of short duration. He called his conduct prudence and filial obedience—and those are virtues —thus concealing its naked atrocity by a seemly covering. His letters grew briefer, and their interval greater to the lady of his love—his visits became frequent to the lady of wealth. But why dwell on an occurrence so common in the world, the casting away of virtue and beauty for the worship of riches, though the devil gives them? He married; found the lady's fortune a great deal less, and the lady a great deal worse than he had anticipated; went to town irritated and disappointed, with the consciousness of having merited his fate; sunk part of his fortune in idle parade to satisfy his wife; and, his affairs being embarrassed by the lady's extravagance, he was, at length, compelled to sell out of the army, and retire to economize in the country.

Malthus had not yet enlightened the world. Every succeeding year[1] he reluctantly registered in the family bible the birth of a living burthen. He cursed my mother's fertility, and the butcher's and baker's bills. He grew gloomy and desponding.

A bequest fell to him, and he seriously set about amassing money, which was henceforth the leading passion of his life. He became what is called a prudent man. If a poor relation applied to him, he talked of his duty to his wife and children; and when richest, complained most of his poverty, of extortion, and of the unconscionable price of every thing. He contended that he could not afford to send his children to school; learning was too dear; it was unnecessary, for his education at Westminster had proved of no benefit, as he had never since looked into the Greek, Latin, and all the books he had read there by compulsion; yet he was not more ignorant than his neighbours. He knew the importance of money, still more of accumulating it, and could calculate the value of learning. Perhaps he believed exclusively in the doctrine of innate talent. Knowledge, in his opinion, would come when called for. It would be time enough when our professions were determined on, to learn what was indispensable; and as my brother's and mine would be that of arms, very little was necessary. He hated superfluity in any thing; besides, he had observed that those in his regiment who were addicted to books were the most troublesome, and their learning was no step to their advancement.

CHAPTER II

And oft
In wantonness of spirit, plunging down
Into their green and glassy gulphs, and making
My way to shells and sea-weed, all unseen
By those above, till they wax'd fearful; then
Returning with my grasp full of such tokens
As shewed that I had searched the deep, exulting
With a far-dashing stroke, and drawing deep
The long suspended breath, again I spurn'd
The foam which broke around me, and pursued
My track like a sea-bird.

BYRON

FROM my earliest days I gave indications of the energy, the un-shaken resolution and the fierce obstinacy which marked my career through life. My brother was of a different disposition, tractable, mild, and uncomplaining. I was in continual scrapes. I insisted on following the bent of my inclinations; and opposition only sharpened my desires. We were not allowed, among the many petty restrictions of our unkind governor, to stray off the gravelled paths in the garden. My brother submitted to this; while I sought for compensation in our neighbour's gardens, returning from them with fruits and flowers in abundance. My brother was contented with his daily walk upon the common or the road; I, with my pockets well filled with bread and apples, climbed the cliffs, or descended them to learn swimming in the sea. I hated all that thwarted me, parsons, pastors, and masters. Every thing I was directed cautiously to shun, as dangerous or wrong, I sought with avidity, as giving the most pleasure. Had I been treated with affection, or even with the shew of it, I believe that I also should have been tractable, mild, and uncomplaining. Punishment and severity of all kinds were the only marks of paternal love that fell to my share, from my earliest remembrance.

My father had a fancy for a raven,[1] that, with ragged wings, and a grave antique aspect, used to wander solitarily about the garden. He abhorred children; and whenever he saw any of us, he used to chase us out of his walks. I was then five years old. Had the raven pitched on any other spot than the one he selected, the fruit-

garden, I certainly should never have disputed his right of possession. As it was, we had all, from the time we could walk, considered
him and my father the two most powerful, awful, and tyrannical
persons on earth. The raven was getting into years; he had a gray
and grisly look; he halted on one leg; his joints were stiff, his legs
rough as the bark of a cork-tree, and he was covered with large
warts: his eyes had a bleared and sinister expression; and he
passed most of his time idling in the sun under a south wall, against
which grew the delicious plums of the garden. Many were the
stratagems we used to lure him from this spot; the garbage, on
which he gloated, was offered in vain. His moroseness and ferocity,
and our difficulty in getting fruit, were insupportable. We tried
to intimidate him with sticks, but were too weak to make the least
impression on his weather-hardened carcase; and we got the worst
of it. I used, when I could do so slily, to throw stones at him, but
this had no effect. Thus things continued. I had in vain sought
for redress from the gardener and servants: they laughed at us,
and jeered us.

One day I had a little girl for my companion, whom I had en-
ticed from the nursery to go with me to get some fruit clandestinely.
We slunk out, and entered the garden unobserved. Just as we were
congratulating ourselves under a cherry-tree, up comes the accursed
monster of a raven. It was no longer to be endured. He seized hold
of the little girl's frock; she was too frightened to scream; I did
not hesitate an instant. I told her not to be afraid, and threw myself upon him. He let her go, and attacked me with bill and talon.
I got hold of him by the neck, and, heavily lifting him up, struck
his body against the tree and the ground; but nothing seemed to
hurt him. He was hard as a rock. Thus we struggled, I evidently
the weaker party. The little girl, who was my favourite, said, 'I'll
go and call the gardener!'

I said, 'No; he will tell my father; I will hang the old fellow'
(meaning the raven, not my father); 'give me your sash!'

She did so, and with great exertion I succeeded, though I was
dreadfully mauled, in fastening one end round the old tyrant's
neck and the other round a tree. Then I climbed the tree, and,
holding one end of the sash, I put it round a horizontal branch,
and, jumping on the ground, I fairly succeeded in suspending
my foe.

At this moment my brother came running towards me. When

he saw the plight I was in, he was alarmed; but, on beholding our old enemy swinging in the air, he shouted for joy. Fastening the end of the sash, we commenced stoning him to death. After we were tired of that sport, and as he was, to all appearance, dead, we let him down. He fell on his side, when I seized hold of a raspberry-stake, to make sure of him by belabouring his head. To our utter amazement and consternation, he sprung up with a hoarse scream, and caught hold of me. Our first impulse was to run; but he withheld me, so I again fell on him, calling to my brother for assistance, and bidding him lay fast hold of the ribbon, and to climb the tree. I attempted to prevent his escape. His look was now most terrifying: one eye was hanging out of his head, the blood coming from his mouth, his wings flapping the earth in disorder, and with a ragged tail, which I had half plucked by pulling at him during his first execution. He made a horrible struggle for existence, and I was bleeding all over. Now, with the aid of my brother, and as the raven was exhausted by exertion and wounds, we succeeded in gibbeting him again; and then with sticks we cudgelled him to death, beating his head to pieces. Afterwards we tied a stone to him, and sunk him in a duck-pond.

This was the first and most fearful duel I ever had. I mention it, childish though it be, not only because it lives vividly in my memory, but as it was an event that, in reviewing my after-life, seems evidently the first ring on which the links of a long chain have been formed. It shews how long I could endure annoyance and oppression, and that when at last excited, I never tried half measures, but proceeded to extremities, without stop or pause. This was my grievous fault, and grievously have I repented it; for I have destroyed, where, in justice, I was justified, but where, in mercy, I ought only to have corrected; and thus the standers-by have considered that, which I only thought a fair retaliation, revenge.

CHAPTER III

There arose
From the near school-room voices that, alas!
Were but one echo from a world of woes,
The harsh and grating strife of tyrants and of foes.

SHELLEY

Phrenzied with new woes,
Unus'd to bend, by hard compulsion bent.

KEATS

IN compliance with my father's notions respecting the inutility of early education, I was not sent to school till I was between nine and ten years old. I was then an unusually great, bony, awkward boy. Whilst my parents were in their daily discussion of the question as to the period at which the schooling of their sons was to commence, a trivial occurrence decided the question. I was perched on an apple tree, throwing the fruit down to my brother, when our father came on us suddenly. Every trifle put him in a passion. Commanding us to follow him, he walked rapidly on through the grounds, into the road, without entering the house. He led us towards the town and through the streets, without uttering a syllable, a distance of two miles. I followed with dogged indifference, yet at times inquired of my brother what he thought would be the probable result, but he made no reply. Arriving at the further extremity of the town, my father stopped, asked some questions inaudible to us, and stalked forward to a walled and dreary building. We followed our dignified father up a long passage; he rung at a prison-looking entrance-gate; we were admitted into a court; then crossing a spacious dark hall, we were conducted into a small parlour, when the door was shut, and the servant left us. In ten minutes, which seemed an eternity, entered a dapper little man, carrying his head high in the air, with large bright silver buckles in his shoes, a stock buckled tightly round his neck, spectacled, and powdered. There was a formal precision about him, most fearful to a boy. A hasty glance from his hawk's eye, first at our father, and then at us, gave him an insight into the affair. With repeated bows to our father, he requested him to take a chair, and pointed with his finger for us to do the same. There was an impatience and rapidity in every thing he said; which indicated that he liked doing and not talking.

'Sir,' said our parent, 'I believe you are Mr. Sayers?'[1]

'Yes, Sir.'

'Have you any vacancies in your school?'

'Yes, Sir.'

'Well, Sir, will you undertake the charge of these ungovernable vagabonds? I can do nothing with them. Why, Sir, this fellow' (meaning me) 'does more mischief in my house than your sixty boys can possibly commit in yours.'

At this the pedagogue, moving his spectacles towards the sharpened tip of his nose, peered over them, measuring me from head to foot; and clenching his hand, as if, in imagination, it already grasped the birch, gave an oblique nod, to intimate that he would subdue me. My inauguration proceeded—

'He is savage, incorrigible! Sir, he will come to the gallows, if you do not scourge the devil out of him. I have this morning detected him in an act of felony, for which he deserves a halter. My elder son, Sir, was instigated by him to be an accomplice; for naturally he is of a better disposition.' With this, my father, after arranging what was indispensable, bowed to Mr. Sayers, and without noticing us, withdrew.

Consider the outrage to my feelings. Torn from my home, without notice or preparation, delivered, in bitter words, an outcast, into the power of a stranger, and, a minute afterwards, to find myself in a slip of ground, dedicated to play, but, by its high walls and fastnesses, looking more like a prison-yard. Thirty or forty boys, from five to fifteen years of age, stood around us, making comments, and asking questions. I wished the earth to open and bury me, and hide the torturing emotions with which my bosom swelled. Now that I look back, I repeat that wish with my whole soul; and could I have known the future, or but have dreamed of the destiny that awaited me, boy as I was, I would have dashed my brains out against the wall, where I leaned in sullenness and silence. My brother's disposition enabled him to bear his fate in comparative calmness; but the red spots on his cheeks, the heavy eye-lid, the suppressed voice, shewed our feelings, though differing in acuteness, to be the same.

Miserable as I was during my school-days, the first was the bitterest. At supper, I remember, I was so choaked with my feelings, that I could not swallow my dog-like food, arranged in scanty portions; and my first relief was when, in my beggarly pallet, the rush-lights extinguished, and surrounded by the snoring of the wearied boys, to me a sound of comfort, I could give vent to my overcharged heart in tears. I sobbed aloud; but on any one's moving, as if awake, I held my breath till re-assured. Thus I sobbed on, and was not heard; till the night was far advanced, and my pillow bathed in tears, when, outworn, I fell into a sleep, from which I was rudely shaken, unrefreshed, at seven in the morning. I then descended to the school-room.

Boys, acting under the oppression of their absolute masters, are cruel, and delight in cruelty. All that is evil in them is called forth; all that is good repressed. They remember what they endured when consigned as bond-slaves; the tricks, all brutish, that were played on them; the gibes at their simplicity; their being pilfered by the cunning, and beaten by the strong; and they will not allow a new comer to escape from the ordeal. Boys at school are taught cruelty, cunning, and selfishness; and he is their victim and fool who retains a touch of kindliness.

The master entered. He was one of those pedagogues of, what is called, the old school. He had implicit faith in his divining rod, which he kept in continual exercise, applying it on all doubtful occasions. It seemed more like a house of correction than an academy of learning; and when I thought on my father's injunction not to spare the rod, my heart sickened.

As my school-life was one scene of suffering, I am impelled to hasten it over as briefly as possible; more particularly as the abuses, of which I complain, are, if not altogether remedied, at least mitigated. I was flogged seldom more than once a day, or caned more than once an hour. After I had become inured to it, I was callous; and was considered by the master the most obdurate, violent, and incorrigible rascal that had ever fallen under his hands. Every variation of punishment was inflicted on me, without effect. As to kindness, it never entered into his speculations to essay it, since he, possibly, had not heard of such a thing.

In a short while I grew indifferent to shame and fear. Every kind and gentle feeling of my naturally affectionate disposition seemed subdued by the harsh and savage treatment of my master; and I was sullen, vindictive, or insensible. Vain efforts, for they were ever vain, to avoid the disgrace of punishment, occupied

C

the minds of others. I began by venting my rage on the boys, and soon gained that respect by fear, which I would not obtain by application to my book. I thus had my first lesson as to the necessity of depending on myself; and the spirit in me was gathering strength, in despite of every endeavour to destroy it, like a young pine flourishing in the cleft of a bed of granite.

CHAPTER IV

The relationship of father and son
Is no more valid than a silken leash
Where lions tug adverse; if love grow not
From interchanged love through many years.
KEATS' MS.

He has cast nature off, which was his shield,
And nature casts him off, who is her shame.
SHELLEY

As my bodily strength increased, I became, out of school, the leader in all sports and mischief; but, in school, I was in the lowest class. I was determined not to apply to learning, and to defy punishment. Indeed I do not recollect that any of the boys acquired useful knowledge there. When satisfied with the ascendancy I had gained over my school-fellows, I turned my whole thoughts to the possibility of revenging myself on the master. I first tried my hand on his under-strapper. Having formed a party of the most daring of my myrmidons, I planned and executed a castigation for our tutor. Once a week we were refreshed by long country-walks; in the course of one of these the tutor sat down to rest himself; the boys, not acquainted with the plot, were busy gathering nuts; my chosen band loitered near, preparing rods; when I, backed by three of the strongest, fell suddenly upon our enemy. I got my hand round his dirty cravat, which I continued twisting; the others seized his arms and legs, and threw him on his back. A halloo brought six or seven more. He several times nearly succeeded in shaking us off; but I never resigned my hold, and when his struggles had driven away one boy, another took his place; till, completely overcome, he entreated us, as well as he could articulate, to have mercy, and not to strangle him. I griped him the tighter, till the sweat dropped from his brow like rain from the eave of a pig's-sty. We then unbreeched him and gave him a sample of flogging he could never forget.

The upshot of this is told in a few words. On my return to school, our pastor and master, (for he was clerical,) began to have an inkling of what I and his pupils were capable. The dreadful narrative which the usher gave of my violence awakened a dread that the sacredness of his vocation, and sacerdotal robes, had been alone respected by our despair of successful opposition; that having once tasted of the sweets of victory, we might be presumptuous enough flatly to refuse obedience to his commands; that my influence and example encouraged others, and that he would daily lose ground in his authority. This castigation of the usher astonished him. He opened his eyes to the necessity of using more decisive steps, and of making an example of me, before I was so hardened in my audacity, as perhaps to attempt or execute some plot against him! His caution came too late. He called me to him, standing three steps above me on a raised platform. The boys, like young horses, when they learn their power, were unruly. I stood not as I had done, drooping before his angry glances, but upright, and full of confidence, looking him in the face without quailing. He accused me—I pleaded my justification—he grew angry—my blood mounted to my forehead—he struck me—and I, with one sudden exertion, seized him by the legs, when he fell heavily on the back of his head. The usher, writing-master, and others, came to his aid; but all the boys sat silent and exulting, awaiting the result in wonder. I, unwilling to be seized by the usher, who, between fear of the boys and duty to his employer, stood irresolute, rushed out of the school-room into the garden, and there was I in triumph. I resolved that nothing should or could compel me to continue in the school, which determination I should long before have made, but from awe of my father's dreadful severity. I had borne two years of such suffering as few could have sustained; nature could endure no more. I was now desperate, and therefore without hope or fear. I received a message, by one of the servants, to go into the house. After some hesitation I went. I was confined in a bed-room by myself, and at supper-time bread and water was brought—spare diet certainly, but not much worse than the usual fare. I saw no one but the servant. Next day the same solitude—the same spare diet. At night a bit of candle was left to light me to bed; I know not what impelled me, I suppose the hope of release, not revenge—I set fire to the bed-curtains. The bed was in a bright flame, the smoke arose in clouds: without a thought of escape I viewed their progress with boyish delight; the wainscot and wood-work were beginning to burn, the fire crackling up the walls, while I could hardly breathe for smoke. The servant returned for the candle, and as the door opened the draught augmented the flame. I cried out, 'Look here, George, I have lighted a fire myself, you said I should have none, though it was so cold.' The man's shrieks gave the alarm. There was little furniture in this condemned hold, and the fire was extinguished. I was removed to another room, where a man sat up all night with me in custody; and I remember I exulted in the dread they all had of me. They called it arson, treason, and blasphemy—these accusations made some impression, because I was ignorant of their meaning. I did not see my reverend preceptor—perhaps his head ached; nor was I permitted to see any of my comrades,—the latter pained me; nay, I was not permitted to see my brother, lest I should infect him.

The next morning I was despatched home under a guard. My father was—O happy chance!—absent. An unexpected and considerable fortune had been bequeathed to him. He returned, and, either softened by his good luck, or from good policy, he never opened his lips to me on the subject. But he said to my mother, 'You seem to have influence over your son. I give him up. If you can induce him to act rationally, be it so; if not, he must find another home.' I was then about eleven years old.

To give an idea of the progress I made at this birchen school, my father, one day after dinner, conversing with my mother on the monstrous price of learning, and hinting that a parish-school in the village, to which he was compelled to contribute, would have done as well, said, turning to me, 'Come, Sir, what have you learnt?'

'Learnt!' I ejaculated, speaking in a hesitating voice, for my mind misgave me as to what was to follow.

'Is that the way to address me? Speak out, you dunce! and say, *Sir!* Do you take me for a foot-boy?' raising his voice to a roar, which utterly drove out of my head what little the school-master had, with incredible toil and perseverance, driven into it. 'What have you learnt, you raggamuffin? What do you know?'

'Not much, Sir!'

'What do you know in Latin?'

'Latin, Sir? I don't know Latin, Sir!'

'Not Latin, you idiot! Why, I thought they taught nothing but Latin.'

'Yes, Sir;—cyphering.'

'Well, how far did you proceed in arithmetic?'

'No, Sir!—they taught me cyphering and writing.'

My father looked grave. 'Can you work the rule of three, you dunce?'

'Rule of three, Sir!'

'Do you know subtraction? Come, you blockhead, answer me! Can you tell me, if five are taken from fifteen, how many remain?'

'Five and fifteen, Sir, are—' counting on my fingers, but missing my thumb, 'are—are—nineteen, Sir!'

'What! You incorrigible fool!—Can you repeat your multiplication table?'

'What table, Sir?'

Then turning to my mother, he said: 'Your son is a downright idiot, Madam,—perhaps knows not his own name. Write your name, you dolt!'

'Write, Sir! I can't write with that pen, Sir; it is not my pen.'

'Then spell your name, you ignorant savage!'

'Spell, Sir?' I was so confounded that I misplaced the vowels. He arose in wrath, overturned the table, and bruised his shins in attempting to kick me, as I dodged him, and rushed out of the room.

CHAPTER V

Oh, gold! why call we misers miserable?
   Theirs is the pleasure that can never pall;
Theirs is the best bower-anchor, the chain cable
   Which holds fast other pleasures, great and small.
Ye who but see the saving man at table,
   And scorn his temperate board, as none at all,
And wonder how the wealthy can be sparing,
Know not what visions spring from each cheese-paring.

BYRON

MY father, notwithstanding his increased fortune, did not increase his expenditure; nay, he established, if possible a stricter system of economy. He had experienced greater enjoyment in the accumulation of wealth than in the pleasures of social life. The only symptom he ever shewed of imagination, was in castle-building; but his fabrications were founded on a more solid basis than is usually to be met with among the visions of day-dreamers. No unreal mockery of fairy scenes of bliss found a resting-place in his bosom. Ingots, money, lands, houses and tenements, constituted his dreams. He became a mighty arithmetician, by the aid of a ready reckoner, his pocket companion; he set down to a fraction, the *sterling* value of all his, and his wife's relations, their heirs at law, their nearest of kin, their ages, and the state of their constitutions. The insurance-table was examined to calculate the value of their lives; to this he added the probable chances arising from diseases, hereditary and acquired, always forgetting his own gout. He then determined to regulate his conduct accordingly; to maintain the most friendly intercourse with his wealthy connections, and to keep aloof from poor ones. Having no occasion to borrow, his aversion to lending amounted to antipathy. All his discourses, with those whom he suspected to be needy, were interlarded with the wise sayings of the prudent and niggardly; and the distrust and horror he expressed at the slightest allusion to loans, unbacked by security and interest, had the effect of making the most impudent and adventurous desist from essaying him, and continue in their necessities, or beg, or rob, or starve, in preference to urging their wants to him. Till he was rich, he had not been so obdurate on this point.

We never sat down to table without a lecture on economy. It was a natural consequence that I, thwarted on all sides till I had acquired a spirit of contradiction, should be incorrigibly free and generous. I was stirred up to evade, by cunning, his parsimony towards myself and others. I was detected in many thefts, having little respect for personal property, which is generally the vice of those who have none. Eatables were extracted from the pantry; sundry somethings of bread and ham from the cupboard; wine, sweetmeats, and fruit, as I had a particular relish for them, owing to their being almost interdicted, strangely vanished. But at last I was convicted of a heinous sin, which appeared of so monstrous and unprecedented a character, that it was never forgiven or forgotten. My father cursed his fate at having such a degenerate son; and that I might not infect others with my example, and utterly ruin him, he resolved forthwith to get rid of me.

The sin I had committed was stealing, and giving to a beggar-woman, an entire pigeon-pie, dish and all. Perhaps the offence would never have been discovered, if the officiously conscientious old woman had not returned with the empty pie-dish. I hated her honesty, and never afterwards could endure old women. The poor creature was summoned by my father; she heard his threats of the stocks, and the house of correction, of a charge of felony, and transportation, without betraying me; nor do I think he could have elicited the truth, had I not stepped forward and confessed the fact. I shall never forget my father's wrath. He said, I was not only a thief, but a hardened one; and vented some portion of his rage in cuffs and kicks. I stood firmly, as I had done to my school-master, for I had learnt to endure, and my hide had grown thick and horny from blows. I neither wept nor asked for mercy. When his hands and feet were weary, he said,

'Get out of my sight, you scoundrel!' I moved not a foot, but looked at him scowlingly and undauntedly.

Lest it should be imagined there was something particularly evil in me, requiring the utmost severity, I must add that my father ruled my brother and sisters with the same iron-rod; the only difference was, it could not rule me, and therefore I was not to be endured. Let one instance of his ferocity suffice—one which happened several years after this, when he was residing in London.

It was his custom to appropriate a room in the house to the conservation of those things he loved,—choice wines, foreign preserves, cordials. This sanctum sanctorum was a room on the ground floor, under a sky-light. Our next-door neighbours' pastime happened to be a game of balls, when one of them lodged on the leaded roof of this consecrated room. Two of my sisters of the ages of fourteen and sixteen, though, in appearance, they were women, ran from the drawing-room back window to seek for the ball; and slipping on the leads, the younger fell through the sky-light, on the bottles and jars upon the table below. She was dreadfully bruised, and her hands, legs, and face were cut; so much so, that she still retains the scars. Her sister gave the alarm. My mother was called; she went to the door of the store-room; her child screamed out, for God's sake to open the door, she was bleeding to death. She continued to scream, while my mother endeavoured to comfort her, but dared not break the lock, as my father had prohibited any one from entering this, his blue chamber; and, what was worse, he had the key. Other keys were tried, but none could open the door. Had I been there, my foot should have picked the lock. Will it be believed that, in that state, my sister was compelled to await my father's return from the House of Commons, of which he was a member? What an admirable legislator! At last, when he returned, my mother informed him of the accident, and tried to allay the wrath which she saw gathering on his brow. He took no notice of her, but paced forward to the closet, where the delinquent, awed by his dreadful voice, hushed her sobs. He opened the door and found her there, scarcely able to stand, trembling and weeping. Without speaking a word, he kicked and cuffed her out of the room, and then gloomily decanted what wine remained in the broken bottles.

CHAPTER VI

And now I'm in the world alone,
Upon the wide, wide sea;
But why should I for others groan,
When none will sigh for me?

BYRON

THERE was some talk of my going to Oxford, as one of my uncles had livings in his gift, which my father could not, without pain, contemplate as property out of the family. I was consulted; but the decided manner in which I declined priesthood, left no hopes of my ever being guided by self-interest.

Soon after this I was taken to Portsmouth, and shipped on board a line of battle ship, the Superb,[1] as passenger to join one of Nelson's squadron. She was commanded by Captain Keates; and thence we sailed to Plymouth to take on board Admiral Duckworth, who hoisted his flag, and detained the ship three days to get mutton and potatoes from Cornwall. By this delay we unfortunately fell in with the Nelson fleet off Trafalgar, two days after his deathless victory.

Young as I was, I shall never forget our falling in with the Pickle schooner off Trafalgar, carrying the first despatches of the battle and death of its hero. We had chaced her many hours out of our course, and but that our ship sailed well, and the wind was fresh, we should not have brought her to. Her commander, burning with impatience to be the first to convey the news to England, was compelled to heave to, and come on board us. Captain Keates received him on the deck, and when he heard the news, I was by his side. Silence reigned throughout the ship; some great event was anticipated; the officers stood in groups, watching, with intense anxiety, the two commanders, who walked apart: battle,—Nelson,—ships,—were the only audible words which could be gathered from this conversation. I saw the blood rush into Keates's face; he stamped the deck, walked hurriedly, and spoke as in a passion. I marvelled, for I had never before seen him much moved; he had appeared cool, firm, and collected on all occasions, and it struck me that some awful event had taken place, or was at hand.

The admiral was still in his cabin, eager for news from the Nelson fleet. He was an irritable and violent man; and had been much incensed at the schooner's having disobeyed his signal, until she was compelled. After a few minutes, swelling with wrath, he sent an order to Keates; who, possibly heard it not, but staggered along the deck, struck to the heart by the news, and, for the first time in his life, forgot his respect to his superior in rank; muttering, as it seemed, curses on his fate that, by the admiral's delay, he had not participated in the most glorious battle in naval history. Another messenger enforced him, such is discipline, to descend in haste to the admiral, who was high in rage and impatience.

Keates, for I followed him, on entering the admiral's cabin, said, in a subdued voice, as if he were choking: 'A great battle has been fought, two days ago, off Trafalgar. The combined fleets of France and Spain are annihilated, and Nelson is no more!' He then murmured,—'Had we not been detained, we should have been there. The captain of the schooner entreats you, Sir, not to detain him, and destroy his hopes, as you have destroyed ours.'

Duckworth answered not, conscience-struck, but stalked on deck. He seemed ever to avoid the look of his captain, and turned to converse with the commander of the schooner, who replied, in sulky brevity, 'yes,' or 'no.' Then dismissing him, he ordered all sail to be set, and walked the quarter-deck alone. A death-like stillness pervaded the ship, broken at intervals by the low murmurs of the crew and officers, when 'battle' and 'Nelson,' could alone be distinguished. Sorrow and discontent were painted on every face; and I sympathised in the feeling without a clear knowledge of the cause.

On the following morning we fell in with a portion of the victorious fleet. It was blowing a gale, and they lay wrecks on the sea. Our admiral communicated with them, and then joining Collingwood, had six sail of the line put under his command, with orders to pursue that part of the enemy's fleet which had escaped; and I joined the ship to which I was appointed, the Colossus, Captain Morris.[1] It is unnecessary to dwell on the miseries of a cockpit life; I found it more tolerable than my school, and little worse than my home. Besides, I was treated with exceeding kindness, and I began to be delighted with the profession. We returned to Portsmouth. The captain wrote to my father to know what he should do with me, as his ship was about to be paid off. My father, in his reply, determined not to have me at home, ordered that I should instantly be sent to Dr. Burney's navigation school.[2] I was horror-stricken at this news, thinking I had done with schools; and, supposing they were all like my former one, I anticipated a state of suffering.

We had had a rough passage, being five or six sail of the line in company, some totally, and others partially dismasted. Our ship, having been not only dismasted, but razed by the enemy's shots (that is, the upper deck almost cut away,) our passage home was boisterous. The gallant ship, whose lofty canvass, a few days before, had fluttered almost amidst the clouds, as she bore down on the combined fleets, vauntingly called the Invincible, now, though her torn banner still waved aloft victorious, was crippled, jury-mast, and shattered, a wreck labouring in the trough of the sea, and driven about at the mercy of the wild waves and winds. With infinite toil and peril, amidst the shouts and reverberated hurrahs from successive ships, we passed on, towed into safe moorings at Spithead.

What a scene of joy then took place. From the ship to the shore one might have walked on a bridge of boats, struggling to get alongside. Some, breathless with anxiety, eagerly demanded the fate of brothers, sons, or fathers, which was followed by joyous clasping and wringing of hands, and some returned to the shore, pale, haggard, and heart-stricken. Then came the extortionary Jew, chuckling with ecstacy at the usury he was about to realize from anticipated prize-money, proffering his gold with a niggard's hand, and demanding monstrous security and interest for his monies. Huge bomboats, filled with fresh provisions, and a circle of boats hung round us, crammed with sailor's wives, children, and doxies, thick as locusts. These last poured in so fast, that of the eight thousand said to belong at that period to Portsmouth and Gosport, I hardly think they could have left eight on shore. In a short period they seem to have achieved what the combined enemies' fleets had vauntingly threatened—to have taken entire possession of the Trafalgar squadron. I remember, the following day, while the ship was dismantling, these scarlet sinners hove out the three first thirty-two pound guns; I think there were not less than three or four hundred of them heaving at the capstan.

Our captain, suffering from a severe wound, went on shore, and gave me, with two youngsters like myself, in very particular charge to one of the master's mates, who shortly after crossed over with us to Gosport. He had orders to convey us to Dr. Burney's.

CHAPTER VII

If any person should presume to assert
This story is not moral, first, I pray,
That they will not cry out before they're hurt.

BYRON

OLD Noah and his heterogenous family felt not greater pleasure in setting their feet on terra firma than we did. The mate's face, which had been, by long habit of obedience and command, settled into a wooden sort of gravity, now relaxed, and became animated as a merry-andrew's.[1] Looking about as if he had taken entire possession of the island, and as if he considered it treason and blasphemy in any of his subjects to appear malecontent, he turned sharply to me, and said, 'Holla! my lad, what's the matter? Why, you are as chop-fallen as if it was Sunday, and the prayer-bell was ringing. You don't take me for that lubberly school-mastering parson on board, do you?'

He had nearly hit it. The accursed school had crossed my mind, and I guessed he was taking us there. However, I said nothing, and he continued, 'Never go to church on shore or in soundings. At sea can't help it sometimes. Besides, then there is something to pray for—fair weather and prize-money—don't want to pray for any thing on shore. Come, my lads, keep a sharp look out for the Crown and Anchor. It should be somewhere in these latitudes if it has not driven or slipped its moorings.'

'A reprieve!' thought I; 'he has forgotten the school, and we are bound to the tavern!' I stepped out like an unbitted colt as I descried the glittering crown in the only place I ever wish to see it, swinging over a tavern-door. I pointed it out, and he was just taking us in, when he suddenly stopped, and rubbing his brow, said, 'Hold fast, my lads! Let me see—let me see—didn't the captain tell me to—to—take these lads—to—where the devil is it? I say, lads, where are you to go?'

'Go!' we repeated.

'Ay, I was ordered to take you somewhere. Damned odd you don't know, and I can't remember. O, ay, I have it!—to Dr.—somebody at Gosport. Ay, ay, I've heard of the fellow. Remember they would have sent me there once—too sharp for 'em—keep too good a look out—not such a lubber as that comes to. But must obey orders—humph!—but I've liberty now—not under the pennant—do as I like. Well, lads, what do you say? Will you go to the school, or—come, you're looking round the offing, as if you were thinking of cutting and running!'—(which was indeed true.) 'Well, my lads, we can talk over this with a glass of grog. Lots of time—I've three days' liberty! So, if you obey orders, why I sha'n't disobey mine, if I see your names entered on the doctor's books before I report myself on board. So heave a-head, my lads!'

On the waiter's shewing us into a room bustling about, and waiting for orders, our commodore asked us what we would have, and, turning to the waiter, who was stirring the fire, vociferated, 'What a damned dust you are kicking up! If you don't bring some grog to clear our coppers, I'll see if a kick astern won't freshen your way. Hold fast!' stopping him. 'Come, my lads, don't you feel the land wind getting into your orlop deck? Has it struck seven bells?'

'No, Sir,' said the waiter; 'it's only ten o'clock.'

'No matter; let's have some grub.'

'What would you like, Sir?—very nice cold round of beef and ham in the house.'

'No, damn that! What, do you want to give us the scurvy, you lubberly scoundrel?'

'Would you like a cutlet, Sir, or beef steak?'

'Ay, ay, that will do. Come, why don't you move your stumps, you landsman.—Hold fast! Can't you grill some fowls?'

'Yes, Sir, there's a nice chicken in the larder.'

'Damn your chicken! Grill a hen-coop full of fowls, I say, and be quick. And mind, if they ar'n't here in five minutes, tell Mother —what d'ye call her?—the landlady, I'll be damned if I don't come and grill her. Well, why don't you move? Hold fast!—why, where the devil is the grog?—ordered it an hour ago.' He then shyed his gold-laced cocked hat, and drove the waiter out of the room.

After a monstrous meal, diluted with an unsparing hand, ships and schools clear out of our memory, we all sallied out, our pilot taking us into a variety of shops, in every one of which he ordered something, or made some purchase, and told us to take any thing we wanted, for he would pay for it, observing that these fellows knew him, and would not humbug him as they would us. He made a point of penetrating into their little back-parlours, to see their wives and daughters, and get a glass of grog.

During this cruize, as he called it, he invited every messmate, as well as every person he had seen before, to dine with him at two o'clock at the tavern; and he made appointments with all the girls of his acquaintance, which were not a few, ordering them to go home, like good girls, sweep the decks, put their cabins in order, clean themselves, meet him at the theatre, and tell their old mothers to see their case-bottles properly filled,—no marines[1] among them,—with plenty of grog in their lockers, as he intended to take a round among them all and come to an anchor where there was the best holding ground and safest laying. He then, for he was very provident and systematic in his arrangements, went to the theatre, engaged two or three boxes, and returned to the Crown and Anchor, complaining of his 'dry duty.'

His straggling acquaintances were soon dropping in. Wild, rough, and unruly were their greetings. The dinner came, and the viands miraculously vanished. The bottles flew about, the empty dishes were cleared away, and dried fruit, and wines of all kinds, with sundry cut glass bottles of brandy, hollands, shrub,[1] and rum, garnished the board. Toasts, songs, and unclerical jests wended away the time, till our methodical master's mate, who was president, said,

'Ye sea-whelps, stopper your jaw, or I'll hand ye, youngsters, over to the doctor;—you understand me! Now, my hearties, what say you to a turn out? It's time for the play; and you know to church and play-houses we must go sober—in respect to parsons and ladies. It's unofficer-like to get drunk before sunset; it's not correct, and I shan't allow it. So, come, I've only one more toast to give,—then I hoist the blue Peter, and you must consider your-selves under sailing orders.' Here he was interrupted by the noise in the room. 'Silence! I say ye sons of bitches! now, gentlemen, fill your glasses! No heel-taps, for I am going to give a solemn toast —and those who don't drink it with all their hearts, I pray, (lifting up his hands) 'Heaven will most particularly well damn! but, gentlemen, I am very sorry to observe that, from the neglect of duty of these lubberly landsmen, there's nothing but marines and bottoms on the table. Therefore, I command that you all gripe a marine by the stock, and prepare to break their necks.' The waiter remonstrated, and begged the president to spare the bottles. 'Lads!' he vociferated, 'a mutiny! Stand by your com-manding officer! Waiter, go below,—leave the quarter-deck. Oh, you won't? Now, lads, one—two—and when I say—three, remember that is your target,'—pointing to the waiter, and break *his* neck!'

The scared serving-man withdrew at the critical instant, and every empty bottle was smashed against the door. The memory of Nelson was then pledged, and we all sallied into the High-street. I thought the air was impregnated with alcohol, for, when I got out, I felt the first symptoms of drunkenness.

I remember nothing more of the theatre than that the audience was exclusively composed of sailors and their trulls. Had the great bell of St. Paul's been sounding, instead of the tinkling music between the acts, it would not have been heard. About midnight we supped in the same manner we had dined, and again turned out. Watchmen, dockyard-men, and red coats were assaulted wherever we fell in with them. The master's mate, notwithstanding the enormous quantity of liquors of all sorts contained in his body, had a head no more affected by them than the wooden bung of a rum-puncheon. But this being my first drunken bout, I cannot say I saw very clearly; for the houses appeared to roll and pitch like ships. Neither could I walk very well, for in the broadest street I broke my shins against the curb-stones on each side of the way. As I grounded on every tack I made, beating it up, I thought the street had neither beginning nor end. But the master's mate kept stragglers together, till we arrived at, what he called, head-quarters. He there entrusted me and the two others into the custody of a fiery-faced, flaming, old harridan, with strict in-junctions regarding her treatment of us; to which she replied she would take as much care of us as of her own children. In the mean while he went out to survey the coast, promising to return, and ordering a bed, a warming-pan, a woman, a red herring, and a bowl of punch, to be all in readiness by his return.

Our careful, obedient, and moral hostess, with more than a mother's care, ordered a bed to be prepared for each of us strip-lings, mixed each of us a glass of strong waters, and then sagely observing that late hours were bad for young blood, led me to bed first. She put one of her own caps on my head, tied it under my chin with a blue riband, closed the curtains, called me a sweet creature, tucked me up, slobbered my cheek, and parted from me with—'Be a good boy, now; and mind you say your prayers before you go to sleep!'

About daylight I woke from unquiet and suffocating dreams. Had I been previously acquainted with that phantom, the night-mare, I might have imagined myself under its influence; but my astonishment was great to find myself in my small couch under a real night-mare, a monstrously fat woman, snorting, blowing, and sweltering from the effects of drink. She smelt like a gin-shop. I was dry as a rusk, and got out of bed to search for water. The steam of my body (it being a frosty morning) arose like that of a mail coach horse. The nymphs of the house, it appeared, were not

water nymphs; for not a drop could I find. The door locked, all
fast asleep in the house, and a cold shivering coming over me,
I could do nothing but return to the bed. My cold limbs disturbed
the huge creature within for she cast herself abroad. Again I
slept and when I awoke I stared in wonder. Where was I? At
last I remembered the night-mare, and turning round, found the
vulture had fled. There was a huge indenture amongst the feathers
still hot as an oven, which showed her flight was recent. Soiled
ribbands, torn caps, rent stays, pieces of combs, and linen not as
white as the snow, which glistened on an opposite roof, were
strewed about the room. While endeavouring to distinctly re-
collect how I got there, the maid of the tenement appeared, and
the mystery was solved. She was officiously kind but, it struck me,
somewhat unchaste in her talk.

I therefore, after some delay in procuring the necessaries for
a morning ablution, dressed; and, directed by the mate's well-
known voice, entered the parlour, ashamed, foolish, and dreading
his rebukes, not knowing, or not then considering him as the cause.

Though he was very methodical, he was no methodist, at least
in preaching. His and their practice may be near akin. There he
sat, like an emperor, or Abyssinian prince, (according to Bruce,[1])
his august person occupying the old hostess's honoured arm-
chair, and in exclusive possession of the fire. Cups, sawcerless and
chipped, a handleless tea-pot, a piece of salt butter wrapped in
brown paper, sugar on a broken plate, and soddened buttered
toast, half eaten, and tooth-marked, were scattered about, with
fat of ham and sausage. Three of the nymphs were attending on
the master's mate. Two seated each on a knee, were feeding him
alternately, one with red herring, the other with gobbets of cold
plum pudding, both occasionally patting his rough cheeks, with
other fondling endearments; while the third was on her knees,
changing his stockings; and besides them, the queen of the mansion
herself was proffering him a notched teacup of blue ruin.[2]

These my first sins ought to find a place in my last will and testament; but to whom am I to bequeath them? to my father? the
captain? or the master's mate? Surely the most malicious enemy
can never cast in my teeth nor even the devil himself heap burning
coals on my head for what I committed at about twelve years old.

A day or two after this, our master's mate conducted us to
Dr. Burney, and delivered us over in precise terms, behaving with

greater gravity than the doctor himself; who was so pleased with his modest carriage and address, as to ask him to dinner. He excused himself, under the plea of ship-duty, and returned, I suppose, to 'headquarters;' not, however, before he had slipped a couple of guineas into each of our hands, which he wrung heartily, telling us to apply to him for anything we wanted, and to say nothing to the old hunkses[1] about the past. Thus we lost sight of him for ever.

CHAPTER VIII

A barren soil, where nature's germs, confined,
To stern sterility can stint the mind;
Whose thistle well betrays the niggard earth,
Emblem of all to whom the land gives birth.
Each genial influence nurtured to resist,
A land of meanness, sophistry, and mist.

BYRON

MANY of the boys in the school, like myself, had been to sea. There were considerably more than a hundred, the discipline very lax, the boys very independent, and therefore little was taught. I was never corrected. Indeed it was understood that I was only to remain there until appointed to a ship.

One circumstance alone connected with this school lives freshly in my memory. Captain Morris had given me a letter to forward to my father; and, on my way to the post-office, I was accompanied by a school-fellow, a lad of about sixteen, who had been two years at sea. He asked to look at the letter, handled it, felt something, peeped into it, and exclaimed, 'A prize, by God!' He inquired who had given it to me, and upon hearing that it came from the captain, instantly guessed at its contents. 'O! then,' said he, 'it is a balance of the money your father gave him for you. Why, you won't be such a greenhorn as to send it, will you?'

I answered, 'Certainly!'

'Lord! what nonsense!' he continued, 'it is your own! And with this you can get everything you want—women, a gun, wine!' —which was precisely what he wanted.

Then he jeered me for being pennyless; and went on till I

D

began to reflect on my father's niggardliness, and that I might never meet with such another opportunity. I listened to his argument that, at any rate I had a right to a portion of the money, because a boy ought to have money in his pocket. While talking, he broke the seal, and cried out; 'See, it is open by accident, quite by accident; and here is the money!' A sight of the enclosure, as he foresaw, was more effective than his oratory. The sum was indeed a very small one, though I thought it inexhaustible. By my comrade's kind assistance it was quickly expended, my share being swallowed up in the purchase of a gun, powder, and shot; he had the larger portion.

The ensuing morning we went out a-birding. My companion let me have the first shot, and then, as we had agreed to fire alternately, I gave him the gun. Here I was foiled, for he insisted on retaining the gun. I entreated him to let me have my turn, but in vain; I taxed him with his breach of word, and murmured that it was my gun; upon which the muzzle of the gun was pointed at me, and I was kicked. Thus we went on, till weary of finding nothing to kill, or, which is the same, being unable to kill anything, towards noon we were both hungry, when he ordered me to part with my last crown to buy refreshment from a farm-house. There was no choice; he, with the gun, was my master. After this, growing insolent, his commands were, that I should put up my hat for him to have a shot at it. I at first refused; but he swore that he would permit me to have the second fire at my own hat, and then, if I did not put as many shot in it as he did, I was to lose the crown. To this I agreed; he fired, and gave me the gun loaded. The instant it was in my hand I pointed it, not at my hat, but at the hat on his head, exclaiming, 'Hat for hat!' and pulled the trigger. He looked aghast, and screamed out, 'You will shoot me!' I told him I intended as much, and snapped again. It was not primed. Luckily his cunning for once saved his life. He ran off; I primed the gun and followed him; he had got forty or fifty yards a-head; when, as he was jumping a hedge, I stopped and fired. He fell; and my rage instantly turned into sorrow. He lay on his face, shrieking out he was killed; I put the gun down, which was now offensive to his sight, and went up to him. He was dreadfully frightened, and a little hurt, begging me not to do him further harm, and declaring he should die. Good-luck had directed the shot exactly to the part where he merited the birch. On repeated assurances that he was not much hurt, I persuaded him to let me lead him home. Before he arrived at the school he was much better. He then complained to the master, contrary to the terms I had bound him to by oath. The master without appealing to me, laid a deodand on the gun, and placed me under confinement.

At the expiration of two days I was sent for, lectured, and informed that a letter from my father directed my being sent on board a frigate then fitting for sea. On the following morning I went on board. We went to sea[1] in a few days, and cruized off Havre-de-Grace. The captain was intimately acquainted with my family. He was a red-gilled, sycophantic Scotchman, the son of an attorney, and had bowed and smirked himself into the notice of royalty. His first lieutenant was a Guernsey-man, a low-bred, mean-spirited, malicious scoundrel, who disliked all who were better than himself, and that was everyone. However, there was a fine set of boys for my messmates, so that the time passed on tolerably well at first. Yet I now saw the navy was not suited to me. The captain being intrusted with unlimited power, it depended on his humours to make a heaven or hell of his ship. I was no studier of men's humours, no truckler to those in power, consequently I was hated. I was soon dissatisfied, and longed for freedom. Then, in the navy, I had looked forward to active service and fighting; here was none, nor the probability of any, while many told me they had been all their lives at sea, without seeing a shot fired. In short, the battle of Trafalgar seemed the last act of naval warfare, and old Duckworth's passion for Cornish mutton and potatoes had prevented my initiation into the profession with glory, which might have urged me to persevere.

Nothing is so slavish and abject as the deportment of junior officers on board a man of war. You must not even look at your superior with discontent. Your hat must be ever in your hand, bowing in token of submission to all above you. Then if the captain, or any of the lieutenants happen to dislike you, so utterly are you in their power, that existence becomes scarcely endurable. How much soever you may be in the right, it matters not; for your superiors, like majesty, can do no wrong, and opposition is fruitless.

This may be necessary to the effective discipline of the navy, or not. No one can deny it is an evil; and this is certain, that all, whilst in subordinate situations, complain of it as an evil, and resolve, when they possess the power, to remedy it. But, good intentions, when the period arrives for executing them, are forgotten, or no longer considered good. To make alterations is then called a dangerous innovation, a bad precedent, an impossibility. They expound their new creed in specious common-places: 'we must do as others do; things go on well as they are; it is presumption to attempt change;' thus glossing over their own natural desire to tyrannize in their turn, often strongest in those who have been most severely treated. They continue following the beaten track, and perpetuating a system, no matter how corrupt; and if they live only for themselves, they act, as the world calls it, prudently, if not wisely. As Bacon says of the ant, 'It is a wise creature for itself, but a shrewd thing in an orchard or garden.' For every one opposes with hate every one that purposes an alteration, because it implies that every one has hitherto been in error, and, what is equally humiliating, has not been consulted. Reformers, in all ages, whatever has been their object, have been unpitied martyrs; and the multitude have evinced a savage exultation in their sacrifice. 'Let in the light upon a nest of young owls, and they cry out against the injury you have done them.' Men of mediocrity are young owls: when you present them with strong and brilliant ideas, they exclaim against them as false, dangerous, and deserving of punishment: 'Every abuse attempted to be reformed is the patrimony of those who have more influence than the reformers.'

CHAPTER IX

And from that hour did I, with earnest thought,
    Heap knowledge from forbidden mines of lore,
Yet nothing that my tyrants knew or taught
    I cared to learn, but from that secret store
    Wrought linked armour for my soul, before
It might walk forth to war among mankind.

SHELLEY

HAD it been optional, I would now have left the navy; notwithstanding, my passion for the sea was undiminished. I felt it was not in my nature to submit to a long apprenticeship of servitude. Before I could possibly be a master, fourteen or more years must elapse ere I could arrive at that height; and fourteen years then seemed to me a long life. From that time forward, I brooded exclusively on the possibility of breaking my indentures, and seeking my own fortunes, as tales and histories tell us people did in the olden times. But then my friendless situation, and ignorance of the world, appeared an effectual bar; and still my heart yearned at the recollection of my mother, whom I then almost worshipped, and of my sisters. A thousand tender remembrances of early life clung to my heart and moistened my eyes; while the continued persecution of my fate, long absence, neglect, and the memory of my stern and unforgiving father, made me of a desponding and unhappy disposition. But to continue my narrative.

At this period of my life an involuntary passion was awakened in my bosom for reading; so that I seized on every occasion for the purchase of books, and every leisure moment for reading them. Old plays, voyages and travels were my principal study; and I almost learned by heart Captain Bligh's narrative of his voyage to the south-sea islands, and of the mutiny of his crew: his partial account did not deceive me. I detested him for his tyranny, and Christian was my hero. I wished his fate had been mine, and longed to emulate him. It left an impression on my mind which has had a marked influence on my life.

Our captain's clerk, seeing I had a good store of books, with no place to put them in, thought they would be an ornament to his cabin, for he never read. He proposed to take care of them for me, offering me the use of his cabin, where I might read them. I gladly acquiesced in what I, simple fool that I then was, thought a most kind offer; and, for a few days, we got on very well together. One day I went for a book; he was angry about something or nothing, and had the impudence to say, 'You may read here if you like; but I will not permit any books to be taken out of my cabin.'

'Are they not mine?' I asked.

'Not now;' he replied.

'What!' I then asked, 'do you intend to keep possession of my books?'

To this I received no other answer than,—'Come,—none of your insolence!'

Upon this, I said, 'Give me my books; I will leave them here no longer, now I see your object.' He dared me to touch them;

I snatched one from the shelf; he struck me; I returned the blow. It was then harmless as the unweaned colt's not (it had afterwards been) like a full grown horse's.

My opponent was two or three and twenty, strong and thick set; I a tall slim boy of fourteen. The presumption of my returning his blow so astonished his cowardly nature, that, for a moment, he hesitated what to do. But some of the youngsters had collected round the door, and cried out, 'Well done, my boy!' which incensed the paltry, dirty scrawler. He seized hold of me, and vociferating, 'You young rascal, I will tame you!' gave me a blow with a ruler, which he broke over my head; then jammed me up against the bulk-head, so that I could not escape, and belaboured me without mercy. As long as my strength lasted, I opposed him. The lookers-on were encouraging me, and exclaiming shame on him. My head grew dizzy from blows; my mouth and nose were bleeding profusely; my body was subdued, but not my spirit. I asked not for mercy, but defied him; and on his attempting to kick me out of the cabin, I increased his fury, by declaring I would not leave it, till he had given me my books. We were thus contending, he to force me out, and I to remain in, when he kicked me in the stomach, and I lay motionless; while he roared and sputtered,—'Get out, you rascal! or I'll knock the life out of you!'

I felt I could no longer resist. I was in despair. The being beaten like a hound by a dastardly brute, and the insulting and triumphant language the fellow used, made me mad. My eye caught, by chance, something glittering close to me. The table was capsised, and a penknife within my grasp. The prospect of revenge renewed my strength. I seized it, and, repeating his words of knocking the life out of me, I added, as I held up the weapon, 'Coward! look out for your own!'

I was then on one knee, struggling to get up. On seeing the knife, and my wild look haggard with passion, the mender of pens shrunk back. After this, all I remember is, that I stabbed him in several places, and that he shut his eyes, held his hands up to his face, and screamed out in terror for mercy. Some one then called to me, with 'Holloa! what are you at?'—I turned round, and replied, 'This cowardly ruffian was beating me to death, and I have killed him!'—I then threw down the knife, took up my book, and walked out of the cabin.

Presently a serjeant of marines was sent down, with an order to bring me on deck. The captain was there surrounded by his officers. He inquired of the first lieutenant what was the matter; and the answer was,

'This youngster went into your clerk's cabin, Sir, with a carving knife, and has killed him.'

The captain looked at me with horror, and, without asking a question, said, 'Kill my clerk! put the murderer in irons, and handcuff him. Kill my clerk!'—I attempted to speak; but was stopped with, 'Gag him! Take him down below instantly. Not a word, Sir! Kill my clerk!'

As the serjeant attempted to collar me, I said, 'Hands off!' looked fiercely, for I now thought myself a man, and walked slowly down the hatchway. A sentinel was put over me, and the master-at-arms brought the irons. But, I suppose, the captain, by that time, had heard a different version of the story; for a midshipman, named Murray, came down, and countermanded the manacling part of the sentence; and then, addressing himself to me, said, 'Don't mind, they can't hurt you. We will tell the truth. You have acted like a man. Keep up your spirits.'

'Never fear me!' I replied.

Some hours after, the captain came to me, and said: 'Are you not ashamed of your conduct, Sir?'

I answered, 'No!'

'What, Sir! is that the way to answer me? Get up, Sir, and take off your hat.' I told him I was waiting for the irons. I, however, stood up.

'You will be hanged, Sir, for murder!'

I replied, 'I had rather be hanged, than kicked by your servants.'

'Why, are you mad, Sir?'

'Yes! your ill-treatment has made me so. You, and your French lieutenant, are always punishing and abusing me without cause, and I will not submit to it. I came into the navy, an officer and a gentleman, and I am treated like a dog. Put me on shore! I will do no more duty; and I will allow neither you nor your domestics to abuse and beat me.'

With that I advanced a step towards him, from what motive I know not. He seized me by the collar, and bade me sit down on the gun-carriage. 'No!' I contended, 'you told me never to sit down in your presence, and I will not!'

'Will not!' said he, holding me tightly, and nearly strangling me with his grasp. I could not speak, but put my hand up to release myself; upon which, repeating the words, 'you will not!' he gave me a violent blow in the face, and I, with another 'no!' had the audacity to spit in his.

His flushed brow turned from deep scarlet to almost black in an instant. He could not articulate a word; but, dashing me from him with all his might, turned into his cabin, choking with rage. Many of the officers, particularly the midshipmen, had gathered round—I got up from the gun-carriage on which I had fallen. Two of my messmates, Murray and Napier, came up to me and said, 'Well done, my lad, don't be afraid.'

'Do I look so?' was my reply.

At sunset I was told I might go below; but I was never to shew myself on deck. I never saw the gorbellied Scotch captain afterwards.

All the rest of the cruise was holiday to me. I got my books, and endeavoured, by reading, to make up for my want of education. The clerk recovered, and, though he took care to give me a wide-berth, when obliged to pass near me, I was malicious enough to say, pointing to a large scar on his cheek, 'Though you are a clerk, don't cabbage books, or kick a gentleman.' He was the son of our noble captain's tailor, and his preferment was a Scotch device to pay his father's bill.

CHAPTER X

The ocean with its vastness, its blue green,
  Its ships, its rocks, its caves, its hopes, its fears,
  Its voice mysterious, which whoso hears
Must think on what will be, or what has been.

KEATS

ON our return to an English port, I was drafted[1] on board a guard-ship at Spithead; and, without hearing a word from my father, was shortly redrafted on board a frigate fitting out for the East Indies. Whether my former captain had intimated in his account to my father my threat to leave the navy when I got ashore, I know not; but this I know, I was not permitted to go ashore. So that finding I was serving in the navy on compulsion, detestation of it increased and determined me to take the first occasion of leaving it. Though young, I had pride enough to forbear useless remonstrances or whining complaints, and philosophy enough to endure. From my childhood I had been inured to commands forced upon me, so I tried to look with indifference, and knitted my brows to stifle my emotions.

Hitherto I had at least been consigned into the hands of men who knew my family; but now I was suddenly drafted into a ship where all were utter strangers, without money, and ill provided with necessaries. For I was not a 'carefu' prudent bairn,' as a Scotch midshipman was, whose parents had sent him to sea, with a very small supply of clothes for his back, but with a head crammed with scroundrelly Scotch maxims, such as 'a bawbee saved is a bawbee got,' and 'mony a little makes a mickle.' This haggis-fed, sandy-haired sharper had extracted most of my traps out of my chest on board the guard-ship, in which I was incarcerated till appointed to a ship. Some one detecting him with a bundle of stray articles, old tooth-brushes, bits of soap, foul linen, &c., in the act of depositing them in his bag, asked him what he was at; and he replied, 'anly picking up the wee things about the deck.' This Caledonian lurcher had the effrontery to confess he had three or four dozen of shirts, with every one a different mark; the scoundrel having pilfered thirty or forty boys. He had too much prudence, I too little. No one troubled himself to inquire into my wants, and to sea I went again in a sloop of war.

We proceeded to Cadiz, Lisbon, South America, and the coast of Africa. We were eighteen months absent, and had visited the four quarters of the world; so that I picked up a little practical geography whilst going over thirty thousand miles.

Our commander was a surveying captain, a little, pert, pragmatical fellow; and, like most little fellows, thought himself a very great man. The only thing I can remember of this small commander is, that he used to twist and screw his head aside to look up at me, and snarl; and then, with words too big to find utterance from his diminutive mouth, shrilly say, 'You overgrown monster, you logger-headed fellow, without nerve or feeling, what are you idling here for, instead of attending to my commands?'

He hated me because I was framed like a man, and I despised him because he so little resembled one. Sometimes he would jump on a carronade-slide to box the men's heads.

As, in after-life, I revisited most of the world in detail, with
expanded faculties and awakened feelings, I shall not inflict on
the reader my puerile detail of events. I loathe the prattle of talka-
tive gawky boys, and mothers' talented darlings; it is as irksome
as a dedication in the 'Spectator,' or as Addison's drunkenly-
inspired, mawkish, moral papers.

On returning to England, our circumnavigating commander
communicated with my father; who, nothing softened by time,
therefore harder than stone or iron, re-issued his high and abhorred behest that I should be re-drafted[1] into another ship,
fitting out for the East Indies.

We were soon ready for sea. I say little of my feelings. Who can
paint in words what I felt. Imagine me torn from my native country,
destined to cross the wide ocean, to a wild region, cut off from
every tie, or possibility of communication, transported like a felon
as it were, for life, for, at that period, few ships returned under
seven or more years. I was torn away, not seeing my mother, or
brother, or sisters, or one familiar face; no voice to speak a word
of comfort, or to inspire me with the smallest hope that any thing
human took an interest in me. Had a servant of our house, nay,
had the old mastiff, the companion of my childhood, come to
me for one hour, I could have hugged him for joy, and my breast
would have been softened to parental love instead of hardening
indifference. From that period, my affections, imperceptibly, were
alienated from my family and kindred, and sought the love of
strangers in the wide world. Again, to be separated from my
messmates, whom I had learnt to love—these are things which
some may feel, but none can delineate. The invisible spirit which
bore me up, under such a weight of sorrows, is still a mystery,
even now that my passions are subdued by reason, time, or exhaustion. The intense fire which burned in my brain is extinguished, leaving no trace but the deep lines prematurely stamped
on my brow. Yet even now the mere memory of what I suffered
rekindles the flame, and I burn with indignation.

I could no longer conceal from myself the painful conviction
that I was an utter outcast; that my parent had thrust me from his
threshold, in the hope that I should not again cross it. My mother's
intercessions (if indeed she made any) were unavailing: I was
left to shift for myself. The only indication of my father's considering he had still a duty to perform towards me, was in an

annual allowance, to which either his conscience or his pride impelled him. Perhaps, having done this, he said, with other good and prudent men,—'I have provided for my son. If he distinguishes himself, and returns, as a man, high in rank and honour, I can say,—he is my son, and I made him what he is! His daring and fearless character may succeed in the navy.' He left me to my fate, with as little remorse as he would have ordered a litter of blind puppies to be drowned.

Forced from England in this friendless state, I was sick and sad; every thing in prospect being gloomy, even in imagination. Notwithstanding my extreme youth, my buoyant spirit, my naturally sanguine disposition, I could see no bright spot to lure me on to the smallest hope of brighter days.

We had been at sea two or three days, when the captain, who was angry with one of the lieutenants, turned round to me, being in the same watch, and said, '*You* had better take care of yourself here; and remember, I have heard from Captain A——¹ of the atrocity you were guilty of in his ship.' I replied, 'I was guilty of none.'

'What!' he continued, for he wanted to expend the remnant of his passion on some one more helpless than a commissioned officer, 'what, Sir! do you think stabbing people is nothing? I will convince you to the contrary; and the very first complaint I hear of you, I'll turn you out of the ship.' This threat of vengeance, as to get on shore was the height of my most ardent longings, made me smile. He perhaps considered it contempt, and turned away with anger.

But I soon found out he was not a bad man—merely a weak and choleric one. He had been many years on half-pay, and, brought up in the country, he had imbibed a farmer's taste for dirt and dung, which his naval profession had interrupted, but not erased. During the long interval which had elapsed from his promotion to the command of a ship, he resumed the natural bent of his inclinations, by setting to, in right good earnest, as a cultivator of his paternal soil; and felt more pride in viewing his fat hogs and sheep, and ploughing ground for his Swedish turnips, than ploughing the Indian sea in a dashing frigate. His appointment to her was an honour unsought; for an honourable member of his family, in the Admiralty, scandalized at his degenerate occupations, officiously thrust greatness upon him, by ordering him on service.

He reluctantly left what he could not take with him,—his house and lands; he wept over his child and its mother—possibly with sincere regret as she was a mistress not a wife; and his heart almost burst with emotion on contemplating the glorious and magnificent mountain of the richest compost, he was compelled to leave behind. As for the live stock, pigs, sheep, and poultry, it was too painful to be separated from them, after having expended more time, money, and patience on their nurture and education, than most parents do on their children; so he brought them on board with him, and the ship's resemblance to a farm-yard was to him a source of delight. Most of his time was occupied with these his adopted children; and the first lieutenant was left in charge of the ship, with only one little check to his pleasure, that of receiving a portion of the ill-humour, which vented itself on the quarter-deck, in abuse of the officers, whenever our farmer-captain was irritated by some mishap to his live stock, such as must arise in blowing weather, from sickness, death, and broken limbs. On the whole, we, the midshipmen, used to annoy him more than he annoyed us. One of our tricks, I remember, was, to run a fine needle into the brain of a fowl or two every night, when, their bodies being ordered to be thrown overboard, on the supposition that they had died of disease, we used to be on the look-out to save them, and a grill was our reward. He was, in the usual sense of the phrase, a good sort of man; that is, neither good enough, nor bad enough for any thing; and it was equally impossible to love him, respect him, hate him, or despise him.

CHAPTER XI

> Rock'd in his cradle by the roaring wind,
> The tempest-born in body and in mind,
> His young eyes opening on the ocean foam,
> Had from that moment deem'd the deep his home.
>
> BYRON

HAVING fully made up my mind to quit the navy, I paid some attention to my duty. I began to study drawing and navigation, read every thing I could lay my hand on, and collected from the officers and sailors every information regarding India, and her countless islands. We went in the old track: touched at St. Helena, and the Cape of Good Hope, and, without any thing remarkable, anchored in the harbour of Bombay.

The only circumstance connected with my after-history, which I have occasion to relate here, is, that I formed, during my passage, a lasting friendship with the junior lieutenant, Aston.[1] I had been in his watch, and, through the tedious nights, he had dived into my real character, so as to discover that I was not what I seemed to be. His kindness had drawn me out from the shell in which I shrunk, when strangers, who appeared as enemies to me, drew near. He awakened those feelings which had become torpid, and called others forth that I had never felt. He became my champion with those above me.

One circumstance had, he told me, often impressed him with admiration, considering my youth. On our passage, a second-lieutenant, a keen, sharp, cunning, and villainous Scotchman, whose sole delight was in torturing those he commanded, when questioning me one day on a point of duty, said: 'When you address me, Sir, tak off your hat!'

I replied, 'I have saluted you as I do the captain, in putting my hand to my hat.'

He then came up to me, with—'Tak your hat off, Sir, whilst you address your superior!'

'I have none.'

'What, Sir! am I not your superior officer?'

'Yes, Sir,—you are that.'

'Well, then, why don't you tak your hat off?'

'I never do, Sir.'

'Off wi' your hat, Sir!' exalting his voice.

'No, I will not.'

'What! will not?'

'No,—to no one but God!'—and then recollecting I had done so to the king, I added,—'and the king!'

This parasite considered (at least one would think so, by the use he made of it) that the only utility of a hat was to be pointed, as an index of his base grovelling nature, to the ground, not as a covering for the head. Though he had bowed and fawned himself into the good graces of the captain, his complaint could not be comprehended, when he accused me of mutinous disobedience of orders. His rage, in this instance, being rendered impotent, he revenged himself by heaping on me a greater portion of petty spites, which I treasured in my memory, to be summed up and paid. I did so, and with interest.

Another occurrence, admired by Aston, happened while coasting between Madras and Bombay on the pirate coast of Goa. A suspicious-looking vessel, having tried all day to avoid us, got becalmed, and three boats were ordered to board her. I was sent in the one commanded by the Scotch lieutenant. She was the fastest pulling boat, and the best manned and armed. Aston was in the next best boat, and kept in our wake. The supposed pirate craft kept sweeping towards the land; and, as it appeared, from the ship, we could not come up to her till she run on shore, and a light breeze springing up, besides the general orders of the navy in India to destroy, but not to board the Malay pirates, the frigate fired a gun and hoisted the recal-pennant. We were then within two gun-shots of the craft; she had got inside the reefs, and the armed natives were crowding down to the beach. On the signal-gun's being heard by our boat, the lieutenant declared we must return, and ordered the men to lay on their oars till Aston's cutter came alongside, whom he hailed, and said: 'Aston, you see the recal-signal—we maun return to the ship.'

Aston answered, 'What signal!—I don't see it.'

'If you look, you will,' said the lieutenant.

'I don't intend to look,' was the next reply. 'We were ordered to see what craft that is; and I shall do so. Give way, my lads!'

I requested Aston to lay on his oars a moment, and then, turning to the Scotchman, I asked, respectfully, if he were going on, as I was steering the barge. He said 'No!' and ordered me to return to the ship. On this I let go the tiller and jumped overboard, and, calling to Aston to pick me up, swam to his boat. The lieutenant, with the snarl of a hyena, said, 'I shall report your conduct, Sir!'

Aston ordered his men to pull in shore; and in ten minutes we were on board the Malay. I was in the bow of the boat, on fire to realise my ardent love of fighting; and, the instant our boat touched the bow of the Malay, I swung myself on board, by seizing a rope with one hand, when, before my foot was on the deck, I cut a fellow across the head; and then, followed by two or three sailors, we cut and slashed away without mercy. The Malays to a man jumped overboard. I was so heated as not to observe whether they resisted or not; but, excited by my own violence, and furious at any of them escaping, I thought of our fire-arms, seized a musket, and was about to fire at a fellow in the water, when Aston laid hold of me, and exclaimed: 'Don't you hear? I have been roaring to you till I'm hoarse. Why, what are you at? Are you mad?—your example has made all my men so. Put down the musquet. You have no right to touch these people.'

I inquired, in surprise, if she was not a Malay. 'How can I tell,' he replied, 'what she is? You should have waited for my orders. Perhaps she is a harmless country-vessel.'

I then began to imagine I had been too precipitate, too rash; and my ardour was cooled in thinking I might have compromised Aston. It was therefore with inexpressible delight that I beheld the savages on the beach open a fire from match-locks on us, and saw them launching their canoes full of armed people. However, while they were delayed in picking up their country-men, we scuttled the craft, leaped into our boats, and the frigate, having stood in, picked us up. Two of the wounded Malays Aston took with him.-

After the skirmish I tried to appease Aston's anger by my coolness and activity; so that, having lectured me, he represented my conduct in such favourable terms to the first lieutenant, that the Scotchman's account obtained nothing worse for me than a simple reprimand. He now detested me; but, under the protection of Aston's wing, I was safe. Besides, his pusillanimity was a source of ridicule; and the sailors, who all look on courage as the highest attribute, applauded me.

CHAPTER XII

Long in misery
I wasted, ere in one extremest fit
I plunged for life or death.

KEATS

BEFORE this, I had gained respect in the ship by a reckless daring. My indifference and neglect of all the ordinary duties were in some degree tolerated, owing to my unwearied diligence and anxiety in every case of difficulty, danger, or sudden squalls. In the Indian seas a squall is not to be trifled with; when the masts are bending like fishing-rods, the light sails fluttering in ribbons, the sailors swinging to and fro on the bow; bent yards, the ship thrown on her beam-ends, the wild roar of the sea and wind, and no other light than the red and rapid lightning. Then I used to rouse myself from dozing on the carronade-slide, springing aloft ere my eyes were half open, when the only reply to Aston's trumpet was my voice. I felt at home amidst the conflict of the elements. It was a kind of war; and the danger suited me. The more furious the storm, the greater my delight. My contempt of the danger insured my safety; while the solemn and methodical disciplinarians, who prided themselves on the exact performance of their separate duties at their respective stations, beheld with astonishment the youngster, whom they were always abusing for neglect of duty, voluntarily thrusting himself into every arduous and perilous undertaking, ere they could decide on the possibility or prudence of its being attempted. The sailors liked me for this, and prognosticated I should yet turn out a thorough sailor. Even the officers, who had hitherto looked on me as a useless idler, viewed my conduct with gaping wonder, and entertained better hopes of me.

But these hopes died away with the bustling scenes in which they were begotten; and, during the fine and calm weather, I lost the reputation I had acquired in storms and battles. Among my messmates I was decidedly a favourite. What I principally prided myself in was protecting the weak from the strong. I permitted none to tyrannise. I had grown prematurely very tall and strong; and was of so unyielding a disposition, that in my struggles with those, who were not much more than my equals in strength, though above me in years, I wore them out with pertinacity. My rashness and impetuosity bore down all before them. None liked to contend with me; for I never acknowledged myself beaten, but renewed the quarrel, without respect to time or place. Yet what my messmates chiefly lauded and respected was the fearless independence with which I treated those above me.

The utmost of their power had been wreaked against me; yet, had the rack been added, they could not have intimidated me. Indeed, from very wantonness, I went beyond their inflictions. For instance, the common punishment was sending us to the mast-head for four or five hours. Immediately I was ordered thither, I used to lie along the cross-trees, as if perfectly at my ease, and either feign to sleep, or, if it was hot, really go to sleep. They were

alarmed at the chance of my falling from so hazardous a perch;
and to prevent, as it was thought, the possibility of my sleeping,
the Scotchman one day, during a heavy sea with little wind, ordered
me, in his anger, to go to the extreme end of the top-sail yard-
arm, and remain there for four hours. I murmured, but, obliged
to comply, up I went; and walking along the yard on the dizzy
height, got hold of the top-sail lift, laid myself down between the
yard and studding-sail-boom, and pretended to sleep as usual.
The lieutenant frequently hailed me, bidding me to keep awake,
or I should fall overboard. This repeated caution suggested to
me the means of putting an end to this sort of annoyance, by
antedating his fears, and falling overboard;—not, however, with
the idea of drowning, as few in the ship could swim so well as
myself. I had seen a man jump from the lower yard in sport, and
had determined to try the experiment. Besides, the roll of the ship
was in my favour; so, watching my opportunity, when the officers
and crew were at their quarters at sunset, I took advantage of a
heavy roll of the ship, and dropped on the crest of a monstrous
wave. I sunk deep into its bosom, and the agony of suppressed
respiration, after the fall, was horrible. Had I not taken the precaution to maintain my poise, by keeping my hands over my
head, preserving an erect posture in my descent, and moving my
limbs in the air, I should inevitably have lost my life. As it was,
I was insensible to every thing but a swelling sensation in my chest,
to bursting; and the frightful conviction of going downwards,
with the rapidity of a thunder-bolt, notwithstanding my convulsive
struggles to rise, was torture such as it is vain to describe. A death-
like torpidness came over me; then I heard a din of voices, and a
noise on the sea, and within it, like a hurricane; my head and
breast seemed to be splitting. After which I thought I saw a confused crowd of faces bent over me; and I felt a loathsome sickness.
A cold shivering shook my limbs, and I gnashed my teeth, imagining myself still struggling as in the last efforts at escape from drowning. This impression must have continued for a long time. The
first circumstance I can distinctly remember was Aston's voice,
saying, 'How are you now?' I tried to speak, but in vain; my lips
moved without a word. He told me, I was now safe on board.
I looked round; but a sensation of water rushing in my mouth,
ears, and nostrils, still made me think I was amidst the waves.
For eight and forty hours I suffered inexpressible pain; a thousand

E

times greater, in my restoration to life, than before I lost my recollection.

But what signifies what I endured?—I gained my point. The Scotch lieutenant was severely reprimanded for his unjustifiable conduct in sending me to so dangerous a place for punishment. The captain's heart was moved to order a fowl to be killed for soup; and he sent me a bottle of wine. I had the one grilled, and the other mulled, holding an antipathy to every thing insipid. I was never sent to the mast-head again; nor could any one suspect even me of such a mad freak as to run a hazard of drowning, to rid myself of a trifling annoyance, which others bore unrepiningly.

In taxing the Scotch lieutenant with pusillanimity, in the adventure of the Malay craft off the pirate coast, it is necessary to explain, that an officer, ordered on such an adventure, must be vested with discretionary power, implied by the nature of the service, though not expressly set down. The recal-signal was made under the impression that the Malay vessel would get on shore; and that, by the support of the natives, for such is their character, she might make a desperate resistance. Commanding officers are very properly instructed to be economical in expending the material of the ship,—that is, the men,—in quixotic adventures; not from womanish and tender feelings of humanity, but on more solid grounds,—the sterling value, in pounds, shillings, and pence, of every able seaman, taken to a foreign country and inured to its climate, besides the difficulty of replacing him. Thus the captain, seeing a probability of losing some of his crew, for the trifling object of destroying a few savages, and no prospect of prize-money, hoisted the recal-signal; by doing which, he washed his hands of the consequences, if they were unsuccessful, leaving the officer commanding the boats to act on his own responsibility. This, of course, is an understood thing. If the ship, making such a signal, happens to be rather distant, and the boats are in the vicinity of their object, they can better calculate on the attempt; then if the probability of success, backed by the sailor's ardent love of fighting, and hopes of promotion, out-weighs the risk, they keep their backs to the signal, and push on to the fight. But, on the other hand, if no recal-signal is made, however hazardous the service, they must attempt its accomplishment. Therefore the general impression throughout the ship was against our Scotch lieutenant.

CHAPTER XIII

I, alas!
Have lived but on this earth a few sad years,
And so my lot was ordered, that a father
First turned the moments of awakening life
To drops, each poisoning youth's sweet hope.

SHELLEY

BESIDES Aston, there were several of my messmates I particularly
liked. One of them, about my own age, whose name was Walter,
was my ordinary associate; not that there was much resemblance
in our tastes and characters, but his father had treated him with
even a worse brutality than I had endured from mine. Perhaps
indeed he had, in conscientious minds, merited his father's hatred,
from having made his appearance on the stage of life in an unlawful
and unorthodox manner. Relations and guardians had not been
duly consulted; the church had been invaded in its rights, insulted in its discipline, its ministers defrauded of their fees; no
merry peal of village-bells, or circle of feasting friends, had united
their harmonious voices in giving the unbidden stranger a welcome
into the world. Instead of these joyful omens, he and his mother
were smuggled into the obscure environs of a great city; and as
much artifice and precaution used, and as many bribes given, to
conceal his birth, as if a murder had been committed. This was
the only mark of his father's care,—at least he had never heard of
any other. His mother was one of the million of simple girls, who,
seduced under a promise of marriage, believe in the protestations
and oaths of lords;—as if a lord could love any thing so dearly as
his own coronet! or that he would hesitate to sacrifice a world of
ignoble inferiors, rather than be guilty, like base plebeians, of
keeping his vows, and acknowledging his offspring, with a blot on
his escutcheon!

Walter was educated at a charity-school, the Blue-coat school,
a royal foundation for the maintenance and education of poor and
fatherless children; and who so poor and fatherless as this son of
a man whose rental was forty thousand pounds? This institution,
and many others, are admirable nurseries for the bastards of
aristocrats; and the country must be proud of its high and dis-

tinguished privilege in expending hard-earned wealth for the support and instruction of the offsets of our high-mettled lords and masters. It would be sacrilege if one drop of their noble blood should be spilt on the ground.

His mother exerted herself to the utmost, and, by some means, placed him in the navy. Poor and unprotected, save by her, he led but a sorry life, and underwent a series of vexatious persecutions, which seemed perpetuated under the Scotch lieutenant. These made him gloomy; he shunned our mirth and sports; and, while we were carousing, he generally was reading. I felt much for him; and several times took on myself the punishment for his neglect of duty. This won his heart.

To turn the recreant Scotchman into ridicule, I made a caricature, representing his obedience to the recal-signal, while the two other boats were hastening to the Malay. Walter had a better talent for drawing, and I persuaded him to execute an improved copy of it; then watching my opportunity, when all the officers were assembled at their mess, I dropped it down the hatchway on the table. There was a burst of laughter, and it was some time before the person, who figured as the principal character, discovered it; but when he did, his long colourless face turned to a bright lemon-hue, and, festering with suppressed bile, he had an attack of jaundice. He spared no pains in finding out the author of this satire. I should have added, that we had annexed, by way of explanation, a doggrel poem, which, perhaps from the vanity of authorship, or from the example of ancient bards and a modern poet, I was particularly fond of singing, with little attention to time and place, so that very soon it became as common with the sailors, as 'Cease, rude Boreas,' 'Tom Bowling,' &c., and, to my critical taste, it was much superior. I was not then aware that the celebrated author[1] of the latter of these national songs had obtained a pension, or I certainly should have put in my claim. All I got was abuse for the noise I made, together with increased persecution from the hero I was so indefatigable in immortalizing. His ingratitude, like Brutus's dagger, was the unkindest cut of all.

Some time afterwards he discovered that the drawing was by Walter. 'I thought that fellow' (meaning me) 'had done it,' said he, 'and he is a cheald of the deil, capable of any atrocity; besides, he cares for no one, and is protected in his insolence by Aston and the first lieutenant. But as for that pale-faced, sickly boy, Walter,

whom every body kicks about, by God, I'll make him drown himsel
before he is a week older!'

Well, he strove to keep his word. By cunning, lying, and treachery, he persecuted the captain and first lieutenant with such un-
ceasing complaints against him, that poor Walter was punished
and abused till he became desperate from oppression; and then,
replying in hasty words and anger, he was degraded from the
situation of an officer, turned before the mast, and stationed in
the mizen-top. In spite of orders to the contrary, I was always
talking to him, and cheering him. His gentle heart was bruised,
he sunk into gloom, and I feared would have verified the lieutenant's prediction. He paid little attention to what I said, till
I confided to him my determination of leaving the ship and navy
the first port we entered, counselled him to do the same, and
pointed out the exquisite treat we should have in buffeting his
enemy to death. The hope of this wild justice did what no other
hope could do—it made him calm. He even feigned to do his
duty with alacrity.

His persecutor harassed him with unrelenting brutality. He was
compelled to do duty with the mizen-top boys; his former messmates were interdicted from speaking to him; he was obliged to
put on the dress of the sailors and mess with them; and the Scotchman had exerted his utmost influence to blast his name by the
abhorrent infliction of corporeal punishment; but the captain,
though hitherto cajoled, would not consent.

CHAPTER XIV

> Young hearts which languished for some sunny isle,
> Where summer years and summer women smile;
> Men without country, who, too long estranged,
> Had found no native home, or found it changed,
> And, half-uncivilized, preferr'd the cave
> Of some soft savage to the uncertain wave.
>
> BYRON

WHEN on duty, particularly in the night-watches, I used to
accompany him into the top, where I allayed his piteous moanings
at his fate by prospects of ample vengeance. I pointed out to him
the facility with which the thing was to be achieved; I told him

we were now men; that we had the power of shaking off the fetters which bound us; that our ship was not the world, nor were we galley-slaves chained to the oar for life; that if the English conspired against our liberty, they were little more than tyrants of the sea-shore, and India, with her thousand kings, was open to us; that there was hope in our very despair of the present; that lower in the scale of misery we could not sink, and that any change must, to us, be good.

'Yes! let us go,' said he, 'where no Europeans have yet been, and where they dare not follow! Let us cast off a country, where we have no patrimony, no parents, no ties. Let us change our country and caste, and find a home amidst the children of Nature. I have read of such things; I have heard they are true. And who so fit to make the trial as oppressed outcasts like ourselves? The leprous and despised pariah, loathed by all, to my mind, lives in bliss, compared to what I have endured and still endure.'

'As for leprosy,' I answered, 'it's out of the question, as I intend that my limbs shall do me good service. They are the only friends I have, and the true philosophers in the East set a juster value on the gifts of nature than the English; among whom unfinished abortions, with resemblance of form, and intellect enough to class themselves with human beings, are raised by lying, pimping, and hypocrisy, to such a height, that we, who could crush them like fleas between a thumb and finger, are compelled to stand bareheaded before them! Now, with the natives here, there is no such infamous degradation. Strength is power; and the scales of justice are biassed by the sword.'

Walter would kindle up his spell-bound spirit, burst forth in ardent and passionate words, transporting himself, in imagination, to one of the countless isles of the Indian archipelago, and exult in his bow and arrow, his fishing-rod, and canoe. 'No, no canoe!' he then exclaimed; 'for never will I look on salt-water—my blood would curdle at it. No, I will find out some sheltered ravine, some river's bank, shadowed by trees, and there will I live in brotherhood with the natives.'

'By taking their sisters,' I observed.

He went on; 'I'll marry, and have children, and build a hut.'

'And be tattooed and naked?' I asked.

'Yes,' said he; 'no matter; what they do, that will I.'

Thus we would wile away the time, building castles in the air, almost possessing them, and forgetting all things else, until our pastoral, innocent, romantic fabric was suddenly annihilated by the accursed, croaking, querulous, sycophantic, broad, vulgar accents of the Scotch lieutenant, bawling out, 'Haud your tongues, ye wearisome rascals in the mizen-top, there; or I wull ha' ye all down to the rope's end of the boatswain's mate, I wull, ye ragamuffins!'

We then, such is the force of habit, slunk down the rigging, crept into our hammocks, and awoke to a repetition of our abject slavery during the day, and a continuation of our romance at night; till, I believe, we both looked forward to the night-watches with equal anxiety. As to Aston, he never ceased to treat Walter otherwise than as a gentleman; and the men, observing his conduct, with the ready cunning of slaves, followed his example.

I have narrated events on board this frigate, as they chanced to recur to my memory, not as they happened in order of time. After staying a short time at Bombay, we sailed to Madras, and then returned to the former place, with secret instructions[1] from the admiral.

On our passage from Bombay to Madras, on a fine day, as I was sleeping in one of the quarter-boats, there was a wild halloo throughout the ship. The first burst of Bligh's mutiny came across my mind. Such a commotion I never witnessed on board a man of war: the men came rushing over each other on deck, up every hatchway; discipline was at an end; the lieutenant commanding the deck stood astounded and aghast; the captain and most of the officers were struggling through the dense mass of sailors, questioning and commanding; but all control was lost, and they were huddled and wedged together without distinction. I soon observed it was despair, and not ferocity, that was painted on the rough and weather-beaten brows of the men. At last the secret burst forth in every voice at once, of 'Fire! fire! Fire in the fore-magazine!'

That awful sound effected what nothing else mortal could have done; it made the stout, the hardy, the valiant sailor break through the well-organised drilling of an entire life; and he was seized with an irresistible dread of the only element he could shrink from contending with—fire, and in the powder magazine! An instant, and bodies would be mangled and mingled in the air, without distinction of rank or station. Habit or instinct roused the officers, who, at the first cry, seemed to participate in the one unanimous feeling. None moved but with a flushed brow; and their eyes were glaringly bent on the fore hatchway, awaiting a fate they could not avoid. We were out of sight of land; not a sail in view, nor a speck on the horizon; the only cloud was the black, dense smoke, which burst from the hatchway; and there being no wind, it ascended in an unbroken mass aloft, we anticipating soon to follow it.

A dead silence reigned throughout the gallant frigate; then a confused murmur; and presently the men, without combination, yet simultaneously, rushed aft to the quarter-boats; others crowded to the sides of the ship, straining their eyes in the vain hope of espying some means of escape; some tremblingly crept up the rigging; while a small band of iron-nerved veterans alone stood undauntedly—men grown grisled from storms, battles, and hardships, not from years. During this movement I started at the loud, clear, trumpet-like voice of Aston, commanding the firemen to get their buckets, the marines to come aft with their arms, and the officers to follow his example. With that he drew a cutlass from the stand, and now the first lieutenant and other officers, as if awakened to their duty, drove the men from the boats, and out of the chains.

The moment I heard Aston's voice I went up to him, and said, 'I will go down to the magazine, if you will send the gunners there and hand down water.'

I rushed forward down the main hatchway, hurried along the abandoned lower deck, seized a rope, and descended through the smoke directly into the magazine. In the fore-part, which was darker than the blackest night, it was impossible to distinguish whence the fire came. I groped about, and found my hands and head burning, and a difficulty of respiration from the smoke. Then I stumbled over a man, either dead, or dead drunk, I knew not which; and tore down bundles of matches, which were on fire. In doing this, the blue-lights, used for signals, were ignited, upon which I heard some men, who were coming down to assist me, cry out, 'She is going!' and they hurried back to the deck, where there arose another hopeless cry of 'She is going!' and then all was hushed.

One glance, as the blue-lights flamed, cleared up the mystery. The gunner's mate lay prostrate at my feet, with a broken pipe stuck in his mouth, and the only sign he gave of life was puffing.

The ready-primed matches for the guns, had caught fire from his carelessness. The slow smouldering fire from hundreds of these, had alone caused the smoke, and the danger was in their proximity to the powder. I grasped hold of the blue-lights, fire-proof in my ardour, which the probability of saving the ship gave me.

While endeavouring to hand them up, I called out for more men. At this instant Aston was jumping down. 'Don't come down,' I said; 'but hand these damned things up, and then—a dozen buckets of water—and all is right.' Aston called to one of the men who followed him, bidding him go on deck, tell the captain there was no danger, and that all we wanted was water.

The first bucket which was handed down, Aston threw over me, saying, 'By God, you are on fire!' My hair and shirt were burning. This, and the smoke, I suppose, were the cause of my falling down insensible. Aston took my place. The fresh air soon restored me. In a few seconds the magazine was inundated by the buckets and all was safe.

I was sent for on deck, and went there, my features begrimed with wet powder—nothing on but my trowsers—my hair and eye-brows burnt, my hands and face scorched, and my whole appearance, I imagine, exhibiting a lively picture of a fire-demon fresh from hell. All the officers smiled; but they seemed, at the same time, to highly laud my presence of mind; I say *seemed*, for it is against the general custom of the navy to express more. Thanking me would have been reprimanding themselves. However, I was content; the impression could not be erased; they could not call me a useless idler, though I took care to be a complete idler for a long time after, on the plea of my burning and bruising, and they said, 'Well! poor fellow, he deserves a little indulgence!'

CHAPTER XV

ON the ship's mooring in any harbour, I watched the first opportunity of getting on shore, and till the Blue Peter was hoisted, and the fore-top-sail loose, there was little chance of seeing me on board. The instant we entered, for the second time, the harbour of Bombay, I was, as usual, under some plea or other, in a shore-boat; and presently had established my favourite headquarters in the town—to wit, in a tavern, where I plunged headlong into extravagant pleasures. What time I could spare from women and wine I devoted to galloping about the country, rioting in the bazars, and playing at the billiard-table. As in the ship, so it was on shore, every commotion and disturbance was generally traced to me. In India Europeans lord it over the conquered natives with a high hand. Every outrage may be committed almost with impunity, and their ready flexibility of temperament has acquired a servile subordination. Resistance, or even complaint, they scarcely urge; and the greatest kindness from Europeans, for long and faithful services, never exceeded what is shewn to dogs— they were patted when their masters were in good humour, and beaten when they were vexed—at least it was so when I was there. As long as you refrained from political interference, and presumed not to question the omnipotency of the Holy of Holies, the East India Company, and their servants, as they are pleased to designate the governor and all in office, you could do no wrong. If you treated the decrees of these merchant-sultans with due deference, and expressed your servility by arrogance and cruelty to their slaves, the only consideration was, that the heat of the climate made it a porter's task, and you were considered by the old stagers as a greenhorn, horse-whipping the wretches during the sultry hours of the day.

I kept up a communication with Walter by notes and messages, and had arranged that he should not desert the ship, till she was on the point of sailing. I was then to engage a catamaran to lie near the ship at night, and he was to drop himself over the bow-port, and swim to her. As for the lieutenant I was to deal with him, for I had now grown tall and strong, and there were few men with whom I would have hesitated to cope.

At the tavern where I took up my abode, I commenced an intimacy with a merchant. In youth we form friendship in days, which, at a more advanced age, require years. So with this man; from a game or two at billiards, eating together, and walking together, we had become boon companions. Many of the naval officers used to come in parties to the tavern to see me, when we often sallied about the town, and played a thousand mad pranks. My friend, the stranger, as he was called, seemed to seek the society of naval officers, and take great interest in the different accounts of their cruises, the ships they belonged to, their rate of sailing, and the peculiarities which distinguished their respective commanders. His conversation was principally confined to questions, and, as people, for the most part, prefer talking to listening, he was liked the better. He frequently, in company with me, visited the men-of-war in the harbour; the only one I objected to introduce him to was my own frigate, but to make him amends, I gave every information he wished regarding her.

Though he then called himself De Witt, I shall speak of him at once under his real name, De Ruyter.[1] He mentioned to me that he was waiting for a passage to Batavia; he seemed perfectly acquainted with India and its seas. He spoke most of the European languages, nor had he the slightest foreign accent in his pronunciation of the English. In walking about the bazars, commonly at night, he sometimes met me, and took me with him. He was familiar with all the out-of-the-way corners of the most irregular of towns, and entered into many dark abodes without ceremony. He conversed, on these occasions, with the natives, in their varied tongues with equal ease, whether in the guttural, brute-like grunting of the Malay, the more humanized Hindostanee, or the softer and harmonious Persian. What struck me most at the time, was, the great deference these people paid him; even the proud, fat, swelling, and pompous Armenian merchants stopped their palanquins, and got out to converse with him, apparently delighted at their meeting. These and other circumstances made me wonder, but nothing more; at seventeen we do not suspect every man to be a rogue as we do at thirty. There was a self-possession and decision about De Ruyter's ordinary acts, with a general information, that made me feel what, I suppose, I should not have thanked any one for remarking, as, at that age, we are loth to allow any to be our superior. Perhaps I might not have felt this so strongly, had he not been as much my superior in physical as in mental endowments. In stature he was majestic, the length and fine proportion of his limbs, and the shortness and roundness of his body, gave to his appearance a lightness and elasticity seldom seen but in the natives of the east. It was only on close examination you discovered, that under the slim form of the date-tree was disguised the solid strength of the oak. His face wanted breadth to please an artist's eye, but it added to the effect of his high, clear, bold, unwrinkled forehead, as smooth, though not as white, as sculptured marble. His hair was dark and abundant, his features well defined. The greatest peculiarity was his eye; it was ever so varying that it was impossible to distinguish its colour; like the hue of the cameleon it had no one fixed, but shewed, as in a mirror, the reflection of his mind. In a state of rest it was overcast with a hazy film, like a gray cloud; but when he was excited by the vehemence of his feelings, the mist evaporated, and it gradually brightened, till its rays, like the sun, became so intense, that your own were dazzled beholding it. His eye-lashes were jet-black; he had thick, straight, and prominent eye-brows, with a habit of knitting them together, contracted from exposure to the intense heat of an eastern sun, leaving an infinity of minuter lines, traced at the corners of the eyes, but unlike the deep furrows of age or debauchery in northern climates. The lines of his mouth were boldly and clearly cut; it was muscular, full of expression, and the upper lip, which was prominent, had a convulsive action when he spoke, independent of its companion; his jaw was full, and gave him the air of invincible determination. Though naturally not of so dark a complexion as myself, those parts of his person exposed were not merely sun-burnt, but appeared to be seared to the very bone. He was approaching his thirtieth year.

I am thus minute in describing De Ruyter, to account in part for the extraordinary influence he gained, on so short an acquaintance, over my mind and imagination. He became my model.

The height of my ambition was to imitate him, even in his defects. My emulation was awakened. For the first time I was impressed with the superiority of a human being. To keep on an equality with him was unattainable. In every trifling action he evinced a manner so off-hand, free, and noble, that it looked as if it sprung new and fresh from his own individuality; and every thing else shrunk into an apish imitation.

The enervating influence of a long residence in a tropical climate had not affected him; his strength and energies seemed insurmountable; the maddening fever of the jungles tainted not his blood; the sun-stroke fell innocuous on his bare head; and he alone went the round of his ordinary occupations, regardless of time or temperature. But then I observed he drank little, slept little, and ate sparingly. While we were carousing, and keeping midnight orgies, he often joined us, drank his coffee, and smoked his hooka. He exceeded the youngest of us in the enjoyment of the present hour; even with the sedative aid of the mocha-berry, he could scarcely reduce his high spirits to a level with ours, when fired by the juice of the grape, or maddened by arrack-punch. Without effort he caught the tone of mind among his associates; thus marking the toleration of his own, as he had the power of bending the most stubborn and thoughtless to his will, of directing them, and of moulding them into any form which pleased his fancy. But he chose rather to draw out others' characters, to view them in their natural hues, and to relieve the tension of his own high-wrought imagination by resuming the thoughts and feelings of boyhood. By putting himself on a par with us, he gained that influence, which Solomon, in all his wisdom and wise sayings, could not have accomplished.

CHAPTER XVI

Do ye forget the blow, the buffets vile?
Are ye not smitten by a youngling arm?

KEATS

TREATED as an equal by a being of such superior intelligence and years, I felt a pride, an importance I had never before known. By this conduct he gained my unlimited confidence, and imperceptibly drew from me my most secret thoughts. I told him I was resolute to leave a profession, in which I failed to realize those ardent and ambitious prospects of glory it had portrayed in my imagination. Instead of encouraging me in this, he ever urged me to do nothing prematurely, or in passion. I spoke of the neglect and contumely I had suffered, of the despondency of my views in life, in consequence of my hopeless situation with my family; and concluded with a firm determination to shake off the fetters which galled my spirit, and bound down my aspirations; declaring that, if I could do nothing better, I would go into the jungles, and herd with wild buffaloes and tigers, where I should at least be a free agent, however short my life, rather than longer submit to the iron despotism, which held my very thoughts in bondage. 'Is it not written,' I exclaimed vehemently, 'in the code of our naval law, that you shall not, in look or gesture, signify that you are dissatisfied with those who govern you by holding the lash of correction over your head? If gods were to rule us by brutal intimidation, who would not rebel? And if we must have a master, why not enter the service of demons and devils, on fair terms, and with fair words?'

'Nay,' said De Ruyter, 'you are running yourself a-ground now. Restrain your passion; view things in their real colours, not as disfigured by the sickly yellow of your jaundiced conceptions. We cannot all be masters; nor can the best commander content every one beneath him. Your mind has received a warp from the neglect and folly of weak, but not evil men. You, who have endured so much from the narrow-minded views of others, should learn to reason justly and tolerantly; and distinguish between ignorance and malice in those who have sinned against you. Now, the only case you have made out of malice amounts to little; and the object is too insignificant to waste a thought upon;—I mean the Scotch lieutenant you told me about.'

'Little!' replied I; 'do you call that little?—the utter ruin and degradation he has heaped on my friend Walter? And as I am the cause, so am I bound amply to revenge his injuries. May every evil in life be concentrated exclusively on my head—may the pariah scoff and spit at me, and the wild dogs hunt me through the jungles, if I forgive that malignant—'

As his hated name was trembling on my lips, the scoundrel himself, and alone, entered the billiard-room where we were talking. He looked at my flushed and heated brow, and hesitated what he should do, slink back, or advance. He chose to advance, assuming his most cajoling look, with smirks and smiles, and that little enginery, by which he had wormed his way through the world, wrecking the hopes of true and honest men. I should mention that he had often visited this tavern whilst I was there; and that on shore he was affable as he was overbearing on board. As I was under his command, perhaps he considered me still in his power; so stepping towards me, he said, 'Well! when are you going on board? The ship is ordered to sail to-morrow, and all the officers are to be on board by daylight.'

'Is it so?' said I, in a slow and suppressed voice, to hide the fierceness of my purpose, while every fibre of my frame swelled in action, and my blood seemed ignited, and then congealed to ice; 'then the time is come to settle my accounts; and most providentially my principal creditor is here.'

'What do you mean?' he asked.

'Once,' I answered, 'you told me never to stand in your presence with my hat on. I now, for the last time, obey you!' and, with the word, I dashed my hat in his face.

As he stood gaping in amaze, I stripped off the only remaining badge of servitude upon me, and, trampling on it, exclaimed, 'Now, Mr. Lieutenant, I am free! You are no longer my superior officer! If I must acknowledge you my superior as a man, prove it with your sword!' Then placing myself between him and the door, I added, 'Draw! This gentleman and the billiard marker shall see fair play.'

He attempted to pass, muttering, 'What do you mean?—are you in your senses?' Seizing him by the collar, I swung him into the middle of the room, and said: 'There is no escape! Defend your life!'

He then went towards De Ruyter, and appealed to him for protection, swearing he was ignorant of what I meant, or what I wanted. De Ruyter continued calmly smoking, and answered: 'Why, it seems pretty clear what he wants. I have nothing to do with your quarrel. You had better draw and fight it out; he is but a boy, and you should be a man by your beard.'

The lieutenant, whose fears then took entire possession of his mind, humbled himself to me; he protested he had never intended me any wrong; that if I thought so, he was sorry, and asked my pardon; he entreated I would put up my sword, and go on board with him, promising, with an oath, that he would never take advantage of what had passed. Disgusted at his meanness, I struck him from me, and, spitting at him, vociferated, 'Remember Walter! cowardly, malignant ruffian! What! you white-livered scoundrel, can no words move you?—then blows shall!' and I struck him with the hilt of my sword in his mouth, and kicked him, and trampled on him. I tore his coat off, I rent it to fragments, saying, 'This is the first time such a poltroon has disgraced this true colour!' His screams and protestations, while they increased my contempt, added fuel to my anger, for I was furious that such a pitiful wretch should have lorded it over me so long. I roared out, 'For the wrongs you have done me, I am satisfied. Yet nothing but your currish blood can atone for your atrocities to Walter!'

Having broken my own sword at the onset, I drew his from beneath his prostrate carcass, and should inevitably have despatched him on the spot, had not a stronger hand griped hold of my arm. It was De Ruyter's; and he said, in a low, quiet voice, 'Come, no killing. Here!' (giving me a broken billiard cue,) 'a stick is a fitter weapon to chastise a coward with. Don't rust good steel.'

It was useless to gainsay him, for he had taken the sword out of my hand. I therefore belaboured the rascal: his yells were dreadful; he was wild with terror, and looked like a maniac. I never ceased till I had broken the butt-end of the cue over him, and till he was motionless.

De Ruyter, though I was not aware of it at the time, had stood sentinel at the door to bar intrusion. He now left it, and a shoal of blacks and whites rushed in.

CHAPTER XVII

Bring forth the horse!—the horse was brought,
  In truth he was a noble steed,
  A Tartar of the Ukrain breed,
Who look'd as though the speed of thought
Were in his limbs.

　　*　　*　　*　　*　　*　　*

And snorting with erected mane,
And struggling fiercely, but in vain,
In the full foam of wrath and dread,
To me the desert-born was led.

                                        BYRON

AT the head of these intruders, to my astonishment, appeared
Walter. His wonder was as great at the scene before him,—the
man he most loathed lying, as dead, at his feet. He gazed on him
with a sort of triumph; his lips quivered, and his face became at
first scarlet, and then pallid. He raised his eyes to mine, and, seeing
me panting and speechless with rage, together with the broken
sword on the floor, the truth flashed on his mind. His inquiring
gaze then caught De Ruyter, who not only understood him, but
seemed to know who he was, for he asked him if his name was not
Walter. Upon being informed it was,—'Well, then,' said he, 'there
lies your enemy, whose breath, I think, your friend has stopped.
I wish he would keep some measure in his passion.'

'I hope,' replied Walter, 'he has not killed him.'

De Ruyter, being in doubt, got up and felt the lieutenant's
pulse. He then said: 'No; he is not quite dead. Here!—take him
out.'

The servants lifted him up; he opened his eyes; the blood was
running out of his mouth; and some of his teeth were jammed in.
He was a most pitiable object, and blubbered like a boy. As soon
as he regained his senses, he saw Walter, which increased his
panic; and Walter, with a flushed brow, restrained himself with
difficulty; for, on hearing from De Ruyter that I had not broken
the sword in his body, but on it, he imagined he was more frightened
than hurt. But De Ruyter assured him to the contrary, and observed, 'Why, he is as difficult to be killed as the tiger-cat. I have
never seen a fellow endure such a mauling in my life. Come,

F

youngsters, he has had enough; and too much, if you are got hold of to answer for it. Your way of discharging yourself from the service may not be considered as an unexceptionable precedent; and therefore, before the alarm is given, and the town-gate closed, by the affair being made known, had you not better cut and run? As to you, Walter,—have you followed your friend's example in doffing the blue? What means this red sign? Have you shifted your colours in good earnest, or is it a mere frolic?'

I had observed, with surprise, that Walter was in a military uniform. 'Thank God, and my mother!' he exclaimed, 'I have a commission in the company's service, and was discharged this morning from the ship. So eager was I to pay that fellow the debt I owe him, (fortunately one of the officers going to England has made over his traps to me,) that, as the frigate sails to-morrow, I came here to surprise you, and consult how we were to get hold of the infernal villain. I heard you in wrath as I entered the house, little imagining you had forestalled me in my revenge; but good fortune never comes single-handed.'

De Ruyter interrupted him with—'Come, be off, like the wind! You'll have time to discuss these matters on a fitter occasion. Time presses on. Go,'—(he continued, sinking his voice into a whisper,) 'go to the bungalo I showed you the other day, near the village of Punee. You know the road. Walter or I will be with you as soon as the frigate has sailed, and this affair has blown over. Now, no more words. Off! I say.'

My horse was brought. He was a vicious-looking brute, with an ambiguity in his eye, that gave him an uncommon sinister expression. He had been brought in from the country, and having succeeded in throwing several of the naval officers, no one would mount him; so that, when first offered to me, he was enjoying a sort of sinecure. Never having met with any one or any thing as obstinate as myself, I liked him. I had a fellow feeling for his independent spirit, took him under my especial protection, and found the excitement of contention a delight. A restive and violent horse, in the sweltering climate of the tropic, is considered any thing but the means of recreation; but I loved to stem the stream, and never followed the footsteps of the prudent, who keep the high-beaten track of the world. My horse and I became a show-lion to the sober natives; and an interest was created to see which would conquer. Every day I was in the habit of galloping about the narrow streets, to the imminent peril of men, women, and brats. Countless were the complaints made of stalls up-set, bruises, and fractures; and I believe there was one unanimous wish throughout the entire district, notwithstanding its hundred conflicting castes, joined to a hearty curse, against me. If curses could have unhorsed me, and directed the brute's hoofs to my head, not one among them, heathen or christian, would have stirred an inch to arrest the visitation of so just a judgment. Thanks to a Turkish bit and saddle, which I had substituted for the mockery of English ones, I, drunk or sober, kept my seat, and diminished, though I could not subdue, the spirit of the horse, till we began to understand each other; and, when wearied of contention in private, jogged on together in public, like decent married people. On this animal I mounted, in a white jacket of De Ruyter's, speeding towards the gate, under the excitation of drubbing the lieutenant, not at all allayed by drinking two bottles of claret with Walter. The guard of sepoys was drawn up, beneath the arch of the town-gate, on some point of duty. My antipathy to the hired badge of servitude extended to all who wore it. In altitude and strength I thought myself augmented; and to shew off my newly-acquired freedom, in which feeling my mischievous horse, as if instigated by the same impulse, most willingly coincided, I dashed through the guard with the rapidity of thought, and, with a wild triumphal hurrah, scampered on to the plain of sand, which lies immediately on the outside of the town.

Here I gave vent to my joy, and played as many antics as a madman broke loose from his chains. I spurred my willing horse on to the centre of the sandy waste, hallooing and screaming myself hoarse with rapture. I drew the sabre De Ruyter had given me, and flourished it about, regardless of my horse's head and ears. As I lost sight of the town gate, I pulled in my foaming steed; then looking around, and seeing nothing human, I dismounted, when patting the horse's reeking neck, I exclaimed: 'Here we are, thou only honest creature, free at last! The spell of my bondage is broken! Who shall command me now? I will obey no one: I will have no other guide than my instinct; no one's will shall be mine; I am for my own free impulses! Who dare attempt to replace the yoke around my neck? Let them come here! I'll not move from this spot, though pursued by all the men in the fleet and garrison!'

CHAPTER XVIII

The sun was sinking—still I lay
   Chain'd to the still and stiffening steed,
I thought to mingle there our clay;
   And my dim eyes of death had need—
   No hope arose of being freed.

BYRON

THUS I continued my idle vaunting to the winds; my bosom swelled with the free beatings of my heart; to roam at liberty, unchecked by churlish superiors, was exstacy. I had thrown off my cap, though the sky looked like molten gold or brass; and was proceeding to tear off my clothes, though the white sand sparkled fiercely, and pierced the soles of my feet like fire, so abhorrent to me was every vestige or sign of slavery,—or, which was the same thing at that moment, of civilization. During the paroxysm, I should have unsaddled and unbridled my horse, to give him also freedom; but, at this period, I beheld some commotion at a distance.

My first impression of its being some one in pursuit subsided, on discovering that I was between it and the tower. I endeavoured to distinguish what it was, but all I could see was a silvery cloud of sand rising in a bright circle, and a dark object, at intervals, discernible. I mounted, and galloped towards it. As I advanced, I saw it was a horse, running incessantly in a round. I went on, and, amidst the clouds of sand, I saw that the lunging and plunging of the horse was every instant more violent. My own threw up his crest, replied to his loud neighings, and pressed on; but, on approaching the object, my astonishment was raised to the highest pitch at a voice hailing me, and at beholding a man, in a cavalry uniform, half covered with sand, while the sweat and blood were trickling down from his close-cropped poll to his forehead and face. I shouted out,—'What is the matter?' when the horse came towards me. His large eye and expanded nostrils were of deep crimson, and the blood from several gashes on his head, neck, and flanks, mingled with the white foam on his bright black skin. With erect mane and tail, and open mouth, he came to within a few yards of me. I pulled up, and drew my sabre. He then wheeled round, and, making several circles within each other in rapid

motion, he flung out his hind legs at the prostrate soldier, whose
sword defended him with difficulty. The horse endeavoured to
avoid being cut, by alertness and rapidity. The saddle and hous-
ings, lying by the man, in some measure protected him. On being
foiled in striking with his hind feet, the horse turned round short
on his haunches, and, with startling ferocity, plunged in head
foremost, like a tiger, striking with his fore feet right out, and
even trying to get hold of the man with his teeth.

Here was a revolution,—the horse attempting to kill his rider,
and using his armed hoofs against his head! In compliance with
my spirit of freedom, I should have aided the horse, or remained
neuter; but instinct impelled me to side with the biped. Pushing
in to the rescue, I endeavoured to get between the two, but it
was no easy matter; for the horse made no attack on me; on the
contrary, he used every effort to avoid my interference. I hallooed,
and tried to drive him off. He retreated a hundred yards, when
as, once or twice, I was dismounting to succour the apparently
exhausted man, he returned to the charge. However, from exertion
and loss of blood, he waxed weak and less wary; so that, after many
abortive attempts, I succeeded in ham-stringing him. He now
gave one loud bellow, and strove, with a staggering gait, to gallop
off, frequently falling. I followed, and had several cuts at him,
till, faint from the loss of blood, he fell, unable to rise.

I left him there, and went back to the man, who seemed in little
better condition than the horse. All I could distinguish, in answer
to my speaking to him, was—'Water!—water!—water!'—but I
had none, nor was there any near us. The man's mouth was clotted,
almost cemented with blood and sand; I wiped it and his nostrils
with my jacket. Partly by signs, and partly by words, he directed
me to open the holsters on his saddle. I did so, and found old
Falstaff's substitute for a pistol, a bottle—not indeed of sack, but
—of arrack. I gave him some, and rubbed his face and head with
the remainder. This restored him, when I asked him to get up
and ride my horse, till we should arrive at some hut. He waved
his hand, and said,

'No! I have had enough of horses to-day.'

'Well, will you walk?'

'How can I?' he replied, 'my leg and my left arm are cracked;
or you would not have found me beaten by that brute. If you had
not come up, he would have finished me. I was nearly done.

I never heard of such a thing before, though I have been a rough rider to the regiment for sixteen years, and crossed all sorts and breeds of cross-grained cattle. Never, till now, could one throw me from his back, without rearing, on a clean field. Then to come in upon me, like a wild beast, with hoof and tooth!—he must be mad. I hope you have killed him.'

Dungaree was the nearest village. I mounted, rode thither, pressed a palanquin into service, and returned to the soldier. He was in great pain, but calmer. He told me, the horse belonged to the colonel of the regiment. He had been purchased, at a great price, of an Arab; was quiet at first, but afterwards became so vicious and violent, that none could mount him. 'I,' he continued, 'undertook to tame him, or kill him. I have done my best. I tried in vain to work down his mettle; he was not to be beaten. Deprived of his food, he was only the more furious, and watched, with wonderful cunning, every occasion of kicking and biting me. Once he got hold of me by the back, and lifted me into his manger; and if I had not been tolerably strong, and assisted by others, he would have killed me. Whenever I rode him, he used every artifice to throw me; which he had never been able to achieve till to-day, when, by violent lungings and lashings-out, he worked the saddle down to his loins, and, in that situation, set off at full speed, and succeeded in shaking me off. As I was lying doubled up, he broke my arm, and, I believe, my leg. Then, after going a short distance, he stopped, and wheeled round to renew the blow. I had, with great difficulty, drawn my sword; and till you, Sir, came up, which was but a few minutes, he was attacking me in the way you found him. Though I had wounded him with my sabre in many places, the devil only grew more savage. I was frightened more at his looks than at any thing else; and I do verily believe, Sir, he was the devil.'

'Do you?' said I, 'then it is some consolation, my man, to see he is dead.'

With that I sent him into Bombay, directing the men to the hospital, giving them money, and promising more, provided they made haste.

CHAPTER XIX

Whether she was a 'mother,' I know not,
　Or whether they were 'maids' who called her mother,
But this is her seraglio's title, got
　I know not how, but good as any other;
So Cantemir can tell you, or De Tott:
　Her office was to keep aloof or smother
All bad propensities in fifteen hundred
Young women, and correct them when they blundered.

BYRON

AT sunset I returned to the village, determined to conclude a busy day by a noisy night. This village is set apart by the government in its thoughtful morality, to provide for the wants of its subjects, and for the exclusive residence of that sect of females who emulate in matters of love, their version of the golden age. Here they formed a little Utopia, liberal in their opinions, and unfettered by the narrow views of those whose doctrine is, that each individual ought to select one of the other sex, no matter how worthless, and with churlish egotism, behold all others, however beautiful and good, with cold indifference. These ladies were so averse to such maxims, that they founded their republic on precepts in direct contradiction to those of the vestals. Indeed they were a loose caste, for with a star-pagoda in one's pocket, —(not a heavenly star not a pagoda of bricks and mortar,—but a shining little, fat, golden coin,) there was the talisman, the *open sesame*, unlocking all doors and hearts at the same time. Protestations, ogling, sighing, vows, and oaths, together with the flimsy paper medium of love making in civilized life, found no credit. Paper had no chance against gold here. And what is most extraordinary, this great radical change was effected by people who had never read or heard of Cobbett's book on the subject.[1]

I put my horse up, and made a round to examine the motley live stock in the different mud-built and bamboo huts. The well-greased and black beauties of Madagascar first presented themselves. 'Aye,' said their governess, 'I see, sir, you know what is what. You some taste to like black rose; it smell sweet; white rose no smell at all, or smell like not fresh fish. You feel how soft this young lady skin.' I caught hold but she slipped through my fingers.

At the next shop there was but a small assortment. The sample produced was a ferret-eyed, amber-hued, thick-set Japanese. The mistress, in handing her forth for my inspection, said 'What you tink of my sun-flower? She shine like gold.'

'Melt her down and coin her then,' I replied, 'for you'll have no gold of mine.'

I passed on from house to house, till I stood before the filthiest hovel in the place, a den for English Jezebels, ancient camp-followers, born in ditches and bred in the trenches, vermin attached to a garrison, who, after preying on various regiments, and maiming and consigning more to the hospitals than the wars, had become themselves incurable, and, as such, turned out into the world.

Looking at these unsexed and most disgusting brutes filled me with loathing and disgust, and, what no moral sermonising could have done, they turned me from my purpose. Two of them sat sweltering on the steps, mopping their reeking necks; and an odour exhaled from them and their hovel worse than that from the disturbed sewer of a city. Yet such was their vanity, flourishing amidst the desolation of all other feelings and senses that the remnants of their noses were drawn up in disdain at my preference of the natives. To distinguish themselves from sows, far less impure, their flaming and soddened faces, and blood shot eyes, were surmounted by a rag and flaunting scarlet ribbon, which once had been an English cap, their deeply creased and collapsed bosoms were supported on their knees; and frowsy linen, soiled check aprons, and shoes worn slipshod were their whole attire. With gross and bestial words they hailed me as I passed. I spat and went on.

The abode of an ancient friend of mine received me. She was the female Schaich of the tribe, deeply versed in the mysteries of her vocation. Her dwelling was pre-eminent, being distinguished by a second story, with verandahs. This was the chief resort of the Europeans, in compliment to whom she had mounted a sort of English head-dress above her mahogany visage. She united in her person the characteristics of the buffalo of the jungles, its ball-proof hide of dingy hue, decorated with bristly straggling hair, sunken eye, and horny face, with the splay feet and hump of the dromedary. She was a monstrous hag, that looked coeval with Sin.

After drenching my parched thirst with a jar of toddy, fresh from the tree, I commanded old mother Ebony to exhibit her stock in trade, which was indeed abundant. Her frail tenement of mud, sand, and matting, shook to its foundation with the noise my arrival occasioned. I sat myself down on a mat, like a sultan, ordering the ladies to be presented according to the etiquette which the old mother had established. Then I heard the little patterings of their baby feet, and presently the jingling of their bangles and rings. Arms, wrists, ancles, toes, and fingers, glittered with brass, silver, and glass, making most harmonious music, as from aloft they descended a faery-looking bamboo ladder, like a continuous stream of ants down an old wall. With flowing trowsers, and scanty cotton vest, each one was starred on the forehead with yellow or red ochre. There was every gradation of colour and caste, muddy, olive, leaden, copper, and all the family of browns, from the dusky-red scaly cock-roach of India, till it became lost in the shining jet black beetle of my own country. There were all ages, and every degree of stature: from nine to (what the old Hecate appeared to be) ninety; and from the height of my pipe-stick to that of the palm-tree. There was the light and pliant-limbed Kubshee coupled with the swollen and blubbered Hottentot, moving like a porpoise; the Hindoo girl, with eyes like the stag, and form like the antelope; the fair, oily, moon-faced, and fleshy Armenian, fashioned like a turtle; and the soft and fondling Parsee, like a turtle-dove. Among these were the Cheechees, a race of the mingled blood of Europe and India— a compound of fire and frost—with the tallowy whiteness of the English joined to the dark hair of the east; and, though wanting the roseate tints of their western sires, yet were they amply compensated by the bright and glowing brilliancy of their mother's eyes, unalloyed by the dead and fish-like colour of the north.

I rioted in the wantonness of imagination; I felt pampered at the feast of the senses; yet the apparent impossibility of being dissatisfied made me so. There was too great an abundance, and the difficulty of choosing begot satiety; besides I had not recovered from the nausea produced in my way through the village, by my own delectable countrywomen. Then again, the most prodigal superfluity is poor whilst aught, however worthless, is with-held. The triumph of the antique dromedary made me indignant, as she continued to repeat that she had brought together for my selection, every specimen of the district. 'No,' said I, 'it is a feast without salt. Where is my Malay?—she is the only girl who can make a chillam, or light a hooka.' The hag raised her hump in astonishment, and exclaimed:—'What! dat ass-eared, ring-snouted beast! Faugh! How can you tink of her?' Then, mumbling incantations between her horny lips, she continued,—'You had better send for de English women next,—stink like de rotten dog-fish, soft as de prickly pear.'

I grew peremptory that the Malay girl, Moosoo, should be produced; and the jingling girls slunk off in wonder and contempt at my unclean and unaccountably bad taste.

On entering the hut I had ordered an ample supply of the ingredients for composing what doctors designate by the name of liquid fire, but which the unlearned call punch. Of this I poured so much down my throat to allay the consuming thirst and retrieve the loss of animal moisture, that it nearly deprived me of my senses. 'Come, Antiquity! Come old mother Hump!' said I, 'hand out my little smutty!'

'I say, she not here. She gone to cocoa-nut grove, to set de toddy pots.'

'That's a lie, old Sycorax! I want her upstairs, she is beautifying herself with cocoa-nut oil not fetching toddy.'

'Why you no believe me? I never tell lie.'

'Truth, you mean—old Damnable! Come—here goes!'

As I staggered toward the ladder, old mother Midnight stood before me to prevent my going up, when I sent her reeling into the room, snatched up a piece of blazing pine-wood, and ascended into a sort of loft. This was the ante-chamber of the nymphs, where they were squatted down on their heels like a bed of toad-stools. Half a score of the house sprouted up to mar my further progress. This would have impelled me on, had I been sober; but, with the pertinacity of drunkenness, I was about to do more, for I cried out,—'Keep off! you devil's kittens, or I'll see if you are true-bred salamanders, or not!' and was applying the fire to the cane-work of the hut.

They fell back with a discordant croak, and I rolled into the sacred gynecaeum, wrenching away the matting which enclosed it, when a rough voice bawled out, 'Hold fast there, you young dog!'

'Holla, old Hoofs!' I exclaimed, recognising the voice of my late Captain, and saluting him with his nickname among us, from the preposterous dimensions of his feet; 'Holla! old clod-hopper; you here! and by all that's holy, in bed with my Malay!'

'Get out, Sir! What do you mean by this audacity? Why are you not aboard, Sir? Don't you know the orders?'

'Get out!—and leave you in bed with my—sister! No, I won't; and I don't intend going on board again. I am discharged, most potent Signor!'

'I see you are drunk, Sir.'

'I drunk! Come, old commodore, what the devil do you mean by turning in with my sister? By the blood of all our tribe, I'll unman you if you don't make reparation!'

'What do you mean, you scoundrel?'

'Mean! Why you must marry my sister, leave the accursed ship, and be my bailiff; for I am going to turn agriculturalist, and make manure of old mother Rubbish here. Say, are you satisfied, Captain Turnip? But you look like a skuttle-fish, white and dry about the gills. Hoist up there a tank full of drink! Come rig yourself, old Hoofs! I'll make 'em treat you with proper respect.'

With that I put his coat and gold-laced hat on the hump-backed harridan, and insisted that he should get up and drink.

He, seeing I was not to be balked in my humour, gave way to me, and indeed, not being a very austere character, he entered into the frolic; besides, though not drunk, he was not sober.

We sat over our punch, while I sung, or rather roared, the song of the 'Old Commodore,'

> 'Blast the old Commodore!
> The bullets and the gout
> Have so knocked his hull about,
> He'll no longer be fit for sea.'

Then in return for his kindness in playing the parson, when he read prayers every Sunday, out of soundings, I treated him with a sermon, expatiating on his manifold sins and iniquities, especially with the Malay, and the awful injury committed against me, her brother, and against his own lady at home, the affectionate mother of his innocent and sucking babes. Yet, notwithstanding the orthodoxy of my doctrine, and the courtesy with which maiden speeches and sermons are attended to, the old Commodore was as impatient to be off, as if he had been seated on lunar caustic.

While I could distinguish him from the old mother, I barred all egress. He plied me with grog, till the last glimmerings of my reasoning faculties were flickering in the socket, then another beaker,—and I could not distinguish his hoof from her hump and every thing became quadrupled. Some Nâch girls dancing in the room, and shaking their bangles, looked like devils; while the volcanic fire within my body, together with the oven-like closeness of the room, impressed me with a notion that I was in hell. The Captain stole away during the time I was dragging down a bamboo rafter, with which I demolished the cudgeree-pots, and all within its swing. The hag grew furious at the destruction of her household gods and goods, and called out for the Burkandazers, (police-officers of the village.) Thus backed, she made a furious attack upon me, the old Fiend-skin calling out 'You more like tiger, not than man. You no go my house. I make sepoys come kill you. I never see such *obstroperousness* when I live.'

CHAPTER XX

The last of human sounds which rose,
As I was darted from my foes,
Was the wild shout of savage laughter,
Which on the wind came roaring after
A moment from the rabble rout;
With sudden wrath I wrenched my head,
And writhing half my form about,
Howl'd back my curse.

* * * * *

Away!—away!—my breath was gone—
I saw not where he hurried on:
'Twas scarcely yet the break of day,
And on he foamed—away!—away!

BYRON

THE hubbub within soon brought up some sepoys from without. On seeing a fellow's pike peering above the ladder, my blood began to rise, and my passion to sober me. Hecate and her witches were hanging on me like a pack of terriers on a badger. I now first missed the Captain; and surmising he had sent a guard of Sepoys, I shook off, with a sudden effort, the lethargic effect of drink, as well as the old and young devil stickers, as the tiger does his parasite providers, the jackalls, when he himself is hunted. Regaining the bamboo, I drove them down the ladder; in their confusion, their weight, with the addition of the flabby governante, broke the ladder, when they fell, and formed a cone-like hill below, of which she was the apex; she plumped down like a Dutch dogger out of the slips, sepoy and all vanishing beneath her ample beam. Great was the uproar which succeeded. A dense crowd had collected outside, with a sprinkling of peons, sepoys, and police.

I now thought it time to remove myself. One wick of the shattered lamp was still burning; with that I lighted some cotton dipped in oil, and fired the house in several places. Its dry and combustible materials rapidly brightened up into a fierce flame. A wild shout from without-side proclaimed the event. I had no time to lose. Amidst the burning and crackling, I precipitated myself from the window, and luckily alighted on the sepoy-halbadier. I was not hurt, but he was. Springing up, I seized his pike, which had fallen from his hand, used it as a quarter-staff and cleared my way, till I gained the shed in which my horse was tethered. I clapped the bit in his mouth; but in the darkness and hurry not finding my saddle, I mounted without it, and took the field.

Determined on seeing the fire, I turned round on the sepoys and others, who were close at my heels; and putting my spear in the rest, like a knight of old, I dashed full tilt down the narrow lane, broke through them, and spitted one against a small mud temple, well nigh immolating him as an offering to the god Bramah; while my vicious and sacrilegious horse thrust his impious hoofs into the very penetralia of the piscina, a little nich, with a pipkin-bellied idol, and a cudgeree-pot of perfumed rice, which were dashed to atoms. They yelled curses at us,—'Yaoar! Dog!' but, under the dark wing of night, we escaped the missiles which were hurled after us, and we heeded not words. We now sprang into the middle of the crowd gathered before the conflagration, and created much havoc. I came upon them in great wrath, for I had but a little time to stay. The mob fled before me like wild ducks. As old Muckery was busying herself, with a long bamboo, in fishing out her traps, I applied the sharp end of my pike to her nether parts, and goaded her into the embers. She grasped a number of flaming bamboos, and, missing me, burnt the horse; upon which he rushed forward, kicking and rearing with ungovernable fury. I could neither stop, nor check him. We cleared the village.

Away we went as free and fast as the wind. My head became
dizzy; and rushing through the fresh air, after a heated room,
made me death-like sick. With difficulty I clung to my seat, un-
assisted by saddle. All around me was darkness and gloom.
I crossed a wide jeel, where my sagacious Bucephalus plumped
into a ford, and waded and swam to the opposite bank. With my
head laid down on his neck, I held on by his long, shaggy mane.
As I knew I was receding from the fort, I cared not whither he
bore me. Fain would I have pulled up, for I was overcome by a
drunken drowsiness, but one of the reins had given way, and my
mettled courser speeded on, reeling, and floundering, and blowing like a grampus, I know not how long, for I was hardly sensible.
He made towards a glimmering light: it belonged to a chokey, and
striking there against something, the shock was like that of a ship
against a rock. He gave two or three heavy rolls and fell on me,
as I had fallen on the sepoy. I became insensible; and long I must
have continued so.

On opening my eyes, I gazed around with astonishment, and
felt as after a trance. A group of people, squatted on their haunches,
encircled me. A thin and wizard-visaged old man, with the peeta
of a Bramin, seemed mumbling incantations; all I could distinguish
was,—'*Topee Sahib!*'—'*Ram, ram, ram!*'—and '*Dum, dum, dum!*'
A better looking, and better garmented man, with a grisly beard,
said nothing but—'*Il' Allah!*'

I tried to sit up, and signed to give me water; they shook their
heads. My mouth was glued, I could not speak, and was faint with
thirst. I found I was lying on a mat, under the shade of a bunyan's
shop, with verandahs. He came out on hearing I was alive, and
spoke to me in English;—no music was ever so harmonious. He
brought me a cudgeree-pot of toddy, which revived me; no drink
was ever so delicious. Close to me stood a bheestie, gazing and
gaping with wonder; a bamboo was poised across his shoulder,
supporting two buckets of palmetta-leaf, full of water. He had
been entreated by my gestures to let me have some, but he grinned
refusal. I now grasped hold of the rim of the bucket, and tilted it
over my head. The water hissed on my burning temples; instantly
I felt a thrilling sensation of pleasure; and I sat up.

Then I discovered I was at a village near the road to Callian.
It was long ere I could recollect the events of the passed day. My
bones ached as if I had been beaten to a mummy; and my face,

head, and hands were cut. The horse was first recalled to my mind by a lock from his long mane, which was entwined in my fingers, still clenched. I went into the shop, and, lying down again, fell into a profound sleep. I awoke, when the sun was sinking in the west, drenched with perspiration. After eating some fruit, I went to a tank, bathed, and felt as man new made.

Ruminating on my situation, and remembering I was to meet De Ruyter at the bungalo, I inquired for my horse. They knew nothing of him. I had been carried by some cooleys from the chokey, and laid in the bazaar. By the advice of the shop-keepers, I hired a buffaloe-hackerie, and proceeded towards the rendezvous.

CHAPTER XXI

> There is a pleasure in the pathless woods,
>   There is a rapture on the lonely shore,
> There is society where none intrudes
>   By the deep sea, and music in its roar:
>   I love not man the less but nature more,
> From these our interviews, in which I steal
>   From all I may be, or have been before,
> To mingle with the universe, and feel
>   What I can ne'er express, yet cannot well conceal.
>
> BYRON

An author, justly celebrated for his knowledge of human nature, observes: 'Let a man be ever so honest, the account of his own conduct will, in spite of himself, be so very favourable, that his vices will come purified through his lips; for though the facts themselves may appear, yet so different will be the motives, circumstances, and consequences, when a man tells his own story, and when his enemy tells it, that we can scarce recognise the facts to be one and the same thing.'

In twenty hours I arrived at a small village, on the frontiers of the Deccan; and there, having discharged my hackerie, I picked up a couple of cooleys, passed through some paddy and Indian corn-fields, crossed a ford, and reached De Ruyter's bungalo, which I knew by land-marks he had given me, and by the compass. It was prettily situated on a rising ground at the foot of a mountain, in a retired nook, hid in a grove of cocoa-trees, which love a light and shingly soil, and sheltered by hills to the north, east, and west. There was a wild garden, overgrown with guava, mango, and pomegranate trees, and surrounded by a high and impervious fence of prickly pear. The inside of the house was painted in blue and white stripes to look like a tent, the roof of the centre room being supported by upright bamboos, on which were suspended arms, guns, and spears for the chace. Two sleeping apartments adjoining to this were divided by split bamboos and matting. It was furnished with a tent-table, beds, and other conveniences; a few books and drawing-materials; with rough but spirited sketches of ships, and of lion and tiger-hunts, hanging on the wall. A small open space before the door, studded with banana and lemon-trees, drooping with fruit, sloped down to a large tank, used as a bath, encircled with rose, jessamine, and geranium. An old peasant, in charge of the place, said, 'You see, master, it is *ungregi*,—English fashion.' On the east side of the bungalo, canopied by a magnificent sago-palm, was a long, low shed, which served for kitchen; and under the same roof dwelt the peasant, with his wife and family, and a yâk, or little cow, which was squabbling with the children about some fruit.

This yâk was remarkably small and wiry haired. The man told me she was good, strong to ride, and that his malek (master) had brought her *out from the sea*.

'A sea-monster!' I said with a laugh, 'come, then, we'll have a swim together!' and was going to turn her into the tank.

'No, no, she like go up mountain; no like go down water.'

I inquired if he had seen his malek lately. 'No,' he replied, 'but he had sent, two days back, much things for huzoor,' another name for master.

'Did he not write?' Upon which he took a scanty rag turban from his pate, and extracted from its folds, where it was carefully enveloped, a plaintain leaf, doubled up and secured with a piece of coir twine. I cast off the leaf, and found a note from De Ruyter.

'Why the devil,' I asked, 'did you not give me this before?'

'You not tell me to.'

'No, for how could I know you had it?'

'Yes, malek know everything; poor gaowala-man know nothing at all.'

This made me comprehend why no eatables had been offered to me, while I was ravenous as a wolf in winter, notwithstanding

I had kept my jaws in perpetual motion with all sorts of fruit. I therefore ordered tiffin, and returned to the house to read the letter; by which I learned that the frigate had sailed, after some little inquiry for me at my usual quarters. This was a great relief, and my heart leaped with joy. 'Aye,' thought I, 'thanks to my having trapped the old Commodore in a bordello and made him drunk. A lucky hit! Though it was not designed. He recollected my ballad with a caricature and feared another for himself.'

De Ruyter concluded his letter by saying he had been detained by Walter, who was placed under arrest while the affair of the Scotch lieutenant was investigated; and notwithstanding every lie had been invented to implicate Walter, De Ruyter's evidence acquitted him. The ship was delayed one day, to inquire into the affair, and to remove the Scotchman on board; for he was very ill, spitting blood, with two of his ribs stove in; so that, together with the dislocation of his jaw, and loss of ivory, I considered my debt to him handsomely cancelled, and sponged the rascal from my memory, I thought for ever. Walter had offered him satisfaction, but he was surfeited with what he had already received. I afterwards learned that he never ventured on shore at Bombay, saying that malaria, musquitoes, and scorpions, made it worse than hell; but what he dreaded more than the cobra-di-capella itself, was the sight of Walter there.

I sent a cooley to bring me a hooka, and a girl from the village, bathed in the tank, and, with a book, the 'Life of Paul Jones,' lay under the trees, eating my dessert after an abundant Indian lunch. A lightness, elasticity, and exuberance of joy, never felt before, thrilled through me. It was the first day I could number of entire happiness; nor did I then, as in more mature years we do, dash the present hour with thinking on the ensuing one. The only happy life appeared to be a peasant's; and his limited wants the cause of his being happy. Forthwith I essayed it, threw my torn and soiled garments from me, twisted a piece of striped cotton, as cummerbund, round my waist, and put a turban on my head. Thus, barefooted, with a cocoa-knife in my hand, and well greased with cocoa-nut oil, I sallied into the grove, and, with the peasant's family, ascended the trees, learnt how to tap them, and how to hang the toddy-pots. This and gardening made my time pass on so smoothly, that, on the third day, when I received

notice of De Ruyter's being on the road, I felt it as an inter-
ruption on my quiet and my solitude.

However I mounted the yâk, a bamboo in one hand and my
knife in the other, and went forth, preceded by two coolies, to
meet him. Suddenly turning a tope of neem trees, he was before
me, occupied in narrating a history of lion-hunting to Walter,
and so complete was my metamorphosis, that he was passing on
without recognition, until his quick eye rested on his own yâk.
I hailed him with, — 'Holloa! De Ruyter, — what cheer, ho!' They
pulled up in astonishment; and, after surveying me an instant,
they set up such a wild roar of laughter that I thought them out
of their senses. De Ruyter rolled off his horse, and held his sides,
exclaiming, 'By Heaven, you'll kill me, you mad-cap!'

Looking very serious, I observed, 'I am not aware of any thing
sufficiently ludicrous to excite your merriment. I am rigged in
the fashion of the country; and it is best adapted to the climate, —
is it not? If you like to have some fresh toddy, here are these
fellows with my cudgeree-pots full of the freshest, and of my
own tapping.'

We sat down on the bank, talked, and, when they were weary
of their mirth, I remounted my yâk, preceding them to the bungalo.

We passed two days of unalloyed happiness. We climbed the
hills, we chased the jackalls, regardless of heat or toil; we sung
and danced, not as in the days of slavery from the excitement of
drink, for we were drunk with joy.

De Ruyter and I were both, from choice, of plain and simple
habits. He never committed any excesses, and those I was guilty
of arose from my volcanic materials, which were fired like powder,
from any accidental spark, though struck by an ass's hoof. In
everything I undertook, no matter how ridiculous, I must out-
herod Herod, brooking no compeer. My brow now burns with
shame in remembering how many follies (to give them the mild-
est term,) I then, and afterwards committed. Severity and constant thwarting had accumulated within me so much of the subtle
spirit of opposition and obstinacy, that it has mingled itself with
every action of my life; while my judgment and better feelings
have in vain struggled to stem the stream that bore me on. False
lights have distorted the fairest and brightest scenes of my existence; converting that which was really good and beautiful to
blackness, and leading me to act the characters I most despised.

Thus I have played the drunkard, the glutton, the braggart, and the bully. My wrong view of things must have been the effect of education and example, for by nature I was the reverse of all this, and when acting on sudden impulses, I have seldom erred.

CHAPTER XXII

The kings of Inde their jewel-sceptres veil,
And from their treasures scatter pearled hail;
Great Bramah from his mystic heaven groans,
And all his priesthood moans.   KEATS

He felt assured
Of happy times, when all he had endured
Would seem a feather to the mighty prize.

Ib.

AFTER the second day Walter was compelled to return to his regiment. As he was delighted with his new profession, so was he determined to be exemplary in the fulfilment of his duty. Though we had talked day and night with little intermission, we could not afford time to say a word either of the past, or of our plans for the future. We therefore agreed to have a speedy meeting to discuss these points. On the morning of his departure he said, 'You are now a free agent and an idler. We are encamped on the artillery-ground. Come to my tent. What I have, you may command. I wish to Heaven you would procure a commission in our regiment —you could do so.'

'No, no, Walter; the badge of servitude, blue or red, I have shaken off for ever. King nor Company shall bribe me with their gold, their honours, or their frippery, to give up my birthright of free agency. And for what?—bread?—I can find its substitute on every bush.'

'Ay,' he replied; 'but you love glory, and cannot live without broils and fighting.'

'If so I can find enough of it in the world, and choose my own ground and cause, not fight like a butcher's dog, on compulsion, because I am fed on my master's offal, and feed with sixpence a day. You, Walter, will be slipped like a dog from his collar against these subdued and trampled-on slaves. Your masters foment disunion and enmity among them, and then despatch their myrmidons to seize upon their wealth and country, to make them helots, or exterminate them as rebels and traitors. Is this glory? Now, if I want fighting, I shall most assuredly change my colours, and battle against tyrants and oppressors wherever they are to be found—and where are they not?'

To this he said, 'Do not let us disturb these few last minutes at parting with discussion. Perhaps I think with you—perhaps you know that such are my sentiments; but I am not made of the same tough stuff as you are. Alas! my poor mother has known nothing but sorrow and disappointment! Her existence has been cheerless. In my helpless years no hand but her's caressed me— I knew no resting-place but on her bosom—and when I could distinguish one from another, I never left her dear presence. When I was ill she lulled me to sleep by singing and by her harp, and sealed my eye-lids with kisses and tears. Once, in the wild spirit of healthy boyhood, I asked her—heaven knows how innocently!—for my father. She laid her head on the table, and the room shook with her convulsive sobs!'

Walter turned away his head, struggling in vain to speak without sobbing aloud. At length, with an effort, he continued, 'You may think me a boy still to talk thus, for you do not know the pure and intense love which two hearts united, and indifferent to all others, can feel—a friendless mother and her orphan child! How can I, knowing that the dear angel has stinted herself, perhaps of the necessaries of life, in order to remove me from a situation in which she thought I suffered—for I forbore to tell her so directly —how can I, now that her exertions and prayers have been heard, destroy her fondest hopes? At least I am removed to a comparative state of happiness, and after two years, I shall be allowed leave of absence to go to England, and then—but tell me, can I—would you—deny such a parent any thing?'

I had followed his example in turning away my face, for I could not reply. So it is in civilized life!—we were ashamed of our feelings when natural, and glory, if not in atrocity, in assumed apathy.

He then added, 'Come to me, and that speedily. We will talk over your plans, and remember, whatever you do, or I do, we are always brothers. Here, take this book—it has almost unfitted me for my new profession—it is written for you, and for men with souls like yours. I must try to forget it, but who can estrange his mind from truth?'

He wrung my hand, and was out of sight. When I looked towards De Ruyter, who had been calmly smoking his hooka under a tree, I perceived he was rubbing his eyes with his rough and red hand. 'That Walter,' said he, 'will make women of us all. Now, I loved my mother too—but cannot talk of her. And like him, I had no father—at least I never knew him!' He then, as was his custom when moved, bent his head to the ground, and smoked with redoubled violence. After a pause, he went on with, 'That is a good-hearted fellow, but he has sucked too much of his mother's milk—it has almost made him a girl. What book is that he has given you?—his mother's bible—or a drawling psalter?—or a cookery book?—or an army list?' He took it out of my hand. 'Ha!' he cried out, 'Volney's *Ruins of Empires and Laws of Nature!*[1] By the God of Nature the fellow has some soul! Had I known this sooner, I would have worked him to a better purpose!' But, after a moment's reflection, he said, 'No! a crooked stick, though straightened, is ever struggling to resume its natural bend. I confide in men like yourself, men naturally upright and resolved. They may be warped too by their humours, or by force; but, in the end, they will resume their uprightness, or be broken. Come, I must return to town to-morrow; and in ten days I am going to sea. What do you intend to do?'

'Why, I have not yet,' I answered, 'given it a thought. I like this sort of quiet life.'

At this he smiled, and said: 'Well, my dear fellow, don't balk your wishes. The bungalo is yours, if you like it. Let me see,—there are sixteen cocoa-nut trees,—the devil's in it if they and the garden won't keep you and your yâk in your natural state; for old Saboo there keeps himself, and frow, and half a score of young ones, with half their number. Think of their value: from their sap you have toddy; toddy fermented becomes arrack; the fruit, with rice, is an excellent curry; and compressed, you have abundance of oil to brighten your skin, and lighten your darkness; then of every shell you can make a cup; the husks will furnish you with bedding, twine, cordage, ropes, and cables; and the tree itself, when old, may be formed into a canoe. Some of these commodities you can barter for rice and ghee.'

'So I will; besides, I can live on fruit, and hunt, and shoot.'

'Do so, my lad. Only, as the most exquisite luxuries do pall, and become nauseous from possession, so may these, all exquisite as they are. Remember I have a lovely little craft, well armed and formed for peace or war, as occasion serves, merely lacking an enterprising commander; such a one as I once thought you would prove,—but I was mistaken.'

'Where, De Ruyter, is she? You never told me of this. Come, where is she?'

'You forget your toddy, your cudgeree-pots, and pastoral life.'

'Oh, no, I don't! But, let us just have a look at the craft. How is she rigged? Where does she lie? How many tons? How many men? What is she to be employed in?'

'By no means. You appear so admirably adapted for a baboo life, you had better go on with old Saboo. Perhaps next year you may like to take a tour among the islands, and pick up a few Persian and Hindoo girls, for the propagation of peasantry;—is that in your law of nature?'

Thus he went on, bantering and laughing, but would give no reply to my questions regarding the vessel. As he was in the habit of journeying in the night, as soon as the great bear shone on the verge of the Heavens, he shook my hand, threw a bag of pagodas on the table, bade me deny myself nothing money could procure, promised to be with me in a few days, and returned to Bombay.

CHAPTER XXIII

> I could not choose but gaze; a fascination
> Dwelt in that moon, and sky, and clouds, which drew
> My fancy thither, and, in expectation
> Of what I knew not, I remained.
>
>   SHELLEY

THE night was such as is often seen in the east. Every near object, fruit and flower, illumined by the bright, deep, and liquid light of the moon and stars, was, in shape and colour, as distinguishable and clear as by day. The pale and softened tints, the bland and gentle air, fanning the drooping trees, formed a delightful contrast to the flaming and red-hot glare of the day, when the eyes are dazzled, and we gasp, as if under suffocation, in the hot atmosphere.

I sat down on the green slope, listened to the hooting of the owls and watched the flitting of the large vampyre bats round the tank, until I fell asleep. My dreams were of De Ruyter, of the Indian islands, of Walter; but at last I started up at the abhorred voice of the Scotch lieutenant, saying,—'How now, Sir!—asleep on your watch!—gae to the mast head and waken yoursel!' Looking up, I beheld not that snarling cur, but honest old Saboo, who was waking me with this warning,—'No good sleep in sun; make sick; house good to sleep.' I was cold and cramped. The sun was up. Ordering some toddy, I went down to the tank, plunged in, and was myself again.

The quiet and happy time I passed here was uncontaminated by disgust. However, I had resumed a jacket and trowsers, my skin not being musquito proof; and, having inadvertently trampled on a nest of young centipedes, I was glad to replace my shoes.

From my earliest remembrance, I was subject to occasional melancholy; but not of the gloomy kind; rather a pleasing and soothing sensation than otherwise. This solitude was well-adapted to awaken the shadowy phantoms that are created in the imagination. Mingled with these, realities forced themselves upon me, and at last I began to ponder on my singular position. There was a strangeness and mystery in the actions and pursuits of De Ruyter, which I could not develope, and which fascinated and spell-bound my spirit. The rapidity with which he had gained an influence over me was marvellous. His frankness, courage, and generosity—the nobleness of his nature—his liberal and en-lightened sentiments, so unlike the merchants and money-traders I had seen, convinced me he was none of them. After reflecting on his words, and what I had witnessed of his conduct, I concluded he was commander of a private ship of war. But then neither the English nor the Americans had any in India; the French indeed had something of the sort; but, if under their flag, what did he in an English port, and apparently on friendly terms there? My next conclusion was that he was an agent of some of the Rajahs, who still were independent sovereigns, although the Company were drawing their circles within circles around them, till they became driven from their fastnesses to the plain, to fall on any prey. These princes, whether at peace or war, were known to have secret agents in the presidencies, to transmit to them early intelligence of the movements and policy of the Company's residents. De Ruyter seemed admirably fitted for this service; though he could not, or did not care always to disguise his indignation at what, he thought, the barbarous policy, intolerance, and arrogance of the Anglo-Indian dictation in India. His brow used to darken, his lip to quiver, and his eye to dilate, as he narrated, with thundering voice, instances of its cruelty, extortion, and presumption. Yet he liked England, and individuals of that nation, though he preferred those of America, his adopted country. He observed: 'It is curious that all nations who are blessed with the greatest portion of liberty at home, govern their colonies with the most remorseless and unmeasured despotism.' Then he would add: 'Fortunately for mankind it is so; it forms the only hope of freedom's being ever universal. When goaded past endurance, the most patient animal will turn, armed with the invincibility which despair gives;—the wild cat will do so against the tiger,—I have seen him do it.'

This, and much more, which I now remembered of De Ruyter, convinced me he was not what he seemed, but left me still in doubt as to what he really was. If my surmises were well grounded, I felt I should like him the better; and I entertained not the slightest hesitation in placing myself under his pilotage, from every thing I had seen of him. He was after my own heart.

He sent me frequent notes and messages; and as his departure was protracted, I could no longer refuse Walter's pressing invitation; so that one evening I mounted a horse he had provided for me, and on the following night I was canopied under his comfortable tent. He took a boyish delight in pointing out and particularising all his comforts and advantages, contrasting them with his early privations and sufferings. As not a particle of envy was in my disposition, I participated in his feelings. He had already become a favourite with the officers; and having told them part of my story, we were hail-fellows-well-met the first night I passed in the camp. Escorted by a party of them, I returned in a palanquin to my old quarters in Bombay.

My time passed agreeably, either in the camp, or at the bungalo, where I made parties, or at the tavern in Bombay; De Ruyter joining us when not employed about his affairs,—or business, as he called it.

CHAPTER XXIV

Man, who man would be,
Must rule the empire of himself; in it
Must be supreme, establishing his throne
On vanquished will, quelling the anarchy
Of hopes and fears, being himself alone.

SHELLEY

DE RUYTER now took me on board of an Arab grab brig, remarkable for its lean, wedge-like, and elongated bow. She was rigged
as a hermaphrodite; and, as is the custom with the Arabs, she had
disproportionate square yards. Her crew were partly Arabs; and
the remainder, by their colour and dress, shewed they were of
various castes. She was unloading a cargo of cotton and spices,
purchased, I was told, by the Company. De Ruyter very seldom
went on board of her; but her captain, called the Rais, was daily
with him. They generally met on board a small and very singular
craft, called a dow. She was chiefly manned with Arabs; but to
my surprise the sprinkling among them was of European seamen,
Danes and Swedes, with two or three Americans. These were
secreted on board, for what purpose I did not then know; but
I was especially cautioned not to mention the circumstance on
shore. This dow had a large mast forward, and gigger-mast aft.
She was the clumsiest and most unsightly craft I had ever seen in
India. Her head and stern, raised and raking, were of light bamboo
work. She seemed crank, and to have little hold of the water. On
De Ruyter's asking me if I should like to have the command of
her, I answered, 'Yes; when I cannot get a catamaran, or masuli
boat, I may possibly hazard my carcase on board her.'

'I see you are particular,' said he. 'Now though I have my
choice, I shall, from preference, go to sea in her. Perhaps you,
being fastidious, may prefer the grab?'

'Why,' I replied, 'knock the shark's head off her, and ship a
bowsprit in its place, with a lick of tar and paint, I should be well
content to take a cruise in her. Besides, I like the look of those
Arabs, and of those savage, lean, wild-eyed fellows, with their red
caps, jackets and turbans. I never saw cleaner or lighter made
fellows to fly aloft in a squall, or board an enemy in battle.'

'Yes, they are our best men, and come from Dacca; and they'll fight a bit, I can tell you.'

'But then I should like to have something to fight with.'

'O, she has guns!'

'I hate those pea-shooter-looking things on her gunnels. A few twelves, or short twenty-fours, would not be too much for her. She has a beautiful water line, and a run aft like a schooner. Her bow is of the leanest, and her beam being so far aft, I doubt she pitches damnably in a swell. Nevertheless there is a varment and knowing look about her which I like.'

'Well, will you run her down the coast to Goa. I'll follow in the old dow. When the sun sets, get on board, and weigh with the land wind. You see she is already removed into the roadstead, and ready for sea. At daylight I shall get under weigh. I have told the Rais that you are going in the grab, and to obey you. I'll give you a few notes, in case of an accident separating us, though it is not probable. Come along. Remember you are a passenger to Goa. Not a word more to Walter! When we get into blue water, you shall know every thing. Are you satisfied?'

'I am. I should not have held on so long without questioning, had I not entire confidence in you, De Ruyter. Where you go, never doubt but I'll follow. I have not a very squeamish stomach, and am no changeling.'

'Very well! But have one thing uppermost in your mind. Before you can govern others, you must be perfect master of yourself. That you may be so, do not, like a girl, let words or gestures betray your purpose. A loose word spoken in passion, or an embarrassed look, may mar your designs, however ably planned. Above all things do not indulge in wine; for that, they say, opens the heart, and who but a fool would betray himself, perhaps to those on the watch to entrap him?'

'You know I drink but little.'

'True; but now I wish you not to drink at all.'

On my staring at him, he smiled, and said: 'That is, for the present. If you do indulge, do so with tried friends only. But you had better not drink; for I know you can more easily abstain altogether, than follow a middle course. Is it not so?'

'I believe you are in the right.'

After our return on shore, stopping near the tavern, he said: 'Give your orders to those boatmen as to the things you want.

You'll find almost every thing you can have occasion for on board;
and that is lucky for you, as you are a most heedless person.'

Just before the sun had sunk to rest, I received De Ruyter's
parting instructions, shook hands with him, and leapt into the
boat. The Rais, who spoke English very well, received me on
board, and shewed me into the cabin. I gave him a letter from De
Ruyter; he put it to his forehead, read it, and asked me at what
time I wished to get under weigh, as he was referred to me.
I answered, at twelve; such were my instructions. I bade him hoist
the boats in, stow them, and have every thing prepared for sea.

While he executed these orders, I looked over De Ruyter's
pencilled memorandums. Though I certainly understood I was
to have the command of the vessel, if I wished it, I could not
account for the strange way in which it was enforced upon me.
The Rais would do nothing without my orders. 'Well,' thought
I, 'with all my heart! To-morrow we shall meet the dow, and then
De Ruyter will enlighten me.'

Mine had been such a dog's life in those situations in which
my guardians had placed me, that I could not possibly, seeking
my fortunes blindfold, stumble on any thing more miserable; so
that not only without hesitation, but with a joyful alacrity, my
mind was instantly made up to execute any thing De Ruyter, the
only person who seemed interested in my fate, thought fit to
employ me in. I took a hasty turn or two on the deck, with a firm
step and proud glance, which command gives; and spoke with
kindness to the Serang and others, as a man does in the fresh
bloom of office.

Though the vessel was in a disorderly trade-like trim, she was
not deficient in the essentials of defensive, if not offensive warfare.
Her masts and sails, with the coir running rigging, had a slovenly
look to a man of war-man's eye; and, from the want of tar and
paint, she had a bronze hue. Notwithstanding, on a close inspection, you could see she had been fitted up with great care in all
essential points, and with many of the modern European improvements. In measurement she was about three hundred tons, but
could stow little more than half. She had a deep waist, pierced
with portholes for guns, but battened in, except the two forward
and four after ones, which had six long nine pounders. Her gunnels
were armed with swivels. Her forecastle was raised; and abaft
she had a low poop, or half deck, under which was the principal

cabin. As the last stroke on the gong sounded eight o'clock, the sailors' supper time, I instinctively returned to this after-cabin; the grave, which time had dug in my stomach since mid-day, yawning to be filled up. Swarms of men, with the same intention, hastened from below, squatted on their heels in small circles, divided by caste, and turned to with their messala (messes), of rice, ghee, dried bumbalo, curry, fresh fruit, and dried chillies.

Having filled up the aforesaid vacuum, I laid down on the couch, smoked De Ruyter's hooka, and took an inventory of the cabin. It was low, but roomy; and well lighted and cooled from the stern ports. There were two sleeping births on the opposite sides; and in the spaces between them and the upper deck were two stars of pistols; that is, fourteen or sixteen pistols in each, with their muzzles together, their butts forming the radii. The fore bulk-head was closely ribbed with bamboo spars; the outer portion was ranged with musquets; and there was a garnish of bayonets, and jagged Malayan creeses, arrayed in most fanciful forms. This was the 'fitting for war,' as De Ruyter called it. Then the after part was certainly dedicated to peace, its shelves being crammed with books, writing materials, and nautical instruments; and the ceiling, low as it was, had a number of rolled charts suspended between the beams; while in the middle of the centre-beam swung the transversed compass. In other nooks and corners were telescopes; and, though less picturesque, yet equally indispensable, such articles as I had called in requisition for my supper.

Not being forbidden to sleep, nor having the fear of punishment over my head for neglect of duty, I was wakeful and alert. My mind was occupied by the responsibility with which my friend had intrusted me. I walked the deck, gazing at the dog-vane, to see it wooed by the land wind; but, as De Ruyter said, it was near twelve before this took place. Then I ordered the Rais to get under weigh, and, if possible, without noise. The first, he said, was easy work; but the last impossible. We weighed our anchor, and went to sea.

CHAPTER XXV

With thee, my bark, I'll swiftly go
    Athwart the foaming brine;
Nor care what land thou bear'st me to,
    So not again to mine.

Welcome, welcome, ye dark blue waves!
    And, when you fail my sight,
Welcome ye deserts and ye caves!
    My native land, good night!

BYRON

ALL whose physical and mental powers, no matter of what metal they are composed, when forced into premature developement by artificial means, or by the communication of cities, attain the rapid and wire-drawn growth of plants and herbs in the dense shelter of a forest. Early they put forth their leaves and buds, but seldom if ever more; or if they do produce fruit, it is unwholesome and nauseous. When transplanted from their shelter into the open spaces of the world, the first frost or storm destroys them. So it is with animals: the power of the high-bred racer, forced by exciting food and clothing, does indeed give an early promise of strength, but never realised. He is cut off in the dawn of his prime, with all the symptoms of age and decay.

There are in the north some few men, and women too, who, without this care and culture, spring up into their full growth with the marvellous rapidity of the east; and the germs of life and hardiness within them are not to be subdued, perceptibly, by time or toil; so that, at the age when ordinary beings become extinguished, these iron ones yet hold their ground, sturdy and upright. Such were the patriarchs of the olden time; and now that the world is more ripe with war, disease and adventure, diminishing their numbers, yet such beings are to be found, who outlive all kin and kind, who cease to count time by years, but refer to the page of history and past events, and wonder of what malady a brother died at fourscore.

Though not one of these granite pillars, I gave token, not artificially, of belonging to their hardy breed, for, at this period of my life, I had attained the attributes of perfect manhood. I was six feet in stature, robust, and bony, almost to gauntness; and, with the strength of maturity, I had the flexibility of limb which youth alone can give. Naturally of a dark hue, my complexion readily taking a darker from the sun, I was now completely bronzed. My hair was black, and my features perfectly Arab. At seventeen I looked to be seven and twenty. Then, having in extreme youth, been left to jostle my way through the crowd, I had made a proportionate advance in, what is called, worldly knowledge, which experience alone, not years, can teach.

In the way I have related the course of my first acquaintance and subsequent friendship with De Ruyter, I am fearful that some may be impressed with an erroneous idea that he was selfishly working on the malleability of my youth. I can speak now with proof of his having been assayed on the touchstone of time, and found true gold. De Ruyter himself was in reality a friendless wanderer; a man self-exiled, from out the pale of civilization and its ties; and with a highly wrought imagination, and cultivated mind, it was natural he should seek objects to lavish his affections on, and who could sympathise with him. Such were not easy to be found where he was, and in his unsettled way of life. With the semibarbarians of the East it was out of the question; and the European adventurers were scattered about, busy in the accumulation of wealth, or exclusively engaged in their own separate views of ambition. The few renegado sailors he could pick up from time to time were either deserters, or deserted for their worthlessness. A few associates he had liked were removed by death, or, what is the same thing, distance. He was not formed for an ascetic: his free and buoyant nature impelled him to seek companionship; and having perhaps no predilection at that period, as accident cast me in his way, his feelings were interested in my behalf. He had perfectly seen through me during that period, though short yet full of matter; and nothing doubted but that, with a little time and guidance, I should become what he wished me to be. He perceived that added to the fresh and warm feelings of youth, I possessed honesty, sincerity, and courage, not yet soiled and way-worn by journeying through the sloughs of the world, which few can pass without defilement. The step he took therefore was not so preposterous as superficial lookers-on might conclude. From the hour in which I had consummated my revenge on the lieutenant, in a manner which cut off the possibility of my return to the navy, De Ruyter, seeing I was utterly friendless, became my friend in its true sense, and ever after treated me as such, so that if fathers followed his example, we should have less of that eternal and mawkish cant about filial disobedience, dull as it is false, spawned on society by dry and drawling priests, and incubated by the barren sect of mouldy, virgin blues.[1] His disposition, or restlessness, caused his to be a life of adventure, and consequently of peril. I was a scion of the same stock; my inclinations homogenial; and whether I had met with him or not, I should have run my destined course, though not on the same ground.

As I am writing more for my own gratification, and to beguile the now weary hours, than for strangers, they must be content to give me cable and range enough, while narrating this part of my history, which, however dry and tedious to them, is to me the most interesting. And who that lives, and has a heart not grown sabre-proof, does not glow with pleasure at the remembrance of what he did and felt from seventeen to twenty? With some, both earlier and later remembrances may be equally delightful. Not so with me; for at twenty-one I was like a young steer taken from the pasture to the shambles; or like the wild horse, selected from the herd, and *lazoed* by the South American *gauchoes* in the midst of my career. The fatal noose was cast around my neck, my proud crest humbled to the dust, the bloody bit thrust into my mouth, my shaggy mane trimmed, my hitherto untrammelled back bent with a weight I could neither endure nor shake off, my light and springy action changed into a painful amble,—in short, I was married; and married to—but I must not antedate my European adventures. For the present I must endeavour to forget it, that I may relate my actions in India with the open and fiery spirit which freedom gives; not in the subdued tone of a shackled, care-worn, and spirit-broken married man of the civilized west.

We gently glided out of the port, with just enough of air, as sailors express it, to lull the sails to sleep. At daylight, the port and harbour still in sight on our lea-beam, we discerned the sluggardly old dow under weigh, creeping along the land like a tortoise. At noon a breeze sprung up from the S.W.; and at sunset, relieved by distance from all apprehension of our movements being watched by the port, I bore up, ran some leagues in shore, shortened sail, and hove to. As I had anticipated, with the earliest dawn, when the grey mists evaporated and left a clear line of horizon, it was first broken, as I swept it round with a telescope, by the old dow, like a black spot on the light blue sea, on the bow. I ordered the helmsman to bear up; and with a press of sail we came down on her at eight o'clock. I hailed her, and De Ruyter came on board. We again hauled our wind, and continued our course along the land.

De Ruyter then retired with me to breakfast in the cabin, inquiring of me what I thought of the grab. 'She seems to move,' I said, 'independently of the wind. We passed a man-of-war brig yesterday, as if she were a rock.'

'Yes, in such a light air as this, nothing will come near her. In a heavy head-sea, she does indeed pitch heavily. But if not overpressed, she is light, buoyant, and holds a good wind. Therefore, don't press sail on her, or she will be buried.'

CHAPTER XXVI

Half ignorant they turned an easy wheel,
That set sharp racks at work, to pinch and peel.

Why were they proud? Because their marble founts
   Gush'd with more pride than do a wretch's tears?
Why were they proud? Because fair orange mounts
   Were of more soft ascent than lazar stairs?
Why were they proud? Because red-lined accounts
   Were richer than the songs of Grecian years?
Why were they proud? again we ask aloud,
Why in the name of Glory were they proud?

KEATS

DE RUYTER, after some other nautical talk, veered round to the point of the compass I desired, commencing with,—'What I told you at Bombay was true;—I was a merchant there. Now, having concluded my mercantile task, I am ready for freighting or fighting; but I am generally compelled to begin with the latter. I pursue no invariable line of action; both I and the grab are transmutable.'

'How are we to shape our course now?'

'Why, in this wide sea, and amidst the conflicting broils and wars of European adventurers, and native princes, and rajahs,—

besotted barbarians, worrying and flying at each other's throats in contention about the pasture, while English wolves steal in and walk off with the cattle,—there can be no lack of employment, though it requires consideration to decide. First, we must run down the coast to Goa, where, having settled some business, and laid up the dow, we shall afterwards be together; and then it will be time enough to decide on our after-movements. How old are you?'

'I have turned seventeen.'

'That's odd!—I took you for twenty. Well,—no matter your age. A green trunk often produces the ripest and richest fruit. A little more experience, which you will soon pick up in our bustling life, and a great deal more of command over your passions, and you will lack little of the essential qualifications to fit you for any thing on sea or on shore. The choice is entirely yours. If you like land-work, I have some friends scattered about, who, for your own sake, as well as mine, will be glad to employ you. If you stay with me, I need not say that you are most welcome. But mine is a rough life; and if you are to judge of my actions by the common canting sophistry of public opinion, you may pronounce their legality as something more than questionable, and had better not hazard your—reputation.'

'Damn that!' I replied; 'with your permission I shall stay where I am. I told you before I wished to stay with you, and I repeat it. I don't want to know your plans till I have experience enough to aid you with my counsel.'

'No; you are a man in intellect, and have more firmness than most men I have had to deal with. For some things I have done, those devouring locusts of Europe have denounced me a bucanier. These sordid fellows, who would squeeze their fathers' eyes out without compunction, if they were nutmegs, will let no man warm his blood with spice, or cool it with tea, unless they have their profit, or, as it is called, their *dustoory*. They would monopolise every thing, and wherever there is gain, let them but once hit on the scent, they'll hunt it out through blood and mire, and admit no sharers in the spoil. Now I like spice and tea too; and their system of exclusive right not suiting with my ideas of things, I began to open a trade for myself. They denounced me, seized my vessel, and left me bankrupt. Well! I did not rot in a jail, nor sit down in abject despair, nor waste my breath in beggarly petitions.

H

I am not one of those spiritless cravens. I went forth again, alone like the lion, no longer circumscribed within the narrow limits of a paltry burgher, but determined on making reprisals, and returning blow for blow, no matter whence it came. In the interval, however, between my ruin and return to the sea, I gratified my longing to see the interior of India, and traversed the greatest part of it. I sojourned some time with Tippoo Sahib.[1] He alone had the ingredients of greatness in his composition. I accompanied him to some of his principal battles,—but you know his fate. I was, at that time, one of those visionary enthusiasts, impelled, by an ardent love of liberty, to try to breast the stream which heaves the weak onward unresistingly. Like a petty mountain-torrent contending with a mighty river, I foamed and struggled to maintain my purpose; but in vain.—I was borne on like the rest, till mingled with them I became lost in the wide ocean. Foolishly I thought that men might be induced to lay aside their paltry interests for a season, and let their passions sleep, like scorpions in the winter, till the sun of freedom dawned, and gave them leisure, undisturbed by foreign invasion, to resume their civil and religious discord. I conjured princes and priests (the world's attorneys,) to relax their gripe on each other's throat, till the general enemy were driven from the shore to the sea from whence they came. But truth is a sword in a child's hand, dangerous to himself alone. My doctrine was thought damnable. I narrowly escaped adding my name to the list of martyrs. Every where throughout the east I saw the necessity of a great moral revolution. The old system is there in all the grey and hoary frightfulness of desolation and decay; and will remain dreary and hideous, till an entirely new one shall spring up. Time alone can effect this; and the efforts of hands like mine to hasten his tortoise-steps are puerile.'

'It seems to me,' I observed, 'that we have not much to brag of in Europe. There is room for alteration; and men's minds, and hands too, are already at the work of regeneration.'

'Ay, but for themselves alone, as among the natives here. Europe is an old man's child, an unnaturally begotten and wrinkled abortion, created out of the shattered fragments of the wreck of the east, pieced and joined ingeniously together, but without solidity. It is an antique bronze, patched and smeared with white-wash, a plaster miniature copy from a granite statue. The finger of destruction is already upon it, like a Spartan mother's on her puny offspring. Thus thinking, I was aroused from my dreams of reformation; and having expended my gold, and wanting bread, I turned round, resolved henceforth to go with the stream, and say, with the wise philosopher, ancient Pistol,—"The world's mine oyster, which I with sword will open." I returned to the sea, went to the Mauritius, fitted out an armed vessel on credit, and quadrupled my former capital;—it was but fair I should have interest for my money. My person is not much known; however, I seldom trust myself in any of the residencies. My visit to Bombay was to achieve an important object,—not to dispose of the paltry cargo of the grab. Yet,' laughing, he continued, 'if they had grabbed me there! Why, what do you think? That very cargo they have paid for—once at least, as I have vouchers for that—and perhaps twice, if the original venders have not been robbed of it. Six months ago, cruising in this grab, under French colours, I cut off a lazy Company's ship from Amboyna, lagging astern of her convoy,— that was her cargo! I have intelligence of some more of them loading at Banda, and perhaps we may fall in with them. When they are swollen up like leeches, I know where to put my thumb on them, and squeeze them till they disgorge. What say you?'

'With all my heart!' I answered. 'But, till I came here, I always heard that our colonies were for the protection of the poor devils, they not being able to take care of themselves, and for their conversion to christianity;—then, when baptized and civilized, emancipation will follow.'

'Truly, so it will,—when they are converted. It is curious, though now so few stomachs are gross enough to retain cant or castor oil, that every quack thinks he has a method of insinuating either of them down the throat without nausea. We are drenched whether we will or no, with oil of cant, as a panacea for all complaints. This is certainly the age of gold, for who values any thing else? Women, saints, and philosophers squabble now for nothing but loaves and fishes. Who speculates on any other subject than how to fill his purse? And what is not to be attained by gold, from kingdoms to mitres and maidens? This merchant-company say they have an exclusive right (which is a general wrong) to the entire produce of this great empire. On what a grand scale is robbery now carried on! Petty plundering is out of fashion, and put to shame. The mighty thieves have now enclosed that beautiful island,—I wonder we are allowed to inhale its fragrant odours!'

'What! Ceylon!'

'Yes; they have there a ring-fence of posts, in which the King of Candy is enmeshed. He calls the English *beach-masters*, but soon will they be his masters. Jungle, reptiles, nor fever can hold back those led on by insatiable avarice, till glutted with entire possession. The other spice-islands will follow. Then no rock so bare but they will covet, and convert to their own purposes. Yet their reign will be but as a day; the time of just retribution will come, and that speedily.'

'You are too sweeping in your strictures, De Ruyter. At least, they make a shew of doing some good. They have established schools, built churches, started newspapers,—which are the banners of freedom.'

'It is but show and sound! The schools are for their own offsets; the churches to provide for knaves; and their printing, being entirely under their own censorship, is one of cut and dried lies for exportation. As for priests,—better the plague had crossed the equator! They are a well-sifted compound of bigots and fools, of knaves, jesuits, presbyterians, moravians, and the bilious tribe of croaking, beetle-browed, ravenous, obscure dissenters. We had venomous reptiles enough before they were let loose on us.'

'You are now growing scurrilous, if not blasphemous. Remember they have made converts, even of some of your own men.'

'They have converted honest men into scoundrels and hypocrites, like themselves; but if I catch any more on board, I'll keel-hale them. As long as there are beggars and outcasts, and they give rice and arrack, a sprinkling of water on the forehead won't stand in the way of a meal and a glass of grog down their throats.'

'A few honest men there must be among them.'

'Perhaps so; but their being here is no proof of their wisdom. And what can they do? Before they have become seasoned to the climate, and have learnt the language, most of them drop off. The rest devote themselves, not to saving souls from being damned, but to preaching damnation on each other. If their sacerdotal cloaks cover aught but hypocrisy, the Company know how to slake their holy zeal by letting them plainly see their labour is in vain. The vagabonds they do baptize are left on their hands, unsaleable as rotten sheep; for none of the Company's servants are permitted to employ them; nay, if before employed, they lose their bread with their caste, lest they should taint the obedient flock. Merchants know that the many-faced and many-handed Bramah is a better god for slaves than Jesus; they know also that they may keep their ground while the multitudinous conflicting castes of superstitious idolatry shall endure; and that their tenure would be of little worth, if the natives were united in one religion. —But no matter what Christian or Mahometan the sun is sinking in the eave; and by its bloody mantle, and by the mares' tails streaming in the sky, we shall surely have a breeze. I have only this to add: I am no hungry dog, to stand patiently by, in the hope of picking a bone, which these lordly merchants, in general, pretty successfully blanch before they leave it. Let them gorge themselves undisturbed till, like the vulture, their weight is too heavy for their wings; then we, like hawks, after hovering in watchfulness, will pounce upon them. No harm in despoiling robbers! A convoy of Company's country craft, protected by their own cruisers,—whom I hold as trash for aping ships of war,— has sailed for the spice islands. By the by, you must transform your body, with an abbah, into an Arab's,—when the devil can't detect you. I have written full instructions. Continue your course to Goa, where I will follow. On no account go on shore till my arrival. The Parsee merchant, for whom I have prepared a letter, will do all you want. See, the breeze is springing up! Haul the boat alongside!'

He shook my hand, jumped into the boat, and returned to the old dow.

CHAPTER XXVII

We can escape even now,
So we take fleet occasion by the hair.

SHELLEY

NOTHING particular occurred till our arrival at Goa. I had rigged myself in loose dark trowsers, and purple vest, with a high black cap of Astracan lamb's skin, a cashmere shawl round my waist, and a small creese stuck in it. My long dark elf-locks were shaven off, with the exception of one, on the crown, by which the black-eyed houris were to haul me into paradise. A roll of beetle nut, properly chinammed, stuck in, or was rather sticking out of my cheek. My teeth were dyed in the bright red colour of chess-men; and my bare neck, arms, and ancles were well greased and highly polished. The men gathered around in congratulation, declared unanimously that I must be, that I was decidedly Arab, and even went so far as to demand who was my father, and of what tribe.

I lay to, off the point of Cape Ramas, all night awaiting the dow, passed under the fort of Aguada, and anchored in the harbour of Goa. The sun rose magnificently, glittering on the marble monasteries, and on the ruined arches and colleges of the old town, spread over an extent which shewed it had once been a flourishing city. The bunder, or pier, was breached by the sea, and in the harbour was nothing but a motley assemblage of country small craft. I sent the Rais on shore with the ship's papers and the letter to the merchant. In the evening the dow came to an anchor under our stern; and at night-fall De Ruyter was again with me.

On the following day he went up the country to meet some agents of the Rajah of Mysore and a Mahrattah prince; leaving me at Goa to discharge the remaining part of the cargo, consisting of coffee and rice, and to take in ballast, and to complete our water. When he returned to Goa, I saw with him a Greek and a Portuguese, whom I believed to be spies in his employment. They used to meet in the ruins of a monastery or college in the old town, close to the sea, always at night. On these occasions De Ruyter came on board for one of the grab's boats, which landed him there. Their conferences were from twelve to two, A.M. The crew of the boat were even selected by De Ruyter.

Having got everything ready for sea, we removed all the men, and what else was useful, from the old dow, which was here given up to her owners. I warped outside the harbour, and every night at sunset, I hoisted the boats in, and hove short, lying in readiness to move on the instant. On the tenth day after our arrival, one hour after midnight, I observed, by the phosphoric light sparkling on the black surface of the water, something approaching us with unusual rapidity. The hallooing and distant turmoil in the harbour was hushed; the moving lights on the shore had been some time extinguished, but just then I thought I descried some commotion on the pier. As the sound was borne off by the light air from the land, I distinctly heard some one hailing a boat in the port. This was repeated louder and louder. Lights then re-appeared along the beach, and I heard the noise of oars, and spars, and boats, as if moving from amongst others to the shore. The noise growing

higher, I turned towards the first object which had caught my
attention in the other quarter; and, though all was silent there,
I still distinguished the sparkling ripple in the waters, and the
long arrowy line of light, such as a shooting star leaves in the
heavens, or the wake of a boat darting on a calm sea in this climate.
By the muffled sound of oars, and by the long and heavy strokes
which De Ruyter had taught the men in his favourite boat, I
knew her, and marvelled at her returning before the wonted
hour, and at the rapidity with which she approached. The noise
in the harbour augmented. My mind misgave me that all was not
right. I felt my heart flutter with anxiety of I knew not what.
I called the Serang, who was asleep, (the Rais being with the boat,)
told him to rouse the men, and, in my impatience, kicked them
up myself.

Ordering them to man the capstan, loose the jib and fore-top-
sail, and cast off the lashings of the fore and aft main-sail, I returned to the gangway, where, now seeing our boat, I hailed her.
Instead of the usual reply of 'Acbar,' a voice answered in a low
and suppressed tone, 'Yup! Yup!' (silence! silence!) I had been
instructed regarding this signal, and rushing to the bow, I seized
the axe lying by its side in readiness, then, ordering the jib to be
hoisted to pay her round, cut the cable, together with a chip from
an Arab's leg, who was standing by it.

De Ruyter then came forward, and said: 'That was right, my
boy, in cutting the cable; but be cool,—you have wounded this
poor fellow,—send him into the cabin. Clap all the canvass on her
instantly. I'll go aft. The blood-hounds have hit on a scent; they
think to find us like jungle-fowls at roost; but they shall find a
panther, and he is never caught sleeping!'

He sprang aft. We wore slowly round, and as I was cursing the
length of her kelstow, and the lightness of the breeze, which made
her so tardy in paying round, De Ruyter put his hand on my
shoulder, and said, 'Arm the men,—but only with their spears.
Let no boat come alongside of us, or attempt it. Speak them fair,
but if a man puts his hand on the ladder, spear him as you would
a wild boar. There is no occasion for saltpetre, it makes a noise,
and has a bad smell. Harpoon them! but not till I tell you. I must
keep back, and not be seen. If they question you about De Witt,
the merchant, say you know him not.'

Two boats were approaching, and the foremost hailed us with

—'Grab, ahoy!' I answered. They commanded me to heave to, as they wished to see the captain. I ordered the Serang to let the mainsail fall, and loose the top-gallant-sails, and replied—'We are going to sea. I have got my port clearances, and ship's papers, all regularly signed at the proper offices. I can't lose this breeze. What do you want?'

'Heave to, Sir, instantly, or we shall fire!'

'You had better not,' I said.

We had not yet got weigh enough on her to distance the first boat, which belonged to the captain of the port. De Ruyter ordered the men to lie down on deck. He stood at the helm. He was just calling to me to keep under cover, when, with a flash of light from the boat, a ball whizzed by my head, and went into the mast. In obedience to De Ruyter's orders, I did not return it, much against my inclination. Soon after, as the boat was shooting up to board us on the gangway, De Ruyter, bearing away, brought them under the lee quarter. Not being able to board us there, they lost some time, by falling astern, before they could re-use their oars. In this way (the breeze now freshening a little) we kept them off some time, during which not a word was spoken. De Ruyter remained at the helm, and I, with a party of men, stood ready, all armed with spears, to prevent their boarding us. The other boat was nearing us, and both had fired many musquets; but we, sheltered by the bulk-heads of the deep waist, were untouched. The foremost boat now got hold of the lee chains, and they were very coolly coming on board. De Ruyter said, 'Cheelo, chae!' (Advance boys!) when we thrust our spears through the port-holes, and three or four, with their leader, fell back, spitted, into the boat, yelling with pain. Notwithstanding an officer's commanding them to hold on, they would not; but as the other boat was coming up under the stern, I cast off one of the after guns, ran it out of the stern port, and hailing both the boats, I said, 'If you pull another stroke in our wake, or play your fire-works off under our stern, you shall hear the roar of this brazen serpent. Command where you have power to enforce obedience; you have none here.'

I blew the cotton match; they saw the bright brass muzzle of the gun depressed to a line with the boat, when I could have blown them to pieces. They lay on their oars; and their oaths and threats, mingled with the rippling of the waves, died away, while we, crowded with sail, majestically receded from the port, and beheld them returning from their bootless expedition to the shore.

CHAPTER XXVIII

The slim canoe
Of feather'd Indian darts about, as through
The delicatest air.

KEATS

AFTER taking the bearings of the land, De Ruyter patted me on the back, and said, 'Those who fight under the banner of silence are victorious, whilst noise and threats end in defeat. The force of air or fire, when concentrated and confined, is irresistible. Women, and weak people, and boys before they have learnt to bite, bluster and threaten. A silent man, with a drawn weapon, is to be dreaded, because he is determined. When a man vaunts or menaces, he is either afraid, or he wavers in his purpose;—I have ever found it so. Come, you have made a proper beginning!— why, your wariness exceeds that of the oldest and most experienced. What induced you to keep so much on the alert, that you were prepared to be under weigh before I even hailed you? I thought the night-owls on shore had anticipated me, and were alongside of you.'

I told him the reasons which had impressed me with an idea that all was not right. 'Well!' he added, 'I had great confidence in you, and anticipated much when your judgment should be perfected by experience. But, in some natures, quickness of perception is intuition, like instinct,—it is strange. But go, my lad, you have worked hard, and when overwrought we must have rest. Go to sleep; I will keep the watch to-night.'

He shook me as I lay half dozing, with my head on the hatchway, saying, 'The night dew, with a land wind, is here as venomous as the serpent's bite; it is heavy with the vapours from the jungles. Good night!' Notwithstanding my objections to leave the deck, complaining of the heat, and urging that we might still be pursued, he was peremptory that I should go below. 'No fear,' said he; 'before daylight the eye of the eagle will not descry us, though perched on the highest rock. Good night!'

The change of atmosphere, which takes place an hour before the night is seen to break into day, awoke me. I stumbled up the ladder on deck, and was only thoroughly roused by breaking my shins against a gun-bolt. De Ruyter was standing on a gun-carriage, looking over the stern with a night-glass; the moon was reflected on his face; he looked haggard with watching, and his hair and moustaches were dank with dew. Saluting him, I requested he would go to rest, and apologized for my long sleep. 'I only wonder,' was his answer, 'you are up so early; but the young and happy rest when the sun withdraws his light, and awaken when he unfolds his curtains. At my age you will keep company with the moon, and prefer the shadowy silence of night to the glaring day, which is the prelude of never ending, and never useful toil.'

We were standing to the southward and westward, under a press of canvass. The watch were sleeping in groups under cover of the half-decks. As the day broke, De Ruyter looked carefully around the horizon, and ordered the watch to be awakened to their necessary duties, never ending on board a ship, and he ascertained the only sails in sight to be country vessels. Our distance from the harbour and land was such as to blend all minute points into an undefined mass, its dark outline broken by the fleecy clouds of morning, and enveloped in transparent vapours. We took our departure from the land, and De Ruyter retired to the cabin, pricked her run of the night on the chart, gave me directions how to steer, and when to call him, covered himself in his capote, and slept. Hauling up as he directed, I kept a S.E. course, to make the southern-most of the Lacadive Islands.

In getting into the latitude of these islands, we were many days becalmed. My mind was then too elastic to be oppressed with weariness. I loved the sea in all its moods. During the day the duties of the ship occupied me, and, notwithstanding the grab remained as stationary as if she had taken root, time seemed to keep pace with the swallow. My inclinations and duty were, for the first time, blended together, and, from a drowsy boy, I all at once, as if by magic, became transformed into a most active and energetic man.

De Ruyter wished to give his vessel a more warlike trim. We hoisted up four verdigrised brass nine-pounders, secreted under the ballast on the kelstow, and mounted them. We fitted and filled shot-lockers on deck, made cartridges, and prepared two furnaces for heating shot red-hot. We put the magazine in order, made rockets and blue-lights, cleaned and whitewashed between decks, mustered and quartered the men, exercised them, and practised the guns and small arms, and I learnt to use the spear and creese, under the tuition of the Rais.

We had fourteen Europeans, chiefly from the dow; they were Swedes, Dutch, Portuguese and French together with a few Americans. Then we had samples of almost all the sea-faring natives of India; Arabs, Mussulmans, Daccamen, Cooleys, and Lascars. Our steward and purser was a mongrel Frenchman, the cabin-boy, English, the surgeon, Dutch, and the armourer and master-of-arms, Germans. De Ruyter was indifferent as to where his men were born, or of what caste they were; he distinguished them by their worth alone. I was astonished at such dissimilar and incongruous ingredients being mingled together with so little contention; but it was the consummate art of the master-hand, his cool and collected manner which regulated all; before a murmur was heard, he forestalled every complaint by a timely remedy. He himself was the most active and unwearied in toil, the first in every danger, and every thing he did was done quicker and better than it could have been by any other person. In short, he would have been, amidst an undistinguished throng of adventurers, in any situation of peril or enterprise, by a unanimous voice, their chosen leader. The most unforeseen calamity, which struck the hardiest aghast, when all looked in hopeless despair, he was pre-pared to meet, not by submitting to it, but by an opposition equal to the emergency. This, however, must be shewn in his actions, and I proceed with our voyage.

On the fourth day, the sameness of the scene, the blue sky and blue sea, underwent a change. Masses of clouds began to move and meet until the horizon was overcast with gloom. We took in our light canvass, and double-reefed the top-sails. Cat's paws, or light airs, came scudding along the waters from all points of the compass, amidst pale streaks of lightning and low thunder. Then the rain fell in torrents, and the rippling of the sea, borne by the eddy-winds into puny waves contending for sway, subsided, and now, bending all one way, was accompanied by a steady breeze, instead of a violent gale, which we had expected. The clouds evaporated in rain; and, borne by a steady wind from the N.E., at daylight we came in sight of the Lacadive islands.

The canoes of the natives here astonished me. They are called by Europeans, owing to the wonderful rapidity with which they sail, *flying proas*. One of them hull down on our lee beam, we going under a staggering top-gallant breeze eleven knots an hour, came up to windward of us, standing two points nearer the wind, and passed us as if we had been stationary. There was a short breaking sea; two or three of her men, standing on her outriggers, looked as if they flew on the waters. She dashed not over, but through the sea, and at times was quite enveloped in the spray, resembling the reaction of a water-spout after its breaking.

De Ruyter drew a sketch, and gave me a description of the boat. 'These untaught people,' he said, 'have achieved, in the construction of that vessel, the triumph and perfection of naval architecture, in which we, with all our learning, study, and encouragement, have not gone beyond our ABC, as far as concerns swiftness, dexterity in change of direction, the making no lee-way, and, above all, simplicity of working. They have done all this; consequently the construction of their proa is, in every part, in contradistinction to our ideas of naval architecture. We build the head and stern of a vessel as dissimilar as possible; they construct them precisely of the same form and proportions. The sides of our vessels, on the other hand, are precisely the same; but in the proa you see the sides altogether different. The proa never tacks, sailing indifferently with either end foremost, as occasion serves; but the same side is constantly the weather one. The left, or lee-side is flat as a plumb line can make it; consequently she would capsize, the weather-side being rounded, and from her great length and narrow beam; but, to prevent this, on the lee-side, an outrigger, made of bamboos, projects considerably into the sea, and supports a heavy log of cocoa wood, shaped like a solid canoe. This gives her an immense artificial beam, without opposing much resistance to the water. Between this outrigger and the flat side of the proa the water passes without obstruction, and is the cause both of her celerity, and that no lee-way is made. The proa itself, or body of the boat, is merely a few planks sewed together, and wadded between the seams with coir-oakum. Not a nail, nor a bit of metal is about her. The sail is matting, the mast and yards are of bamboo. When they want to go about, they bear away and bring what is then the stern to the wind, move the heel of the triangular sail till they fix it on the opposite end, and at the same time shift the boom into the opposite direction; so that what was the stern is then the head, and a man to steer always remains at each of the extremities. It may be said of them that they keep pace with the wind. No European vessel, in any weather, ever had a chance with them. They are admirably adapted for the navigation of islands situated in the latitude of the trade-winds, being enabled to cross on a wind from one to the other, with as unerring a flight as a crane; while, in our vessels, if we miss the object steered for, by making lee-way, we have great difficulty, and lose time in beating up. True it is they are of small capacity, adapted solely to the simple commerce of bartering superfluous productions for absolute necessaries. The ordinary Indian canoe would not serve their purpose; it either foundered in sudden squalls, or was driven to leeward of its destined port. By their ingenuity they invented this simple alteration and addition, and attained the important results I have pointed out.'

CHAPTER XXIX

> And first one universal shriek there rush'd,
>   Louder than the loud ocean, like a crash
> Of echoing thunder; and then all was hush'd
>   Save the wild wind, and the remorseless dash
> Of billows; but at intervals there gush'd,
>   Accompanied with a convulsive splash,
> A solitary shriek,—the bubbling cry
> Of some strong swimmer in his agony.
>
>   BYRON

ON nearing one of these islands, I went on shore to see the natives, and obtain fruit. In the night the breeze again died away. At daylight we saw two or three square-rigged vessels, about two leagues to the westward of us, lying becalmed. I boarded one of them, in a boat with ten men well armed; and her Rais, who was in great apprehension, told me he had been boarded off the Persian Gulf, by a large Malay brig, full of men. They had not only plundered him and two other vessels in his company, but killed several of his men, using them with great cruelty. He added, that this Malay had been cruizing at the entrance of the gulf, and had rifled a vast number of vessels.

I brought the captain and some of his crew on board the grab. After De Ruyter had satisfied himself that the man's story, with all the particulars was true, he instantly determined to look after the Malay. The Persians told him she was full of gold, and that her cargo was so rich, she had cast rich bales of Persian silk into the sea, not having room to stow them.

In the evening a light breeze sprung up, and we made a long stretch to the northward and westward, anticipating to fall in with her before she entered the straights of Malacca. We made a capital run in the ensuing days, kept a good lookout, and daily boarded many country boats and vessels, hoping to learn intelligence of the pirate. Day and night we were most vigilant, and hourly our hopes were excited by some passing stranger, whom we all swore was the Malay, whom we chased, and then were as often chagrined at finding our hopes deceived, or rather at their deceiving us.

De Ruyter's patience was now exhausted. He had important despatches for the Isle of France, and would brook no longer detention. We therefore reluctantly altered our course again to the southward, and after running twenty or thirty leagues in that direction, at daylight, when the horizon was particularly clear, before the sun arose with his misty mantle, the man at the mast-head called out, 'A large sail on the lee-bow!'

Fearing she might be a man of war, I took a glass up to the mast-head; where, after straining my eyes to make her out, De Ruyter hailed me with, 'Well, what is she?'

I replied with confidence, 'The Malay!'

'Which way is she standing?'

'She has not yet seen us, and her course is to the northward.'

Then I described her, and De Ruyter said, 'Very possibly you are right.'

I came on the deck. The horizon became misty, and as they had neglected to keep a look-out, we trusted we should get much nearer, ere she discovered us. We bore down on her under every stitch of sail we could spread. The studding-sails we wetted with an engine for that purpose, to make them hold the light breeze better; and at eight o'clock she saw us, and bore away. We had gained considerably on her; the head of her lower yards were then visible from our deck; and De Ruyter said, 'If the breeze holds till mid-day, she cannot escape us.'

There was an alacrity and a buzz of joy throughout our crew, intent for plunder. We pumped the water out, lightened her by throwing some tons of ballast overboard, winged and shifted the iron shot, cleared the decks for action, got the arms and boats ready for service and for hoisting out, and watched and antedated all the motions of the enemy, as the hawk does the curlew.

At noon the breeze freshened, and we gained rapidly on her; nevertheless it was six P.M. before we came within long shot. We then kept up a fire from the bow-chasers. For some time she disregarded this. We had hoisted a French tricoloured flag, De Ruyter indeed having a French letter of marque's[1] commission, which he now produced for me to read, as the only person among the officers ignorant of that fact. The shots now falling over and on board of the Malay, her top-gallant sails were lowered; and we ran up under her lee-quarter, shortened sail, and backed the top-sail.

A Malay on board of us was desired to hail her. Her deck swarmed with men. We ordered her to send a boat with her papers on board of us, and seeing they paid no attention to this order, De Ruyter again fired a shot over her. She returned this with a volley from four cannonades, divers small swivels on her gunwales, and twenty or thirty match-lock musquets, when the pieces of old iron, glass, and nails, with which they were loaded, rattled against our rigging, and three of our men were wounded. 'Damn their impudence!' exclaimed De Ruyter, 'they shall have enough of it!'

We opened and kept up such a heavy, low, and well-directed fire, manœuvring with our broad-side on her stern and quarters, that, in ten minutes, De Ruyter called out to cease firing, as we had not only silenced her fire, but entirely cleared her deck, cut her rigging to pieces, and shot away her rudder. Our boats were then ordered to be hoisted out, and, with thirty men in three boats, I shoved off to board her; De Ruyter cautioning me to be particularly careful against their cunning and treachery. 'They must have been,' said he, laughing, 'a colony founded by the ancient Greeks, for they have all the characteristics of my modern friend at Goa.'

We approached her warily. Not the smallest impediment was opposed to us. Indeed nothing gave token that there was a being on board of her. I ordered the Rais, who commanded one boat, to board her on the bow with his Arabs; whilst I, with a party, chiefly Europeans, and a gallant set of fellows they were, climbed up her ornamented quarters and bamboo stern. On getting on board, we saw many dead and wounded on her deck, but nothing else. She was only about two-thirds decked, having an open waist, latticed with bamboo, and covered with mats. Her sails and yards were hanging about in confusion. We were now all on deck, and a party of men was preparing to descend between decks; when, while replying to De Ruyter's questions, I was suddenly startled at hearing a wild and tumultuous war-whoop, and springing forwards, I saw a grove of spears thrust up from below, which, passing through the matting, wounded many of our men. I was certainly as much astonished at this novel mode of warfare as Macbeth at the walking wood of Dunsinane. Running round the solid portion of the deck, several spears were thrust at me, which I with difficulty escaped. Some of my men had retreated; I ordered them to fire down below, through the open work. Most of the men belonging to the Rais, who were not wounded, had jumped overboard to regain their boat.

Hailing De Ruyter, I informed him how the affair stood. He desired me to make fast a halser, which he would send me, to the ring-bolts of her bob-stays, secure it to her bowsprit, and that then we should all return to the grab; he being very careful of the lives of his men, and knowing that these pirates, when once they have made up their minds not to be taken, will abide by their resolution. I told him that if he had any hand-grenades, or fire balls, I would rout them out. Though we had already made considerable havoc among them, I was very anxious, as were all the Europeans, to go below at every hazard, but our native crew were opposed to this; and seven or eight of us could have had little chance, unable, in the dark, to see our enemies, who would spear us from their lurking places, without endangering themselves.

The crew were busy in handing our wounded men down into the boat. A Swedish lad, whom I valued for being an excellent sailor, had been wounded by a spear, driven through his foot, and was suffering great pain. Hastening forward to see him handed into the boat, I stepped over a dying Malay, shot through the body before we boarded her. I had previously, in passing him, caught a glance at his peculiarly ferocious look, and the malignant expression of his broad and brutish face. His coarse, black, straight hair was clotted with blood from a wound in his head, apparently by a splinter. As I now stepped over him, I was arrested by his eye, surrounded by a rigid lid, and deeply imbedded above his high cheek-bone, the sunken pupil still glaring like a glow-worm in a dark vault. My foot slipped in the gore, and I fell on him; when, as I was recovering myself, he griped me with his bony hand, and made a horrible effort to rise, but his extremities were stiff. He drew a small creese from his bosom, and with a last effort tried to bury it in my breast. The passion of revenge had outlived his physical powers; its sharp point slightly grazed me, and he fell dead from the exertion, dragging me down, his hand still clenching like a vice. I could only extricate myself by slipping my arm out of my vest, and leaving it in his ghastly hand. 'Such men as these,' I cried out, 'are not to be conquered even by death! Their very spirits fight and stab at us!'

De Ruyter became peremptory for our instant return, as the night was now coming on, and the Malays below had again opened a fire on us with their match-locks. With rage and disappointment I returned.

We had now altogether eight wounded. On reaching the grab, De Ruyter observed, 'There is no help for it! We must try to tow her towards the land; when near the shore, they will perhaps escape by swimming. But I fear we shall not succeed in capturing her.'

As we filled our sails and towed her, a gang of men stood at our stern to fire at any object they could see moving on board of her. We found it difficult to tow her: not being steered, she yawed about, and in less than an hour they had contrived to cut the tow-rope. Under a cover of musquetry we again made fast another, and kept up a continual fire on her bows. Nothing living was seen on her decks, yet again the halser was cut. We hailed her, as we often had done, but no answer was given.

At daylight, De Ruyter came to the determination of sinking her; which we reluctantly did, by opening a fire with our largest guns, and red-hot shot, which had been prepared during the night. Symptoms of fire from below soon made their appearance; smoke slowly arose; several explosions of powder took place; the smoke arose darker, and in masses; at last we saw the savages themselves crawling up on all-fours upon deck. Their guns having been thrown overboard by us, they could make no defence; yet they had the hardihood to fire a few scattered shots more in bravo than to do us hurt. We picked them off as they appeared. Streams of fire now burst out of her hatchways and port-holes. On the

O

balls going through her, our Arabs swore they saw the gold-dust, and pearls, and rubies, fly out of her on the opposite side. I cannot say I did; nor could I smell the atta of roses, which they affirmed was running out of her scuppers like a fountain. I saw nothing but the dense flames and smoke, and the poor devils swarming up and jumping into the waves, preferring death by water to fire and balls,—for they had no other choice. Though we lowered our boats to pick them up, not one approached them; and the boats did not near the vessel, fearing her blowing up. She appeared to have an immense number of men; not less than two hundred and fifty to three hundred.

Having given over firing, we lay at some distance, intently gazing at her. After an explosion, louder than the loudest thunder, which vibrated through the air, we could see nothing but a black cloud on the waters, enveloping all around, like a pall, and darkening the heavens; and where the pirate had been was only to be distinguished by the bubbling commotion and dashing ripple of the sea, like the meeting of the tides, or where a whale has been harpooned, and sunk. Huge fragments of the ship, masts, tackling, and men, all shattered and rent, lay mingled around in a wide circle. Some dark heads, still above the surface, awaiting, as it were, the utmost of our malice, faintly yelled their last war-cry in defiance; then a few bubbles shewed where they had been. Her hull was driven down stern-foremost, and her grave filled up on the instant.

Even the wind became hushed from the concussion of the explosion; and I started as our sails flapped heavily against the mast, and the grab's hull shook as in terror. The black cloud cleared away, and slowly swept along the surface of the sea; then ascended and hung aloft in the air, concentrated in a dense mass. As I gazed on it, methought the pirate ship was changed, but not destroyed, and that her demon crew had resumed their vocation in the clouds. De Ruyter said: 'It has been an awful and painful sight!—but they deserved their fate. Come, set our gaping crew to work! Hoist the boats in, and make all sail on our proper course.'[1]

CHAPTER XXX

This is the way physicians mend or end us,
    Secundum artem; but although we sneer
In health,—when ill, we call them to attend us,
    Without the least propensity to jeer.
                                    BYRON

Two days after, one of our wounded Arabs died, and his companions committed him to the deep with their usual mystic ceremonies. His body was washed with great attention; his head was carefully shaved and cleaned; his mouth, nostrils, ears, and eyes were stuffed with cotton saturated in camphor, with which his body was also anointed; the joints of his legs and arms were broken, and then tightly bandaged in the mummy form; and, with a twelve-pound shot fixed to his lower extremities, the mutilated carcase was launched into the ocean. Upon inquiring why they broke his joints, I was answered that it was to prevent his following the ship; because, had they neglected to fulfil this sacred duty, his body would float on the waters, and his spirit pursue them for ever.

It did not appear that the Malays had, in this instance, poisoned their spears; for the men rapidly recovered from their wounds, except the Swedish boy, whose wound was of such a nature that, had not De Ruyter added to his other chieftain's qualifications surgical knowledge, superior to many of the diploma'd butchers, we should have lost him. De Ruyter gave up his own state-cabin to him, where we both attended to his wants, without a thought of saving ourselves trouble by permitting the doctor, for the sake of practice, to lop off the limb, which most of the faculty would have done, and of which he strongly urged the necessity.

Van Scolpvelt, our surgeon, had been engaged out of a Dutch East Indiaman, where he was surgeon's-assistant, and grown old, hoping to see service, and be a surgeon. But the muddy mettle of those burghers could be stirred by nothing but the prospect of gain; and their antipathy to powder was as great as that of Quakers, so that he became weary for want of practice, and the instruments of his trade grew dull and rusty. All the practice he had on board of her was in administering an emetocatharticus, an enema, or

simple dejectors, to the swag-bellied Hollanders, after gormandising had disarranged the gastric functions. His dignity—and moreover the dignity of his profession—which he alone revered, he
thought compromised by this degrading application of science.
He therefore gladly closed with De Ruyter's proposition, and had
now accompanied him in several voyages.

He said, 'De Ruyter is a considerate creature, and generally
keeps me tolerably employed. He has only one great blemish in
his character, unaccountable in a man so liberally-minded and
humane, and that is, in siding with the heathenish prejudices of
his barbarous crew, and opposing, in all cases, amputation. On
this point,' addressing himself to me, 'you Englishmen are the
most enlightened people on earth. Your government, too, with
providential care, fearing that surgeons, like others, untinctured
by the love of science, may not like gratuitous work, give (I have
been told) a premium for every limb or shoot pruned off from the
parent trunk; thus, from the multitude of the maimed, their
knives don't rust, and it must make a very pretty addition to their
salaries. Then not only the operator, but the operatee, is bounti-
fully compensated, getting more by his limb off than he ever
earned by it on. Why I,' he exclaimed with unusual energy,
'I, Van Scolpvelt, assisted in taking off a man's leg in an English
frigate, and it was the pleasantest operation I ever attended. It
was a compound fracture: the man had fallen from the mast, so
that the knee-bone was forced through the integuments into the
deck. The next day the man recovered his faculties, and we commenced upon him. It would have done your heart good to see
him,—I wish you had,—he was a glorious subject! No one could
have witnessed the operation without astonished delight! He
never squealed, or made a wry face, or spoke a word till it was
over; and then, turning his quid, he only asked for a glass of
grog;—if there had been but one bottle in the world, he should
have had it!—I loved him! They are good people, and feel no
more than the log of wood that carpenter is now adzing;—no
patient ought! Now this boy in the cabin,—they would not speak
one word to him, but take off his leg, and then ask him how he
feels. Afterwards he would be sent to the hospital for life,—or he
dies,—no more!—while I shall be three or four months in curing
him, and he, all the time, eating and drinking, and doing no work.
De Ruyter does not think of this! You are an Englishman; go and

persuade him, that's a good lad!—go and tell him I do it with very little pain.'

I stopped his cajoling whine with—'If my leg was hanging by a remnant of skin, and any doctor clipped it, I would stab him with one of his own probes!'

He stared at me with unutterable wonder, and, putting the case of instruments, on which he had been descanting, in his pocket, he shuffled away, making a noise like a shark's fin flapping on the deck, which his flat feet resembled.

As De Ruyter called him to answer some questions, I could not refrain from running my eye over his extraordinary figure. He had a small, dry, sapless body, then stripped for operating, which I could compare to nothing but a gigantic russet-haired caterpillar. His wizzened face was puckered up like a withered shaddock, or Chinese mandarin. His pate was bald, hedged round with long, wiry, reddish grey hair. The hair, that should have been on his eye-brows, eye-lids, and beard, having entirely deserted its several posts, was dotted about on his lank cheeks, chin, and neck, the latter of which was long as a heron's, and seemed covered with scorched parchment. Four or five irregular, yellow-crusted tusks boomed from his jaw, like the wild hog's; and his capacious mouth, and thin, fishy lips, were like a John Dory's. His eyes were small and sunken, with a mixture of light red, green, and yellow.

Yet, notwithstanding his immoderate love of practice, and this preposterous exterior, he was not deficient in a certain sort of ability, and was an enthusiast in his mystery. When not actively engaged, his recreation consisted in poring over old Dutch surgical works, chiefly manuscripts, or, if not, closely interlined and annotated, throughout the margins, by his own hand, and illuminated with disgusting representations of appalling operations in their horrible preternatural colours. His dress, on ordinary occasions, was composed of such stray articles as he picked up in the sickward, or plucked from the corpse of a savage. As to his age, it was impossible to form a guess at it, for he looked like the resurrection of an Egyptian mummy, yet he was active, always awake, (as far as we knew,) and his faculties were unimpaired.

He was in animated discussion with De Ruyter as they returned to where I stood, with his hand extended, of which he was somewhat vain. It was long and narrow, like the claw of a bird of prey, so utterly devoid of flesh, that on meeting him at night with a candle shaded between his palms, the light shone so clearly through them that I asked him to let me have the loan of the signal lanthorn he was carrying. But he valued his hand from its useful properties. 'For,' as he said, 'where a ball goes there I can follow it,' stretching out a long ghastly finger, adorned with the only ornament he wore, a huge silver-mounted, antique, carbuncle ring, embossed with cabalistic characters.

I went below with the doctor to see the wounded, where he proceeded to business without delay, using his probe with the same sort of indifference as a man does a pipe-stopper. When he had probed, and cut, and fingered those who had mere flesh wounds, De Ruyter insisted on his looking at the scratch on my breast. He did so, and pointed out to the standers-by the physiology of the part, descanting on the action and effect of Indian poison, and on the subtlety with which it infuses itself by absorption into the whole animal economy, through the circulation of the blood and nervous system. 'That is, to be plain,' said he, 'having taken the outposts, having poisoned, paralyzed, and wormed its way through the husk and shell, it eats into the kernel. Then, beginning with the extremities, which it destroys, it gathers and concentrates its power, till the venom touching the heart, the patient is seized with convulsions, and dies.'

Such was the tune the Dutch doctor sung in my ears, as he was preparing a red-hot iron, which, with the gloating look of a sensualist, he applied to my breast. Whether this prevented the agreeable voyage of the poison through my system, I know not; but it certainly converted a slight scratch into a spreading and ulcerating sore, which troubled me for a long time.

When he came to examine, for the second time, the really bad wound of the boy, the water oozed from his flabby lips like a hungry dog's while his master is eating. He revelled in his description of the muscles and tendons torn and wounded in the instep. Gangrene and mortification were the least that must ensue: he declared that unless amputation above the ankle took place, in four-and-twenty hours he might be compelled to remove the entire quarter up to the hip, and yet with little probability of saving his life, as a patient generally expired under the operation.

The poor boy cried, and petitioned first the doctor and then me. I called De Ruyter, who absolutely forbad the operation. To compensate in some measure for this, the surgeon, after having the boy held, set to work on him with as much ingenuity as an Indian when flaying a staked enemy; and when the boy happily became insensible from the excruciating torture, the doctor looked at him, then round in astonishment, and said; 'Why does he groan and faint like a little girl? Why, you see I merely scrape the bone!'

De Ruyter then came down into the cabin, and told him to bind up the wound and poultice it. 'Doctor,' said he, 'you are like the old cook, who put live eels into a pasty, and knocked them over the pate with the rolling-pin, exclaiming, "lie down, ye wantons!"'

When the boy came to his senses, De Ruyter gave him a glass of brandy, which restored him; and afterwards would never allow the wound to be dressed unless he or I was present; when, in spite of the doctor's predictions, he did recover, though slowly. This boy is mentioned particularly, as I shall have to narrate his melancholy fate.

CHAPTER XXXI

The sky became
Stagnate with heat, so that each cloud and blast
Languish'd and died; the thirsting air did claim
All moisture.
SHELLEY

OUR progress was slow; frequent calms—but, not to be tedious, my time was fully occupied, and we practised a thousand amusements. The abstemiousness and temperance of the natives rendered it a less arduous task to govern them, than a crew, however small, of Europeans. Those of the latter which we had, were picked up with great caution, all holding responsible situations in the ship, and were also fully occupied. De Ruyter was not only a high-spirited and excellent commander, but an admirable companion; so that I had nothing to complain of.

After leaving the Lacadive islands, we put into one called Diego Rayes, for wood and water. We then passed a long cluster called the Brothers; and, keeping more to the south, took a fresh departure from Roquepez island. Some days after, between the great bank of Garagos and the St. Brandon islands, the man at the mast-head called out—'A strange sail to the westward!'—and then—'Another!'

They were in our course; we stood on. A heavy squall of mist and rain coming on, we lost sight of them for some time. On this clearing away, the strangers were visible from the deck; and the instant I saw them, I called De Ruyter from the cabin, being then one o'clock, P.M., telling him they were certainly two frigates—perhaps French ones, from Port St. Louis, in the Isle of France.

'They may be so,' said he, 'but I doubt it. Give me the glass.' He looked at them attentively, and muttered—'Too high out of the water;—canvass too dark;—hull too short;—and the yards not square enough for Frenchmen. No, they are not French. Haul down the studding sails, and bring her up on the larboard tack, close to the wind.'

On doing this, the headmost stranger hauled his wind, and shortly after tacked too; the sternmost held the same course. The wind was light, and we all kept turning to windward. The headmost frigate sailed remarkably well, and left her companion hull-down to leeward; but yet she was no match for us. All we feared was the wind changing, or losing it altogether, which we did at sunset.

During the night we were on the alert; no light was allowed, fearing they might see us; our decks were cleared for action; the guns, double shotted, and the small arms were got up in readiness; not in the vain hope of contending with the frigate, but as a measure of precaution against any possible attempt at boarding us with boats. After the middle watch, a light air came out of the channel of Garagos, and we made a long stretch to the eastward. The wind then varied, with intervals of calm; the night was dark; the frigates shewed no lights, nor did we see any thing to form a guess of how they were standing. Our object was to get among the group of islands, the Brothers; by which means we might elude their seeing us again, as we thought they would, in all probability, retain their position between us and the port, which, by the course we were steering when they first discovered us, we were evidently bound to. But the breeze had been so scanty during the night, that we had made but little way. The night, too, had been cloudy, so that our night-glasses were of no use; and we began to feel anxious for the dawn of day.

At last the sombre clouds broke in the east, changing their colour to purple, which speedily became fringed with an orange hue, and the circle of the horizon was enlarged. Still the frigates were not to be seen, and every face was brightening up with the appearance of day. De Ruyter stood on a gun, watching a hazy bank of misty clouds on our lee quarter, which were slowly evaporating, and he suddenly exclaimed—'There she is!'

I looked, and saw one of the frigates looming in the vapour, in which she was enveloped, like an island. She must soon after this have seen us, for she tacked in our wake, and crowded on all the light canvass she had. She was not more than nine or ten miles astern, and four to leeward of us. Her consort we saw at a great distance, hull down. We turned all our attention now to trimming the grab, and we clapped every inch of canvass on her; then all the deck-lumber was turned overboard. After watching the frigate for some time, De Ruyter said, 'By Heaven! she is a crack sailer! I think she almost holds her way with us; and that is what no other vessel can do in these seas. She must be some new frigate, fresh from Europe. Besides, in this trim and rig, the grab is not herself. I don't like the look of the weather; when the sun gets up, the breeze will die away. Get all the sweeps in readiness.'

Two hours after this, the water became of a glassy smoothness. The sun rose like a globe of fire, and looked terrible; its piercing rays hardly could be endured; they seared to the very brain; and I was obliged occasionally to close my eyes in relief from the dazzling glitter, which I thought would have deprived me of sight. Yet in this heat the frigate ventured to hoist out her boats, at about ten, A.M., and give us chace. De Ruyter admired their hardiness.

For the last hour we had been sweeping; yet, from our size, and the disadvantage of labouring with the thermometer at a hundred and eight in the cabin window, we made little progress. We therefore made every preparation to meet the worst; but De Ruyter observed—'Those fellows toil in vain! At mid-day we shall have a sea-breeze; then they may hoist in their boats, by which they will lose time.'

As he predicted, a little after noon, flaws of wind began lightly to ripple the glassy surface to seaward; and then a faint current of air raised the feathered dog-vane. We held up the palms of our hands towards it, as in supplication. The light cotton sails aloft first caught it; when, instead of sticking, as if glued, to the spars, they swelled out to their arched form.

On my telling De Ruyter that one would imagine he held com-
munion with the elements, he interpreted them so truly—'And
so I do,' was his reply; 'all my life have I studied them; but life
is too short to comprehend their mystery! They are a book a sailor
should ever keep his eye on; and it is ever unfolded before him.
Those who do not, are unfit to command, and have charge of the
lives and properties of others.'

We saw the frigate hoist the recal signal to her boats, and tele-
graph to her companion, to stand off and on, to intercept us if
we should attempt to bear up during the night for the Isle of
France. De Ruyter had copies both of the Admiralty and private
signals of ships of war, as well as their telegraphic signals; which
did him good service on many occasions.

We continued beating up to the weathermost island, and then
the breeze gradually freshened, till we were compelled to take in
our light canvass. The headmost frigate, as she continued to carry
hers, rather gained on us. De Ruyter grew impatient at finding
that the grab did not distance her pursuers, as she had been wont
to do. He said she was cramped in her movements; and, to ease
her, the stays and backstays were slackened; we cut away the
stern-boat; got the anchors pressing on her lean-bow further aft;
and lightened her forwards. We then shifted ballast in her wings,
and, to try her in different trims, he ordered all the men, with
eighteen-pound shot in each hand, to come aft; then he removed
them from place to place; but still we could hardly hold her on.
He remarked that her copper was foul with the accursed slime of
Bombay. 'Ay,' I added, 'and the frigate is a clipper.'

The sun sank to rest, cloudless, red, and fiery, as it had risen.
The breeze still freshened, and having neared the land by eleven
o'clock P.M., De Ruyter determined on bearing away, getting to
leeward of the island, and anchoring; which we did, trusting that
the frigate would stand on to windward, and so lose us. Still, however, we were on the alert during the night; or those sleeping had
their arms in readiness: our cannonades were loaded with bags
of musquet-balls.

CHAPTER XXXII

The morning watch was come; the vessel lay
Her course, and gently made her liquid way;
The cloven billow flash'd from off her prow
In furrows form'd by that majestic plough.

BYRON

THE doctor, who had as keen a scent for blood as the carrion-kite, after having made a platform of gratings in the hold for the antici- pated wounded, thrust his head up the hatchway from time to time, to ask when the slaughter was likely to commence, and to solicit two of the boys as his assistants. At night, when we had anchored, he ventured up, trailing a bandage as long as the log- line, which he was adroitly rolling up. 'Now, my dear fellow,' said he to me, 'it's time I should instruct you. Just sit down on this gun-slide for one moment, while I shew you how to apply a tourni- quet.' With these words he lugged one out from his waistband.

'Nonsense, doctor, I have other things to attend to than to do your duty.'

'Oh! you are young and wilful! Every man should know how to apply that, for if not done at the critical moment, I lose my patient, and the wounded man his life.'

As I was called off to attend to something aft, he went to De Ruyter, whom he was beseeching to be instructed how to apply cross and double-cross bandages. He was answered somewhat harshly, and went below, muttering, 'Want of sleep creates fever, fever delirium, and then madness!'

He soon after made his appearance with a small bottle and glass, and insisted that De Ruyter and I, and the whole crew should take a glass of his water. He said it was a natural, cooling draught, would allay the heat of the body, and be as refreshing as sleep. De Ruyter, who was sorry for having spoken unkindly to him, took the glass, and saying it was nothing but nitric acid and soda, drank it.

Van Scolpvelt, finding him so pliant, again lugged out some fathoms of bandage; but De Ruyter laughed, and walked away.

Then I was attacked, and, in succession, most of the crew; but he could not, with all his eloquence, dispose of another drop of his cooling draught on deck; so that in despair, and that it might not be lost, he took a bumper himself, and only refrained from emptying the bottle by remembering his actual patients below, whom he accordingly drenched.

Wearied and jaded as I was, I looked for daylight with great anxiety. Older seamen, habituated to such scenes, lay down at their posts, and soundly slept. De Ruyter paced the deck with a night-glass in his hand. I bathed in the chains, by having buckets of water thrown over me, to keep my eyelids from closing, till De Ruyter entreated me to lie down for an hour.

At the first glimpse of daylight we were all astonished, as the object which caught our sight was the frigate at anchor, and not three miles from us. Her lying close under the high land, and her hull being hid from us by some high rocks, projecting into the sea, together with the shadow of the mountain, had prevented us from seeing her during the night. The quick and piercing eye of De Ruyter was aware of her, before she had espied us; and our cable was cut, and we were again under a crowd of sail, with the rapidity of thought.

She soon followed us; but she had to work round the dark coral reef, which lay like a huge alligator; so that we got a good start of her, considering there was but a very light air stirring. We again lightened her by throwing lumber and ballast overboard; but De Ruyter fearing we should be calmed, set himself to work in seriously preparing for battle. The sweeps were got out under the hot sun; the breeze again died away; and, at ten, the frigate being about four miles astern, began to prepare her boats. With what little air there was, and with sweeping, we continued to drop the frigate; which she observing, hoisted her boats out, and we counted seven which shoved off in pursuit of us.

De Ruyter saw there were no hopes of wind till the evening; and in despite of our utmost exertions at the sweeps, we could not prevent the frigate's boats coming up with us in three or four hours. His clear brow became overcast with thought, and his look anxious, but without fear.

He called me to him, and said: 'You see that precipitous rock, jutting out boldly into the sea, bleached by the sun and storms to a grayish white, and sapped and undermined into caverns. There is not a symptom of vegetation on it, or in its neighbourhood. It stands like a watch-tower, overlooking the island. You observe,

by the colour and stillness of the water at its base, that it is pro-
foundly deep on this side; and you see a long dotted line, like the
floats of a fishing sean, stretching round in the form of a half
crescent;—that is a low ridge of white coral, with which the sea,
near this island abounds. Now I want the grab to be swept round
that rock; but you must keep her well out, to clear the outermost
point; therefore place men on the extremity of our bow, and on
the fore-yard, to look out for breakers. There we shall find a little
sandy nook, sheltered from the trade wind that blows at this time
of the year, which can be entered only in very smooth water, and
by no vessel with much greater beam than ours. All around is so
thickly studded with reefs and rocks, eddies and currents, that
no one, imperfectly acquainted with its intricacies, would venture
to approach it, even in a calm like this. But with the slightest wind
stirring, or from the swell left after a breeze, all about is in commotion, and hazardous even for a life-boat, for coral cuts like steel.
In a moderate gale of wind, such as I once witnessed in that very
place, the most foolhardy in sea-daring would not venture within
leagues of the shore. The heavy swell, which gets up between this
island and the great bank of Baragos, is tremendous; the mountain
waves rolling in here are opposed and broken (as regular armies
are sometimes by guerillas), by those countless rocks, whose
heads you just see peering above the water. Then, though impeded
and broken, yet not stopped, the sea is white with rage, and covers
half the island with spray and foam. On this side, there being no
impediment, the roar and dash of the surge drowns the loudest
thunder. In the gap leading to that,—it looks no bigger than an
albatros' nest,—we will place the grab athwart, to give these
fellows (who fight for love with more ferocity than others do in
hate), a meeting. With our men I might indeed meet them on
fairer ground, without dreading the result; but the days of chivalry
are past; craft and cunning are now called the art of war, and a
commander is stigmatized who gives a chance, when he can avoid
it. Besides, I now wish to spare the effusion of blood; still I must
defend, and will defend the grab against all odds, even if the
frigate herself came alongside of us. The savage Malays have
taught us that death is preferable to dungeons;—if all men thought
so, there would be none. What think you, my boy?'

'I love fighting, and hate foul air.'

'But they are your ——'

'I am sorry for it. But bull-dogs, you know, will fight against their own kind and kin; and I am no mongrel. I'll shew my breed.'

He smiled, and I went to cheer the men at the sweeps, and place the look-outs, whilst he directed the helmsman.

CHAPTER XXXIII

Death doing in a turban'd masquerade.
                              KEATS' MS.

A victory!
* * * * * it will pluck out all grey hairs;
It is the best physician for the spleen;
The courtliest inviter to a feast;
The subtelest excuser of small faults;
And a nice judge in the age and smack of wine.
                                        Ibid.

AT two P.M. we were sweeping round the reef, in accordance with De Ruyter's plan. The frigate lay becalmed under the northern extremity of the island. Her boats were gaining on us fast. When we were embayed amongst the shoals, and closed in by the shore to the south, we lost sight of them all, hidden by a massy abutment of rock, stretching out in lonely grandeur. We furled all our sails, took up our position at the inner entrance leading to the little cove, got halsers from our bow and stern, and made them fast with some difficulty to the rocks. We mustered our men; there were only fifty-four fit to bear arms, and many untried men amongst them.

All being in readiness, an awful pause took place while awaiting the boats' weathering the point. Even I, fond of fighting and reckless as I then was, felt a queer sensation in this sudden transition of circumstances, finding myself leagued with dusky moors in opposition to my fair-haired countrymen. Then, when one of the boats reappeared, and we heard their cheering hurrah repeated from boat to boat, till it died away in echoes on the hollow shore, I felt my heart beating impetuously against my bosom, and the cold drops trickling down my burning brow. There was a stillness in the grab I had never witnessed before; unpleasant thoughts were gathering in my brain; but they instantly took flight at the full and clear tones, unembarrassed look, and firm step, with which De Ruyter advanced, saying to his men: 'Come, return them the Arab war-cry! You were not wont to be so silent. And try if that headmost boat is in range of the guns.'

I fired accordingly. 'That gun,' said he, 'is too much elevated. I'll try this;—here, bring a match. Ay, that will do.'

The ball went in a right line, struck the water, bounding like a cricket ball, or, as it is technically termed, ricochetting, and passed clean over the headmost boat. She lay on her oars till it passed, cheering the other boats to advance. I omitted to mention that, with the first shot, our French colours were hoisted; each of their boats had the Union Jack flying.

On their uniting, we observed them in consultation; and then separating in two divisions, they advanced along the inside of the reef. We kept up a steady fire upon them; but nothing daunted they replied to every gun with a cheer, and quickened their advance upon us. 'Look, De Ruyter!' said I, perhaps with some degree of exultation at their heroic courage,—'one of their boats was struck with that last shot, and she is sinking; and see they have only left a boat to pick the men up, drowning every mischance with a jovial hurrah, as if they were rejoicing at a feast!'

His answer was, 'Prize money, promotion, and habit will do much. Now let's give them a volley of cannister. We must cripple their leaders.'

From this period I continued at my station forward; most of the Europeans were under my command; and De Ruyter having given me his last injunctions, went and remained aft, surrounded by his Arabs, over whom he had great influence. Another boat, which took the lead, was swamped; and, whilst they were picking up the men, though they opened a cross fire from swivels and musquets, their loss in men was obviously so appalling, that we heard them hailing each other. Rash as they certainly were, they were brought to a stand-still, and paused as if hesitating in what way to advance; for as to retreat,—the word had fallen into disuse among men grown presumptuous with success. The heaviest boat, their launch, with an eighteen-pound carronade, and crowded with mariners, now came with their barge. We heard the order —'Give way, my lads!' and, under a steady quick fire, which did some small damage on board of us, they dashed on with redoubled cheers, suffering severely from our commanding fire, though they were partly sheltered by some points of rock. They had undergone immense toil; the little air stirring scorched as that from the mouth of a blast-furnace; and it was evident they had not anticipated so warm a reception and unequal a combat. Desperation and their characteristic gallantry seemed to urge them on. Five of their little squadron laid us alongside, while the groans of the dying were mingled with their comrades' loud cheers and sharp fire.

We now took to our spears and small arms. Some of the most active, however, soon got up into our chains; and, though frequently repulsed, renewed their endeavours to get on board. While we were all intent on repelling them on our exposed side, the barge got across the bow; when a breeze and slight swell swinging the grab's bow in shore, many threw themselves on our deck from the land side. This calling us off, small parties boarded us in other directions.

I saw a Lascar, whom I had before reproved for skulking behind the mast, attempting to shirk down the hatchway. All the hatches were battened down, except the main one, under which the doctor was to operate. De Ruyter, fearing some of his Bombay sailors might run below, had ordered Van Scolpvelt to allow none but the wounded and powder-boys to go down or up; adding, with a smile, 'Clip the limbs off, doctor, from any cravens who desert their quarters!' to which Van Scolpvelt grinned a pleased assent, and answered, 'Never fear, Captain!' Aware of the evil example of cowardice, and how rapidly a panic takes place, I instantly shot the Lascar, who fell down the hatchway on the doctor, who was lugging at his leg.

At this moment I received a wound from a cutlass, and a pistol was thrust into my mouth with such force as to cut my lips, though, perhaps from the lock being wet, it did not take fire. De Ruyter swept the deck with his Arabs, and called out to me to look out on the starboard bow. Our opponents never had a shadow of chance in their favour, though they fought with the most foolhardy valour. Many of them, severely wounded, still held on by the rigging, and fought manfully; and when we had driven them headlong into the boats or the sea, they struggled to climb up again. Our loss was great in wounded; my veins seemed to run with burning lava; I felt a thrilling excitement that almost made me mad; though slashed and maimed in several parts of my body, I was totally insensible to pain; and my men fought, generally, if not with the same impetuosity, with equal courage.

Two more of the boats were lost by being stove and swamped alongside. Those of the enemy, who yet remained on board, were sullenly submitting, or rather had discontinued their hopeless resistance; one of them observing, 'Damn me, if I strike to a Negur, howsomever they sarve us!'

To quiet these fellows' scrupulous delicacy on that score, I addressed them with,—'Come, my lads, give up your arms; and you shall have what is more use to you now,—a piece of salt junk, and a glass of stiff grog.'

'Why,' said one to the other, 'it's all over, Tom! And though he ben't rigged, yet he speaks like a christian.'

Those who remained forward, many of them wounded, came to me, and gave up their arms.

De Ruyter told me, after the action, that as soon as Van Scolp-velt had learnt it was I who had inflicted summary justice on the Lascar, he came on deck, in the thick of the fight, to complain of my having, in disregard of orders, unjustifiably robbed him of an excellent patient, on whom he ardently wished to try some new instrument he had himself invented, which he held in his hand, and called a hexagonal, transverse, treble-toothed saw, rapidly revolving on its own axis, and cutting without pain or splinters. In vain he was reminded of the necessity of continuing at his station; he went on complaining, that, either in contempt of science, or from a plot, there seemed to be a general combination on board, a malevolent and wicked design to blast, destroy, and render abortive all the fondly cherished hopes of his philanthropic life. De Ruyter insisting on not being further interrupted, he stood in mournful and abstracted contemplation of his horrid instru-ment, when a sailor, struck by a ball in the heart, was spinning his death-round near him. Van whipt hold of him, ere he fell, by the arms, doubled up his body in the form of a Z, and with miracu-lous strength trotted off with him, saying, 'If I cannot have a living patient, I will essay my saw on a dead subject, and that forthwith!'

K

CHAPTER XXXIV

Pick'd like a red stag from the fallow herd
Of prisoners.
                              KEATS' MS.

The fight was o'er; the flashing through the gloom
Which robes the cannon as he wings a tomb,
Had ceased.
                              SHELLEY

WE had ordered parties to take possession of their boat and barge
alongside, while a cutter and gig were shoving off with some of
the officers and men, whom we had driven overboard. At the same
time a handful of men, led on by an officer, seeing his boat seized,
cut his way aft to get at De Ruyter, with whom he seemed determined to try his hand, or, if compelled, to surrender himself only
to the commander, not to his dusky crew. De Ruyter saw his
purpose, and called out to his men, who were struggling to oppose
him, but who could hardly use their weapons on account of the
dense crowd, 'Stand back, Arabs! Let him pass; but alone!'

My attention thus arrested, I looked aft, but instead, as I expected, of seeing him surrender his sword, he attacked De Ruyter
with great impetuosity. In bulk and stature I thought him the
most powerful man I had ever seen. De Ruyter seemed to think
he had found his match, and to be glad of it; for his form dilated,
and his piercing and full eye became fixed and contracted. He had
a pistol in his left hand, and a short, slightly curved sword in his
right. He several times ordered his men, who were pressing on,
to hold back, or advance at their peril. The stranger's common
ship's cutlass, made of the worst of metal, bent like a hoop as it
struck the sword-guard of De Ruyter, who stood alone on the
defensive. At this critical juncture, the cook, a Madagascar black,
was in the act of plunging his long knife into the stranger's side.
De Ruyter shifted his position, and pistolled the fellow; and said
to the stranger,—'Come, lieutenant, you have done every thing
the bravest could, and it is too hot to be thrusting carte and tierce.
You forget you are amongst old friends here. The game of fighting
has been long up; chance has decided for us. Come, cast away that
worthless weapon.'

I then went aft, and said, 'What! Aston!'

He threw his sword on the deck, and gazed on me with wonder. As soon as he could recognize me through my coating of blood, powder, and sweat, 'Ha!' said he, 'I see it all! The well known De Ruyter, that was De Witt, the plodding merchant at Bombay, —and—' (looking at me) 'and—you!'

He looked half reproachfully as he continued, 'Well, it is strange! And with two such fellows, and a crew composed of the same stuff, what chance had we? Then, to attempt to take you in such a position as this, to sacrifice the finest fellows in our ship in such a wild-goose venture, it was folly or madness, I know not which to call it!'

Some of the frigate's men were still endeavouring to escape; and two of the boats which had, in the confusion, shoved off, were now attempting to retake a third boat from some of our men, who had possession of her, when a desultory fire was kept up. De Ruyter was waxing wrathful, and came up to Aston with a hurried step, saying, 'Sir, I entreat you—speak to your men! If they are to expect the usages of war, let them desist from useless efforts at further opposition. It is mere wantonness, and I can no longer control my people, if yours are permitted, after they have struck their flag, to attempt to regain their boats. My only wish is to spare a greater effusion of blood.'

Aston sprung forward, commanded the men, struggling in the barge, to desist, and come on board, and those on board to go below. 'As for those boats already shoved off,' he said, 'they must take their chance.'

'Let them!' replied De Ruyter, 'I shall not impede their flight. I do not want boats or prisoners. Nevertheless I must do my duty in keeping those I have got, though I am sorry to have them. It is the most unprofitable victory I ever gained. I have lost some of my best men, and the services of others that are wounded.'

'Continued success,' observed Aston, 'makes us perhaps too confident, and this is the result.'

'No,' said De Ruyter, 'it is that confidence which insures your success in almost all you undertake. All nations have had their turn: while they thought themselves invulnerable, they were so; when they began to doubt it, no longer were they victorious. People become what they believe they are. The flags of Europe are faded, old, and rent, successively decaying. Those stars and stripes' (pointing to an American flag covering the hatchway) 'must,—it is their station,—soar aloft! But,' (turning to me) 'shew your friend below, and make him welcome. There is much to be done. Yet what? holla! what is the matter? Why, you denied being wounded!'

From toil, exhaustion, and loss of blood, I dropped so suddenly on the deck, as if shot, that De Ruyter could not catch me, though he contrived to break my fall.

Van Scolpvelt had been some time on deck, looking over and summing up, with satisfaction, his rich harvest of patients. He viewed, with a malignant glance, an assistant surgeon, who had accompanied Aston in his boat, and was bandaging a wound on the lieutenant's leg, having obtained De Ruyter's sanction to attend exclusively on his own wounded, which were by far the more numerous. These were by no means prepossessed in favour of Van Scolpvelt; on the contrary, as he was busily scanning amongst them for a case of amputation, in order to make a trial of his newly-invented instrument, its horrid appearance, in such hands, made the stout hearts of these hardy sailors quail. I heard one of them say, 'Blast my heart, Tom, here's an Indian devil of a cannibal going to cast off our head-matting,' (that is, scalp us,) 'cut us up into junk, and sarve us out, like so much salt pork, to the ship's messes!'

'I'll be damned,' replied the other, 'if old Nick brings his hell fork here to ship me into the harness cask, I'll sarve him out with a long spoon!' At the same time he picked up one of the shot-ladles.

The offended amputator complained of this mutinous conduct to De Ruyter, just before I fainted; and then said, leaning over me, 'I thought how it would be! He laughed when I offered to dress the contusion on his face; but he won't laugh now!' (taking out his case of instruments.) 'Yes! he knows better than the doctor! I would sooner smoke my *meershaum* in the powder-magazine than have him to cure; for he is self-willed and obstinate as the she-kind are. He killed my patient, too! Could he not have left the man to me? So fond of shooting people, this is a judgment on him! But for him, I should have had the best case!'

During this soliloquy, which Aston repeated to me, they carried me into the cabin, where Scolpvelt loosened my shawl-sash, and, on taking off my stained shirt, found two other wounds, one from a ball through the small part of my arm, the other a contusion on my side, from the butt end of a musquet. 'A judgment,' he continued, 'for the most atrocious of crimes—deceiving his surgeon! He would not learn how to put on a tourniquet either; what foolish and irrational people the English are! I don't doubt but that he would rather lose his life than his obstinacy. To cheat and rob his doctor of a pa-ti-e-n-t!' (here he was scooping about, and shoving tow into the wound,) 'Oh, ho! he don't like that! I thought he had no feeling.'

Aston told me I was roused into motion by his applications; then, being called on by a dozen different messengers, he hastily dressed and bound up my wounds, and went to attend on his numerous patients.

CHAPTER XXXV

In stern reproach demanded where
Was now his grateful sense of former care?
Where all his hopes to see his name aspire
And blazon Briton's thousand glories higher?
His feverish lips thus broke the gloomy spell.
                                BYRON

ON recovering my senses, I found Aston stooping over me, sponging my face and breast with vinegar and water. It was some time before I understood where I was; for Aston's face reminded me of my drowning frolic. 'I have been dreaming,' I said; 'is that Aston? where am I?'

'Where I am sorry to find you. Under any flag but this, I could have forgiven you!'

This recalled my flitting remembrances together, and I said, 'You will allow I had cause to be disgusted with the former. Now I fight under De Ruyter. Shew me a braver man, and I'll leave him; but there is none braver or nobler.'

'Ay, he is well known for a gallant fellow, and I have found him so; but that is not to the purpose.'

'Well, Aston, you know how I was situated; what better could I do? What, in my case, would you have done?'

He thought a moment, and taking my hand, said kindly, 'By

heaven, I believe the same!' But then added, 'when I was at your age.'

'Ah! if you knew him as well as I do, you might go farther, and say at any age. I know I would; so let's say no more about it. I want to know how things are going on upon deck. It seems a dark night, and we're in a devilish queer place. What! is that the surf breaking against us?'

'No, against the rocks. Who would have ventured in such an anchorage as this but De Ruyter? I see his object, to prevent our ship's getting alongside of him. It is wonderful! I should as soon have thought of anchoring on the sand-heads in a tiffoon.'

'Rest satisfied; he knows what he is at. 'Tis not the first time he has lain here; he told me so. But come, boy, hand out the grub and grog. I must supply the loss of this red liquor; I am dry as a sponge. What the devil has old Scolpvelt been at with my side? I feel the print of his cursed talons festering in my flesh. That fellow is ready made for chief torturer in hell. I wish, Aston, you would let your doctor overhaul me, for Van has spoiled my appetite.'

Aston sent for him, and said: 'That doctor of yours has certainly an extraordinary look. I can't say I like the cut of his jib.'

'Not half so bad as the feel of his paws; they burn like blue stone.'

Aston's surgeon now came down. As doctors never openly censure individuals of their tribe, except by direct implication— that is, by always undoing what another has done—so did he. Some soothing liniment was applied, and the accursed tow plugs were removed; which gave me as much relief as drawing a splinter out of a wound, in which it had been long rankling. Thus eased, I resumed my talk with Aston, shook hands with him, asked him about our old ship, and why he had quitted her; for I knew she was not the one which had chased us.

He told me a friend of his had just come out in command of the present frigate, and had got him appointed as first lieutenant. Having received intelligence of two French frigates, they had gone in all haste to report the same to the admiral at Madras; and he had ordered them, and another frigate, to go and look after, and by no means lose sight of the Frenchmen. They had discovered them lying in Port Louis, which they had been some days blockading. 'Besides that,' said he, 'we had intelligence that De Ruyter was out in his corvette; with orders to endeavour to cut him off in his return to port. Not the smallest idea had we of finding him here in the grab. We all mistook him for an Arab. I thought I had seen her somewhere, forgetting it was at Bombay. But then, I had not the slightest reason to suppose De Ruyter had any concern with her, or even De Witt; much less that they were one and the same person. He has done more harm to the Company's trade than all the French men of war together; and his head is worth a frigate's ransom. It is wonderful how long he has kept clear of the traps set for him, clever as he is.'

De Ruyter having made his arrangements on deck, came down, shook Aston by the hand, and said: 'This mischance of your falling into our hands will be no great evil. You can better afford it than I. What mercy should I have if the merchant inquisitors had me in their gripe? I would rather feel the elephant's knee, when in wrath, on my breast.'

He then added: 'to put you as much at ease as circumstances will allow, I have only to say that I leave the disposition of your men to your judgment, satisfied with your word of honour. How many men had you in the boats?'

'With officers and marines, sixty or more.'

'Well, while your ship is in the neighbourhood, your men may be impatient and troublesome. She will be off here in the morning, and you may send the doctor on board with the badly wounded; they will be better attended to there for we are lumbered up here, and altogether unprepared for such unexpected guests. I had no idea of any of your cruizers being off here. If you have any letters to write, get them ready.'

He returned on deck, Aston wrote, and I slept till the ensuing morning. I was then well enough, with a stick, to scramble on deck. A look-out, whom we had placed on a point of rock on shore, gave us notice of the frigate's motions. Soon after day-break she stood in as far as she could with safety, to where we lay, with a top gallant breeze. We sent our long boat on board her with a flag of truce, the wounded, under the care of the surgeon, and with letters from Aston.

The Captain of the frigate returned his thanks, but promised, notwithstanding De Ruyter's gentlemanly and humane conduct, to rout him out of his lurking-place.

To this effect every expedient was used. But De Ruyter knew, by the signal made to the other frigate, that she was on no account to quit the blockade of Port Louis. She having lost her boats, could do nothing, it being impossible for her to get within gun-shot of the grab. Her only chance was in blockading him; but on account of the frequent storms prevalent at that time of year, she could not do that effectually; so that De Ruyter felt little uneasiness. 'As to the rest,' said he, 'I shall sleep better, and eat better with a slight excitement to help my digestion, and keep that portion of my blood, which is Dutch, from stagnating.'

To avoid tediousness, should I have been hitherto fortunate enough to shun that rock on which so many writers have wrecked themselves and their readers' hopes, I shall borrow an extract from De Ruyter's abrupt and succinct journal:

'Ten P.M. dark and cloudy; lightning; heavy showers of rain; got under weigh; warped out from our anchorage; wind fresh from the land; aided by the lightning, kept clear of the breakers; at one A.M. made sail; turned to windward of the island, which had been our refuge.'

This was on the third day after our action with the boats. We stretched over to Diego Garcia, and got out of the track of the frigates, having my friend Aston, and twenty six of his men on board.

CHAPTER XXXVI

There's nought, no doubt, so much the spirit calms,
As rum and true religion.
BYRON

DE RUYTER was willing to emancipate Aston, but the latter would not hear of it. He said he disdained to evade the natural and merited consequences of failure in his attempt. Had he been successful, he hoped he should have wished to be generous as De Ruyter; but his power would have been limited. Consequently, now that the reverse had happened, he readily submitted to the usages of war; entreating De Ruyter not to hazard his own reputation, and the allegiance he owed to the sovereign under whose flag he was fighting, by stretching his power to save him from, he trusted, a short incarceration, however severe;—short, because, as there were so many French prisoners in India, an exchange would readily be effected.

'It shall be as you think best,' said De Ruyter. 'Only be sure of this: I have power enough at least to promise you that, if the name of prisoner does not gall your patience, you shall not feel any of its indignities. If I thought otherwise, you should be none, where I command. My allegiance is of ink, not of blood;—I owe the Frenchman none. Our compact is (as all should be, if intended to endure) one of mutual interest; which ceasing, either party would break it without an instant's hesitation. The scum that the French revolution has boiled up, domineers at the Isle of France, a Botany Bay to which France transports her lawless felons. There they are frivolous, fickle, and violent as the monsoon gales in Port Louis, where the wind blows from every quarter of the compass between sunrise and sunset. But they dare not trifle with me. I say, dare not; for, with all their trumpet-tongued vaunting, they are neither brave nor noble at heart. Their courage is but lip-deep, their rage but as a hurricane in petticoats. They will hate you, because you are brave, and have so often plucked their borrowed plumes, exhibiting them in their naked gull-like form; or they will hate you, because you are taller, have a better coat, or beard, or button. They are envious, malicious, cruel, and dastardly, as is the mowing and chattering tribe of Madagascar monkeys; noisy and filthy as the draggletailed dysenteric cockatoo; vain, conceited, libidinous, and bestial as the ourang-outang of Borneo.'

Aston looked in amaze, and I laughed at this tirade.

He continued: 'I tell you this, because I wish you to understand I am serving not them but myself. I despise them as a nation, though there are a few redeeming characters among them. With all their vaunted civilization they would treat you with indignity. So seldom have they an opportunity of heaving up their accumulated bile on an English prisoner, they would play all sorts of fantastic tricks on you. But they shall not. Let them choke with their own venom, ere I permit an Englishman, and my prisoner, to be even looked at with contempt. So now we understand each other. Come, my lads, let us see what shot remains in the locker. I am afraid our cookery and crockery have suffered since these rude visitors boarded us. But this cool and cloudy weather does not need the aid of shaddock-bitters to sharpen the edge of appetite. Go down;—I'll just give a look round, and follow you.'

As we went down I called out for our steward, Louis, telling him we were hungry as hyenas. 'Yet who the devil,' said I, 'can masticate the dry junk and rotten salt fish on the table? Come, old boy, fork out something better than this; or I shall be obliged to make a devil of Van Scolp, and grill him.'

Louis replied, 'He once in, you never eat more. I rather eat a horse's hoof.'

Scolpvelt himself then came down the ladder to look at my wounds. 'No, no, old Van,' I said, 'no caustic plugs for me! Sit down, and fill out some of the loose skin hanging about you, like a shrivelled tarpaulin.'

'What!' he exclaimed, 'you must not eat! I have ordered the boy to make you some congee.'

'Curse your rice water! Go, Louis, go up to the cook, and tell him to grill us a couple of fowls, with a piece of pork. I want something solid.'

Van would have countermanded this, had I not clapped my hand as a stopper on his jaw-tackle. Then pouring a bottle of Madeira into a slop-basin, I was about to empty it down my throat, but he struggled hard against me, declaring I should not, while his patient, commit suicide, and stigmatise his system. He called his boy, and told him to bring a bottle of his concentrated lemon juice. 'Unless you drink congee gruel,' said he, feeling my pulse, 'the lemon, with your febrile symptoms, is your only fluid. It is the fruit of the citrus, of the class polyadelphia, order, icosandria. It is the chief ingredient in citric acid, valuable for pharmaceutic uses on shore, and would be a thousand times of more use on shipboard, where it is never to be had. But I,—I, Van Scolpvelt, have long been labouring to make it applicable by condensation. Hitherto, among the chymists, it has shewn symptoms of decomposition. But by the aid of a valuable old manuscript of mine, written by the learned Winschotan, the preceptor of the immortal Boerhaave,[1] bearing date 1673, together with some small additions of my own, I have at last succeeded in preserving it in the concrete form. It is now sixteen months old; and you shall see it better and fresher than when plucked from the tree. Here, boy, give it me!'

As he turned to the boy, he forgot the Madeira, which I swallowed at a draught. He gave me one look, put the concrete essence in his pocket, hastened on deck, and told De Ruyter he washed his hands of me, that he had not been accustomed to attend mad people, and recommended a strait-waistcoat.

After supper Louis handed out a dusty-looking stone bottle

of the right bamboo-coloured skedam. We satisfied ourselves it had the true zest, or, according to Louis's dainty observation, it had the taste and colour of flame, mellowed with smoke of the juniper-tree.

'Come, Louis, devil us a biscuit. You are the only useful man on board—no one can equal your curried devil. It will bring out the oily and delicious odour of the juniper-smoke.'

As Louis toddled on deck, Aston inquired, 'What is Louis? He seems every thing here—purser, steward, clerk—and now you are adding cook to his other vocations.'

'He is, in fact,' I answered, 'a double man—Dutch stock crossed by a Frenchman—a nondescript fellow, born at the Mauritius. He unites the characteristics of the two nations—the portentous belly and square beam of the Hollander, with the wiry arms and legs of the Frenchman, like a hogshead of skedam on stilts. His face is a ludicrous compound of both parents; full and round as the pumpkin, and rubicund withal, with a Gallic nose, like a ripe red fig, the stalk uppermost, a mouth from ear to ear like the bat's, and heavy, flabby, moist lips, which, when gathered up in talk, display a long double row of ebonies, similar to the piles at the entrance of a Dutch dike or canal, and, like that, ever ready to receive whatever is offered. His natural chin is ridiculously short, but, like his stomach, of a prolific nature, for it has shaken three reefs out—a mass of fat stuck on a thorough-bred French neck, long, bony, and arched out in the dromedary fashion. His head seems formed for nothing but a golden crown, as no covering with less ballast can stay on it in a breeze of wind, and, indeed, he goes by the name of *Louis le Grand*. Here he comes—look at him, and say if I have exaggerated.'

When the devil and grilled fowls were placed on the table, I bade Louis come to an anchor on the locker, and explain to Aston how he came to be promoted to the office of purser.

'Vy, Sir, de last purser die.'

'Come, I know that; but how did he die?'

He then commenced a history in his broken English, shewing how the late purser, in his too great love of economy, was about to put on the cabin-table the leather-like rind of a dry, over-salted, Dutch cheese; how he, Louis, objected to it as uneatable; how the other abused him for growing dainty and wasteful, affirming that the cheese was a good cheese; how to convict Louis, whom he called an obstinate half-bred Dutch hog, he splintered off a ragged fragment, and attempted to bolt it; how it stuck in his throat like the horns of a goat when swallowed whole by a boa; how Scolpvelt was on shore; and how Louis, as a kind friend, smacked the poor purser on his back till he died, and then stepped into his shoes.

CHAPTER XXXVII

Few things surpass old wine, and they may preach
Who please, the more because they preach in vain;
Let us have wine and women, mirth and laughter,
Sermons and soda-water the day after.
BYRON

WE all laughed at Louis, though there was no one on board that did not feel indebted to him for his good services. He was indefatigably industrious, and having a stomach himself, like a chronometer, he never missed the hour of serving out the rations; besides, he was scrupulously honest in weight and measure. Under the abundant and well-organized system of this conscientious purser we rarely had cause to complain; and he used to pride himself on the crew's increase of power and weight since his appointment; the only exception, which gave him infinite pain, was Van Scolpvelt. He said, 'I believe he de devil! He live on physic and smoke—he smoke all day and night—eat noting—sleep noting!—he must be de devil or noting! Is he not?'

While conversing on the admirable purveyorship of Louis, De Ruyter joined us, and spoke highly in his favour. 'Nothing,' said he, 'is of such importance in a commander as feeding his men well. Sailors are really very little eaters; but if they are stinted, they are ungovernable and savage as beasts of prey, which, even lions, when surfeited, are innoxious. Your fleet,' turning to Aston, 'once mutinied;'—men that never rebelled before took your wooden walls from you, because you stinted them in provisions, when the united riches of the world could not have seduced them from their duty. Your soldiers too break through all discipline, and cease to be soldiers, when deprived of their rations. With us, who only hold our command by the suffrages of those under us, nothing puts our rule in such jeopardy as when surrounded by half-starved men. Hunger is deaf to reason, to fear, and to the iron curb of habit. The only thing requisite on board a ship is to prevent waste and drunkenness,—which last is, in its effects, akin to hunger. Come, old Louis, let us have another flash of the liquid lightning, for good cheer is as necessary as a good compass on board a ship; and then, as our fellows have had hard work, go on deck, and splice the main brace. You have corrupted our men's orthodoxy; your eloquence has overcome their scruples regarding gin;—so easy is it to make converts on a point of faith tallying with our desires! This Louis has persuaded my Mussulman crew that gin was not, and is not forbidden by Mahomet; on the contrary, he interdicted wine, in order that nothing but gin might be drunk in the world, in compliance to a miraculous vision, wherein an angel presented him with a stone-bottle full, brought as a sample from Heaven,—or Holland!'

Louis went on deck, and presently returned to tell us there was a blue shark in our wake, reminding us at the same time that our fresh provisions were exhausted. Then, as he hauled a shark-hook out of the locker, he said: 'I go catch him. He very good to eat, in de vay I cook him.'

At this we all turned up, and having baited the hook with a fowl's entrails, the greedy monster hardly let it touch the water, ere he darted on, turned quickly round, and without benizon or grace, gulped the garbage, regardless of the barbed iron. We soon succeeded in hauling him on deck; he was a gigantic one; and notwithstanding the remains of a sailor's jacket was found within him, Louis instantly employed his knife, and a plentiful dish of cutlets was carved out of his sirloin.

This wiled away the evening. The watch was set. De Ruyter went to pore over his volume of Shakspeare; and I leant over the hammock nettings, ruminating on the past, the present, and marvelling at what was to come.

Henceforth everything went on pleasantly and merrily; or if interrupted by untoward occurrences, such as are inseparable from a sea-life, where men are huddled up like herrings in a barrel, and will sometimes ferment, still they passed over as the summer clouds, leaving the sky yet clearer than before. Time lagged not on board the grab. I was associated with the two men I most admired and loved. I wanted but Walter;—and then if a deluge had swallowed up all the world, and the grab had been our ark,

I should have lost nothing to weep for, so narrow and selfish were my views in this my dawn of life. Those I loved were all the world to me; to all else I was totally indifferent. My affections were germinating, yet unexpanded. My passions and feelings were in embryo, except those awakened into being by Aston and De Ruyter. They were in fact alike; though, from education and country, habits had so grown on them, and encrusted them, that, to a casual observer, no two men could seem more dissimilar. But at the core they were the same, they had the same stability of character, heroic courage, gentle and affectionate manners, and open manly bearing. They soon grew fast friends.

Sailors consider the sea as their country, and all true bred sons of Neptune as their foster-brothers. National prejudices are washed and rubbed off by the elements. In a ship intimacies are formed in an hour, which would require years on shore; and what is never done on land is freely done at sea, when shipmates share purses, and give more frankly than the nearest of kin lend,—a word not in the vocabulary of a sailor. Sea-air ripens friendship quicker than the hot-bed of a city. Good fellowship, sincerity, and generosity seem to have flown for refuge to the ocean.

After a few days, we descried a strange sail to the westward. She bore down on us, and we, finding we outran her, shortened sail, till she came near enough for us to make her out. De Ruyter then knew her to be a French corvette. We hoisted a private signal, which they answered. We hove to. At sunset she came under our quarters; and after some conversation with the captain, De Ruyter went on board, where he had a long conference. On his return we altered our course for the island of Madagascar.

Several of our wounded died. Not having sufficient room for our prisoners, De Ruyter, first consulting Aston, and being well acquainted with the French commander, who was a humane and honourable man, removed them under the direction of one of their own midshipmen, and a marine lieutenant, to the corvette, with the exception of Aston, and four of the men, who intreated permission to remain with their officer. This permission, through my intercession, was easily obtained.

CHAPTER XXXVIII

Afric is all the sun's, and, as her earth,
Her human clay is kindled; full of power
For good or evil; burning from its birth,
The Moorish blood partakes the planet's hour,
And like the soil beneath it will bring forth.

BYRON

WE then understood from De Ruyter that the corvette had been
sent to examine into an act of piracy, committed, it was supposed,
by the Maratti, a formidable nest of brigands, on the north point
of the island of Madagascar. The Portuguese and French had
several times attempted to settle there, but had always been compelled to abandon the place with great loss, the natives having
harassed them unceasingly, day and night; till at last they declared
the climate to be pernicious, and the settlement of no use, and they
decamped in the night (that is, those who could), with such pre-
cipitation, that they left the buildings they had erected, and some
temporary fortifications, to be occupied by the Maratti, together
with other lawless bands.

These Maratti, an ancient horde of pirates, formerly dwelt on
the east side of Madagascar, where they became a terror to the
early settlers in the neighbouring islands; especially by their
junction with the pirates of Nossi Ibrahim, afterwards called St.
Mary's. They cut off the supplies of cattle and provisions furnished by Madagascar; and even landed, burned, and slaughtered
the inhabitants of the Mauritius and the island of Bourbon. The
Dutch, then in possession of the Mauritius, were so straitened for
provisions, and tormented by these hornets, that eventually they
were compelled to abandon the island. Like the Portuguese, they
too had their ready excuse, and pleaded locusts and rats as the
cause of their abandonment; but there are, as old Shylock says,
'land-rats and water-rats,' and these last were the rats who drove
out the Dutch. They retired to the Cape of Good Hope, where
they found the brute-like Hottentot a far less noxious animal than
the water-rats—Pirates, I mean.

The French settled in the island of Bourbon, close at hand,
instantly took advantage of this; and, like the cuckoo, took posses-

sion of the Dutchman's nest ere it grew cool. Port Louis was then a miserable hamlet; for the Dutch love mud and wood, of which, as elsewhere, their dwellings were exclusively composed.

Soon after, the French, Portuguese, and Dutch companies formed an armament to exterminate the Maratti, who committed great havock on their trade. They attacked the pirates in their strongholds of Nossi Ibrahim and other posts, and, with immense loss on their part, destroyed a great portion of their war-canoes, and drove the pirates for refuge to the hills of Nossi Ibrahim, and the mountains of Madagascar.

Now the Maratti, after driving off, or rather doing as they had been done by,—exterminating a French settlement which the Company had planted in the bay of Antongil, had re-established themselves on the coast of Madagascar, near Cape St. Sebastian, where they grew formidable in numbers. They were encouraged by the natives, who found them a less nuisance than the Europeans, who plundered their coast, and massacred them, whenever they wanted a sallad or a fresh egg. Here the Maratti, hardy and desperate, became adventurous from success, having defeated several attempts to suppress them; and they were widely spreading the circle of devastation. By their robberies on the Indian seas, they had already depopulated the Comoro, Mayotta, Mohilla, and other islands in their vicinity, by seizing the inhabitants, and selling them to the European slave-merchants; though prior to their expulsion from Nossi Ibrahim, they never could be induced to enter into the slave trade. So abhorrent was it to them at that period, that they invariably massacred the crew of every vessel they found carrying on this loathsome traffic, to which their own, as pirates, was comparatively just and honourable. This was the principal cause of the combination among the European merchant companies, to annihilate them, as unchristian barbarians, without light enough to see their own interest. At St. Sebastian (I suppose the patron saint of slaves), they speedily gave indications of being less heathenishly inclined; for there they entered, with true christian zeal, into all the ramifications of slave-dealing, and monopolised that trade in the east, with the same system of exclusiveness as the Dutch had methodised for spice, and the English for tea. They learned statistics, mapped the islands, counted their population, divided them into districts, calculated their power of breeding, and every spring and autumn sent out a fleet of proas, visiting the different islands in rotation. They considerately refrained from pouncing on the same island for three or four, or sometimes more years. The young and able-bodied were selected, from the age of ten to twenty-five, marked on the buttocks with a hot iron and black powder, and carried to St. Sebastian, where they remained till an occasion offered for disposing of them to the French, Dutch, Portuguese, or English. This was a better method, more profitable, and attended with less difficulty than Malthus and his heterodox mode of stopping pro-creation for which a very honest woman once told me he was sure to go to the devil who would hand him over to be well mauled by old maids and their apes.

The Maratti learnt another lesson from the Europeans: they left no means untried to foment disunion and hatred among the natives of Madagascar, and enlightened them as to the advantage of selling their prisoners through them, out of which they deducted a very pretty interest, in the way of dustoory. As long as they restricted themselves to kidnapping and selling slaves, however obtained, whether from their own kin and kind, whether they were sons sold by fathers, or brothers and sisters by the first born, all was fair and honest traffic. But a French schooner, having plun-dered a village of sheep and poultry, and beaten the inhabitants, was pursued by the Maratti in their war-canoes, boarded, taken, and, ere the French had time to cut the throats of the sheep, they themselves were slaughtered, and the innocent sheep released, and restored to their pasture. The representatives of the grand nation at the Mauritius were struck with horror at this daring atrocity; and if unatoned for by an ample massacre, their honour would be compromised. A total extermination of the natives of Madagascar was first contemplated. These ideas of severity were, however, mitigated, owing to the unlucky circumstance of their only disposable force, two frigates, being blockaded in the port by two much smaller English frigates, or, generally, by no more than one. At last a corvette arrived in the port, to windward of the island, and she was sent with ample orders, but with very limited means, to execute them. This was the vessel we fell in with.

The commander, a young man of engaging manners, the next morning came on board, rejoiced at the opportunity of getting information from De Ruyter. He used every argument to induce

L

him to join the expedition; and insisted on his dining on board the corvette, with Aston and myself, at four, by which time De Ruyter promised to give a final answer.

CHAPTER XXXIX

How speed the outlaws? Stand they well prepared
Their plundered wealth, and robber rock to guard?
Dream they of this our preparation, doom'd
To view with fire their scorpion's nest consumed?

BYRON

THAT evening De Ruyter told the French commander that he had only one difficulty to get over, and, if that could be mastered, it would please him well to keep company with him till the blockade of Port Louis was raised. 'But,' said he, 'you must be aware that, with our force, we can literally do nothing; unless, perhaps, to ascertain who the pirates were, wherefore they had attacked the French flag, and whether the schooner had given cause for that attack. For,' he added, 'I am sorry to say we are somewhat too hasty, overbearing, and unjust in our dealings with the natives of these islands. Therefore let us first discover who were the aggressors, and then we may find a time to punish them.'

The captain replied he had boarded several vessels, which had been recently plundered by the long war-canoes of St. Sebastian.

'I doubt little,' said De Ruyter, 'of their being the Maratti. But you know they seldom go to sea, unless in the south-west monsoon; and what can we do against their numbers?'

To this the captain answered, 'From every thing I hear they are now out; but where, I cannot learn. We must first think of your despatches; and I believe we shall not be long without an opportunity of sending them; for I expect every day to fall in with some of our cattle-boats.'

From this time we continued in company. The weather being particularly fine, with little wind stirring, we passed our time very pleasantly, in giving parties alternately on board the corvette and the grab. Aston, who had been a prisoner in France when a midshipman, spoke French as perfectly as De Ruyter. At daylight we used to separate, and keep a look-out to windward; and towards sunset we bore down, and remained together during the night. The first vessel we fell in with was a schooner, which, after a long chace, we made out to be an American. As soon as she discovered we were French, she hove to. She was a beautiful vessel, long, low in the water, with lofty raking masts, which tapered away till they were almost too fine to be distinguished, and the swallow-tailed vanes above fluttered like fire-flies. The starred flag waved over her taffrail. As she filled and hauled on a wind, to cross under our stern, with a fresh breeze to which she gently heeled, I thought there was nothing so beautiful as the arrowy sharpness of her bow, and the gradually receding fineness of her quarters. She looked and moved like an Arab horse on the desart, and was as obedient to command. There was a lightness and bird-like buoyancy about her, that exclusively belongs to this class of vessels. America has the merit of having perfected this nautical wonder, as far surpassing all other vessels in exquisite proportion and beauty, as the gazelle excels all animated nature. Even to this day no other country has succeeded in either the building or the working of these vessels, in comparison with America.

A light and fairy-looking boat, akin to the Nautilus, was now launched over the gunwale. It appeared a marvel how she could support the four herculean mariners that jumped into her. Two or three strokes of her long wooden fins brought her instantly alongside of us, and De Ruyter was overjoyed at meeting with his countrymen; for though his father was Dutch, he was a naturalised American, and he had known no other home. He wrung the captain of the schooner by the hand, talked of nothing but Boston, his birth-place, and the port whence the schooner had last sailed. She had touched at St. Malo's, and was bound to the Mauritius.

This was one of the fast-sailing schooners, which drove what was called a forced trade for drugs and spices. They were principally Americans, selected for their matchless sailing. After leaving America, they touched at some French port, got French papers, and sometimes had commissions and lettres de marques. They were armed and well manned; and all on board being allowed a portion of the profits on the freightage, they were interested in its success. They had a nominal French captain, a mere cipher, but necessary, as America was then at peace with England.

This schooner had a cargo, to my mind richer than gold, of cognac, claret, sauterne, and a variety of European luxuries;

which, when she had discharged at the Mauritius, were to be exchanged for spices. She had run the gauntlet through the English squadron in the Bay of Biscay, and at the Cape of Good Hope; and had we not given her information of the blockade at the Mauritius, she would have run another risk of being captured. De Ruyter advised her to put into the port to windward of the Mauritius, gave our despatches, and wrote some letters. She, in return, let us have a pipe of claret, a hogshead of cognac, and good store of edibles.

The corvette now coming up, we separated from the American, and kept our course for St. Sebastian. Soon after we fell in with, and boarded some Arab trading-vessels. They had been plundered: the greater part of their cargoes and crews were taken out, leaving merely a few old men to work the vessels, with a little water and rice. This was committed by a fleet of eighteen Maratti proas, each having from eighteen to forty men on board. It appeared that this fleet was bound to some of the islands in the Mosambique channel.

De Ruyter now conferred with the French commander; and his advice was that we should, in the absence of the greatest part of the pirates, effect a landing at St. Sebastian, surprise them during the night, plunder and destroy their fortifications, burn their town, and rescue their prisoners; for doubtless they were loaded there, as they had kept possession of two of the largest of the Arab traders. This was agreed to; and the corvette supplied us with two of her brass guns, and lent us fifteen of her soldiers.

Without any thing particular happening, we got into 15° 20′ south latitude, ran on till we saw the high land of Madagascar, and kept to the north-east side of the island, till we had run well in shore; when we sent a boat, and brought off some fishermen, who gave us information. We then crept round the land, to the north, at night, De Ruyter piloting, being in sight of the north point of Cape St. Sebastian, which stretches far out to sea, in the form of an estuary. Taking advantage of the twilight, De Ruyter piloted us through a narrow channel in the reefs; and, before mid-night, we brought to as close to the rocks as we could on the east side, having the cape between us and the town, by which means we were unobserved.

It was a cloudy night, with frequent showers of rain. We got out our boats, and landed a hundred and twenty officers and men well armed: eighty from the corvette, and forty from the grab. To do the Frenchman justice, he felt no envy of De Ruyter's superior knowledge; on the contrary, he insisted on his taking the command, and gave his officers orders to implicitly obey De Ruyter in every particular, he himself staying on board the corvette.

On landing, De Ruyter divided the men into three parties, retaining to himself and the first officer the strongest, consisting of fifty men, armed with muskets and bayonets; a French lieutenant commanded thirty-five, and I thirty. I had a part of De Ruyter's favourite band of Arabs, armed with their lances, and short carbines. We kept on together, till we got round the cape; then De Ruyter ordered me to ascend the rocks, and keep round the hill, nearly at the foot of which the pirates' town was situated, till I arrived immediately above it. The lieutenant was directed to keep along the beach, till he was in a line with me; while De Ruyter, with the main body, went directly forward. We were all to march as near as possible, and by every precaution to avoid discovery. When we had taken up our respective positions, we were to conceal ourselves till just before the dawn of day, when the main body would fire a rocket, which, on being answered by us, was to be the signal for a simultaneous advance and attack. We were to make what observations we could, under cover of the night, as to the readiest means of getting into the town, which was defended by low mud walls, having three entrance-ports. On taking possession of these entrances, we were each to leave a party to keep them, who were to kill or make prisoners all who attempted to escape, whilst the remainder attacked those within. If any of us should be previously discovered, or if we should be attacked, we were to retreat to the main body. After some other instructions, De Ruyter commanded us to kill none, at our peril, but those with arms in their hands; and particularly to avoid doing injury to the women, children, and prisoners.

CHAPTER XL

With a nimble savageness attacks,
Escapes, makes fiercer onset, then anew
Eludes death, giving death to most that dare
Trespass within the circuit of his sword.

KEATS' MS.

MY party had some distance to go, and up a rugged and precipitous path, where we were suddenly stopped by a black and deep
ravine or chasm, at the bottom of which we heard the dashing of
water. It would have been folly to attempt to cross here; for a
couple of men, on the other side, might have perhaps opposed us
with success. We therefore went lower down the mountain; and
it was with great toil, and loss of time, that we crossed to the
opposite side. My impetuosity spurred me on; and when it wanted
little more than half an hour to dawn, our scouts in advance gave
us the welcome intelligence of being near our destination. I now
halted our party, and advanced with two men. We descended a
narrow sheep-path, amidst broken and stony ground, overgrown
with prickly pears, low shrubs, and clumps of the palm cocoa.
We heard distinctly the surf breaking on the beach, with the
monotonous regularity of the ticking of a clock at night. The
ground became smoother, and we discerned, close under us, the
low huts of the town, huddled together, and looking like a multitude of large white ant-hills, or bee-hives. We then came to some
ruins, on a conical hill, up which one of the Arabs climbed on all
fours, like a jackall, and found it was deserted. I sent the other
man back, to bring up our party, as this was a capital post to occupy,
in case of surprise. With great caution I then descended to the
wall of the town; it was low, and in a crumbling state, till I came
to two or three palm trees, where a mud hut was built on the
wall, like a swallow's nest. Below there was an entrance, or rather
a hole, which evidently led to the interior. Having examined the
place well, we hastily returned. The clouds gave indications of
breaking in the east. The rain was still falling. I crept down with
ten men, and advanced under the shadow of the wall, till within
pistol-shot of the entrance. There taking our position, we im-
patiently awaited the concerted signal from De Ruyter.

The night was tardily withdrawing her dusky canopy, and the morning advanced gloomily. The hushed stillness was ominously broken by the whizzing noise of the rocket-signal, flying like a meteor over the devoted Maratti town. It evidently came, not as it should have done, from De Ruyter, but from the lieutenant, being exactly opposite to my position, which shewed that the lieutenant's party was discovered, or anticipated discovery. I replied to it; and nearly at the same moment another rocket ascended from De Ruyter. This commanded an immediate attack; and scarcely had it risen to the height of the lance I held in my hand, ere I had forced the trifling impediments at the entrance; and, in my haste, stumbled over something on the ground. The man, for such it was, essayed to rise. I dropped my lance, and grappled him by the throat. The greater part of my Arabs rushed in. I called out to force open the inner entrance; which done, the faint light shewed us four or five of the Maratti rising from the ground, commencing their war-cry. These were despatched quickly. The man I held scarcely needed the aid of the creese, which I forced through his breast into the sandy floor.

A commotion was now raised within. We got through the rude out-works into the interior. The remainder of my men were dropping down inside the wall, which, with the aid of their lances, they had scaled. A noise of the assault on the other side was growing high; and presently we heard the sharp report of fire-arms. I left a portion of my men to guard the entrance, and advanced, as previously arranged, to the centre of the habitations; the inmates of which—for the surprise was complete—came out in twos and threes, in great confusion and terror. Those who crossed our path we speared; and those seeking to save themselves by flight we fired at. We gave them not an instant to rally, till we arrived at the ruins of a considerable building in the centre, which had been erected as a magazine and court of guard by the Portuguese or Dutch. Here having taken possession, we halted. Presently the lieutenant, and then De Ruyter, came up; he said, 'Well done, my lad! always first in danger.' Then leaving an officer and twenty men to keep this place, we advanced in three parties, dividing the men equally, with strict injunctions to make all the prisoners we could, and send them in to this post.

De Ruyter told me to go round to the port I had entered, as there would be an attempt to escape that way to the mountains;

and while he was speaking, a sharp fire was opened from that quarter. I hastened thither, amidst a scattering fire of muskets and match-locks, and the yells and shrieks of men, women, and children, running about in all directions. The war-cry of the Arabs, and the *allons!* and *vive!* of the French were so loud, that I could not hear either my own voice, or distinguish the report of my own carbine. On nearing the place at which we had entered, we saw a mingled heap of naked savages, of all ages, men and women, armed with creeses, guns, knives, and bamboo spears; others with their children, and many loaded with their goods, all rushing on. I stopped my men, and gave them a volley; and as they were facing about, we charged them with our lances. They stood on their defence with the fierceness of desperation, and a few of our men dropped; but they resisted without method, impeded by their own numbers, and a panic seizing on them, they separated to escape. A great many were butchered, and no prisoners made; for blood is like wine, the more we have the more we crave, till, excited to madness, one excess leads to another; and it is easier to persuade a drunken man to desist from drinking whilst he can hold his glass, than a man, whose hands are reeking with blood, to desist from shedding more.

My fellows rushed about in ungovernable disorder, destroying all whom they met; and I was obliged to remain myself at the outlet, until I had enforced ten or twelve of them to keep that post. As the light grew clearer, objects became distinct, and I beheld the confusion and slaughter going on within. My senses were dizzy with the blood I had shed, and seen shed. The Maratti, environed in their own walls, essayed every outlet, sought every means to provide for the escape of their women and their children, and, finding none, they fought with the fearlessness or heedlessness of ensnared tigers. They ran from gate to gate with blind fury, and threw themselves headlong on the bayonets and lances. They had never heard of mercy, yielding, or asking for quarter. There were no such words in their language. They had been accustomed to shed blood from their childhood, whether of men or monkies, with equal indifference; and they believed all the world to be of the selfsame nature. As for Europeans, they were always treated by them, if they fell into their hands, like fish—hanged up in the sun to dry. Old men, women, and children, therefore, preferred to die fighting; and, thus far, we had not a single prisoner. They would have succeeded in forcing my position, had not De Ruyter come to my aid. I feel extreme pain and shame at remembering the horrible ferocity with which I slaughtered these besotted bar-barians, and more at the savage and inhuman delight with which I did so. It would have ended in their total extermination, had they not effected several outlets in their mouldering walls.

The only wound I received was in the leg, from a woman, who attempted to hamstring me, as, in hurrying along, I stepped on her body; and the first symptom of my returning reason was, on discovering her sex, instead of crushing her with my uplifted foot, to have her carried to the main guard; this was the first prisoner we had taken. It was then De Ruyter came to me, and said, 'We have had blood enough. Call our people off, and let the poor devils go. Seize what prisoners you can, but take no more lives: and lead your men to the huts on that sand-hill;—there you will find their Arab and other prisoners; take care they are not sacrificed in the fray; and send them to the guard. Bandage your leg—you are bleeding fast.'

CHAPTER XLI

> She was born at midnight in an Indian wild,
> Her mother's screams with the striped tigers' blent,
> While the torch-bearing slaves a halloo sent
> Into the jungles; and her palanquin,
> Rested amid the desert's dreariment,
> Shook with her agony, till fair were seen
> The little Bertha's eyes ope on the stars serene.
>
> KEATS' MS.

> How beautiful, if sorrow had not made
> Sorrow more beautiful than beauty's self.
>
> KEATS

I DID so, and went as directed to the sand-hill. It was well I did, or we should not have had a prisoner to release; for the women were killing them, as they lay bound hand and foot on the ground in heaps. These dark hags were despatched. Then entering a small matted tent, affixed to a larger one, the first object which struck me was a naked, gaunt Arab, bound and fastened to a short stake driven into the earth. He was covered with stabs, weltering in his own blood; yet though bound, helpless, and dying, his unsubdued spirit still shone like a chieftain's. An aged, a decrepit she-devil was lying on his prostrate body, she having slipped in the gore, and with a cocoa-nut knife in her hand, was hacking at him with feeble blows. Her fallen victim held fast her left hand in his teeth; and at his feet, huddled up in a corner, was a young girl, almost naked, screaming in affright,—'Oh! father, father, let me get up!'—with her bound hands stretched out, struggling to rise, but pressed down by the strong limbs of the man, who thus sheltered her from the fiendish old woman. I seized on the cloth band round the Hecate's loins, and, lifting her withered carcase up in the air, I dashed her down with such force, that she never stirred more, but lay sprawling like a crushed toad, the faint sparks of life being extinguished without even a groan escaping her.

This scene exhibited to my view the worst of cruelty, in its most diabolical shape, and filled me with horror and pity. I bade an Arab unbind the father, who lay motionless watching me, as I proceeded to liberate his daughter. He seemed perfectly reckless of himself, and hesitating how to act, doubting my designs. In vain he endeavoured to sit up, for the ground was slippery with his blood. I saw his fears, and, to dispel them, instantly placed him in a sitting posture, and drew my creese from my belt. His eyes glared ferociously. I put the weapon into his hand, and said, —'We are friends, father!—fear not!' He tried to speak, but the blood oozed from his mouth, and the words died on his lips.

His child, now unbound, over whom I threw a mantle, crawled to her father's side, and kissing his incrimsoned hands and eyes, bent over him in speechless and indescribable anguish. The old man's desperate look relaxed; his eye lost its fierceness, then became clouded and dim. I knelt, subdued by the scene, on the side opposite his child, supporting him. He, with an effort, took my hand in his; I felt its clammy moisture; he put it to his lips; then, with great difficulty, he removed a ring from his finger, and placed it on mine; and, laying my hand on his child's, he alternately looked at us both, and convulsively squeezed our hands together, muttering some words. My eyes were wet with tears, which dropped on his bosom. His head and frame shook as with an ague-fit; his fingers grew cold as ice, his eye stony, fixed, and glazed, and his limbs rigid. I could no longer uphold his increasing weight. His spirit fled its earthly tenement. Yet still our hands were bound together so fixedly in his, that I could not release them; and he still seemed to gaze on us both with intense anxiety.

Motionless as a form of marble, his child bent over him. She neither wept, nor even appeared to breathe. This recalled me to my senses. I thought she was dead too; and unclenching his death-gripe, I freed myself, arose, and went to her. She appeared to awaken, when I tried gently to remove her, as from a trance, threw her arms round her father's neck, and clung to him with convulsive strength. I cleared the tent of the gazers-on, who were not unmoved, for they gave vent to their feelings in vows of vengeance; then placing two Arabs, in whom I could confide, at the entrance, to let no one pass, I went into the open air, to recover from the faintness that was creeping over me.

I slung my carbine over my shoulder, and now used all my efforts to stop the slaughter. A general pillage was going on. The grab's and the corvette's long-boats were attending on the beach, the vessels themselves not being able to get round the reef, as it was perfectly calm. These boats, therefore, and some canoes lying on the beach we commenced loading with the booty, which was considerable; gold, spices, bales of Chinese silk, the muslins of India, cloths and shawls from the Persian Gulf, bags of armlets and anklets, silver and gold ornaments, maize, corn, rice, salt fish, turtle, rackee, and an infinity of arms and apparel, besides slaves, male and female, of all ages and countries. Every eye glistened, and every back was bent with a costly burden.

Yet so greedy and insatiable were our men, who were at first fastidious in their selection, that at last they regarded everything with a jealous eye, and became so gross in their avaricious desires, that they would fain have borne off garbage which the wild dog would have passed heedless by; rotten fish, mouldy rice, rancid ghee, broken pots and pans, cast-off apparel, mats and tents, nothing so villainously worthless or nauseous, but had some value in their inordinate avidity for plunder. What they could not carry on their backs they did in their bellies: they gorged themselves, like the ostrich, till they could scarcely move.

Van Scolpvelt and the steward now appeared in the field, and took their ground, intent on very different objects. Van seemed distracted with the rich variety of patients before him. As he hurried about the encampment, with his shirt sleeves tucked up, his skinny arms, bare, bony, and hairy, a case of glittering and appalling instruments in one hand, and in the other a monstrous pair of scissors, rounded into the form of a crescent; he realised, in his appearance, the most damnable picture of an avenging demon, presiding over the tortures in hell, that ever was conceived by saintly painter or poet. Some, not quite dead, feebly shook their creeses at him, others screamed with horror as he stopped to examine their wounds, and a few actually gave up the ghost as he approached.

The steward, on the other hand, grinned from ear to ear, as he contemplated the huge mass of plunder, and the destruction of the pirates, whom he hated, because they had repeatedly intercepted the cattle trade to the Mauritius. But his joy was presently checked, and he said to me in sadness, and in worse English than I give him, 'Oh, Captain, can you let these improvident savages waste so much? Look, the earth is covered with grain and flour as if it had snowed! And do you see these lively turtles? They are of the most delicious kind, and the most beautiful creatures I ever saw: what beastly savages to leave them here! Make the men throw away the lumber they are carrying on board; we don't want it; do you? and load the boats with these. Of what use are those black savages you are sending in the boats? One of these' (pointing to a turtle,) 'is worth an island of them. Nobody can eat them; can you? Bah! I hate savages, and doat on turtle; don't you? We have enough of the one sort on board; but where have you ever seen such lovely creatures as these? I have not for years; have you?'

Intent on this, which now solely occupied him, by threats and entreaties he endeavoured to induce the men to assist him in bearing off the turtle. At last growing desperate at the Arabs, who loathe them, (which Louis said proved they were without human palates,) he set about loading the slaves and women with them, the latter of whom he declared he never saw usefully employed before; then turning to me, asked, in his peculiar voice, which began in the deep hollow tones of a muffled drum, and ended with the tinkling jingle of a matin bell, 'Have you?'

De Ruyter now came up, accompanied by Aston, who had just come on shore to see the place. I told them of the scene I had witnessed in the slave tent, when Aston's gentle heart was moved, and he reproved me for having left the girl. My reply was, that I had done so, thinking it was better she should be left alone, to give vent to the first burst of sorrow.

VOLUME II

CHAPTER I

The Moslem daughter went with her protector,
For she was harmless, houseless, helpless; all
Her friends, like the sad family of Hector
Had perished in the field or by the wall:
Her very place of birth was but a spectre
Of what it had been; there the Muezzin's call
To prayer was heard no more!

BYRON

'But,' said De Ruyter, 'there is not now an instant to lose. We must hasten aboard; for these fellows outside will assuredly rally, and, aided by the Madagascarenes, assault us in our turn. So call the stragglers together. The prisoners are embarked, and we must embark forthwith.'

'Come, Aston,' I said, 'assist me in getting this poor orphan girl on board.'

We proceeded together to the tent, where we found her making loud wailings. Then she would break off, and cry, 'Father, arise, —we are free! The strangers are good; and see! they come to free us. The old woman has not killed me; I am well, and she herself is dead. Oh! father, get up!—look, I have bound up your wounds,—you don't bleed now!' And indeed she had carefully bandaged him with the only remaining rag on her person.

Taking her hand, I said, 'Come, dear sister; you are free. We must leave these cruel Maratti.'

Without looking at me, she went on,—'See, how my father sleeps! They would not let him sleep or eat, and he is weary and hungry.'

'Come, dear,' I said, 'we must go.'

'Go!' she replied, 'how can we?—our father sleeps!—and I cannot awake him! Oh, awake him, that I may feed him! See, I have got some beautiful fruit, and his lips are dry. Oh, these

cruel Maratti will come again when you are gone, and kill him!
Awake, my father! His eyes are open, but he can't move. He is
old, and feeble from hunger; he wants food; his lips are cold
with hunger!' At this she kissed him, and rubbed his head, and
squeezed pomegranate juice in his mouth.

'Come!' said Aston, 'they are calling you. We must be off.
I cannot bear this sight. I'll take her to the boat.'

I entreated him to do so; then gently loosed her hands, covered
her with my abbah, and told her I would take care of her father.
Aston snatched her up, and bore her off. Her screams were appalling. She called on the name of her father to save her; and Aston
shook, but not with his light burden. I was in little better trim.
Sending some Arabs down to the beach with Aston, I returned to
De Ruyter, who was drawing off the men with great difficulty.

Louis, whose bad English I must continue to make better, as
Aston passed him, exclaimed to me, 'What is he carrying away?
What! a girl! What use is she? Why, he could carry this great
turtle, which else must be abandoned, for no one here can lift
him,—can you? And she might carry that little one,—it will make
very good soup; and is very pretty,—much more so than a little
girl?'

I passed on, ordering him instantly to come on board, or the
Maratti would soupify him. 'What!' he ejaculated, 'leave that
turtle, worth all the rest we have taken!' and he wrung his hands
in anguish.

Armed men were now appearing on the hills; and De Ruyter
grew furious at the tardy movements of his men. Many of the
Frenchmen were drunk, and could not be got out of the tents.
The shouts on the hills augmented, and we were obliged to move.
De Ruyter went out of the gate, and I staid some time longer with
the Arabs, to collect stragglers, and then followed him. I omitted
to mention that we had fired the town in many places, and burnt
two Arab vessels which were grounded, with seven or eight canoes
on the beach.

The natives were hurrying towards the town; and soon after
we saw bodies of them armed, skirting along the side of the river
we had to cross, and descending as if to attack us there. We hastened
on, preparing our arms. When we arrived there, keeping as near
the sea as possible, we heard a firing, and saw De Ruyter crossing
the river. He left a party to keep the opposite bank, went on to the

boats, fearing they might be attacked, and sent a messenger to me, to hasten me on. But before I could arrive there, being detained by the difficulty in getting on the drunken Frenchmen, the natives had increased till their numbers were formidable. They grew bold, and attacked the party on the opposite bank; then wading down the stream, and closing on our rear, they became troublesome. We kept our ground firmly, and I continued on the bank till our party had crossed. Just as I was following with my Arabs, I heard some shots in our rear, and now appeared, emerging from behind a sand-bank, a monstrous figure, a Patagonian, in (what I thought, as the sun shone on him,) bright scaled armour. It was the steward, with the turtle on his shoulders, accompanied by a Dutch soldier. I roared out to them to come on quickly, for every moment became more perilous. As they staggered towards us, I could hardly refrain from laughing. Louis, when I could with difficulty make out to be a human figure, looked like a hippopotamus, as, reeling like a drunken man, he bent under the weight of the huge fish, which I thought he had left behind. The other fellow, the Dutchman, who came staggering on in his wake, was bulged out into preposterous proportions; his red Guernsey frock and ample Dutch trowsers, secured at the wrists and knees, were crammed with stowage of gold and jewels, which he had discovered after one of the houses had been pulled down. He looked like a woolsack, and moved like a Dutch dogger, which his broad beam resembled, labouring in a head sea. I told them to cast their slough, if they valued their lives, and commenced crossing the river by a sand-bank, thrown up by the tide, the only passable ford.

The natives pressed more closely on our rear; the difficulty in using our arms in the water made them bold; and but for our men stationed on the opposite bank, we should have had little chance of escape; for they, in a great degree, checked their advance, and kept the space clear before us. Still we were compelled to hurry on. At this moment I heard something flounder in the water, and a savage yell, as of triumph, from the natives. I looked round, and the Dutch soldier, who was in my rear, was missing. Overballasted by his treasure, he lost his footing on the ford, and sunk in the stream, borne down by the weight about his body, which it was impossible for him to shake off. I only got a glimpse of his person, when my attention was called off by the steward, who either from fear, or from having been caught hold of by his fallen countryman, who was close to him, had also fallen. I ran back, and holding the shaft of a spear to him, he grasped it tight, while the huge monster he had been carrying tumbled into the water, and flapped his heavy fins in triumph, as he regained his native element.

When Louis had recovered himself on the bank, he exclaimed, with a rueful look,—'But where is my turtle? Oh, don't mind me, Captain!—save the turtle!'

'Damn the turtle! I wish he was down your throat!'

'Oh! so do I, Captain!—that's all I want! Oh, where's my turtle?' As he vociferated this demand, up it rose to the surface, in mockery of his enemy; and the instant its bright shell glistened in the sun, Louis seemed inclined to rush down the stream after it, bawling out, 'There he is! Oh, save him!'

Thinking he meant the soldier, I looked, and inquired, 'Where?'

'Why, there!' he replied, pointing to the turtle. 'Oh, Captain, I told you how lively he was! I cut his throat two hours ago; but he won't die till sunset; they never do; and then he will be lost, —won't he?'

I had ordered two of my men to drag him along; and so loth was he to leave the turtle, that with his eyes strained down the stream, he came reluctantly in a sidelong motion, like a crab.

Once or twice I was compelled to turn round on our pursuers, and drive them off, before we reached the other side. We hastened to regain our boats. Four of our men were slightly wounded in this retreat; besides the loss of the Dutch soldier, and the deeply lamented turtle. Wherever the ground was broken, or where there was a cover of rocks or shrubs, the Madagascarenes closed in on our flank and rear. I therefore retired close to the sea, and skirted its margin. There was one very dangerous pass; it was the rough abutment of ragged rocks jutting out into the sea, half a mile on the other side of which were our boats. The natives were ranged along the ridges in files, and there was already a sharp firing going on there. While wondering that De Ruyter should have deserted me under such circumstances, and hesitating as to the best mode of proceeding, I espied on the extreme point his swallow-tailed flag. We now ran on, and were hailed by our ship-mates; who seeing this post was possessed by the enemy, had driven them up, and opened a passage for us. Yet every inch was obstinately disputed, and here three of our men were left dead; for the natives, under cover of the rocks, and lying down with their long match-locks, had a great advantage, while we could not get a shot at them. The boats approached; and the French soldiers were drawn up on the beach, which being open, the natives dared not advance, though they kept up a scattering fire. We embarked amidst the wild yells of the savages, who, the moment we shoved off, came down like a countless flock of crows; and with as much noise and din they even followed us into the water, and their arrows, stones, and balls fell about us like a hail-storm.

CHAPTER II

Ay! at set of sun;
The breeze will freshen when the day is done.

*   *   *   *   *

The vessel lay
Her course, and gently made her liquid way;
The cloven billow flash'd from off her prow
In furrows form'd by that majestic plough;
The waters with their world were all before,
Behind the South Sea's many an islet shore.
BYRON

ALL of us, I believe, were glad to regain our ships. We then towed them out, it being a dead calm; awaited the land breeze at night; and ran directly from the land, shaping our course for the island of Bourbon.

On computing our loss on board the two ships, the killed and missing amounted to only fourteen, but we had twenty-eight wounded, most of them, however, slightly. I observed to De Ruyter, as I was entering these particulars in the log-book, 'It appears to me, considering the service we were on, and the numbers against us, this is a very small loss.'

'No, it was a very large one!' cried out Louis, who had just come down the ladder, 'you'll never see so fine a one again. I'd rather have lost every man and thing than that;—would not you?'

'What do you mean, Louis?'

'Mean!—why, the turtle, to be sure. You saw it, Sir, and might have saved it,—could you not? But you think of nothing but little girls,—my turtle was worth all the girls in the world;—was it not?'—turning, as he always did, at his repeated interrogations,

M

sharp round, and shoving his expanded nostrils right in one's face.

'This fellow,' said de Ruyter, 'is a Hindoo; and believes the world is supported on the back of an enormous turtle.'

'And I should not wonder,' I added, 'if he makes a voyage to the Pole, not for the benefit of navigation, but to extract its calliopash and calliopee. What luxury, Louis, to let your entire carcass wallow in such a sea of green fat!—would it not?'—mimicking him.

'Yes;' he replied; 'but there is no turtle there; nothing but walrusses, white bears, and whales.'

Van Scolpvelt now came down with some splinters of bone in his palm, and said, holding out his saw in the other hand, 'See here! I have trepanned a skull; and look, what I told you is true; feel the edges of the bone, they are smooth as ivory, and have a gloss, a polish on them, quite beautiful. I have extracted a ball, and the cerebrum is uninjured, the weight of a hair not having compressed it.' He was proceeding to say the man never felt it, when an assistant came to tell him the man was dying. 'That's a lie!' he exclaimed, and rushed on deck after the messenger, who was frightened at the outstretched instrument. As the doctor followed him up the ladder, it tickled him on the breech, and made him spring on the deck, as if a white hot iron had been applied.

Soon after, under the superintendance of Louis, a feast, that might well be termed a turtle one, was served up. A huge tub of soup, where a fleet of canoes might have almost fought a battle, the steward himself put on the table; and, mopping his reeky brows, said—'Taste that, and you'll live for ever! Why, the odour itself is a feast for a burgomaster, or a king! I never smelt any thing so beautiful;—did you?'

Then came calliopash and calliopee, and stewed, and steaked, and minced, and balled, and grilled; and when all these were cleared away, leaving us well nigh surfeited, quoth Louis le Grand —'Now here are two dishes which I have invented, and no one has the secret of them; though burgomasters and foreign ambassadors have been sent to me with great offers to discover it. But I never would; because this secret makes me greater than all the kings in the world, for they cannot purchase them with a kingdom, nor would I give them in exchange for a kingdom;—would you? All I shall tell you is this—and it is more than I ever told any one before—the soft eggs, and head, and heart, and entrails, are all there!—but there are many other things, which I shall not, must not, speak of.'

Casting his eye on my plate, and seeing the green fat left, he inquired in astonishment why I did not eat it. I answered him, 'I can't; I don't like it.' 'Can't!' he exclaimed—'why, if I were dying, and had but strength enough to open my mouth, I would devour that divine food! And not like it!—then you are no Christian!—is he? But it is impossible,—I don't believe him;—do you?'

Madagascar is one of the largest and most fertile islands in the world; nearly nine hundred miles in length, and three hundred and fifty in its greatest breadth. There is a chain of glorious mountains, winding through its entire length, of varied height, whence many large and navigable rivers take their source. The interior of this vast island, and its inhabitants, are little known; but those parts on the coast which, at that time and afterwards, I have frequently visited, give abundant indications that nature has here scattered her riches with no stinting hand. Nothing seems wanting but knowledge to place this magnificent island in the foremost rank of great and powerful empires. When I was there, the line, distinguishing the man from the animal, was hardly visible.

The evening was singularly beautiful, the sea calm and clear as a mirror, and our crew sinking into rest, outworn by the unwonted toil of this busy day. De Ruyter was in the cabin; I was keeping the watch, and Aston bore me company. He lay along the raised stern, and I leant over the taffrail, gazing on the land. The forms in the distant range of mountains were growing dark and indistinct. The transparent, glassy, and deep blue of the sea faded into a dusky olive, subdivided by an infinity of mazy, glimmering bars, as if embroidered with diamond heads, traced by the varied, wandering airs, and sporting like the lion's whelps on their mother's quiet bosom; while he, their mighty parent, lay hushed within his lair, the caverned shore, torpid from toil and devastation. Over the land the glowing sun hastened to his cool sea-couch; his expiring rays stained the lucid sky with bright, fading colours, —deep ruby tints changing to purple; then emerald green, barred and streaked with azure, white, and yellow; and as the sun was dipping, the whole firmament was dyed in crimson, and blazed; then left the western sky brighter than molten gold, till the sun's last rays were extinguished. When the moon came forth with her

silvery, gleaming light, all the gay colours faded, leaving a few
fleecy and dappled specks, like lambs grazing on the hills in
heaven. The change was like life in youth and beauty suddenly
extinguished; white and misty death, with his pallid winding-
sheet, enveloped all around. As the grab's stern swung round,
and as my eye caught our companion, the corvette, her black hull
and white wings alone broke the line of the moon-lit horizon, like
a sea-sprite reposing on the boundless waters. Enwrapped in our
contemplation of the wonderful beauty of an eastern night, we
remained hours in silence; and after the turmoil of the day, this
stillness had a preternatural, or magic effect on the mind, more
soothing than sleep. The helmsman, in his sleep, from habit,
called out—'Steady! steady!' and even the customary forms of
changing the watches had been neglected; while the sentinels,
unconscious that their time of duty was expired, dozed on their
posts of guard over the prisoners; and the balm of sleep medicined
the wounded, and made free the captive, who, perhaps, dreaming
of hunting on his native mountains, or fondling with his young
barbarians, or their mother, was destined to awake, fettered and
bound with festering manacles, chained, like a wild beast, in the
worst of dungeons, under the sea, in a ship's hold, doomed to
death or slavery.

CHAPTER III

And we prolonged calm talk beneath the sphere
Of the calm moon, when suddenly was blended
With our repose a nameless sense of fear;
  *   *   *   I seemed to hear
Sounds gathering upwards, accents incomplete,
And stifled shrieks; and now, more near and near,
A tumult and a rush of thronging feet.

                                        SHELLEY

A SOUND, as of some one moving, caught my ear, instantly succeeded by a rattling noise, as of stifling, and a gurgling flow, as
of water, followed. Aston and myself started up. He inquired,
'What is that?' as a heavy weight tumbled on the deck, in the bow
of the grab. Ere any one could answer, a dark and naked figure
approached us with a hurried step. Instinctively I griped hold of

the small creese I always wore in my sash. As he stopped, a few paces before us, I said, 'Holla! Torra, is that you?' (He was a Madagascarene-slave, whom De Ruyter had emancipated, and who had been much favoured by him and me.) 'What do you want? What noise was that just now forward?'

He replied,—'Only Torra kill his bad brother with this.' And he extended his black bare arm, his hand clutching a broad knife.

'Killed what?'

He repeated, 'My brother—bad brother Shrondoo.'

'What brother? You are mad or drunk!' For I knew of no brother he had.

'No, massa. Torra no mad, and no drink.'

An alarm now took place in the forecastle; and the helmsman, opening his eyes, said, 'Steady! Steady!' Torra looked round, and, seeing the men coming aft, said, 'You no hear me now, massa. Torra say all when day come.'

The men recoiled on coming near him, seeing his knife. He observed it, and told them—'No fear Torra. No do bad. Torra only kill bad brother;'—and he cast the weapon into the sea. 'Massa, you good man. You friend to poor black slave; won't let them kill Torra, now night. When morrow come, Torra say all. He wish to die then. No wish to live. Go to his father in good land; no slave there; no bad white man come buy poor black one, for make slave.'

Thinking him mad, I ordered him to be seized, handcuffed, and ironed. He stood motionless, only again saying,—

'No kill Torra, night. Kill Torra morning. Torra must tell all.'

I hastened forward, asking—'What has he done? Who is killed?' And as I advanced, my naked feet felt something wet and slippery. Looking down I beheld a dark liquid stream running to the scupper holes. Something lay huddled up, from which it flowed, an undistinguishable mass, covered with a stained white cotton garment, at the breech of the bow-gun carriage. A man lifted it partly up, and said, 'Here he is!' The gazers-on said, 'Allah! Il Allah!' and it again fell heavily; when, at the sound, they all stepped back. The light of the moon, then unshaded, fell on the corpse of a dark naked man; its covering had fallen; the head was nearly separated from the trunk by a frightful gash across the throat. Again I demanded, who it was; but none could answer. I then recognized it as the body of one of the prisoners lately captured.

As life was extinct, I ordered the corpse to be laid on a grating, and brought aft, and a sentinel to be placed over the assassin.

This horrid sight seemed to have banished sleep. The men stood about in disordered groups, startled at their own voices, which sounded low and husky; and fellows whose hands and garments were still moist and dabbled from the morning's slaughter, stood appalled at a solitary night-murder. They gathered round to gaze on Torra, the assassin, as he sat on his heels, shadowed by the bulk-head. His irons jangled, and the gazers-on shrunk back; the same men who, a few hours before, had assaulted unhesitatingly a walled camp of desperate men, of ten times their number.

Aston and De Ruyter were conferring together, when I observed a light air stealing along from the land. I called out, 'All hands trim sails!' The crew started, and then I went on giving directions to shorten sail, to reef top-sails, and to make sail again. De Ruyter came up to me, and said, 'Why all hands? There is no squall that I can see.'

'Nor I either,' I replied; 'but a panic seems to have taken possession of the whole crew; and I want, by finding employment, to shake it off. They appeared spell-bound; and if a squall had come, we should have lost our masts, ere they regained their faculties.'

'Well thought of, my lad!'

Having turned the tide in the sailors' minds, by making as great a commotion as if we were in a storm, they replied to my orders, and moved with their wonted alacrity, regardless of the continued stillness of the weather. At any other period I should have insured to myself a thousand muttering, sullen curses. This done, I left De Ruyter in charge of the deck; and in despite of what had taken place, the stiffness of my limbs, and the smarting of my cut leg, with shooting pains from former wounds, which seemed breaking out again, so heavy were my eyes that, while endeavouring to recal the events of the day, without troubling myself to unrig, I tumbled into a berth, and slept as soon as my head touched the pillow, as if by enchantment. Perhaps it was a magic pillow;— I wish I had it now.

CHAPTER IV

I am a guilty, miserable wretch;
I have said all I know, now let me die.
SHELLEY

In a youthful, well-formed frame, which is health and strength, and wherein a good heart naturally seeks to dwell, for it must have room to expand, in order that its glowing impulses may rush through every channel, unimpeded, like lightning, ere it cools,— in such a frame the soul or spirit which governs us is strongly engendered, is born, and lives for ever; but when forced and crammed into narrow, dark, and dreary bosoms, from want of air and room, its feeble flame dimly flickers in the lamp of life, till it is almost or wholly extinguished. The philanthropist Owen of Lanark,[1] or the sage and saintly Hannah More,[2] and her tribe, scrawl and jabber about education, and of that alone constituting the difference between man and man, and of nature having sent us into the world equally disposed for good or evil. Shakspeare and Bacon thought otherwise; and they were deep and wise, as the others are shallow and foolish. Bacon says, 'Deformed persons are commonly even with nature; for as nature hath done ill by them, so do they by nature, being for the most part (as the scripture saith,) *void of natural affection*; and so they have their revenge of nature.' And as ill-finished, dwarfish, or shrivelled half-abortions sometimes strive against their nature to attain goodness, so do the well-formed (for I talk not of beauty), in some instances, incline to evil, from choice against their nature.

I have been led into this digression by the memory of Aston and De Ruyter, whose noble and majestic persons, free and graceful movements, lofty spirits, and gentle and loving hearts, first awakened in my nature feelings, which had been trampled on but not annihilated, of friendship and benevolence; for I had begun to think the world was peopled with demons, and that I was confined in a dark and dreary hell. How fondly do I dwell on those days, and gladly pay them this tribute, poor as it is, in return for such content, and happiness as I experienced in their dear presence, when the sun seemed always shining, and the world one great garden of fruits and flowers! I would not then have given up this world, such as it was to me, for paradise, such as it is painted by saintly enthusiasts, even though I could have gone thither, without passing through the dread ordeal leading to it.

Yet mine was then a life of almost unexampled toil and peril, of pain from wounds, and sometimes of greater suffering from hunger and thirst. I have seen the time when I would have freely exchanged my blood, or given both my hands full of gold for enough water to fill one of my palms; when my lips have been glued together, and thirst, like a malignant fever, gnawed at the vitals of life. Abundance came, and my sufferings were forgotten on the instant, or only remembered to give a keener appetite, a more exquisite relish to things, which, grown too common by use, are almost considered useless,—bread and water. Often with my head pillowed on a shot-locker, for iron served my turn then better than the softest down does now, covered with a tarpaulin to break the fury of the rain and spray, in which I was well nigh floating, plunged and tossed on what might be well called a sea-coffin, on a lee and dangerous shore, amidst thunder and lightning, in a tempest which would have torn up a cedar, as easily as man up-roots a blade of corn,—thus, and in such a scene, I have slept sounder than a wearied child upon its mother's lap, hushed with song and gentle rocking. If I could endure these hardships and privations uncomplainingly, how unnaturally must I have been dealt with in my earlier days by parents and guardians, to be so disgusted with life, as to seriously ponder on self-destruction! Yet not only did I think on it, but, at the age of fourteen, I was on the point of carrying it into execution. It was then that I collected all the authorities, ancient and modern, within my reach, in its defence and justification. I am induced to mention this, on account of having found that paper a few days since. But soon after Aston, Walter, and then De Ruyter bound me to the world by the gentle chains of friendship. Thus was I rescued from a fate, which, but for their love, would assuredly have been mine.

It was near noon ere I was awaked by the doctor's boy with a bottle of camphor and oil to apply externally, and a mixture to take internally. Louis was standing by, giving directions for serv-ing up a second repast of turtle, and commenced an angry alterca-tion with the fellow. 'What is camphor good for,' said he, 'but to stuff dead Arabs? I hate the smell;—don't you? The doctor would make every man live on poison, like himself, the scorpions, and the centipedes. The captain wants to fill his body, not to rub his legs. The soup is ready; and I warrant that will go down to his toe-nails, and circulate through his corns, if he has any. It will cure every thing;—won't it?'

I answered, for I was hungry as a bird in a hard frost, 'I think it will.' So the boy was chased up the ladder, and a repetition of turtle laid on the table. When De Ruyter and Aston came down, I inquired what had been done with Torra.

'He is as you left him.'

'Well, have you found out the mystery? For he must have been governed by some strong impulse, to enact so bloody a tragedy, as he has always appeared a good and quiet man.'

'Yes,' observed De Ruyter; 'but I have ever found these very quiet men the most dangerous, revengeful and bloody. They execute, whilst brawling fellows satisfy themselves with talking. Did you not see him, in the morning's slaughter, dyed like a red Indian in blood?'

'Certainly I did; he startled me. He rushed wherever they were thickest, armed with nothing but two long knives. I began to think he had a propensity for cannibalism. But he is kind-hearted as bold: you remember the other day, when my favourite bird, the loorie, was knocked overboard, in a squall, by the topsail halliards; he leaped into the sea, and saved him. And he was very honest; for he was continually down here, where dollars are more plentiful in the lockers than biscuits, and spirits than either, yet he never took one of the first, nor helped himself to a glass of the latter. Besides, Louis knows him to be the most trust-worthy man in the ship.'

'Oh,' said Louis, 'I am sure of that! I'd trust him with all the gold in the world; for nothing can tempt him to steal. Only re-collect when, off Ceylon, I picked up that pretty little turtlet, which you all contended was a log of wood,—but I knew he was a turtle. Why, I can see a turtle twenty miles off, when he shews no more shell above water than that ladle; that is, when they sleep, for then they like to feel the sun on their backs,—don't you? Well, do you remember how I took him up in the boat, so gently, with-out waking him, like a little child! And then, when I was insinuat-ing my knife between his shell, he just popped out his pretty little head, looked me in the face, and felt my knife tickle him; and he had only time to draw it in again, before he felt himself in the pot on the fire. Oh! the black man is honest and brave!—for he knocked down one of the men who wanted to put his spoon into that soup! And though I left it to him to watch, he didn't even put his finger in to have one lick. Oh! he is the most honest man in the world! —for any body else would have had one lick,—would not you? I'd trust this man in bed with my wife; wouldn't you Captain? Because a black man, quite different from a white man, steals nothing, not so much as a lick at the soup. I like a black man for that;—don't you?'

'Come,' said De Ruyter, 'hand out the long corks, and clear the decks.'

This done, Louis withdrew himself into his berth, where we heard him feeding like a cormorant, and bolting green fat, as a turkey bolts barley-meal balls. 'If the ship were on fire,' said Aston, 'he would not move from his moorings; he is fast. So, De Ruyter, tell us about Torra.'

'It is soon done,' said he, 'but I must first tell you what I knew of him previously to last night.'

CHAPTER V

I do not feel as if I were a man,
But like a fiend appointed to chastise
The offences of some unremembered world.
                        SHELLEY

Thou wert a weapon in the hand of God
To a just use.
                        Ibid.

'EIGHTEEN months since I put into the Island of Rodriguez for wood and water; and, shooting in a jungle there, I sprung this fellow from a lurking-place among the rocks. He was one of the most wild and hungry——'

'What!' bawled out Louis, not getting up, but thrusting his enormous head forwards, the perspiration running from his forehead, the turtle-fat oozing from his jaws, and his eyes, like a lobster's, protruding, 'What! hungry!—If he's hungry, I'll give him some of this. I can't eat it all, and there's plenty on board now; and I love him, because he's an honest man.'

Our laughter compelled him to withdraw, when De Ruyter continued: 'Having a rifle in my hand, he could not escape. I beckoned him towards me, and when he came I questioned him. As well as I could comprehend him, he gave me a dreadful account of what he had suffered from a Dutch overseer (for he was a slave), and that he had been employed, with others, on the northern part of the island, in salting fish and catching turtle, to be sent to the Isle of France. He ran away just as the party were taking their departure before the S.W. monsoon was over, for Macao; and ever since he had lived alone in the woods, subsisting on eggs, fish and fruit. Well, though his was an old tale, I pitied him, and took him on board; since which, as you have seen, he has always behaved extremely well.'

Louis, now surfeited, again made his appearance, recommending us strongly to take a glass of skedam, just to keep the turtle quiet. 'For,' said he, 'though you have got him in your bellies, he'll not die till sunset, because he was killed this morning; for now Torra is gone, I have nobody able to assist me. A turtle should always have his throat cut at sunset, and then they die directly. Torra knows this; but all the rest on board are fools, and know nothing, —do they? Just let this little drop go down, it will turn him, he'll stay quiet till sunset, and you'll hear nothing more of him. That French wine is only good for soup, when there is no Madeira.'

As he could not persuade us that smoky Hollands was better than the best Bourdeaux, he, to comfort himself, half filled a cocoa-nut shell, which he called a sail-maker's thimble, opened his dry dock gate, and let the water in.

De Ruyter, who oftener encouraged than interrupted him, proceeded,—'After you were asleep, I went to Torra. On my questioning him, he related his story. I'll give it, as well as my memory serves, in his own words.'

'Do,' I said; 'but not with your usual brevity. You are a most unmerciful clipper down of other men's stories. And I wish much to know every thing about the fellow; for, as Louis says, I like him, and shall be sorry to find I have been deceived in him.'

'I will be more honest,' said De Ruyter, 'than most translators are; for, if I don't give it literally, you shall have the matter un-biassed by my opinions, and free from the chaff of canting moral digression, either as episode, preface, note, or annotation, all which one fool makes, thinking many fools will read.

'"I was born," said Torra, "at a fishing village, on the north-east part of Madagascar, in the Bay of Antongil. My father was a poor man, and took one wife. She had only one child, a boy, sickly, and not good for much. She would not let him work, nor would she have another child; and as she grew old, she grew cross. So, you see, the same species of women flourish here as in Europe. In courtship they give us their furred paw, and we think it soft as velvet. We wed them; and then the contracted talons are unfolded, and their gentle purring is changed to a threatening hiss." '

I looked at Aston, and we smiled at De Ruyter's having so soon forgotten his promise at starting. He observed this, and said,— 'By Heaven! this is only a liberal translation, or imitation, of a simile he actually did make. Hear his own words: "In youth a woman is like a green gourd; her shell is soft and pliant; but, when old, harder than iron-wood. My father talks not to his wife, it is of no use; but, like a wise man, he goes and buys another wife, and gets three children by her. The first wife likes not this, and lets him not bring her home. So he goes to the other side of the water and builds a new house. Here he catches more fish, and trades with the white men who come there. He now sees not his old wife. Her son is big enough to work, and he gives him a canoe, a fishing-net, and a spear. But he likes not work, and they are very poor.

'"When I grew strong, I was a good fisherman. My father loves me. Sometimes I give my brother fish; and when I have no fish, I give him couries. Then the white men," (here Torra meant the Frenchmen from the Isle of France,) "seeing the place was good, speak kindly to my father, and a great many come and live there. Soon after they quarrel with my father. They want his land, where he grows his bread, to build a strong place. My father likes not to give it; and they kill him, and take it, and take my mother and my sisters, and make them slaves.

'"I run up to the mountains, and then I cross to Nossi Ibrahim. There they are a very brave people, and hate the whites. They steal on the water, not on the land, and make no slaves. When I tell them the white men came and killed my old father, who was a good friend to them, they all say they are glad of it, for my father was wrong to have white friends. But when I tell them they took my mother and my sisters, and made them slaves, they say that was very bad. Then they call a war-talk, and say they would speak with these white men. And then an old man who was a friend to my father says, 'No! it is not good to speak with them. Their words are white as morning, but their deeds are black as night. It is not good to speak with them. It is good to kill them all.' And after much more talk, they agree with the wise old man.

'"They get many great war-canoes. They all sail over in the night. There was no moon, and the night was dark. The old man likes the black night. 'For the white man,' he says, 'is afraid, and likes not to fight in the dark. A black man is the owl that sees them in the night; but they the wild turkey that sees nothing. Their thunders strike not.'

'"The white men made a feast; for it was the great day of their good spirit; and in the poor black man's country they are all drunk. And when we hear they sing no more, we know they sleep; and we come down the hills and kill them every one.

'"My friends take all they can find, and go away. I like not to stay there, now that my father is dead. I take my mother and sisters, and go to the other side, where my father first lived. Our father gone, my brother seems very sorry; so we are all good friends, and I work for them all. My brother goes many times away, we know not whither; and stays many days.

'"Four moons after, I go to Nossi Ibrahim, to see the old man; for he was a good friend, and more moons older than I can tell. When I come back, I go to my house, and find no one there, though it is night. I go to my brother; and he nearly dies with grief. He tells me that, when I went away, the Maratti came in their war-canoes, took my mother and sisters, and because his old mother talked to them, and she not being good for much, they killed her. 'Now,' he says, 'I want to make fire to burn her.' In grief we go, and build a pile, and the body is burnt.

'"Then my brother says to me, 'It is not good to weep. Thy tears will not bring back the women.'

'"And I say, 'why did they not take thee?'

'"Oh," he says, "I ran up the mountain, and they saw me not."

'"I was going back to the old man at Nossi Ibrahim, to ask counsel. But my brother says, No; that people is few and poor, and they sell not slaves. The Maratti are a very great people, and they make many slaves. They hate each other like bad brothers. In the Maratti there are some good men; let us go to them; one of them is my uncle; he will get back what you have lost, for he loves me; let us go and talk with him."'

CHAPTER VI

The ghastly spectres, which were doomed at last
To tell as true a tale of dangers past,
As ever the dark annals of the deep
Disclosed for man to dread, or woman weep.

BYRON

The boat was one curved shell of hollow pearl
Almost translucent.

SHELLEY

'THE conclusion,' continued De Ruyter, 'you may surmise. The simple fool, Torra, was kidnapped and sold by his crafty brother. He being the eldest, inherited paternal rights over the youngest; and had, by their laws, the power, of which he took advantage, to sell them all. His old mother, having less of the devil in her, or through fear, opposed him; upon which he himself killed her. Torra was sent in slavery to Rodriguez; and the women to the Isle of France. You already know the rest of Torra's tragic history, and his summary code of laws. There is no more to remark on but this: yesterday morning, when we had landed, he swam on shore, with his knives; and it seems he joined your party.'

To this I replied, 'Torra indeed surprised me. When we were stumbling about in the dark, seeking to cross the ravine, it was he that led us forward to a place lower down. He was afterwards of infinite use in directing us to the walls and the gate. Indeed I had a suspicion, from his extraordinary officiousness, that he intended some stratagem, and therefore I kept an eye on him. But on our entering, when the signal was made in the morning, all doubt vanished; for the fellow was by far the most active of us all. Though he puzzled me then, you have now made me understand his feelings of revenge against the Maratti. While I was losing time in holding a fellow by the throat, to prevent his giving an alarm to those within, Torra had most expeditiously, as well as more effectually, silenced the three others—I verily believe, before they were awake. He then burst open the other entrance, which led to the interior. After which I lost sight of him, till I caught his figure, crimsoned from head to foot, rushing from hut to hut. Wherever he was, the air was rent with piercing shrieks and screams, till all was silent. I thought the fellow mad, and at last fired a shot across his bow, for it was useless to talk to him; and thus I stopped his triumphant war-yells.'

'But,' said Aston, 'you have told us nothing regarding his meeting with his brother.'

'Oh,' said De Ruyter, 'it was truly fraternal. But I had forgot, he is a dreamer, and has visions. Never remembering my own dreams, no wonder I should forget friend Torra's. By the Lord it is most miraculous, deserves to be recorded, and ought to follow next after the great Nabucodonosor's. Thus saith Torra:

'"In the town of the Maratti I seek, in every place, to find my bad brother; but I find him not. So I feel my head and blood like fire. I kill all I find. I too wish to die, but no one fights with me. All run away from Torra, one man with nothing but a knife; while they have swords, and darts, and guns. Iron strikes me and hurts me not; guns wound not Torra.

'"When I come on board I am sick and hot, and lie down on the hammock-nettings of the forecastle, but not to sleep. I have too much pain to sleep. I lie down, looking at the sea: and then I see my old father rise up from the bottom, in a great fish-shell, with his fishing-net in his hand. He looks at me, and says, 'Torra, my son!'

'"I try to answer, but cannot.

'"Then he says, 'Thy mother, thy sisters, where are they?'

'"I try to say, they are slaves to the white men.

'"He understands me, and says, 'No, Torra, they are free; look here! thou art a slave, my son, but they are with me!' And I see them all three in the shell.

'"Then he says, 'Thy brother, where is he?'

'"I try to answer, 'I know not!' when an old and wrinkled white man, who lives in the dark clouds, comes with a long spear of fire, and says, 'Where is he?'

'"My father shakes his fishing-net, and again says, 'Where is he? Torra, thou art a bad son, and a false brother to thy sisters, not to send thy bad brother to the evil Spirit, who bids me cast my net for him; and till I catch him, we are to have no rest, no peace, condemned to follow him; and now I find he is in the ship with thee, and he alone of all my blood can sleep. Torra hath forsaken and forgotten the law of his father's land, blood for blood!'

'"My father then throws his net again and again, and the white demon of the cloud shakes his spear, calling on the name of my brother,—Shrondoo.

'"I turn and look the other way, and see my brother, as my father said, asleep. I go down on the deck; I stand over him; and when I am certain it is he, I kill him. And I look through the port on the waters, and see my father catch his spirit in the net, and the white demon take it on his spear. They all scream and clap their hands; the shell sinks in the sea; and the white demon is seen no more!"

'Such was Torra's vision—what think you of it? I promise you the fellow is in earnest, for he entreats me to let him go overboard to his father; but I think the conch-shell is sufficiently charged already.'

'Poor fellow!' said Aston, 'he has been hardly used, and misfortune has extinguished what little intellect he had.'

'By God!' I exclaimed, 'I don't know what you call little; the wisest of the ancients would have lost their senses in such a case. As to killing his brother, if he had slaughtered a myriad of such fellows, he ought to be rewarded, not punished.'

'Very true; but men's prejudices,' observed De Ruyter, 'must influence the scales of justice. Our crew would become mutinous, if I were to pardon Torra. His brother, as the first-born, had his patriarchal rights, and might sell all his kin and kind. The command of the father, though but in a dream, might, on the other hand, justify Torra in killing him; but, as the father is not here to give evidence, Torra's blood must now atone for that which he has shed.'

'Surely,' I eagerly asked, 'you don't intend it?'

'Surely I do not,' was his reply; 'but we must make a shew as if we did, and use some occasion of letting him escape when we get near land.'

However this was unnecessary; for, two days after, Torra going towards the bow of the vessel, handcuffed, and with a sentinel guarding him, looked at the sea, cried,—'There he is, waiting for me! I come, father!' and sprung over the bow, and the ship passed over him. It was useless to make any attempt to save him, as the weight of his manacles dragged him down like lead.

This poor fellow's story, and melancholy fate, made us all sad for some time. Aston, who had a shade of a sailor's faith in dreams and omens, was at some trouble, on our arrival at the Isle of France, to find out if that part of Torra's dream or vision, relating to the death of his mother and sisters, had actually happened. There being a government office, where the deaths of slaves were registered, he discovered it not only verified, but, on comparing our log-book with the register, that they had all died within the four-and-twenty hours, in which Torra had seen them on the sea; they having been drowned in a boat as they were being conveyed to the Isle of Bourbon. I need not add that Aston's faith, after this, was not to be shaken.

CHAPTER VII

> Whereat a narrow Flemish glass he took,
> That since belonged to Admiral De Witt,
> Admired it with a connoisseuring look,
> And with the ripest claret crowned it;
> And, ere the lively bead could burst or flit,
> He turn'd it quickly, nimbly, upside down,
> His mouth being held conveniently fit
> To catch the treasure: 'Best in all the town!'
> He said, smack'd his moist lips, and gave a pleasant frown.
>
> KEATS' MS.

WE were in the west trade-wind, and scudded merrily along in company with the corvette, having determined to run into Port Bourbon, in the Mauritius, on the south-east coast, as the English frigates were blockading the port on the north-west. 'Port Bourbon,' said De Ruyter, 'is the best to get into, being on the windward side, but difficult to get out of. However, it is a beautiful harbour, and we shall have to lie out the north-west monsoon, which is on the eve of commencing. Besides, we shall then be nearer my home, and in quiet, as there are few ships and little commerce in Port Bourbon, that being carried on to leeward at Port Louis.'

Having been now some days at sea, I thought of visiting my little female captive; not that I had neglected her hitherto, having given her my own, comparatively, comfortable cabin, and ordered the good old Rais to find out those of her father's tribe, or followers, on board. Besides, I sent him, privileged by his age and rank, to see her, talk to her, and assure her she should want nothing,

N

and that all her wishes should be granted. He told me that three women, who had been with her in her father's ship, were already with her; that he had collected and given them what articles they wanted, and that in a few days she would be better. Indeed the old Rais, in respect of her father's having been, not only an Arab, but a schaich, of a tribe in the Persian Gulf, near his own country, had anticipated all my wishes. He said, 'I must do the same for her as for my own child; for we are all brothers.'

De Ruyter, who heard our conversation, as he stood by, began to talk with the Rais, addressing him by the name of 'Father;' for so he called him, the commander of his Arabs, and one who had been long with him. He consulted the Rais on every point connected with his men, and never opposed the fulfilment of their customs. On his secret expeditions to the English ports, the entire command, in appearance, devolved on the old Arab, while De Ruyter took the character of a merchant, Parsee, Armenian, or American—they were all the same to him, as occasion served. 'I have been telling this youngster of mine, Father,' said he, 'that the Arab girl is now lawfully his wife, in the most sacred manner, according to the customs of your country. Is it not so? Inform him.'

The old Rais had heard all the particulars from the men present at the father's death, and said, 'Most assuredly, malik; who can doubt it? Yet strange it sounded in my ears when I was told it. It is the first time, old as I am, that I ever heard of an Arab schaich, whose generations are countless as the grains of sand on the great desert, giving his daughter, and mingling the blood of the ancestors of the human race with one of the infidels of a country, so newly discovered, that our fathers knew not of it, nor could her father have heard of its existence; a Yaoor!'

'Bah!' replied De Ruyter. 'No more a Christian than you are. Why, the father knew him for an Arab, to be sure. What else? Does he look like a Christian? Has he not the Koran in his cabin? And where is his Bible? Come,' (addressing me,) 'say your *Namaz*. You are circumcised!'

'Wise are you, malik,' said the Rais; 'that is the truth. It is not strange her father should have so thought; and I am an ignorant man if his father was not an Arab born, or Arab descended; for I never saw any of your western people sun-dyed and featured like this boy. He is honest and brave, loves our people, fights with our weapons, and uses our customs. You see nature will break out.

Now that he has, by the blessing of Mahomet, our Holy Prophet, an Arab wife, I hope he will find out the tribe of his ancestors; and not, like unto his foolish father, go from his own country, to dwell on white rocks in the sea.'

This was spoken so seriously, and De Ruyter, checking his ready laugh, conversed so learnedly on the subject, that I began to entertain doubts of my mother's chastity and my own identity.

Moreover the Rais argued that the father had joined our hands, when under the shadow of death; at which period, though distant things become indistinct, things near are miraculously unfolded, when connected with the secrets of the other world, which, to us living, are visionary as spectres in a dream, but, when flitting between life and death, are made distinct and clear. 'Therefore,' said he, 'her father could not have been deceived in that moment. He knew into whose hands he was giving his daughter, the hopes of his house, and the care of his children.'

'What children?' inquired Aston; 'has he other children?'

Already I began to think in what a devilish predicament I was placed;—wife, children, and Heaven knew what else!

'Children!' said the Rais; 'oh, yes! but not many. For he was a brave and desperate warrior; and most of his tribe have been cut off in wars with people like these Maratti, who pillaged his village, and killed them almost all. Now he has not more than twenty or thirty.'

'Enough too!' exclaimed Aston.

'I think quite enough,' added De Ruyter, mimicking Louis,— 'don't you?'

I suppose I looked little animated at this discourse, now that I began to find it in earnest; and, perhaps, as chap-fallen as one of Louis's lively turtle, after his throat is cut. However, I was a little comforted by discovering that his children were not of his body, they having been removed by the creeses of his enemies, but his tribe—as the Rais called all the Arabs on board his children; sometimes, when he was pleased, including De Ruyter and myself. De Ruyter assured me, on his honour, casting jesting aside, that, strictly speaking, every thing the old Rais had said was true as the Koran. 'But then,' he added, 'the Koran is nothing to you, and the Arab law is not yours.'

'True; but how will it affect her?' I inquired.

'Only that, as her father affianced her to you, she can marry no one else. From duty, therefore, as well as humanity, you must provide for her, and convey her, with her Arabs, to her own country. I know you have feeling as well as honour, and that, whatever course you are destined to steer, they will never quit the helm. I never have, nor ever will, my dear boy, thrust officious counsel down your throat, which, like iron, is only to be digested by the power of an ostrich's stomach. Besides, you are not one of those who arrogate exclusively to themselves, their sect, or country, (as too many of your countrymen do,) all the good and virtue under the sun. The light is not less bright, because unobscured by, what is falsely called, civilization, on the sands of these wild children of the desert. Though they are not warmed and cooled by the same summer and winter, as old Shylock says, as Jews and Christians are, yet if you prick them, they bleed,—and so forth. You understand me. So, come down, and having discussed this, let us discuss a cup of claret; the making of which, and of barbers, dancers, fiddlers, cooks, pimps, and courtezans, are the only real benefits France has conferred on the world, as Voltaire has fully proved in his "Lettre aux Welches."[1] If any Frenchman expects to go to heaven, it must be by virtue of one of these pleas alone.'

Aston afterwards inquired of me what I intended doing in this affair. 'Doing!' I replied; 'why, did you not hear?—it is all ready done, man.'

'What done?'

'Why, I am married,—without banns, or babbling about the business. It is but like the first shock in bathing; the timid suffer most by creeping in by degrees; the bold, by plunging in head foremost, hardly feel it. I am no stickler. If I must go in, give me deep water, and a height to leap from;—then I shall neither cut my foot, nor feel the shock.'

'But consider, my lad, she is but a baby; and you have scarcely seen her.'

'Well, what Arab does till after he is married?'

'How can you take her home? You don't intend passing all your life with Arabs?'

'Why not? I have no home. Old father Rais says this is my country; and I like it very well,—I like the sun better than snow. Aston! don't be puckering up your face, like a libidinous parson in the pulpit, exhorting his parishioners against the sin of the flesh and the devil. Come, shake those wrinkles out with claret.

Have you not heard this is my wedding-day? Let us spend it in rejoicings! I hate preaching, and like wine.'

So with callians, sharoots, and claret we passed the time; De Ruyter and Aston bantering me about my novel marriage. My spirits were too good to be dashed by such a trifle, as I then thought marriage. When Louis heard of it, he said, 'I had a frow too once; but she was never good for much. When I went to sea, she drank all my gin. I never could keep a drop of good skedam in the house. I did not like that;—would you? She grew very big, and every one said she was with child; but I knew, if she had any thing, it must be young kegs of hollands for she took nothing else. Afterwards the doctors thought the same; for they—what they call—tapped her many times. But she loved the liquor too much to let it out,—they got nothing but water. This I could not have believed if I had not tasted it—would you? For I never saw her touch water in my life; she could not abide the sight of it, and said it gave her a cold in the stomach. So I left her, and went to sea, —I knew she'd not follow me on the water; and she was sad, and sick, and melancholy, from grief, poor woman!—because she got no more gin. I took all with me.'

CHAPTER VIII

For your gaping gulph and your gullet wide,
The ravine is ready on every side;
There is boiled meat, and roast meat, and meat from the coal,
You may chop it, and tear it, and mash it.

SHELLEY

VAN SCOLPVELT then came down, with the list of sick and wounded. His hands were so full of business, that we seldom saw him,—except his head, which he occasionally shoved up the hatchway for air, as a grampus does his above the water. He expounded to us the law regarding murderers, whose bodies, in all civilized countries, were given for dissection; therefore, he continued, by benefiting science, they did a great deal more good than evil in the world, and that it was a pity so few murders were committed. Then he accused us of a conspiracy to paralyse the efforts of scientific men, not only by opposing amputation, but by conniving at a felonious fraud in depriving him of a post-mortem dissection. 'Had you acted,' said he, 'in a summary manner, which you do on other occasions, with Torra,—who was a very fine subject,—you would have hanged him instantly, and given me his body. I thought he was an honest man, but find him like every one else, conspiring to cheat the doctor,—which he has done by throwing himself away to the fishes, when he was my lawful perquisite. I therefore wish there were a hell for his sake.'

With this Christian wish and a glass out of Louis's bottle, he returned to his patients. 'Ah!' said Louis, 'if I did not see him drink this now and then, and smoke his pipe, I'd not believe him a live man. But any man may live on this,'—(holding up the bottle,)—'could not you? For it is like oil and spirit at once; the one keeps the body, the other the soul;—don't they?'

'Yes, with the addition of a turtle, now and then, I think I might. Do you think, Louis, they have turtle in heaven?'

'I am positive they have,' was his reply; 'or who would wish to go there?—would you? It is no paradise without turtle;—is it? Then there is plenty of water in the moon, or where does the rain come from?—so there must be gin there as well, to keep the damp out.'

I went on deck to keep the first watch. From Louis and turtle my thoughts reverted to my own little turtle-dove in her cage. Then, only looking at the sunny side of things, all was bright. I seemed to expand in bulk and stature. My thoughts ran nearly in the same channel with those of Alnaschar,[1] the prattling barber's brother, the fabled glass-merchant, of imaginative renown; for, like him, my fancy ran wild. I determined to be, at first, a kind and loving husband, then austere and severe, or kind and cruel by turns. Certainly, though I thought of every thing the most preposterous, not a single ray of light, useful or rational, shone on my midnight reveries. The gong sounded twelve; I was relieved from duty. The cares of married life not once disturbed my sleep. I wonder now I slept so soundly.

At last I was awakened by Van's shaking my leg. I sprung up in an instant, stamping it on the ground, in fear that he had been operating on it in my sleep. 'What's the matter, Van? Damn it! you were at your devil's work! By God! I'll throw your infernal saws and knives to hell.'

'What are you talking about? One of the prisoners, an Arab, is dying. He wants to see you.'

I dashed my head into a bucket of salt water, and followed the doctor. Notwithstanding I met Louis in the way, with a hot turtle-steak, which he urged me to eat first, as it was hazardous to go into the sick berth with an empty stomach, down I went; the man, who was badly wounded, only wanted to tell me to be kind to his father's child; to let him see her before he died, in order that he might take any message to her father, with whom he should soon be again, for he saw the blue angel of death hovering over him, in haste to spring aloft; to urge me to be a father to his two wives and five children, and to tell them they must, Ishallah! (please God!) continue their war for ever with the Maratti; because, whilst one remained alive, their father's spirit would be kept out of the heavens; and lastly, to see him put into the sea with all the customary rites of his country, not allowing that white Indian with his long knife, pointing to Van Scolpvelt, to scalp him, or cut him. 'For,' said he, 'if he cut any thing away from me here to eat it, I am no more fit for a warrior in the other land.'

Van gathered up his visage into a compound of horror, astonishment, and ferocity, and growled and snarled like a hyena. I believe the fear of Van Scolpvelt hastened the Arab's spirit, which, by the glassiness of his eye, was already on the wing, for it took flight, while I was endeavouring to appease the doctor's wrath.

I bade his Arab comrades take charge of the body. They erected a canvass berth, placed it within, and repeated the same ceremonies I have before narrated—only that now I was obliged to be an actor in their mysteries.

Here was I transformed, as by magic, from a friendless, outcast, reckless boy of the west, without tie or home, into sea Schaich, Arab, Mussulman—married! To give some idea of how much these transitions (at least the last, which governed the rest) weighed on my mind, I should not have known my wife from any other girl or woman. I had been so occupied with the father, and her head and face having been, for the most part, veiled, that I had not seen, or observed her features. I had not even yet inquired her name. It is true I had a Koran; but I knew not where was my adopted country.

The first step I took was, I then thought, and think still, the right one—to obtain information regarding the lady. I therefore ascertained, to begin in a business-like way, that her name was Zela.[1] That, engraved on my memory then in faint characters, will be found deeply, indelibly impressed on my heart when I die. Should any curious Van Scolpvelt desire to pry into my body, I freely give him leave, but more readily to Van himself, should he then live, to shew him that I have not that unmeasured hatred of science, with which he has so often taxed me. He shall find, annexed to my last testament, a codicil, in which I have expressly set down that my body shall be sent to Amsterdam, (where he was when I last heard of him,) conserved in a hogshead of right skedam—the body for the scientific Van Scolpvelt, the fluid for honest Louis's frow, if recovered from her dropsy.

After I had breakfasted, and fulfilled the injunctions of the dying Arab, by witnessing the consignment of his body to the deep, my thoughts again veered round to the right point of the compass—my virgin bride. I was schooled into the proper guttural pronunciation of her name; no easy task, for I was compelled to repeat the Z a hundred times, ere the old duenna who tutored me was satisfied with its hissing aspiration. Then she proceeded to impress on my memory ten thousand ceremonies and cautions to be used; I was not to touch the lady's veil, or person, or garments, or talk too much, or ask questions, or stay too long. For the lady Zela's thoughts were communing with her father's spirit; all her love was dead with him; her eyes, which outshone the stars, when she was happy, were now lustreless as her dead father's; her face, fairer than the moon, was now darkened by the clouds of grief; her lips, redder than henna, were pale with sorrow; all her loveliness was under eclipse, for tears had been her only food, and peace and sleep had fled her pillow, since her father's spirit had gone away, and left her alone in the world. She then added, 'Oh! stranger, be good to her, and all good will be yours in possessing her!'

CHAPTER IX

She like a moon in wane,
Faded before him, cower'd, nor could restrain
Her fearful sobs, self-folding like a flower
That faints into itself at evening hour.

KEATS

This ring　＊　＊　＊　＊　＊　＊
'Tis chosen, I hear, from Hymen's jewelry.

KEATS' MS.

SHE went to prepare the lady Zela, and, had I been a hot and impatient lover, she left me time to cool. Possibly the very thought that I was not going to woo, but was already fast wedded, helped to make the hour and a half, before she returned, appear neither more nor less than ninety minutes. Nor did I make any pretty invocations to time, with leaden or swallow wings. It might be that about this time of the day, I had a particular relish for smoking my callian, and sipping my coffee. I have never quitted this vice, or rather virtue; for, at this very time, I am as surly, if called away in the morning ere I have had my pipe and coffee, as a judge, when a jury finds a verdict according to their conscience, and against his summing up; or, as a bull-dog with his bone, when an impudent cur offers to knab it; or as a woman, detecting her wearied husband in the act of moving her new bonnet off the sofa to repose himself.

I sat inhaling the last whiff of the fragrant tombacae of Shiraz, through rose-water from Benares. I filled my lungs with a delicious cloud, which seemed to circulate throughout my body; and I sent it forth again like a jet of water, or frankincense burning from an altar, or from a swinging chalice, or like the spiral wreath from a cottage chimney,—for I was comparing it to all these; and so intently wrapt in watching and admiring the rainbow-like tints, borrowed from the sun, glittering upon the vapour, as I eked it out from my compressed lips and nostrils, with my cheeks swollen like a trumpeter's, that I had not seen the old Arab woman return. I suppose her beauties too were, like the moon, under a cloud, or in an eclipse; for her dark figure startled me, and I thought of the tale of the fisherman, and that the smoke had condensed itself into a black witch. She informed me that the lady Zela had been awaiting me with coffee and sweetmeats, till the one was cold, and the other turned sour.

'No one has been here,' I replied, 'to tell me she was ready.'

She looked sour enough to have spoilt the sweetmeats at a glance, as she said querulously, 'I have been standing here so long, that, see—my feet are grown to the wood!'

I laughed; for she was so far right that the sun and heat of her foot had melted the pitch; and she had some difficulty, as the vessel was heeling over, to keep her balance, while she disengaged her hoof. Saying all I could to soften her, down we went together.

The cabin-door was opened by a little Malayan slave girl, from the coast of Malabar, whom I had sent as my first gift, and I entered. The lady-mine was seated cross-legged on a low couch, so shrouded and enveloped in white drapery, the mourning of her country, that I could distinguish nothing of those wondrous beauties the old Arab woman had talked of. On my entrance I thought her one of those marble figures I had heard of in Egyptian temples; but I found she was alive. Her feet were bare; she rose and placed them in embroidered slippers, which lay on the deck of the cabin; she took my hand, put it to her forehead, then to her lips: I entreated her to be seated. She resumed her position, and remained motionless, her arms drooping listlessly down; her little rosy feet nestled under her, like tiny birds under the mother's wing. Her hair, the only part now visible, covered her like a jet black cloud. I had felt the pressure of her tremulous lips; and imagination, or perhaps some faint outline which fancy had left graved on my hand, pictured her mouth exquisitely soft and small,—(I loathe a large and hard one;) and I think now, this silent pressure wove the first link of that diamond chain which time nor use could ever break or wear away. I seemed entranced. We both sat silent; and I felt it a relief when the old Arab woman returned with coffee, and mangastene and guava jelly. She again rose, which I would have prevented, but the old woman signed me to sit still. She took a minute cup, in a fillagree silver stand, and presented it to me. I was so intently gazing on her tapering, delicately formed fingers, that I upset the coffee, and, putting the cup to my mouth, was going to swallow that; which indeed, as it was not bigger than the spicy shell of mace that holds the nutmeg, I might have done without choking. The old woman told me afterwards this was a bad omen. She then presented the conserves, and, returning the stand to the woman, resumed her seat.

Taking from my hand a ring of gold, with an Arabic inscription, and hooped with two circles of camel's hair, the same her expiring father had placed on my finger, I held it towards her. The low and suppressed moans she made on my entrance broke out into sobs, so violent that I could see her loose vest agitated by the beating of her heart. I was about to remove this object, which awakened such painful remembrances, when she grasped it, pressed it to her lips, and wept over it some time. The woman then said something to her; and, without the guidance of her eyes, she again put forth her tapering little fingers, and replaced the ring. It was indeed the antique signet of her father's tribe; and, like the seal of princes, it made right wrong, or wrong right, and gave, and took away, and made, and unmade laws, obeying the will of its wearer. She put it on the fore finger of my right hand; and again pressed my hand to her head and lips.

Upon this I took a ring I had selected from De Ruyter's store of baubles; it was a deep ruby, of the shape and size of a wild grape, hooped and massy with virgin gold, and, by its size, seemed to have been worn by a fairy. Gently disengaging her hand from the drapery as it lay motionless by her side, I placed this ring on the fore finger of her right hand;—the old woman smiled. Then I put her little palm to my lips, and repeatedly kissed it;—the old woman's brow darkened, or rather the wrinkles on her brow deepened, for her colour, by time and the sun, was fixed into an indelible bronze. However, taking the hint, I let go the hand, and it dropped by her side.

This interchange of rings was a definite acknowledgment of our union. I now asked the lady if I could do any thing to add to her comfort on board the ship. I told her I had collected and released all I could find of the tribe of her father; that they should be kindly attended to; that I was a stranger, and ignorant of many of their customs, entreating that she would direct me; that our Rais was a good man, and would love her like a father. Her sobs now became more violent. Catching the infection of melancholy, I put my hand to my heart, and said, 'Dear sister, moderate your grief. Command me in all things; for am I not your happy slave?' She did nothing but weep, and I withdrew.

CHAPTER X

The simplest flowers
In the world's herbal;—this fair lily blanched,
Still with the dews of piety; this meek lady
Here sitting, like an angel newly shent,
Who veils his snowy wings and grows all pale.
KEATS' MS.

THUS passed my first visit, and many successive ones. It was long
ere I heard the music of her voice. I thought she was mute as well
as motionless; but, distracted by the busy turmoil of our now
crowded vessel, my visits to the silent lady were not irksome.
I culled every thing I thought would amuse or please her; made
strict search, amidst the heaps of plunder we had taken from the
Maratti, for every thing belonging to her, her father, and his
people, which was restored; and I was unwearied in attempt to
win her regard. Yet so long she remained insensible, that I thought
I might as well have worshipped a mummy from the pyramids;
and had not my impatience been listened to, and soothed, by the
kind-hearted Aston, I should have expressed my dissatisfaction to
the lady herself, and totally have withdrawn from her, as my
presence seemed offensive.

Perhaps that would have been no easy task. For though I could
never interchange speech with Zela, the old Arab woman was not
so reserved. She would stop in the midst of every errand, as she
crossed the deck, and talk of nothing but her lady Zela. At first
I cursed her garrulity, as my legs grew weary with standing;
I thought she would have talked them off, for nothing would
induce her to be seated. No! she must not sit in the presence of
her malik; besides, her mistress was waiting for water, coffee,
sweetmeats, or something else. Methought her mistress must
be wonderous patient, for the moon wasted ere her discourse
concluded.

At last she instilled into me hopes that Zela was not insensible
of my kindness; that she said I was very good,—I must be, for
her people said so; that it was a pity I spoke her language so imperfectly, and was a stranger of a far distant tribe; she was sorry
the great kala panee (black water) was between our fathers' lands;

but I was gentle, kind, beautiful as a zebra, and she liked to hear my voice.

This delicious poison relumed my expiring hopes; the dark old woman grew bright and entertaining, and her harsh voice sounded sweet. My night watches seemed miraculously diminished. Yet I had seen no more of Zela than her foot and head; the tone of her voice I was as yet a stranger to.

How then could I love her? I had never felt, or seen, or dreamt of the strange power of love. Indeed I know not when, or why, or where, or how he found entrance even in my thoughts. It appeared to me I was only fulfilling a duty, sacred from its having been laid on me by the impressive energy of a dying parent, consigning to me, with his last breath, his friendless child. In the crystal purity of youth, this was the first impressive scene, in which I had been the principal actor, in which the emphatic appeal was made to the good feelings of my heart, a sealed fountain, then broken; and pity, and sorrow, and now love were flowing from it like a swollen torrent, which bears down all before it. The poor little captive bird was building her nest in my bosom's cove, whilst I thought her quietly caged in my cabin below. My visits grew longer and more frequent. I retained her passive hand in mine, till I felt its warmth restored, and fancied it glowing with mine. The very air about her seemed to grow heavy with fragrant odour. Even the touch of her insensible hair, more graceful than the willow's pendent boughs, as it kissed my cheek, filled my soul with passion. All my senses seemed exquisitely refined, and a world of new thoughts and delicate fancies to have birth within me. As I at last caught the full radiant brightness of her large dark eye, my limbs shook, my voice trembled, and my heart beat convulsively, and fast. Holding her hand, I gazed in speechless ecstacy. Whether she observed, I know not; but she removed her hand, and veiled the brightness of her eyes. It was enough; they had thrilled through me, and the fire was inextinguishable. She had murmured some words in a broken voice, which buzzed in my ears like a honied bee's, or like the warbling of the humming-bird, that lives in the cinnamon groves, and her breath was sweeter than the trees on which it lives. My senses ached with the intensity of the new world of delight which opened to me.

And love was thus ignited in my breast, pure, ardent, deep, and imperishable. Zela, from that day, was the star I was destined to worship; the deity at whose altar I was to offer up all the fragrant incense of my first virgin affections, feelings, and passions. Nor did ever saintly votary dedicate himself to his god with intenser devotion than I consecrated my heart to Zela. When dull mortality returns to dust, when the spirit bursts its charnel-vault, and wings its way, like a dove, it will find no resting-place, or olive branch of peace, till re-united with Zela's; then will they blend, two sun-beams together, shining onward to eternity.

CHAPTER XI

And then he went on shore without delay,
  Having no custom-house nor quarantine
To ask him awkward questions on the way,
  About the times and place where he had been:
He left his ship to be hove down next day,
  With orders to the people to careen,
So that all hands were busy beyond measure,
  In getting out goods, ballast, guns, and treasure.

BYRON

No other circumstance, of any importance, dwells on my mind during this eventful cruise. We were now in the latitude of the Mauritius, thirty-two leagues N.W. of the Isle of Bourbon. The Mauritius was first called by the Portuguese, on their visit in 1521, Swan Island, from being a favourite resort of that bird. The grasping Dutch were the first to lay their hands on it, yet not till long after, somewhere about 1600. They named it the Mauritius, complimenting, in this appellation, the Admiral of the United Provinces. The French, as I have already related, succeeded them, and called it the Isle of France; and it was the rallying point and rendezvous of all their cruisers. Nearly in the track of the Company's homeward and outward bound Indian fleets, of the departure of which care was taken to procure early intelligence, they sent their ships of war to cruise for them in the latitudes of their usual route. But it was from private ships of war, with commissions of lettres de marque, that the English merchant-fleet principally suffered. Against the large French ships they were protected by efficient convoy of their own men-of-war; but the smaller, fast-sailing French cruisers, filled with desperate adventurers, hung round

their fleets, like the wandering Arabs on the desert round a caravan; while the English men-of-war were withheld from pursuing
them, fearful of losing sight of the merchantmen, and of their
being attacked by others in their absence. The Frenchmen rarely
ventured near them during the day, or when it was fine weather,
unless supported by some of their own frigates, following them
in the hope of cutting off stragglers. In bad weather, during dark
nights, they deceived them, by making false signals to lure them
off; or during the heavy and sudden squalls which prevail in those
latitudes, in the event of any accident happening, such as losing
a mast, or, what frequently was the case, losing sight of their
convoy, they were certain of attack from one or more of the French
privateers. But being all well armed, and very large ships, they
sometimes succeeded in defending themselves, not only from the
private ships-of-war, but, on more than one occasion, they gallantly beat off a French squadron.

The French found the Mauritius of essential importance;
enabling them to harass the English commerce, and to preserve
a footing in India. They spared no expense in fortifying it; and,
to confess the truth, they were not backward in improving it, by
rendering it useful and productive. They introduced, and cultivated with success, most of the spices and fruits of India, with
rice, and all sorts of corn from Bourbon, Cochin China, and
Madagascar. But the island being small, not more than nineteen
leagues in circumference, of course all this was on a proportionally
limited scale. The Dutch, by their neglect, had allowed the most
valuable port, on the N.W. coast to be choked with their own
filth, and mud and stones washed down by the torrents from the
mountains rising close to it. The French, under a clever and
enterprising governor, cleared this harbour, built a good wall,
and made a superb basin for their ships of war, sheltered from all
winds, which are here occasionally terrific.

We made the land of Bourbon, then hauled up to the Mauritius,
which we soon after got sight of. This island is of an oval form, and
that part we now coasted, on the N.W. was grand and rugged,
with occasional verdant cover. De Ruyter observed that this side
of it had been turned topsy-turvy by the agency of volcanoes;
and that it was thought, by observers in these matters, to have
been formerly united with the Isle of Bourbon, but torn asunder
by the convulsion of internal fire. We saw many huge, arched

caverns, into which the sea was rolling with a hollow, thundering voice. Grey and ragged fragments of calcined rocks were piled on each other in fantastic disorder. The land then rose gradually from the cliffs to the centre of the island, terminating in a mountain, which rose like a dome. De Ruyter told us this was an elevated plain, thirteen hundred feet above the sea; and though, from this side, it appeared a precipitous mountain, on the other side, at Port St. Louis, the ascent was so gradual, that a horse might gallop up nearly to the summit, which was pointed like a sugar-loaf, called *Piton du milieu*, and surrounded by a plain. We saw seven other mountains, looking like seven giants seated in conference. Many low capes stretched out into the sea, and, winding their rocky roots yet farther, formed beautiful bays, with white sandy beaches, and narrow valleys, often intersected by streams or rivers, verdant and wooded, and thickly set with shrubs and flowers.

As Aston and myself stood watching these with our glasses, I said, 'How quiet and exquisitely beautiful is that! O, let us go and dwell there!' Then, as that shut in, and another opened far more beautiful, and then another, and another still, I reiterated the same exclamation. We all three loved nature, and De Ruyter took delight in pointing out to us every minute change in the scenery. 'Surely,' I cried, 'this island is a paradise of the eastern poets! Who but a fool, once on this land, would leave it? O, let us forsake the never-certain ocean, which, with its treacherous smiles, lures us on to sickness, disappointment, pain, and death!'

Aston was not less delighted than myself; and there was a willing alacrity and lightness in the movements of all on board. Joy spread in every countenance, every source of discontent was forgotten, and all was union and harmony. As we let the anchor go, the men flew aloft like birds, and the sails were furled in an instant. Canoes, almost sinking with their cargoes of fresh fish, fruit, and vegetables, were hovering round us.

The pleasure which filled my heart was augmented to overflowing by the dear presence of my little eastern fairy Zela, who, yielding to my earnest prayers, had allowed me to lead her on deck. As the gentle air waved her light gauzy robes aside, or pressed them closer to her, played with her hair, and shewed her youthful form, which seemed almost suspended in its own lightness, Aston gazed at her with astonishment, and compared her to a young fawn by the side of a stag. De Ruyter, who spoke her language perfectly, took her hand, but was so surprised at her beauty, that it was some time before he could utter a word, though she was then pallid and wan, and her lips colourless. He talked to her in his most soothing manner; then, turning to me, said, 'This is some little eastern sprite, too delicate and frail to be touched by human hands! I may now congratulate you with all my heart; nor lives there a man so cold as not to envy your good fortune. By God! I thought you were making a sacrifice, and I find you have a jewel, which kings, if they had hearts, would give their crowns to possess! Knowing this, if you do not treasure her as such, may happiness forsake you for ever! Fortune can never again give any thing so far above comparison.'

She looked round like a frighted antelope, with wonder at finding herself surrounded by so many strangers, all gazing on her; and her face was crimsoned like the morning clouds. She would have returned below, but her hand was shackled in mine. I sent for a carpet and cushions, and she sat down on deck, encircled with women.

CHAPTER XII

Worse than a bloody hand is a hard heart.
SHELLEY

Thou bitter mischief, venomous, bad priest!
KEATS' MS.

DE RUYTER went on board the corvette, to tell her captain that the English frigates had left their blockade of the leeward port. This was occasioned by the loss of their men and boats, and in order to return to Madras before the S.W. monsoon set in. Besides, as the homeward-bound fleet was supposed to have passed the latitudes of these islands, their object in blockading was effected. It was then determined that the corvette, after getting a supply of water and fresh provisions, was to go round to Port St. Louis; and that De Ruyter, by crossing over land, was to meet the captain there, and give their despatches to the French general commanding.

This done, he returned on board, when we sent all our prisoners

o

and wounded on board the corvette, and De Ruyter went on shore to provide accommodations for his own sick, and procure supplies. The next morning he left us for the town and port of St. Louis. He gave me directions what to do in his absence, and promised to be with us at latest in three days. We shook hands and parted.

It was arranged that when the grab was cleared, we should lay her up, and proceed to De Ruyter's country house; he possessed a considerable estate in the interior of the island.

It is worthy of remark that, regarding climate, this island has a peculiarity I never remember to have found in any other in India. Other islands are comparatively cool and pleasant on the coasts, and close and unhealthy in the interior, unless on the heights. Here it is reversed: the entire coast is so scorchingly hot, and the air so bad, that at Port St. Louis, and other places round, no one dares venture out in the daytime during six months of the year, as he may be almost certain of having a sun-stroke, which occasions a brain-fever, the malignant fever, cholera morbus, or dysentery; while, at the same period, in the interior, particularly on the windward side, the air is temperate and salubrious. For six months in the year, from November to April, the town of St. Louis is insufferably and noxiously hot; scarcely any one but the slaves could be induced to remain there, the free inhabitants departing for the interior. Then again, the dry months at Port St. Louis are the rainy ones in the central parts; and, whilst the fiercest hurricanes are raging on the coast, a few miles in-land all is calm and sunshine. I have repeatedly witnessed this; and it is strange in so small an island.

With a nature ardent, active, and enterprising, my soul was in what I undertook, and with unwearied diligence I executed De Ruyter's behests. Watching and toil were to me pleasure, for my body was strong, and my spirits winged. Magazines of spars, planks, and matting were speedily erected on the shore; every article not pertaining to the vessel was landed and daily sent round on the backs of mules, asses, and slaves,—(the last, I shame to say, were the chief animals of burthen on the island,)—and transported, with proper precautions, to the town of Port St. Louis.

De Ruyter had made great exertions and sacrifices in the importation of buffaloes and asses, to supersede the use of slaves, in the degrading and painful toil of bearing burthens in a climate of almost insufferable heat. But the cold indifference with which men,

solely devoted to mercenary pursuits, treated his humane propositions, made it up-hill work. These heartless traffickers could
neither see nor hear of any plan, except such as tended to their
own immediate profit. With them the common organs of nature
became brutalised; their views of things were narrowed into the
circumference of actual sight; and as the wasp, with an eye like
a lens, magnifying into bulk the minutest objects within an inch
of its optics, cannot distinguish, at the distance of a yard, a wall
from a wall-flower, so was it with these fellows. There was no
use in talking of to-morrow, of what could be then done with
mules and buffaloes, because with slaves they could realise a
profit to-day. As to human suffering, they not being touched with
human feeling, how could that influence them? 'Is that the law?
—I cannot find it, 'tis not in my bond,'—is the sum of their ready
reply to the advocates of humanity. To every appeal they are deaf
as crocodiles; and while you are talking of humanity, they will lash,
or order to be goaded the bare and festered back of an overloaded
female slave, her tender nature one animated mass of ulcers and
cancers, half consumed alive by flies and maggots, antedating
their destined prey. Then, what the free and happy most fear—
death, is her only hope and refuge, and comes like a bridegroom;
when the corrupted mass is cast uncoffined into the sea, or in a
ditch, where the dog-fish, or the wild dog, famishing, will turn
from it,—the worms' leavings. Thus it is with her, and with
harder and more enduring man. I have seen their spines knotted
as a pine tree, and their skins as scaled and callous, with the flesh
cracked into chasms, from which blood oozed out like gum, as
hundreds of them, poor wretches! underwent their daily toil in
the dock-yard at Port St. Louis, under a sun so scorching, that
their task-masters, shaded, sheltered, and reclining, have gasped
as from suffocation; and when, from the mere exertion of moving
a few yards, at a snail's pace, to give commands, their bodies have
reeked with moisture, and larded the earth, like a horse's after a
race in July. The pity and pain I felt, at the sight of these poor
slaves, could only be equalled by the deep and overwhelming damnation I invoked on the heads of their inhuman oppressors, them
and their kind for ever! Surely monsters like these are annihilated,
—they cannot be immortal! Yet they should be so, with an eternity
to torture them in. They should have justice and their bond;
what they have done to others should be done to them; and I defy

the invention of hell's fabled demons to be more cunning in cruelty than themselves.

This barbarous treatment of the slaves, though not to the extent which I afterwards witnessed on the other side of the island, impelled me on, if a spur was wanting, to despatch my business in Port Bourbon, that I might hasten to the secluded, wild, and wooded hill, De Ruyter had pointed out as the place of his residence. There, I knew, where he had power, pain and oppression would be softened, if not driven away altogether.

At the appointed period De Ruyter returned. Active and energetic as he was in all he did, he was surprised at our expedition. The burthened hull and lofty-rigged vessel, which, a few days before, had come into the port half buried by her weight, with clouds of canvass on her, now floated as light as a sea-bird sleeping, her canvass unbent, masts and yards struck, dismantled, and moored close to the shore.

De Ruyter informed Aston that he had obtained permission for himself, and the four men belonging to the frigate, whom we had kept on board, to remain with him, on his parole for himself and them.

We were discoursing of the slaves when he came in. He told us this tale, in his pithy and abrupt manner: 'Two days ago I went to the door-way (for I never venture farther) of a church they were consecrating, to seek for a slave-dealer, with whom I had business. He is a cruel villain, but a punctilious, sanctimonious, and sour church-goer; a fellow who, if there remained but one man besides himself in the island, and if their faiths differed but in the breadth of a hair, would, by force or stratagem, stake or burn him. You shall hear: the church, flagged with white pavement, was blotted by half a score of black priests. There was a mass of people to see the ceremony; and these priests looked like the smutted ears bound up with a sheaf of corn. I was going away, for I grew sick, from the filthy compound smell of frankincense, sweat and garlic, all mingled. An ignorant, converted slave entered, who, seeing some muddy water in a stone basin at the portal, concluded it was for ablution. He, therefore, laved his tarred and begrimed arms in it, up to the elbows. A missionary priest observing this, struck him over the pate with the cross, on which was bedaubed, as if in mockery, a gory Christ. The cross, being of the same materials as the priest's heart, iron-wood and ebony, was heavy. The priest was strong and malignant. It crushed the fellow's bare head, and entered the brain;—the first good act a bigoted priest committed, —for the slave was emancipated.'

'What did they with the assassin?' exclaimed Aston.

'I know,' answered De Ruyter, 'what they would have done with you, if they had heard you so call him. Why, they drowned the victim's death-scream with bellowing *Te Deum*, mopped their sweating brows, and went and feasted at the slave-butcher's house. As to poor *negur* man, I saw his carcase to-day, as I rode along at high water-mark, a banquet for the land-crabs. These are the staunch upholders of Christ's bloody banner, and these the arguments used for the conversion of unbelievers. At Rome is the main spring of this faith, which I liken to a banian tree: for every branch from the main body throws out its own roots, at first in small tender fibres, but continually growing thicker, by gradual descent, they get within the surface of the earth; where, sticking in, they increase to large trunks, and each becomes a parent tree, throwing out new branches from the top; these, in times, suspend their root, and receiving nourishment, swell into trunks, and shoot forth other branches; thus continuing in a state of progression, so long as the first parent of them all supplies its sustenance.'

'No more of this!' said I; 'let us hasten to our quarters on the hill, away from priests and slaves!'

CHAPTER XIII

> Soft mossy lawns
> Beneath these canopies extend their swells,
> Fragrant with perfumed herbs, and eyed with blooms,
> Minute yet beautiful.
> SHELLEY

> No tumbling water ever spake romance,
> But when my eyes with thine thereon could dance,
> No woods were green enough, no bower divine,
> Until thou liftedst up thine eyelids fine.
> KEATS

IN a few days more, all our arrangements being made, and the Rais left on board in command, De Ruyter, Aston, and myself, with the gentle Zela, and her attendants, went on shore as the day broke. We commenced our journey in-land, with mules,

ponies, and asses. We went some distance along the pebbly margin
of the shore, beautifully tesselated with a variety of shells, of all
colours and shapes. Then crossing an arid plain, we wound up
a rocky, rugged ascent, on a path with only room for one mule.
I walked by the side of Zela's little horse, and pointed out to her
the sublime beauty of the scenery. As the grey mist was evaporating, the tops of the cone-like hills were left bare, while their bases
were still hidden by the vapours. They looked like a group of
beautiful islands, or black swans, floating in a calm and silent
lake, some feathered to the very crest with shrubs and bushes;
some with majestic timber, the palm and cedar; and others blasted
by volcanic fire.

Zela had the blood of a fearless race. She had been bred and
schooled amidst peril, always at hand. Not having learnt to affect
what she did not feel, she crossed ravines, wound along precipices,
and waded through streams and rivers, not only without impeding
us by enacting a pantomimic representation of fears, tears, entreaties, prayers, screaming, and fainting, but she was such a
simpleton as not even to notice them, unless, in the usual sweet,
low tone of her voice, to remark that they were delightful places
to sit in, during the sultry part of the day; or she would stop her
pony over a precipice to gather some curious flowers, drooping
from a natural arch; or to pluck the pendant and waving boughs
of the most graceful of Indian trees, the imperial mimosa, sensitive and sacred as love, shrinking from the touch of the profane.

'Put this,' she said, holding out a branch, 'in your turban; for
I am sure in some of these hollow caves and dreary chasms the
ogres live; they feed their young with human blood, and they love
to give them the young and beautiful. Put it in your turban,
brother,—since you say I must not call you master;—and never
frown,—I do not like to see it, for then you are not so handsome,—
I mean, good, as when you smile. Do not laugh, but take it. It will
preserve you from every spell and magic. Nothing bad dares come
near it.'

While crossing a sandy level, suddenly she started, as her eye
caught some object. Without stopping her horse, which was
ambling along, she sprang off, and ran up a sand hill, like a white
doe. Never having witnessed any thing like this before, I was so
astonished that she was returning, ere I could overtake her to
ask if an ogre had lured her with his evil eye. 'O, no,' she cried,—

'look here! You like flowers, but did you ever see any one so lovely as this? Smell it,—'tis so sweet, that the rose, if growing near it, loses its beauty and fragrance, from envy of its rival.'

Certainly I thought she was bewitched. It was a glaring, large, red bough, full of blowzy blossoms, and yellow berries, with a musky fœtid odour. 'Why,' I exclaimed, 'you have as much reason to be jealous of old Kamalia, your nurse, as the rose to be jealous of such a scraggy bramble as this! Faugh! the smell makes me sick.'

I suppose I was instigated to make this rude speech by her fondling and kissing it. Her dark eyes expanded; and she seemed, for an instant, to view me with astonishment, then with sorrow; as they closed, I perceived that their brightness was gone, and the long jetty fringe, which arched upwards as it pressed her cheek, was covered with little pearly dew-drops. The branch fell from her hand under my feet, her sprightly form drooped, and the tones of her voice reminded me of the time when she hung over her dying parent, as she said,—'Pardon me, stranger! I had forgotten you are not of my father's land. This tree covered my father's tent, sheltered us from the sun, and kept away the flies, when we slept in the day. Our virgins wreathe it in their hair, and, if they die, it is strewed over their graves. So, I can't help loving it better than any thing. But, since you say it makes you sick, I won't love it, or gather it any more.' Then her words became almost inarticulate from sobbing, as she added,—'Why should I wear it now? I belong to a stranger! My father is gone!'

I need scarcely say that I not only returned the flowers, and pleaded my ignorance, but I went up the hill, and pulled up the tree by the roots. 'Sweet sister,' said I, 'I was only angry with it because you abused the favoured tree of our country, the rose. But now, as the sun shines on it, and I see it nearer,'—looking at her,—'I do think the rose may envy it, as the loveliest of my countrywomen might envy you. I'll plant it in our garden.'

'O, how good you are!' she exclaimed; 'and I'll plant a rose tree near it, and they shall mingle their sweets; for our love and care of them will make them live together without envy. Every thing should love each other. I love every tree, and fruit, and flower.'

Still I observed, as her thin robes were disarranged, that her little downy bosom fluttered like an imprisoned bird panting for liberty; and, to turn her thoughts from what had pained her,

I said,—'Do not fear, dear Zela. That is the last stream we have to cross; and then we shall ride over that beautiful plain.'

'O, stranger!' she replied, 'Zela never feared any thing, but her father, when angry; and then, those who feared not to gaze on the lightning, when all the world appeared to be on fire, feared to look in his face. Then his voice was louder than the thunder, and his lance deadlier than the thunder-bolt. Last evening, when you talked to that tall man, who is so gentle, you looked like my father; and I thought you were going to kill him, and I wanted to tell you not; for I have read his eyes, and he loves you much. It is very bad to be angry with those that love us.'

'Oh, you mean Aston! No, dear, I was not angry with him. I love him too. We were talking of the horrid cruelties practised on the poor slaves here; and I was angry at that.'

'I wish I knew your language! How I should have loved to hear you! And then I should have slept; but being ignorant of that, I did nothing but weep, because I thought I saw you angry with one that loves you.'

De Ruyter now came up, and we suddenly stood on the elevated plain, called Vacois, in the centre of the island. Our ascent had been very abrupt, winding, and rugged. Before us, in the middle of the plain, on which we now rode, was the pyramidical mountain I have already noticed, under the name of *Piton du Milieu*. Inclining to our right was the port and town of St. Louis. To the south were large plains, in rich vegetation, divided by a fine river, with one solitary hill. To the north were other plains, inclining to the sea, white as if the briny waters had recently receded from them, and only partially cultivated with sugar-canes, indigo, and, in the marshy spots, with rice. From south to east it was volcanic and mountainous, with jungle and ancient forests. The north-east was, for the most part, level. The plain, where we were, was full of little sheets of deep water, forming themselves into pretty lakes; which, overflowing during the heavy rains, at times made the plain swampy, and ever overgrown with canes, reeds, and gigantic grass. Such was the diversified and beautiful scenery now disclosed, as the sun, having risen above the mountain in the east, dissipated the yellow mists, and laid bare the hitherto obscured beauties of this divine island, like a virgin unrobed for bathing.

We alighted under the shade of a group of the rose-apple trees, which seemed to have drawn a charmed circle round a solitary oak, on the brink of a lake, clear as a diamond, and apparently of amazing depth, the golden Chinese fish sporting on its surface, and green, yellow, and blue dragon-flies darting here and there above it. The modest wood-pigeon and dove, disturbed in their morning ablutions, flew away to the woods. The gray partridge ran into the vacour, which stood in thick lines on the brink, impenetrable from its long fibrous leaves, standing out like a phalanx of lances. The water-hens dived, and the parrots chattered on the trees, as if they had been peopled with scolding married women; whilst the sluggish baboon sat, with portly belly, gormandising with the voracity and gravity of a monk, regardless of all but the stuffing of his insatiable maw with bananas.

We were told that there were, in this lake, prawns as big as lobsters, and eels of incredible size, from fifteen to twenty feet long. The two principal rivers took their rise from this plain, augmenting in their course by the tribute of an infinity of streamlets; till swollen into bulk and strength, like two rival monarchs, they ran parallel for a while, trying to outvie each other in pomp and velocity, springing over their rocky beds. After some distance they separated to the right and left, and passed through their different districts, to pay, in their turn, tribute to the mightier ocean.

CHAPTER XIV

The oak
Expanding its immeasurable arms
Embraces the light beech. The pyramids
Of the tall cedar, over-arching, frame
Most solemn domes within; and far below,
Like clouds suspended in an emerald sky,
The ash and the acacia floating hang
Tremulous and pale. The parasites,
Starr'd with ten thousand blossoms flow around
The grey trunks.
                              SHELLEY

AFTER the senses were satiated by the matchless beauties of nature, our grosser appetites prevailed, craving some of her solid bounties. Fish, fruits, and other simple fare, a sailor's greatest luxury, were spread out in abundance. We devoured them with truly sacerdotal zeal. Meanwhile the odour of citrons, raspberries, guavas, wild mangoes, and strawberries, with countless herbs and aromatic plants and shrubs, ascending up the valley with the morning dew, filled us with exquisite sensations of delight. My limbs, light and elastic, impelled me to believe I could have outrun the deer, which, from time to time, we saw crossing the opening glades, and dashing into the coverts.

A portion of the pleasure I felt infused itself into the mind of Zela. This was the first time we had eaten bread and salt together. As I remarked it to her, she smiled, and said, 'Yes, now we must be friends! And, if you keep our country's customs, you must not even frown on me, your guest, till the sun shall set, and again dawn.'

While strolling together, and gathering flowers, I questioned her respecting their classification,—not the botanical, but the oriental one of love; but De Ruyter soon halooed us to horse.

We left the lake on our right, skirted the base of *Piton du Milieu*, over a volcanic soil of pulverized cinders, and, by gentle descents, proceeded towards the south. Again we were among mountains, passing green lawns, and marshes overgrown with vitti-vert, (which is used for thatching,) fern, marsh-mallows, waving bamboos, and wild tobacco. We saw plantations of the manioc, (breadfruit,) maize, sweet potatoes, the cotton-tree, the sugar-cane, coffee, and cloves. Then we crossed rocky channels of clear rippling water, hedged by dwarf oaks and the dusky-coloured olive, underneath which flourished the dark-green fig-tree, with its strawberry-red marrowy fruit, bared by the bursting of its emerald-green rind. Here the majestic palmiste towered grandly alone, crowned with its first, tardy, and only fruit; and when deprived of that diadem, like earthly monarchs, it perishes. We penetrated the wild native woods, where grew the iron-wood tree, the oak, the black cinnamon, the apple, the acacia, the tamarind, and the nutmeg. Our path was arched by wild vines, jessamine, and a multitude of deep scarlet-blossomed creepers, so thickly interlaced in their living cordage, that neither sun nor storm could penetrate them; or if a wandering beam found entrance through the thick natural trellice-work, it was only enough to cover some little tuft of violets or strawberries, its own offspring, growing up in its genial warmth with a strength and vigour pre-eminent amidst the pale and sickly brood of the neglected children of the shade. Nothing I had ever imagined of the loveliness of nature equalled the reality of these scenes. Among such fairy haunts, created for a sylvan people, we appeared intruders; and, for the first time, methought De Ruyter's and Aston's voices were harsh, and their manly figures and weather-strained brows, out of keeping: they would be more in their places, I thought, on the armed deck of a ship, or leading men to battle. I could in no manner so group them as to make them keep tone, or preserve the harmony of the scene. The most favourable view that could be taken of them, was to regard them as wood-demons, *jungle admee*, (wild men,) ouran-outangs, or centaurs. The old nurse, Kamalia, who, with two black slaves, brought up the rear, I was so convinced was a sybil or sorceress, with her attendant demons, ready to execute her horrible enchantments, that I began to wish myself out of the gloom of the forests, and to long once more to be in the sun, however scorching; and when Zela pulled in her horse, and the old dark hag approached with her blacks, I grasped hold of his bridle, and urged him on, anticipating every instant to see Zela transformed into a white fawn, bounding into the density of the woods, and myself and all the others into great black dogs, doomed to hunt her, without pause, for a hundred moons. My fears were a little dissipated, as, clinging firmer on her horse, for its sudden motion, as she was looking up, had almost thrown her, she said, 'O, let me go—I shall fall!—and I want to speak to old Kamalia, to ask her what these beautiful red flowers are on the top of that tree. And, see! they are not blossoms, but little scarlet birds, and you have frightened them all away!'

I, laughingly, acquainted Zela with my thoughts. She laughed too, and inquired—

'But what do you think I am?'

'You, dear, are the gentle Ariel, the fairy sprite of the place. This wood should be your dwelling-place, your empire: nothing human, for every thing human is dashed with evil, should find an entrance. Elemental walls should incage you, and you should live, like the bee and those bright birds, on the sweets of herbs and flowers.'

'Yes, but I should not wish to live alone; nor could I be happy if imprisoned, though in the sweetest place, for then it would be no longer sweet.'

'Then, dearest, I would attend on you as your slave.'

'O no, no, no, there shall be no slaves: did you not say so?'

Our path now became wider and lighter, and we emerged from dark shade into an open plain, almost blinding us with dazzling brightness. As we crossed a river, by a rustic bridge, I thought I recognized De Ruyter's hand in the construction. Again ascending a zig-zag path, we mounted, amongst groups of trees and shrubs, to an elevated platform, on which stood the house and gardens of De Ruyter. I shouted with delight to Aston, who was behind me—

'See, here it is—here is our house: it must be so, for who but De Ruyter would have ever discovered so matchless a spot to build a dwelling on? I told you so: every thing we have hitherto passed is nothing in beauty to this; and, possessing this, what else can a man desire; for here is every beauty in nature drawn together to make it perfect.'

'It is indeed!' answered Aston, looking at the situation, and gazing round at the extensive view over the island, 'it is perfection!'

'Come, come, dismount,' said De Ruyter; 'you'll have time enough to examine this. It is now the hottest hour of the day. Your husband,' turning to Zela, 'is fit only for a wandering santon of the desert: see, he has selected the most unsheltered place he could find, to have the full benefit of the fierce sun. Look at him, he is unturbaning! He would be a saint among the Raypoots— the sun's offspring!'

Zela came up to my side, and gently said, 'Do not stand in the sun, for it is very bad now. Look! all the blossoms and flowers shrink from it, and, shutting their eyes, they sink into the shadow of the leaves;—and they too droop despondingly. And all the pretty birds and insects are gone to sleep in the woods. No animal is stirring abroad, when the sun is in the middle of heaven. Every thing sleeps; even the wind is gone to sleep, in those holes and caverns we saw on the shore. Nothing but the malignant little fly is awake; he now collects his venom in the poisonous exhalations, to torment the night with his war-cry, whilst he stabs with his lance, and frightens sleep away. He is the bad spirit, and sleep is the good. Come away; the captain says so, and you mind him more than me.'

A very pretty description of the sand-fly tribe, thought I, as we dismounted under a viranda, and were led by De Ruyter into the house. It had a double row of Persian blinds all round, which completely excluded the sun, and let in the air. The centre hall, comprising nearly half the house, had a flag pavement, with a

stream of the clearest water, hurrying through a little channel,
which filled an oval basin in the middle, and then a large bathing
tank in the garden-grounds, serving also for irrigation. It afterwards formed a cascade, and leaped from crag to crag, till it
reached its parent-river, whose waters could be heard from the
window, murmuring beneath us. De Ruyter had cut, upwards in
the mountain, to the source of one of the springs, which he thus
brought down into his house and grounds. Round the centre hall
were low, broad, cushioned seats; and on its walls Indian and
European weapons of the chace, mingled with drawings and rustic
implements. Zela and her attendants were shewn into one of the
wings, over which was written, in Persian characters, '*The Zennanah.*' 'This was a whim of the artist,' said De Ruyter, 'who
arranged and painted the interior; for your lady is the first who,
as far as I know, ever entered it.'

Then shewing Aston his room, he turned to me, and continued:
'As for you, a walled room cannot contain your wandering spirit.
So we must leave you to rove about after your restless fashion;—
I know you will do so, whether permitted or not. If you want any
thing, clap your hands; then, if they are real wants, they will be
satisfied. As to luxuries, I have avoided the taint of the climate;
yet nothing is prohibited, for that defeats its object, and sets a
value on shadows. When the gong sounds one, you will find tiffin
in the hall.'

CHAPTER XV

> We gaze and turn away, and know not where,
> Dazzled and drunk with beauty, till the heart
> Reels with its fulness.
> > BYRON

WITH these words he left us to ourselves, and Aston exclaimed:
'What can he mean by luxuries? Can the world produce such as
these, to my mind the most exquisite that man can conceive?'

'I think we may contrive,' I replied, 'not being very fastidious
in these matters, to rough it here.'

'Yes,' he rejoined; 'and when we leave it, every thing else will
appear rough and musky as an Irish hut.'

Thus chatting, strolling about the hall, and just sallying out, the gong sounded. All but Zela appeared. 'We shall find you,' said De Ruyter to me, 'but a droning sort of comrade, unless the queen bee makes her appearance; so let her be entreated to wave the customs of her country, and follow ours,—at least in this. In most others I like her's best.'

A woman was called and sent to her. After some demur Zela entered, and, placing her on a couch, for she had never sat on a chair, I placed myself by her. Admirable were her little tapering fingers in eating. Their beauty was destroyed by an ugly iron prong, which she essayed in vain to use. I begged her to teach me her way; but, instead of separating grains of rice, as she could, with fingers, it was impossible to separate the rice from the wing of fowl in a curry. I was compelled to shovel them both in my mouth together.

Zela, with still some difficulty, consented to accompany us in our evening stroll. She retired, and we reclined on the couches round the hall, with coffee and callians, gazing on the water, which, in its shadowed channel, looked like a mirror in a marble frame. Too happy to express our feelings, we did not talk, but sat musing, till we found relief in sleep.

On awaking, we washed in basins placed on stone benches by the stream. A drink was brought, of iced water, with the compressed juice of the freshly plucked pomegranate; and a little filagreed basket of fruit and sweetmeats. Then again restoring the fine tone of the palate with coffee, whose fragrance filled the hall, we once more smoked our callians, till the sun was sinking behind a mountain, and the breeze came from the sea, when we sent for Zela.

At her appearance we went into the grounds about the house, and ascended, by a gentle aclivity, in shaded and embowered paths, to a summer-room, exactly of the form and colour of a markee. Here was a commanding view of the principal beauties of the island, the sea, and the entire port of Bourbon. Zela cried out, 'There is the ship!—close below us,—not more than five miles off!' And, with the telescope, I fancied I could see Louis le Grand busily handling the turtle, under the awning on deck.

I sat down on a projecting crag, above a deep chasm, with my eyes rivetted on the light and winged movements of Zela, who was flitting about, like a bee or bird, from tree to flower, examining nicely into each scent and quality. Elegant motion, graceful bearing, and bashful yet unembarrassed address are to be found in perfection in the east. Nature, as if fearing the rivalry of art, or indignant at its presumption, or disdaining to contend with so feeble a foe, or disgusted that her choicest, best gifts are despised, tortured, and distorted into unseemly shapes in what is called civilized communities, has withdrawn from populous cities to the desert and the lonely mountains, her own loved haunts; and there she dwells sporting with her favoured offspring, the ring-dove, the antelope, and the barb. A child of the desert is like a vine in the wilderness, spreading its leafy tendrils in profusion; although, in comparison to the same plant cultivated and pruned, it yields but a scanty vintage, it is more beautiful, hanging in flowing ring-lets on the heads of forest trees, than clipped and confined to hedge-stakes. The vine and the olive are children of the hills and sands, nurtured by sunbeams. The desert-horse and antelope are the fleetest and most beautiful. That majestic king of birds, the plumage of which waves over the jewelled diadems of human kings, and nods in triumph over a royal hearse, inhabits the sandy wastes. The richest fruits, the sweetest flowers, the balmiest air, the brightest and purest water, are found amidst rocks and sands, nursed in solitude and liberty; and there man communes with God and nature till, in love and worship, his feelings are almost divine. There too I have seen her virgins, and Zela was one of these, untaught as her wildest children, whose exquisite loveliness shamed the Grecian sculptor's art, his measured lines and cold proportions, by beauties such as inspiration, with the perfection of science, could never dream to trace. I have gazed on their forms, features, and expression, blending and harmonizing to-gether, till the over-excited senses, all concentrated into one, have so fascinated my being, that I have become faint with unendurable delight, and my heart, overflowing with its delicious sensations, sought relief in sighs and tears. What eye so stony, that meets their arrowy glance, darting through the brain, could scrutinize its colour or measure its lines, to see if it were of the Grecian or Roman mould? The owl might as well attempt to gaze undazzled at the sun.

It was only in Zela's absence that I could dwell on her por-traiture. She had just turned her fourteenth year; and though certainly not considered, even in the east, as matured, yet, forced like a flower, fanned by the sultry west wind, into early development, her form, like its petals bursting through the bud, gave promise of the rarest beauty and sweetness. Nurtured in the shade, her hue was pale, but contrasted with the date-coloured women about her, the soft and transparent clearness of her complexion was striking; and it was heightened by clouds of the darkest hair. She looked like a solitary star unveiled in the night. The breadth and depth of her clear and smooth forehead were partly hidden by the even silky line from which the hair arose, fell over in rich profusion, and added to its brightness; as did the glossy, well-defined eye-brow, boldly crossing the forehead, slightly waved at the outer extremities, but not arched. Her eyes were full, even for an orientalist, but neither sparkling nor prominent, soft as the thrush's. It was only when moved by joy, surprise, or sorrow, that the star-like iris dilated and glistened, and then its effect was most eloquent and magical. The distinct ebon-lashes which curtained them were singularly long and beautiful; and when she slept they pressed against her pale cheeks, and were arched upwards.

That portion of the eye, generally of a pearly whiteness, in hers was tinted with a light shade of blue, like the bloom on a purple grape, or the sky seen through the morning mist. Her mouth was harmony and love; her face was small and oval, with a wavy outline of ineffable grace descending to her smooth and unruffled neck, thence swelling at her bosom, which was high, and just developing into form. Her limbs were long, full, and rounded, her motion was quick, but not springy, light as a zephyr. As she then stood canopied beneath the dense shade of that sacred Hindoo tree, with its drooping foliage hanging in clusters round her, in every clasped and sensitive leaf of which a fairy is said to dwell, I fancied she was their queen, and must have dropped from one of the leaves, to gambol and wanton among the flowers below. Running to her, I caught her in my arms, and said, 'I watched your fall, and have you now, dear sprite, and will keep you here!'—pressing her to my bosom.

'Oh, put me down! You hurt me,—I have not fallen,—oh, let me go!'

'Will you promise then not to take flight to your leafy dwelling, in that your fairy-kingdom-tree?'

'What do you mean? Oh, let me go,—you'll crush me!'

I gently placed her on the ground, and told her my fears. The instant I unclutched her, she ran to her old attendant, scared like a young leveret; and this was my first embrace of my Arab maid.

That it may not be considered I exaggerate, when speaking of the Arabs in India generally, I must refer the reader to what a recent, learned, and unprejudiced traveller[1] says of them: 'The Arabs are numerous in India; their comparative fairness, their fine, bony, and muscular figures, their noble countenances, and picturesque dress, intelligent, bold, and active,' &c.

Zela's father was all this, and her mother a celebrated beauty brought from the Georgian Caucasus, and twice made captive by the chance of war. After giving birth to Zela, she looked, and saw her own image in her child, blessed it, and yielded up her mortality. Is it to be marvelled at, that the offspring of such parents was as I have described, or rather what I have attempted to describe? For I am little skilled in words, or words are insufficient to represent what the eye sees, and the heart feels.

CHAPTER XVI

There's not a breath
Will mingle kindly with the meadow air,
Till it has panted round and stolen a share
Of passion from the heart.   KEATS

ON my return to De Ruyter and Aston, they were determining on the necessity of our calling on the commandant at Port St. Louis, and agreed to ride thither on the ensuing day. I begged off, under plea of having the ship's duty to attend to. We continued in the open air till supper was announced, and our evening terminated as agreeably as the day had begun, wanting nothing but the presence of Zela. As we were to rise long before the sun, to enjoy the cool morning air, we retired early to our couches.

My restless spirit could not be hushed to sleep. After tossing about for an hour, I returned to the summer-house, where they found me in the morning. I then went to the bath, which refreshed me more than sleep. After coffee, and smoking our callians, we went round with De Ruyter to look at his plants and shrubs, which he had brought from different islands in the Indian archipelago; for he had a strong passion for gardening, building, and planting,

P

and loved this island for its climate and soil, where every thing flourished. He said, 'I have questioned all sorts of people, up to princes and tyrants, and find that gardeners are the most contented, and therefore the happiest people in the world. I confess, if I had not been a sailor from chance, I should have been a gardener from choice. But we have no voice in these matters, compelled, like the beetle and the bat, blindly on, in the earth, or in the air.'

I could hardly remember a fruit or flower I had ever seen in Europe or India which he had not collected together here; and there were many I had never seen, or never taken note of before, besides the aboriginal trees of the island. Except the platform on which the house was built, all the ground round about was wild and broken. The timber found on the spot had been partially cleared away; small groups, and single forest trees were left. The house consisted of a single story, with a projecting front and roof, and was colonaded. The front was to the south, and looked down on a small plain; the sea was to the north-west; and to the east, mountains, forests, rocks and precipices diversified the scenery. With the exception of a portion of the plain below, nothing indicated cultivation or inhabitants. There was a large plantation, with several small ones, divided by avenues of trees and paths between, and white-washed wooden cottages, whence De Ruyter drew all his supplies, making it a point to produce every article he consumed in abundance.

'It would be more advantageous,' said he, 'in a worldly point of view, to cultivate that alone, in large quantities, which is best adapted to the peculiarity of the soil; and, by turning the overplus into specie, to purchase what necessaries or luxuries I might fancy. But, besides the satisfaction I feel in my plan, for what I lose in profit I gain in pleasure, health, and occupation, it enables me to meliorate the hard fate of those suffering under a detestable system,—which I abhor, but cannot remedy,—I mean that of slavery. What I could, I have done. You will find no slave on my property. The bread you eat may not be the whitest or the lightest; but it is not stained by the blood and sweat of the galled and over-toiled captive, or leavened in execrations. Some score of slaves that I have redeemed, or found free, are my tenants. I have a tithe of their produce; I take it in kind. One is to supply me annually with corn, another with coffee, and so on to rice, sugar, spices, cotton, tobacco, wine, oil, spirit, and what else the ground will

produce. What is superfluous I dispose of. Every thing you eat
and drink here is by free, not by forced labour; and I think we
shall not relish our homely fare the less from knowing it is so.
I am not one of those heavy-beamed Christian moralists who
preach, but hang astern from practice; fellows who scrutinize into
the doctrine of a tailor before they venture into a pair of breeches
of his making, without a thought of payment; I rather look at
the goodness of their work, than at their godliness. I am better
served by free people, working with all their hearts, than by the
hands of heartless slaves.'

The ride to the commandant being postponed to the following
day, we all proceeded to employ ourselves after our own fancies.
De Ruyter made a drawing of a wing he wished to add to his
dwelling, as a zennanah for the women. Aston unearthed sweet
potatoes, yams, and herbs for dinner. I formed an harbour of
bamboos amidst the shrubs, where I planted the mystic tree, the
yakoonoo, that caused Zela's tears to flow on our journey. As
I lay down under the shade of a rose-apple, not having slept at
night, I fell into a sound nap; from which I was awakened by
feeling, as the sun ascended over the trees, the rays stealing up
my limbs like flame. I knew I should be burnt out of my post in
a few minutes; yet this enhanced the pleasure of those moments,
and I contentedly endured the fiery martyrdom of my lower
extremities. At this moment I heard a gentle rustling noise
approaching. What could it be? I was stretched out in such listless
indolence, that I could neither move nor look, though I continued
to listen intently. I felt I ought to rouse myself, for as it came on,
it struck me it was a serpent; but then I instantly recollected that
De Ruyter told us there was not a single venomous reptile on the
island. Oh, no! thought I, I know the sound; I am confident it is
only a lizard or two, fly-catching. Then I was conscious of something being lightly placed above me, which rustled in its motion;
and, opening my eyes, I beheld Zela, with her little Malayan girl,
Adoo, shadowing me with part of a talypot palm-leaf,—for an
entire one is sometimes thirty feet in circumference. She was
running away when she perceived me awake; but I caught hold
of the hem of her loose, embroidered trowsers. 'Why,' said she,
'do you lie in the sun? Don't you know it is worse than the bite of
the chichta?—and its blow on the uncovered brow more fatal
than the bahr's?'

'Sweet Zela! what brought you here?'

'Oh, to gather fruit!'

'Why did you bring the palm-leaf? There's none of them near this place.'

Her eye then caught the tree I had planted, and she asked, 'What do you think for? How could I know you were sleeping in the sun? We got the leaf to cover this yakoonoo.'

'How did you know it was planted there, for I told no one of it?'

I thought I read in her eyes, and in the varying expression of her features, the mirror of her mind, that I was not, as heretofore, indifferent to her. With a step almost as light as her's, I returned with her to the house.

CHAPTER XVII

> Sublime tobacco! which, from east to west,
> Cheers the tar's labour, or the Turkman's rest;
> Which on the Moslem's ottoman divides
> His hours, and rivals opium and his brides;
> Magnificent in Stamboul, but less grand,
> Though not less loved in Wapping, or the Strand;
> Divine in hookahs, glorious in a pipe,
> When tipp'd with amber, mellow, rich, and ripe.
>
> BYRON

> And on the sand would I make signs to range
> These woofs, as they were woven of my thought;
> Clear, elemental shapes, whose smallest change
> A subtler language within language wrought.
>
> SHELLEY

WE were met by De Ruyter, who said, 'Lady, I was about to pay you a visit, for a cup of old Kamalia's coffee.'

'I beseech you do, captain,' she answered; 'she makes it better than any one; her sherbet, too, and her arekee are excellent. She knows many other things; and can read the old books of our country, and the stars.'

'By her antique look,' observed De Ruyter, 'she must have studied from the papyrus; and it would not surprise me if she could clear up the mystery of hieroglyphics.'

On entering the zennanah, the old governante, Kamalia, having counted us on her four skinny fingers, proceeded to fulfil that sacred rite, never omitted in the east, of presenting refreshments; without the heartless and niggardly ceremony of appealing to the guests, as is wont in Europe, to learn whether they will take them or not, looking on those who receive them with an evil eye. I followed Kamalia to know how the genuine oriental coffee is made. Good mussulmans can alone make good coffee; for, being interdicted from the use of ardent spirits, their palate is more exquisite and their relish greater.

Thus it is.—A bright charcoal fire was burning in a small stove. She first took, for four persons, four handsful of the small, pale, mocha berry, little bigger than barley. These had been carefully picked and cleaned. She put them into an iron vessel, where, with admirable quickness and dexterity, they were roasted till their colour was somewhat darkened, and the moisture not exhaled. The over-roasted ones were picked out, and the remainder, while very hot, put into a large wooden mortar, where they were instantly pounded by another woman. This done, Kamalia passed the powder through a camel's-hair cloth; and then repassed it through a finer cloth. Meanwhile a coffee-pot, containing exactly four cups of water, was boiling. This was taken off, one cup of water poured out, and three cups full of the powder, after she had ascertained its impalpability between her finger and thumb, were stirred in with a stick of cinnamon. When replaced on the fire, on the point of over-boiling, it was taken off, the heel of the pot struck against the hob, and again put on the fire. This was repeated five or six times. I forgot to mention she added a very minute piece of mace, not enough to make its flavour distinguishable; and that the coffee-pot must be of tin, and uncovered, or it cannot form a thick cream on the surface, which it ought to do. After it was taken, for the last time, from the fire, the cup of water, which had been poured from it, was returned. It was then carried into the room, without being disturbed, and instantly poured into the cups, where it retained its rich cream at the top.

Thus made, its fragrance filled the room, and nothing could be more delicious to the palate. So far from its being a long and tedious process, as it may appear in narrating, old Kamalia allowed herself only two minutes for each person; so that from the time of her leaving the room to her return, no more than eight minutes had elapsed.

Zela herself handed it to her guests, the little Malayan girl following with sweetmeats and water. Zela then brought me a cheboukche (Turkish pipe); it being the custom for the wife, in her apartment, to fill and light it, but only for a father or husband. She removed the pale-coloured amber from her ruby lips, and, presenting it to me, crossed her hands on her forehead. She then left me to see her other guests served by her women.

Pallid amber, not transparent, tinged with the lightest shade of violet, or, as the Mussulmans say, like the hue of a fair virgin's brow just as the life has fled, is by far the most precious. Next to that, in their estimation, ranks the lightest of the lemon shade, cloudless and unspotted, but not transparent.

The only admissible beverage to preserve the sensibility of the palate, whilst inhaling the vapour of that exquisite and inestimable leaf, which grows at Shiraz, on an estuary, the eastern side of the Persian Gulf, (said to have been Adam's Paradise, and I believe it!) if you would voluptuize in the full luxuriance of its perfect flavour, is either coffee, such as I have described, or the juices of fresh fruits compressed in water, or the pure element, or Tonkin or Souchong tea, gathered whilst the dew was on the leaf; let the best be selected, and infused with a liberal hand in water, the instant ere it boils,—not stewed, as in Europe. Just as the leaves are unfolding themselves, the infusion is pungent and aromatic, without being bitter and vapid. It should then be sweetened with the clearest candied sugar. All fermented liquors are held in Mahometan abhorrence by refined smokers, as blunting the delicate sense of the palate, and destroying the mental relish.

Zela's father was deeply versed in the art of smoking, and had initiated her theoretically in its most hidden mysteries, as an indispensable part of female education; and De Ruyter, little inferior in his practical knowledge, used to say, 'I consider European accomplishments as mere springes to catch woodcocks. Useful knowledge they have none. All their pride is in their feathers and ornaments, like the coloured muckarunga, or the flaunting peacock, or the motley jay, stupid, presumptuous, and chattering. Whilst these Arab maids, whom they scoff at as barbarians, because they alone value what is useful, can manufacture cloth of all sorts, fashion it into dresses, sow the corn, bruise it, and make it into bread, hunt and spear the flying antelope, or ostrich, and cook either in a variety of modes. Then their plighted faith was never broken; and their watchful quickness and devoted courage are a shield on their husband's bosom, when his eyes are closed in the nest of danger; for then treason or force cannot reach their lords, unless through their faithful breasts. As to female beauty, who is to decide on the general standard? They are all classed together, and so are the lily and the garlic; yet what can be more dissimilar. In Siam and Arracan long ears and black teeth are thought charming; in China and Tartary, large lips and long nails. In some parts of Europe the points of beauty are considered similar to those of the horse,—breadth, bone, height, and solidity of structure. In England there is an Amazonian breed arrived at perfection, together with the horse, the bullock, and the oak. But those who love dainty, delicate, and feminine forms, must seek them in the lands where flourish the crimsoned-blossomed ceiba, the date, and waving bamboo, which love nature's wildest nooks, and refuse to mingle their beauties with the crowded jungle or cultivated plantation.'

On the ensuing morning De Ruyter and Aston went to the town of St. Louis on a visit to the commandant; and I amused myself in gardening. Zela was becoming accustomed to be with me, and I could hardly live a moment out of her presence. Her calm features became dimpled and animated by smiles. We were both unlearned in love. Though we could converse on common topics, notwithstanding my mistakes in the Arabic, without any great difficulty, yet were we equally novices in the language of the heart. The fierceness of my passions, which usually hurried me on impetuously, was now checked by the acutest sensibility. I could find no words to express my new feelings, while their violence craved the perfection of eloquence to delineate them. But words died on my lips; and, as we sat down on a carpet, under the shade of a tree, we communed in the antique characters of her country, which, for lovers, far excel the alphabet of Cadmus. We drew figures, on the red sandy soil, of birds, ships, and houses, and to these hieroglyphics we added the mute language of fruits and flowers. These, with her large dark eyes, the sweet movement of her lips, their touch, and our fingers twined together, as our young hearts beat tumultuously, seemed to me most eloquent and intelligible. Time past rapidly, as the little gusts of wind, flying over the silvery surface of the tank of water at our feet, or as they bent the flowers and passed on. Then we strolled about, and ravaged the garden of its ripest and richest fruits, when the greatest contention that ever passed between us was,—who culled the best? and which was the best? She grew animated in panegyrics on the fresh and luscious date, and I declared it nothing in comparison with the downy nectarine, and the lordly-crested pine-apple; while Aston, close behind us, gave it against us both in favour of the mangostein, in which he contended were united the flavours of the nectarine, the date, and the pine-apple, in addition to its own.

'Holla!' I exclaimed,—'Aston! I thought you were gone to call on the commandant. It is too late now,—the sun is hot,—I feel my blood boiling. Why did you not go with De Ruyter?—he has been off this hour.'

'You are dreaming,' answered Aston; 'De Ruyter and myself went off six hours ago, and here we are returned. It is now mid-day, and we have been seeking you every where. Dinner is waiting.'

'Nonsense! Zela and I came out here while you and De Ruyter were drinking your coffee, and talking of going into town. Certainly that's not more than an hour ago.'

'Awake, you dreamer!' he said, 'and look at the sun. Don't you see it has passed the south, and is now above your head? Surely it must have affected your brain! But come, get up; we, who count time by our appetites and the calendar, want something more solid than the dainty food of love.'

Amazed at the unwonted rapidity with which the day had flown, we returned to the house. Zela, ignorant of all artifice, could only assure De Ruyter, in reply to his bantering, that she did not know it was so late, that she feared she had unconsciously dozed away the time, and that as we had eaten of so many fruits, neither of us was hungry, and we had never thought of dinner.

CHAPTER XVIII

And are you really, truly, now a Turk?

*   *   *   *   *

Is't true they use their fingers for a fork?
Well, that's the prettiest shawl, as I'm alive!
You'll give it me? They say you eat no pork.

BYRON

THE commandant, I was informed, was anxious to see me, and had requested us all to dine with him. Aston had been very kindly received.

Consequently, a few days after this, before the break of day, we returned by the same route by which we had come to the elevated plain, passed the *Piton,* and, by a tolerable road, and a very agreeable descent, arrived at the town of St. Louis. On this side the mountains slope as smoothly down to the sea, as they rise abruptly and precipitously on the other side. The lands near the town were highly cultivated. Groups of pretty cottages, with green virandahs, were scattered about on the plantations, which were separated from each other by double avenues of trees. These were vacours, impenetrable from the dense mass of barbed and pointed leaves, and the beautiful scarlet and white blossomed rose-apple, growing in the form of an olive; and under their shade was the coffee-tree. We saw a great variety of bananas, fields of pine-apple, hedged by peach-trees, Persian roses, and a beautiful Indian shrub, called netshouly; while the willow-like bamboo hung his head over the clear river, as if enamoured of his own graceful form.

On arriving at the town, built close to the harbour, at the mouth of the delightful valley through which we had descended, and which was overhung by a lofty mountain, we passed some tolerable houses in the suburbs, having gardens filled with fruits and flowers. We then wound through some narrow, dirty, unpaved streets of wooden and mud tenements. As we approached the harbour, near the quay, we came to the commandant's house, which looked like a magnificent palace amidst the dwarf hovels around.

The commandant received us with that urbanity and equality which the French so readily put on; and which are so striking when compared with the dog-like surliness of the rude and stiff-backed Englishman in power, who looks at every stranger as an intruder that ought to be attacked. He swells with paltry pride, puts on the air of a muzzled bear, or vicious mule, and pats his dog, the emblem of his master, that struggles to break his chain and fly at your throat, while you are growlingly asked,—'What's your business, Sir?' If, forcing his nature, he sulkily asks you to walk in, and if his wife happens to be caught unprepared to receive you, she reddens with anger, and with some gentle hint to her husband, bounces out of the room like a fury. Unless you find some means to appease her, for the whole day her temper is discomposed, and you are ever after considered as an intruder; or, if of high caste, she treats you with blank indifference.

With our French commandant it was different, he went to the other extreme and loaded us with welcomes. While refreshments were preparing, he took me into his lady's dressing-room, and saying,—'I have brought you a young Arab chieftain,'—left us.

She made me sit by her on the couch, and asked me all sorts of questions, never doubting I was not what I seemed. She told me I was handsome, and my shawls were handsomer, wished to know if they came from Cashmire, why I shaved my head, if I believed in the Virgin Mary, if I had ever loved, and if I would be christened. Her hands kept pace with her tongue till she almost stripped me to examine my apparel. My skin, she said, was very smooth, not very black, and she asked if Arab women were handsome, and if I liked the French women. Then she told me she was returning shortly to France, because she could no longer endure the heat, the barbarous people, the want of society, the want of an opera, of every necessary of life,—except the real ones, which she allowed were good and abundant,—but these she did not want. Here she was interrupted by De Ruyter, a great favourite of hers. She called him the only real gentleman on the island, as he had passed many of his early years in France and at Paris. Upon which she talked unceasingly of Paris. 'Dear De Ruyter,' she said, 'does this boy belong to you? Where did you get him? I have taken a great fancy to him, and positively I am determined to take him to Paris. Only think what a sensation he will make there! Well! it is wonderful these people, who live on the sands, with the lions and tigers, should have such a distinguished air, and carry themselves so well! And then, my dear De Ruyter, only think what he will be when he has passed a winter in Paris, and learnt to waltz! Well, you are a dear creature,—and remember you have given him to me. How beautifully he puts on his turban, and—what is your name? Come, shew me how you fold your turban. Every one in Paris will be dying in love with—your turban and shawls.'

She ran on in this style till wearied; then vowing I should remain with her, and that she could not bear me out of her presence an instant, she threw herself on a couch, and pointed to me to get a punka and fan. 'Ah! who would live here,' she ejaculated, 'where the heat is so insufferable that a person cannot say a single word of welcome to an old friend, without being ready to expire! I declare I have not spoken three sentences this month. And this boy must be wearied too. You know our house, De Ruyter; and do—that's a dear creature—send some of my women,—and reach me that Eau de Cologne.'

After a sumptuous tiffin, the commandant conducted us, together with the captain and some of the officers of the corvette, which was then lying in Port St. Louis, to a reading room, which the merchants had built for literary pursuits and the improvement of the island. There we found all the principal persons assembled, military, civil, and mercantile. The commandant was requested to read an address of thanks to the captain of the corvette, De Ruyter, and their officers and crews, for the important benefit they had effected in the extinction of the pirates at St. Sebastian. The French captain added that their success was to be attributed to De Ruyter's skill and intrepidity. The commandant then presented the two captains with handsome swords, and the first lieutenant of the corvette and myself, with silver-gilt goblets, bearing inscriptions. The commandant, in compliance with De Ruyter's wish, previously made known, from delicacy to Aston and me, did not refer to the affair with the English frigate.

We then separated, after a renewal of refreshments, and looking over the books and newspapers. On returning to the commandant's house, where there was to be a public dinner, his lady insisted on our all sleeping during the heat of the day; but I made my escape, and went to look at the ships in the port. The beautiful American schooner was there, and I could have passed the day in gazing on her symmetry and the exquisiteness of her model; but the groans of the slaves, staggering under their burthens, their sweaty brows, wan eyes, and galled backs covered with flies, drove me away. I then wandered about the town. Out of a population of seventeen or eighteen thousand, there were not more than seven or eight hundred Europeans; and these were a motley crew of all nations. Consequently the proportion of slaves was immense. They were chiefly from Mosambique and Madagascar, and the islands scattered about. Some of them were free, and excellent mechanics, very good and industrious. Most of them spoke French, and many spoke English. They were admirable accountants and linguists. I saw neither horses nor carts; slaves and buffaloes were the only animals employed; these did all the work. I wandered about the suburbs, where the natives exclusively reside, went into their hovels, and talked with them, till I thought it time to return to the commandant's.

After bathing, I dined with a large party there. The conversation ran principally on *la grande nation*, the pirates, and Paris; only one of which I had seen, wished to see, or cared about. I remember a gawky, convex-bellied, bilious, hawking Frenchman, with a mouth as large and deep as a horse's, eyes yellow as topazes, no forehead, no complexion, no hair, with a nose like a squashed fig, the usual characteristics of his nation, and he asserted that London was as inferior to Paris as the black town of the isle of France was to Calcutta. I was rejoiced to get away from these vain, gasconading harlequins, and accompany the commandant on horseback to a magnificent open space, planted with trees, in the outskirts of the town, surrounded by hills, with summer cottages of every description. We then, to my great delight, returned towards our home, the commandant accompanying us part of the way.

CHAPTER XIX

And, oh! that quickening of the heart, that beat
How much it costs us! Yet each rising throb
Is in its cause, as its effects, so sweet,
That wisdom, ever on the watch to rob
Joy of its alchemy, and to repeat
Fine truths—

BYRON

IN my impatience to be at home, I took little notice of the scenery. De Ruyter asking me what I thought of the lady, I replied, 'I think her a little angel! She is so gentle, of so heavenly a disposition, with such noble sentiments, and high courage! And though she is extremely silent, that arises from timidity and thoughtfulness; for such eyes and such a mouth were never meaningless!'

'Take a turn there, my lad!—you have said enough. I will allow you she has all the beauty pertaining to her nation,—that is, youth and dress. As to all the other charms you have enumerated, I have not discovered the smallest indication of their existence, neither in her, nor in her nation,—and I have lived among them. The four cardinal virtues which they hold in the highest estimation are cooking, drawing, pimping, and hair-dressing. What do you mean by timidity?—the air and carriage of a courtezan! As to her thoughtfulness, you may as well call these noisy, screaming parrots contemplative. Then her extreme silence!—I would rather lie in a whirlpool, with a hurricane over my head, or be condemned to the galleys for life, than endure the torture of a French woman's tongue an hour a day in a tropical climate!'

'A French woman!' I exclaimed; 'who do you mean?'

'Mean! who should I mean but the woman we have passed the day with!'

'Oh! I had quite forgotten her! I was talking of Zela!'

'Ha! ha!' he replied laughing, 'you are the lad who—

'Wrote to his father ending with this line,
'My dearest Zela, I am ever thine!'

I thought you had more of the eagle's aspirations than to stoop so low. It is rightly called *falling* in love, for a man can fall no lower.

Great spirits are never enslaved by so grovelling and feeble a foe. You are greedily gloating on a poison, which will destroy all the noble feelings and energies of your character. You have now as inextinguishable a fire in your bosom as that which is burning in the dome of this mountain; and, mark me! it will destroy you as it will that hill, granite though it be. Poor boy, I pity you! for I see you have resigned yourself, a willing slave, to the worst and most enervating of human passions. Women are like parasitical plants, casting their wild tendrils from one tree to another, till, swollen into tough cordage, they strangle those they embrace, and luxuriate in their decay. That broad and open forehead indicates a judgment, which, when matured to fullness, ought, with its iron grasp, to crush the reptile passion, soon as it has birth. Men like you are for nobler uses, for actions that may benefit mankind, not to be dedicated to the narrow, paltry, selfish views and gratifications of a solitary individual, however worthy. What! devote yourself to the childish pastime of fondling a tawdry toy, a baby's doll!' Seeing me silent and sad, he ended by quoting his favourite authority, on all questions, but, like all others, quoting only for his own purpose:

> 'Rouse yourself; and the weak wanton Cupid
> Shall from your neck unloose his amorous fold,
> And, like a dew-drop from the lion's mane,
> Be shook to air.'

Soon after he added, by way of softening the pain his taunts had given me, 'I do not mean to censure you for loving Zela. She is your wife, dependent on you, and most worthy to be loved. But I object to your exclusively loving her, and withdrawing your affections from others, together with your time and talents which can be beneficially employed.'

He then talked on other subjects, and endeavoured to awaken that interest which heretofore I had taken regarding general topics, as well as in those connected with my own particular duties.

Perhaps to avoid further discussion, I spurred on a long way before De Ruyter. On ascending the eminence on which our dwelling stood, I was surprised at observing all the blinds and windows closed of the centre room. It was the cool time of the evening, the sun had dipped behind the western hill, and the sea-breeze was blowing freshly. I feared something was wrong,— some accident. As Zela was alone in my thoughts, notwithstanding

De Ruyter's censure on love, I hastened round to the back of the house, forced one of the blinds, and jumped into the large room. The sudden transition from light to gloom prevented me from distinguishing any thing; but calling out 'Who is there?'—a voice replied, 'Close the window,—he will escape! Shut the window, —they will escape!'

As I advanced, I stumbled into the water channel, the voice still vociferating,—'Shut the window,—oh, they will escape! they will escape!'

Recovering my footing, and looking up, a ghost-like, lean, and shadowy figure came towards me. I soon recognised the sound of the flabby foot on the pavement, and then distinguished, by the aid of a small lamp held in a horny hand, the light reflecting through it, the unearthly visage of Van Scolpvelt. In his left hand he held a long white bamboo, which he waved like a wand, pre-paratory to an incantation. He passed, without noticing me, his eyes strained almost out of their sockets, staring towards the ceiling. He shut the blinds with his wand, then kept waving it aloft, and muttered: 'They have not escaped me,—there they are!—and the air has done them good. They were merely some-what vertiginous, and have resumed their vivaciousness. Well, it is wonderful! Look—is that you, captain?—I thought it was one of the blacks,—I am glad you are come; for you will be delighted with these gay, sprightly quadrupeds, wantoning about in the air.'

'What do you mean? I see no quadrupeds. I believe you are the devil, or you could not stand the suffocating heat of this room.'

'Heat! I feel no heat. Now, don't open the windows,—you will destroy me. I shall be satisfied in a few minutes more. Do look at them!'

'I see them, and hear their faint cries. What are you at with these birds? Are you conjuring with them, or what?'

'Birds! Humph! I thought you must be very ignorant, on account of your opposing science. Birds!—they are no more birds than I am. They are viviparous, classed in the same order of animals as yourself. You threw my Spallanzani[1] away the other day, when I sent it you, or you would not be so ignorant as to call a bat a bird.'

'Come, Van, open the windows, I am sick.'

'Sick! what consequence is that? Am not I here? I wish you to witness the success of the experiment. Would you not, observing

their motions, conclude they had the use of their visual orbs?
Would you imagine the cornea had been burnt out?'

'Burnt out!'

'Yes, this half hour.'

'What brute did it?'

Zela, the window being now open, came in weeping, and said,
'I am glad you are returned,—that horrid yellow Indian has been
catching all the poor creatures he could, and putting out their
eyes with hot needles.'

Van, it appeared, coming to see De Ruyter, found some bats in
the ruined wall of an old well. He had caught three, blinded two
with a hot wire, and scooped out the eyes of the third. Then he
let them loose in the room to see if they could direct their flight
with the same rapidity and precision as before they were thus
horribly deprived of sight.

He termed it an interesting, delightful, and satisfactory experiment. 'Spallanzani,' said he, 'essayed it on the common bat, but
I on the vampyre and spectre species. To-night I will determine
another question. It is asserted they are such admirable phle-
botomists as to insinuate their tongues, which are aculeated like
the finest lancets, insensibly into the veins of persons asleep,
using their long wings as a fan to soothe their slumbers, and thus
extract an immense quantity of blood. They prefer the veins on
the back of the neck, or on the temples. Sometimes the victim
insensibly bleeds to death. Now,' turning to me, 'you are young,
heated, feverish,—and your veins are large and full,—will you
repose by the old well to-night? I will regulate the quantity, and
stop the after bleeding,—which is the only danger. Think of the
advantage you will confer on science, as well as the benefit to
yourself! For, if it is true, cupping-glasses, leeches, and other
means of bleeding may be advantageously superseded by this
inestimable phlebotomist. Then, in the morning, we will proceed
to the examination of the physiological construction of its tongue;
as that may throw some new light by which the lancet may be
improved.'

Van warmed with the idea, and grew eloquent. I knew how
vain it was to contend with him on these points, and therefore
contented myself with giving him a flat denial, and expressing my
abhorrence of what he had already done. Upon this he tried to
coax De Ruyter and Aston to submit to the experiment; but,

finding them deaf, he put on his most whining look, and was shuffling towards Zela,—she ran off like a hare. Spluttering about the ignorance of womankind, and the prejudice of mankind, he declared that he himself would have his bed by the well-side, which he actually directed to be done.

CHAPTER XX

> Grim reader! did you ever see a ghost?
> No; but you've heard;—I understand—be dumb—
> And don't regret the time you may have lost,
> For you have got that pleasure still to come.
>
>   BYRON

ASTON and I vowed we should practise some trick on Scolpvelt, in return for his cruelty to the bats, and quickly decided on our operations. While De Ruyter accompanied him to supper, I went, with a couple of black boys, to survey the localities of the well. It was built in the eastern manner, broad and deep, with steps leading to the bottom. With difficulty I descended, the steps being broken and worn away, the sides overgrown with dark and rank vegetation, night-flowers, and creepers, and towards the bottom blackened and clogged with the dung of bats, and slippery from the slime of toads, which raised a hoarse and discordant clamour as I thrust a bamboo down to try the depth of the water. Satisfied there were only two or three feet, and having partly cleared the bushes away, I ascended and made my arrangements. A cot of De Ruyter's having been brought, we placed it with the head towards the steps of the well, passed a rope through the rings at the two ends, and then a loose lashing round it, to haul-taut when we had turned in. A large pepul tree grew near, with one of its branches crossing the mouth of the well, and darkening it with its dense foliage. On this bough a block was lashed, and the rope rove through it. Having instructed the boys in the parts they were to play, I returned to the house to equip them properly.

As I entered the room to call De Ruyter away, it having been agreed that Aston was to be left to entertain Van till he chose to retire to his berth, I could not refrain tarrying an instant in admiration of his discourse. 'I wish,' he exclaimed, 'my mother had not

Q

brought me into the world, or that I had been born a thousand years antecedent to this dark age, in which I behold the sun setting on science. Had men been wise, had they encouraged it to the utmost, it would progressively have advanced, till it ascended above the dark clouds enveloping us, and the chemist, with his galvanic battery, would be no longer destroying, but creating. New planets with immortal beings might then by science have been created, as by science they have been created out of pre-existing matter. Oh! my mother, had you lived to this dark period when I cannot find a man rational enough to sleep by a well! You, my mother, who loved and honoured nothing but science, and me, your only child, for my devotion to it, you knew how long and ardently the Scolpvelts had pursued their god-like profession; and when, from intense study, your eye became diseased, and I told you it would end in cancer, if not removed, you said,—"My son, remove it." On the instant I did so, and she uttered not a groan, but leant back unconfined in her arm-chair, smiling approbation at my unshaken nerves!' Then exultingly he added,—'And where will you find such a woman now?'

He lit his *ecume de mer*, offended at our laughter, which he at all times abhorred, and went and laid himself down in his cot by the well. Aston had promised to give a look to Van every hour.

We now proceeded to fit the black boys for their parts. De Ruyter mixed up some chenam and lime, with which he drew lines on their bodies, leaving the form of a skeleton distinctly marked out,—a white one on a black ground. This, together with Malayan bows, covered with blackened paper, streaked with white, and attached to their backs as wings, gave them a complete spectral appearance. We then armed them with small needles, bound together with thread, leaving a minute portion of their points bare, and separated from each other, such as sailors use for tattooing their skins.

A little after midnight Aston and De Ruyter placed themselves at the end of the tackle, to be hoisted at a given signal; I crawled, unperceived, under the pepul tree; and the spectre-boys occupied stations among the bushes on each side of the cot. There was actually several of the dusky, monstrous, obscure bats flitting round and round the well, while others were attached by their long thin claws to the branches of the pepul, hanging with their heads downward, immediately over Scolpvelt, who lay on his back, and seemed anxiously watching them. He looked like an ancient mummy partially unrolled. He was furnished with a bandage to stop the bleeding, when he should, in quality of physician, cry—'Hold, enough!' When I gave the signal, the boys rose from the bushes with a shrill cry, flapped their skeleton wings, enclosed him in the flaps of the cot, and hauled the lashing taut in an instant. The signal to hoist was then made, and Van ascended. I bore the cot over the mouth of the well, and made the signal to lower away. The boys, playing all sorts of antics, caught hold of the rope, jumped on the cot, and pricked Van all over with needles, thickly as the stings of a swarm of wild wasps. Meanwhile the cot was lowered as fast as possible, when the bats, disturbed in their haunts, sprung out in multitudes, flapping their wings in disorder; and the toads and rats, of which there was an abundance, increased the din. When the cot was landed at the bottom of the well, and the boys had cast off the rope, and cut the lashing, we ran them up. We then all joined in the shrill cry of the American Indians, by screaming and patting the mouth with the hand, at which the affrighted inhabitants of the well, undisturbed for centuries, beasts, birds, and all the tribe of reptiles and vermin, burst from their dark abodes, appalled at the unwonted summons.

To us, who were only looking down, it was a fearful sight; to Van at the bottom it must have appeared horrible. We began to repent of our frolic; but De Ruyter said, 'No, he has the heart of a stoic. Either his philosophy, or his fear, or both,—for they are not, though they ought to be, incompatible,—prevent his calling for aid.'

'Hush!' I whispered, 'I hear his fin going in the water. He is moving,—and hark! his croak rises above the toad's.'

We heard him muttering and stumbling about, groping his way; then a splash in the water, as if he had slipped his fin and undergone a ducking. Satisfied he was in no immediate danger, but wishing to punish him for his barbarity, we left him till the expiration of the hour. Aston then went, feigned surprise at not finding him, and walked about the garden halooing his name. I, who had followed, heard him floundering in the water, cursing the hour in which his mother had brought him into the world, the island, the bats, the well, and all the devils in it, in Dutch, Latin, and English. At last Aston deigned to hear him; and, after allowing some time to elapse, we proceeded with ropes and lights to release him. A boy lowered into the well lashed a rope round his body, and we ran him up to the pepul-bough with such force that his trowsers and shirt were torn, and he looked like a felon hung in chains with his rags fluttering in the wind. When lowered on the ground, he was too exhausted to articulate. The resurrection of Lazarus conveys but a faint idea of him as he stood before us, with our lanthorns thrust in his face. His head shook as if palsied, his thin legs knocked together like bamboos in a gale, his skin was stained with bat's dung and green slime, his face was of a clay-cold blue mottled with spots of blood, and his long thin hair hung down like a mermaid's. With grizzled eye-brows standing right out, he was sullen and snarling as a jackall entrapped. Not a word was uttered in reply to our incessant interrogatories, as we followed him to the house. He scowled malignantly at me, as I persecuted him with questions respecting the vampyres, how they got him down into the well, and if they had bled him. A tumbler of skedam, a dry shirt, and a bed were prepared for him in the hall. He sullenly and silently lay down.

CHAPTER XXI

> When snouted wild boars routing tender corn
> Anger our huntsman.
>   KEATS

ON the morrow Aston and I took our boar-spears, and ascended the woody part of the mountain. After wandering for some time, we followed the course of a small stream, almost consumed by the long drought. Its scanty waters laboured in tortuous windings under the shade of trees and shrubs, which, still verdant from the moisture, in grateful homage bent over their feeble nurse, paying their tribute of shade. The burning sun, like fire, seemed to be destroying all around. The hardy oak and lofty pine, the giant palm and the majestic teak, rising like chieftains above the forest, with scorched and seared heads, appeared drooping in anguish. Their shrivelled and red-spotted foliage, and withered fruits dropped from their sapless branches without a breath of air to move them, and cracked under our feet. The noisy parrot tribe was stilled; and the restless monkeys, half-dozing in listless apathy, hung on the branches, and let us pass unnoticed; or, if I awakened their attention by casting my spear or a stone, slowly and sullenly they ascended a few feet higher, or merely shifted their posts to the other side. No other animal was to be seen. Yet, with the nerve and sinew of youth, health, and strength, we seemed sun-proof, as we bounded along regardless of all impediments of bush, bamboo, or briar, clearing the path with our spears, and forcing a passage, like the wild-boar which we were seeking, and only reminded by our appetites of the approaching hour of noon.

Then, crossing the streamlet, we descended towards the house, when we were surprised at the report of a musquet close to us, loud as a cannon, owing to the stillness around, and echoing from rock to rock. In an instant the wood was in an uproar with its alarmed inhabitants. As we hastened to the spot, whence the gun was fired, a wild sow burst out of the hollow trunk of a broken tree, followed by her litter of young, filling up the concert with their most sweet voices. Aston and I gave a loud holloa, and sprang after them. The mother, brutish as she was, turned at bay, and opposed her breast to our pointed weapons, forgetting all but her children. I wish my good mother would sometimes think of hers; it is so long since she gave them birth, that perhaps she may not remember she ever had any. In my eagerness I got before Aston, and heedlessly rushing on, the shaft of my spear snapped, as the weapon, ill-directed, glanced off from the sow's hard and wrinkled hide, and, the ground being dry and slippery, I fell before her. She gave me no pause to rise; I grasped the small creese in my bosom, and lost not my presence of mind; though her small and fiery eye, her wrinkled snout and huge tusks looked terrific as she was dashing in on me. Aston exclaimed,—'Lie still!—don't move!' and I felt his lance glide over me, as he forced it under the sow's left shoulder through the heart, and almost through the body, which fell dead upon me.

Another voice then exclaimed,—'He'll make excellent hams! I'll carry him down, and salt, and cure him!' upon which I found my limbs were caught hold of.

'I'll be hanged if you do!' I answered, as I got up, and confronted Louis, who had that morning arrived at the house with provisions.

'Oh!' said he, 'I did not see two, I thought there was only one!' —then stooping down, and handling the swine, he chuckled over it with delight, as he feasted, in imagination, on its carcase; till, catching the sound of the little grunters, squeeling and running about in quest of their dam, 'Ah!' he cried out, 'she has little ones, —has she? Why didn't you tell me that?'

We succeeded in catching the greater part of the litter. Louis fondled, kissed, and hugged them, called them his pretty dears, bade them not cry, promised to take as much care of them as their own mother had done, and then, turning to us, inquired if we were hungry, and if he should light a fire and roast a couple of them, by way of tiffin, to give us an appetite for dinner. We asked him what he had been firing at. 'Oh, I had quite forgot!' he replied; 'first let me tie these lovely little creatures, two and two, by the legs, and I'll shew you what I've been shooting;—it is not dead yet.'

He led us a few paces off, under a large tree, from one of the horizontal branches of which was suspended a huge baboon. His entrails were hanging out, and the blood was running down in a stream, yet, in pain and agony, clinging with his hind feet to the branch, he mowed and chattered at us. Louis forthwith reloaded his long gun, and as he pointed the barrel upwards, the poor brute seemed sensible of his impending fate. His rage gave way to fear; he cast one piteous glance, made a last effort to move from his perilous and exposed situation, and, ere the gun was fired, dropped down lifeless. Louis promptly seized him by the nape of the neck, and cut his throat. It looked so like a human murder that I shuddered, and said, 'Come along,—leave him there,—leave him!'

'What for?' said Louis. 'I'll not leave him; it is the best eating in the world! If you don't know that, you know nothing.'

'Bah!' said Aston, 'the fellow's a cannibal; come along.'

We left him, promising to send some servants to bring down the wild sow, and hastened down the hill. We found Van Scolpvelt seated under a prickly pear hedge; he had a large, old, musty folio spread out before him, and was intently occupied in looking at something with a magnifying glass. He took no notice of our approach, but resumed working with a small knife; and I discovered he was (still untamed in his cruelty) at what he termed vivisection on an unfortunate hedgehog. He said to Aston, with asperity, 'Take a lesson here! Look at this heroic little animal,' (drawing his knife across him,) 'you see he is alive, has muscles and nerves, yet he neither moves nor makes a noise!'

CHAPTER XXII

ENTERING the house we saw De Ruyter busy with his books and journals. He asked me to look over the ship's books and letters; when my attention was called off by a discussion between Aston and De Ruyter. The former was urging the latter to publish some journals he had written, and permitted us to read. I was struck with De Ruyter's reply. 'If,' said he, 'I were ambitious of an immortal name, and had genius enough to insure it by writing, I would not write. Action, when pure, bright, and unsullied, is the nobler sort of immortality; and writing, unless our actions correspond with it, is to be remembered but as Seneca's. How few of the ancient Greek and Roman heroes were authors, yet how many live to us in their deeds. Æschylus, Sophocles and Homer are read; but Socrates, Timoleon, Leonidas, Brutus, Portia and Aria are known. Signal actions of heroism, devotion and generosity have saved them from oblivion. Immortality, conferred by action, is fully as honourable, and infinitely more universal than that conferred by writing. For millions are incapable of comprehending the ideas of a great author, who are warmed and made to glow at the narration of a noble or generous deed. Content, during my life, to be thought well of by those I love; to the world in general, now and hereafter, I am indifferent. I value your good opinion beyond the approbation of the French government. They have written me here that you are to be—(but it is a general order)—imprisoned until exchanged. But I, selfishly inclined to live in your good opinion, give you your liberty unconditionally; and will procure you a passage to one of your ports, when you grow tired of our dull life here.'

'If I am to wait till then,' answered Aston, 'it will never be; for, till the present period, I have hardly ever enjoyed rational pleasure, or felt a delight in my existence, such as I now feel. I am perfectly content here; I have not a wish ungratified; and my happiness would be complete, but from the uncertainty of its duration. So that I must candidly confess my lips would belie my heart, if I thank you for this news.'

'Then spare your thanks, and stay where you are,' he said, getting up and wringing his hand. 'Stay where you are, and leave the rest to me. I will manage the commandant; and from what you have told me of your affairs, it cannot injure you in your own service.'

'Curse the service!' said Aston, as De Ruyter went out of the room. 'I was a silly boy when I entered it, and have been a be-sotted fool to continue in it, till I am unfitted for any rational pursuit, by which I might earn my bread. I have been in it from ten years old till now that I am five-and-twenty, never three months on shore, my skin nearly burnt black by the sun, and my hair grizzled with storms; this, with a sprinkling of scars, occasional rheumatic twitches, and the rank of lieutenant, is all I have yet got, or am likely to get.'

'Yes,' I added, 'you will get a snug berth in Greenwich Hospi-tal,[1] — a nice little cabin there, six feet by five, all to yourself, with grubbery, free of rent and taxes, a cabbage-garden to ruralize in, and three half-pence a day—backee money! What can man wish more?'

Aston went on bewailing his hard destiny, and I dosing him with consolation derived from the hospital. However, it ended with my persuading him to continue for some time where he was, and to wait for an opportunity of our putting him on board one of the country vessels, or of landing him on the coast near one of the English settlements. I must confess I often urged him, with all the warmth of my character, and my friendship for him, to re-linquish a service where he was hopeless of promotion, and, as he was destitute of fortune, to join with us; by which means he would, after a few years, in all probability, be enabled to return to his own country, or to any other, with the means of enjoying, his sole ambition, a country life. 'For,' I continued, 'a man without money has no country. Besides, Aston, you are a Canadian born; and if you go to England without money, remember there are certain unsightly boards at the entrances of the towns, neatly painted, and swung gibbet-fashion, intimating some awkward, ungentlemanly sort of hint to persons without money—something to this effect— *Vagrants are not admitted here*. So that Greenwich—' Here he stopped me, by taking down a boar-spear, and I jumped out of the window.

Nor would he ever seriously listen to my propositions on this subject; he was not to be moved. As to De Ruyter, I believe, he never thought of such a thing; though he and Aston were firm and inseparable friends.

I went down to the port where the grab lay, paid the men a considerable share of prize-money, and discharged the greater number, merely leaving sufficient to take care of her, under the command of the good old Rais. I made an arrangement with him that I should go on board the grab twice a week, and that he should come up to us on two or three of the other days. Thus having settled every thing regarding her, I gave up mind, body, heart, and soul to the full enjoyment of our rural life. Nearly every day I explored the island in some new direction, discovered where game most abounded, and in what rivers and lakes were the finest fish, sometimes with De Ruyter, at other times with Aston. On good sporting days we all went together, taking provisions with us, and dining in the woods; when Louis, who had little to do on board, was our caterer. When the weather was favourable for working in the garden we were occupied there; when it was wet or stormy we fenced, read, wrote, or employed ourselves in drawing. We went as seldom as possible to the town, notwithstanding the almost daily solicitations from the commandant's lady, officers, and merchants. De Ruyter, and indeed all of us, hated what is called society. He had therefore chosen a place for his house, well nigh inaccessible during the rainy season; thus artfully avoiding intrusion on his solitude by frivolous, idle, and troublesome visitors, such as swarm in every garrisoned town, quoting the words of the French philosopher Morin,[1] 'Those that come to see me, do me honour; and those that stay away, do me a favour.' When some of them did venture, their whole discourse was about the perils they had passed in fording rivers and swamps; while De Ruyter provokingly pointed out with what facility it might be remedied, and talked, after his next voyage, of looking to it. But when they had left us, he would say, 'I wonder how they managed to get here so easily. We must dam the water up to increase the swamp and the torrent, and add to the vibration of the bamboo-bridge.'

Yet he was no churl. All worthy men were welcome; he himself would be their guide; and, as the door flew open at their approach, he clasped their hands, and every feature in his face expressed how heartily they were welcome. He felt, and he made them feel, that their acceptance of his hospitality was a proof of their great friendship for him. The longer they stayed, the more he was obliged; and if they left him before their affairs compelled them to be gone, his brow darkened with unquiet thoughts. In few houses where I have lived, (married men's, of course, out of the question,) did every guest, as well as the host, enjoy so much liberty as in De Ruyter's. If fellows, calling themselves gentlemen, resembled him, they would require no slang dialect, no polish to their boots, or starch to their shirts, to point them out.

My little orphan bride, thank heaven! knew nothing of civilization. Her shyness was that of the wood-pigeon, not the coquette's. She, poor simple thing, thought her husband alone should dwell in her thoughts; and imagined not that fashion had made that a crime in my country, more heinous than adultery. The circumstances of our first meeting, our ship-life, then our dwelling together in scenes formed for love, perfected in a few months what years would have perhaps been too short for in ordinary situations. Besides, the custom of her country was in our favour, where courtship is wisely dispensed with. I say—wisely, because while youth and beauty are wooed, judgment is blinded by passion. In the east these matters are better contrived; the process is summary; parents, whose judgments are matured, and whose passions are withered, conclude the necessary preliminaries; and the bride and bridegroom meet, and are married in the same hour. 'For,' said the old Rais, and he was wise, 'young men and women are like fire and gunpowder; they should therefore be carefully kept apart from each other, as on board the grab.' It is notorious that, in Europe, diplomatic mothers know how much, for their own interest, is to be effected by dress and address, importunity and opportunity, with young persons. There the unmarried talk of domestic happiness and conjugal affection; at which, I have observed, the married wince, as the horse does under the torture of the firing iron;—some, indeed, with heads as hard as rams, and hides wife-proof, endure the yoke with magnanimity. It is in the east that wedded love reigns triumphant; where the unmarried alone are the poor, the houseless, and the despised.

Zela, though young, was familiar with death, and as grief for her lost parent faded, her affections were re-awakened by me, their only claimant, and mine were all dedicated to her. I taught her my language, and learnt more of hers,—it was all she knew. Our breath mingled as I bent over her, our lips met, and our hearts beat together. She was an apt scholar, though her only punishment for idleness or neglect was the infliction of kisses, which were so long and ardent, that our lips seemed to grow together. She became the companion of my rambles, and, with a light hunting spear, followed me through the woods, and up the mountains. Her fairy form was endued with wonderful strength and agility. If stopped by a torrent, or a rugged ravine, I bore her in my arms; and, in the jungles, cleared the path before her. Our happiness could admit of no augmentation; it was perfect. In these our halcyon days, we thought no more of what others were about in the world, than of what was doing in the moon or stars. Those who dwelt with us occupied the small portion of our thoughts and affections, which could be spared from our deep and overwhelming devotion to each other; and Aston always, and afterwards De Ruyter, sympathised with our feelings, and glowed with admiration at witnessing such strange and matchless love.

CHAPTER XXIII

> Rapt in the fond forgetfulness of life,
> Neuha, the South Sea girl, was all a wife;
> With no distracting world to call her off
> From love; with no society to scoff
> At the new transient flame; no babbling crowd
> Of coxcombry in admiration loud,
> Or with adulterous whisper, to alloy
> Her duty, and her glory, and her joy.
>
> BYRON

WE had now been some months luxuriating in a tranquil life, little disturbed or marked by events worth recording, every moment of which lives fresh in my memory, when De Ruyter received intelligence that determined him to prepare for sea. His spirit knew no pause when an object was to be obtained. His mind, like a lens, concentrated its power into one piercing ray. From the instant he arrived on shore he had doffed his sea-garb, put on that of a planter, and with it the character. They both sat on him so well that a stranger would have thought he never had worn any other. Horticulture and agriculture, pruning and planting, exclusively occupied him, hand and heart. He never went down to the port, detested the smell of tar, said the sight of the sea made him qualmish, and cursed the sea-breeze for uprooting his sugar-canes, and destroying his young plantations. He interdicted the use of nautical phrases, and forbade salt junk to be brought into his house.

So that one day when he hailed me from the balcony, as I was at work in the garden, with—'Holloa! my lad,—heave ahead!— you're wanted!' I threw down my spade and entered the house, ready to tax him with his sea-slang. But I was stopped, on entering the room, by observing the floor covered with charts, a case of instruments lying open, and himself kneeling and measuring distances with a scale and compasses. The tall spare form of the Arab Rais leaned over him, pointing with a sea-bleached hand to a group of islands in the Mosambique channel. As De Ruyter was too intently occupied to perceive me, I looked for a while first at one, and then at the other. The hazy film which hung on his eyes when he was calm had evaporated, and they sparkled; all his face was lighted up, and its muscles in motion. I then looked at the Rais; but his features were as little subject to change as a ship's head, stained with tar and tempests; his face was like an antique sun-dial, with its surface corroded and effaced, no longer marking the passing hour. 'Ha! my boy,' said De Ruyter, 'we must be stirring. Order out our cattle. We must go down to the port.'

He then rose up, took off his white jacket, and shipped a blue one. I asked no questions, but followed his example, and off we started. His little acheenian pony kept not pace with his rider's impatience. 'Come,' he said, 'let us leave these ambling stumbling brutes, only fit for monks, and cross the hills on foot by the compass.'

We gave them to a servant, climbed the hills, and made our path as straight, and our flight almost as rapid, as the crane's. Arrived at the port, we pushed off in a canoe. The instant he was on board of the grab, he resumed his command with a stamp on the deck, when the idle Arabs, who were listlessly lying in the sun, jumped up, and all was life and motion. As he went about giving orders, the new masts, spars, and sails, which had been preparing, were now completing. The copper bottom of the vessel was careened; the elongated bow was unshipped; the upper works lowered; and the grab was about to be converted into a corvette.

When De Ruyter had instructed me in what he wished to be done, he went on shore with the Rais, and crossed the land to Port St. Louis, to recruit his crew, complete his stores, and arrange his other affairs. Immediately it was known he wanted volunteers, sailors of all countries, and all sorts of adventurers flocked to him. His name was enough; every man shipped for a cruise with him thought his fortune made; and instead of slinking about to avoid his creditors, he was again to be found carousing and brawling in wine-shops, and lolling on shop-boards and benches. The hollow in his cheek was again filled with a quid, and his inconstant womankind now his constant companion. But De Ruyter was fastidious in the selection of men, particularly of Europeans, whom indeed he employed as sparingly as he could, knowing the difficulty of governing such lawless outcasts, and left the old Rais in charge to make up the number of his crew from Arabs, and various natives of India, which, in the crowded port of this island, was no great difficulty.

Mean time we worked hard, day and night, on board the grab, —as I shall still designate her, for she underwent many trans-formations. In a few days, from looking like a floating hulk, she became like a winged thing of life; and, in a few days more, like a ship of war. We painted her sides of different colours, one entirely black, the other with a broad white streak.

De Ruyter had given me to understand that he should proceed to sea alone. He also informed me of the design he had in view; which was to intercept some English vessels in the Mosambique channel; and that he should not be absent more than a month or six weeks. 'In the mean time,' he said, 'you can amuse yourself in overlooking the plantations, and completing the improvements we were about. You seem so perfectly happy here, are become such a good planter, and there are so many things that require a master's eye, that it is better, since one of us must remain, that it should be your lot. Besides, Aston must not be left alone. On my return,

I have more important designs in view. We will then refit, and all embark; when we can put Aston ashore in one of the English settlements.'

These and other reasons induced me willingly to consent; and when De Ruyter had completed his water and provisions, we had a carouse on board the grab, shook hands, and parted. He weighed with the land-wind; and in the morning, at break of day, from a height, which Aston and I had ascended, we saw her dark hull and white canvass, skimming the water like an albatross.

I continued the same sort of active, yet quiet and happy life. My love for Zela knew no diminution. Every day I discovered some new quality to admire in her. She was my inseparable companion. I could hardly endure her out of my sight an instant; and our bliss was as perfect as it was uninterrupted. My love was too deep to fear satiety; nor did ever my imagination wander from her, to compare her with any other woman. She had wound herself about my heart till she became a part of me. Our extreme youth, ardent nature, and solitude, had wrought our feeling of affection towards each other to an intensity that perhaps was never equalled, assuredly never surpassed. I went to the town only when affairs called me thither, or to visit the commandant, with whom De Ruyter had pointed out it was necessary to keep on a friendly footing. His lady, who was really a good creature, preserved her liking for me, and wished me much to put Zela under her tuition; that she might be instructed in, what this lady called, the rules of civilized society, declaring she would be a gem of the first water, if set and polished. Little as I had seen of polished and accomplished ladies, that little was enough to disgust me. Even in their extreme youth their beauties are soiled by the pawing and officious hands of dancing masters, music masters, and French masters, whose breath is the essence of garlic. Then, when properly drilled, and the necessity of hypocrisy and lying inculcated by their mothers and governesses, they are thrust into the stream (not a crystal one) of fashionable life, rudely stared on, and examined, point by point, by those, exclusively denominated gentlemen, who earn the title from doing little but wenching, drinking, and gambling. If the girl has money, some sinking gamester seizes on the occasion to keep himself afloat by marrying her; if she is poor, some old lechers, their dormant passions rekindled, beset her; and if she escapes either of these snares, a season or two of fashionable dissipation, day-beds, fetid air, nightly waltzes and quadrilles, rob her of youth; when, with a mind tainted by vicious converse, her rose-coloured cheeks now yellow, her bosom collapsed like an ancient matron's, she could not, had she lived in the stews, have suffered more, or gained less, from her bringing up and bringing out. Something I had already seen of this, which determined me, from the first, to leave Zela wild and unreclaimed as she came from the deserts; and I carried my dread of any innovation in her country's customs, so far that, had cannibalism been one of them, I do not think I should have permitted her to change it.

CHAPTER XXIV

A sail!—a sail—a promised prize to hope!
Her nation—flag—how speaks the telescope?
She walks the waters like a thing of life,
And seems to dare the elements to strife.
Who would not brave the battle-fire—the wreck,
To move the monarch of her peopled deck?

BYRON

DE RUYTER had been absent little more than five weeks, when I was aroused, before the day, by a messenger with news of the grab's lying at anchor in Port St. Louis. I sprang from my couch, asked no questions of the messenger, but hurried through the gloomy wood, ascended the *Piton du Milieu*, with the fleetness of a roebuck, regardless of falls and broken bones. When on the height over the port, there still was not light enough to distinguish the vessels: I could see only a confused mass of hulls and masts. I hastened on. The morning gun announced the daylight, when, running up a high bank, I saw the grab's dark, long, low hull, and her masts towering above all the other ships. She was lying outside the harbour; she was in the act of hoisting her flag. A cable's length astern of her, my eye caught the beautiful American schooner, floating buoyantly on the short and breaking sea, (for it had been blowing freshly during the night,) like a sea-gull. What could she be doing there? She had left the Mauritius for Manilla, and then to return to Europe. I was the more astonished at observing her hoisting a French flag, and an English ensign

unfolding itself beneath. What could it mean? Certainly she had
come in with De Ruyter. I descended the bank, and my pace was
not slackened by this first excitement. I thought I should never
arrive at the port; and when there, I was in despair at the few
minutes which elapsed ere I could get a boat to take me on board.
I passed one of the grab's boats going on shore, but would not
delay an instant in speaking her. I seized hold of the stroke-oar,
and pulled as if each stroke was for my life. The clear and deep
voice of De Ruyter struck my ear, and in an instant our hands
were clasped together. His left hand was suspended in a sling:
I pointed to it, not having yet recovered my breath. He smiled,
and, in return, pointed to the schooner.

'What do you mean?' I exclaimed.

'Come down, my lad, and I'll tell you. After cruising some time
on the northern coast of the Mosambique channel, I received
intelligence of an English frigate's having run into Mocha in a
gale of wind. To avoid her, I stretched over to the Amiranti
islands, between them and the amber shoal, during a tempestuous
night. I observed, or rather, I imagined, for amidst the lightning
it was difficult to distinguish them, blue lights and signal rockets
to leeward. I kept my wind as well as I could, thinking it might
possibly be the frigate. Towards daylight the wind lulled, and
I soon after discovered, to my great surprise, as well as joy, a sail
on our lee-quarter, certainly not the frigate. She was to the northward and eastward; and as we had been standing to the eastward,
I could only make out she was a fore-and-aft, and not a square-
rigged vessel. I got my top-gallant masts up, and bore down to
make her out better. We neared her fast, for she was lying to,
having, as it afterwards appeared, been struck by lightning, with
the head of her foremast badly wounded. As we neared her, I
discovered, by her hull and raking masts, (for who that has once
seen, can mistake her,) our Boston schooner. Now doubly anxious
to get to her aid, I buried the grab's lean bow in the still heavy
swell, by crowding canvass on her, till I thought I should have
been dismasted too. The puny spars bent like bamboos, and the
kiar backstays, strong and elastic as they are, snapped like cast
iron—not from having too much wind, but too little. On shewing
my flag, I observed some commotion on board of her, and marvelled at seeing her soon after, despite of her crippled state,
making sail, and bearing up. You know the grab's point of sailing

is not before the wind; nor is the schooner's, luckily. However, she got her square sail up, and, with her immense main-sail, she seemed to hold her ground with us. In this juncture, a man at the mast-head called out, "Another strange sail to—leeward!" Pondering on what this could mean, I saw the Boston schooner's main-sail jib; and as she broached to, the head of her foremast went by the board. I pressed more sail on the grab; and ere she could clear, or rather cut away the wreck, which soon after floated past us, I was within gun-shot of her. I then fired my bow-chaser, but without shot, to make her shew her colours; but she did not shew them till a second, with shot, was fired over her, and a third into her. The mystery was then explained by her shewing an English ensign. She had been captured by the frigate which was to leeward of her. They had been separated by the gale during the night. There was no time to lose. The frigate, though a long way to leeward, was in sight; yet it was probable, from her great distance, and from our being smaller objects than she was, that she had not yet seen us. The courage of Englishmen is not to be subdued, under whatever circumstances they are encountered. Having cleared herself of the wreck of the foremast, she bore down on her consort, and kept up a fire on us with every gun she could get to bear. Soon along side of her, I was compelled to give her several broadsides; and, keeping to leeward of her, we cut off all possibility of escape. She then struck, and I took possession of her. I found she had been—.'

'But,' I said, 'you have not yet told me what loss you suffered, and what is the matter with your arm.'

'We had one man killed, two wounded, and my fin shattered by a splinter.'

'Not much damaged, I hope?'

'Oh, no;—nothing.'

'What!' said my old friend Van, who came into the cabin with plaster and scissors, 'what do you call nothing? I, that have practised for nearly half a century, never saw a worse contused wound. Were not two out of the three digital branches of the ulnar artery lacerated?—the bone denuded under the flexor profundus of the mid finger?—the first phalanx of the index finger shattered, even to the socket of the metacarpal?'

'Bah!' said De Ruyter, 'a feeler or two smashed and jammed together.'

R

'Yes,' answered Van, looking at me with triumph, and then with complacency on the swollen and disfigured hand, which, having unbandaged, he laid on the table, and examined;—'had I not amputated that index finger, and removed every particle of splintered bone,—had you been under any other surgeon's hand than mine,—you would not have lost a mere finger, but the entire hand up to the wrist. And now you call it nothing! But wounds are nothing, when I am by to heal them;—such is my art! I operate so gently,' (applying a strong wash of blue stone,) 'that my patients are more inclined to sleep than groan.'

Perceiving that De Ruyter winced, I said, 'Yes, Scolpvelt, you torture your patients into insensibility.'

Without noticing this, he watched De Ruyter, and said, 'I feel pleasure that you feel pain.'

'The devil you do!'

'Oh, yes! I am delighted; for it shews that the sensibility of the part is restored. I also observe that the muscle is granulating. Now we have only to use fomentations to subdue the swelling, and keep down the proud flesh with lunar caustic. It will soon be well.'

I greeted old Louis, who inquired kindly after the turtle he had left with Zela; and, while breakfast was preparing, I went on deck to shake hands with the Rais, and my old shipmates.

CHAPTER XXV

Ay, we like the ocean patriarch roam,
Or only know on land the Tartar's home!
My tent on shore, my galley on the sea,
Are more than cities and serais to me;
Across the desert, or before the gale,
Bound where thou wilt, my barb! or glide my prow!
But be the star that guides the wanderer, thou!
Thou, my Zuleika!
                                              BYRON

AFTER breakfast De Ruyter related the conclusion of his cruise. He found that all but five of the Americans, who were ill of the fever, had been removed on board the frigate; that seventeen men, with two junior officers of the frigate, had been put on board of her, with orders to keep company; but, as has been mentioned, she was separated in the squall. 'I sent these men on board the grab,' said De Ruyter, 'replaced them with a strong party of my best, took her in tow, and set about repairing her damage with some of our spars. The frigate chased us, and kept in sight two days, till I got among the Amaranti islands. There (for I knew them well, which they did not) I baffled her by anchoring, during the night, under the lee of one of them. I saw no more of the frigate, put a jury mast in the schooner, and here I am, my boy.

'Now take a boat, and go on board of her; let us work into the harbour; or—stop—you had better remain in the grab,—the wind is dying away. I must go on shore. Do you moor them close together in our old berth. I'll return in two or three hours. I must go and talk to the commandant, get our prisoners landed, and see the merchants to whom the Boston was consigned. Though taken by the English, she was not yet condemned by them, when I retook her; so I suppose I am only entitled to salvage on her and her cargo;—but that will be a heavy one.'

This news a little damped my pleasure; for I had regarded the prize as ours, and doubted not having the command of her, to obtain which was the climax of my most aspiring wishes, and certainly I should have preferred her to a dukedom. From our first meeting her at sea, and especially when I afterwards examined her in port, I had viewed her with a longing and jealous eye. The apparent impossibility of possessing her made me covet her the more. I would not only have sacrificed my birthright, but a joint of my body to boot, with all I had in the world, except what was alone more estimable—Zela, to obtain her. De Ruyter had often bantered me on this; and now that my wish seemed within my grasp, I could not comprehend his law of salvage. He had possession, and that was the only law I considered just or rational.

I awaited his return with impatience, but when he came, my impatience was left unsatisfied; for he was to meet the merchants in the evening. Next day brought the same story, and so on for many days. I loathe the tardy transactions of these grovelling serpents. I hate arithmetical calculations; they do more mischief than earthquakes in destroying badly founded fabrics; they are like a Mameluke's bit to a fiery and impatient horse. I was, however, like the horse, compelled to submission.

Much time was thus wantonly wasted, ere De Ruyter had concluded arrangements to pay, instead of receiving, certain sums, and give securities, and enter into certain bonds, and sign deeds, all preliminary to retaining possession of the schooner. However, it was accomplished; and, in less than a month after his arrival, I was installed in my heart's desire. Aided by De Ruyter, I set about refitting the schooner for sea. Whilst at work on board, Zela stayed with me. We all made occasional holidays at the villa, which was left in charge of Aston.

When the grab and schooner were ready for sea, De Ruyter gave me his instructions. In company we weighed our anchors. De Ruyter had pretty well recovered the use of his hand. The Americans, who had been left on board, and the four English sailors, taken with Aston, had entered voluntarily to serve on board the schooner. My crew had been completed by De Ruyter, and was a tolerably good one. I was armed with six twelve pound carronades, and four long six pounders. We had provisions and water for ten weeks. Zela, whom nothing but force could have induced to remain behind, and that I had no inclination to essay, was with me, and Aston was permitted to go on his parole not to serve till exchanged.

Thus, with all my wishes gratified, my joy was boundless as the element on which I floated; and I thought it would be as everlasting,—thanks to my being no arithmetician, and not being gifted with the prescience even of an hour. Accursed foresight! which turns enjoyment into misery by calculating on what is to ensue! I never did so; but went to sea with an exulting heart, fearless and free as the lion, when he leaves his lair in the jungles to hunt on the plains.

We steered to the northward, intending to make the island of St. Brandon, thence to a group called the Six Islands, and cruise in the northern Indian Ocean, crossing the track of the vessels which run from Madras to Bombay in the south-west monsoon. The first days were passed in trying our respective rate of sailing, and getting the vessels in their best trim. The grab beat everything in India, except indeed dead before the wind; with a heavy swell nothing hitherto had any chance with her but the schooner. We now found, on repeated experiments, that, in short tacks, we could beat her close on a wind; but in every other point of sailing she had the advantage, though so small as still to leave a doubt about it.

We ran by the island of St. Brandon without meeting with any particular event. Shortly after I gave chase to a brig, which I brought to. She proved to be French, from the island of Diego Garcia, bound to the Mauritius. Her captain told us he was employed in running to and from that island, for fish and fresh turtle, which abounded in its vicinity. It was uninhabited; but some merchants had sent him with a party of slaves thither; while taking in his cargo, an English ship of war had nearly surprised him: and, though he escaped, the slaves and his cargo had fallen into their hands.

When De Ruyter heard this, we consulted with the captain on the possibility of recovering the slaves and cargo. De Ruyter, who was as fertile in plans as daring in execution, soon determined on a stratagem to be carried into effect by him and me. The brig, not being a very crack sailer, he recommended to go into a port, which he pointed out by his chart, in one of the Six Islands, which had previously been agreed upon as our rendezvous, in case of separation. This arranged, we made all sail, running down, with a rattling trade-wind, to Diego Garcia. The form of this island is that of a crescent, containing within its band a very small island, which, serving as a break-water, afforded a spacious and secure harbour behind. On making the island, and observing the frigate at anchor there, we, in running down on the land, kept the little island between us and her, which prevented our being seen. We there anchored; and the next day getting under weigh together, the grab ran down to leeward, disguised like a slave ship, and appeared at the mouth of the harbour, as if ignorant of there being any vessel there; till, opening the frigate, which instantly got sight of her, she wore round, and made sail as if to escape.

The frigate, under the prompt and rapid hands of English sailors, slipped her cable, and made sail in chase. Yet time enough elapsed to give the grab a good offing, and time for me to keep out of sight, by working up to windward. I had landed a man on the little island to make signals of the frigate's motions, and timed it so well that, as she shut in the port, by rounding the projecting angle of the island, I weathered the extreme point of the little island, ran into the bay, hove to close to the shore, and landed with a strong party of men.

The contrivance was so well managed, and so rapid, that I surprised a party of the frigate's men, with the slaves in custody, and others employed in cutting wood. We embarked the slaves, and as much fish which had been cured, and turtle as we could during the four hours I ventured to lie there. The remainder we destroyed. As to my countrymen, their case seemed so vexatiously hard,—I left them; yet not before I made them declare I was the blastedest good fellow in the world,—but then I had made them all drunk. Besides, I had cheated them, hoisting yankee colours, and they knew the schooner must be of that country; so that, instead of escaping to the woods and hills, by running a hundred yards, they had awaited our landing without suspicion, discussing the amount of anticipated prize-money, and disappointed at having been left by the frigate, when in pursuit of a flying French-man, as they were certain the strange sail was, by her leanness and fleetness. We parted such good friends that, as I left the shore, they gave me three cheers, in return for three bottles of rum I left with them.

CHAPTER XXVI

No dread of death, if with us die our foes,
Save that it seems even duller than repose;
Come when it will, we snatch the life of life;
When lost—what recks it—by disease or strife?

BYRON

I THEN rounded the northern point of the island, and, with a flowing sheet, scudded gallantly along towards the port where we had engaged to meet; nothing doubting the success of De Ruyter's stratagem to draw the frigate off, and, after dodging her about to give me time, to escape in the gloom of night.

The weather had been hazy, with violent squalls of wind and rain, which was a favourable circumstance. We had a speedy run down to the destined islands; and the grab and schooner almost simultaneously appeared to the north and west, as entering the channel between the centre of the cluster. We anchored together in a small but secure port, sheltered from the winds, as well as from observation, by a high and projecting bank stretching into the sea, in the form of a bent arm.

Next morning the brig made her appearance off the island; and soon after came to an anchor. I left De Ruyter to settle the business he came about respecting the return of the slaves, and went on shore. I remember nothing particular of the natives, except that they were a simple-hearted, hospitable people, chiefly fishermen. We procured goats, fish, fowl, and vegetables; and then took our departure, standing towards the Maldive Islands, to get on the Malabar coast before the north east monsoon, which was approaching, should set in.

We soon after boarded and plundered several vessels, having English papers. Among these there was one with a Dutch frow on board, whose beam was nearly as large as the vessel's. She had a considerable investment of goods belonging to herself, with which she was trading, between Madras and Bombay, on her own bottom. Her late husband had been in the employment of the English Company, which was enough for me to condemn her as lawful prize. After culling out some of the most valuable portion of the cargo, and throwing overboard the most worthless, I recollected we were in want of water. There were five or six butts of that element on her deck. While I was waiting to get out the long-boat to send them on board the schooner, the Dutch monster of a woman was smiling, ogling and coaxing me to come down in her cabin, praying and entreating I would not take the water. I assured her, though we had boarded the vessel, we had no intention of ravishing; besides, said I, 'It is infernally hot, and I want water. Hand a bucket here!' (catching hold of a half empty cask.)

'Oh, that's not good,' quoth the oily frow; 'here, boy, get some water out of the cabin. Oh, don't drink that, captain! I'll get you some wine,—Constantia, from the Cape itself!'

'Come,' I ordered to one of the men, 'knock out the bung from this cask.'

One was trying to wrench it out with his knife, and the Dutch woman was entreating him to broach one of the others, declaring that to be brackish. 'How comes it then, you old frow, abroach? Damn it I think you've got Constantia here! If so, I'll take it on board.'

I seized on a crow-bar, and forced out the bung, marvelling at the frow's eagerness to withhold me, and withdraw my attention. I really believed there was something uncommonly good in it, skedam or wine, owing to her protestations to the contrary. The bung out, I held a bucket as a man tilted over the cask; and, while the clear water rushed out, and while I was laughing at the bedlam's pertinacity, she gave a scream, and I a shout of surprise, at what I first thought was some animal, but was soon distinguished to be the end of a pearl necklace. The frow's red face, as I pulled it out, and held it up to her, became redder than a string of cornelians, which next plumped into the bucket.

'Out with the head, and start the water!—A lucky prize! Hands off,—or I'll cut them off! Put the baubles into the bucket.'

We fished out a superb haul of rings, pearls, corals, and cornelians,—a private spec of the Dutch frow, who, during the chase, had thus cunningly secreted them. But for my having taken a particular fancy to diving into that cask, not wishing to broach a full one, we should have missed this pearl fishery.

We made a stricter search, but discovered nothing else. Giving back to the frow a ring, not one of the worst, which she, with an oath, assured me was her grandame's, together with a kiss, as I placed it on her fat, stubby finger, I said, 'Don't grieve, my young frow; for this is a marriage contract in the Arab country, and you're my wife. When we meet again I'll consummate the rite, and, till then, take care of your dower.'

I then shoved off to the grab, putting the plunder on board her, as we had little stowage on board the schooner. I told Louis of the affair with his countrywoman, and added: 'She is certainly your frow, by the description you have given me of her, in search of you;—the identical woman, depend upon it.'

Louis looked grave, but presently cheered up, and said,—'My wife has no jewels, nor any rings on her fingers; she gave her wedding-ring for a bottle of skedam, the first time I refused her a dollar to buy one.'

We fell in with a fleet of country vessels from Ceylon and Pondicherry, convoyed by a Company's brig of war. De Ruyter telegraphed me to bring to, and examine the vessels, while he gave chase to the Company's cruiser. I soon came up with the country craft; they were of all sorts, shapes and rigs,—snows, grabs, padamas. The Company's vessels, discovering us to be enemies, made sail, and left them to shift for themselves. As soon as I was near enough to get a gun to bear, I fired a shot amongst them, when they separated like a flight of wild ducks, driving away in the direction of every point of the compass; while I pursued them as the beneta does the flying fish, and kept them as well together, by running round them, as a huntsman, or rather a whipper-in controls a pack of hounds. Some few, indeed, gave me the slip; but I got the main body together. We boarded them successively, with little for our pains; they were principally loaded with bumbalow, paddy, beetle-nut, ghee, pepper, arrack, and salt. However, there was a sprinkling of silks, muslins, and a few shawls; and, with infinite industry, I contrived to realize a few bags of gold mores, and rupees.

De Ruyter was now a long way to leeward; and by occasional reports of cannon, I knew she was keeping up a running fire on the brig, which seemed to be a remarkably fast sailer. Leaving the small craft, I bore away, crowding every inch of canvass, to rejoin the grab. In the direction they were running there was a group of three rocks raising their crests high out of the water. There was a passage between them, and the Company's brig seemed making for them. Her object I could not guess at; but when she neared them, being much cut up in her rigging, and finding she had no chance of escape, she hauled her wind, and, after shortening sail, hove to, and commenced an engagement with De Ruyter. I was all on fire to be in it. As I approached, a signal from De Ruyter directed me to run to leeward of the rocks, to prevent the possibility of her escape; and, judging from appearances, the grab had already so much the advantage of her opponent, that I could only have diminished my friend's glory, without gaining any myself. But, before I could obey the signal, the brig had drifted on the rocks, designedly to destroy her, and then struck her flag.

Instantly, in conjunction with the grab, we got all our boats out, boarded her, and endeavoured to tow her off. She was a fine vessel, armed with sixteen eighteen-pound carronades, and had eighty or ninety men and officers on board. She had not been engaged more than ten or fifteen minutes; yet her hull, as well as rigging, was a good deal cut up. She had only seven or eight men wounded, and one killed; the grab had two or three wounded, and one killed by an accident. As he was in the chains, ramming down a cartridge, (the gun not having been sponged, and the vent stopped,) it exploded as the man was standing before it. The old Rais told me, in his unmoved way, 'I looked out of the port-hole, and ordered the man, who was loading the gun, to take care not to carry away the dead eyes of the standing rigging;—for he was too hot and hasty. The gun going off prevented his replying. I looked again;

the man was no longer there; but a piece of his red cap, or red head, was floating on the water. I never saw anything more of him.'

'It was Dan Murphy,—poor fellow!'

'Yes,' replied the Rais; 'he was always in a hurry, never attending to orders. And look at the dead eyes,—he has carried them away with his foolish head.'

We secured the Europeans in the prize, took some of her stores and arms, put on board our sick men, with all the plunder we had accumulated, and draughted twenty men, two quarter-masters, a prize-agent and master. After repairing her during that night and the ensuing day, (for we hove her off the rocks, without much damage, it being calm weather,) we sent her to the Isle of France. Her Lascars and native sailors, in a few days after, we shipped in a country vessel, giving them their liberty; with the exception of eight or ten, who entered with De Ruyter. More would have followed their example, had we wanted them.

CHAPTER XXVII

But feast to-night!—to-morrow we depart;
Strike up the dance, the cava bowl fill high,
Drain every drop!—to-morrow we may die.

BYRON

DE RUYTER determined on running through the straits of Sunda, while I was to run through the straits of Molacca, and procure intelligence of the English ships,—consequently we separated. We were to meet, after a certain date, at an island near the great Island of Borneo. De Ruyter gave me full instructions, from which he made me promise not to deviate.

He then took an affectionate leave of Aston, pressed on him presents of curious arms, in which Aston was an amateur, and both of them struggled, by indifferent words, to hide their emotions. De Ruyter then laid his last solemn injunctions on me, kissed Zela's brow, shook hands, and returned on board the grab.

We made sail, steering different courses. As soon as I was sufficiently near the entrance of the straits, I stood over on the Malay coast, which is very high and bold. Getting into a large bay, formed by a bite of land, I anchored in a secure berth, between a small island and the main. There I opened a communication with the natives; and with some difficulty, procured a large and very fast pulling proa; which, I thought, was the safest way of taking Aston to Pulo-penang, lying at the entrance of the straits, and in the possession of the English. Pulling along the Malay shore, in one of their own fashioned canoes, I should neither be remarked by the natives, nor suspected, if seen, by the English. Thus I might land on any part of the island I pleased.

Pulo-penang was purchased by the English East-India Company from the Malays on the opposite coast, and is now called Prince of Wales's Island. It is small, but exceedingly fertile, and very beautiful. It runs parallel with the Malay coast, which is very high; and the intermediate channel forms a magnificent harbour.

Determined to accompany Aston, I manned the proa with six Arabs and two Malays, (their arms secreted,) with three days provisions and water. Aston and I embarked; he in a white jacket and trowsers, I in an Arab sailor's dress. We shoved off from the schooner, left in charge of the first mate, an American, who had been a second mate on board of her when she was taken. He had recovered from his fever, and De Ruyter had recommended him to me fervently. He was an active, intelligent fellow; a thorough sailor, born and bred at Shrewsbury[1] in the south of England. His name was Strong, a short, thick-set man, powerful as a Suffolk horse. One of my own country, who had been captain of the forecastle in Aston's frigate, was my second mate. He had all the characteristics of a man-of-war's man, taciturn, obedient, brave, and hardy. He had also a sailor's predilection for grog. The captain of the hold, his messmate, having bulled an empty rum cask, that is, immediately after the spirit is started, put in a gallon of water, there to remain, with an occasional roll, for twenty-four hours, when it turns out good stiff grog, our forecastle captain swilled too freely of this wash, and failed in his respect to a superior officer. The boatswain, jealous of this man's better seamanship, and hating the deference that was paid him, was the cause of the man's being flogged. This disgrace preyed on his mind, and was the motive for gladly entering with me. Besides, as he argued, he had been twenty years serving the king in the West and East Indies, with nothing but two days liberty on shore, the yellow fever, many wounds, one drunken bout while on duty, and a flogging.

To return to my story, after shoving off in the proa. It was calm, with a sun that seared to the bone. We kept along the Malay shore; and in the evening, were off the Malay town of Prya, defended by a fort. Having got into conversation with some Malays in a fishing-boat, at night we crossed over in company with them to Penang river, lying to the southward of George Town, on the Prince of Wales's Island. As it was a run of less than two miles, Aston and I recreated ourselves with swallowing the delicious oysters, so celebrated on this coast. On attempting the river, we found our proa was too large to cross the bank; so he and I landed. I directed the proa to go into the harbour, with some fishing-canoes, taking fish to town in the morning.

We slept in a fisherman's hut. Just before daylight, we started for the town; and crossed several streams, flowing from the mountains into the river. The hills were covered with magnificent timber, and our path was fragrant with the odour of flowers and spices; which seemed ten times more exquisite to us, just landed from a small and crowded vessel, any thing but fragrant. Near the town, on the margin of the sea, was a wide extent of plain, of a light sandy-looking soil, as thick with pine-apples as the most prolific soil in England could be with turnips. Like boys, always hungry, we walked along, scooping their hearts out with our knives; and daintily plucked and cast away twenty, ere we were satisfied with the flavour of one.

We entered the town unquestioned, and went to a recently established hotel. Aston there rigged himself, waited on the Resident, and told as much of his story, as we had previously agreed on, was necessary for him to know, or for us to divulge. He said he had been landed from an American vessel, lower down the coast, and brought to the town by a Malayan proa.

The Resident, a military man, was very kind; he requested him to take up his quarters in his house, till some man-of-war or English ship should come into port. Aston thought it prudent to comply; merely requesting permission to stay at the hotel for a day or two, till his apparel and other necessaries should be furnished.

He then returned to me; and as I was to go back to my proa that night, we were resolved to make a day of it beforehand, which we forthwith commenced by a tiffin, and an order for a sumptuous dinner.

Aston took this opportunity of again counselling me to return to the navy, and pointed out the consequences of my serving under an enemy's flag, urging me, at all events, to remain at the Isle of France, neutral, and not act offensively against my own countrymen.

'When I have realized a competency,' I said, 'it was always my intention, following our old captain's example, to become agriculturist: but I must first have money, for, you know, I am getting into years, have a wife, and shall have a family. Oh, I must be provident, and provide for them! Now, if I were a single man, like you, Aston, young and thoughtless, it would be another thing.'

'Get out, you mad-headed boy. Why, the united ages of yourself and family would scarcely amount to the proper age of manhood—thirty!'

'Thirty! Whew! A man is then old, decrepit, grisled like a worn-out mastiff!'

This was while we were playing at billiards. Weary of the game, I sauntered forth, surveyed the port, and set down in my memory every vessel lying there. I marked, too, my proa, lying astern of an Arab vessel, a little to the westward of the town, near a landing-place which led to a slip where a large country vessel had been built. Not thinking it prudent to attract notice, I returned to the tavern. We dined; and what with sangaree before dinner, craftily qualified with Madeira, and claret, well brandied, after dinner, I cannot affirm I was as sober as a parson should be, or as silent as a quaker affects to be: yet I was not drunk; and to avoid being so, I proposed we should sally out for a 'lark'.

When in the open air, I yawed about a little wildly, and was taken aback now and then, by keeping too much in the wind's eye; but I soon became steady. We wandered for some time through crooked streets, and among sun-burnt mud-huts, till we fell in with a place called Bamboo-square. It was an open space, with an irregular range of shops, sheltered all round from the sun by bamboos and mats. A beating of drums and tinkling of instruments led us on to a row of huts exclusively occupied by Nâch girls. Aston was fond of music, and an admirer of dancing-girls, whom I, as all married men should do, had forsworn. Besides, the smell of rancid oil, ghee, and garlic was not to my taste. I therefore left him, and strolled on to a range of shops called the Jewellers' Bazaar.

CHAPTER XXVIII

So I drew
My knife, and with one impulse, suddenly
All unaware, three of their number slew,
And grasp'd a fourth by the throat.

SHELLEY

IT was thronged with people, and illuminated with coloured-paper lamps. I stood before one of these shed-built shops: it was the best, and kept by a parsee. He was shewing a woman, who was veiled from her feet to her snout, some ear and nose rings, nearly the circumference of a boy's hoop, and descanting on their neatness and elegance. When they had agreed on the price, she removed part of her head-drapery, and exhibited her nostril and part of her ear: the latter was almost as big and flat as a plate, and hung down like a sow's. The jeweller, placing his thumb to keep the slit in it open, suspended the huge ring, which looked like a chandelier. She had no occasion for a mirror, for, turning her head a little towards her shoulder, she pulled the lap of her ear forwards, and grinned with delight, shewing a double row of deeply orange-dyed teeth, more numerous than a garden-rake's, and as sharp-pointed. The jeweller, struck with these beauties, exclaimed, 'What an angel!'

She then asked him for a betel box. He produced four or five of gold, declaring that no baser metal ought to touch her lovely hand. They were handsomely made; and as it had just before crossed my mind that I should present some token of friendship to Aston, who had given me his watch in the morning, I took hold of two of the boxes. I then weighed them in my hand, without attending to the price he named, for I hated bargaining and haggling, put the boxes into the folds of my shawl round my loins, and gave him, without counting, what I considered to be the value in gold mores. He counted them, and seeing me so free with my gold, became urgent for more. He declared I had only paid for one. To this I answered, 'That's a lie!'—rolled up a leaf with chinam, deposited it in my mouth, and was going away. The jeweller called me a robber, and stretched out his hand to detain me. He got hold of the end of my turban, which was hanging down, and pulled it off. I turned round, and giving him a blow on the head, he fell among his glass jewel-boxes. A Parsee never forgives a blow—who does? He stabbed at me with a knife, or weapon of some sort, the moment he recovered his feet: but he was in his shop, and I out of it, so that by stepping back I avoided his weapon; and my blood now rising, more at what I thought the fellow's audacity than at his endeavour to stab me, I seized on a jewel-box, and dashed it at his head.

Several persons, both in and out of the shop, interfered in the business, and sided with the Parsee. The row spread through the bazaar. The jeweller, with his head and face bleeding, and phrensied with passion, called me thief, robber, and vociferated to those about me (for the clamour had now drawn all idlers to us) to seize me, to take me to prison, or to kill me, if I resisted. As the crowd increased, many pressed about me; and the infuriated jeweller, grown desperate, made another effort to lay hold of me.

Danger perfectly restored my senses; and I was enabled to rally that presence of mind with which I was gifted. I drew from my sash a pistol and creese, the two best weapons for close quarters; but not till I had seen several men close to me draw their arms. Still I refrained from using mine; for, in cases of this sort, men will bluster, draw, and threaten, but yet hesitate to strike an armed and resolute man, ready to oppose them; but the instant a blow is struck, all strike, when the weaker party must fall, unless by the intervention of some unforeseen event, some lucky chance. In this momentary pause, on which hung my fate, as by a hair, my eye glanced round, and I saw the impossibility of escape in the front, which was crowded. To be killed on the spot was preferable to being detained and made a prisoner. I seized the only outlet of escape, by retreating into the den of my enemy, the jeweller,— not to solicit his mercy. My movements were so rapid that those in the shop could not oppose me; I stabbed one, struck the jeweller down, and forced away, suddenly exerting my utmost strength, the two upright bamboos, which supported his tent-like shed. Down the roof fell between me and the people, and I escaped into a narrow and obscure passage at the back of the bazaar.

The deep guttural curses of the Malays, and the Parsee's loud threats of vengeance reached my ear. It was better to retreat than brave the fury of incensed numbers; not forgetting who I was, and the consequences of being discovered. Had I been wise, I should

have immediately retreated to the outside of the port, where my
proa lay, and embarked; but the desire of seeing and taking leave
of Aston withheld me. I therefore cautiously threaded the crooked
and dingy passage, which led from the bazaar, surprised at not
being pursued. Nevertheless I hurried on; and to avoid being
recognised, made alterations in my dress. There was much difficulty, through a labyrinth of dark lanes, in finding the tavern,
which was near the port.

I entered and reached my room unnoticed; but was annoyed
at Aston's not having returned. Thinking it possible he might be
concerned in the fray; I determined on changing my dress, and
seeing him. I put on a white jacket and trowsers belonging to him,
and could not forbear smiling, as I went out of the house, at the
man who had attended us at dinner, when I saw him puzzled to
conjecture who I was. But that triumphant smile, I had afterwards
reason to believe, betrayed me.

I proceeded directly to the bazaar. There I saw Aston's tall
figure, a head and shoulders above the crowd, which was still
before the jeweller's door,—or rather, on the threshhold, for it
was all door now, an empty space. But I observed the crowd did
not consist of the same persons, but of sepoys and police officers.
Aston and one of the officers seemed listening to an account of the
affair. The jeweller, haggard and ghastly, stood before them, narrating his injuries. Several of his family and friends were about
him. He pointed to the place where his shop had stood, now a gap
in the bazaar, stamped on the roof, as low as the foundation, and,
as he finished his vehement discourse, tore the turban from his
head, and rent his robes to fragments. And then, without heeding
those who addressed him, he disappeared.

CHAPTER XXIX

Cry a reward to him who shall first bring
News of that vanished Arabian.

KEATS' MS.

To avoid observation, and not wishing to be questioned, I went
back to the tavern. Aston soon joined me, and, shaking my hand,
said, 'I am glad to find you here. There has been a serious row in
the bazaar, and I feared you might have been concerned in it.'

'What was it?' I inquired.

'I was drawn to the spot, by seeing the people run that way. There was a shop, or shed, belonging to a goldsmith, pulled down, when the mob began to plunder it, while himself and a few others attempted to defend his property. But all the scoundrels from the port were there, and I don't think they have left the poor fellow a gold more. It was too late when I arrived there, nor had I my sword with me; but I did what I could. I knocked down some of the fellows, and procured the sepoy guard from the gates.'

'But how did it originate?'

'With an Arab; and, as far as I can understand, it is no unfrequent occurrence here, though seldom done so openly. The bazaar was full of people, and while the jeweller was shewing some valuable trinkets to a woman, who is supposed to be an accomplice, an Arab came, seized every thing he could lay his hands on, stabbed one of the men in the shop, knocked the jeweller down, and, assisted by others on the outside, rushed through the shop, which was then torn down, and a set of miscreants commenced plundering.'

'Do they suspect any one in particular?'

'I don't know; they have some of the thieves in custody.'

'Come, light your sharoot, and I'll tell you all about it.'

His surprise was great at hearing I was the person denominated the Arab robber; and, in much grief, he censured my folly and rashness. 'Besides,' he added, 'the jeweller said he could recognise the man who first attacked him amidst a thousand; and, casting from him the few things he had saved, swore by his religion he would fast till he was revenged.'

'If he keeps his word,' I answered, 'his rhamadan may last for ever; for I shall go to sea with the land-wind.'

But as the devil willed it, the weather was so bad I could not embark that night. I had no reason, however, to imagine that I was, or could be suspected; especially in a town where brawls were common events, and where a man dead, or missing, was of little account, amidst a population of armed and blood-thirsty Malays, (who, of all eastern nations, and all human beings, except kings, hold human life in least respect,) and Arabs, with whom, if precedents and time can make a thing lawful, killing is no murder, and robbery no crime, for they are coeval with their race. Besides, the Parsee's brother was not dead.

S

Aston went early in the morning to the Resident; and I went out, taking the precaution to wear an arrican cap instead of a turban, and loitered down to the port to glean information. Afterwards I visited the shops to purchase some trifling things I wanted; besides which, I had several important commissions to execute for De Ruyter, in procuring information, and forwarding letters to the interior of Hindostan. This I did through an agent of the French government, who had spies, I believe, in every port in India. Once or twice during the forenoon I thought I was watched, and evaded my imagined pursuer; and, on more than one occasion, the waiter at the hotel surprised me by some observations he made on the affair of the preceding night; which struck me the more, because another servant had told us this same jeweller was in the habit of bringing his trinkets to the hotel, when there were strangers there.

We passed this day in the same way as the preceding one; not that I was altogether quite at ease in being delayed. The affair of the jeweller troubled me little, compared to the hazard of personal discovery. Some of the vessels I had plundered at sea might be in this port; and notwithstanding the difference in my dress, some person or other might recollect me. My mind then reverted to the schooner; for however secure she might be in her present berth for a day or two, some accident might discover her; and she was only in comparative safety when in motion, with a good offing. Then there was a magnet, stronger than all these prudential considerations to hasten my departure,—my own little turtle dove, Zela, who, I knew, would outwatch the stars, and find no rest while I was absent. This determined me to embark that night, in despite of wind and weather, which was still cloudy and unsettled; and, what is often the case in these latitudes, the day-breeze went down with the sun.

I pass over my parting with Aston; indeed, to avoid some portion of the pain, I took advantage of his absence, and wrote him a short adieu, leaving the fifty or sixty gold mores I had about me in the sleeve of his jacket, so that he could not fail to find them.

I made no mention of my departure to any one in the house. As to baggage, it consisted of nothing but my abbah, which the occasional showers made no burthen. Modern frippery of combs, razors, brushes, and linen, which prevents a man from sleeping out of his own house without the incumbrance of the best part of a haberdasher's shop, I never dreamed of. My teeth were as strong and white as a hound's without the aid of hog's bristles. My head was not, as before, shaved, but thickly sprouting like a bramble bush, and was left to its natural growth with as little care and cultivation as is bestowed on that most fondly remembered fruit-tree. I say so, because, in common with all young urchins, I re-collect the time when, spurned like a dog from the vicinity of every other fruit-tree, I solaced myself under the friendly bramble, and its beloved companion, the beautiful hazel. Sacred haunts! unprotected by churlish guardians, and where, by the by, we eat without having planted. This must be the reason why starving poets call nature and mother earth bountiful,—there can be no other; for only be detected in extracting a turnip, and hear what a magistrate will say, particularly if he is clerical. You will then find mother earth the worst of step-mothers, and have enough of her in the colonies.

CHAPTER XXX

The waning moon,
And like a dying lady, lean and pale,
Who totters forth, wrapt in a gauzy veil,
Out of her chamber, led by the insane
And feeble wanderings of her fading brain.
SHELLEY

He dies! 'Tis well she do not advertise
The caitiff of the cold steel at his back.
KEATS' MS.

THUS unincumbered, a little before midnight, and avoiding the most populous parts of the town, I walked as fast as possible; but the night, and the narrow, dirty lanes, considerably impeded my progress. At length I reached the open space near the now quiet port, in my way to the outside of the town, where was a rude sort of half-finished dock-yard, off one of the slips of which lay my proa. The weather was favourable; what wind there was, I ob-served, by the occasional gusts, was not stationary, but shifting about in all quarters. Dark and white masses of clouds seemed jostling together; and, every now and then, as they met in con-tention over the moon, the world was left in almost total darkness.

Men from the shore hallooing their vessels to send boats, and the 'All's well!' of the sepoy sentinels, were the only voices I heard. When out of the town, my heart became lighter, and my stride longer, as I beheld the free expanse of sea on my right, and the mountains before me; either of them would have been a refuge, had I been pursued; however, I now considered myself out of danger. I came on a little line of huts, and a wooden fence, which I had not observed before. A sentinel, standing under the lee of a hut, stepped forward, as I was passing, and said, 'Who goes there?—stop!'

How near the guard was I knew not; therefore, to prevent his giving an alarm, which he would have done had I not stopped, I obeyed, and, to preserve my Indian character, answered in Hindostanee, 'A friend.'

He then questioned me, in the usual manner, about where I was going, and upon what business. On my replying, he said, 'You can't pass here without an order.'

'I know that,' I answered; 'I have one;'—I fumbled in my dress for a letter or paper. I took one out, and, with great appearance of simplicity, advanced towards him, and said, 'Here, Sir, it is!'

He bade me keep off, and was bringing his musquet down, when I sprang in upon him, griped him by the throat, which prevented his giving the alarm, and laid him on his back in an instant. His musquet fell from his hands; and this little irascible Bombay soldier struggled hard to loosen my hold, and lay hands on me; but he had no more chance than a cat with a mastiff. I held him till he was almost strangled; then, the moon being again hidden by the clouds, I cast his bayonet one way, his musquet another, let him go, arose, and bolted off in the direction I had come, as if returning to the town. But I took the contrary direction, and, giving the arsenal a wide berth, went through some Indian corn fields. When at a sufficient distance, I again slanted down towards the sea. More than once, it seemed, I was followed. I stopped, and turned round. As I regained the beaten track, I fancied I saw a figure skulking along, his shadow reflected on a wall. I drew my creese, and, turning back, sought vainly for the object. The changing and uncertain light made my efforts fruitless; I concluded it was a shadow created by my excited imagination, and went on.

As the moon again shone forth, I saw, between me and the sea, a building close on the beach, in a bite of the bay, which I knew to be a public slaughter-house. A little farther on was an enclosed slip, in which a vessel had been built or repaired. Half a mile onward, off at sea, lay my proa expecting me.

I stopped on a little mound of sand, looking to seaward, if I could make out the boat. One of the walls of the slaughter-house was by the side of this, and I leaned on it. At this moment, with a gleam of moonlight behind me, my shadow was reflected slant-ingly on the white ground, when a huge arm uplifting a weapon, large (such it appeared in shadow,) as a spear, was in the act of stabbing. I turned, and thrust my left hand, in which my cloak was gathered, to ward off the blow, for it was a man with a creese in the very act of despatching me. The blow pierced through many folds of the strong camel's hair, but the point of the weapon was turned, and glanced on my loins. I gave a shout, started back, presented a small pistol Aston had given me, and snapped it in the fellow's face. The Birmingham toy was not made for use; it missed fire; I cursed its manufacturer, threw it away, and drew my creese, in the use of which, thanks to the Rais, I was perfect. I having the upper ground, the assassin could not repeat his blow. He believed the first had wounded me; and, knowing his weapon to be poisoned, and if the skin was but scratched, it was enough, he endeavoured to escape.

Instantly I was at his heels. He was swift of foot, and so was I. By the turnings and twistings he made, he seemed acquainted with the localities of the ground, over which I repeatedly stumbled. Yet I pressed him so hard, calling out, 'Stop,—or I'll fire!' (though I had no fire-arms,) that he suddenly turned through a gap in a wall, a loose stone of which I caught up, and hurled at him. Follow-ing close upon him I found, by the spars and timber which impeded me, that I was in the temporary dock. It had, I remembered, a high fence on each side; for I had been down there twice to speak with my men. The deep slip, or channel, which had been cut to float a vessel in, now almost free from water, lay in front. I there-fore thought him embayed here. However, the man went straight on, then turned, and hesitated an instant. I imagined he was about to turn round, and again attack me. The night had become a little lighter, but I could distinguish no features in his dusky face, except the eyes glaring on me. As I was now rushing on him, he eluded my grasp by stepping aside, for he was on the very verge of the deep chasm, and walking, as it at that moment appeared, in the air; whence he turned his head towards me, and exclaimed, —'Robber and murderer, you dare come no farther!'

The moon, again unveiled, explained the mystery. The shaft of an unbarked tree, the larger part towards the side on which I stood, lay horizontally across the chasm; and the man, steadying himself, and clinging with his bare feet, was cautiously crossing on it.

He paused to defy and execrate me; and I, hesitating what to do, said,—'Cowardly slave! who are you?—and why have you attacked me?'

With his ghastly face towards me, he replied, 'I am the jeweller you robbed, the brother of him you stabbed! But I am revenged!'

'You lie,—you are not!'

'Fool!' said he, holding up a creese, 'if this did not go deep, the poison on it will!'

'Will it?' I cried, and, without more hesitation, having shaken off my shoes, I sprang along the spar. He jumped on it, perhaps to increase the vibration, or to cross it, or to turn,—I know not. My action was so rapid that, quick as lightning runs along an iron rod, I closed with him. He was surprised, if not panic-struck. The impetus with which we met destroyed our equilibrium, and we fell together, neither making the vain effort of using the dagger. The jeweller, who was on a smaller and more rounded portion of the spar, and, I believe, in the act of turning, made a desperate effort, as he fell, to catch hold of me, when we should have been precipitated together in the dark gulf. But it was not so decreed; for he only clutched my dress, which rent asunder, and I heard him fall heavily beneath.

I had fallen on my face, and clung round the spar with my legs and one arm, for in the fall I seemed to have dislocated the other. My body was light, and my limbs long and sinewy. I contrived, though I hardly know how, to thus support and save myself; but I remember what toil and peril I had in crawling along, hand and foot, on this dangerous bridge, which now, to my mind, was as difficult to cross as the bridge which Mahomet calls *al Sirat*, finer than a hair, and sharper than the edge of a sword, with the gulf of hell gaping below.

It was strange that, when the jeweller caught at me, and rent my vest, the gold boxes, the source of all this mischief, dropped from my bosom, (for, after what had occurred, I did not think it right to give them to Aston,) and I saw them glittering, as I imagined, on the man's head.

CHAPTER XXXI

A bitter death, a suffocating death,
A muffled death, ensnared in horrid silence,
Suck'd to my grave amid a dreary calm!

KEATS' MS.

ON regaining the brink of the chasm, breathless and almost exhausted, suffering from a contusion on my head and wrist, I sat down on the margin of that deep and dismal gulf, which gaped like a charnel-vault beneath me, and looked the more deep and terrific under the clear moonlight. Then the noise from below, which the Parsee made, struggling for life; for at the bottom of the canal was a little stagnant water, dammed up with sand from the sea, and sludge washed down by the torrents, with all the accumulated filth from the slaughter-house—being a consistency in which no man could long float, or immediately sink; but every struggle made it worse. The man had sunk deep the first plunge, and his hard efforts to rise were apparent from the speechless agony with which he toiled, and the quick and stifling noise he made, as if half suffocated by the slimy composition. He panted, gasped, and floundered on the surface. I could perceive no more than an indistinct mass thus writhing and groaning in torture. It was a horrible sight, and, though not very nervous, my flesh quivered, and my whole frame shook as in sympathy with his sufferings.

I gazed round in the vain endeavour of seeking something to aid me in rescuing him; but though the moon shone brightly, it only shewed me the hopelessness of the man's situation. I tried to keep my eyes off, but, as if fascinated, I could not. I had almost determined to give the alarm, by calling for assistance, (as I supposed a sentinel could not be very far,) regardless of consequences to myself.

The struggle now became feeble, and the noise indistinct, rattling, and hoarse. I looked, and the dark mass was slowly sinking beneath the slimy surface; and, as he sunk for ever, I thought I saw an arm still holding its serpentine weapon, which seemed (as it might have been from his convulsive death), quivering while it gradually sunk—shaking, as it were, still in defiance!

I remembered he had told me it was poisoned, and his last action reminded me of a venomous serpent I had killed the day before, which, whilst expiring with its emerald-green eye sparkling, and inflated hood, yet shot forth its forked tongue, as if in revengeful rage not to be subdued.

My eyes were riveted on the spot where the man had disappeared. The bubbling and disturbed surface was subsiding into smoothness, when I was suddenly so startled as nearly to lose my balance and fall down headlong, at hearing a voice at my ear call out—'All's well!'

It was the voice of a distant sentinel, borne on the wind while my head was on the ground near the fatal spar which crossed the chasm, and which acted as a conductor. This, and the extreme stillness of the night, made the voice seem close to me, and certainly alarmed me more than I had ever been alarmed.

I sprang on my feet, and looked round fearfully; but all was again still. Daylight was approaching, and every moment precious. I cast a last look at the spot where the man had sunk, and a pang of remorse came over me as I recalled the occurrences of the two last days, in which I had been the cause of the destruction of this man's property, perhaps of his brother's life, and then of himself. What havoc and sorrow had I caused in his family; what curses must fall on my head!—What demon of mischief urged me on? His death-cries long haunted me.

It appeared to me, on after-reflection, that the waiter, or some other person in the tavern, had suspected me as concerned in the jeweller's affair—that he had acquainted him with his suspicions —that, during my morning walk, the jeweller had seen and recognized me—that he had afterwards followed and kept sight of me down to the place where my boat lay.

Had he given notice to the authorities, and charged me with being the principal in the attack on his shop, he perhaps was aware of, or had experienced the tardy and corrupt proceedings of courts, and the little justice to be got by law: besides, there are wrongs which cannot be righted by law, and for which men seek redress in vengeance. Feelings of this sort must have determined him on attempting to kill me. If he had indeed known who I really was, his revenge would have been effectually executed by simply informing against me; but of this he had no suspicion.

I hastened down to the beach, as if pursued; and, descrying the proa, I was about to hail her, when I called to mind the vicinity of the sentinel. My left wrist was strained or dislocated—the hot blood was trickling down my face, and I was suffused with a clammy heat. I looked anxiously along the margin of the sea for a boat, but could discover none that would serve my turn. Every instant of delay augmented the hazard of detection: I therefore secured the few things which would be destroyed by water, in my cap, and walked into the sea, which was smooth, with a breeze from the land. I swam as fast as I could, having the use of but one paddle. There was no difficulty in this to one like me, who could swim nearly as well as walk, and whose daily pastime, when at Madras, had been in buffeting through the tremendous surf in which no European boat can live. But the danger I ran was from sharks and alligators, which were multitudinous about this island, the latter of which I knew used to swarm round the outlet from the slaughter-house, attracted by the smell of offal. Perhaps they were then banqueting on the wretched jeweller.

CHAPTER XXXII

> As past the pebbly beach the boat did flee,
> On sidelong wing, into a silent cove,
> Where ebon pines a shade under the starlight wove.
> SHELLEY

> With shatter'd boat, oar snapt, and canvass rent,
> I slowly sail, scarce knowing my intent.
> KEATS

HAPPILY I got on board the proa; and, having silently weighed our grapnel, we all lay down, and let the boat drift out in the channel, till the fishing canoes ran out, when we paddled amongst them, hoisted our mat-sail, and ran over to the Malabar shore; there being little wind during the day, we paddled along the shore; and as the clouds towards evening again threatened a squally night, we went into a little open cove, not having any visage of being inhabited.

There we beached our boat, and prepared to sup and sleep under the shelter of some pine-trees, growing close to the sea. Meanwhile two Malays speared fish from the rocks, and others lighted a fire against a huge teak-tree, which, as I afterwards learnt, had crept into the forest, and continued burning for seven or eight months. Wearied and worn out, after having placed two men as outposts some distance from us, and appointed a strict watch to be kept, I selected a soft stone as a pillow for my head, and with my feet to the fire, wrapped in the boat's sail, I slept so soundly that neither the wind nor rain, which came on in the night, awakened me.

An hour before daylight I was called. My limbs were cold and stiff. Coffee and smoking, my never-failing remedies in the morning, refreshed me. We launched our boat, and, with a breeze still from the land, made good way through the water, keeping well out to meet the sea-breeze. After mid-day the weather became clear and bright, and about midnight, we ran along the north-east side of the island, at which the schooner was moored. We did not see her, so snug was her berth, until we rounded an estuary. A man on the look-out on shore, belonging to the schooner, des-cried us. As we approached, I perceived Zela, with my pocket telescope, looking through one of the ship's glasses.

Springing over the schooner's low gunwale, I lifted her up by the waist, which had outgrown my span. I pressed her to my bosom in rapture, carried her down the hatchway and placed her on the cabin table. Then, turning to my mate, I said, 'Strong, have you seen any strangers in the offing?'

'Only country craft, Sir.'

'No matter. Get under weigh, and let us make a stretch to the eastward.'

I should have mentioned that I had previously examined the place which I thought the jeweller's creese had grazed, but could discover no wound. The loose and thick folds of my camel-haired abbah, and the shawls round my waist had saved me. My eyes were both blackened by the blow on my brow, and my left wrist was swollen and painful.

My abbah I had picked up, so there was not the minutest clue by which the jeweller's friends could trace him or me. Whether the sentinel, with whom I had the scuffle, gave an alarm, or made a report, I know not. Probably, as he had committed a fault in permitting me to come near him, without giving an alarm, he was silent.

Zela's paramana (nurse), old Kamalia, doctored my wounds; and Zela chafed my temples, and rubbed my stiffened limbs with cajeput oil and camphor. Whether it was this hot oil, or the hand acting in animal magnetism, or roast fowls and claret, or my callian and coffee, or guava jelly and sweeter lips to kiss, that restored me, is a mystery. But certain it is that these external and internal applications restored my body's health. My arm I was obliged to keep some time in a sling; and I hardly think it ever regained its former strength.

De Ruyter having told me he should go through the straits of Sunda, and touch at Java, I proceeded to Borneo. I passed the straits of Drion; but anxious to get through these, I did not run out of my way to board any of the country vessels, which I occasionally fell in with. The first vessel I boarded was some time after this, at the dawn of day. She was a singularly constructed and rigged vessel, coming right down on us, apparently of less than a hundred tons burthen, with two masts, snow-fashion; her ropes were principally of a dark grass, her sails of purple and white cotton, though some looked like matting; her hull was high out of the water, bleached to a whitish brown; her bottom (for I could almost see the kelston as she rolled heavily, more from want of ballast, and the weight above board, than from any swell of the sea) was overgrown with barnacles, sea-weed, and green slime. She yawed so widely about, owing to bad steering, that I could scarcely keep clear of her. I fired a musquet for her to heave to, which she did in so lubberly a manner, by heaving up in the wind, that she was nearly dismasted. A strange antediluvian crew of almost naked savages, the most uncouth and wild I had ever seen, tattooed from head to foot, were groping about her deck and rigging. A ragged piece of painted cloth was hoisted by way of ensign. Who or what she was, whence come or whither going, it was impossible to guess. Her upper works were so broken and gaping, that you could see both into her and through her; this with her rent and ragged trim made her look as if she had been floating about ever since the flood, and yet the wonder was how she was kept afloat an hour.

They were attempting to hoist out an old and ornamented canoe; but, to save time, and anxious to examine her, more from curiosity than hope of plunder, I lowered a small dingy from our stern, and went to board her. On nearing her I was more astonished at her wild appearance; and, having with great exertion climbed up her projecting bamboo outworks, I found the interior far surpassing the exterior. Her upper deck was thatched over with coir, held together with twined grass cordage. The savage crew had palmetta-leaf coverings on their heads, and Adamite inexpressibles.[1] A very tall, thin and bony man came forward to receive me. He was distinguished from the savage group, that crowded around, by his comparative fairness and fierceness, besides having more covering to his person. His features were prominent, his complexion a reddish brown, his hair somewhat darker; and he would have been strikingly handsome in figure and bearing, were it not for the extraordinary and grotesque manner in which he was tattooed on his face, arms, and breast, which were bare. The figure of a hideous serpent was wreathed around his throat, as if in the act of strangling him, with its head and lancet-like tongue traced on the lower lip, as if, killing two-fold, it was darting into his mouth. The bright green eye and red tongue of the serpent were so cunningly tattooed in colours, that, with the movement of the lower jaw, they appeared in motion. Yet there was a placid expression of the eye and brow which did not correspond with his wild attire. I had no time to examine farther, for this captain, or chieftain, came forward in a most courteous and affable manner, and with a strange accent, but in tolerable English said,—'You are English, Sir?' (I had shewn English colours.)

'And who are you, Sir?' I asked.

'I, Sir, am from the Island of Zaoo.'

'What!—where is that? I never heard of such an island.'

He informed me it was in the direction of the Sooloo archipelago. 'But it is strange,' I said, for his manner struck me more than his appearance; 'are you of those islands?'

'Yes, Sir.'

'What! a native?'

'No, Sir.'

'Who are you then?'

He paused for a moment, and then answered,—'An Englishman, Sir.'

'Indeed! How the devil then came you there, or rather here, in this trim?'

'If you'll walk down in the cabin, I'll tell you, Sir; I'm afraid I've little refreshment to offer you.'

Just as we were at the hatchway, I heard a woman's cries below. He stopped, and said, 'I had forgot,—we cannot go down there.'

'Is there any one ill?'

'Yes, Sir; one of my wives is lying in, and I believe, before her time. Her labour is brought on by sea-sickness. She is suffering dreadfully.'

I sent for old Kamalia, telling him I had a wife on board, and that her nurse, as I had understood, was learned in these cases. Zela's paramana soon came on board; when, not to interrupt them, we sat apart on the deck, near the stern, where the stranger thus began:—'It is so long since I've spoken my mother tongue, and the circumstances I am going to relate happened so many years ago, that I shall make a bungling story of it, and am afraid you'll not understand me.'

'Well,' said I, 'it is almost calm, and we have time; so don't hurry yourself. And as you seem not very well found in the grub-bery line, I'll send for something to freshen your memory, while you recal old times.'

We were soon supplied from the schooner with beef, ham, claret and brandy. Englishmen hate each other till they have eaten together. Eating made us friends, and drinking opened our hearts. The only remnant of civilization, which still marked him a gentleman, was that he smoked without intermission. When our callians were lighted, he commenced his narrative; but in so strange an idiom, and with so many breaks and stops, that, at first, I had great difficulty in comprehending his meaning. For the benefit of others, I take the liberty of amending his phraseology.

CHAPTER XXXIII

Nelson was once Britannia's god of war,
And still should be so, but the tide is turn'd;
There's no more to be said of Trafalgar,
'Tis with our hero quietly inurn'd.

BYRON

'SEVEN or eight years ago,' he said, 'I left England in an East India Company's ship, with convoy, bound to Canton. The first officer, who had mercantile transactions with my father, and was considerably his debtor for prior investments, induced him to furnish him with a still larger investment than usual, upon condition that I, who was a clerk in my father's house, was to be shipped as a midshipman, and to receive a certain portion of the profits, on my father's account, arising from the investment. Properly instructed in this, I was to make the voyage, and, if I liked it, to continue in the service; if not, to return to the counting-house. At the age of fifteen I need not say how gladly I quitted debiting and crediting, invoice books, journals, and ledgers, to go to a country of which I had heard so much, and to rank among those aspirants, who used to give themselves such airs, and appear so happy, when they were on shore;—not knowing then that the cause of their joy on shore was the being released from a tyrannical subjection on board those worst of prison-ships, East Indiamen. However, under the patronage of the first officer, my initiation into the service might be supposed favourable.

'But we had not long sailed from the Downs, when I experienced a visible alteration for the worse. For, besides the degrading and abject services in which the class I belonged to was employed, the first mate, my patron, in whose watch I was, turned suddenly upon me, without any fault on my part, and reviled and abused me. From that time, he treated me, on all occasions, with mockery and contempt. Not satisfied with making me do the most menial offices, he punished me for his sport; for I gave him no cause. He one day told me, in his passion, that my usurious old Jew of a father had hooked me on him as a spy, to defraud him of his freightage; adding, "He made me give a bond too as security, but I'll be damned if I don't make a bond-slave of you!" It is needless to tell you what a miserable life I led.

'Our captain lived apart, as a sort of deity, and so I believe he thought himself. He associated with none but two or three of the passengers of the highest rank, and issued all his orders through the first officer. One night, off Madeira, it was blowing hard, when a man called out,—"A strange sail on the weather bow!" I was standing near him, and answered,—"Very well, I'll report it;"— though I saw nothing but what seemed a great black cloud, and proceeded aft to acquaint the first officer with it, who had charge of the watch. I beheld him asleep on the carronade slide; a new feeling awoke in my bosom,—revenge!'

'What,' I asked, 'did you stab the fellow, and throw his carcase overboard?'

'Oh, no; it was but a boyish spite;—if I were to meet him now, perhaps I might do as you say. I left him asleep, and went down to the captain, whom I awoke with,—"There is a large ship just under our lee-bow!"

'He started up, saying, "Where is the officer of the watch?"

'I cannot find him, Sir.'

'"Not find him!"' and up rushed the captain. The officer was sleeping close to the companion ladder; so that, on the captain's putting his foot on the deck, he stood before him, and called out his name. The affrighted sleeper sprung up at the well-known voice of his stern commander. But there was no time to waste in words; it was blowing a hard gale, and the sea running high; the dark and moving mass which, an instant before, I had thought a cloud or land, now in the form of an immense ship dismasted, came driving towards us. Our captain roared out to put the helm down, and turn the hands up; but it seemed too late. A voice, trying to make itself heard through a trumpet, hailed us as from a tower, for so she loomed, as she drifted before the wind, borne on by a gigantic sea, which lifted her above us. The blue lights burning on her forecastle were reflected on our close-reefed top-sail. It appeared inevitable that, as she replunged in the deep trough of the sea, in which we lay, becalmed by her monstrous hull, we should be crushed, or cut in two. Our sails struck against the masts with a thundering sound; and the crew, scrambling up the hatchways in their shirts, but half awake, involuntarily screamed at the sight of the immense ship coming upon us. Panic-struck we could do nothing; and she, impelled by the fury of the sea and winds, was borne on, rolling and plunging, without sail or mast to steer or steady her. It was a scene that appalled the most hardy; some held out their arms widely, and shrieked; others fell on their knees; and more threw themselves headlong down the hatchways; and though it was but a moment, such a moment makes a boy an old man. A loud and more distinctly heard voice, speaking through a trumpet, again hailed us,—it seemed our death summons,— "Starboard your helm, or we shall run you down!"

'As the wave was lifting us up, the stranger struck us. There was a frightful crash. Then I heard the loud shrieks of our men, and, giving myself up for lost, convulsively griped hold of the shrouds, and awaited my fate. My eyes were riveted on the stranger; she passed, as I thought, over us, and then lay, like a gigantic rock, immoveable, close on our lee-quarter. The gale, unimpeded, again roared among our shrouds, and the sea broke over us. After a horrible pause, the bustle and the noise of the winds, waves, and voices recalled me to my senses. The stranger had struck us on our quarter, and carried away our quarter-gallery, stern-boat, and main-boom;—nothing more,—and we were safe. The ship again hailed us, and asked our name. She then ordered us to keep close to her during the night, and added that she was his Britannic Majesty's ship, Victory.[1]

'That night nothing was said to the first officer; but he was put under close arrest. Indeed the panic was so great that, for a long time, every one seemed under a spell, and our captain and officers were only recalled to their duty by the frequent night-signals from the Victory, with the roar of her immense guns to enforce attention to them, and to keep us in our station on her lee-quarter; for they feared we should give them the slip during the night.

'In the morning, when I went on deck, I found we had lost our convoy; and the Victory, still close to us, was making signals for us to take her in tow. For this purpose, as there was more swell than a boat could live in, we veered an empty cask astern, with a rope attached to it, for her to take on board. This done, she fastened halsers, as big as our cables, to the rope; and we hauled them on board over the taffrail, secured them to our main-mast, made all the sail we could carry, and bore up for the Island of Madeira. Our situation was most perilous; for, notwithstanding the great length of the halsers by which we were towing, the weight and size of the Victory, then the largest ship in the world, gave us dreadful shocks as we lifted up trembling on the crest of a wave, and she sank beneath us in its hollow,—she seemed dragging us stern foremost downward; then again when we laboured, becalmed in the deep trough, and she was lifted up, she appeared plunging down directly on us. Sometimes the tow ropes, though nearly the size of my body, snapped like rotten twine; and we had again the difficult and dangerous task of getting her tow-ropes on board. Luckily that night the wind abated, or, I think, we should both have foundered. The strain on our ship was so great, that besides the danger of carrying away our main-mast, the seams of our deck opened, and the sea broke over us, sweeping away all before it, and threatened destruction by filling us with water. Our captain hailed the Victory, and represented our danger: the only reply was, "If you cast off the tow-rope, we will sink you."

'On board the Victory, they had eased her by throwing overboard the guns on her upper deck, setting storm-sails on the stumps of her lower masts, and by every means in their power. The next day the gale was considerably abated, though the sea was still heavy. We brought to a large West India ship bound to Madeira, and she was compelled to take our place.

'Our captain then went on board the late admiral's ship, when her commander, after reprimanding him for his bad look-out during the night, said he should pass over his conduct in consideration of the service he had done in having been the means of saving to his majesty and his country the most valuable of their ships that bore the triumphant flag of Nelson, and that was then bearing his body.

'He gave our captain a certificate to this effect. This somewhat appeased our proud commander; and, the danger over, his wrath was allayed against the delinquent officer, whom he had threatened, in his passion, to annihilate. Besides, they were relations, or at least of the same name—Patterson; and you know, Sir, Scotchmen are clansmen, and care not if all the world goes to wreck, so that their own particular clan escapes, and profits by the general loss. But I ask your pardon, Sir—there may be some very good men amongst them.'

'Come, come,' I said, 'I hoped you had lived long enough among savages to forget to lie. You know there is not one honest man among them. I hate them all. They come amongst us like locusts or rats and devour up everything while we get nothing in return but lice, fleas, and the itch. I wish the vermin were crushed, or

T

blockaded amidst their barren mountains, to browse on heath and peat till the rot carried them off. But let us forget the rascals; and do you go on with your story concerning those two particular ones.'

CHAPTER XXXIV

That boat and ship shall never meet again!

BYRON

Thou must hold water in a witch's sieve
And be liege lord of all the elves and fays,
To venture so.

KEATS

'THE first officer,' he continued, 'returned to his duty, and had no difficulty in tracing the origin of his disgrace to me. I need not say my condition was not improved by this event. Oh, how I envied the life of the most ill-used chimney-sweeper or outcast beggar! Their existence seemed passed in bliss compared to mine! Besides, they could fly from a heartless beadle or cruel master, while I (for so I then thought) was a hopeless slave. But, Sir, I am detaining you.'

'Oh, no,' I replied—'go on;' for the similarity of this man's fate with Walter's doubly interested me, and I already felt a friendship for the narrator. By gazing on his features, as he spoke, I was soon familiarised to the sight of the frightful figures portrayed on his skin, and 'saw his visage in his mind.'

'At length,' said he, 'by the usual passage, we entered the China seas. One night, the ship being anchored off an island, (for what purpose, I forget,) I was ordered in the boat which lay astern, to take care of her. Suddenly the thought crossed my mind that I might take advantage of this and escape. Without for a moment weighing the hazards of such an enterprize, I gave myself up to the impulse. There was a mast, a sail, and a keg of water in the boat, for she had been employed in landing on the island to leeward of us, to seek for water. This determined me. It did not then occur to me there were so many things necessary, especially bread. I had only brought my supper of biscuit and beef with me: compass and charts I never thought of. The night was dark, a steady breeze blowing out of the gulf, and the sea tolerably smooth.

I took a favourable opportunity of all being quiet on board, slipped the painter which held the boat, and, after drifting astern in fearful suspense for a short time, got the mast up, veered round, and soon lost sight of the ship.

'An hour elapsed, when I thought I saw a lantern hoisted by her, and afterwards plainly distinguished a blue-light. I hauled in towards the island, that, by running to leeward of it, I might be screened when daylight should appear. Thanks to my having been born near a dock-yard, and to my fondness for boating, I had learnt to manage a boat very well.

'But only, Sir, think an instant on the alteration a few months had made in my fate, and more particularly that of a few hours; yet the last I could not regret. My heart, however, misgave me when at sunset the next evening I pondered on my desolate condition—alone in a little boat, without compass, or the means of existence, on the wide ocean, the wild waters all around me, and the cloudy and then starless sky above me. My folly struck me to the heart. I wished myself on board the ship again. I wept bitter tears, resigned the helm in despair, and left the boat to be drifted at the mercy of the sea and winds. Hunger long kept my eyes open: however, at last, after drinking some water, I slept, overcome by toil and fasting. My sleep was long and troubled: it was near day when I awoke, and the sky was clear. I again loosened the sail to the breeze, and ran before the wind. I endeavoured to think what course I was in. From the direction of the wind and the north star, I concluded I was running towards the islands in the Sooloo archipelago, and that the high land which I saw in the morning was Borneo. I was steering nearly due south, and the island of Paragua, near which I had left the ship, must have been nearly astern. The breeze continued fresh, and my little bark went fast through the water. There was no vessel of any kind in sight. I detected myself unconsciously nibbling round the rim of my only remaining biscuit. I considered if I should haul in for Borneo; but the wind veered several points, and, finding I should have to beat up to it, I was forced to proceed.

'The fear of starvation already made me feel starving: yet the wind freshened, and I knew I could not be long without making one of the countless islands which lay before me. I was determined to run slap ashore on the first I could. This day I passed in torture from hunger: I felt sick and desponding. The day passed, when

I saw no land ahead, and lost sight of the land astern. At night I became wild and feverish, and arraigned Providence for having abandoned me. The night was clear, almost as light as day, and as I sat sullenly at the helm, I heard something fall splashingly into the boat, and sprang up for joy as I eagerly grasped hold of it— a bright silvery-scaled fish, nearly a pound in weight. My joy cooled on reflecting that I had no fire to cook it—not even a knife to scale it, so ill was I provided. I threw it down in the boat, and resumed my desponding station at the helm. My eye now caught something dark floating on the surface of the water: I edged the boat that way, and stretching out my arms, lifted what I thought a small log of wood, but which proved to be a turtle. I threw it in the bottom of the boat. These two god-sends, by lengthening the distance between me and starvation, re-assured my mind, and, lashing the helm, I again fell asleep.

'But I was soon awakened by the water rushing over the gun-wale of the boat, which heeling over on the side I was lying, it covered me. I believed she was swamping, but had recollection enough to cast off the sheet, when the boat righted, though up to the thwarts in water. Securing the sail, I turned to with my cap, and baled. The wind had freshened, the sea was getting up, and the weather lowered threateningly. Still the night was light. I reefed the sail, again set it, the boat scudded at a great rate, and I felt confident of seeing some land in the morning.

'I now became so hungry that I sought out the fish, and, from biting and sucking at the tail, I proceeded upwards towards the head. It was so deliciously refreshing, so far superior to any I had ever eaten before, that I wondered people spoiled them by cooking. However, I had forbearance to stop when I came to the thick part, to reserve it for a relish on the morrow: but this served rather to sharpen my appetite, than appease my hunger. I began to look longingly and greedily on the turtle, which was flapping about, and, remembering it had nearly escaped when the water came into the boat, I lashed it by the fins. The remainder of the night was passed in thinking how I could open its shell, to get at the meat; and I cursed my improvidence again and again, in not having provided myself with a knife, a compass, a quadrant, and a Nory.[1] It seemed I only wanted these four articles to fit me for circumnavigating the globe: for you know, Sir, a man feels full of confidence after a good supper.'

CHAPTER XXXV

With dizzy swiftness, round, and round, and round,
Ridge after ridge the straining boat arose,
Till on the verge of the extremest curve,
Where through an opening of the rocky bank
The waters overflow, and a smooth spot
Of glassy quiet mid those battling tides
Is left, the boat paused shuddering.

SHELLEY

'THAT night I ran a great distance. As the day broke, I watched with intense anxiety to discover land ahead. There was as much sea running as my small boat could live in, and I was kept almost constantly baling. My life seemed to depend on making land quickly; and I cannot describe my disappointment and horror, when the day did appear, to see I had run past several small islands in the dark, and the wide sea before me, without a solitary speck on the horizon. The remainder of the fish—I could not help it—I had devoured during the night. I made a vain attempt to haul my wind, and fetch one of the islands I had passed; but the wind and sea were too high, and if I had not instantly again put the boat before the wind, I should have been swamped.

'A few hours after, notwithstanding every effort to keep my eyes on the horizon ahead, that I might catch the first appearance of land, and shape my course so as not again to get to leeward of it, fierce famine again so gnawed my stomach, that, in spite of every endeavour to the contrary, from occasional wanderings, my eye became fixed and riveted on the turtle. I could attend to nothing else. If I exerted myself to slue my head in another direction, it was only like shaking a compass—the turtle acting on my eye-ball as the pole on the magnetic needle, bringing it always round again to the same point. My thoughts, too, were absorbed in imagining the possible means of opening its shell. I unlashed it, brought it aft, and pored over the mazy, coloured lines and divisions marked on its back, as if I had been studying a chart. Never had I seen any thing so well secured, except the iron-chest in my father's counting-house, to open either of which without iron appeared impossible. Then I studied the structure of the boat, till I could have built one, to discover if a bolt or nail might be safely subtracted; but in vain. The extremities of the turtle, indeed, seemed more in my power; but one end was fast locked by its horny head and bony fins, and the other by his fins and a substance tougher than the sole of my shoe. As to its head, as if aware of my purpose, it never even put it out. I then tried to crack the shell, by beating it against the gunwale of the boat; but the boat was stove, without the slightest fracture in the shell. After many fruitless attempts, I succeeded in grasping hold of its head, when I secured it with a rope-yarn, and, making use of the last expedient, at length I killed it.'

'But how?' I asked.

'By gnawing through the skin of the throat, though my eyes were well nigh beaten out by the fins. Then I thrust my fingers into the breast, forced off the fins, and so got into it. But, in my haste, or from ignorance, for I knew nothing about the matter, I suppose I burst the gall; for though I washed the flesh well, it was very bitter. The eggs, of which it was full, though they were very small, were the best part. However, my appetite was appeased; and I now turned my attention to look out for land; when I shouted with rapture as I discerned it on my starboard bow.'

While describing his contention with the turtle, his looks and gestures became so fiercely vehement, that I shoved over to him the remains of the meat on the table; and kept my throat at a respectable distance from his vulture-like claws, which the black lines tattooed on them made them resemble.

'At the sight of land,' said he, 'my expiring energies were awakened. The breeze was still increasing, and, fearful a gale was coming on, I exerted myself to make the island quickly. Although the boat almost flew through the water, so that the spray dashed right over me, I thought, in my impatience, she lay like a log. I saw several other islands to the south of this. The sun was nearly sinking, when I had approached the land so as to see the surf breaking on the rocks. In my anxiety to be on shore, I heedlessly let the boat run on, and neglected to run along the shore to seek a beach or landing place, and avoid the shoals and rocks. Blindly I scudded on even to where the surf was highest, and found my- self suddenly embayed amidst rocks, over which the waves were furiously and unceasingly breaking. In my too great eagerness to escape from sea-perils, I was devoting myself to destruction on the far more dangerous rocks. I let go the sheet which held the sail; it fluttered wildly in the wind. The sea-birds flew screaming over me. My little bark, almost buried in the spray, which beat on me like a hail-storm, was tossed, wheeled, and whirled about, with so much water in her, that I hardly knew if I still floated in her, or in the sea. Just as she was borne by a high wave madly against a rock to be dashed to pieces, the wave, not breaking, bounded back like a ball, and hurried her against the opposite rocks, and then rebounded, as if in play. The noise of the winds and waves, breaking all about, was deafening. The space between me and the shore was white and frothy as milk when overboiling, and seemed close to me, without a chance of my arriving at it. Suddenly the boat disappeared from under me. Though I could swim, my efforts were vain; for after I had, with all my strength, approached within an arm's length of some of the rocks, the reaction of the swell drove me back again, mocking my exertions. At length worn out, and bleeding all over from wounds inflicted by the lancet-like points of the coral reefs, against which I was driven from time to time, I felt myself going down. I believed it was all over with me, and must say that death by drowning is not so frightful as it is represented. Perhaps my previous exertions, hunger, loss of blood, exhaustion, and the hopeless situation I might be in, if I were landed, made it the less bitter. However that may be, a calm sensation, almost amounting to pleasure, came over me as the water closed over my head. After that I even remember, as I still mechanically or convulsively struggled for a few moments, that I seemed suspended under the water, not sinking. Then came a pang, as if my heart had burst, and life was fled.'

CHAPTER XXXVI

The gentle island, and the genial soil,
The friendly hearts, and feasts without a toil,
The courteous manners, but from nature caught,
The wealth unhoarded, and the love unbought;
Could these have charms for rudest sea-boys, driven
Before the mast by every wind of heaven.

BYRON

HE paused to fill his callian, and then proceeded in his story. 'How long I remained under the water I know not. A sensation of dreaming and trying to awake, of which I have a faint recollection, was what I next felt, and then of suffocation. I thought people were endeavouring to stifle me, by holding me under the waters of a torrent, and that its noise drowned my cries. At last my senses were partly restored. I distinguished some figures leaning over me. I was giddy, sick, and shivering with cold. The people looked very strange, and talked to me; but I could not understand them. They were very kind, for they were chafing my body with their hands, to recal me to life. But I hasten over this, Sir, to tell you of my astonishment, when, so far recovered, I could comprehend things about me.

'I lay on the ground with mats under me, and cotton cloths above me. There were three women, nearly naked; but I afterwards found their being so was owing to their having covered me with their garments, not from the custom of the country. Their faces, arms, and necks were covered with black lines. They had gold rings in their nostrils, and on their arms and ancles. They were very young, and were it not, as it then struck me, for the strange marks which disfigured them, handsome, and not very dark. They screamed when I spoke and moved to sit up. Dreadful hunger had again taken possession of me. I made signs to this effect, when they all ran away, but soon returned with fruits. Greedily were they devoured, one after the other, as they gave them; while they were frightened at the ferocity with which I ate.

'My hunger satisfied, I gazed round to see where I was, and found myself on the brink of a little river, smooth and transparent; yet I was startled at hearing the loud surf breaking near me. It was not in sight, for a high screen of rocks lay between me and the sea. It afterwards appeared that when I had sunk, a strong under-ground eddying current had carried me, along its windings, into the mouth of this little river, calm as a pond, being completely sheltered from the wind, and not visible from the sea, though running into it from a jungle. Three girls, who had just come down to this river's mouth in a canoe, to be in readiness to spear fish in the night, always plentiful during boisterous weather at sea, must have arrived at the instant my body came up to the surface. Neither surprise nor fear prevented them from dragging me to the shore. For a long time they considered me dead. To decoy the fish they lighted a fire, near which they had laid me; a happy chance, as I conjecture, to which I owed my life. My first symptoms of breath and motion, as they occasionally came to look at me, were sufficient to excite them to do all they could to preserve me, which, though little, was enough.

'I am now, Sir, speaking of the ensuing morning; for I remained there all the night under their care. Then I was enough recovered to stand on my legs, and they led me down to the canoe, which they launched in the river. I had a strong repugnance, a dread of the water; but we all embarked. They seated me down in the bottom, and commenced with their paddles to urge the boat along.

'When we left the little open pool, formed by the river, hedged round with rocks, cocoa-nut trees, and yellow moss, and ascended the stream, the trees and bamboos were so thick on each side, as, in many parts, to meet together overhead, and exclude both sun and light. On these trees were hanging in clusters, like living fruit, little black monkeys not bigger than an apple. The sweet smell of the trees and blossoms, and the kind looks of the girls who conducted me, went far towards restoring me. The river turned about a good deal, and, at times, narrowed. In many places it had burst through its banks, and formed streamlets, of which you could trace the course by the loftier and brighter trees, and by the luxuriant vegetation. In about two hours we came to one of these streamlets; its mouth was larger and deeper than those I had observed before; they turned their canoe into this, and made signs for me to land. I did so: the vegetation was so thick here, that there was scarcely sufficient space for us to stand upon; nor could I see any path, where the canoe was landed, amongst the long wild grass.

'They made signs for me to follow them; and they walked down in the shallow part of the stream for a few minutes; then, after a turn, they came to a path, still by the stream. Here, amidst a grove of tall trees, entirely cleared from underwood, there was a multitude of little huts, built of wood, and covered with leaves. They led me into one of two or three, the largest and nigh together, fenced by a prickly pear-hedge.

'On clapping their hands, a number of old women, and young naked children came out of different holes and corners. After staring at me, they asked a thousand questions of the girls who had conducted me thither; then they came and scrutinized me, touched my hair and hands, and returned to listen again to my story. Soon after all the old women of the village, in like manner, visited and examined me.

'Mean time my hostesses supplied me with abundance of provisions, flesh broiled, rice, Indian corn roasted, and fruits. What astonished me most was that I saw no men, except two or three decrepid ones. But,' said my narrator, 'the night is coming on, and therefore I'll hasten over my tale of years; for all seem but as yesterday, since few events have marked them.

'I found a refuge amongst the kindest-hearted and most simple-minded people in the world. When I arrived, the men of the village, as I afterwards learned, were gone to attend the king on a great hunting and fishing tour, through and round the island, which takes place twice every year. The three girls who had gone fishing down the river, and preserved me, were this king's daughters. At night when I retired to sleep, my surprise was great when the eldest of the girls, after making up for me a comfortable bed of reeds and mats, conferred a few minutes with her sisters, and then came, and lay down by my side.'

On my laughing, the Zaoo Englishman seemed annoyed, and said, 'Sir, it is the custom of the country for the eldest unmarried female of the family to sleep with the stranger.'

'Go on; I approve of the custom very much. It is admirable, especially for us travellers; and I wish such sort of hospitality were universal.'

'From that time,' he added, 'this girl became my wife.'

That, thought I, alters the case, and I looked grave. 'The king,' continued he, 'returned with his people, and expressed his surprise and joy at finding me one of his family. By degrees I became accustomed to their manners, and spoke their language. I had naturally a mechanical turn, improved by my vicinity to a dock-yard in England, so that I was useful to the old king, who soon loved me as a son, and gave me his two other daughters for wives, at their own earnest request. Then I went into a separate house, a gift from the king; but he could not long endure my absence. You may see, Sir, I have lost every vestige of civilization, and am, as it were, a native of the island.'

'But,' said I, as he concluded, 'you have not told me whither you are bound.'

'Oh,' he replied, 'as you are English, I believe there is no harm in my telling you. Why, Sir, within these few years, several vessels of the Spaniards and Dutch have touched on our island; and, besides plundering our coasts, they have seized some of the un-armed people to make slaves of them. They come from the Philippine Islands. I am going, Sir, to petition the aid of the English government in India, and to purchase arms and ammunition for a battery, or——'

I interrupted him with,—'The latter is wise; but as to your petition,—don't think of such a thing. What have you to induce the Company to interfere?'

'A valuable pearl fishery,' he said, 'which neither they nor any European is aware of except myself.'

I placed my hand on his mouth, and exclaimed, 'Never again mention it to a living being, or your island will be wrested from you! Collect your pearls in secret, and barter them for arms, or let them lie quietly where they are.'

This advice I impressed so seriously on him that, I believe, he has followed it, and I have been careful not to betray him. 'But still,' he said, 'I must go to Calcutta; for there I hope to hear of my family, and I wish to let them know where I am living, and that I am perfectly content. Return to Europe I never will! Besides that I have wives and children here, and am beloved by every one, what could I do in Europe with the marks of my savage life branded on my face and body? Here they exact reverence, as they shew I am the son of a king; there they would make me stared at, and hooted wherever I went, like a wild beast.'

CHAPTER XXXVII

As to the christian creed, if true
  Or false, I never question'd it:
I took it as the vulgar do.
  For my vext soul had leisure yet
To doubt the things men say, or deem
That they are other than they seem.
                    SHELLEY

'BUT where, in the name of old Neptune,' I asked, 'did you get this antique-looking vessel? Or is this the pearl oyster bank raised up, and set afloat?'

'Seventeen or eighteen months ago,' he replied, 'when I was out with a number of canoes, pulling round the south-west part of the island, we discovered this vessel, dismasted and drifting towards the land. I approached her, and, seeing no one, went on board. I found her entirely abandoned. On opening her hatches, and going below, dreadful exhalations arose as from putrid bodies; of which, indeed, we found a heap lying huddled up together, in an undistinguishable mass. By a few vestiges we believed them to be Lascars or Arabs, or both. There was a large ring-tailed cat, together with some great water-rats, tearing at and feeding on the corrupted bodies. My people said, and I suppose they were right, that it was a country vessel, which had been attacked by pirates, and the crew massacred. Every thing valuable or portable, that could be come at, had been taken from her. We towed her into a little port in the island, cleaned her, and repaired what we could. I have been a year about her, and you see how little I have been able to do, having neither proper tools, iron, cordage, tar, paint, canvass, anchor, nor cable. Such shifts as I have been put to you perceive. Whether I shall proceed, or obey the dictates of common sense, and go back, I cannot tell. Your opinion, Sir, as you seem kindly interested in my behalf, and are my countryman, shall decide on my movements.'

I shook hands with him, and professed that, in either event, I would do all in my power for him. But, as it was then late, I returned to the schooner, with a promise to lie by him that night, and to visit him early on the morrow, accompanied by my carpenter and boatswain, that his vessel might be properly surveyed, to see if she was sea worthy.

Accordingly, the next morning, a careful examination took place, and I received rather a favourable report. After consulting with his highness, the Prince of Zaoo, and having listened to all his motives for wishing to visit an European port, where he could procure arms and supplies, and a variety of articles he wanted, I recommended him to run along the Malabar coast, with the land and sea breezes, and go to Pulo Penang, where his vessel would be repaired, and put into better sailing trim; and thence to go on to Bengal, as there alone he could procure the supplies he wanted.

In reply to my questions regarding the island and its inhabitants, he told me the island is small and low, with the exception of one rugged mountain nearly in the centre, which the natives informed him had, according to tradition, been once all on fire. 'I therefore conjecture,' observed the prince, 'it has been a volcano, possibly thrown up from the bottom of the sea, and then enlarged, as it is now increasing, by the living coral. You know how rapid vegetation is in this climate. They add that the village, where the king now resides, was formerly close to the sea; and by the sand and sea shells, found on digging, it seems it has been so. The whole island is now covered with large timber and impenetrable jungle, except towards the summit of the mountain, and in those places, near the rivers and the streams, which have been cleared by the natives for their dwellings. We have wild and tame hogs, goats, deer, monkeys, and poultry; then there are yams, kladi, and a variety of roots and herbs, mangoes, plantains, cocoa-nuts, and other fruits, while the sea coast swarms with shell and other fish. Where Providence does so much, we do little but fish and hunt. The inhabitants are wise in contenting themselves with what they have, never toiling and sweating for more. What is forced and wrung from the earth by hard labour is embittered by the pain with which it is purchased. The women are very industrious, attending to household affairs.

'Our people are spread about the island in villages, governed by their own laws, which are simple, equitable, and summary. A great council is held twice a year, at which the king presides, hears complaints, and settles all disputes. Women have their full share of liberty. Every one may marry whom she likes, and return to her family, if ill used by her husband. Before marriage they may indulge in sexual intercourse with the unmarried and un-betrothed; but when married, it is considered so infamous, that both parties are branded and turned out of the community. Poly-gamy is allowed, though none but chiefs are permitted to have more than two wives. As every woman is obliged to do the work of her own house and family she is not only content that her husband should take another wife, but generally provides him with one herself, either a favourite sister or friend, for there are neither slaves nor servants among them.

'The women are well made, gentle, and remarkably attached to their families. They are clean in their persons, attired in a cloth made of the bark of a tree, which is both soft and durable, and dyed of all colours. Our houses are raised a story on bamboos, the lower part serving as a magazine for provisions. The tobacco you are now smoking grows on the island; our people all use it. They manufacture these wooden pipes out of a sort of jessamine creeper, by forcing the pith out when green; and the bowls are made of a hard wood burnt. They make their own spears and knives, the handles of which are ornamented with carving. There is a remarkable diversity in the features and complexion of the people. Occasionally there has been a little commerce, by way of barter, (for money is not known,) with small vessels from Borneo; which brought iron, hatchets, wire, coarse cloths, brass, and old musquets; and in return received a variety of gums and resins, cocoa-nut oil, sandal and kiabouka wood. But the approach to the island is dangerous, owing to the strong under-ground currents, and the immense coral reefs, on which the sea is perpetually break-ing. Then there is only one port, very small, and not very secure.'

Upon my inquiring if they had any religion, and what it was, he said, 'Yes, we have our superstitions, but no priests. Our chiefs preside on particular ceremonies, sing prayers, and make offerings to the evil spirits.'

'But,' I asked, 'what is their faith?'

'Oh, it is founded on the same as yours at home;—a belief in a good spirit which is above the earth, and in an evil one which is beneath it.'

His highness had victualled his ship with paddy, deer and goat's flesh, in slices of about the size of cutlets, dipped in salt water, and dried in the sun, and fish cured in the same way. Besides, he had great store of cocoa-nuts, and a fiery sort of arrack made from the sap of the tree fermented, with melons, pumpkins, onions, and an extraordinary supply of tobacco, which was large and thick leaved, but of an excellent flavour. He gave me a boat-load of it, and one of his pipes; the latter I still preserve in memory of this strange being; grotesque and wild figures of non-descript animals are deeply chased on it.

During the day one of his princesses miscarried of a prince; and to my astonishment, shortly after, made her appearance on deck, with the intention of bathing in the sea.

Having already expended more time than was warranted with him, I gave him a chart and compass, a few bottles of brandy, a bag of biscuits, and what was of more importance, I repaired his rudder, and put his vessel in a better trim. He was profuse in thanks, and pressed a small bag of pearls on me; which, as it was a plentiful product of his island, I accepted. I then promised, if possible, to visit his island; when we cordially embraced, and made sail on our different courses.

CHAPTER XXXVIII

> Or could say
> The ship would swim an hour, which, by good luck,
> Still swam, though not exactly like a duck.
>> BYRON
>
> It may be easily supposed, while this
> Was going on, some people were unquiet;
> That passengers would find it much amiss
> To lose their lives, as well as spoil their diet.
>> *Ibid.*

CONTINUALLY in chase of something, I fell in, among other coasting and country craft, with a Chinese junk, drifted out of her course, on her return from Borneo. She looked like a huge tea-chest afloat, and sailed about as well. She was flat-bottomed and flat-sided; decorations of green and yellow dragons were painted and gilded all over her; she had four or five masts, bamboo yards, mat sails and coir rigging, double galleries all round, with ornamented head and stern, high as my main top, and was six hundred tons burthen. Her interior was a complete bazaar;

swarms of people were on board, and every individual, having a portion of tonnage in measured space, had partitioned off his own, and converted it into a shop or warehouse; they were like the countless cells of a bee-hive, and must have amounted to some hundreds. All sorts of handicraft trades were going on, as if on shore, from iron forging to making paper of rice straw, and glass of rice, chasing ivory fans, embroidering gold on muslins, barbacuing fat pigs, and carrying them about on bamboos for sale. In one cabin a voluptuous Tartar and a tun-bellied Chinese had joined their dainties together; a fat dog, rosted entire, stuffed with turmeric, rice, suet, and garlic, and larded with hog's grease, the real, delectable, and celebrated sea-slug, or sea swallow's nest, shark's fins stewed to a jelly, salted eggs, and yellow dyed pilaff formed their repast. A mighty china bowl of hot arrack punch stood in the centre of the table, from which a boy was continually ladling out its contents. Such voracious feeders I never beheld; they wielded their chop-sticks with the rapidity and incessant motion of a juggler with his balls. The little, black, greedy twinkling eye of the Chinese, almost buried in mounds of fat, glistened like a fly flapping in a firkin of butter. The Tartar, with a mouth the size of the ship's hatchway, seemed to have a proportionate hold for stowage. Understanding these were the two principal merchants on board, I had come to speak to them; but like hogs, buried up to the eyes in a savoury waste of garbage, there was no moving them from the dainties they gloated on. A sailor, who had conducted me, whispered his Tartar owner who I was; he grunted out some reply, and with a greasy paw, placed several handfuls of boiled rice on a corner of the table, indented it with his fist, poured into the hollow some of the hog's lardings out of the platter containing the roast dog, and then, adding five or six hard boiled salt eggs, motioned me to sit down and eat.

Driven away by the sweat and stink of these unclean brutes, I went into the Tartar captain's cabin, built over the rudder. He was stretched on a mat, smoking opium through a small reed, watching the card of the compass, and chaunting out, 'Kie! Hooé! —Kie! Chee!' Finding I might as well ask questions of the rudder as of him, I hailed the schooner to send a strong party of men.

We then commenced a general search, forcing our way into every cabin, when such a scene of confusion, chattering, and noise followed, as I never had heard before. Added to this there

were the mowing and gibbering of monkies, apes, parrots, parro-
quets, loories, mackaws, hundreds of ducks, fish-divers, pigs, and
divers other beasts and birds, hundreds of which were in this
Mackow ark. The consternation and panic among the motley
ship's crew, and merchant-passengers, are neither to be imagined
nor described. They never had dreamed that a ship, under the
sacred flag of the Emperor of the Universe, the King of Kings,
the Sun of God which enlightens the World, the father and mother
of all mankind, could, and in his seas, be thus assailed and overhauled. They exclaimed, 'Who are you?—Whence did you come?
—What do you here?' Scarcely deigning to look at the little
schooner, whose low, black hull, as she lay athwart the junk's
stern, looked like a boat or a water-snake, they wondered at so
many armed and ferocious fellows, not believing they could be
stowed in so insignificant a vessel, whose hull scarcely emerged
from the water. A Hong[1] silk merchant, while his bales were
handed into one of our boats, offered us a handkerchief a piece,
but protested against our taking his great bales, when we could
not possibly have room for them.

A few grew refractory, and called out for aid to defend their
property. Some Tartar soldiers, got together with their arms; and
the big-mouthed Tartar and his comrade, swollen out with their
feed of roast dog and sea-slug, armed themselves, and came blowing and sputtering towards me. I caught the Tartar by his mus-
tachios, which hung down to his knees; in return he snapped a
musquet in my face; it missed fire; his jaw was expanded, and
I stopped it for ever with my pistol. The ball entered his mouth,
(how could it miss it?) and he fell, not so gracefully as Cæsar, but
like a fat ox knocked on the head by a sledge-hammer. The Chinese
have as much antipathy to villanous salt-petre, except in fire-
works, as Hotspur's neat and trimly dressed lord; and their
Emperor, the Light of the Universe, is as unforgiving and revengeful towards those who kill his subjects, as our landed proprietors
are towards those who slaughter their birds. An English earl told
me the other day he could see no difference between the crime of
killing a hare on his property, and a man on his property, arguing
that the punishment should be the same for both. However,
I have killed many of the earl's hares, and a leash or two of Chinese
in my time, instigated to commit these heinous crimes by the same
excitement,—that of their being forbidden and guarded against
by vindictive threats of pains and penalties.

U

But to return to the junk. We had a skirmish on the deck for a minute or two, a few shots were fired, and a life or two more lost in the fray. The schooner sent us more men, and no further opposition was made. Then, instead of gleaning a few of the most valuable articles, and permitting them to redeem the remainder of the cargo by paying a sum of money, as the rogues had resisted, I condemned her as lawful prize. We therefore began a regular pillage, and almost turned her inside out. Every nook, hole, and corner were searched; every bale cut, and every chest broken open. The bulky part of her cargo, which consisted of camphor, woods for dyeing, drugs, spices, and pigs of iron and tin, we left; but silks, copper, selected drugs, a considerable quantity of gold dust, a few diamonds, and tiger-skins were ours; and, not forgetting Louis, who had entreated me to look out for sea-slug, I found some bags of it in the cabin of my late friend, the defunct merchant. Neither did I neglect the salted eggs, which, with rice and jars of melted fat, victualled the ship. I took some thousands of these eggs, a new and excellent sort of provision for my ship's company. The Chinese preserve them by merely boiling them in salt and water till they are hard; the salt penetrates the shell, and thus they will keep for years.

The philosophic captain, whose business it was to attend to the navigation and pilotage of the junk, having nothing to do with the men or cargo, continued to inhale the narcotic drug. His heavy eye was still fixed on the compass, and his drowsy voice called out, 'Kie! Hooè!—Kie! Chee!' Though I repeatedly asked him whither he was bound, his invariable answer was, 'Kie! Hooè!—Kie! Chee!' I pointed my cutlas to his breast, but his eyes remained fixed on the compass. I cut the bowl from the stem of his pipe, but he continued drawing at the reed, and repeating, 'Kie! Hooè! —Kie! Chee!' On shoving off, as I passed under the stern, I cut the tiller ropes, and the junk broached up in the wind, but I still heard the fellow singing out, from time to time, 'Kie! Hooè!— Kie! Chee!'

We had altogether a glorious haul out of the Chinaman. Every part of our little vessel was crammed with merchandize. Our men exchanged their tarred rags for shirts and trowsers of various coloured silks, and looked more like horse-jockeys than sailors. Nay, a few days after I roused a lazy and luxurious old Chinese sow from the midst of a bale of purple silk, where she was reclining; perhaps she thought she had the best right to it, as it might have belonged to her master, or because she was one of the junk's crew, or probably she was the owner himself transmigrated into this shape,—there needed little alteration. I also got some curious arms, particularly the musquet, or fowling-piece, which, had it obeyed its master's intention, would have finished my career. The barrel, lock, and stock are deeply chased all over with roses and figures of solid gold worked in. I preserve it now, and it has recalled the circumstance by which it came into my possession; otherwise, it might have been driven, like many others of greater moment, from my memory, by the lapse of time, and by more recent events.

CHAPTER XXXIX

Not a star
Shone, not a sound was heard; the very winds,
Danger's grim playmates, on that precipice
Slept clasp'd in his embrace.
SHELLEY

BEING now on the south-east side of the island of Borneo, and the time for meeting De Ruyter drawing nigh, I made the best of my way to our rendezvous, a little group of islands close to Borneo; but just as I got sight of land, it fell a dead calm, which lasted three or four days, during which I lost one of my best men. Slung in the bite of a rope, and lowered over the bow, he was nailing on a sheet of copper that had become loose from the heads of the nails being worn off. I was on deck, and, hearing a dreadful noise and scream, I ran to the bow from which it proceeded. A monstrous ground-shark had got hold of the man's leg, and, while his fins and tail lashed the water into a white foam, was tugging to draw the man under water. Secured under the arm-pits with a strong rope, and holding on the chain-plates, the man struggled violently to save himself. When he saw me, he cried out, 'Oh, Captain, save me!' I hallooed to the men who were gathering round, to bring the harpoons and boarding pikes, and to lower the stern-boat; and with the promptness of sailors, fearless when a comrade is in danger, they attacked the monster. A brother of the man even jumped overboard, armed with a knife. The foam on the water was dyed with blood, and the greedy and ferocious sea-devil received many wounds, and was harpooned ere he relinquished his gripe; but the line, from want of giving him scope enough, was broken, and he escaped. Meantime, the man, now insensible, was hauled on deck: his leg was frightfully mangled, the flesh from above the calf being drawn down like a stocking, and the bone left bare. We had a sort of surgeon, whom Van Scolpvelt had picked up at the Isle of France, but he turned out to be an idle and drunken fellow, though not ignorant. The man died a few days after: I suppose his wound was past the art of surgery.

An unlooked-for death on board a ship makes a great and awful sensation. Sailors are as untaught, and have as little communication with the enlightened world, as the Arabs imprisoned in their deserts. The one studies the sea of waters, and the other his sandy wastes, the winds and their stars, like magic-books, not to be decyphered; and who, ignorant of their causes, can contemplate these mysterious powers, daily witnessing their wonderful changes and effects, without becoming superstitious? Certainly not Arabs and sailors, whose firm faith in signs and omens is as old and boundless as the sands and sea. It is curious that so many superstitions belonging to the sea should be general throughout the world; for instance, seamen of all countries and religions, from Lord Nelson, and the Capetan Pacha commanding the Ottoman navy, to the Mainotte corsair and the Arab rais, all think it a dread omen of evil to begin a voyage on a Friday, the Moslem's sabbath and the Christian's day of the crucifixion. I had begun my last voyage from the island near Pulo-Penang on that fatal day; and it is remarkable that the second mate, my countryman, and two men, brothers, all admirable sailors and very good men, when they heard me give the order to weigh the anchor, were dissatisfied, and murmured. I frequently laughed at them about it: they always answered, 'You will see, Sir—we are not returned to port yet.' It was one of these brothers who lost his life by the shark, and the other, shortly afterwards, lost his life in as strange a manner.

Becalmed off Borneo, I one day pulled in-shore to look at a small bay at the mouth of a river, and then pulled some way up the river. We let go the grapnel to dine; and in the cool of the evening the men bathed. The brother of the man who lost his life by the shark, an excellent swimmer, challenged a Malay (whom I had brought as interpreter, in case I met with any of that nation) to try which could dive the deeper, and remain the longer under water. I was just out of the water, and dressing. They plunged in together, and were so long under water as to alarm me. At last, up came the dark head of the Indian: he was astonished at being beaten, and said the white man must be the devil, for no one else could beat him. Our anxiety became intense: every eye was strained as if its glance could penetrate the deep and turbid stream. The unfortunate diver never again appeared. We dragged and searched in every possible manner, but in vain. The night came on, and compelled us to return to the ship.

The strange deaths of these brothers, within a month of each other, made a strong impression. Matted vegetation, or a sunken tree, might have entangled him, or the cramp might have paralysed his efforts to rise,—or, more probably, the jaws of an alligator. Some, indeed, thought that grief at his brother's death, which certainly had deeply affected him, made his own death voluntary. Their fate threw a melancholy and gloom over the ship's crew, beyond what the loss of the greater part in broil or battle would have done.

As we slowly crept along the south-east coast, towards the appointed port, the weather was, and had been for a length of time, unusually clear and bright, with calms and gentle airs. One evening, just before sunset, I observed the first appearance of a cloud for many days. Thin misty vapours, of a gauze-like transparency, began to envelope the mountains to the westward; and suddenly, as the sun disappeared behind them, a bar of bright flame shot along their summits, then wreathed itself around the dreary dome of the highest peak, and remained there for some moments, glittering like a crown of rubies. The moon was of a dusky red, the sea changed its colour, and was unusually clear and transparent. I started at seeing the rocks, the fish, and the shells at its bottom; we sounded, and there were twelve fathoms water. The atmosphere was hot and heavy; the flame of a candle, burning on deck, arose as clear as in a vault. I ordered the sails to be furled, and the anchor to be let go, as we were evidently drifting in shore, determined to get under weigh with the first appearance of wind. I remarked to the second mate, who had the watch, 'Well, now we are anchored, the charm is broken; is it not?'

The man replied sulkily, 'We are not in port yet, Sir.'

CHAPTER XL

Hark! tis the rushing of a wind that sweeps
Earth and the ocean. See! the lightnings yawn
Deluging heaven with fire, and the lashed deeps
Glitter and boil beneath.

SHELLEY

THE shore nearest to us was low, and appeared like a huge swamp, overgrown with monstrous reeds, which waved about, though we had not a breath of air. There was the abode of wild elephants, tigers, serpents, and fevers. We thought we heard the roar of the tigers in the stillness of the night. I watched eagerly for the lightest air, to enable us to remove from this dreary spot. The country evidently was not habitable for man; yet, as the night advanced, we saw lights flickering about on the surface of the morass, like the lights used by fishermen; others were stationary, as from a village.

There were no clouds visible to leeward, yet not a single star shone. At length the lightning began to play about the mountains inland. I was sitting with Zela on deck, watching these unusual signs, which filled us both with melancholy bodings; and she was telling me what strange fires, simooms, and whirlwinds she had witnessed on her own wild sands, when, at that instant, I heard a strange noise, such as comes before the thunder breaks. 'Hush!' I said, 'what is that?' and sprung on my feet. The blow was struck before I had time to turn the hands up, for the men were sleeping on deck. We were dismasted. I looked aloft, and by the light of the sheet-lightning, saw nothing standing but two bare poles. All our loftier spars, yards, and rigging were flying away, borne up by the wind, as if they had been thistle-down. The sea was all white with foam, and flew about, covering us as if under a cataract. Our ports, and a great part of the gangways, were blown clear away; the gun-bolts were drawn, and the guns broke loose. Our little vessel plunged madly into the sea, and for a time we were actually under its surface. I grasped hold of Zela and the shrouds, and with difficulty retained my grasp against the weight of the waters. The cable parted, or we should inevitably have foundered.

I first drew my breath on seeing the bow of the vessel re-appear above the water. I called to the men, but none answered, and I thought they were all swept into the sea. At length, speechless, panting, and panic-struck, some straggling individuals came crawling aft. 'Are there any men overboard?' I inquired, and looking anxiously over the stern, a voice called to me from the sea, 'Oh, Captain!' It was clearer far than mid-day; the flashes of bright sheet-lightning were without interval, almost blinding me. The sea, too, was white as snow, and I thought I could distinguish many dark heads feebly and vainly struggling in it. The voice that called on me I recognised as my favourite Swedish boy's, and fancied I saw his despairing and piteous look.

The fatal blast of the simoom was over. I loosened Zela, who had clung to me in agony, and placed her in safety, accompanied by the American mate, who had seized the helm. We rushed to a light whale-boat, lying on the gangway—for the one astern was washed away—and seeing it had escaped the wreck, I called on the men to save their comrades. For a moment they hesitated, scarcely knowing if they themselves were saved. I then called, by name, some of my own countrymen, and said, 'What! shall our shipmates perish for want of a boat, or a rope? Not a hand to throw them even a rope! Get out the boat, and where is Strong? By God! he is overboard, or he would not have needed to be called! Heave together, my lads;—she is afloat;—now take care she don't get adrift or swamp;—that's well;—now the four best men on board get into her;—I'll go with you;—I know where they are; —come, no more hands' (for now all seemed eager); 'and you, Sir, keep her in the wind;—hoist lights;—have ropes ready!'

We shoved off; the wind had as suddenly lulled as it had burst, but the sea was dashing, jostling, and tumbling about, like a river where it empties itself into the sea. The lightning, too, died away into faint and indistinct flashes, and it was dark and awfully gloomy. As soon as we had drifted astern, we picked up two men, who had saved themselves by holding on the drifting spars, which were towing astern. We saved two others, floating near them. Then, after halooing, and pulling about in the direction where the squall had struck us, in search of the man-of-war's-man, my second mate, and the Swedish boy, both of whom were certainly missing, and how many more we knew not, till we ourselves were in danger of losing our vessel, we were compelled to return.

Wind and rain succeeded, and the night looked horrible. It was with infinite toil we neared, and at last got under the lee of the vessel, drifting rapidly out to sea. As the boat shot up under her quarter, not being fended off, while the men were scrambling to get on board the schooner, she gave a heavy lurch, swamped the boat, and left me, with six others, floating on the sea. I struck out to keep clear of any one's catching hold of me. Curses and screams were mingled. As we fell into the wake of the schooner, shooting from us, I heard the men in her crowding aft, and throwing ropes, none of which reached us, and calling to us to lay hold of the wrecked spars, but they were lying out of our grasp, foul of the bottom of the schooner, and to windward, the ship then drifting bodily to leeward. I called out distinctly, 'A rope, or we are lost!' for I knew that our only remaining boat could not be got out. I thought my hour was come, when I perceived something white on board the schooner, and heard a voice, which thrilled through my frame, and arose above the wind, the sea, and the cries of the drowning. It exclaimed, 'There is a rope! Oh, God! give it him, or take me!' The extreme bite of a small white rope fell almost in my hand, it was clutched; so unerring was the eye that directed, and the hand, heart-impelled, that cast it. Zela, that hand was thine! Thy little arm and tiny hand, at that moment, possessed more strength than the sturdiest seaman's, and saved five lives, which could not have been preserved five minutes later.

I can hardly see the paper I write on! The long lapse of years which have passed since that time, appear but as many minutes, so vividly is that overwhelming instant graven on my heart. And oh, blessed angel! have you not since, hovering over me in battle, preserved me when I have wildly rushed on death, (for why should I fear or shun what is?) to re-unite myself to you? And have you not, protecting spirit! turned aside the cowardly assassins' balls directed at the heart consecrated to you, and guided them through my body, balmed the wounds, mortal to human remedies, unclenched the gripe of death, when I have felt his icy fingers in my breast, and restored me to health by most miraculous means?

CHAPTER XLI

Angela the old
Died palsy twitch'd, with meagre face deform.
KEATS

BUT, slave of my feelings, I must go back to my narrative. Zela, who had not left the deck, (indeed she never did, but on compulsion, when I was in danger,) witnessed the whole calamity. She was, as I have said, of a fearless race, and her fragile form contained a spirit almost unearthly. She had pointed to the sailors on board —for the eye of love pierces through the darkest night—where to throw the ropes; but, not relying on them, she seized on the deep-sea-lead-line, which luckily had no lead bent to it, and unreeling a long coil, she ran out on the foot-ropes of the main-boom. The man swore she ran on it like a spirit. When at the extreme end, she was directed by my voice, and threw the coil of line in her hand, with all her strength. Fearing it might not reach me, she had fastened the other end, purposing, in that event, to jump into the sea to bring it me; but finding that I had it, she threw the end on board. Four out of the six men with me grappled and got hold of it. Being not much thicker than whip-cord, it was miraculous that it held us; but the schooner was now getting stern-way on her, so that other ropes being thrown, our safety was insured. Two men, either entangled in the ropes of the boat, or not being able to swim, (and it is a fact that very few sailors can swim,) never rose after the boat was stove.

Zela rushed into my arms, but spoke not a word. Her lips were cold as ice. I seated her down by the Malay girl, in the hatchway. 'Oh, God!' I cried, as her inanimate form was upheld by the girl, 'she is dead!'

Then the old Paramana, Kamalia, who was bed-ridden in the cabin, called out—

'No!—Death is indeed come; but not yet for her. When next he comes, the noble tribe of Beni-Bedar-K'urcish, which is coeval with the sands, is extinct for ever! When the destroying salt wave reaches the root of the date-tree of the desert, it dies, and its fruits and leaves die too. It is written so by the Prophet. I ransom her life with mine. I swore, when he took her mother, that when he next called on the spirits of our house, he should take old Kamalia. Blue fiend! the Prophet heard me, and thou must obey him!'

These words were followed by a stifling noise, as if the poor nurse was drowning. As I knew the cabin had been full of water, though I had forgotten her, I called for a lantern, and ordered the Malay girl and two of the men to go down, and bring the old woman, who had been rapidly declining in strength, on deck. There was not a dry rag on board; I could only press Zela to my bosom, which was but an icy pillow, and breathe on her eyes; yet I thought I felt symptoms of returning life. The men called out from below, that the old nurse was dead, stiff, and cold as a stone!

The water being cleared out of the cabin, I carried Zela down, and, when I saw she lived, left her in the Malay girl's lap, and hastened on deck. We had enough, in clearing the wreck, to occupy our hands and minds till daylight, without inquiries into the number of men we had lost. The Malay girl's screams recalled me into the cabin. I found Zela in what I then believed the con-vulsions of death. She writhed for a long time in extreme agony, and pain seemed to have restored her senses. Before the morning her struggles ceased. She had been seized with premature labour, and brought a dead child into the world. But I was happy, for she lived. I forced her to drink some strong hot brandy and water, and she fell into a deep and tranquil sleep. Her before cold and pallid brow became warm and moist, and at that moment she looked so exquisitely beautiful, that I gazed on her, spell-bound, still throbbing with agitation in reflecting how nearly I had lost her, and determining in my own mind that henceforth I would cherish her with tenfold care.

Fearful, when she awoke, that she might hear of Kamalia's death, and perhaps see her body, I went to the place where the faithful and good old creature lay. I held the lantern to her face: it had undergone no change; a mummy that I had seen at the Isle of France, of Cleopatra's era, nearly two thousand years entombed, looked not more antique than old Kamalia, and it bore as much appearance of animal moisture and flesh and blood as did her shrivelled, withered, and dried-up remains. The worms were defrauded of their prey. Her livid-blue skin covered nothing but dry and sapless bones: a pale crimson streak, the last small drop of blood, stained a vein on her temple; a little tuft of grey hair, like hoary moss on a withered tree, or, as if a spider had spun his web on her skull, alone sheltered the bare bone: her arms and body were rigid to brittleness. Wrapping her remains in her own barakan, I lifted the body, and conveyed it to a separate cabin. She weighed no more than a bundle of rushes. I closed her stony eye and skinny mouth.

Daylight was approaching: a man called out, 'Breakers a-head!' —yet we had no soundings. Spite of her crippled state, the schooner, on which we had now some canvass, went round them, when we saw the surf breaking on sunken rocks. As the day dawned, the weather resumed its previous tranquillity: the sun arose in all its brightness; a vapoury veil of mist hung over the now distant low line of shore, from which we had been driven as if by a hurricane, like an eagle descending to its nest, was sinking to repose in its own desolate region, the abode of everlasting rain and tempests. This vast and dreary swamp extending deep into the island, occupies more than a hundred miles along the shore, and is exactly under the equator. We had cause to be thankful we were driven, though a wreck, from it, instead of being wrecked on it. The builder would not have recognized the schooner. The Zaoo Prince would not have exchanged his rotten and worthless bark for our now less safe-looking vessel. Battered, dismasted, and broken, we lay a complete wreck on the waters, at the mercy of waves and winds which we should have laughed at the day before. Our plunder, and great part of our provisions, were damaged.

Giving the necessary directions, and leaving the deck in charge of the mate, I went to my cabin, after having mustered the crew. We had lost the second mate, the steward, the Swedish boy, and seven men.

I found Zela still asleep, and, putting chairs by the side of her couch, I placed my arms around her waist, pressed her gently to my breast, and fell into a deep sleep. I dreamed of undergoing every kind of horrible death; of being torn to pieces by sharks, by tigers,—of suffocation by drowning, and of my skull being cracked and crushed like a nut between the huge jaws of a croco-dile. In my struggles to escape, I capsised the chairs, and fell heavily on the deck of the cabin, dragging Zela with me. In terror she asked what was the matter! The perspiration was pouring down my brow: she wiped my face, and, kissing my lips, said, 'You were dreaming, dearest! and I was trying to waken you, for your sleep seemed dreadful.'

It was some time ere I recollected where I was, and could recal the events of the night. Then, overjoyed to find Zela recovered, I kissed her a thousand times, and shook off my heavy drowsiness and sickness with cold water and coffee.

Retarded by light winds and want of canvass, we were four or five days reaching our destined port. Finding De Ruyter there with two prizes, our sufferings were instantly forgotten, and we brought to, under the grab's stern, singing and cheering, as if we had returned from a most prosperous voyage; so completely can a ray of joy dispel the remembrance of the longest and dreariest sufferings.

De Ruyter hastened on board, not knowing what to think, beholding our crippled and weather-beaten appearance. 'Halloo, my lads!' he said, as he came alongside, 'have you cruized to the north pole, and been locked up in an iceberg for a hundred years?'

'No,' I answered, 'we have merely turned the schooner into a diving-bell, or torpedo, to cruize under water.'

'What has happened?' he said, as, standing on deck, his keen eye glanced over the tempest-stricken wreck; 'you have been battling with the simoom! No human engines could have done this. Ha! and I miss some familiar faces!' For De Ruyter had the gift, which kings are said to have, of never forgetting faces.

He came wondering down in our cabin, and I told him our disastrous history. 'Well!' he added, 'you have had a miraculous escape. It cannot be helped. We must do the best we can to set you to rights again. I hope you are all right under water. We have spars enough here; and I can make a shift to supply you with rope and canvass. I have been more successful, among a convoy of coasting craft in the Straits of Sunda. We dismasted a lubberly Company's cruizer, and took two of her convoy, charged with naval and military stores and provisions, run them into Java, where we sold them and their cargoes to advantage. Since which we have picked up two private traders on our way hither; one loaded for Macoa with cases of opium, better than dollars, for the markets are high; and the other with oil, coffee, sugar-candy and sundries. You see them both in the port. Besides which, I have done some service to the people here, Beajus, or wild men, as they are called by the Moors, for which they have made me king of the island. Here am I, King Prospero, with a thousand Calibans for my subjects! See, now they are bringing wood and water; and they have shewn me—

> 'All the qualities o' the isle
> The fresh springs, brine pits, barren place, and fertile.'

'What can you mean?' I inquired.

'Near the uninhabited Tamboe islands, I was surprised at discovering a fleet of proas. Taking them to be pirates, I ran in amongst them. They were lying close to the shore, and most of their crews escaped. Some got under weigh, and attempted to get out; but, with the exception of two or three, I compelled them to return; when their crews also jumped overboard, and swam on shore. I boarded their boats, and found, as I had predicted, they were Malayan and Moorish pirates. They had been to the south-east side of Borneo, where they surprised the natives; who, as their country is swamped during the rainy season, and for some time after, live in floating houses, which are moored to trees. They could not escape, for these fellows went along side of them in their shallops, and made prisoners of them, their wives and children, who could neither fight nor fly. Then, with their living cargo, they put to sea, and had run into the Tamboe islands for water and provisions; when I happily, in turn, and as unexpectedly, surprised them, and released the captives, of whom I found nearly two hundred in the different proas. These proas I placed in their possession, brought them here, and landed my Beajus near their own country.'

I must observe that we were now anchored in a port on the south of the Island of Borneo, in a bay formed by three very small islands, which were not inhabited, nor indeed habitable, the largest being less than a mile in circumference, and having a scanty supply of water. The channel between us and the main was scarcely a mile broad, and the passage blocked by an extensive shoal, on which the sea was always in an agitated state, and generally breaking. The grab lay completely land-locked; I had been beating about some days ere I could discover the place, although De Ruyter had been most particular in laying it down, with written and minute directions.

To add to the calamities of the schooner, many of our men had been suddenly seized with putrid fever, and dysentry, attributed to the pestilential atmosphere on the night when we were anchored off the fatal shore of the morass. Some died within four and twenty hours after they were attacked; and the instant their last struggles were over, we were compelled to throw their bodies in the sea, to be rid of the stench exhaling from them, which was insufferable before they died. And all these misfortunes were imputed to having begun our voyage on a Friday! Every individual in the schooner firmly believed in this, except myself. But superstitions believed in, are, in their effects, truths; therefore I never went to sea again on a Friday.

VOLUME III

CHAPTER I

A long, long kiss, a kiss of youth and love,
And beauty, all concentrating like rays
Into one focus, kindled from above;
Such kisses as belong to early days,
When heart, and soul, and sense, in concert move,
And the blood's lava, and the pulse a blaze,
Each kiss a heart-quake;—for a kiss's strength,
I think it must be reckon'd by its length.

BYRON

THE Beajus are supposed to be part of the aborigines of the immense island of Borneo. They have been driven to the interior, which is composed of hills and huge mountains, dark, rugged and precipitous. A chain of these mountains approached that part of the island, off which we lay; and stretching their roots, as it were, far out into the sea, rendered the approach dangerous. Had it not been for the little islands, like excrescences or suckers from the roots, which sheltered us, we could have found no anchorage there, nor within many leagues. The sea lies on both sides without port or pasturage, while the immense morass and high mountains form a barrier in-land, so that, with the exception of occasional marauders pillaging in proas a few scattered villages on a plain bordering on the morass, the Beajus here live undisturbed, in consideration of a tribute paid to a Malay settlement on the western coast. Left to be governed by their own chiefs, they live in patriarchal simplicity. Hunting and fishing are their principal occupations; nevertheless they have a sufficient quantity of rice, Indian corn, and some other grain, with abundance of fruits, roots, and herbs. The rainy season begins in April, and continues for more than half the year; and on the great morass, the boundary of their territory, it rains for ever, with frightful storms, thunder and lightning. Nothing living dares to enter, except wild beasts, which sometimes prowl thither. It was called the land of the destroying power, and believed to be peopled by demons, who there prepared all the evils in the world, and then directed their flight with them, whither they listed. To assuage the wrath of these destroyers, the Beajus made sacrifices and offerings. They believed in a good and greater power, but as he never did harm, they did not attempt to bribe him with offerings, or invoke his clemency. Their chiefs were elected by the old people. Every head of a family was despotic, and answerable for those belonging to him. Only for great crimes they were cited before a general assembly; and adultery, in either party, was considered the most heinous, and punished with death.

The good office De Ruyter had done these people was not forgotten. Their gratitude knew no limit. The two hundred, whom he had liberated, considered themselves his bond-slaves, doing him every service in their power, and rejecting payment. Some of them were continually alongside, and on board us, supplying fruits, fish, goats, poultry, and what else their country produced. They erected convenient huts, on the largest of the islands, for our sick and maimed, which were numerous in both vessels, under the superintendence of Scolpvelt, who always took care to be well supplied with medicines. Besides, he was a herbalist himself, and devoted his leisure hours to prowling about in search of herbs and plants, to distilling, making decoctions, and gathering balsams and gums, for which Borneo is famous. One of the Beajus' canoes was at his command, with which he made daily excursions on the coast.

For some time I was exclusively occupied in refitting the schooner; for which purpose I searched the woods, in the country of the Malays, for spars. The difficulty was in procuring those which possessed the requisite qualities of lightness, strength and elasticity; for, as to timber, there was enough to build fleets. One day, having pulled far along the coast, I landed in a small creek, within a little valley, inaccessible on the land side, owing to an abrupt mountain, and the number of very high trees, undergrown with jungle; while the bushes and canes were so woven together by enormous creepers, that it seemed as if nothing larger than a rat could pass. But seeing some pines, or a species of fir, which struck me would answer my purpose, provided I could arrive at them, I landed with Zela, and sent the boat on board to bring the carpenters with their tools. Although the schooner lay at some distance, the boat had a leading wind both ways, and, as she sailed remarkably well, I calculated she would return in three hours.

In the mean time we first examined the spot, to find an outlet, but in vain. We then strolled on the margin of the sea, in the small space which was open, gathering oysters and muscles; for abutments of overhanging rocks, impossible to climb, shut us in on both sides. While Zela was preparing coffee, I lay on the rocks, lulled by the monotonous waves, the crowing of the jungle cock, and the distant voice of the faoo, screaming shrilly in complaining notes. All who have mingled in the busy turmoil of life have felt the exquisite luxury, for there is none like it in the world's enjoyments, the balmy sensation while reposing alone, or, doubly sweet, with one loved companion, in a sheltered and secluded nook. There we can unpack the burthen with which our hearts are loaded, by thinking aloud, secure from observing eyes, unmocked by triumphant pity, or sneering self-conceited friends,— those officious prophets who foresee our misfortunes, warn us to avoid what is inevitable, and abandon us on finding them irremediable, salving their consciences with, 'Well! he rejected our counsel, and must take the consequences of his headstrong proceedings!'

Having finished our coffee, Zela laid her head on my arm, and pointed out a white speck on the waters, which she said was a canoe, and I contended it was our boat. We were betting which it would turn out to be. But, that I may not be accused thus early of a propensity for gambling, I must record that our stakes were only kisses; so that, whichever it was, boat or canoe, it only made the difference between giving and receiving,—yet a very great and important distinction there is between giving and receiving. Having been accounted learned and proficient in this abstruse branch of study, my opinion on this controverted question may be pronounced decisive. Certainly I was indefatigable in my application to the mystery; and had I followed mathematics or astronomy instead of kissing, (not that their utility to mankind admits a comparison,) Sir Isaac Newton and Napier would have been considered but as pioneers in science, clearing the path for my superior genius. Some curious arithmetician has demonstrated that a man, taking snuff once in ten minutes during the day, for the space of thirty years, will have been four years perpetually snuffing. Not only did I kiss every ten minutes during the day, but all night long, sleeping not to be subtracted; so that more than

X

half of my early life was dedicated to, what I then thought, the only thing very well worth doing, without grudging or grumbling, purely from instinct. I therefore, declaring it was our boat, insisted on Zela's kissing me; but, on nearing us, we perceived it was Van's canoe; upon which I was about to pay her kisses back again, when I heard a rustling amongst the jungle, and prepared my carbine, being concealed by a projection of rock. The faoo came nigher to us, and Zela whispered, 'Be cautious,—it is a tiger! for that bird always gives notice of his approach.'

CHAPTER II

Upon a weeded rock this old man sat,
And his white hair was awful, and a mat
Of weeds were cold beneath his cold thin feet.

*   *   *   *   *

Then up he rose, like one whose tedious toil
Had watched for years in forlorn hermitage.

KEATS

I PUT a ball, over the large shot, in my carbine, and making a rest on the rocks for my gun, I determined not to fire till he attacked us; then, if I missed killing him, we were to swim out to the boat, which was rapidly approaching. Still as we were hidden, I hoped we should escape undiscovered. Taking my cap off, I peeped over the rock; the rustling noise in the bushes continued; when, to my astonishment, I saw, not a tiger, but a gray, hairy old man. He removed the bushes, and, after cautiously surveying the place, stooped down, and came out at the opening of the little creek. I was about to rise, but Zela held me down, and signed to me not to move or speak. When he stood up, he was the strangest looking figure I had ever seen, tall, lean and emaciated, not at all resembling any people within my knowledge. He was remarkably long limbed, and had no other weapon than a large club, such as is used by the South Sea Islanders. His face was black, with grisly hair, and deeply furrowed with wrinkles. His figure seemed bent with age and infirmities, yet he walked with long strides over the rough ground. There was a wild and sullen malignity of expression in his eyes, more like those of a demon than of a man. When he came to the margin of the sea, in an opposite direction to us, he seated himself on a rock, took up a sharp stone, knocked off the limpets and muscles, and swallowed them fast and voraciously. After this, he gathered a large leaf, put a heap of oysters and muscles on it, and folded it up. Then, looking towards the sea, with his eyes fixed for some time on the boat, he washed his hands, and returned, somewhat more nimbly, to the place whence he had issued, and disappeared.

'I'll follow him!' I cried, and jumped up.

Zela urged me to forbear; 'For,' said she, 'he is a *jungle admee*, more dangerous, cunning, and cruel than any wild beast.'

'He is alone,' I replied, 'and surely I am a match for him. Besides, I shall find a path which will be useful.'

Saying this, I went after him, and discovered, upon crawling under the thick kantak bush, a narrow winding path, a good deal foot-worn. I heard the grisled old savage before me; and, unseen myself, from time to time, caught glimpses of him. Several branches of trees, under which he could not pass without stooping, he beat down, or broke off with a blow of his club. Zela, who could not be induced to stay, followed close at my heels. We tracked him for a short distance through the wood in silence. He then branched off to the right, in the direction of the great morass, passed the channel of a mountain-stream, ascended a bank, and then, coming to a rock fifteen or sixteen feet in perpendicular height, he climbed up an old moss-grown pine-tree. When he had mounted the stem of the tree, somewhat higher than the rock, he clung with his arms and legs to a horizontal branch; and, as a sailor works himself along the stays of a mast, by alternately shifting his limbs, he arrived above the summit of the rock, when, suspending his body by his hands, he let himself gently down, and walked on.

We followed in the same manner, cautiously avoiding his seeing or hearing us. He crossed a ridge of rocks, comparatively open. It was here grew the pine-trees that I wanted. There was little or no underwood. The old man stopped, and looking attentively at a huge pine which had fallen from age, out of which, in its half-decomposed prostrate trunk, grew a line of young pines, thus perpetuating its species, he appeared to be measuring their length with a stick. He pulled up four of them by the roots, stripped them of their branches, secured them together with a fillet of wire-grass, put them on his left shoulder, and proceeded onwards to a small space, in which were the wild mango and benana. He examined the fruit of them, and smelt them to find if they were ripe; and gathering a plantain, which did not readily peel, he threw it away. He now made many turns, we following him as close as we could, without risking discovery, till he came to an open piece of ground, which had been neatly levelled, the grass, weeds, and bushes cleared away, and in one corner, under the shelter of a remarkably thick and beautiful tree covered with white blossoms, I observed a neat hut, built of canes wattled together.

I looked round with admiration, marvelling at the good taste with which the recluse had selected a place for his hermitage. On one side was a rocky bank, covered with tamarind and wild-nutmeg, perfuming the air. There was an excavation in the lower part of the bank, partially screened by three tall, straight-stemmed betel-trees, with their shining, silvery-white bark; they shone resplendently-beautiful, and looked like the Graces of the forest. At the back of the hermitage was a wild waste of jungle, in which I distinguished tamarind, nutmeg, cactus, acacia, banyans, toon, and the dark foliage of the bamboo.

The old man, having laid the bundle of young fir-trees against his dwelling, stooped down and entered the low door on his hands and knees; for the palmetta-leaved roof came down to within two feet of the ground. While I was attentively surveying and marking the spot, determined on visiting it again, and endeavouring to look into the hut, under cover of a thick bush on the margin of the cleared space, a rustle among the bushes made me turn my eyes to the ground, when I saw the diamond-like eye, sparkling from the black, square head, of a cobra-di-capella. It was crossing the path immediately where Zela stood, and seemed to have stopped to gaze at her. Forgetting everything but her danger, I shouted out, and caught her up in my arms. The snake, without appearing alarmed, slowly retreated into the opposite bushes. Zela exclaimed, 'Oh! *jungle admee!*'

Placing her down, I turned round, and was startled at seeing him advance with his club firmly clenched in both hands, and swinging over his head, like a quarter-staff. The gaunt old man, by the increased malignancy of his eye, the grinding of his teeth, and the wrinkles on his narrow brow, was evidently proceeding to attack me. My carbine, cocked, was in my left hand, but ere I could get it to my shoulder, he made one huge stride, and his club was descending on my head, when, stepping a pace back, I discharged my piece under his left arm-pit, lodging the whole contents in his body. He sprung up into the air, and, before I could retire, fell slap upon me. I thought, as I fell prostrate, that the brute would certainly finish me, and called out to Zela to run to the boat and save herself; but she was forcing a boar-spear into his side, and answered, 'He is quite dead; he don't move; get up!'

With some difficulty I extricated myself, and saw that my ball had passed right through him, entering his heart, as I suppose, which had caused that convulsive spring. He bled profusely.

We then went into his house. It differed little in the interior from those of the other natives of the island, only it had a greater degree of neatness and appearance of comfort. At one end of it was a partition, very ingeniously fastened, as a security, I conjectured, against thieves when he was absent. There was good store of roots and fruits, carefully spread out to prevent their rotting. It might have been mistaken for the abode of a mangy mongrel Scotch philosopher.

Hearing musquets discharged, and voices hallooing, I was surprised at finding we were much nearer the sea than I had anticipated; but on retracing our steps, I accounted for it, by the circuitous path the *jungle admee* had taken us to his abode. We hastened back to the beach, and found Van and his canoe. He had been directed to the spot by the men of our boat, which was now drawing nigh, induced to come from what they said of it; then, alarmed at not seeing us, together with the report of my carbine, he ordered musquets to be fired.

'Well met, Van,' said I, 'here I have procured you a magnificent subject to work upon.' I then told him of my encounter with the wild man.

'Where is he?' exclaimed Van.

As I led him to the spot, he eagerly followed close at my heels, and, when he approached the body, cried out, 'What! that? Why, that is not one of the order Bimana,—of the genus *homo*, or man; but of the second order, Quadrumana,—one of the tribe of *Simeæ* —apes, monkeys, baboons;—narrow pelvis, lengthened falx, long arms, short thumbs, flat buttocks. 'This,' continued Van, as he turned him over, 'is an orang-outang; the first full-grown one I ever saw, and really very like the genus *homo*. But feel,—he has thirteen ribs. There is little other distinction between him and

you: Buffon[1] says they have no sentiment of religion, and what
have you? they are as brave and fierce as you are; and are very
ingenious, which you are not. Besides, they are a reflective and
considerate set of beings; and have the best government in the
world: they divide a country into districts; are never guilty of
invasion; and never infringe on the rights of others. All this is
because they have no meddling priests, kings, or aristocrats. They
are ruled by democratic chiefs, go about in bodies, build houses,
and live well. This one has been refractory—a heavy sinner; and
see, he is diseased, has ulcers and a goitre on his throat. There are
also many wounds on his body;—yes, he has been refractory, and
doubtless banished from the community of his fellow creatures.
I'll preserve his skeleton, and present it to the chemical college
at Amsterdam. It is a rare species.'

Leaving Van to work on the orang-outang we went to examine
the timber, and cleared a path to the beach. At sunset we returned
to our boats, as the place was declared by the natives to be infested
by tigers and serpents.

CHAPTER III

Millions there lift, at Freedom's thrilling call,
Ten thousand standards wide; they load the blast,
Which bears one sound of many voices past,
And startles on his throne their sceptered foe.

SHELLEY

BOTH nations and individuals, possessing qualities most particularly to be admired, I have remarked are most generally hated
and abused. The mass are exclusively occupied in loving and benefiting themselves, in slandering the characters of others, and
extracting something from their wealth. All who are ambitious of
their good word, must lie to them, fool with them, and do them
homage:

'Desert does nothing; valiant, wise, and virtuous,
Are things that walk by without bread or breeches.'

The Malays, scattered about on the sea-coast of India, and its finest islands, are, by the general voice, pronounced to be the most fierce, treacherous, ignorant, and inflexible of barbarians;

'Which any print of goodness will not take,
Being capable of all ill.'

De Ruyter, who had no faith in public clamour, and was never biassed by the opinions of others, when it was possible to judge for himself, soon set me right in regard to the character of this much abused people. I found he did them but justice in saying they were true to their words, generous to prodigality, and of invincible courage. All the attempts of European and Indian kings to subdue this people have failed. If any portion of their country is wrung from them by superior force, with spirits unsubdued they abandon it, maintaining their unconquerable love of personal freedom, and gain a footing by conquest in neighbouring states or islands. On the coast of Malabar, and the three great Sunda islands, they are the most numerous. They are the only people in India who have preserved their national character and liberty amidst contending powers; and it arises from their love of liberty being greater than their love of any particular spot of earth which has chanced to be their birth-place. There, where they can be free, be it rock or sandy waste, is their country. They are simple in their wants, hardy, brave, and adventurous; such a race can find few parts of the world where they will not contrive to exist. Like the cocoa-nut, they are never far from the sea; and, like the Arabs, they are not over scrupulous in appropriating the superfluities of wealthy strangers to their own uses. Who that lives in want does not desire to supply himself from the rich?—cowards beg, the cunning pilfer, a brave man takes by force. The wealth of India and Asia, obtained by force and stratagem, is conveyed along the shores of the Malays towards Europe; and they would be the most besotted of barbarians, if they did not help themselves to a portion of it. They do so; and though they have been pursued, massacred by thousands, their country ravaged, their vessels destroyed, yet their numbers augment, and their piracies, as they are called, increase instead of being diminished, for their war-canoes are widely spread over the Indian ocean. They have several settlements on the western shore of Borneo, which lies very conveniently for marauding on the Chinese trade. Portuguese, Dutch, English, and others have, from time to time, formed settlements on various parts of the island, the King of Borneo protecting them the while, as the industrious bee is protected; but when they had established a factory, and filled it with treasures, they were smoked out, and plundered. They are now abandoned to their fate by church missionary and merchant militant, the island having no roads, few ports, and plenty of swamps, jungle, rivers and mountains.

The Moorish king, who resides at the capital of the island, Borneo Proper, has neither command nor influence beyond his own province. Chinese, Macassars, Javanese, and adventurers from many other lands, have also established themselves there, and live independently; while the Chinese have monopolised most of the trade of the island. To return to my friends, the Malays; —a settlement of these neighboured the part of the coast where we were lying, and as De Ruyter was partial to them, having many of that nation in his vessel, we were soon on the best terms; for we were weary of the Beajus, a far inferior race.

A Malay chieftain was frequently with us, and, on our expressing a wish for a tiger hunt, he willingly assented, though it is not common with them to seek tigers for sport, as they merely attack them in their own defence, or to preserve their property. For this sport I had long been eager; and, being now in a country in which they most abounded, I could hardly restrain my impatience.

I must observe that, while we were lying here, De Ruyter occasionally got the grab under weigh, and went out to see if he could pick up any thing, or gain intelligence of any thing at sea. Meantime our repairs on board the schooner, (thanks to my friend, the orang,) proceeded rapidly, as I had found spars. We sometimes made hunting parties on shore, to kill deer, wild hogs, goats, and, at times, buffaloes, in order to supply our vessels with fresh meat, and not to infringe on our sea-stock. Besides which, there was an abundance of fine fish on the coast; a party of men was every day sent to haul the sean—so that we lived well and free of expense. Rice, coffee, tobacco, Indian corn, and other grains, we procured, by barter, from the natives. De Ruyter's intention was to await the sailing of the China fleet homeward bound, and, if possible, to attack them.

Having time on our hands, we were anxious to see the interior of the island. We had heard the natives frequently talk of the ruins of an ancient city, skirting the great morass, and that it was the abode of tigers and other wild beasts. An excursion to that place was quickly planned. We always kept our vessels in the best order, and omitted no precaution against surprise, by sea or land. In general, either he or I remained in charge of the vessels. On the island, where we had landed our sick, we had mounted two guns and built a battery, which commanded the schooner. All our men were kept constantly employed. Discontent, drunken brawls, and, sometimes, quarrels with the natives, gave us considerable vexation. But De Ruyter was better qualified than any man in the world for the service in which he was engaged; for, either by lenity, or by severe and summary punishment, he overawed the refractory, and tranquillised the discontented. He had a quick eye to see into the characters of men, and he employed great art in controlling them; a portion of which I acquired.

We now made preparations for our tiger hunt. The Malay chieftain was to accompany us, with a party of his followers; and he engaged to supply us with elephants. De Ruyter took twenty of the most untractable of his crew, well armed; and I a few picked men out of the schooner.

CHAPTER IV

> I saw a fury whetting a death-dart.
>
> KEATS

> Around, around, in ceaseless circles wheeling,
> With clang of wings and scream, the eagle sailed
> Incessantly, sometimes on high concealing
> Its lessening orbs, sometimes as if it failed
> Drooped through the air; and still it shrieked and wailed,
> And, casting back its eager head, with beak
> And talon unremittingly assailed
> The wreathed serpent, who did ever seek
> Upon his enemy's heart a mortal wound to wreak.
>
> SHELLEY

THERE is more of the spirit of chivalry among the Malays than among any other people. They are devoted to war, and to its inseparable accompaniment, women; these, with hawking and cock-fighting, formed the principal recreations of our Malay chieftain. One of the peculiarities of his character was a punctilious observance of the Malayan code of retaliation, surpassing the Jewish law of 'an eye for an eye, and a tooth for a tooth.' Indeed I doubt whether any thing in the records of the most heroic periods of chivalry, when crazy red-cross-knights ran tilting among the Saracens, dyeing their yellow sands red, can compete with our Hotspur of the east. In one of his voyages he touched at Batavia, to dispose of a cargo, when under the government of the Dutch, who are particular about the cleanliness of their houses, but as lousy and filthy as the Scotch in their persons and habits. A Hollander, in his arm-chair, with a yard of baked clay, well saturated with the essential oil of tobacco, and filled with No. 11 canestre, with a pottle of smoky skedam, experiences all he can imagine of paradise; and, ever careful to avoid polluting his dwelling, spits into the street. An unlucky delivery of this sort, out of the window of a Dutch house, fell, not refreshing as the dew of heaven, on the face of our chieftain, as he passed under the dwelling. He sought in vain the source whence his defilement sprung, 'and passion having his best judgment collied,' he drew his creese, and ran a-muck through the streets, attacking all he met. Many a bayonet of a Dutch sepoy let him blood; the garrison was in arms; when, after stabbing fifteen or sixteen persons, he threw himself into the sea, regained his proa, and escaped.

Another time a vessel from Bombay had anchored off the coast where his father was chieftain, who bartered with its owner the produce of the country for Birmingham musquets, warranted to endure for ever, hatchets, adzes, and other tools. Ere the vessel sailed, one of the musquets, on the first discharge, burst in his father's hands, and a piece of the barrel, entering his brain, killed him. His dutiful son called together the immediate followers of his father's house, boarded the vessel in the night, and succeeded in taking possession of her; when, with his own hand, and his father's knife, he severed the heads from every individual of the crew, made a funeral pile, placed his father's body on it, bedecked with a triple crown of thirty heads, and fired it.

To one of the feats I was witness, on his first day of our march. A brutal follower, a Tiroon, acting as mahout (conductor) to the little elephant on which Zela was seated, while in the rear of the party, made a sign to the sagacious beast, as he was passing a wretched man, who came out of the ruins of a tank to beg, to kill him. The elephant did so. I was talking to the chieftain, when Zela's voice made me turn round. She pointed to the object, which I had not before observed; it was a foul and hideous leper, the body perforated thick as a honeycomb with ulcers, so bloated, swollen, and plastered with leaves and filthy rags, that it bore no resemblance to a human being, with the exception of the face, the lineaments of which were spared by the fell disease, and shewed that he was thus struck and blasted in the dawn of manhood.

The Tiroon mahout was of a race who delighted in shedding blood. They make human sacrifices to their gods, and to the ladies of their love. No Tiroon can marry until he has presented his bride with a gory head, no matter whose, friend's or foe's, taken in battle, or pilfered from a sleeping guest; a head must be the first gift. A fiery lover who presents a bouquet of heads to a blushing fair one is not to be resisted. I suppose this to be a natural feeling among gentle women, as it is a general one, from the Roman ladies who viewed in ecstacy the wounds and agonies of expiring gladiators, to our modern fair ones, who are always to be won by fighting.

But to return to my friend the chieftain. As soon as he was made acquainted with the wanton murder committed by the Tiroon on the outcast and despised leper, he seized on a mahout's stick, and began beating him with it. The wild Tiroon drew a poisoned arrow from his belt, and attempted to stab his chastiser, who, on seeing it, became infuriated. He struck the arrow from his hand, drew his own creese, forced the fellow back against a tree, held him there in an erect posture with his left hand, and continually stabbed him with the weapon in his right, even long after life was extinct. His fury was indescribable; and himself, covered with the Tiroon's blood, glistening on his raven hair and fiery face, looked like an avenging demon.

I said to De Ruyter, who had drawn near me, 'My carbine must be in readiness;—the fellow is mad with rage, and will be running a-muck here.'

The chieftain, wearied with stabbing, cast the mangled body of the Tiroon beside the leper; then looking up to the air, he gave a yell of delight, pointed his crimsoned creese upwards, and exclaimed, 'There they are!—Did I not say so?'

Looking up, I saw a long-winged haggard hawk, of the largest species, battling with a raven, which had been attracted by the scent of blood to the spot where we were. His watchful foe had espied him, and taken the field against him. The chieftain averred the hawk was the leper's spirit, the raven the Tiroon's, and watched the conflict with intense interest. Both, wheeling upwards, ascended till they were scarcely distinguishable. They looked no bigger than the motes in a sun-beam; but the eagle-eyed chieftain vociferated, 'Now the leper is uppermost, and is descending on the spirit of his black assassin!'

The hawk, having in spiral motion achieved the upper flight, fell like a thunder-bolt on the raven, stunned him with the blow, clutched him in his talons, folded him in his wings, and, the hawk undermost, they tumbled down like a black ball, till within a short distance from the earth. The hawk then unfolded his wings, but loosened not his talons till close to the ground, when the force of the air, acting on the wings, brought the hawk uppermost, and the raven fell on the earth motionless, but, as it seemed by his low harsh croaking, not quite dead. The chieftain clapped his hands, went to the spot close by the dead bodies, took up a stone, and smashed the raven's scull. The hawk took flight, and perched triumphantly on the top branch of a very high tree, and appeared as if awaiting our departure to begin his feast.

Under the conduct of this fiery chieftain we had placed ourselves. I must remark that the issue of the battle perfectly tranquillised him; and we resumed our march in harmony. With the exception of these gusts of passion, he was kind-hearted, courteous, affable, and exceedingly attentive to us his guests. He had great natural sagacity in overcoming every difficulty which impeded us, held his followers in complete subjection, and took every precaution not to be surprised by the people through whose districts we were passing. His instincts were exquisitely acute from constant exercise, as the civilized are dull from want of use. He could distinguish objects correctly, ere our eyes could reach them; and his hearing was quicker than a dog's. Our progress, however, was slow; the elephants were often compelled to clear us a path through the jungle, and we lost entire days in searching for passes round or through the swamps, and pathless forests. There were few signs of the abodes of man, and there was neither corn nor culture; but we had an ever-varying succession of beasts and birds.

CHAPTER V

There the large olive rains its amber store
In marble fonts; there grain, and flower, and fruit,
Gush from the earth until the land runs o'er;
But there too many a poison-tree has root,
And midnight listens to the lion's roar,
And long, long deserts scorch the camel's foot,
Or heaving whelm the helpless caravan,
And as the soil is, so the heart of man.

BYRON

DURING the heat of the day, and in the evening, while lying by, we practised with single ball on deer, wild hogs, and wild pea-cocks, which last flew over our heads in thousands, to seek their roosting-places in the woods. On the fifth day we drew near our sporting-ground, on the south-east side of the island. While in this neighbourhood, De Ruyter cautioned us to smoke incessantly; and knowing its efficacy, I made Zela smoke a small hooka. My argola was never allowed to go out; I was mounted on a huge dromedary, and the mahout, on the animal's neck, carried a pot of live charcoal, and an ample sack of tombackie. During this excursion I witnessed the admirable effects of tobacco as a preventative against fever. All those who did not use it suffered from fever, giddiness, vomiting, spitting of blood, and dysentery. Even those who were not accustomed to it, and could only be induced to occasionally smoke a cigar, had slight attacks of fever. Chewing the weed appeared of little service. The hooka and callian, by continually exciting the action of the lungs, as the smoke must be drawn down to the chest, were effectual preservatives. Then, if possible, we avoided sleeping under trees, or near jungle. The Malays always cut down the jungle, and set it on fire; which both cleared the ground, and purified the atmosphere.

We left the woods, and came to a large extent of plain, with nothing on it but enormous reeds, grass, and nauseously smelling weeds, that grew as high as young fir-trees, mingled thickly with rattans. Paths had been cleared by wild elephants, which enabled us to pass this otherwise impenetrable wilderness. It was bounded by mountains, forests of the most stupendous trees I had ever beheld, and, on our right, by a low ridge of rocks, in which direction we bent our course. From the centre of this ridge there arose a mound of earth, like a green island; and the ridge of rocks branching out on each side, looked like piers built to connect it with the mountains. On this spacious mound were said to be the ruins of an immense Moorish city, once called the city of kings, —but now the city of the tigers. The plain was called the plain of the elephants.

We followed the elephants' tracks for many a weary mile, and saw elk-deer and other animals, but no elephants. At last we came to the ridge of rocks, and, having ascended them, we looked down on a black and fetid morass which extended further than the eye could reach, and lay considerably lower than the plain which we had crossed. The green and wooded hill, to which we were bound, was still a day's march from us. There was a terrible gloom hanging over the black swamp: nothing grew there but dark marsh-reeds, with high and silky tufts of sooty black, which waved to and fro, like the nodding plumes upon a hearse, though there was not a breath of air where we stood. It indeed looked like the murky abode of all evil; and when the night came, and the land-wind arose, and swept over it, illumined by faint, pale-blue lightning, it seemed like a black and agitated sea beneath us. I thought how nearly I had been cast on it, and doomed to inevitable destruction.

After having been threatened with a locked-jaw from tearing and tugging at a half-roasted wild peacock, I lay down in my tent on a tiger-skin, and put my carbine under my head, while Zela nestled by my side, and drew a tanned elk-skin over us. I slept better than those lodged more luxuriously, till towards morning, when I was with difficulty awakened by Zela. Owing to the wild and perilous life she had led from her infancy, she could awake at the smallest noise from the deepest sleep. I have seen her open her eyes at the musquito which I had prevented from alighting on her brow, as it flew, humming in anger, round her head. This night she was awakened by a rustling sound, and, seeing my legs were bare, was about to cover them, when she perceived a large venomous serpent move from under the skin, and leisurely crawl over my stretched-out legs. Fortunately, I slept like death, and felt it not. She had presence of mind, lay leaning on her arm, held her breath, and watched its motions by the light of the lamp, and the glowing embers of a fire, at a little distance from the tent-door, as a preventative against the foul vapours of the morass. The serpent, attracted by the heat, had left its cold bed among the rocks, and passed directly towards it. Had I made the slightest motion, or had she then given the alarm, he would have wounded me, and mortally. When it was a few yards from the tent, she aroused me, and the instant I was made sensible of the danger, I jumped up, fearful that some of the people sleeping without might be attacked. I bade Zela awaken those on the side of the tent, and followed the serpent, which was gliding onwards. It heard my approach, erected its crest, and looked back at me. My carbine was loaded with large shot, and, being close to it, I lodged the contents under its head. A man sleeping close to the spot, sprang up, and then fell prostrate: I thought I had killed him.

The chieftain gave the alarm, and rushed towards me with his followers. I pointed to the writhing monster, struggling amidst the embers. At the report of the gun, he had anticipated a battle of some sort; but when he saw what it was, he appeared disappointed, and said, 'Pshaw! it is only a chickta? It is wrong to waste powder, and awaken people, to kill troublesome worms! Why, there are thousands of them here. This is the way to kill them!' At which he struck his spear through its head, and held it in the embers. The snake wound its body round and round the shaft till its tail came near his hand. The chieftain then unfolded it, and said, 'If you like to hold it here for ten minutes, till well roasted, you'll find it excellent eating!'

When dead, he dropped it into the fire—covered it with the ashes, and saying, 'We'll breakfast on it,' returned with the others to their sleep.

De Ruyter, Zela, and myself, not desirous of being again disturbed by such troublesome interlopers, sat by the fire, and talked the night away. Our conversation, after a while, veered round from the frightful and supernatural aspect of the scene of our encampment, to tiger-hunting. De Ruyter, who had a strong passion for the sport, and had been celebrated for his exploits in the upper provinces of India, said—

'Tiger-hunting, as practised in India, is little better than killing cats; nor are there so many risks attending it as in fox-hunting. The sportsmen, and there are generally twenty of them, with twice that number of elephants, encaged in the houdahs, each of them having half a dozen loaded double-barrelled guns, charged as fast by servants as they can be fired, are perched in the same security as if on a tree, deer-shooting. A mahout sometimes gets a scratch, but it is the noble elephant that bears the brunt of the battle, and every thing depends on his sagacity, courage and steadiness. If he won't stand, becomes frightened, and goes off, then indeed the sportsman's life is in some jeopardy; for a mad bull, or our Malay running a-muck, is nothing to a helmless elephant.'

CHAPTER VI

Cedars, and yews, and pines, whose tangled hair,
Is matted in one solid roof of shade
By the dark ivy's twine. At noonday here
'Tis twilight, and at sunset blackest night.

SHELLEY

The brindled lioness led forth her young,
That she might teach them how they should assuage
Their inborn thirst of blood.

Ibid.

'BUT hunting lions on foot,' continued De Ruyter, 'or lions hunting by themselves, is a noble sight, as I once witnessed. Unlike the crouching and dastardly tiger, they do not lie in ambush to surprise their prey at night, but take the field with the dawn—drag cover, and give chase to the first animal that breaks it, be it what it may, while the forest trembles with their thundering voices. I had been to meet a prince of the family of Bulmar Singh, near Rhotuk,[1] in the neighbourhood of which I was detained some days, attended by a small body of followers, with half a dozen of the little mountain-elephants, on a march towards Kamoon, the country of the Himalaya Mountains, inhabited by a wild race called Sikhs. We went by secret and circuitous paths through an immense tract of country, covered with forest-trees and jungle. I never lived so long without seeing the sun as when toiling through that dreary world of shade. Not a ray could have penetrated it since the creation. Even the winds, wandering vagrants as they are, could find no entrance there. In that everlasting twilight, great owls and vampyre-bats gamboled about all day long, like swallows in spring. The birds and beasts, which were very few, lacked their natural dyes to distinguish them, all partaking of the monotonous hue of the yellow, mossy, and mouldy trees and plants. Fauns, hares, foxes, and jackals were of a brindled grey. There were toad-stools and fungi grouped in knots, which in colour and size so closely resembled lions couching with their cubs, that we, knowing they abounded there, prepared to defend ourselves. Parasitical creepers, gasping, like myself, for air, had plunged their wiry roots in the deep, dingy, vegetable soil, till their trunks swelled to the bulk of the teak-tree, up which they had climbed to redden their heads and spread their scarlet flowers in the sun; then, as if to monopolize all, they extended themselves on the tops of the highest trees, fanned by the air, and basking in sunshine. Oh, how I envied them!

'You have seen this on a smaller scale: imagine, then, my delight when I, accustomed from my youth to a boundless expanse of sea and sky, left this gloomy twilight, and burst from the belt of death—for so it is properly named—into broad, open, unobscured light. I blinked like the owl in the sun, shouted in ecstacy, and respired the free air as you did when you emerged from your plunge off the frigate's yard-arm. The scene looked like a lake fenced by a forest. To the east, the mountains arose to a stupendous height; they bordered the Chinese empire. There was a clear stream winding through this narrow and beautiful valley. After crossing it, we came to the bed of a mountain-torrent, deep, and of great breadth, but at that time dry, with the exception of a few pools of water. In the middle of this bed of gravel, interspersed with pieces of rock, was a small island formed by a rock, and enlarged by fragments which had been brought down by the torrent, and which adhered to it in natural arches, overgrown with moss, flowers, and shrubs. The security of the position, added to its beauty, tempted us to make it our place of halt and repose. I was then young and romantic as you are, and, after passing through the dreary gloom of that forest, thought I could have dwelt there all my life. The night was clear and bright, and long before it was day, I was up smoking my callian, and planning a shooting bungalo.

'The transition from night to day came on so gently that I did not notice it; yet, in the forest, I could see it was midnight. A herd of wild buffaloes, the largest I had ever seen, came out to graze within a little more than musket-shot from us. Suddenly I sprung

Y

on my feet at hearing a confused noise, like the rumbling of a thunder-storm, or distant guns at sea. The woods seemed in motion: jackals, foxes, and dappled deer came bounding out of the forest; the herd of black buffaloes ceased to graze, and turned towards the place whence the noise proceeded. A large flock of glittering peacocks, and other birds, flew screaming over our heads. A pelican that I had watched making prize of a snake, dropped it within a yard of my feet, and flew away. Our little wire-haired elephants, feeding on the shrubs beneath us, looked terri-fied, and their keepers left them, and crawled up the rocks. I watched the opening in the dark forest, which was half screened by thick and thorny bushes, when presently a mohr of the elk-kind burst cover, and, with one long, magnificent bound, appeared in the plain. In his stature he was far beyond those which are known in Europe, and his twisted horns were long as that Malay's spear. At the same instant, a single, clear, deep, terrific roar, like a burst of thunder, announced the hunting lion. He forced his way through bush and briar, with his nose to the ground, followed by four others. On entering the plain, he seemed for some moments endeavouring to catch the scent in silence, his nose always to the ground. Having, as it appeared, hit it, he again gave a roar, which was now echoed by all the others; and, pursuing the track of the stag, he started off at a long gallop, the rest following close in a line at his heels. I remarked, if any of them attempted to break the line, or pass him, he checked them with his voice, which be-came deeper and more growling.

'The elk, taking the upper ground, went at an eagle's speed along the margin of the river, leaving the lions far behind. In attempting to leap the river from a ledge of rock, the opposite bank gave way, and he rolled in; then, wading down, he stopped an instant, as if to bathe and brace his limbs, the voices of the lions now in full chorus nearing him. He ascended a slope, and, crossing, came towards us in the deep, dry channel of the torrent.

'I should have observed that the leading lion, when he passed through the herd of buffaloes, took no other notice of them than as they appeared to have puzzled him in regaining the scent of the stag. The buffaloes stood their ground, without budging to make way for the lions, as if fearless of attack; and my guides assured me these animals are more than a match for the fiercest lion, and that any one of them could kill two or three tigers. However that may be, as the lion passed through the line of these huge oxen, his grisly and erect mane, and shaggy tail, waved above them. It was clear he hunted by scent, and not by sight; instead of crossing the river in the nearest direction to where the stag now was, he nosed him to the spot where he had leaped, then wading to the opposite bank where the stag had fallen, he also followed the course of the stream, ascended the slope, and, ever in the track of his prey, crossed into the torrent's bed.

'In all probability the poor stag had received some injury from his fall. His speed decreased, whilst that of the lions was augmented, and their voices grew louder as they neared the chace. The stag had passed the rocky ledge on which I stood, soon followed by the fell pack. I had a good view of them: the first was an old, gaunt brute, his black skin shining through his thin, starred, reddish hair; his tail was bare and draggled, and the hair on his mane was clotted together; his eyes looked dim and blood-shot; his huge lower jaw was down, and his tongue hung out like a wearied dog's. He, however, kept the lead, followed by a lioness, and three male cubs, almost fully grown. The stag now made attempts to ascend the bank, as if to regain the jungle, but the loose shingle gave way, and he lost much ground. He seemed also, as the chace gained on him, to be panic-struck by their roars; and, again falling when he had ascended three parts of the steep aclivity, he was unable to rise. The roaring of the lions was magnificent, as the head one, erecting his mane, and lashing his sides with his tail, bounded in on him with a mighty spring. Then with one paw on his body, he growled the others off, and leisurely began his breakfast, his family stealing aside with limbs and fragments which he tore away and scattered about.

'But here comes our wild Malay chieftain; so finish your coffee, and let us be moving to the city of kings,—or of wild beasts,—for they are the same. What glorious sport it would be, to hunt tigers with the souls of kings within them!'

CHAPTER VII

Amid the desolation of a city
Which was the cradle, and is now the grave
Of an extinguished people, so that pity
Weeps o'er the shipwrecks of oblivion's wave.

SHELLEY'S MS.

The tigers leap up;
A loud, long, hoarse cry
Bursts at once from their vitals tremendously.

Ibid.

As we approached the hill, there was an undulating ground, the soil red, with low jungle, bearing red and yellow berries in profusion. Bustards, large flocks of cranes, herons, and sea-birds were in the air. Jackals, foxes, and several animals I had not seen before, crossed our path. We had glimpses of herds of wild elephants and buffaloes, grazing on the plain we had passed. At noon we were stopped by a river, broad, muddy, and shallow, which doubtless floods the upper plain during the rainy season; that is, for seven or eight months during the year; it then must force a passage into the morass below. After being a long time detained, the elephants forded it, when we rested for the night; or rather we did not rest, for we were so tormented with stinging vermin that none of us could sleep. The next day we ascended (as it is called) the haunted hill; which the natives hold in such superstitious awe, that, in all probability, we were, for centuries, the first who had disturbed the hallowed precincts of ogres and spirits, confidently reported to reside there. Remnants indeed there were of a city of some sort. De Ruyter said they were Moorish. There were large masses of stone, choked-up tanks, and indications of where wells had once been, but almost entirely concealed by thick bushes, dank weeds, creepers, and other vegetation, flourishing in profusion. Wherever it was penetrable, it bore the foot-prints of so many wild animals, that there was enough to check the hitherto insatiable thirst of dry and musty antiquaries.

We pitched our tents on a rocky part of the hill free from jungle, lighted fires, roasted a young stag, commenced arrangements for the morrow's sport, and slept. Before the dawn, the restless Malay chieftain was calling up his followers, and preparing the elephants, of which he had six. Soon after it was light, every thing was in readiness, and we set forward. Zela, who insisted on accompanying us, was mounted on her small elephant, and encaged in the only covered houdah, ours being all open. We beat about in vain; for though we met with tigers' foot-marks in many of the open places, near pools of standing water, the high grass and thick bushes prevented our tracing them to cover. We found, however, abundance of smaller game; deer, wild hogs, and a variety of birds. De Ruyter having carefully surveyed the neighbourhood, came in at night, and told us he had tracked three tigers to a thick jungle, near which he had found the bones of an elk-deer, recently killed by them.

With this promise of sport, we started in the morning in great glee; and, as we thought, well prepared for the attack. After riding about two miles, we descended to the plain, and came to an exceedingly thick jungle, with thorny bushes and canes. Around us was the plain covered with very high jungle grass, and dank weeds, with bushes scattered here and there, but few timber trees. De Ruyter conducted us to the spot where he had discovered the stag's bones, surrounded by moist and torn-up earth, and trampled grass; thence we had no difficulty in tracing the tiger's huge paws into the patch of jungle. Here De Ruyter divided our party, so as to block up the only apparently accessible outlets, made by wild beasts; and by these openings we were to enter. The greater proportion of our party was on foot, and seemingly as unconcerned as if going in to hunt weasels. I left Zela, seated in her houdah, at the opening of the wood, guarded by four of her own Arabs.

De Ruyter and myself dismounted to clear a passage; the Malays were divided into two parties; and we were backed by our sailors, whom we cautioned to be careful in the use of their fire-arms, as more was to be feared from accidents with them, than from the tigers. De Ruyter expressed great doubts of our elephants' facing the tiger, but it was necessary to try them. In our progress towards the bushes we turned out many deer, hares, and wild cats. We saw also ruins, said to be those of a Moorish palace. Nothing but the sagacity of the elephants could have steered us clear of broken masses of buildings, chasms, and walls overgrown with dank verdure. It was a wild and haunted-looking place, which awed even the sailors in their boisterous mirth, and silenced the ribaldry and obscene threatening of the Malays. The low trumpeting sound and foot-stamping of our elephants gave notice that the tiger's den was near. A vaulted ruin was before us; there was a rustling amongst the bushes; De Ruyter said, 'Be steady, my lad!' and a tiger, the first I had ever faced, finding his passage blocked up, charged us. We fired together, I know not with what effect; for both our elephants slued round, and ran away wild with fear. My mahout threw himself off, and a branch of a tree struck me off. I heard a tremendous war-whoop, and fire kept up on all sides. De Ruyter's elephant fell into a half-choked well; but, with his wonted self-possession, he extricated himself.

Leaving the elephants to their fate, we determined not to lose the sport. De Ruyter thought there were more tigers in the den, and we went on foot to drive them out. We got some of the men together, and proceeded to the spot, to which we were directed by the abominable stench, and the dried bones scattered about. The bushes were cleared away, and we heard, as we drew near, back to back, forcing our way onwards, low muttering growls and sharp snarls. 'Stand close!' exclaimed De Ruyter, 'there is a tigress with her whelps;—have a care;—don't fire, my lads, till she breaks cover, and fire low.'

A whelp, three parts grown, first came forth to charge us. De Ruyter, expecting the old one would follow, reserved his fire, and cautioned me to do the same. The whelp looked frightened, and slunk away, crouching under a thick bush, where it remained snarling, and thither the other whelps followed. The mother's growls became terrific; a shot at one of the whelps brought her out, lashing her sides, and foaming with rage. She rushed right on us; I fired both barrels; we then retreated a few paces. The wounded brute staggered after us, and when rising to spring, De Ruyter, who had still reserved his fire, shot her right through the heart. While I was charging my gun, one of the whelps, already wounded, drove against me, and knocked me down; when De Ruyter, with as much coolness as if he had been pigeon-shooting, put his rifle to its ear, and almost blew its head off. Mean time the sailors kept up a fire, till the balls were flying about our heads, on the remaining whelps, which were stealing away wounded. 'Let us stand behind this rock,' said De Ruyter; 'a sailor uses a musquet as he does a horse,—he bears down all before him.'

A Malay came from the chieftain to tell us the other part of the jungle was alive with tigers—that they had already killed two, and that one of their men was dead. There was now as much noise and confusion as in a naval battle, or at the sacking of a city. I observed, however, that tigers were not such formidable opponents as I had imagined. They lay close and crouching in the long grass, or under the bushes, and were as difficult to get up as cats or quail. It generally required a shot to move them; then they always essayed every means of escape through the thickest cover, and it was only when finding every passage blocked up, and smarting from wounds, that they rushed blindly and madly on their pursuers, forced by despair, like a cat or a rat. With nerve and self-possession, two men with double-barrelled guns would have little to fear, and might boldly go up to the mouth of the den of a tiger. This piece of thick jungle, interspersed with caverns, rocks, and ruins, plenty of water near, a great plain covered with high jungle-grass, and well supplied with a diversity of smaller animals to prey upon, was a favoured abode for tigers; and had they been endowed with reason, they could not have selected a spot on the island so admirably adapted for their residence; while their number and size indicated how well they thrived there. A great many escaped on the plain, where it was impossible to follow them. Several of our men were badly mauled by them, and more by falls: one of the Malays had his spine so injured, that he died in great agony.

CHAPTER VIII

And each hunter, panic-stricken,
Felt his heart with terror sicken,
Hearing the tremendous cry.—

——————Former years
Arise, and bring forbidden tears.
                    SHELLEY

UNEASY at my long absence from Zela, I went alone (for all our people were scattered) to the entrance of the wood, where I had left her guarded. As I approached the place, I was alarmed at a mingled noise of tigers, elephants, and screaming voices. I hastened on as fast as the thick cover and broken ground would permit. The fierce snarlings of tigers became louder. I passed the spot where

I had left Zela, burst through the cover wildly with terror, and, on getting to the open space, beheld a monstrous tiger on the back of her elephant, clinging with his huge claws on the houdah, gnashing his teeth, roaring, and foaming with rage. Zela not visible, methought he had devoured her! I struck my head with my clenched hand, exclaiming, 'Fool! fool!' and for a moment staggered unnerved, while a death-like sickness came over me! It was but a moment: my blood renewed its course through my veins like flame! My carbine not being charged, I cast it from me, and, armed with nothing but a long Malayan creese, fierce and fearless, I rushed by a half-grown limping tiger-whelp, whining and gnawing at something, which I passed unheedingly. The elephant was stamping, squeeling, and struggling desperately to shake off his enemy. The grisly tiger fell; but within his gripe he held a human victim, bent up, and enveloped in a white cotton garment, such as Zela wore. As I came within a few paces of the tiger, holding his victim down with a paw upon his breast, he glared ferociously on me. While I was rushing in on him, a voice above me, faint and tremulous, said, 'Oh, Prophet, guard him!' I heard no more— I was madly striking out my arm, to plunge the weapon into the tiger's throat, while he was in the act of springing on me. The elephant, as if Zela's prayer had been heard, struck the tiger, while his eye was fixed on me, with his hind foot, sent him reeling many paces, and, ere he could recover, I had plunged my creese up to the hilt in his body. A loud shout, drowning the cries of tiger, elephant, and all others, now burst on my ear, and the Malay chieftain came up, in good time, for so tenacious of life is the tiger, that he was still enabled to strike me down with his paw, and as the whelp had come on me, I should have been torn to pieces but for the chieftain's timely aid. He thrust his spear through the whelp, and buried his dagger twenty times in the body of the tiger; then, dragging the lifeless brute from above me, he helped me up, and said, 'Yes, this is very good amusement—I like it! Let's go into the jungle again—there are plenty more of them, and we'll kill them all!' upon which, roaring like a lion, and reeking with sweat and blood, he shook his spear, and darted into the wood again.

My wild and vacant eye fortunately fell on the form of Zela, who was clinging speechless at my feet, or I should have died or gone mad. I endeavoured to raise her, but my strength had left me. I staggered and fell, clasping her, when for a time I was almost insensible. Recovering, I beheld her safe, saw the dead bodies of the tigers, and found all was quiet near us.

'What is that?' I asked, pointing to the bundle of white rags which lay close at my feet.

'That, dearest, is the poor mahout—I fear he is dead!'

'Oh, is it only he! I thought it had been you, and that you were now but a spirit, my elected good one; for you know, by my new Arab creed, I am allowed two, a good one and a bad one.'

My rage was presently directed against Zela's Arabs, who made their appearance from the bushes, whither they had been lured by the cubs of a leopard, one of which they had secured, De Ruyter having shot the dam. I was infuriated at these fellows for having put Zela's life in jeopardy, and gave chase to one, with the determination of shooting him. My pistol was pointed at his breast, and I was in the act of pulling the trigger, when a hand struck up my arm, and the pistol was discharged in the air. I turned round, prepared to fell the intruder with the heavy-capped butt-end of the weapon, when the eye of Zela met mine with a glance that penetrated my breast, and would have restored my reason, had I been mad. In her low piercing accents, she said—

'He is our foster-brother; our milk was the same, so must be our blood. Let us not destroy each other. Has not the Prophet, this day, saved the remnant of our father's house? It is the evil spirit, which pursued my father to his death, that hath now descended on you! His hand is on your heart: beware lest it shall be turned to stone. His shadow is hanging over you, like a cloud over the sun, and makes you appear as black, and fierce, and unforgiving as himself!'

'You are our Malay's hawk, I suppose; but the black shadow of the raven's wing is vanished—the sun is unobscured—the ill-omened bird has left me! I must to the jungle again. What can have become of De Ruyter? Come, mount your elephant: I would rather entrust you to him, than leave you girt round by a thousand Arabs. He is a noble beast.'

Going up to him, I gave Zela some bread and fruit that she might feed him. He seemed abstracted in gloomy contemplation, and gazed with more than human sympathy on the prostrate body of the dying mahout. He noticed us not; and as his eye fell on the dead tiger, he stamped, looked fierce, and made a trumpeting noise, as if in triumph at having avenged his friend's death! Then, as if remembering he had avenged, but not saved, his ears and trunk drooped; and though he himself was torn and bleeding, his moist and thoughtful eye gave token that all his feelings were absorbed in grief for him he had lost. He stood over and watched the Arabs, who were making a sort of hurdle for the purpose of carrying away the dying man; for his breast was torn open, and one of his groins dreadfully mangled. The affectionate beast refused to eat, even after the man was conveyed out of sight. I placed the bamboo ladder against him, and Zela mounted to the houdah: he curled his trunk round, and on recognizing who it was, resumed his former position, and continued to make low moans, as of anguish.

I must remark that the man for whom the elephant was mourning, had long been his provider; and, since the death of the mahout who was killed by the chieftain, had himself become mahout. The elephant did not seem at all concerned at the death of the Tiroon, doubtless owing to his having been a bad and cruel master; for certainly these animals not only have reason, but are more rational than those they serve. In gratitude to his having saved Zela's and my life, I would, had it been possible, have kept, loved, and cherished him. When we parted from him, Zela kissed him, wept, and cut off some of the strong bristly hair near his ears, which I have ever worn, hooped round a ring, engraven with his name.

But again I am wandering from my subject; nor can I restrain myself. I must dwell on those occurrences, however trifling to others, which were written on my memory thus early. Now my brain is like a confused scrawl, crossed and recrossed, blotted, soiled, and torn: it can contain no more, and that which was written in after years is illegible; so that when I come to narrate the latter events of my life, it will be as difficult, and require as much time, toil, and patience, as the unrolling of the antique parchments of Herculaneum, or the Egyptian papyri, and, like them, when decyphered, not worth the trouble.

CHAPTER IX

Most wretched men
And cradled into poetry by wrong;
They learn in suffering what they teach in song.
SHELLEY

And now his limbs were lean, his scattered hair,
Sered by the autumn of strange suffering,
Sung dirges in the wind; his listless hand
Hung like dead bone within its withered skin;
Life, and the lustre that consumed it, shone
As in a furnace burning secretly
From his dark eyes alone.

Ibid.

COLLECTING a party of men, I returned to the jungle in search of De Ruyter, whose long absence alarmed me. At last I heard his well-known voice, hallooing, and calling by name one of his followers. On coming up to him, he inquired anxiously after a Frenchman, his secretary, who had accompanied him to the jungle, and was missing. The wild animals being now driven to the plain, we separated into parties of twos and threes, and explored, in different directions, a wide extent of the thicket, calling out his name, and firing musquets to let him know where we were. But in vain; and the rapid approach of night warning us to leave the gloomy abode of tigers, reptiles and fever, we walked towards our tents, marvelling what could have become of the Frenchman.

He was a young man whom De Ruyter, in compassion for some misfortunes, which had happened to him at the Isle of France, had befriended; and, to dissipate his melancholy, had taken him from the counting-house of De Ruyter's agents, where he was employed, to make this voyage, during which he was to act as supercargo. At the first he fulfilled his duty with exactness; but was hardly ever out of his own cabin in the day time, and never mingled, nor communicated with those on board, De Ruyter excepted. He ate little. Books and writing, which had been, as a poet, his only solace, lost their power to move him. He continued, for days, gloomily entranced in abstracted reveries, only broken by talking, at times, to himself, and monotonously sounding a broken guitar. In my visits to the grab I rarely saw him; and, being piqued at his distant manner, I was fool enough to resent it, not discriminating that he was tongue-tied from sorrow, not from haughtiness. One day he was seated on the taffrail, his favourite seat, and, on my asking him a question, his mind was so abstracted that he did not hear me. Nettled at this, I made some sarcastic comparison,— I forget what. He appeared stung by it, but remained silent, and walked down to his cabin. Van Scolpvelt, who heard this, told me I was very much in the wrong. 'For,' said he, 'he is a hypochondriac, and if he follow not my advice, will assuredly go mad. As he consumes more opium than a Chinese, he may be considered a dreaming philosopher. In the hallucinations, produced by that drug, his faculties are entranced. He is smitten on the brain,— he reads and writes verses! I caught him in the act! Fools might say he was inspired; but I know it is the first and worst symptom of lunacy. All other maniacs have lucid intervals; some are cureable; but the madness of poets, dogs, and musicians, is past hope. Earth possesses no remedy, science no cure.'

That night I lay on deck awaiting De Ruyter, who was on shore. Every one, I believed, was asleep but myself. I saw the young Frenchman come up the hatchway; the bright light of the moon fell on his face, and made him look more pallid than that luminary. He walked steadily two or three times around the deck, as if seeking some person. I thought on Torra; and that, as I had insulted him, he might meditate revenge. Nevertheless I lay still, with just enough of my eyes shut, as he passed, to make him believe I slept. He regarded me, for a moment, steadfastly. If he had held any weapon, I should have sprung up; but his eye looked dull and heavy, and his hands hung listlessly down. He went aft, moved one of the shot-cases, as if going to sit down, and mounted to his usual place, the taffrail. I still kept my eyes fixed on him, and saw his fixed on the moon. He turned to gaze on the water, muttering something which I could not distinguish, when, as if he had lost his balance, he fell into the sea. I sprung up, awakened the sleepers nearest to me, hastened to the spot whence he had fallen, and called out, 'A man overboard!—Drop the boat astern!'

The schooner lay in the grab's wake, and the night was so still that they heard my orders, and I heard them getting into their boat, as I shoved off in ours. I kept steadfastly looking at the spot where the man had sunk, around which the water rippled and sparkled; and after a painful suspense I observed the body, (for the sea was transparent as glass for many fathoms,) as if suspended mid-way. It was bent double, with the face downward; the bright globular buttons on the back of the jacket, such as are worn by dragoons, shone clearly. Forgetting every thing but the man's danger, and knowing this was a critical moment, I plunged in head foremost, so as to bring myself close to him under water. I caught hold of his arm; and the impetus, with which a good swimmer brings himself up, brought us both to the surface. I then endeavoured by shifting my gripe, to lift his head from the water; but his body was rigidly bent, and so extraordinarily heavy, that, notwithstanding the violent exertions I made to keep myself afloat, and the unruffled surface of the sea in my favour, I swallowed so much water that I was half water-logged myself. About to let him go, in order to preserve myself, the schooner's boat reached me an oar; missing that, she passed over us, and forced me under water. However, in imminent peril of drowning, I retained hold of the body. Two men from the boat plunged in, when the young Frenchman, to our surprise, became almost buoyant. We were then all hauled into the boat, and returned to the grab with our rescued man, who shewed no signs of life.

Sick, cramped, with a head as if bursting, I was accosted by Van, who felt my pulse, and said, 'You are in need of medicine; and sea-water is very good for a strong stomach. But you were injudicious in exhibiting so large a dose. I never prescribe more than a tumbler full, to be taken fasting every day, A.M.'

'Go, doctor, and look at your patient below. If I have gulped a barrel, you'll find he has swallowed a butt, and must bulge, if you don't bear a hand and bale him out.'

'How long was he in the water?'

'I can't say;—it seemed to me an hour.'

'No,' said the Rais; 'I turned the minute glass six times.'

'Oh!' replied Van, 'you need not then have been so impatient. You may safely remain under water for twenty minutes, provided I am at hand to restore you. Come,—you shall see.'

Down he stalked into the cabin, where he caused the body to be stripped and laid on a table. Then by means of external warmth, friction, and an artificial inflation of the lungs, faint symptoms of returning life appeared. Louis, who stood by with his stone bottle, now placed it to the man's mouth, and was about to drench him, but Van indignantly pushed it away. Nevertheless Louis pertinaciously insisted on it ever after that he, not the doctor, had saved the man's life, by allowing him to inhale the aroma of the skedam. A small bottle of ether was placed to the man's nose, and afterwards a few drops, diluted, were poured down his throat; but it was some hours before he opened his eyes, or moved his limbs.

But to shorten my story, he recovered; and we ascertained that his design had been to drown himself; that he had taken two double headed cannon shot from the case which lay aft, ready for service, and, with one in each hand, by way of ballast, had dropped himself overboard, having previously assured himself that we were all asleep. From this time forth he sunk into the gloomiest despair, totally indifferent to every thing. He neither spoke, nor ate, unless at De Ruyter's entreaty, and then merely to be rid of his importunity. His aversion to me (since I had saved his life,) appeared to be the only feeling left him. He scowled at me, as in abhorrence, when accident, which seldom occurred, brought us near each other.

It was about a month after this event that we set out for the tiger hunt, when he applied for permission to accompany us, which De Ruyter gladly gave him. He had followed in the rear of our party, and seemed to dread being noticed. It was strictly enjoined by De Ruyter, who himself never lost sight of him, that he should in no way be molested, or intruded on. When we arrived at the hunting-ground, he was more observant and wakeful; I thought he even looked cheerful. On entering the jungle, there was a strange brightness in his eyes, a quickness in his movements. Instead of his wonted scowl, or shudder, and averted look, as I passed him, he appeared as if going to address me, and smiled, with kindness beaming in his aspect. He stood by De Ruyter, when he and I backed into the first tiger's lair; and, though armed with a carbine, he did not attempt to use it. This carbine was afterwards found near the place. During the confusion which ensued he must have withdrawn himself, as from that moment he could not be traced, nor was he ever after heard of.

'I have reason to believe,' said De Ruyter to me, 'from some expressions that dropped from him, that, having pledged his word not to offer violence to himself again, while we were seeking tigers to destroy, he sought them to be destroyed. When urging him against self-destruction, after you had rescued him, he answered me querulously, and half abstractedly, 'Am I a doomed slave, that I cannot dispose of my own body, now that it is a burthen? Why should that fierce Englishman, who destroys every thing opposing him, and delights in cutting off those who cling to life, drag me from my quiet rest under the sea? The coral rocks seemed soft as her bosom! I thought I was sleeping on her lap in heaven! Then that devil brought me back to this hell here,—to me a ten-fold one! There is no quiet but in death; and they have all conspired to keep me, that loathe life, living. But I will defeat their malice, —yet keep my promise!'

For three days we continued our hunting in the jungle, and amidst the ruins, more excited by the hope of ascertaining the fate of the young Frenchman, than by the sport. Indeed the greater portion of the tigers had abandoned this part of the wood; and the accidents, which had occurred, had sobered our enthusiasm. The mysterious disappearance of a person we are interested in impels us strangely on to undergo any toil, or sacrifice, which we fancy may clear it up; but our search was fruitless. Except the carbine, we could neither discover the youth, nor any rag, nor thing that had been his.

There was, indeed, afterwards, the strongest positive evidence, if men's oaths are to be believed, (which I, for one, discredit,) that the suicide-spirit haunted the grab. His complaints were heard muttering in the wind; his shadowy form rested on the taffrail; and, if any one was hardy enough to approach, it plunged into the sea, and followed in the ship's wake, struggling in vain to sink under the surface. The sailors moreover asserted, on their oaths, that he was no living man, when he was first entered on board, that the captain should never have placed him on the ship's books, and that he would pursue them till his body was buried. De Ruyter told me he could not yet get the fellows aft to the main boom at night, and had several times nearly lost it, and had his vessel endangered by their superstition.

CHAPTER X

Alas! what drove him mad?
*   *   *   *   I cannot say.
A lady came with him from France, and when
She left him,   *   *   he wandered then
About yon lonely isles of desert sand,
Till he grew wild.

SHELLEY

Love, jealous grown of so complete a pair,
Hover'd and buzz'd his wings, with fearful roar,
Above the lintel of their chamber door,
And down the passage cast a glow upon the floor.

KEATS

THE history of this youth I learnt from De Ruyter. His agent in
the Isle of France had written to Europe for French clerks; and
some time after, two young persons landed with a recommendation
to him. They called themselves brothers, which was warranted
by a strong family resemblance. The elder was seemingly under
twenty, and the other much younger; both handsome, gentle,
and strikingly elegant, but the younger more particularly so,
being likewise delicate and effeminate in appearance and manner.
An apartment was assigned to them in the merchant's house. The
elder knew very little of business when he came out, the younger
less; their employer was vexed at this, but their unremitting
attention and fidelity soon reconciled him to them, till, by application, they became admirable accountants. They were inseparable,
shunning all intercourse with others, and were utterly different
from the young men he had ever seen. For this conduct they gave
plausible reasons; the delicate health of the younger, their being
orphans, and the injunction of their dying parents.

A malignant fever, then ripe in the country, seized on the
younger, and the other never quitted him. For change of air they
were removed out of the merchant's house, in Port St. Louis, to
a villa. Not having seen or heard of them for some days, the merchant walked out one evening to visit them. On approaching the
villa, he was alarmed at observing, though it was then the hottest
time of the year, and the coolest of the day, the place shut up,
silent and apparently abandoned. After calling and knocking many

times, he forced open a back window, and entered the house. Hearing a low moaning noise in a room over his head, he went up stairs, listened at the door, called the brothers by name, received no answer, tried the door, and found it was secured. He procured instruments, and broke it open. The brothers lay on a mattress on the floor, locked fast in each other's embraces. He thought them both dead; yet having so recently heard the voice of one, he examined them more closely; and uncovering the bodies for that purpose, he was amazed at discovering the younger to be a woman. She had been dead some time. The lover, who was a strong, athletic youth, just on the verge of complete manhood, exhibited faint signs of life.

Examining the room, the merchant found a sealed paper addressed to him, the contents of which deeply affected him, and solved the mystery. It there appeared that the youth, unable to endure the loss of his beloved, and his disease not destroying him as speedily as he desired, (for he too had caught the fever,) had swallowed poison,—opium, that, as in life, so in death their spirits might be inseparable. The merchant, gifted with presence of mind and knowledge, eventually restored the youth to life; the violence of passion neutralizing, or, at least, diminishing the effect of the opium. Still the poison, or grief, the most subtle of destroyers, had penetrated the brain, and he was, for some months, in a state of mental oblivion. Time and care restored his faculties; but the body and mind refused their mutual succour, and warred against each other. While the mind lay torpid, the body gained strength; but, on resuming its faculties, it preyed on the body. Sunk into misery and despondency, he was a mere shadow, and wandered, during the darkness, like a phantom. The man of bales, and ships' bottoms fortunately retained touches of humanity, and did all he could to obliterate, or mitigate such sorrow. But it lay too deep for the surgeon's probe, the leech's drug, or a friend's sympathy. As a last hope, De Ruyter embarked him on board the grab, thinking, if anything could stir him, it would be our bustling and ever varying life.

The letter left by the youth, previously to his taking the opium, explained every thing. They were of a noble family. The young lady had been educated in a convent in Paris, founded for the incarceration of the younger daughters of those proud, unnatural, aristocratic parents, who, to defeat the wise and just ordination of

z

the law of France, by which property is equally apportioned, consign their last offspring to living graves, that they may be robbed of their birth-right. The youth gained admittance there, privileged by ties of consanguinity. Their love was known, for it had grown from youth, though circumstances had separated them. They saw each other, after the lapse of years, when the innocent love of childhood burst into a fierce and uncontrollable passion. Possibly the vestal sisters dreamed not of love's finding an entrance into their holy asylum, much less of what that love might lead to. Besides, love was forbidden there.

> 'The walls are high; the gates are strong; thick set
> The sentinels; but true love never yet
> Was thus constrained.'

Escape was contrived in disguise, and executed. They reached Havre de Grace. A Dutch skipper, bribed with all their wealth, concealed them in his ship. The Argus-eyed police of France was in motion. They were traced, an embargo was laid on the port and every vessel searched, from her truck to her kelston. The skipper knew the consequences of detection, the least of which was restitution of the gold and jewels he had received; while the dread of fine and imprisonment sharpened his wit, and inspired him with cunning, surpassing that of the police. Whilst the embargo continued, and during the heat of the scrutiny on board the ships in the port, he concealed the lovers, whom he believed to be the sons of a conscript of rank, in the vaults of his own smuggling agent. On the vessel's being allowed to leave the port, he re-shipped them, and most providentially, headed them for security in two casks, stowed on deck; for (whether from any suspicion of this particular vessel, or that it was a general practice, is not mentioned,) when the Dutchman had got his vessel under weigh, he was boarded by the police agents, and the search renewed with augmented rigour. It was then that a police officer took the bung out of the cask, in which the girl was concealed, and passed his sword in it, grazing her bosom; while the skipper carelessly observed, 'It's only an empty water cask!' Love, which gives to the gentlest heart the courage of a hero, enabled her to endure this desperate ordeal in silence.

Thus they eluded the searchers, and escaped to Holland, friendless and destitute. The skipper, fearing discovery, and judging from circumstances which had transpired, during the search of the police, that this was not a common case, and that he had risked more than he had bargained for, became extremely uneasy on the subject, anxiously seeking to remove every trace that could implicate him. He knew he had been deceived, but could by no threats or wiles draw from them who or what they really were. At that time the Dutch were employing every means to induce adventurers to go out to their Indian settlements; and our smuggling skipper was one of their agents. The youth proposed that he should procure them situations in one of those settlements, to which he instantly listened, and wondered he had never thought of proposing it himself. To his great joy they were shipped for the Isle of France, recommended to the merchant's house already mentioned; and the skipper, in addition to what he had previously pocketed, realised a handsome premium for procuring two promising and well-educated volunteers. He knew he had little to fear from their being heard of again.

I have been thus minute in setting down this Frenchman's history, as it was the first instance, which I had met with, or which had been related to me in an authenticated shape, of one of that nation loving anything in the world so dearly as himself.

CHAPTER XI

Who would suppose, from Adam's simple ration,
That cookery could have called forth such resources,
As form a science and a nomenclature
From out the commonest demands of nature?
There was a goodly soup.

BYRON

THIS excursion having detained us much longer than we had intended, we returned with all possible haste to the place whence we had started, and embarked, having the satisfaction to find all right on board our vessels, and the schooner nearly ready for sea.

I had brought De Ruyter intelligence, among other news from his agents at Pulo Penang, of an expedition fitting out by the English, destined to attack the pirates at Sambos on this island. The marauders were very numerous there, and had committed great havoc on the Company's private trade, both by sea and land; for, like the Court of Chancery, they endeavoured to get all pro-

perty into their keeping. It was determined to attempt the annihila-
tion of—not the Court of Chancery, but—the comparatively harmless pirates, during the season they were congregated together,
weather-bound in their port of Sambos. De Ruyter resolved to
defeat the expedition, and, but for the crippled state of the schooner,
I was to be immediately despatched in search of French cruizers,
to give them intelligence, and combine measures for an attack on
the Company's force by sea. That not having been possible, De
Ruyter laid his plans, to aid the natives on shore, to whom he
pledged his assistance.

At length I took in my wood and water on board the schooner,
and sailed for Java, with letters and instructions from De Ruyter.
On the same day he took his departure for Sambos. I lent him a
party of my men, and two brass guns. Thus we again separated.
My commission was to deliver despatches to the governor of
Batavia, to purchase stores and provisions, and to meet the grab
again, without loss of time, at our appointed rendezvous. Louis
went with me as negociator for the victualling department.

Nothing particular occurred during my run to Java except the
capture, or rather recapture, (for she had been previously taken
by an English man-of-war,) of a small Spanish vessel, belonging
to merchants at the Philippine Islands, loaded with camphor, and
the celebrated edible birds' nests. There were only six English
sailors and a midshipman in charge of her, although so valuable
a prize; consequently she could attempt no resistance.

A short time before this, an English man-of-war brig had
captured, off the Philippine Islands, a Spanish vessel, containing
a cargo of this sea-slug. On the English officer's boarding her, and
asking what she was loaded with, the Spaniards truly answered,
'Birds' nests.' John Bull, whose ship had recently entered the
Chinese seas, with gaping wonder exclaimed, 'Birds' nests! What,
you rascals, do you take me for a spoony greenhorn? Birds' nests!
I'll birds'-nest you, you lubberly liars! Off with the hatchways!'

Accordingly the hold of the vessel was searched, and the English
sailors were dumbfounded at discovering nothing but sacks of
stinking, dirty, muddy-looking swallows' nests, such as they had
seen sticking under the eaves of houses. They still thought this
slimy compost was merely placed as a skreen or cover, to shelter
something more valuable and threw a great portion of it overboard, in order to arrive at the treasure below—chuckling, and

treating the Spaniards with derision, the Jack-tars cutting many witticisms on Spanish sailors going a birds'-nesting. They cleared down to her kelston, and searched into every nook in vain. Their officer, on his return to the brig, gave the commander an account of what the Spaniards had told him, and that he had verified it with his own eyes; upon which there was a general laugh throughout the ship. 'However,' quoth the greenhorn commander, 'the vessel is Spanish, and we must keep her. Though she is but in ballast, her hull is worth something. They must have been hard up for shingle, where they come from, to put sludge in her,—and in bags!'

He then gave orders that a midshipman, and three or four of his worst men, should take charge of her, and run her into the nearest port. One rational thing he did was to remove the Spanish prisoners to his own brig, or they would have soon retaken her. Thus he left her, and it was not till he himself put into a Chinese port, and accidentally mentioned this occurrence, as a joke against the Spaniards, that he learnt the value of the prize. The edible birds' nests were at that time selling in the Chinese market at thirty-two Spanish dollars a kattie; so that, on a computation of the quantity in the vessel, she was worth from eighty to ninety thousand pounds; and he, poor devil, that had served twenty years without clearing twenty pounds prize-money, would have made a fortune. He raged, and stormed, and went to sea again to look after her. He offered up prayers, for the first time in his life, for her safe arrival in port. But it was otherwise decreed; the few lubberly fellows he had put on board of her, were not sufficient to work her, and she was wrecked on the coast of China. A galleon of gold-dust would not have been such a windfall to the Chinese as was this cargo of sea-slug. The news spread like wild-fire through the country that a vessel had stranded on their coast, containing incalculable wealth. The timid Chinese forgot their fears, and, regardless of winds and seas, rushed through the foaming surf, trampled the strong over the weak, brother over brother, all hurrying on board the wreck; which was so effectually pillaged, that she was left floating like an empty tea-chest, not a grain of her cargo being left sticking to her ribs. During the scramble in the water, and on the wreck—for every handful was fought for— many lives were lost; and the coast, for several miles round was in anarchy and confusion for a long time after.

The capturer of the prize I retook was of the same class of well-informed officers. I had more care of her; and, for security, took my prize in tow. Louis entreated that he might go on board of her as prize-agent; declaring that the only thing he wished was to perfect himself in the mystery of concocting that savoury and glutinous soup, *secundum artem*, so famous in China, that they have a proverb there, which says that if the spirit of life were departing from the nostrils, and the odour of this soup were to salute them, the spirit would reanimate the clay, knowing there is no luxury in paradise to compare with it. 'Besides,' added Louis, 'should I introduce this delicious restorative into Europe, and the no less renowned Chinese arrack-punch, I shall be more deservedly famous than Van Tromp, or the Prince of Orange,—and I will be!'

With these ambitious and glorious aspirations, Louis le Grand, in conjunction with a Chinese cook, went to work, heart and hand; and in the middle of a dark night, off a lee-shore, he hailed me to heave-to, and send a boat, that he might bring me a sample of his triumphant success. He came with it; and, though not at that time, I have tasted this dish. It is certainly a voluptuous relish, but too glutinously rich for any stomach like mine, accustomed to simple fare. In addition to the slimy composition of the nest, which, when dissolved, is like brown jelly, or melted glue, there were the sinews of deer, the feet of pigs, the fins of young sharks, the brawny part of a pig's head, with plovers' eggs, mace, cinnamon, and red peppers. Turtle soup is tasteless after it; and it is a marvel that the numerous gastronomic votaries of Europe have not made this superlative offering to their palates. They are to blame.

One night I was sleeping in the cabin, while Zela, at an opposite couch, was administering to the wants of a woman that was ill, the wife of one of our Arabs. I was awakened from a sound sleep by, as I imagined, the quacking of a duck; for we had brought some from Borneo, which are of an immense size, the finest in the world. I looked up and cried out 'Holla! wring that damned duck's neck off! What does he here?'

Zela laughed, and seemed to hold up the black-looking bird, which continued to annoy me so much with its confounded quack! quack! quack! that I got up in a rage to kill it, when to my utter dismay, I beheld a black child, that had that instant chipped its shell, and come to light. I damned the woman for littering on board the schooner, not being a Lying-in Asylum, and lay down to dream of ducks and little black imps.

CHAPTER XII

But I am Pestilence; hither and thither
I flit about that I may slay and smother:
All lips that I have kiss'd must surely wither,
But Death's,—if thou art he, we'll go to work together.

SHELLEY

Where youth grows pale, and spectre-thin, and dies,
   Where but to think is to be full of sorrow
      And leaden-eyed despair,
Where beauty cannot keep her lustrous eyes,
   Or new love pine at them beyond to-morrow.

KEATS

I TOUCHED at one of the Barlie Islands, which lay in my course, but could get little else there but a couple of sacks of Chinese tobacco, which is excellent. While haggling about the price, I was playing with a pretty, slim, Malay child. 'Come,' said the mother, 'give me the gold more, and you shall have the tobacco, the four fowls, the basket of eggs, the fruit, and my eldest-born child into the bargain,—as you seem to like her.'

I threw down the gold coin, told the men to take the things into the boat, and led away the girl, about eight years old, giving her some fruit to eat, and pice to play with, while neither she nor the affectionate parent exchanged a look of sorrow at parting. The little thing accompanied me on board, perfectly enchanted with her new abode. I gave her to Zela; and in my own mind, lauded the mother, who exhibited so strong a proof of not being influenced by those narrow and illiberal prejudices, which prevail in Europe. All nature teaches us[1] that when the offspring are weaned, and can walk, they ought no longer to be an incumbrance; dogs abandon their puppies, the cow her calf, the ewe her lamb, and christian mothers who are enlightened, abandon their cubs, doubtless prompted by their superior natural instinct. Truly the Malay mother went a step beyond them in making a profit of her produce. In justice to European parents, I must say, at least I believe, they have good sense enough, and certainly know the value of gold well enough, not to throw away that which, had they known of an Eastern market, could have been turned to profit. But in this, like the English commander with the birds' nests, they are greenhorns.

France and Holland were then united under the same dictatorship. Arrived at Batavia, the capital of Java, I was well received by the governor, a Dutch officer. Having delivered my despatches, he ordered the authorities under him to afford me every facility in refitting and provisioning my vessel; and advised me to lose no time in the port, and to communicate as little as possible with the shore, on account of the infectious fever, which was then prevailing. The merchants of the Dutch factory were so officiously hospitable and kind, that they bored me to death with offers of houses, and invitations to feasting and gormandizing. De Ruyter was their hero; and the evident unlimited confidence he reposed in me, the large sums I was commissioned to negociate, and the power I possessed of expending what sum or sums I pleased, had a magical effect. Besides, I had established a private stock of fame, and a name, which served my purpose very well, and passed current for what I then wanted; though detraction has since analysed—not it, but what malignity asserts it was,—and declared the coin was base, and that the stamper of the die deserved a halter,—assertions proceeding from sheer envy and malice. As for gold, I had not then acquired those artificial wants which it can supply.

> 'Our simple life wants little, and true taste
> Hires not the pale drudge, luxury, to waste
> The scene it would adorn.'

Neither was I born with gentlemanly appetites, but, as Louis said, lived more like a 'negur' than a Christian. Like Michael Cassio[1] I had unhappy brains for drinking; my nature was too inflammable tamely to bear the spur of wine in excess. Feasting and swilling, amidst the sweltering and unclean slaves of the mouth, I ever held in Brahminical abhorrence. I therefore shunned the hospitable board of the merchants, expediting my business with them, impatient to regain my own little cabin, which, containing Zela, was spacious enough for all the treasure I possessed or coveted. We were greedy and insatiable in our love, and required little else. We feasted on the same bunch of grapes, a shadock, or a sun-cleft pomegranate. We drank from the same cup, and sat on the same mat. Excess of love was my only excess; and, either from love or temperance in diet, I acquired strength and hardiness, proof against sickness, resisting all contagion. Whilst others writhed and suffered from scratches, the deepest wounds healed with me, unaided by the surgeon; and the Java fever, now raging and destroying with a virulence only to be equalled by the plague, cound not penetrate my strong and healthful frame.

The Europeans, both on board and on shore, declared that the sole effectual preservative was, what they called, living well, and drinking freely; that the fever was like a blustering bully;—

> 'He was a coward to the strong.
> He was a tyrant to the weak.'

I acquiesced in this doctrine, but differed in the premises. They averred that the stimulant of fiery drink was the method of keeping up the languid circulation, the quantity not specified. Water, fruit, rice, vegetables, and all crude substances were interdicted as the worst of poisons. Yet I pursued this diet, and so did my native crew, and we lived; while the Europeans followed their system, and died like murrained sheep. Vessels in the harbour were driven on shore, for want of hands to secure them; others, freighted, could not muster strength to weigh their anchors. A French and a Dutch ship of war, under sailing orders, were in such a state, that they could not leave the port, much less work their ships at sea. If the disease could have been fended off by free living, the European portion of my crew would have been fever-proof. Yet it not only boarded us, but had the audacity to fall foul, exclusively, on the hardy sons of the north, while it respected its own progeny, the children of the sun.

CHAPTER XIII

A mist arose, as from a scummy marsh:
At this, through all his bulk, an agony
Crept gradual, from the feet unto the crown,
Like a lithe serpent vast and muscular
Making slow way, with head and neck convuls'd
From over-strained might.

KEATS

As if to decide the question of diet, the contagion by one fell blow, by one signal example, aimed his shaft at the head and prime organ of his vaunting defiers, and struck Louis. If eating and drinking could have warded off disease, he might have been immortal. He gormandized like a vulture, and on such dainty and nutritive bits, that a whale's liver would not have produced more oil, or an ox's ribs more tallow than Louis le Grand. As to drink, his throat and stomach must have been lined with something as fire-proof as asbestos, or they could not have resisted the burning liquid which he had for so many years insatiably poured down, enough to wear out a dozen copper funnels. From the time the fatal malady commenced its havoc on board the schooner, every hour the ship's glass was turned, and the bell was struck; Louis marked the time by calling out,—'Boy! don't you know the glass is turned, and the fever come on board? Bring the stone bottle to keep him out!' upon which he turned a glass down his coppers. Arnold's chronometer in the cabin kept not better time than Louis with his bottle. So unerring was his palate, that if, by error or neglect, the bell was not struck punctually, he never failed to call out,—'Boy, the bottle!' when, if the urchin pleaded that the bell had not struck, Louis vociferated,—'Then it should have done so;—'tis more than a minute past the hour; tumble up, you idle sea-calf,—give me the bottle!' At last he exclaimed, 'Ha! you young scorpion, what have you been at?—sucking the bottle, and then bulling it with bilge-water? Why, this is not out of my locker; this is beastly stuff,—would make a sea-horse sick.'

The boy asserted it was the same he had always drunk, when Louis waxed wroth, dashed the liquor in his face, and was about to rope's-end him. 'Hold!' said I, 'let me smell it, Louis. Come, I'll swear it's all right.'

'What!' he replied, 'don't I know my own skedam?—the devil himself could never deceive me in that, since I was five years old! Van Sülpke, the great spirit-merchant of Amsterdam declared I could ascertain, better than his spirit-proof, the strength and quality of his liquors; and, besides, I've swallowed as much as would float the schooner,—haven't I?' Here Louis paused, and shewed evident signs of sickness.

'Damned devil-boy!' he went on; 'he has been sucking the bottle, and filled it up with physic,—and I can't abide doctor's stuff! Bring another bottle, devil, thief, liar!'

Another bottle was brought, and he tasted it; but the hitherto genial fluid had lost its flavour on his palate. He spat, and sputtered, and pushed the bottle from him. I observed also that he removed a fresh-lighted pipe from his mouth; and, thinking there must be really something the matter with him, I got up and went over to him. The glow-worm sparkle of his small eager eye was dimmed, his lips were white and frothy, the lower jaw hung down, his head was drooping, and his hands were clenched. 'Holloa, old Louis, what's the matter? Are you ill?'

'Ill?—no, I'm never ill,—I'm only sickish. That damned stuff is like poison in me!' As he said this he made a strong effort to rouse himself.

'Come,' I replied, 'you are ill. Go out of the sun, and lie down aft.'

'No, captain, I'm not such a fool as to be ill. I was never sick like this except once, in the South Seas, at the Island of Otaheite, when those—what do you call them?—missionaries came aboard to preachify with the crew, and cheat them of their dollars. I like a great fool, went ashore with them, and they gave me some cursed stuff they called gin,—such blasphemy I never heard! At first when they told me they had set up a great distillery of gin, I thought them very useful, clever, good men; for you know, captain, any nation might be converted by hollands;—but this was the un-christianest, beastliest liquor I ever tasted, and it made me—as I feel now. Yet the foolish, idiot-people of the island think it very good, because it makes them mad-drunk, and they believe Heaven sent it; but it made me believe the devil had got amongst them.'

Louis broke off his story by complaining of pains all over his body, his head and stomach. I loved Louis, and saw with grief the ravage which the envenomed and ghastly destroyer was tracing on his broad and honest face. I led him down to my own cabin, placed him on my couch, and charged the gentle Zela (who Louis declared was too kind and good to be a woman,) to nurse him, and, if aught human could, to avert the evil power, whose armed hand I beheld striking at his life. But it was written; and the stern decrees of fate, who can turn aside? He struggled convulsively, and foamed, and raved, and then sank into idiotic insensibility, moaning and muttering incoherent words. As the day dawned, (from long habit, outliving both strength of body and mind,) he said, in faint but clear accents, the first intelligible sentence he had spoken for many hours,—'Boy! bring the bottle!' The wearied and dozing boy raised himself from the cabin deck, on which he had sunk, overworn with watching, staggered across the cabin to perform his first diurnal duty for years, and groped at the accustomed locker for the stone bottle. I asked Louis how he was. 'Hot! very hot, and thirsty!—my body is burning hot, parched up, dry as ashes, not a drop of moisture. Why, I am in an oven!—Boy! the bottle!'

I could not resist the supplicating look of his eye, and the trembling eagerness of his hand as he grasped at the glass, which the boy, now thoroughly awakened, held out; but the instant the spirit, which he used to declare was the spirit of life, had touched his white and clammy lips, he shrunk from it, and dashed it from him as if it had been a scorpion. Then, looking wild with horror around, he cried out, 'Oh! God! God! I pray for a sea of water, and a thousand devils all bring me fire! Oh! I am in fire and flame, in hell, red hot and scalding white!'

He continued alternately raving and silently insensible till about noon, when the boy came to tell me he was asleep. So rapid and fierce had been the fever, giving no respite, that my mind misgave me, and I went down into the cabin. I shuddered as I beheld him: the distorted features, pinched and puckered up, expanded nostrils, glassy and half-closed eye, the pallid hue of his skin touched and streaked with blue, the ghastly and collapsed hand, and nerveless arm hanging down, all indicated that he had struck his flag to the grisly pirate-king. Death's gray banner hung drooping over him. I held a mirror to his livid lips,—there was not a breath to stain it. Decay too, as if not brooking an instant's reprieve, had begun its work, ere the spark of fire, which animated his clay, was extinguished. Scarcely had I time, while standing over him, to brush away the moisture gathering on my eyelid with the back of my hand, when the doctor of the frigate, who stood by me, putting his hand on my arm, said: 'Are you deaf, captain? Don't you hear me? I tell you, if you won't cast the body overboard immediately, yours will be prey for the dog-fish to-morrow.'

'What!' I exclaimed, 'the warm hearted, honest, kind, and jovial Louis, the life of the ship's company, the best servant man ever had, food for dog-fish and sharks—thrown overboard like a rotten sheep, ere we are certain that life has totally abandoned him! Feel, —he is yet warm! I'll be damned if it shall be done!'

CHAPTER XIV

And even and morn,
With their hammocks for coffins, the seamen aghast,
Like dead men, the dead limbs of their comrades cast
Down the deep.
                              SHELLEY

THE doctor returned to his ship. At the expiration of a few hours I was convinced the advice he gave, though it sounded harshly at the time, was nevertheless true and good; for the decomposition was miraculously rapid, and the atmosphere of the vessel, previously insufferably close, became tainted. It would have been unsafe, a few hours later, to approach the body; so I gave orders to have it sewed up in a hammock, the sailor's coffin, with a couple of heavy shot secured at the lower extremities. Then, having lowered it in a boat, and covered it with a flag of his country for a pall, I pulled far outside of the harbour to sink it, in compliance with an order that no corpse was to be buried in or near the port. I would have read the burial-service over him, if such a thing as a book of prayer could have been procured; but priests and prayer-books were scarce articles,—indeed not to be come at on board the schooner; and if wandering souls are bored in the other world for passports, as they are in a great part of this, I pity them. We fired three volleys over the remains of Louis, and committed the body to the deep. Watching it, as it sunk, with a heavy heart, I gave the order to pull the boat's bow round, and give way on board; when, with my eye fixed on the rippling, which broke the glassy surface of the sea, I muttered, 'Poor Louis! poor Louis! I would give the world to have thee here ag——ha! what's that? Lie on your oars!' The men turned round, and altogether exclaimed, 'By God! he is up again!'

And so it was. My musings had been interrupted by beholding the body rise on the surface, like a spar, which had been hurled in the sea end foremost from a height, when the reaction sends it back again, almost into the air, and then it lies floating on the waters. The boat was crowded with men, anxious to see the last of him by attending his funeral, for he was a general favourite. We were all so astonished, that the cause of this re-appearance, to wit,—the shot not being properly secured from falling out,— never once occurred to any of us. We pulled round and hurried back to the spot, as eagerly as if it were to rescue a drowning com- rade. Indeed some of the crew were for hauling the body into the boat, to examine if it was not re-animated. On discovering that the ballast had escaped from the lashings, we were at a stand-still what to do. To leave the body afloat is sacrilege among sailors, as depriving it of christian burial. We had nothing but the boat's iron grapnel, heavy enough for the purpose; so we were obliged to expend it. This was securely lashed, and the body again sank, every one, I believe, anticipating its re-appearance; for, as one of the old man-of-war's men sagely and oraculously observed: 'I'll be damned if all the anchors in the dock-yard of Portsmouth would moor that Dutch dogger under water; because as how he never let that stuff enter his scuppers in his life, and it arn't natural to him, howsomever, though he be dead.'

I had laid the schooner as far on the outside of the port as our convenience and security would permit, to be away from the noxious vapours of the land, and to have as much benefit from the sea-breeze as possible. Yet the malady was spreading on board; the symptoms of illness, and, as it turned out, the rapidity of dis- solution, being nearly similar to poor Louis's. During a great part of the night I was attending to the sick; and afterwards I was kept awake revolving in my mind what was best to be done in order to avert the pestilence from spreading;—whether it was not advis- able, leaving my business unfinished, instantly to proceed to some other port for provisions, fearful, if I delayed it, that the alterna- tive of morning or staying would not be left to my decision. My drunken doctor had deserted me; at any other period I should have been glad of it, but I had not yet succeeded in finding another. I had few medicines, and was unlearned in their use; though De Ruyter had taken pains to instruct me in so important a part of my duty. Eight of the crew were very ill. After consulting with the two mates, we came to this conclusion,—to cut and run as soon as daylight appeared. I then retired, harassed and exhausted, to recruit my strength by sleep.

At daybreak the man-of-war's man, to whom I alluded on the previous evening, came down in the cabin, and, disturbing me from a heavy sleep, said, 'Captain, he's afloat again, and alongside. Is he to come aboard, Sir?'

Rubbing my glued eye-lids, I answered, 'Yes,—let him come aboard. Who is it?'

'Why, it be he, Sir.'

'He! Who?'

'The steward, Sir!'

'Steward! What steward?'

'Old Louis, Sir.'

I shook myself, and jumped up, to be certain I was awake; and the mate continued with, 'Didn't I say as how, Sir, he won't *lay* moored under water?'

Accompanying him on deck, he pointed out the canvass-shrouded body of Louis lying across the schooner's bow, seemingly supported by the cable. The men all pressed forward to gaze in wonder and awe. At this apparently miraculous second re-appearance, I was really as much astounded as the crew. The grapnel had been securely lashed, and had often held the boat in a swell, while there had been neither sea nor wind during the night. On examination the mystery was explained: the ground-sharks had been at work, and, by dragging and tearing, had torn the hammock apart to get at the body, which was horribly mauled, and from which a leg had been separated, the canvass having protected the upper part. I now resolved to inter the remains on shore; but they were offensive to handle, and I had no planks for a coffin. After some hesitation, I could contrive nothing better than to tow the body ashore, and inter it in a deep hole, prepared by the second mate, in the sand, above high-water mark. 'For,' said he, 'if he feels the water touch him, call me a land-lubber if he don't slip his cable, get under weigh again, make sail, and get alongside of us, wheresomever we be; so I'll give him a dry, snug berth.' As this was undeniable, we parbuckled Louis into his shore-grave; and, to make assurance doubly sure, we hauled the broken bottom of a wrecked boat, which lay near the spot, to cover the grave with it, so that either from above or below, he was secured against water.

CHAPTER XV

'Tis true they are a lawless brood,
But rough in form, nor mild in mood;
And every creed, and every race,
With them hath found—may find a place.

BYRON

PREPARATORY to going to sea, I called on the governor, and merchants with whom I had business, obtained my clearances, paid my bills and port-charges, had my papers signed, &c. &c.; then loading a couple of shore-boats with all the fresh provisions I could lay my hands on, I returned on board, fired a gun, and hoisted the signal for sailing.

We had been in port only four days, during which there had been a dead calm. The town, like Venice, is intersected by canals, which, being receptacles for all the filth of the crowded population of the place, mud and dead dogs were dammed up at the outlets, and this was the principal cause of the sickness. The interior of the island, and the mountains close to the town, were and are very healthy; but the town itself is almost annually ravaged by what is, *par excellence*, called the Java fever. The young, strong, and florid-complexioned were generally the first attacked, and the soonest despatched. The great feeders and fat-buttocked never escaped. I loathe greasy and haunchy brutes as Moses and Mahomet loathed swine, and rejoice in their extermination—all except honest, honest Louis, whose warm heart no mounds of suet could impede in its free beating, or choke its generous impulses. Gout, apoplexy, dropsy, and the stone, I laud, respect, and salute with my hat off; for they are, in their nature, radicals, the fierce slayers of kings and priests, the grasping wealthy, and the greedy glutton. When the parson robs the poor cottager of his corn and tithe-pigs, though his conscience may never prick him, his great toe often does; and the porkling never ceases to grunt within him, till, incorporated on his ribs, or laying fast hold on his throat, he exhibits apodictical indications of apoplexy. Among us, those of the greyhound race, the broad-chested, long-limbed, bright-eyed, gaunt, and spare-bodied, were rarely pursued or seized on by those blood-hounds, fever and dysentery, no matter what their habits of living were. Our carpenter, a staunch sea-dog, drank, with measured accuracy, half a gallon of arrack a day, and worked like a steam-engine. You might track him along the deck by the moisture exuding from him; and though he had been thus drinking and toiling for years, the first to begin labour, and the last to desist from it, the oldest man on board, and the longest in India, his health and strength were unimpaired—as little affected as a machine by heat and change. Day or night he toiled on, and wondered when others grew sick, died, and abandoned their post. He instanced me as a chip of the same block, and fit to command, for I was always to be found at my duty.

With my mingled, wild, and savage crew, the outcasts of the west, and those who had lost caste in the east—men whom the iron hand of the law could neither hold in subjection nor tame, whose tiger-hearts knew no ties of kindred, home, and country, or, if known, they were rudely rent asunder—my duty was no sinecure. More than once my power was in imminent jeopardy, notwithstanding De Ruyter's precautions in having backed me with a force of old and tried men of his own, the several Europeans I had added to my crew, who were attached to me, and Zela's faithful and devoted Arabs; I say, with all this, such was the unmitigable ferocity of some of my men, that I was frequently in great personal peril, and my destruction was plotted. Zela, by means of the Malay girl I had bought from her affectionate mother, and her Arabs, were my salvation, by putting me on my guard in giving me timely notice of every thing going on. Besides, the first mate, the American, was my firm friend, being bound to De Ruyter by the strict ties of mutual interest—the only hold that man has on man's fidelity. But we had a ruffianly set of lawless Frenchmen, brindled-bearded privateers' men and smugglers, fellows with long knives in their girdles, and of such fiery and irascible tempers, that their hands, as by instinct, were generally on the hafts, while their grey and assassin-like eyes glared ferociously at the slightest provocation. Their jealous and malignant

Aa

natures ill-brooked the partiality they fancied I shewed towards
my countrymen and the natives, and there were continual broils
and civil contentions on board. A leader of this gang had one day
an altercation with the American mate, who was a quiet and somewhat timid man, and threateningly drew his knife on him. I was
in the cabin, and overheard the contention. Having long been
irritated at this man's conduct, (for he was the organ of all the
refractory Frenchmen,) I started from Zela's lap, on which my
head was lying, rushed on deck, and confronted the fellow. He
stood his ground without flinching, his knife still held out. Our
eyes met, gladiator-like, in defiance, as I put my hand to draw the
small creese from my waist, exclaiming, 'A mutiny!—seize the
villain!' We rushed on each other: he called out to his countrymen,
and there was a wild commotion. I felt his knife on my left arm
and ribs, before I could unsheath my weapon. I made no effort to
ward off the blow, but grasped his brawny throat with one hand,
and putting the creese behind his left shoulder, in the Malay
fashion, drove it right down through his heart, and we fell together
on a gun-carriage on the deck.

As I rose, every muscle in my body writhed, like a wounded
serpent, with rage. I killed this man, not from the instigation of
sudden passion, though in passion; for, young and fiery as I was,
I could control myself; but I had premeditated the ruffian's
death, after using every means to conciliate him. He was the boatswain, the hardiest sailor on board, and as insensible to fear as a
buffalo. He hated the English, and I hated him on account of a
story he was in the habit of narrating with savage glee. Once he
had been mate in a small craft running between the Isle of France
and Madagascar, trading for cattle. The vessel was captured by
an English sloop of war, when a midshipman with five or six men
were put in charge of her. This fellow and two of his crew were
left on board, and were imprudently permitted by the midshipman to assist in working the vessel, instead of being confined as
prisoners. One calm midnight, the officer and most of his men
being asleep, he crept into the cabin and cut the midshipman's
throat; then, assisted by the other two, (one an African,) they
massacred all the others, threw their bodies into the sea, and
returned to the Isle of France, glorying in their bloody and successful atrocity. This story I had heard him repeat on the previous
night, and could scarcely then restrain my indignation.

Stretching forth my red hand, with the dripping weapon, I roared out to the gathering Frenchmen, who stood nearest to me and together,—'Go to your duty! There is your mutinous leader;—and thus will I serve all those that dare disobey me!'

Zela stood by my side, holding my sword for me. Her soft eye had changed its hue, and the fire of her race shone in her bright glances. The disorderly Frenchmen sullenly went forward; and the rest of the crew silently leant about in groups. From this time my influence with the men was considerably augmented, the growing insubordination received a check, and my youth, the principal plea urged against me by the refractory, was forgotten.

CHAPTER XVI

It was so calm, that scarce the feathery weed,
Sown by some eagle on the topmost stone,
Swayed in the air.   SHELLEY

WE ran along the eastern coast for a bay, in which, according to my chart, there was anchorage, with the intention of procuring a supply of wood and water. We kept as close in-shore as possible, to be within reach of the land-winds; but, for many days, we lay stationary under the high land, within whose dark shadows I thought we were enchanted; for not a breath of air reached us, either from the land at night, or from the sea in the day. The buoyant rubbish of chips, feathers, and rope-yarn, thrown overboard, remained as stationary as the rubbish cast out of a cottage door. The waters seemed petrified into polished blue marble, tempting one to walk on their treacherous surface. Among the few moving things around were those little azure-tinctured children of the sea, called Portuguese men of war, with sails light as gossamer, and tiny paddles; they manœuvred about us, like a fairy fleet, the largest as big as the chrystal stopper of a decanter, which, except in colour, they resembled. Here and there were scattered the jellied-looking sea-stars; and a singular phenomenon, called the puree, which comes from the bottom to the surface by inflating itself with air, till, from a shrunken, withered, empty thing, it becomes round and plumped out like a blown bladder; after this, it cannot sink for a length of time. We amused ourselves by practising with our carbines at them; and also by lowering the square sail overboard to bathe in, using that method to avoid the ground-sharks, which, in those seas, near the shore, lie like silent watch-dogs in their submerged kennels. The heat was so piercing, that the Raypoots, who worship the sun, fought on the deck for a square foot of the awning's shade. I experienced the greatest relief from anointing my body with oil, and continually, like a duck, plunging my head in water; yet my lips and skin were cracked like a plum-tree. No vessel is so ill adapted for a hot climate as a schooner; she requires a great many men to work her, and has less space than any other vessel wherein to stow them. On coming on deck from below, the men appeared as if they had emerged from a steam-bath.

However, calms at sea, like the calms of life, are transitory and far between; a breeze, a squall, a gale, or a tempest must follow, as certain as the night the day. With us the winds came gentle as a lover's voice to the sleeping canvass, not like the simoom of wedlock, and we glided peacefully along the rich and varied scenery of the shore to our anchorage near Balamhua, withinside the island of Abaran. Here we found an extensive range of sandy beach, a small river, and the wood so abundant, that the trees seemed enamoured of salt water and sea breezes, drooping their heads over its surface, as if they courted the spray, and were nurtured by the briny waves laving their roots. There was a small village of Javanese at the mouth of the river, the chief of which, in consideration of a small supply of powder and brandy, readily gave us permission to procure what we wanted on shore. We landed our empty water-casks, and began to cut wood.

The calms, the excessive heat, the closeness of the atmosphere, all combined to spread the fever and dysentry among the crew; and few days passed without our losing a man. Æther, opium, and calomel were the medicines, by my instructions, to be applied to those attacked; and bark and wine to the convalescent. Something I had learnt of the diseases of the country, yet I regretted I had not been more attentive to Van's medical lectures. Now, without a surgeon, I sweated over one of Van's medical books, and lamented that my old schoolmaster had not succeeded in whipping Latin into my breech. Horses and dogs, thought I, are educated by beating; and why not man, the more obdurate and vicious animal? Latin phrases were hieroglyphics to me. Yet I proceeded to practise, though without wig, amber-headed cane, or stop-watch, as a mask for gross ignorance, and turned to drugging and drenching with as little compunction as the members of the Royal College of Physicians, who write M. D. to their names, which, I shall ever presume, means 'Man Destroyers.'

Preparing for sea, I was annoyed to hear that a fray had happened between some of our men and the villagers. Two of the natives had been wounded by our men firing at them. These disputes were ever recurring in our dealings; nor could our tars comprehend that they were amenable to any law while on shore. They acknowledged themselves shipped, bound to the articles of their duty, and answerable for any neglect or breach of contract, while on board. They belonged to the sea; but, 'it is damned hard if we can't take our full swig on shore. We are ready to pay for what we want,—when we have money; or we are ready to fight for it. For when we haven't money, it an't natural that savages should keep all the shore to themselves; when it is quite sartain the land was made for the christians as well as the sea.' This, or some such reasoning, was all the reply I could get, from my most orthodox christian crew, to my frequent remonstrances on the brutality with which they assailed, robbed, and slaughtered the natives. Nor could I find a remedy for this evil; I restrained them as much as possible, and did what justice was in my power, in the way of recompence, to the wronged. In this instance the Javanese were accused of being the aggressors; yet, though I could not arrive at the facts, I knew some indignity must have been offered to them; and they are neither patient nor forgiving. Dreading therefore some bloody retaliation, and observing they no longer came alongside of us, while a suspension of barter and communication was highly detrimental, I took a few presents for the chief, and went on shore in two armed boats. This method did not succeed; but, by going accompanied by none but my interpreter, after much difficulty and explanation, I succeeded, at least in appearance, in having accommodated the affair, when a renewal of our friendly intercourse took place.

When ready for sea, the chief came on board, and pressed me to accompany him to a hunting station, abounding with deer and wild hogs. He had often heard me express a wish to go thither, but had put it off from time to time, saying it was better to wait till the rains fell, when the animals would be driven down from the mountains. As there had been a violent storm on the previous night, followed by floods of rain, his invitation seemed to be the consequence of his former promise. I readily gave my assent. He cautioned me, with great apparent sincerity, against creating any jealous fears among his people by a train of many armed followers. Then, with other friendly advice on his part, we parted; it being settled that I was to meet him on the ensuing morning before day-light.

CHAPTER XVII

There sat the gentle savage of the wild,
In growth a woman, though in years a child,
As childhood dates within our colder clime,
Where nought is ripen'd rapidly save crime.
BYRON

ALTHOUGH without fear, I did not neglect to use all proper pre-cautions. I went on shore the next morning with fourteen of my trustiest men, well armed. After landing, I ordered the boat, with a smaller one which accompanied us, having a part of their crews, to push off from the shore, lie at their grapnels, and, on no account, to land, or parley with the natives.

The chief was waiting for me, attended by only four or five men, armed with merely their creeses and boar-spears. We penetrated into the interior by following the windings of the little river, now swollen, muddy, and rapid from the late heavy rain. We crossed the stream several times by fords, not without some difficulty, and I failed not to caution our party to preserve their ammunition and arms from getting wet. I had learnt to be watchful and sus-picious, and took note of several apparently trivial circumstances, which might have escaped a less wary person. The Javanese chief frequently held conferences with his men; he sometimes wished us to cross parts of the river which were not fordable, the bottom being muddy, interspersed with deep holes; and, changing the order of our progress, he kept in the rear of the party. Upon this I also fell back, and watched him narrowly. There was awakened a cunning and treacherous expression in the glistening of his small deep-set eye, which startled me. Not to let him imagine he was mistrusted, I determined, as we had already advanced two or three miles, to proceed without pause, keeping near him, and carefully watching his motions. At the same time I accurately noted our road, the localities which marked our progress, and the fords of the river.

I cannot remember to have ever benefited by the advice or example of others. Nothing but a blow from the cyclopean hammer of experience on my head could teach or convince me; and nothing less than the imminent jeopardy in which I had placed Zela, by taking her to the tiger-hunt, contrary to every one's advice and all prudent consideration, could have induced me to leave her on board the schooner, against her own urgent entreaty to accompany me. That I now knew her to be in that safe asylum, by removing every care and fear from my mind, seemed to leave my own body invulnerable. I had yielded, however, to Zela's importunities to take her little, intelligent Malayan girl, Adoo, in whom her mistress placed implicit confidence. Adoo neither cared nor thought about any thing in the world but Zela. Her attachment to me was grounded on my being loved by Zela. Adoo was nearly of the same age as her mistress, but no two creatures could be more dissimilar. The Malayan girl was stunted in growth, broad and bony, low-browed, with hair coarse, straight, and black, hanging over her flat tawny face, like a wild horse's foretop. Her small and deep-set eyes, by their unusual distance, seemed totally independent of each other, and to have power to keep a look-out to the starboard and larboard, the north and the south, at the same instant. They were bright, watchful, and eager as a serpent's, —but there ended the resemblance; for poor little Adoo, far from wile and guile, was the truest and most faithful hand-maiden that ever dedicated herself to a mistress, hand and heart. I was so partial to this little savage, that to keep her about my person, I installed her in the high and important office of Tchibookdgee;[1] and she was matchless in compounding a chilam for a hooka, preparing a callian, or filling a Turkish pipe,—accomplishments not to be despised.

To return to my story. We continued our route by the side of the river for about four miles, when, after ascending an abrupt and rocky eminence, our Javanese leader proposed to stop at two or three small cane-huts, and refresh ourselves with coffee and mangosteens, till some of the people he had sent forward should return to inform us where the game lay. To this I gladly acceded. My suspicions were in a great measure dissipated, seeing no further symptoms to corroborate those which had been lurking in my mind. Milk, fruit, and coffee, which last is of excellent quality in this island, were brought. Adoo, for I was a great epicure in coffee, superintended the making of mine. We were seated in one of the empty huts, to screen us from the sun; and whilst I was smoking my callian, the men were eating and drinking. The chief was sitting on a mat close by me, between me and the door, which was blocked up by Javanese. I was on the point of putting the coffee-cup to my lips with my left hand, as I leaned on my right, and lolled at the full stretch of my limbs, with my head resting against one of the bamboo-supporters of the hut, when my attention was directed to something touching my hand. Turning to see what it was, a low voice on the outside, but close to my ear, said,—'Hush! hush! do not move!' in such accents as evidently indicated terror. Without moving, I glanced my eye in the direction of the voice, and it fell on the keen glance of Adoo, through the matting. I leaned my head close to the spot, when she whispered in my ear,—'Do not drink the coffee;—come out;—bad people!'

Some of our men had complained of sickness immediately after they had drunk the coffee; and I recollected the officiousness of the chief in serving me with it. Instantly it struck me it was poisoned. Happily I had been detained from drinking it, awaiting the somewhat tedious process of preparing, filling, and lighting my Persian water-pipe. The chief, now at the door, was significantly exchanging glances with his men, or every eye was fixed on me; their savage and malign aspects plainly intimated their intentions. There was neither time nor opportunity to form plans or communicate with my men. Suspecting, which was the case, that the chief was waiting for a re-inforcement to attack us, and fearing, from the rising commotion withoutside, they had already arrived, and would, whilst my men were under the paralysing effect of the poison, rush in and butcher us, or fire the huts, and slaughter us as we attempted to escape, I drew a pistol, sprang up, and attempted to gain the entrance. The chief drew his creese, and essayed to detain me. I shot him through the body, and yelled the Arab war-cry, calling out to the men,—'We are betrayed!— follow me!'

So sudden had been my movement that the panic-struck natives rushed down the bank into the jungle. Restraining my men from pursuing them, my orders were to examine if their arms were ready for service, and to fix their bayonets. Adoo told me, from what she had overheard, some fatal or stupifying drug had been administered to the men in their coffee; and that the chief was waiting for a reinforcement. Many of the men were affected, complaining of sickness.

CHAPTER XVIII

Not the eagle more
Loves to beat up against a tyrannous blast
Than I to meet the torrent of my foes.
This is a brag!—be it so; but, if I fall,
Carve it upon my 'scutcheon'd sepulchre.

KEATS' MS.

THE first danger was over, yet was our situation most perilous. We set off, in double quick time, to regain the boats, or to get in sight of the schooner, and give signals of our distress. We regained the river and crossed it. Naturally concluding the natives would lurk in ambush to cut us off, I carefully avoided the route by which we had advanced in the morning, and kept on the highest and the clearest ground. By these precautions we succeeded in retreating three parts of the distance unimpeded, but not unobserved; as, from time to time, we heard the wild war-whoops of the enemy, hanging on our rear. As long as they remained there we had little to fear. Adoo, who ran close at my heels, kept a look-out on both sides, continually pointing at the direction the natives were taking, with extraordinary precision. As we proceeded, in addition to the danger of becoming embogged, was the probability of being attacked at such a disadvantage. At length arriving at an angle of the river, with a swampy morass before us, we were compelled to cross. Whether the strong stimulant of fear, or uncommon physical exertion had neutralized or retarded the effect of the poison, or the inefficacy of the drug itself, was the cause of its effects having disappeared, I know not; but, after the first half-hour, I heard no more about it.

Bent on the one momentous object of regaining our vessel, I led the party across the river, feeling my way and supporting myself with a boar-spear. We secured our cartridges in our caps. The water was shallow, but varying in depth, and the passage difficult from its treacherous coatings of soft, black, and slippery mud. Happily myself and five others achieved a firmer footing and shallower water, after having with difficulty toiled along up to the hips, when Adoo said—'Malik, they are coming!' I lowered my carbine to my shoulder, and called to the remainder of the men to hasten on. The natives, emerging from their ambush, gave a loud yell, fired their matchlocks, and ran tumultuously down to the river's brink. In all savage warfare, the first shout and the first volley are to give themselves courage to advance, and to intimidate and panic-strike their opponents; like yelping dogs, which pursue what flies, but sneak from the sturdy; therefore if the first aimless discharge and war-cry are unshrinkingly replied to and defied, the attack is rendered weak and wavering. The Javanese, seeing we stood firm, and prepared to fire on them, paused on the river's bank. Observing their hesitation we, that were in front, gave them a volley; and, the other men coming up, we shouted, and advanced rapidly to the shore to charge them. They retreated into the jungle, and we succeeded in crossing the ford without the loss of a man.

We hurried down the margin of the stream, the natives following close in our rear, or flanking us, occasionally throwing spears, firing their matchlocks, and yelling obscure curses and threats; to which we replied by a prompt shot the instant any of them became visible. The number of our pursuers was increasing, and, as we approached the sea, the jungle became thinner, when Adoo told me she saw horsemen advancing in our front. At that moment the odour of the sea-beach, impregnated as it was with dead weeds, rotten fish, and briny air, was inhaled by me with far greater rapture than ever fell to the lot of tobacco, or my favourite wines, hock, Bourdeaux, and Tokay. I called out to my men,—'Freshen your way, my boys,—the sea a-head!' and they sped along to the bank on which I stood, with more alacrity than I ever saw them fly up the rigging to catch a view of land after a tedious voyage. When we espied the silken, swallow-tailed vanes, glittering on the trucks of our dark-hulled schooner, although the hull was not visible, we gave a loud hurrah, with a volley of musquetry to our pursuers, and considered, somewhat prematurely, our difficulties over.

On the long line of sandy plain, bordering the sea, a dingy and confused mass stained its surface. A loud shout from the natives, dogging our heels, confirmed what Adoo's hawk's eyes had first descried, and which soon became distinct to us all. A body of native, and nearly naked, horsemen approached us at speed, armed with spears, and mounted on small, but swift and active horses. Their number was not great, but, backed by those who were already nearly surrounding us, they were enough to annihilate the hopes of the wisest, and to turn the thoughts of the best towards Heaven. But I was neither of the wise nor good; all my thoughts were occupied in how best to meet the coming danger.

A bank or bar was formed across the river, of mud and sand; where the salt and fresh water met, and where, in storms, torrents from the mountains and the wild waves joined in conflict depositing their spoils. Old trunks of trees, and pieces of wrecked canoes were firmly imbedded in this bank, through which the current ebbed and flowed in narrow channels, the bottoms of which were deep on both sides of the river. There was a sandy level, a desert waste on our left; close to the sea was the village, interspersed with clumps of the sea-loving cocoa-nut tree; and two or three clumps of these were dotted on our right, intercepting our view of the schooner. We had not time to occupy one of these groves, as the horsemen were rapidly approaching; I therefore promptly took possession of the before-mentioned bar in the river. We accordingly retreated into the water, and, with some difficulty, succeeded in establishing ourselves on the sandy ridges, having a good footing, and the water not deeper than the knees. The bank itself, with the rubbish on it, made a breast-work. I would have also occupied the opposite side, but our party was too small to be divided. I had still my fourteen men, two or three indeed slightly wounded, but not incapacitated from using their fire-arms. Besides other arms, each man had a musquet and bayonet, and our cartouch-boxes were nearly full; for I had economised our ammunition, on which, I knew, every thing depended.

CHAPTER XIX

That Saracenic meteor of the fight!
KEATS' MS.

'Tis a gallant enemy,
How like a comet he goes streaming on.
Ibid.

SHRIEKING and yelling, our foes advanced. We crouched down in silence. These wild and savage-looking horsemen were led on by their prince; mounted on a little fiery courser of a bright red colour, with a mane and tail flying in the air like streamers in a gale. The rider was the only one of the band turbaned, clothed, and armed from head to heel. His tattooed and stained features seemed on fire with impatience to begin the slaughter. The energetic ferocity with which he glanced at our small numbers reminded me of our Borneo friend running a-muck. The horse, inspired by the fiend on his back, kept in perpetual and rapid motion. The prince dashed in the water, fired a pistol at one, threw a lance at another, sprang to the shore, led on the horsemen, wheeled round, yelled at those skulking on shore, drove those on foot with his sword into the river, crossed it himself, recrossed, headed the natives on foot, and then resumed his place, leading, urging, and forcing the horsemen on us, while his horse, foaming and panting, did not for an instant slacken his rapid, springy, and mazy motions. Following him with my eye, and with my carbine resting on the bulk of a tree, behind which I was skreened, I fired several shots at him; but in vain,—a swallow in the air, or a sea-gull riding on a wave, tempest-rocked, would have been as difficult a mark. Yet so favourable was the position we held for defence, and so cool and well directed the fire we kept up, that all the efforts of the natives, impelled on by their meteor-like prince, were unable to dislodge us. But our ammunition was nearly expended, two men were killed, and others of our little band incapacitated by wounds. On the other hand, we had made great havoc amongst the natives, whose exposed situation gave us great advantage. The cavalry, who acted with the highest intrepidity, dashing into the river both above and below us, suffered severely from our fire, but more from the heavy mud on one side, and the deep holes, sunken trees, and spars on the other. Besides, except their prince, they had no fire-arms; but his devil's spirit seemed to be infused in them, and their screams were terrific. However, they could not reach us with their spears, and we slaughtered them in security. It was only by destroying them, or thinning their number, that we could hope to escape.

The time at which it was indispensable to make a desperate effort to land, and endeavour to regain the beach, was at hand. Luckily for us, the only passable ford at this point was where the horsemen could not, from the nature of the ground, oppose us, though a host of villagers withstood our passage. In this predicament, worn with toil, and almost exhausted, I cautiously, one by one, drew my men to the opposite bank, which, when perceived by the natives, they gathered down, and closed on us. The horsemen, whose number was greatly diminished, galloped off towards the sea, as I concluded, to cross and cut off our retreat. We were under the painful necessity of leaving two of the wounded. The first man who landed was killed by a stone from a sling, which was driven into the skull; so that our party was now reduced to nine, including myself. To quench their burning thirst, the men had drunk freely of the brackish water of the stream, which had made them sick; and their standing in the water, under the piercing rays of the sun, had so affected them, that, on their landing, they staggered about as if they were drunk.

It was still about a mile to the sea. Keeping close together, we left the ford, and, skirting the river's bank, proceeded onwards. The natives crossed and dogged our heels in multitudes, which obliged us occasionally to halt, and check their advance by a volley. At last we opened a view of the schooner's hull, and the drooping and staggering men breathed a new life. Our hopes were now sanguine, when a cloud of sand uprose before us, which, partially withdrawn by the wind, exhibited to our view the vampyre-prince, and his bright-red, fiery, and foaming horse, looming through the vapoury mirage of the dazzling white sand, like a centaur.

A small cluster of palms, shadowing the roofless ruins of a mud hut, stood to our left: all around was a sandy waste. To reach this spot was our only hope: thither we ran for our lives, panting as if our hearts would burst, and threw ourselves over the walls of the hut. One of our wounded fell from exhaustion on the road. Hearing a yell, I looked behind, and saw the malignant prince riding over his body, and endeavouring to trample him to death. He then jumped from his horse, and, as if disdaining to use his sword, smashed the man's skull with the butt of his match-lock or musket, sprang on his horse, yelled to his men, and rode to within a hundred yards of us. The horsemen then separated, and galloped round and round the hut, till, nearing us, they hurled their lances, which we returned with a volley. Two or three of the best shots, with myself, singled out the prince, when I observed his horse swerve round, and go off with a staggering gait, while a plume of the bird of Paradise in his turban was scattered in the air. I thought our comrade's death avenged; but no such thing: the prince pulled up, dismounted, shook himself, and after surveying his steed, remounted, and was again in motion; but his ardour appeared to be somewhat cooled.

We now had but a cartridge or two apiece, and were completely surrounded. Desponding and well-nigh exhausted, we prepared to sell our lives dearly, by desperately sallying out. I thought of death—it seemed inevitable. De Ruyter crossed my mind; but Zela's image drove him away, and totally engrossed all my thoughts, which were sad, for I believed they were my last.

The back of the hut was high, and, under its shelter, the natives had approached close to us. We smelt fire, and drove a hole in the wall with our bayonets, when we beheld they had gathered dry reeds and bushes, and had fired it. We drove them off; but to extinguish the flames was out of our power. In the front of the hut there were palm-trees, surrounded by a hedge of vacoua, a strong, prickly, impervious fence. I had several times reproached myself for not having occupied this spot in preference to the hut, being equally secure against the horse, and giving us room to act, with a better view of the proceedings of the natives. Luckily, the front of the hut formed one side of this enclosure, to which it opened as to a court-yard, and had therefore prevented the natives from entering it. The Javanese prince was impelling the savages to close in, and oppose our leaving the hut. My men had been murmuring at the predicament into which I had led them, and followed my injunctions hesitatingly and tardily to form themselves outside the hut in line, to drive the enemy, now close upon us, back with the bayonet.

CHAPTER XX

Because I think, my lord, he is no man,
But a fierce demon 'nointed safe from harm.

KEATS' MS.

AT that moment the low thundering sound of a heavy gun sea-
wards saluted our ears,—it was the schooner's! Its effect was
magical; my gloomy and desponding men brightened up, threw
their caps in the air, and wildly gave tongue like a pack of hounds.
It was the signal of succour nigh,—a sound that restored the dead
to life. Another gun was fired; and while the natives were astounded at its echo from the jungle and the hills, we rushed out amongst
them, drove them panic-struck before us, and threw ourselves
under cover of the palms. With a busy and cheerful alacrity the
men took up their appointed stations, and, shaking hands, swore
to defend themselves against all odds. Yet still the foiled barbarians were forced upon us by their prince and leader, who, with
unslackened courage, urged on his reeking horse from point to
point. We had but five or six cartridges remaining amongst us, and
trusted alone to our bayonets. The natives, observing that no
succour was near us, and that our fire was discontinued, advanced
close to the prickly hedge, and wounded several of our men through
the branches. In reality our situation was more hopeless than ever;
but most of the horsemen had gone towards the sea, and the prince
could not induce his followers to assault us, so much had they
already suffered, or we should have fallen an easy prey. I began to
imagine, what all my men had long believed, that the prince was
the evil spirit, and invulnerable.

Thus encircled like a scorpion girt with fire, we had passed
nearly an hour,—it seemed a thousand!—when my attention was
directed to the margin of the sea by the Javanese, who all turned
that way, and simultaneously yelled. Instantly I heard a fire of
musquetry, and a cloud of doubt, hanging over my mind, was
dispelled. They were my crew, coming to our rescue. Our first
impulse was to rush out and join them; but we could not abandon
the wounded. We shouted, and when I saw, by the crowd of
natives collected in front of us, that our men were approaching in
the right point, up the bank of the river, and as soon as we caught

a glimpse of the scarlet-capped Arabs, I gave signal of our position by firing my carbine; upon which I distinctly heard the war-cry of my Arabs. The prince, with his now diminished troopers, was galloping and wheeling about them; but I knew, by the continued and heavy fire, there was a force sufficient to repel any effort he might make. Yet did this undaunted leader, who, by the swarms gathered around him, seemed to have been reinforced, dispute with wonderful pertinacity their advance, so that they were frequently compelled to halt and fire. At length they approached the bank of the river on our flank, and, spreading in two bodies, advanced to our position. The natives retreated; and in my impatience, I sprung over the enclosure, cap in hand, cheering my gallant crew; when, ere I had proceeded half way to them, a light and bounding figure, with her loose vest and streaming hair flying in the wind, and in speed like a swallow,—(but oh! how infinitely more welcome than that harbinger of spring and flowers!) —came all my joy, my hope, my happiness, my Zela! She sprung into my arms, we clasped each other in speechless exstacy, and there thrilled through my frame a rapture that swelled my heart and veins almost to bursting. The rude seamen forgot their danger, and looked on not unmoved. This, in an instant, was followed by, —'what cheer, captain?'—'where are our messmates?'—and more vociferous cries and questions from Zela's Arabs, mingled, from a multitude of voices, with shouts and blaspheming threats against the Javanese.

Assisting our wounded along, we regained the bank of the river, and continued our march to the shore in good order, small bodies of the natives hovering about us, but not impeding our progress. The prince and the main body of the armed natives were in advance of us, seemingly with the purpose of disputing our embarkation, or attacking the boats previously to our arrival. This urged us on, for I knew the schooner lay too far out to cover the boats with her guns; but my second mate told me he had ordered the boats to lie out at their grapnels, and that the long-boat had a carronade in it. We were worn out with hardship, suffering from hunger, and more from thirst. Zela alone, as a child of the desert, had thought of bringing water, which had been given to the wounded. The boats were evidently kept from the shore by the armed natives on the beach. The schooner was in sight, and getting under weigh to run nearer in. As we approached the beach, I drew up my men, broke the throng before us with a volley, and drove through them with the bayonet; when the boats pushed in to the mouth of the river, and we succeeded in getting the wounded into them. But, as the men were following, the natives renewed their attack, and several of our men were killed in disorderly skirmishes in the water. The long-boat, full of men, was fast grounded in the mud, and the mêlée was hand to hand. The creeses of the natives were better weapons than our musquets; besides, our cartridge-boxes were full of water, and the confusion was so great, there being neither order nor command, that we were in imminent peril. We could not stand on the slimy bottom of the water, stained with mud, and incrimsoned with blood, and, in struggling, the men fell, when the natives stabbed them under water. Having placed Zela in the long-boat, aided by two or three steady men, the natives crowding round and holding on the gunwale, we discharged the carronade loaded with grape-shot. This made them pause, and gave our men time to rally. A second discharge cleared a space on the beach, and enabled us to get the boats afloat.

I was standing in the bow of the boat, with the match in my hand; the bow was hanging on a sand bank, whence the men were shoving her. The natives were scattered, and flying in terror of the cannon, and the beach was strewed with dead and dying, when the invulnerable prince, with unabated fury, headed and led on half-a-dozen horsemen, who stopped on seeing the engine, whose roar they so much dreaded, pointed directly on them. Turning round, the prince spoke some energetic words to them; then, with a shout, and an expression of scorn and daring, he forced his bright red horse along the sand bank, up to the bow of the boat, point-blank before the gun. I blew the match, and touched the priming,—it did not ignite. The prince dashed his turban in my face, and discharged a pistol at me. Whilst I was staggering from the shock, Zela promptly grasped the match, which had dropped from my hand, and fired the gun. A wailing scream arose along the beach from the Javanese. A wounded horse was madly plunging and trampling on his now prostrate rider,—but that was not the prince. Further on, just on the margin of the red surge, lay a mass of mutilated remains, huddled darkly together;—a human leg and a horse's, hands and hoofs, the garments of a man and the garniture of a horse, blackened with powder, and red with blood. Yet was there enough to identify the best horse that warrior ever mounted, and the most heroic warrior that ever led to battle.

Bb

CHAPTER XXI

A little shallop, floating there hard by,
Pointed its beak over the fringed bank;
And soon it lightly dipt, and rose, and sank,
And dipt again with the young couple's weight.

KEATS

I FELT myself severely wounded, without knowing where the
ball had entered. Unable to move my lower extremities, a dull and
torpid sensation crept throughout my frame. On looking downwards, I saw that my garments, from the right side to the hip,
were rent and stained with powder, and that my loose cotton
trowsers were on fire. No bleeding could be discerned. I lay down
on the thwarts of the boat, now afloat, and, the natives having
entirely discontinued their opposition, we left the shore. The
schooner was standing in, keeping up a desultory fire over the
beach. With returning sensibility, the heavy and benumbing
torpor was succeeded by excruciating agony. They laid me in the
after-part of the boat. Zela bent over me, and tried, with gentle
words and soothing attentions, to assuage my agony. 'Zela!'
I said,—'my good spirit!—tell me, was that our evil fate that
struck at my life?—was it Azrael, the red angel of death?—has
he wounded me mortally?'

'Bis Allah!' she answered, 'the good spirit paralysed the warrior's arm, when he aimed at your life. God is strong, and we are
weak. Death strikes the trunk, and not the limbs.'

The ball had entered[1] just below my right groin, inclining
downwards, the prince having been considerably above me when
he fired. The pain augmented, but the wound did not bleed; and
it was not a consolatory reflection at the time that we had no surgeon on board. I was hoisted on the schooner's deck, carried down
into the cabin, and laid on the couch. The prince had been so
close to me that a large portion of the powder had apparently
entered with the ball, and torn and scarified the surrounding flesh,
which was black and livid. Zela applied the yolks of raw eggs over
the wound to draw out the powder;—an Eastern remedy, and
certainly effectual. Nothing was done after this but washing with
hot wine and laying on poultices. For four or five days and nights

the pain was immitigable; except, which I have always experienced with gun-shot wounds, that it was more severe from noon till sun-rise; and no Raypoot ever watched and worshipped the first ray of the rising luminary of day so devoutly as I did. For twelve days I ate nothing, living, like the whale, on suction. What is the strongest impressed on my memory is the unparalleled devotion and unwearied attention of Zela, who, I really believe, suffered mentally more than I did bodily. A friend of our own sex cannot pass through the ordeal of attendance on a sick couch. Friends shrink from the trial; they will share danger,—nay, more, their purses,—they may give their aid, their counsel, and their pity; but they cannot sympathise with one in sorrow or sickness. No, it is the woman who loves,—she alone can soothe, watch with exhaustless affection and patience, endure the waywardness of mind and the vexatious absurdity which arise from sickness or sorrow. Can the friendship of man, however ardent and sincere, be compared with the idolatry with which women give up soul and body to the man consecrated by their virgin affections? Friendship is founded on necessity; it must be planted and cultured with care; it flourishes only on particular soils; whilst love is indigenous throughout the world. Friendship, like bread, is the staff of our existence; but love is the origin and perpetuator of existence itself. Can I think of Zela's care and watchfulness during my sufferings, without digressing on the matchless love of women? If there is a portion I would snatch from the gloomy abyss of my past life to live over again, it should be that month in which I lay wounded, pained, and helpless, nursed with far deeper love than that of the fondest mother when she watches the symptoms of disease, or returning health, over her first-born child.

It should have been remarked that when we got on board, we lost no time in hoisting in the boats and moving directly out to sea, keeping a north-east course, anxious to hasten our junction with the grab, and to have the advantage of Van Scolpvelt's surgical skill. At that time I had not learnt, what experience has since convinced me of, that, in nine cases out of ten, in gun-shot wounds, a surgeon, however skilful, is of little advantage. The probe and plug are discarded; blood enough to avert inflammation generally proceeds from the wound; a few poultices, cleanliness, and bandages are all that nature requires. With healthy and un-corrupted constitutions, nature must be left to use her own inscrutable and wonderous power of healing, recruiting, joining, dove-tailing, and glueing. As I recovered I cannot forget the wolf-like greediness with which I ravenously preyed on a piece of lamb. No words can express the relish with which I gnawed and crunched, with keen eye and sharp tooth, the very bones. The day after, Zela brought me the shoulder of a small kid roasted. It was at noon, and my imagination had been gloated all the morning exclusively on the dinner hour. On its being placed before me, I exclaimed, 'My God! is this all? Now I find the loss of poor Louis! He would not have given me the fragment of a starved kid, —he would have roasted the entire mother, with the kid as a garnish!'

As my appetite returned, my strength was gradually restored; and, with the dignified addition of crutches, I resumed my duty on deck. One of our wounded died, certainly not from the effect of his wound, which was but a scratch, but from the lingering effects of the drug in the coffee, with which he had greedily drenched himself. His comrades, for a long time, complained of the Javanese poison; but their disorder, I believe, arose from their taking the medicine I had prescribed for the sick,—wine. A steady sea-breeze, a moderate temperature, and the methodical regularity of a sea-life, dispelled fever and dysentery, and restored my men to health.

A few words will explain the cause of our receiving the timely succour in Java. Zela, with her younger hand-maiden, had embarked in a small canoe, fancifully denominated her barge, and had pulled along the shore to a sheltered nook, where she might indulge in her favourite recreation of swimming. This had been our diurnal habit, and we were almost amphibious. De Ruyter, at the Isle of France, used to compare me to a shark, and Zela, clothed in striped cotton, to the little blue and white pilot-fish, while she was preceding me in the water, or floating on the surface. At this time, as she was swimming, she caught the sound of musquetry, borne by the land-wind, and conveyed along the sheltered and unbroken surface of the sea; it was distant, low, and indistinct. At first she naturally concluded we were at our sport; but, she said, an indefinable presentiment of evil had crept on her mind. She dressed herself hurriedly; her first impulse was to land, and trace the noise to its source; but reflection forbad her following her inclination, and she paddled the canoe along the beach, towards the mouth of the river, where she had observed the boats were lying, but they were not there. The report of guns then became more distinct; and her exquisite sense of hearing enabled her to distinguish the sound of my carbine, by its sharp and ringing report. Soon after she faintly distinguished the shouts of the natives, which she discovered to be those of war, not of hunting. Hastening on board, she told the mate her fears. He went up to the mast-head, and there caught a glimpse both of the advancing cavalry, and the detached parties of Javanese hurrying from the village. The boats were luckily alongside, the long-boat having the gun in it for the protection of the woodcutters when on shore; they were quickly manned and armed. In spite of every remonstrance, Zela peremptorily insisted on accompanying them; · and, by being conversant in savage warfare, with unerring sagacity directed the party, which otherwise would not have arrived in time; so that I may justly call her the angel of my fate.

CHAPTER XXII

Here the earth's breath is pestilence, and few
But things whose nature is at war with life—
Snakes and ill worms—endure its mortal dew.
                                        SHELLEY

WHAT with calms and squalls treading on each others heels, pursuing the vessels of all nations which awakened the smallest hope of proving lawful prizes, and flying from those for which we were no match, ours was no idle life,—nor was it unprofitable. In India I had always seen those in power make that power subservient to their interests and passions; and thus is it ever with men, unless they are muzzled and chained like dogs, as is wisely enacted in some parts of Europe. I had acquired these rabid propensities, and my power to do wrong was only limited by my means. The gulf of Siam and the Chinese seas long resounded with the depredations of the schooner; and the approach of the horrid hurricanes and water-spouts, so prevalent there, were less dreaded than the sight of our long, low hull; yet, like the devil, we were not of quite so murky a hue as represented. Having faithfully narrated, in my previous history, particular instances of our acts and manner of life, selected from my private journals, I shall add wings to my story, by avoiding henceforth minute details, leading to endless repetition, and the methodical dulness contained in that book of lead,—I mean, a ship's log-book.

We first touched at the island of Caramata for water. Our stowage being principally occupied by plunder, leaving but a narrow space for water, our avarice was often bitterly punished by the severest torture human nature can sustain, when we have been severally limited to a daily modicum of three half pints, or less, of foul and fermenting water; yet, nauseous as it was, the most avaricious among us would have freely exchanged his share of the booty for an unlimited draught. My idea then of perfect happiness was a plunge in a lake of clear, cold water;—a river seemed too small to satisfy my insatiable thirst. We were in this horrible state of drought when we put into Caramata, where we obtained a plentiful supply of water, fruit, and poultry, upon which we renewed our course.

One of the rendezvous for meeting with the grab was in the vicinity of the Philippine Islands. Keeping along the north-east coast of Borneo, we boarded a large Chinese junk, off two burning islands. One of these islands was very small, and shaped like an inverted cone; the smooth edges of the crater were gilded with fire, whence arose a steady column of thin vapour, with occasional sparks. This seemed to be connected by a shoal, probably formed by the lava, to the larger island, which had no fire on its shaggy summit, was of the colour and form of a Persian's cap, and, from a jagged mouth below its top, thick volumes of black smoke were puffed out at intervals. The quarter-master said, 'Look at that lubberly, lazy Turk! what a blasted cool berth he has got, squatting in the sea bare-breeched, to smoke his water-pipe!' I laughed at the fanciful, and not inapplicable comparison. The junk was densely crowded with Chinese, migrating to Borneo as settlers. I bartered some birds'-nests for fresh provisions, ducks, hogs, and fruit, and left the living cargo unmolested to proceed on their voyage.

Some nights after this we were dreadfully alarmed at grazing on a sand-bank. Luckily, there was little wind, and we escaped without any apparent damage; for, had it been blowing weather, we should have been wrecked. We made the Island of Palawan, and brought up in tolerable anchorage off Bookelooyant Point, under the shelter of a group of small islands. Here we remained for two days, and, seeing nothing of De Ruyter, I got under weigh, and steered a northerly course, till I made our second rendezvous, at an island called the Sea-horse. It was uninhabited; and in a certain spot, the situation of which De Ruyter had particularly described, after considerable trouble in searching, I found a letter which he had promised to leave for me, with his further instructions, in the event of his not meeting me there. By this I was directed to run in a parallel line of latitude, therein set down, till I got sight of the coast of Cochin China. I acted accordingly.

Hitherto every thing went on well on board: the weather was remarkably clear and fine, with nights so shining and delightfully cool, that I generally passed them on deck, reading with Zela, or listening to Arab tales. We had been some days becalmed off an island called Andradas, to the westward of which we were slowly drifting, from an under-current, when we observed indications of an approaching change of weather. There was a breathless still-ness in the atmosphere, which was thick with heavy dew: the island became veiled, its outline shadowy and indistinct, the sun seemed blood-shot, and its dimensions considerably augmented; it had lost its wonted fire, and the eye might gaze on it undazzled: the stars were visible long before their hour; they appeared nearer to the sea, and resembled moons, but lustreless. This dismal and melancholy prelude was frightfully reflected in the water, and on the dark faces of my native crew. It was with difficulty that I aroused them from their torpor, to prepare for the battle which it was evident we should soon be compelled to fight with the wild winds and waves.

CHAPTER XXIII

Whilst above the sunless sky,
Big with clouds, hangs heavily,
And behind the tempest fleet
Hurries on with lightning-feet,
Riving sail, and cord and plank,
Till the ship has almost drank
Death from the o'er-brimming deep.
SHELLEY

THE men aloft were sending down the light masts and yards; we on deck were clewing up the sails, and the Arabs and natives drowned their fears in noise and bustle. I watched eagerly all around the horizon: its grey, misty hues were every instant denser and darker. Casting my eyes upwards, a ball of fire, which I thought was a shooting-star, descended perpendicularly from above us, as we lay becalmed and motionless, into the sea, close to our quarter, making the same sort of noise in the water as a red-hot cannon-ball. At the same moment the skies were rent asunder with an appalling crash: our vessel shook as if she had struck upon a rock: rain, wind, lightning and thunder burst over our heads all together, and the sea was lashed up into huge dark billows. The storm, happily, took us right aft; and, under bare poles, with wild and resistless force, rapid as lightning, it drove us before it. Having weathered the first shock, and there being sea-room, we soon recovered from our consternation, and the gale settled in the north-east. We got the storm-sails up, that we might be enabled to bring her to the wind, when the first fury of the gale was spent. Ours was a matchless sea-boat; and, having secured every thing snugly on board, we carefully luffed her up to the wind, and lay to, with a close-reefed fore-storm-staysail. The sky was of a pitchy darkness, the sea white with foam.

I went down in the cabin to see by the chart, as well as, under such circumstances, it was possible, where we were, when I heard a general shout on deck. Wondering what it could mean, I jumped up the hatchway, and, speechless with astonishment, beheld a large ship coming up slap on our weather quarter. She was scudding under bare poles. It was evident she had seen us; and I distinguished the face of a man holding a lanthorn over her bow, when we were asked, through a speaking trumpet, what we were, and then we heard,—'Schooner, a-hoy!—strike, or we will sink you!' Instantly all was in commotion on the deck of the frigate, for such I made her out to be, getting her guns out, and preparing to use them. My surprise prevented my replying, and it was not till her long tier of heavy cannon swept by us, so near that she actually with her main-shrouds grazed our jib-boom, and till a voice again bellowed out,—'Do you strike?'—that I gained my presence of mind, and, calling out,—'Put the helm up!'—we bore away, till I got the wind on my quarter. Several guns were fired at us. Our only hope was in more canvass on the schooner; and as soon as she felt it, and found herself released from the restraint under which she had laboured, with her head to the sea, groaning and staggering from the tremendous blows of the waves, she flew like a grey-hound, when let slip at its prey. She dashed madly through the crests of the foaming billows, which hissed and fumed as if boiling, and left in her wake a line of sparkling light like a meteor in the heavens, brighter from being contrasted with the blackness of the night.

While congratulating myself on our escape, the man, looking out on our fore-rigging, (for the fore-part of the deck was swept clean by every sea), called out,—'The frigate a-head!' We had just time to put the helm up again, when we swept by a ship, which I saw, by a dim lanthorn on her poop, was not the frigate, but a larger vessel. We had scarcely cleared her before we crossed the bow of another, and then another. I was bewildered. The mate said wildly and fearfully,—'These be no real ships, Sir,—but the "Flying Dutchman!"' To which the quarter-master answered,— 'I'll be damned if it be,—it be a China fleet.' The truth of this instantly flashed across my mind;—it was the homeward bound Canton fleet.

When well to leeward of them, we again hauled our wind, and lay to, till daylight should appear. After a dreadful night of anxiety, perplexity, and peril, the darkness, which I thought had lasted an eternity, slowly disappeared; and lurid streaks of light, be-tokening a tempestuous day, barely enabled me to take a survey of the dim and narrow circle of the horizon. What a change a single day had made! On the previous morning a child's paper boat might have swum securely, and now these English ships of colossean size, compared to which we must have appeared a nut-shell, were madly tossed about. Every wave, like a mountain, threatened to overwhelm them. Lashed up by the wind, the sea seemed boiling; and the frothy scum, formed on its surface, filled the air like a snow-storm. The old weather-beaten quarter-master, who had hold of the helm, as with his horny hand he wiped off the spray which was flying over him, and mingling with the tobacco juice down his grisly beard, said,—'Mayhap old Neptune's Mis'ess wants a cup of tea this morning, and has boiled the water, and belike will sarve herself out of those three tea-chests. Three!—ay,—my wife always turned in three spoonsful,—one for I, one for her, and t'other for the pot.'

The three East-Indiamen, which were from twelve to fifteen hundred tons, seemed to have suffered considerable damage. They were lying to, awaiting, as I conjectured, the coming up of their consorts; for it was evident they were part of the convoy I had encountered in the night: consequently concluding I was now both ahead and to leeward of them all, it was necessary I should get the weather-gage before the men-of-war came up, in order to be safe from their pursuit when the violence of the storm should abate. Accordingly, taking advantage of the lull, which generally occurs at break of day, under our storm-sails, we hauled our wind. I have said a better sea-boat never floated than ours: all our light spars were secured on deck, the hatchways and ports were battened down, and, being free from lumber, and in the best trim, we floated on the wild seas in comparative ease as well as security; whilst the huge and unwieldy Indiamen, high out of water, and lumbered up within and without, looked like any thing but swans on a lake. As the light became stronger, the horizon was enlarged; the sun, though at times obscured by dark masses of rapidly-passing clouds, pierced with its wandering beams the vapours hanging over the sea, and I was enabled, with a powerful telescope, to count seven other vessels, among which the most prominent was a line-of-battle ship, distinguished by her broad pennant as the Commodore. She was making signals, as I apprehended, to the frigate from which I had so miraculously escaped —thanks to the gale. Sweeping my glass round the horizon to windward, I observed the frigate bearing down to the leeward ships, seemingly to assist those which had suffered most, the weather ships having borne up and congregated to leeward, except one solitary bark, whose white and reduced main-topsail could alone be distinguished, in the very eye of the wind, or, as sailors say, dead to windward. She, too, altered her course, but not in the track of the others, her object appearing to be to keep near them, but not to go amongst them. I watched her intently: the cut of her sails, her taunt-masts, the celerity of her manœuvres, and the velocity with which she moved, proved her a ship of war, yet every thing denoted she was not English.

'Take the glass,' I said to the old quarter-master, 'I can't make out what the devil craft that is. She is altering her course, and coming down on us: we must wear round, and shew her our stern. Well, what do you make her out to be, quarter-master?'

'Why, Sir,' replied the old seaman, 'did you never see in the Indies three fore-and-aft sails such as she carries? I larnt that cut when I sarved in a New York pilot-boat, and I cut that there canvass, as sartain as my name be Bill Thompson!'

'What!' I exclaimed, 'is it the grab?'

'Sartainly it be,' says Bill.

CHAPTER XXIV

> Blow, swiftly blow, thou keel-compelling gale!
> Till the broad sun withdraws its lessening ray;
> Then must the pennant-bearer slacken sail,
> That lagging barks may make their lazy way.
>
> BYRON

THE welcome news spread through the schooner, and joy beamed from every eye. In an hour she came up alongside of us, when we gave a simultaneous cheer that arose above the noise of the still undiminished gale. My pleasure was indescribable, heightened at its being unexpected and opportune. As no boat could live in the sea, we could only communicate by our private code of signals, by which I was directed to keep close to the grab, and follow her motions.

The gale continued steadily blowing out of the Gulf of Siam, drifting the convoy down towards Borneo. We followed De Ruyter, as he edged down on them. I observed that most of the merchant-ships had suffered more or less damage: one of them had lost her foremast, which, as we afterwards were informed, had been struck by lightning, when twelve or fourteen men were killed—the commodore had her in tow. Another had lost her topmast and jibboom: being a heavy sailer, she was a long way to leeward, and the frigate, under much canvas, considering the weather, was towing her. The other ships were uniting their efforts to keep together, and assist each other: while De Ruyter practised successively every nautical expedient to harass and divide them, in which, with reckless effrontery, I aided and abetted. Day and night we hung on them, like wolves on a sheep-fold, kept at bay by the watch-dogs. Our superiority in sailing gave us the power of annoyance; but, besides the men-of-war, the greater portion of the Merchant-Company's ships overmatched us in number of men and weight of metal, carrying from thirty to forty guns, and from a hundred and fifty to three hundred men. Nevertheless, we impeded their progress so much by day with both feigned and real attacks, and deceived them so much at night by false signals with guns and lights, that they made every effort to destroy or get rid of us. The frigate gave chase to us alternately; but though she was a strong ship, and was handled in the most masterly and seaman-like manner, all her attempts were vain. My temerity frequently put the schooner in jeopardy: once, as she pursued me, out-carrying me with sail, I should inevitably have fallen into her hands, if her jib-boom and fore-topmast had not gone by the board, as she had opened a fire on me from her bow-chasers. Thus we succeeded in embarrassing and impeding the convoy, in despite of their strenuous and unwearied exertions to keep together, we being favoured by the islands, banks, and rocks scattered on their lee, towards which the continuance of the gale, aided by the swell and current, combined to drive them. The ship which the frigate had occasionally in tow, when deprived of that aid, by our keeping her incessantly on the alert, had drifted far astern and to leeward. As the sun set, De Ruyter was alongside of us, considerably ahead of the fleet. He said—

'In twenty-four hours this gale will have expended its strength, not the less violent, in the mean time, on that account. To-night we will make our last effort, which shall be to cut off that sternmost ship. I will prevent the frigate from succouring her till sunset: then she can be of no avail. I will come to windward of you. At nightfall, do you get in her wake, and you shall find me near you.'

With words to this effect De Ruyter left me; and, with even more than his wonted audacity, ran in among the convoy, undauntedly exchanging shots with several of the largest. By the rapidity of his movements he kept the frigate continually on the alert. The Indiamen looked like Chinese junks; and, for the most part, were manned with those outcast, miserable wretches, Lascars. Such a one was the dismasted ship, that De Ruyter and myself, having successfully detached her from the convoy, doubted not would be our prize.

England may be justly proud of her gallant seamen, hardy, fearless, and weather-beaten as the rocks on her own iron-bound coast. The wealth of a single island, paltry and insignificant in itself, maintains more effective ships of war at sea than all Europe combined. To this, however, every thing is sacrificed. Yet it is a singular fact that her vessels engaged in commerce are, without exception, from those employed in the most distant parts to the coasters, the most unsightly, dirtiest, and heaviest sailers in the world, and, during the war, the worst manned, for then the navy impressed all the able seamen. Owing to the injudicious law by which the tonnage-duties are levied, from the measurement of the length of kelson and breadth of beam, not by the tonnage a ship may actually contain, the merchant-ship-builder's study is to diminish the weight of the duty. This they accomplish by continuing the breadth, with little diminution, from the stem to the stern, by projecting the upper works, and sinking the hold to the depth of the well on the desert; so that, by the absurd measurement of our government, a ship, registered at seven hundred and fifty tons, frequently carries a thousand or eleven hundred tons freight. This absurd system can only be equalled by that of the Chinese, which, like other idiotic edicts, they defend on the score of antiquity. They measure the length from the centre of the foremast to the centre of the mizen mast, and the breadth is taken close abaft the mainmast; the length is then multiplied by the breadth, and the product, divided by ten, gives the measurement of the ship. By this method a brig often pays more than a ship, and a ship of one hundred tons half as much as one of a thousand. Yet the English and the Chinese are, in their way, both called wise nations.

CHAPTER XXV

But that sad ship is as a miracle
Of sudden ruin, for it drives so fast,
It seems as if it had arrayed its form
With the headlong storm.
It strikes—I almost feel the shock,—
It stumbles on a jagged rock,—
Sparkles of blood on the white foam are cast.

SHELLEY

A CHANGE in the weather was apparent. The small curled clouds, which hitherto had all scudded one way, congregating to wind-ward, where they remained stationary, arranged in horizontal lines, till incorporated in the dark and rugged bank, as if to supply the laboratory of the tempest with fuel, now no longer hurried on to a particular point, while their hues and forms were changed, being grey and evanescent. Night came on, with occasional showers of rain; and the obscurity was such that I could only at times catch a glimpse of the Indiaman, directed to where she lay by the signals of distress she made to those who could not possibly hear or see her, and, if seen, could not assist her. The gale, though broken, blew fiercely in squalls; and in the intervening lulls, when relieved from the pressure of the gale on the little canvas it was safe to carry, the sullen and tumultuous waves hurled us about, and the water fell on our deck with the noise and shock of an avalanche, every wave threatening to annihilate us. To add to our peril there were shoals and an extensive range of sunken rocks immediately under our lee.

We saw nothing of the grab till towards morning. The weather was then moderated; and De Ruyter informed me that he feared the Indiaman was wrecked; that when he had last seen her she was bound in by sunken rocks; that he had approached to warn her of her danger, and advised her to wear round, and haul her wind, but she had borne away before it, not knowing where she was. 'Now,' said he, 'they must all inevitably perish. Ay, they are firing guns for aid, but it is too late!'

De Ruyter's conjectures, as to her loss, were verified with the earliest break of day. The first object my eye rested on was the huge wreck of the ship, lying along a bed of rocks, fixed within its jagged points as in a cyclopean vice; while the immense waves, lashed into fury by the opposition of the low reef of scattered rocks, assumed their wildest and most destructive forms. Some arose like pyramids, others came sweeping along in continued columns, till, checked by the shoals, their crests flew upwards clear and transparent as glass; then, curling inwards, they hissed and rolled on, till, encountered by the reaction of the eddying swell from other quarters, they successively disappeared in spray and foam. In the very midst of this horrific whirlpool, with the surf thundering on her, as if ejected by the force of a volcano, the doomed wreck lay, like a stranded leviathan.

Not a vestige of the convoy could be descried through the dim veil of misty clouds which hung on the verge of the horizon. The gale, after drawing round to the east, expended its last efforts, and died away at the first ray of the sun. We lay pitching and rolling so heavily that our masts bent like rattans, the knees and timbers of the vessel groaned and shrieked as if torn asunder, and the bulk-heads and deck opened and closed with the violence of the motion. We were already so near the rocks as to fill us with dread. To think of succouring the crew of the wrecked vessel, (should indeed any of them still exist,) was at that period out of the question. With a telescope I could make out that the main-mast with the main-yard, and the stump of the mizen-mast were the only parts of the wreck, over which the sea did not continually break. The fore part of the vessel was bilged, and occasionally under water; so that I knew the decks must have blown up, and her cargo been washed out. Her poop was high out of the water, but the surf played over it like a fountain. It was evident, if any of her crew had escaped, they must be on the weather main-yard-arm, which was topped considerably up, the lee side drooping, and the swell striking against it. Had any sought refuge on the weather side of the yard, it was barely possible they could maintain their hold against the continued shocks to which they were liable.

At nine A.M. the swell had so far abated that, seeing De Ruyter prepare to get a boat out, I followed his example; and succeeded with a light and particularly buoyant whale-boat, with the second-mate and four of my best seamen—my wound confining me on board. De Ruyter having spoken my boat they proceeded to-gether, making a long sweep round the shoals to leeward, as I readily conjectured, to make the desperate attempt at approaching the wreck;—the gallant De Ruyter, the first of seamen, and the first in danger, whether to save or slay!—while I, impotent as a bed-ridden hag, could only curse the paralysed limb, which withheld me from following his noble example.

It was past noon ere I observed the two boats returning round the reef towards the grab. I had been able to distinguish men moving on the main-yard of the wreck, and that the boats had succeeded in getting near enough to induce them to lower themselves by ropes into the sea. Some, I concluded, were saved. The schooner being the lighter vessel, I got her nearer to the boats; and, the swell continuing to go down, they reached us in safety. De Ruyter swung himself on board with a rope; and, as he wrung my hand, his face beamed with joy brighter than I had ever beheld it. 'Had that lubberly ship,' said he, 'kept clear of the rocks, she would have been ours, and I should have cleared forty thousand dollars; yet, I know not why, the rescuing four of her people gives me greater pleasure than if I had made a prize of her, or of tea-chests piled high as the Himmalayan mountains. Poor fellows! they must be endued with the hardiness of otters to have lived through such a night, on such a perch. Hoist them on board, my lads!—but first the father and his son.'

The words were scarcely uttered when a man, with a rent jacket of red camlet and yellow facings, embroidered with silver cord, and the other parts of his dress stained and dripping, came feebly staggering towards me, evidently unable to support himself. A dark stripling, naked to the waist, of a light and muscular form, held him up by the arm. The former was between forty and fifty years of age, a captain in a Bengal regiment, returning to Europe, on leave, after five-and-twenty years' service in India; by which he had acquired a right to full pay for the remainder of his life, amounting to a hundred and eighty pounds per annum. This beggarly stipend, had his habits or the climate been more temperate, he might have lived many years to claim; but incarcerated in the oven-like atmosphere of Calcutta, his liver had enlarged to the same unnatural proportions as that of a Strasburg goose, and by the same means,—heat and stuffing. Bile, not blood, seemed to circulate, or rather to be stagnated throughout his body, dying his skin with the slimy green and yellow hue, encrusting standing water. His annuity was not worth half a year's purchase. The boy was from sixteen to seventeen, his son by a native woman.

Grafted on an indigenous stock he had grown well, and gave promise of goodly fruit. These and other particulars I learnt afterwards, for instantly on their arrival on board I gave them a separate cabin, and had all their wants supplied. Of the other two men saved, one was the third mate, a square athletic north-countryman, inured to wreck and storm, having been brought up in a collier on his own dangerous coast. The other was the serang, or native boatswain; he was the finest looking fellow I ever saw, as good a seaman as he was a brave man—the more remarkable from his caste being stigmatised for dastardly conduct. The gallant youth, who had preserved his father through all the dangers I have described, these men spoke of with wonder and admiration.

CHAPTER XXVI

Then rose from sea to sky the wild farewell;
Then shriek'd the timid, and stood still the brave;
Then some leap'd overboard with dreadful yell,
As eager to anticipate their grave;
And the sea yawned around her like a hell.

BYRON

WHEN refreshed by sleep and food, the third mate told his story of the wreck. His ship, one of the largest, had lost her topmasts, and was otherwise greatly damaged by being taken aback, when first struck by the gale. The frigate had occasionally taken her in tow. She was a very heavy sailer, hardly sea-worthy. Her cargo consisted of tea, silk, and sundries. With women, children, black servants, and others, there were above three hundred souls in her. In the early part of the night she laboured so much from the heavy swell as to become generally leaky; many of the chain-bolts were drawn, and the chain-plates gave way. In bearing up to ease her, two of the guns of the main-deck had broken loose; one of them had stove in a port-hole, which let in the water; upon this the pumps became choked from the tea getting into the well. When the grab had hailed her, and told her of the rocks, she had attempted to wear round, but, for want of head-sail, became ungovernable. Ultimately the wind, swell, and indraught drifted her bodily towards, and then by force through, a narrow channel of the reefs.

There, brought up stern-foremost on a sunken ledge of rocks, in the very midst of the breakers, all the Lascars instantly betook themselves to the rigging and masts. The wailing and screaming were so loud as to drown the uproar of the winds and waves. The spray, sometimes the waves, covered the ship; all thought they were already under water; most of those on the decks were so bewildered that they were washed overboard, before they could take any measures to save themselves. Nothing was visible but the white foam bubbling all around. They were entirely ignorant of where they were, or what they were to do. 'At that moment,' continued the third mate, 'I knew not a single person on board. I swung myself into the main-rigging by a rope; many Lascars and some of the officers were there. I went on the main-top; that also was crowded; none could be heard to speak, from the spray which even reached them there. Soon after I saw the foremast go by the board;—from the noise on it I thought it was covered with men;—they were all lost! Hardly did I know the deck of my own ship; her forecastle seemed entirely under water. I heard a crash; I thought it was the sea working its way between decks, having entered by the hatchways. By a loud report, like thunder, I knew the decks were blown up, and the ship water-logged. Some time afterwards, towards morning, she made a sudden lurch, and fell on her beam-ends to port;—the shock was so sudden and violent that it carried away the mizen mast, on which was the greater part of the Europeans; and it threw most of the men out of the maintop, and the lee main-yard arm;—being in the water, all were swept from it! I and the serang, who had held fast, seeing the top was going to pieces, no longer tenable, crawled out on the weather main-yard, which we found almost abandoned; for the braces, which steadied it, being carried away, and the mainsail, having got loose, had shaken off those which were on it; yet, though the sail was blown away, the yard was swinging about see-saw fashion. I then first came athwart the old captain, clinging like a lobster to a rock, with the young half-cast sticking fast as a barnicle alongside him, both of them lashed on the yard by the gaskins, which the lubbers had cast loose for that purpose, not knowing the sail would get adrift, which had caused so much mischief. Daylight appeared, when I could only count six alive. We were almost exhausted, and without hope, till we saw your boats; but when we looked round, we thought it impossible that any one could near us; for we were shut in by breakers, on which the sea burst so violently that we could scarcely hear each other's voices. Besides, we knew you were French privateers; and when we did observe the boats shove off, pulling towards us, we thought they came to see what plunder they could pick up, not to save us.' Here the mate's hard north-country visage brightened, and his small blue eye glistened from under his high cheek-bones. 'I have seen many brave and good boatmen come off in life-boats, and other shore-boats on our coast, in gales when no ship could shew a rag of canvass, but no man ever saw such a devil's bay as we lay in. The eddying swell whirling round and round, flying up like water-spouts, dead men, tea-chests, casks, bales of silk and cotton, ship-sails, spare boats and oars, men's hammocks, chests, were all tossed topsy-turvy about together. It made me, Sir, very queer to look at it; for they all seemed alive, and the men moved their arms and legs about as if they were drunk. There was in particular an old black nurse holding a white child in her arms, which she seemed trying to re-ship on board us, and then she spun round and round the rocks; and I thought I heard the body squeeling, every time they were dashed against the rocks. A man near me on the yard never took his eyes off her; and, all at once, he called out, as if he were stark mad,—'Ay, ay, old devil, I am coming! I am coming!'—and dashed head foremost amongst 'em; he didn't strike out a stroke, but went down like lead. The old captain told me not to look below; and I did feel my head going round, as if I were top-heavy. A fish or a cork could not float steadily for an instant in that roaring whirlpool, and yet the American captain got near enough, after a number of trials, to throw a lead line on board, when the first man who tried to get hold of it was washed off and drowned. Then it was again thrown, and that young lad, the officer's son, who was as active as a monkey, got hold of it, and I secured the end of a rope to it, which the captain hauled on board. One by one we lowered ourselves down, and were hauled into the boat; and, thank God! though you don't carry English colours, there are some of my countrymen on board,—and that's all I care for. And I must say, though this be a Yankee, I never saw better craft, or better seamen, or kinder to brother tars in distress.'

In the English accounts of this loss it was stated, and never contradicted, that, in a dismasted and leaky state, she had been seen in the dusk of the evening, bearing away, and firing guns of distress. That the men of war, convoying the fleet, could not assist her, as the commodore had already a ship in tow, which, but for his aid, must have been wrecked, being completely dismasted; and the frigate was engaged in keeping off two fast-sailing French privateers, which had been hanging on the convoy during the heaviest gale the oldest seaman had ever witnessed in the China seas; and that the ship missing was supposed to have foundered, or been wrecked on the sunken rocks and sand-banks, which bind the north-east coast of the island of Borneo.

National pride, like the pride of individuals, requires to be well oiled in order to work smoothly; and John Bull, with all his vaunted plainness and honesty, is, in reality, as vain and gullible as the strutting gander after it is stuffed with oil-cake. His dignity would have been compromised at any allusion to the East Indiaman's having been cut off from her convoy, guarded by his omnipotent and invincible ships of war, by a couple of French *Lettres de marque*, and during a tremendous gale, when British tars flatter themselves that they alone have the hardihood to at once contend against its fury, and to act offensively against an enemy.

CHAPTER XXVII

Trust not for freedom to the Franks—
They have a king who buys and sells.
In native swords, and native ranks,
The only hope of courage dwells;
But Turkish force and Latin fraud
Would break your shield, however broad.

BYRON

So from that cry over the boundless hills,
Sudden was caught one universal sound,
Like a volcano's voice, whose thunder fills
Remotest skies.

SHELLEY

As soon as the weather permitted, we steered a north-east course, till we made those small islands off the coast of Borneo, where we had anchored on a former occasion. Here we brought up, repaired our damage, landed our sick, and refreshed ourselves.

I had given De Ruyter an account of every thing I had seen, heard, or done. He was much moved at the account of Louis's death; for Louis, though with an exterior as rough and hard as that of the cocoa-nut, had the genuine stamp of worth, not to be forged or effaced; and he possessed as many good qualities as he was generally useful. 'I do not know,' said De Ruyter, 'how we shall manage without him. He has long had entire control over our money-affairs,—an admirable accountant; and to find another honest man, that is so, to fill his place, will be difficult. There is contagion in the handling of money, and in the knowledge of the science of numbers, which gives too great a facility in the sub-stracting from others to add to ourselves. It makes the mind sordid; the rapacity of money-mongers, commissaries, and pursers is proverbial. We must therefore, despairing to fill his place by any other, share his duty between us.'

After attentively listening to my affair with the Javanese, he exclaimed,—'So, you went a wild goose, or a boar chase, excited, I suppose, by its perilous absurdity! It is true, no one could have extricated himself with greater judgment; but who else would have been guilty of such folly? You are as rash and headstrong as our Malay friend, the hero of Sambas.'

'By the by, De Ruyter,' I replied, 'your alliance with that pre-datory tribe of Malays appears to me as gratuitous an act of un-knightly errantry as my Quixotic expedition at Java.'

He rubbed his hands with glee, his eye brightened, and on his dark and manly features was legibly traced the satisfaction swell-ing at his heart. His lips curled, and his breast dilated, as he said, —'No, my lad;—to harass, burn, sink, and destroy their enemies is a duty I owe to the flag I sail under. I confess I should not so gladly engage in these profitless expeditions, but that I loathe and detest the English-merchant Company,—and all companies, for they are bound together by narrow views and selfish ties. Revenge, or rather retribution, is to me what the Sultan of Borneo says of that matchless diamond he possesses,—like the sun, above all price. A parson-poet of yours exclaims,

> 'What is revenge, but courage to call in
> Our honour's debts?'

—and debts of honour, you know, must be scrupulously paid. I think, for every dollar they once took from me, they have subsequently lost, and by my means, as many thousands. The Company had long sought to obtain a secure footing on that side of Borneo; but the almost total want of harbours, and the opposition everywhere met with from the noble and chivalrous Malays continued to frustrate their attempts. At last they fixed their greedy eyes on the town of Sambas, which has a river; good anchorage, not very distant, and is defended by a fort, besides being situated in the best part of the island for commerce and culture. Perfidious in design as atrocious in act, they gave out that the purpose of their expedition was exclusively to destroy that piratical settlement; when the fact was they had determined to settle there themselves, and lay the foundation-stone of their old system, by which they first take all the produce and trade of the country, and then the country itself.

'The grab being in a secure berth, and our heroic Malay chieftain having pledged himself and people to be under my guidance, I, after completing the necessary arrangements, directed him to embark his followers in their war-proas, when, with a strong party in my boats, we proceeded together along the coast, till we arrived at Tangong point, where we disembarked, and where I left my boats. We then marched overland; the heavy guns and other bulky articles being sent round in the proas. After a very long and distressing journey through forests, over rugged and gigantic mountains, across pathless and almost endless plains, rivers, torrents, and morasses, we came to the banks of the river of Sambas. On one side was a swamp, and on the other an inextricable and interminable jungle. Through intricate paths, guided by the natives, we at last arrived at the town of Sambas, marked out for destruction by the English. Its inhabitants were huddled together in many miserable rattan huts, under cover of a shapeless mass of mud and timber, dignified with the appellation of tower, or fort. Here and there were scattered basket-like habitations, supported, as you are, on crutches, and apparently ready to move to the town, when tempted by business or necessity. Journeying along, I had observed a very capacious, a magnificent bay, shut in by islands, to the eastward of the Malay town, in which, it was evident, the invaders would anchor their vessels, and disembark their troops. I likewise found the native inhabitants were moving their goods, chattels, and war-boats to recesses and fastnesses, prepared to avoid, as it looked, rather than oppose, the threatened invasion of which I had given them notice. At my instigation the chieftain went with his people into the jungle and morasses, ascended to the mountain caverns, to harangue the grey-bearded leaders of the pirate coast, and rally together. At the sound of battle and plunder, the hidden warriors started out like packs of jackals from their retreats; the enterprising spirit of the chieftain inspired every heart, and spread like fire up a mountain in the dry season. Detestation of the Europeans, and emulation of each other, conspired to multiply their numbers, and collect them together. On the second day, while I was putting the fortress into a defensible state, and sinking trees to obstruct the passage of the river, I was startled at the wild war-cry of thousands of these noblest of barbarians. They came pouring down the mountain like a deluge, and I was well pleased to be in possession of the mud-fortress during the first paroxysm of their inflammatory fever. The violence of their gestures, their piercing shrieks, the discharging of their fire-arms, the shaking and clashing of swords and spears, the blasts of their conch-shell trumpets reverberating from rock and ravine,—it seemed as if all the natives of that savage land were running a-muck. My friend, the chieftain, soon came to me, accompanied by the most potent leaders of the various tribes. To these he made me known; and, after the prelude of a plentiful, but not a splendid feast, we proceeded to business. The chieftain, who was a great orator, made a long harangue, in which he magnified my services, and concluded with proposing me as their general director, being best acquainted with European warfare. I separated the respective tribes, and allotted them particular stations, where they were to lie concealed till the enemy had entered the river, and landed the troops. Then they were to be permitted to advance a certain distance, on which a large body of Malays, by shewing themselves on the side of the jungle, should compel them to keep on that side leading to the marshes. When arrived there, they were to be opposed by the natives of the town, who were the best acquainted with its localities. But you may see, in my journal, a map of the place, and a plan of its defence, which was only partially acted on, their sanguinary impetuosity breaking frantically through every restraint.

'When every thing was prepared, we waited the arrival of the flotilla from Bombay. We had placed look-outs all along the coast, and sent fast-sailing proas into the offing. It was so long ere they came, and, when we had sight of them, they were so tardy in their movements, that we well nigh despaired of slaking our unquenchable thirst for vengeance. The soil of India has been crimsoned with the blood of her children; her sultans, her princes, and her warrior-chieftains have been exterminated. India has been subverted by the adventurers of Europe, in their search for gold. To pay off the accumulated arrears of blood, by exacting life for life, is as impossible as to pay off the debt of bankrupt Europe. However, they talk of liquidating that, and India may yet exact a fraction, in the way of dividend, for the myriads of lives so wantonly expended by her prodigal Christian invaders. Would that I might live to behold the eastern ocean red with blood, as was the paltry stream of Sambas, on the day we broke through the marshalled ranks of the Christians, when the fierce and ungovernable Malays breasted the renegade Sepoys' bayonets, with irresistible fury drove them from the muddy banks of the river into its dark waters, and left an ample feast for its swarms of alligators and dog-fish, and for the jackals and vultures on shore! No quarter was given; little plunder acquired. We pursued the fugitives, destroying them as they endeavoured to regain their vessels. Some boats from their shipping were still landing stores, guns, and a few remaining troops; which, by making a stand, facilitated their escape. Yet the slain far outnumbered the rescued,—at least of those who landed. But stop,—I hear our Malay chieftain coming alongside. Let us go up and welcome him.'

The Malays from their proa were soon on board of us. The chieftain rushed towards De Ruyter, knelt and kissed his hand, and then placed it on his heart and head. Afterwards he made a speech, with a voice and action not studied from the school of Demosthenes, but of such violence that the limbs and muscles of his native auditory were set in motion as if by the power of galvanism; which proved, that passionate and untaught eloquence can move the heart of man, as much as, or perhaps more than ever did the learned and commanding diction of that time-serving, subtle Greek philosopher. The purport of his speech was to reiterate their thanks for the repeated services De Ruyter had rendered to their nation, and to express their admiration of him, his courage, and his wisdom;—his words were, 'greater than a lion in fight, and in wisdom a prophet.' They conjured him to stay with them as their prince. They would build him a house on the

gold mountain, at the foot of which runs the river of diamonds;
—this was no oratorical flourish, for a great quantity of gold is
yearly dug from the mountain, and very fine diamonds are fished
from the river. They would give him all they had, and he should
be their father. They only besought of him one small boon; which
was that he would use his influence with the great warriors of his
nation, to go to the little island of great ships, (meaning England,)
and, while the ships were in its ports, awaiting the monsoon to
blow over, that he and his warriors should then burn all the ships,
lay waste the island, and drown all the people. 'Thy son,' (meaning me,) continued the chieftain, 'can stay with us, whilst thou
dost go and do this. Every old man shall be his father, and thy
voice shall be heard and obeyed through him. For is he not of thy
blood?'

De Ruyter, perceiving me smile, said, 'Well, who knows?
Wilder words than these have been spoken ere now, and scoffed
at; yet, in after ages, they have been called prophecies, when
proved, or believed in,—no matter which.'

During our greetings and conversation, a feast had been prepared, of which the chieftain partook, and then told De Ruyter
that every sort of provision should be sent down to him on the
ensuing day, and his wishes complied with, whatever they might
be. He concluded with,—'Thou lovest my people, for thou hast
done more than their fathers and mothers for them;—they gave
them life, but thou hast given them freedom. But my people are
poor, and like presents; I have, however, told them if any accept
the smallest trifle from thy people, I will—' (and here he glanced
fiercely round his own men)—'kill him, even though we had both
come from the same womb, and been suckled by the same bosom.'
They then descended into their proa, and went on shore.

CHAPTER XXVIII

The world is full of woodmen, who expel
Love's gentle dryads from the trees of life,
And vex the nightingales in every dell,
With harsh, rude voices, and unseemly strife.
                                                    SHELLEY

IMPATIENT of confinement, and anxious to see my old friends
in the grab, I went on board of her, accompanied by my little
nurse, Zela, and De Ruyter, who loved her as his child. There we
passed a jovial night, supping and carousing till daylight under
the awning, while the grab's crew danced and sung; for, with
permission, I had brought them a barrel of Java arrack, which is
the best in India.

I must not forget Van Scolpvelt, whom I found nearly the same
as when I left him. My first sight of him was through the skylight
into his pigeon-house-looking dispensary. Near the chinks and
crevices of the beams were several long centipedes crawling about;
and all the cockroches in the ship sought refuge there. Van cared
not for them, provided they did not, which cockroches are liable
to do, when hard pushed for water, creep into his mouth as he
slept. He was perfectly indifferent to their dropping into his soup,
or his tea; perhaps indeed he took the same pleasure in seeing
them scalded to death as did Domitian in viewing the struggles of
the flies, which, for pastime, he cast into spiders' webs. There sat
Van, smoking his meersham, and lugging by its hairy leg, a particular fine, large cockroche out of his tea-cup. The tea not being
hot, the huge beetle was no more than refreshed by its warm bath.
Van, either struck by its extraordinary size, or merely to wile
away the time, after holding it up to the light, spitted it scientifi-
cally, and began to scrutinize it through a magnifying glass. I was
now about to hail him, but De Ruyter put his hand on my mouth.
After Van had satisfied his curiosity, he threw the insect out of
the scuttle, and sipped his beverage. His anatomical propensities
being thus awakened, I saw him fix his eye on the beam, then with
a sudden dash of his long skinny thumb, and with a pressure which
proved him to be no tyro in the art, he pinned the head of a centipede firmly against the timber, the body being concealed in a rent.

The thumb-screw pressure prevented the reptile from using its venom; and the long writhing body, with its hundred quivering legs, fell into the open palm of Van, who forthwith projecting his fore-finger, so as to form a natural forceps, clutched the crushed head. It was the longest and largest I had ever seen. Van, after an attentive examination, put it into a bottle, which contained many more preserved in spirits, where it long writhed about; for it is curious that a centipede, even in that state, will continue wriggling for hours.

De Ruyter now hailed the doctor, who replenished his pipe, put his jacket on, and shuffled up the hatchway. He held out his defiled fin, which, notwithstanding the venom on it, I shook heartily. He then inquired into the particulars of my sick-list, and devoured my discourse as I narrated the ravages of the Java fever. As he heard of the death of poor Louis, he expressed great sorrow, apostrophising, however, on his obduracy with regard to medicine, and eagerly demanded if he had not, during his sufferings, called on his name. To this I answered, 'No.'

'No!' echoed Scolpvelt—'then he died an impious unbeliever! I alone could have saved him!'

When I recounted the death of one of my Arabs from poison, he asked if there was nothing else the matter with him. I mentioned he had been slightly wounded; and, upon his desiring to be informed of the appearance of the wound, I told him the fellow complained it was painful, and it looked reddish.

'What!' said he, 'was it a phagedœnic sloughing sore?—or do you mean an erysipelatous inflammation? Were not the chylopœtic viscera disordered? What did you apply?'

'Apply, Van?—why, I told the fellow to drink congee-water with lemon in it, and to wash his, leg with brandy; but he washed his gullet with the brandy, and the sore with the lemon drink.'

'Did he?—then he proved he knew more of medicine than you did. That fellow should have lived, and you died!'

Scolpvelt vehemently cursed the surgeon who had deserted his post during the battle with an enemy against whom, for the benefit of science, he should have gloried in contending. He then insisted on examining my wound, and observed that, from its appearance, surgeons in general would believe some portion of my garments had entered with the ball, and would prevent the cicatrization by forcing a probe to sound the passage of the ball. 'Now,' he said,

'I know, from a long series of practical experience, which few like me have had, in gun-shot wounds, that, whatever clothing may be shot through, the ball enters the flesh without ever conveying a fibre of it into the wound; unless, indeed, it is a ball almost spent, which can consequently but inflict a superficial wound.'

He wound up his discourse by telling me he saw decided symptoms of jaundice in my eyes and skin.

My old quarter-master, standing by me open-mouthed with astonishment at the puzzling scientific language, from time to time drawled out, 'I wonder what rate that ship may be he is launching now!'—'Thirty years in the navy, and never heard of the *Hajademee* and the *Chylopottic*!—I suppose they be first-raters, Dutch.'—'The *Cockatrice* sloop-of-war I have heard of.'

At last Van turned round with—

'What is the old dog mumbling, eh?—he is rotting with the scurvy—look here!'—at which he applied his hard thumb to the seaman's red and hairy arm: then, pressing on it, he removed his claw, and pointed to the place.

'Look?' said he, 'the indented stamp remains—the collapsed muscles have lost their power and elasticity, from the transudation of the blood in the veins.'

The quarter-master, without noticing the impression on his wiry arm, perhaps because it had no more sensibility than my crutch, said—

'*Collapse*—why, he means the *Colossus* seventy-four, or the *Cyclops*. As to *Ticity* and *Ansudation*, I suppose they too be Dutch craft.'

Van toddled off to see what citric-acid he could spare, saying he should visit the schooner's sick in the morning.

CHAPTER XXIX

I love all waste
And solitary places; where we taste
The pleasure of believing what we see
Is boundless, as we wish our souls to be.

SHELLEY

THE hard features of the old Rais relaxed as he greeted me; and Zela, who loved him for his former kindness, kissed his hand, and, sitting down by him, talked of their country and their tribes. On this topic alone the old Arab was loquacious. They continued, with little intermission, in animated discussion on the matchless beauties of their native countries, till the grey light of morning shone on his dusky form, and illuminated Zela's pallid brow. She dwelt on the magnificence of the town and river of Yedana, its dark mountains, bright waters, and perpetual verdure; the cool breezes from the Persian gulph, and the blue islands of Sohar, of one of which her father had been Schaich. The Rais admitted all this, but warmly protested against their being compared to the riches of Kalat, or the splendour of Rasalhad; then the summits of the Tor mountains touched heaven, and the desert, where he spent his youth, was large as the sea,—but unfortunately there the similarity ended, for it had not a drop of water within its vast circumference. He endeavoured to convince Zela what a paradise was this desert without water or wells, and how peacefully and patriarchally they lived by supplying themselves from the caravans, and exacting tribute from all that passed the inhospitable ocean-bed of sand. By some queries from her he was, indeed, compelled to admit the horrid tortures they sometimes suffered from the want of water; that, it was true, by the parched and shrivelled corpses of perished travellers they used to trace the caravans, which more than compensated them for what they endured—God knew what was best for his children! As he was fondly dwelling on these horrors, I capsized a bucket of water, in which we had cooled our claret, over his head, took Zela by the hand, got into the boat, and returned aboard.

Soon after the schooner was surrounded by country boats, laden with live stock, fish, fruit, and vegetables, enough to have

provisioned a frigate. At the same time the four persons whom De
Ruyter had redeemed from the wreck, went on board the grab,
where there was better accommodation, he promising to embrace
the first opportunity of shipping them to the English settlements.
The bilious captain of the Bengal army continued to suffer from
the hardships he had endured during the wreck of his ship. While
I think of it, I will conclude their history. We shortly after shipped
them for Bombay in a prize we had made, plundered, and liberated. The captain and his son took their passage for England. De
Ruyter and myself, unknown to the father, had insinuated a purse
of gold mores into a trunk of necessaries which they had been
compelled, in their utter destitution of clothing, to accept. Either
at the Cape of Good Hope, or at St. Helena, the father died, and
thereby relieved the Company from the burthen of his annuity.
Of the youth, a lad of noble feelings, and an incomparable son,
I never could gain the slightest intelligence; though I fulfilled my
promise, made to his father at parting, of doing my utmost to find
him out and serve him. Neither did the mate return to England;
for, as I heard, he had a command in the country coasting-trade,
and, probably, the serang continued with him.

During our stay here we hove the schooner down, to examine
if she had sustained any damage by striking on the sand-bank.
There was nothing the matter with her, except that a few sheets of
copper were rubbed off. We then put our vessels into their best
sailing trim, completed our water, cut some spare spars, and
painted both the hulls. The grab was again metamorphosed into
a clumsy, country-looking Arab, with a raised poop and forecastle of painted canvas. The schooner resumed her original
Yankee-cut with broad streaks of bright yellow rosin.

De Ruyter made several excursions into the interior, under the
guidance of the Malay chieftain, being anxious to explore a
country then totally unknown to Europeans. I paddled about the
coast and the islands with Zela in her canoe. We revisited our old
haunts; and, after having designed the plan of a bungalow, I
marked out a garden, calculated the labour of clearing land enough
to yield us corn, rice, and wine, and most methodically made in
my mind every necessary arrangement for establishing a colony,
far surpassing Paradise in purity and bliss, in which we, the happy
founders, were to pass the rest of our days in unruffled tranquillity.
Meanwhile with our own hands we had erected a hut, consisting

of four upright bamboos, thatched with palm-leaves; and, one day, as Zela was, with matchless culinary skill, roasting fish over the live embers, the iron ramrod of my carbine serving as a spit, I, elated at my newly acquired importance as house-holder, and freeholder of land sans limit, stalked over my domain, and said—

'Sweet Zela, under our own wild vine and fig-tree, how much happier we shall be than sweltering in that coffin-like schooner, jammed together, and pitching and tossing, like packed dates on the back of a lame dromedary! How happy—'

Here I was interrupted by the pushing aside of the thick foliage. Hearing some one advance, I began to imagine that the resurrection of my old friend the orang, from the dead, was appearing to dispute my title-deeds to his property; for it was on the ruins of his former dwelling that I had erected mine, which, I must honestly confess, in architectural design, as well as solidity of structure, was far inferior to his. But, instead of the orang's apparition, it was De Ruyter, laughing as if his heart would burst, who thus, for the second time, disturbed my imaginary rural plans, calling out, 'Come along, my lad! The Malay has sent me word that, from their look-out station on the mountain, there is a strange sail in the offing to the north. Come along,—get on board the lame dromedary—ha! ha! ha! The grab is not quite ready for sea. If you once get sight of the stranger, she cannot escape; and if detainable, which she must be, bring her in here.'

In ten minutes I was on board; in five more I was under weigh. With a press of canvass, and with a favourable breeze, we made a clear offing, and, before sunset, were in sight of the stranger. She sailed remarkably well. We lost her during the night, but luckily there was little wind. We regained sight of her next morning; and, a breeze coming out of the gulph, we brought her to, after a hard chace of nine hours. She proved to be a country trader from Bombay, bound to China. Having heard that a French cruizer was off the Cochin China coast, she had, with extreme precaution, kept along the opposite one of Borneo, and thus fell into our hands. She was a beautiful copper-fastened brig, built of Malabar teak by the Parsees of Bombay, freighted with cotton, wool, a few cases of opium, guns, pearls from Arabia, sharks' fins, birds' nests, and oil from the Lackadive islands, with four or five sacks of rupees. This valuable prize consoled us for the failure of our plans on the China fleet, and created general satisfaction amongst the men.

We returned to our anchorage elated with success. A day or two after De Ruyter despatched his Malay friend to Pontiana, a large and wealthy province on the western coast, not long founded by a powerful and wise Arab prince. The capital is situated on the banks of a wide navigable river; there was a branch of the Dutch factory, with which our Malay had extensive dealings. Thither he went for an agent, that we might dispose of the Bombay cargo, as it was adapted for that market; for we could not spare hands to send the prize to a distance. We did not well know how to dispose of the vessel. Her captain, who was part-owner of her, as well as being interested in the cargo, was so fond of her, that he proposed to ransom the hull. While all this was arranging, I rejoiced in the delay, as it enabled me to continue my building and idling on shore with Zela.

CHAPTER XXX

And I
Plied him cup after cup, until the drink
Had warmed his entrails, and he sang aloud,
In concert with my wailing fellow-seamen,
A hideous discord.

SHELLEY.—*Translation*

Ha! ha! ha! I'm full of wine,
Heavy with the joy divine,
With the young feast oversated:
Like a merchant-vessel freighted
To the water's edge, my crop
Is laden to the gullet's top.

SHELLEY, *from Euripides*

As it was necessary that a considerable portion of time should elapse before the disposal of our prize could be accomplished, De Ruyter, leaving instructions for my guidance during his absence, took his departure in the grab to glean the China seas.

I gladly remained. My time was fully occupied in superintending our multifarious occupations. The first mate was placed in charge of the prize, with a party of men, who removed her crew to the small island on which the Malays had built huts for us. The second mate was occupied with a gang of men in curing jerked buffalo and deer-flesh, and salting wild hogs and ducks. I purchased a plentiful supply of rice and maize. What leisure time I had was devoted to my rural occupations, which I pursued with all the zest of novelty, and the zeal of a migrated settler. The little cove, in which I used to bathe with Zela, and where we had encountered the Jungle Admee, or wild man, I constituted my naval arsenal; and spent much of my time there in a tent. This spot was completely barricadoed from the rest of the island by a living wall of jungle. From a high pinnacle of rock, on the east side, we commanded an extensive view to seaward, and overlooked the schooner and her Bombay prize. By a flag-staff placed on its summit I could at all times communicate with the schooner. Towards sunset I always returned to sup and sleep on board, that I might entertain my prize-guests, and be at my post.

One night we were all more than ordinarily disposed for enjoyment, and the deck was thickly strewed with bowls of arrack punch, brandy, Hollands, Bourdeaux, Curaçoa, and various other genial fluids—potent elixirs which prevent the heart from ossifying, and close up the cracks and rents in our clay, laid open by the scorching heat of the sun. The Indians say the sap of the mimosa is an antidote to sorrow; and so it is,—when fermented; and wine can medicine the mind, and 'pluck from the memory a rooted sorrow,' as was exemplified in the person of our captive commander. In the early part of the evening he had been groaning over the loss of his highly prized vessel, and told me that, had it pleased providence to deprive him of his wife and six children, he could have submitted to its heavy dispensation;—

> 'But there, where he had garner'd up his heart,
> Where either he must live, or bear no life,—
> To be discarded thence!'

—meaning from his copper-bottomed brig, not his copper-coloured wife. Yet now that the subtle vinous spirit had touched his soul with its talisman, sorrow fled from him, and his stagnant blood, before jellying into jaundice, flowed from his heart like a fountain. He talked and sung without intermission, wrung my hand, and swore I was the best friend and the best fellow in the world.

Our orgies were interrupted by the old quarter-master's hailing,—'Boat a-hoy!' when the answer 'Hadjee,' (pilgrim,) which was our watch-word, gave token of the approach of a friend.

Dd

A large proa, impelled rapidly by paddles, shot up alongside, and the Malay chieftain appeared on the gangway. Whilst he laboured to explain to me the reason, aided by his powerful gesticulation, for his having so soon returned, altogether inaudible owing to the boatswain-like roar with which the captain was chanting 'Rule, Britannia,' a short, squat, business-like looking man made his appearance, and the Malay shoved him towards me. I arose to receive him. The gravity of his square, flat countenance, with a paunch swelling out like a lowered top-sail bagging-out with the wind, made me laugh. His limbs were preposterously short; or, as the quarter-master said, 'he sailed under jury-masts.' Indeed if that theory is true, which asserts we have all more or less affinity to some bird, beast, or other animal, he was indisputably of the order 'sheep-tick' or if the odour of animals has any thing to do in settling the question, I should perhaps class him with the bug. With measured step and leaden gravity, he saluted me with, —'I am, Sir, Bartholomew Zachariah Jans, an accredited factor of the Dutch Company's establishment at Pontiana, and agent of Van Olaus Swammerdam. Understanding you have a prize to dispose of, I am here to treat and negotiate for the same.'

The captain, I suppose, caught the subject of conversation; for he abruptly stopped his 'Britannia rule the waves!' stared with distended jaw at the accredited agent, and changed his note to the drawling and melancholy tune of 'Poor Tom Bowling!'

Our Dutch factor seated himself on the hatchway without any apparent diminution of altitude. After he had washed his ivories with a cup of skedam, (that would have surprised even Louis,) swallowed, as he observed, to dislodge the night air which he had inhaled, he protested he had never met with such excellent stuff, and, with the addition of a bite of biscuit, would take another toothful. I directed the quarter-master to see the factor's wants supplied, and he went to rouse up the cabin-boy, muttering,— 'Never see'd or heard tell of such a queer-shaped craft as this,— all stowage room! Why, the Temeraire, three-decker, hadn't such a bread-room! Bite of biscuit!—why, a bag of biscuit would float about in his wet dock like peas in the ship's coppers! Why, boy, —turn out!' When he had roused the boy with a kick, I heard an order given to bring on deck all the grub in the locker.

Forthwith appeared a piece of cold pork, one of the immense fat ducks of the island, and half a Dutch pine-apple cheese.

I conversed with the Malay, while the factor, with immoveable taciturnity, battened on the food, and filled up the vacuum in his portentous belly. When he had cleared the platters, and emptied a stone-bottle of gin, he said, 'Captain, it is late. There is no good in talking on business after supper. The night is close;—I will repose here.'

As he spoke this he lay down, not without difficulty, on the main-sail, which was unbent and lying aft to be repaired, covered himself up with a flag, and told the boy to fill his pipe. We soon heard him snoring and puffing away as he slept. Our bacchanalian party followed his example, stretching their relaxed limbs amidst the empty bottles and glasses, and reclining their heavy heads, when slumber soon closed their dizzy eyes.

In the morning, after Bartholomew Zachariah Jans had supplied his loss in animal heat and moisture with salt pork and Hollands, we proceeded together on board the prize. I soon discovered I had a cool, calculating, subtle merchant to contend with. This put me on my mettle; for although I was ignorant and prodigal in money transactions, as far as they affected myself, (for the love of money, like that of olives, is a taste to be acquired, not instinctive,) yet I felt, what many besides Hotspur have expressed, that, in the way of bargain, I could cavil on the ninth part of a hair. In addition to his country's characteristic traits of industry, craft, and patience, this fellow combined the slily-grasping character of the Scotch Lowlander born craven, predetermined to cheat all the world. When the Bombay Captain, with a sailor's frankness, came to treat with the factor about redeeming the hull of his vessel, and talked of the peculiar hardship of his case, reduced, in an instant, from wealth to extreme want, he assumed an impenetrability to human suffering, worse than that of a Hollander, Scot, or the devil himself,—I mean that anomaly in nature, an Irish landlord, with heart of granite, and head of wood. He stared at the bankrupt captain with the blank, remorseless, withering apathy, which, in after-years, was recalled to my memory by one of the aforesaid ruffianly gasconading bullies, as he doggedly listened to the petitions of his squallid and famished tenants; and then our factor resumed his scrutiny of the prize-papers, invoices, and bills of loading. Seeing the captain despair, I comforted him with assurances that he should not be forgotten in the sale. Upon this the factor said, 'I protest against all stipulations. If the captain gives a good price, backed by good security, his tender will be considered; that is, if the factory become the purchasers, or I am the agent; always providing that Van Olaus Swammerdam approves.'

I was then young, and not knowing that such characters are common ones, I felt so disgusted with the tallowy brute, that I not only refused to treat with him, but was about to treat him with a keelhale, or to throw him overboard, and there harpoon him. But, dissuaded from this, I dismissed the wretch with revilings and contempt; which, since then, I have oftener seen merited than inflicted.

CHAPTER XXXI

And she began to moan and sigh,
Because he mused beyond her, knowing well
That but a moment's thought is passion's passing bell.

KEATS

And her, the homicide and husband-killer.

BYRON

DE RUYTER returned, having in tow a small schooner he had picked up; when, without loss of time, we embarked every thing belonging to the vessels, got under weigh, and proceeded to sea. Without any occurrence of moment we anchored at Batavia in the island of Java. The fever had subsided there; and De Ruyter, besides having the prizes to dispose of, had a great deal of business to transact, left unfinished by Louis, and took up his quarters on shore.

We cleared the vessels out, and took in an ample supply of provisions, far superior to what we had been for a long period accustomed to. The vessels being in excellent order, we had, in other respects, little to do; and I made, with Zela, frequent excursions into the mountainous part of this exceedingly rich and populous island. Its productions, timber, grain, and fruit, were of a finer quality than at any of the islands I had visited, with the exception of some portion of Borneo. General Jansens,[1] the governor, an old friend of De Ruyter's, was very civil to me, as he had also been on my former visit. We spent much of our time at his country-house.

In Europe there is or was a rage for golden-haired virgins; but here the mania was for golden complexions. At the same merchant's house where De Ruyter lodged, there lived a very rich widow, a native of the capital of Yug, which was situated on that part of the island still governed by its native princes. She was much admired at Batavia, and had, by the beauties of her person, attracted the beaux of the place, who revolved diurnally about her doors. She was nearly four feet and a half in stature, with a skin so brightly yellow that, when burnished with oil, it reflected the sun's rays like a gilded ball on a cupola, which her rich rotundity resembled. Her little jetty eyes sparkled in a face round and plump as an orange; her nose was minute as the bill of a humming bird; her lips, both in substance and dimensions, betokened her African descent; and the hairs on her globular head, if collected together, would hardly have amounted to the cherished number sprouting from my upper lip. Yet, such as I have described her, she was the beau-ideal of beauty at Java; and suitors from the four quarters of the island thronged to do her homage. In that favoured portion of the world the women enjoy the inestimable privilege of divorcing themselves from their husbands—a law in no danger of becoming obsolete; for the rich and peerless widow, now in her twenty-fourth year, had already been lawfully married to ten different men,—one dead, two killed, six cashiered for neglect of duty, and one missing.

The Javanese are a remarkably dwarfish race, the men seldom exceeding five feet, and the women four and a half. De Ruyter and myself respectively measuring six feet, and of proportionate brawn and bone, loomed titanic, as, with the loose and rolling gait of sailors, we forced our way through the bazaar or crowded lanes, scattering the small human fry right and left, like a couple of benetas among a shoal of flying fish. This manly bearing made a deep impression on the sensibility of the widow. Henceforth she treated the island imps with scorn; and avowed her intention of uniting herself to a man,—no more to fragments of men, as she termed them, fit only for beggars. After a minute scrutiny, and mature deliberation as to which she should take, De Ruyter or me, the golden apple was allotted to me, both as I was younger, and, thanks to the remains of jaundice, far yellower. Nothing doubting my rapturous assent, she, therefore, made a formal proposal in my behalf to De Ruyter, with the offer of an unconditional surrender of her charms, and large possessions of coffee-grounds, sugar, rice and tobacco plantations, houses and tenements, slaves and personals, enough to put me on an equality with the most powerful princes in the province of Yug. De Ruyter, with a suitable and complimentary address, acknowledging the lustre and honour of so condescending a mark of her favour, merely hinted at the trifling impediment of my being already married. This she could not comprehend. A little white-faced, slimly-formed sickly girl she had indeed seen with me, with hair wound round her head like a turban, great eyes, and lips, and mouth ridiculously small, all which every man must hold in abhorrence. Faugh! Truly for a sea-wife she might do; she looked like a fish; and what else can live in water? She then unveiled her dazzling beauties, and said, 'Look at me!' De Ruyter avowed she was the reverse of the sea-girl; but he observed that men had strange and capricious tastes with regard to eating and loving. However, he would inform me of her determination in my favour. 'Ah!' she exclaimed, 'send him to me! Let his eyes judge of me! Let him come and behold beauty, that his soul may be pleased, and his heart scorched!'

A lover of mirth, and delighting in so fair an occasion for its full indulgence, De Ruyter bantered me about this Princess of Yug, and Royal Highnessed me unceasingly. He constituted himself the agent of the widow, and directed her proceedings; he even offered to marry her as proxy for me; and added fuel to her fires by descanting on my merits. The schooner was encumbered with bags of coffee, tobacco, and sugar-candy, besides daily and ample supplies of fresh and preserved fruits, flowers, and provisions, all enforced on my acceptance by the widow of Yug. Meantime our interviews were frequent; for although the Javanese are Mahometans, they conform only to one portion of their religion,—that which in all superstitions is the most attended to,—the external. As to their acts, they have no other limit than the extent of their desires; the women piously fulfilling that precept engraven on their nature,—increase and multiply. I was almost angry with Zela, who, instead of being jealous, was as much amused as De Ruyter, and aided and abetted his practical jokes. In her simple nature and true heart, suspicion could never enter. The torrid blood of her Arabian father was made to keep temperate time in her veins by being mingled with her Abassien mother's; who was born and bred in the chilly valleys of Mount Ellbrus, the highest of that gigantic range, called the Caucasian Mountains, which extend from the Caspian to the Black Sea, and uprear their hoary heads amidst the clouds.

CHAPTER XXXII

While the ship's
Great form is in a watery eclipse,
Obliterated from the ocean's page,
And round the wreck the huge sea-monsters sit,
A horrid conclave, and the whistling wave
Is heaped over its carcase, like a grave.

SHELLEY.—*Translation*

AMONG the innumerable little islands, scattered in the gulph of Sunda, De Ruyter had, in one of his former cruises, been becalmed; and, while exploring and sounding, had accidentally espied, foundered on a bed of rocks, the hull of a small vessel, apparently of European build. He carefully marked on his chart the spot, and took the most minute bearings of the compass and nautical observations, with the design, at a future period, of making an attempt to get her up. The weather, which was now settled, clear and calm, prompted him to proceed in the affair; particularly as he must be still some time detained at Batavia, and the crews were growing rusty and unruly from idleness. Having prepared what was necessary, and provided a gang of the most expert divers, fellows kept in practice by diving under the ships' bottoms at night, to rip off the copper sheets, we got under weigh with the land-wind, and, the ensuing day, lay becalmed off the little group of five islands, which was our destination.

We now got out our boats; after pulling about all day, under a sun so hot that our brains seemed undergoing the process of frying, we happily, before the night set in, hit on the very spot marked by De Ruyter; but, the day closing, we were compelled to desist till daylight. We ran the boats on shore on a pretty island, supped and slept; then, with the earliest dawn, we pushed on our discovery, till we came on the identical foundered wreck. The water was transparent as glass. By sounding on the hull of the wreck, we found there was not more than twenty feet water from her deck; and that, lying on rocks, but little sand had collected near her. We laid down a buoy to indicate the spot, and returned to the vessels, which were drawing near to take us on board, impelled by sweeps; for so still was the wind, that the feathered vanes above the lofty truck drooped motionless.

With lines, halsers, grapnels, and the other necessary materials, not forgetting the divers, we again went towards the submerged vessel. As I gazed below, long and steadily, so perfectly was every portion of her visible, that she forcibly reminded me of those models of ships enclosed in glass-cases—the rough and jagged bed on which she lay resembling the mimic waves which sometimes surround them. Even the heaps of shell-fish that now incrusted and peopled her deck with marine life, and the living sea-verdure of weeds and mosses, might have been as distinctly noted and classed as if exhibited on a table. When the dark divers descended on her decks, the glass-like element, as in a broken mirror, multiplied their forms, till they seemed to be the demons, hidden in her hold, rushing up in multitudes to defend their vessel, assaulted even under the sanctuary of the mighty ocean.

After many fruitless efforts and long-continued toil, we succeeded in getting a purchase on her. Then by sinking butts of water, carefully securing them to the tackle affixed to the wreck, and restoring their buoyancy by pumping out the water from them, at length we moved her, and passed strong halsers under her. On the second day the grab and schooner were placed on each side of her, the number of casks was increased, and we hove on many and complicated purchases, till she was fairly suspended, and, at length, her almost shapeless hull reluctantly arose to the surface. It looked like a huge coffin, in which some antediluvian sea-colossus had been entombed. The light of day shone strangely on her incrusted, hoary, and slimy hull. Sea-stars, crabs, crayfish, and all sorts of shell-fish crawled and clung in and about her, amazed at the transition from the bottom of the cool element, in which they had dwelt, to a fiery death from the sun, whose rays, darting on their scaled armour, transfixed them as with a spear. We turned to, and, by baling, partially cleared her of water; so that it was evident, although she leaked considerably, she was not bilged. The deck and main-hold had been cleared, either by the water or by the people of Sumatra, whose fishing-boats might possibly have come athwart her; but the after-hold, which was battened securely down, protected by a double deck, and bulk-headed off, was untouched. I forgot to mention that, as we were baling, we disturbed a huge water-snake at the bottom of the hold, which the men had mistaken for the bite of a cable, and that he speedily cleared the decks. Either he had a taste for shell-fish, or preferred a wooden kennel to a coral cave. We made a simultaneous and vigorous attack on him with pikes and fire-arms; yet it was not till he was gashed like a crimped cod that he struck his flag, and permitted us to continue our work. The divers said he might have eaten them when they were under water;—I know not that, but can aver that the men, more ferocious and greedy than the snake, did incontinently, now that he was out of water, eat him.

Having towed the wreck towards the island, we grounded her in shoal water, and forced a passage into the after-hold. It was of course filled with water: kegs and casks were floating in it: these were hoisted out, and having baled it dry, we got at the moveables, consisting of sacks of damaged grain, powder-barrels, and a heap of other articles difficult to define, all jammed up together. In poking and raking amongst this mass, according to De Ruyter's prognostication, two small boxes, carefully lashed and sealed, were hauled out, which, on being opened, lightened and repaid us for our toil—they contained above eight thousand Spanish dollars, dyed black with the salt water, as were, more or less, the vessel and every article on board of her. After ransacking every hole and corner, we could find nothing else worth the taking away but five or six brass swivels, not of much value. We abandoned the wreck, and returned to Batavia.

I should observe that the vessel was apparently of Spanish construction, and built of cedar or teak, which, notwithstanding it had lain submerged certainly half a century, and probably much longer, was still of so hard a texture that it turned the edges of the axes. What I considered the best portion of the prize was, not the dollars, but two barrels of Spanish and other wine, and two of arrack. Give me the sea for a cellar! Such delectable fluid never till then moistened the lips, delighted the palate, warmed the heart, and entranced the senses! All grew panegyrical and eloquent on the excellence of this liquor. The old Rais declared the wine resembled the balsam of Koireish, brought from Mecca by the Hajjis—that the shrubs from which the gum exuded sprung

from the blood of the prophet's tribe, slain in battle—and that it
not only cured every malady, and subdued every evil, but had
restored true believers to life!

CHAPTER XXXIII

Fierce, wan,
And tyrannizing was the lady's look,
And over them a gnarled staff she shook.

KEATS

The ghost of folly haunting my sweet dreams.

Ibid.

RUMOUR having arrived at Batavia that we had discovered a
bank of Spanish dollars, by running aground on them, from which
we had loaded our vessels, and that we had fished casks of wine
out of the sea, with the date 1550 marked on them, hooped with
living serpents, the grab was crowded with visitors, all anxious to
drink the wine or arrack. Had either of them been the real elixir
of immortality, it could not have been more devoutly hallowed, or
more greedily swallowed. The greasy Dutch merchants congregated on board, and spent the night in chaunting hallelujahs to
express their delight; so that, had we not at the commencement
substituted other wines and spirits, we should have expended the
real stuff at one bout. As it was, it consoled us afterwards, during
many a weary night of storm and toil, and suppled our joints when
they had become rigid and brittle from heat and drought.

Our prizes were disposed of, and De Ruyter did not neglect the
interests of the Bombay captain, his prisoner. His much-cherished
vessel was once more made over to him at a price below the lowest
estimate, and himself and crew were liberated. This, and what
else was needful, being concluded, we again weighed anchor, and
took our departure from Java.

The widow of Yug was astounded at the intelligence of our
going out of port for an indefinite period. Love overcoming her
antipathy to the sea, she followed us in a row-boat, screaming,
making signals, and scratching—thank Heaven, not me, but
herself! Her melo-dramatic fury augmented to such a pitch, when
she found I did not heave-to for her, that the devilish breeze she

kicked up astern of us seemed to freshen the land-wind. With my telescope I could observe her venting a portion of her wrath on the slaves who rowed the boat, keeping time with the lusty strokes of a bamboo on their naked backs. Aware that a man has no more chance with a woman, armed with the offensive and defensive weapons of tongue, tears, nails, and bamboo, than in a river with an alligator, I, for the first time in my life, acted prudently, and fled the fight. The widow of Yug, had her spirit not been clogged with clay, might possibly have pursued me round the world; but as soon as the boat got into the swell outside the port, and began to pitch and toss, I discovered my princess—or rather, I did not, for she had sunk down in the bottom of the boat, which was slued to the right-about, and without delay vigorously impelled towards the shore; so that I may say of her—

'She loved, and she rowed away.'

I had been so pestered and persecuted by this she-dragon, who one day crammed me with kisses and cakes, and the next would have tattooed me with her nails, that I vowed henceforth never to be lured into a widow's den; for the malignant ferocity of a tiger-cat in a gin, is nothing to a veteran widow balked of her will.

I cannot tell why it was, but as we left the harbour of Batavia and its begrimed water, the clear, pure, deep blue of the Indian ocean, which, since I had commanded the schooner, had always filled my heart with delight, now, on the contrary, overwhelmed me with sadness, that I could neither shake off nor repress. Doubt and dread clouded my mind for the first time. Yet I was well in health, and Zela (for I questioned her) was perfectly well; and this was authenticated by the regularity of her pulse, the bright-ness of her eye, her coral lip, and her breath sweeter than the odour from May-flowers on a spring-morning. What then could it be? not the widow!—her love and her parting curses were for-gotten ere her boat was out of sight. Did her spirit cling to me like a vampyre? I remembered afterwards that, in her maledictions, she had so threatened to haunt me if I abandoned her; and there were rumours, which I laughed at, of her having dealt foully with others. Human life is held cheap in the East; and, at Java, a few rupees sufficed to hire an assassin to stab or poison,—and poison was there indigenous, it flowed from trees and shrubs, nor were the natives inexpert in its application. It did not, however, appear to have been employed on me; and now I was out of its reach. Once, I remember, in the early part of the evening, dosing on the couch, I was awakened by frightful visions. At first the widow was caressing me, and I shrinking from her embraces with repugnance. She faded away, when the wrinkled and withered form of an old yellow hag seized me by the throat, griped me hard, and attempted to force through my clenched teeth a fruit she held in her hand. I struggled to free myself by wrenching back the fiend's icy fingers; but my strength abandoned me, and the fruit was at my lips, when the faithful Adoo appeared, plucked it from me, and exclaimed, 'It is poison!' Then came the fiery Javanese Prince mounted on his blood-red horse; his hoofs were on my head and heart; when Zela, clothed in bright, glittering, white robes, led by a dim spectral figure, black as night,—Zela threw herself on me, and said,— 'I will die!—you shall live!' At this the dark spectre unveiled herself, and I recognized the livid and ghastly features of old Kamalia. With witch-like solemnity she thus addressed me:— 'Stranger, you are foresworn! The best blood of Arabia you have polluted! Your heart is bruised,—my child's you have broken!'

Struggling to rise, I awoke. My head was dizzy, my heart sick at the dreadful vision, which has haunted me through life, and it is in vain I strive to forget it. In my sleep it pursues me, and, ever as it recurs, it is the more frightful, as it assures me of some horrible change. Often since then have I arisen from my bed, haggard, sick, and suffering agonies, such as none but devils or inquisitors can inflict.

On the second day of our leaving port, steering a south-east course, we fell in with two fine French frigates and a three-masted schooner, returning to Batavia from a cruise. The lubberly fellows were elated at having chased an English frigate and brig of war; which, by the by, from what I observed of their sickly, weak, and unsailorlike case, and disorderly condition, might have advantageously brought them to action. By their description of the English vessels I knew the frigate to be the one I had abandoned; and old Hoofs, I had always thought, was fonder of farming than fighting. Like a blustering bully, the French commodore, now that the enemy was out of sight, talked valiantly of what he would have done, had he come up with the Englishmen; adding, 'When we saw you, I thought we had got hold of the John Bulls.'

De Ruyter's curled lip indicated his contempt of the vaunter;

and he observed, as we returned on board our craft, that the fellow had been so accustomed to run away, the having chased, for once in his life, had capsized his brains. 'What a pity,' he said, 'that the French, who excel all other nations in the theory of seamanship, and in practical naval architecture, cannot find men to fight at sea. They are like flying-fish, a prey for every fish that swims, and for every bird that flies. From the oldest records we trace that all other nations, powerful enough to organise a naval force, have produced men able and worthy to command with honour and glory. The naval annals of barbarians, then of Greece, Rome, and Carthage, down to the modern history of Spain, Portugal, Holland, Sweden, Norway, Denmark, and England, have severally teemed with naval heroes, who shed a bright lustre on the countries which gave them birth. France exhibits a solitary exception, a dull obscurity, unenlightened by a single bright page; a blotted chapter in history, a waste log-book; the eye in vain seeks for one spot to rest on, a single star, as a beacon or sea-mark, to guide the lonely pilot, or stimulate to emulation the aspiring sailor-boy!'

I may here remark, that this large and beautiful French frigate was afterwards captured in an action with one of the smallest English frigates, and now carries the British jack. In her first cruise, under the victorious flag of England, she again added to our naval force, by taking, after a very sanguinary and gallant action, another of France's finest frigates in the Indian seas.

We stood along the eastern coast of Java, towards the Sunda islands, and fell in with nothing but the small vessels bound or belonging to that archipelago, burthened with cargoes of coir, oil, jaggeree, ghee, and cocoa-nuts, richer to them than Spanish galleons of gold and silver, but in our eyes, too worthless to waste a thought on.

CHAPTER XXXIV

And their baked lips, with many a bloody crack,
Suck'd in the moisture, which like nectar stream'd;
Their throats were ovens, their swoln tongues were black
As the rich man's in hell, who vainly scream'd
To beg the beggar, who could not rain back
A drop of dew, when every drop had seem'd
To taste of heaven;—if this be true, indeed,
Some christians have a comfortable creed.

BYRON

Hence shalt thou quickly to the watery vast;
And there, ere many days be overpast,
Disabled age shall seize thee; and even then
Thou shalt not go the way of aged men,
But live and wither, cripple, and still breathe.

KEATS

A LONG-CONTINUED gale of wind drove us down towards the coast of New-Holland. When it had broken, and while we were labouring in the heavy swell which followed, we discerned a small boat, evidently in distress, and we wore down to her aid. Owing to the swell, and the wind having moderated, it was some time ere the grab succeeded in getting alongside of her, to take her crew on board, which consisted of four sailors, and a master's-mate. They belonged to an English frigate, which, having captured a small brigantine, had put them on board to take charge of her. The prize had been separated from the frigate by a white squall in the straits of Sunda, damaged in her masts and rigging. A north-wester, against which they could make no head, had driven them a long way to the south-east. In this hapless state, their frail and crazy bark had been struck abaft by a heavy sea, which had loosened her stern-post, and shattered the frame-work of her stern. The water poured in so fast, that it was only by the greatest promptitude and dexterity they had succeeded in getting a clumsy boat, which lay amid-ship, afloat, just as their vessel foundered. They had no time to secure anything but themselves; a boy and two men were drowned, probably in attempting to save something. The boat was as old and worthless as the vessel to which she belonged; and, till she was somewhat seasoned in the water, they were all occupied in baling with their caps, and in stuffing, with rags and coir-oakum, the crevices and rents which the sun had made. Fortunately the boat, as she lay on board, had been used as a receptacle for old spare canvass, oars, light sails, the fag-ends of ropes, and, what was now of far greater importance, a coop with six ducks, an old, grisly he-goat, and a hen, that had demurely laid its egg, as an offering, for its undisturbed sanctuary in the sheltered part of the bow, where it had probably roosted for years in solitary security. The seamen thanked Providence as they beheld their live-stock. Being up to their knees in water, dripping with water, water having destroyed their vessel, and now threatening to overwhelm them in its foaming billows, and with an ocean of water all around them, some time elapsed ere the awful words were uttered, 'There is no fresh water in the boat!' Every voice echoed, in preternatural sounds, 'There is no fresh water!' Every eye wildly glanced at the boat, and around the sea, and again was despondingly muttered, 'There is no water! Oh, God! we must perish!'

Soon anticipated thirst parched their lips, and their stout hearts quailed. Other dangers, past and present, were forgotten. A leaky, rent, mis-shapen boat, hardly big enough to contain their diminished crew, as it lay floundering in the trough of the sea, like a harpooned porpoise, was nothing,—if they had but water. Fortunately their officer, though the youngest among them, was the ablest and manliest, at least in mind; by which boon, nature had amply compensated him for a somewhat slender and delicate form. He had a spirit greater than was contained in the broad breasts of the brawniest and the bulkiest. Evil fortune had persecuted him in many shapes; she kept him at the bottom of her wheel, but could not crush him. He rallied the sunken spirits of his men; he told them they were near land; they had sails; there was wind enough to fill them; the boat, though broken, was buoyant; they were few in number; thirst could be borne for days; besides, they had live-stock, and their blood was nearly as refreshing as water; and the clouds gave promise of rain. The men knew their officer, and had confidence in him. His calmness and fearless bearing did more than his words. The hopes he had so confidently expressed seemed realised. They grew calm, and their reason and obedience were restored.

The mate having succeeded, if not in rendering his boat water-tight, yet in diminishing the leaks, so that it required but occasional baling, next set about putting sail on the boat. For this purpose he selected an old flying jib, and, with a broken studding-sail-boom for a mast, contrived the best and safest form of carrying canvass that could possibly be contrived, representing, what sailors call, a shoulder-of-mutton rig, the larger part (or the body of the sail) being in the body of the boat. To be driven into the South Indian ocean, a desert world of waters, was certain and inevitable destruction. In order to avoid this, it was necessary, at all risks, to haul his wind as much as possible to the eastward, with an oar for a rudder. With consummate skill he, in some degree, effected this; but it required an unerring eye and steady hand to keep his ricketty and rudderless boat from being buried beneath the threatening waves, or capsized by the furious blasts which swept over it. They had neither compass, chart, nor instruments to guide them on their lonely way; nothing but the stars and sun—the latter, glaring and fiery, they hardly dared to look at. Their only hope was to make one of the Sunda islands, or, failing in that, the coast of New Holland, or to be met by some wandering bark.

Thus day and night they toiled on, laving, at long intervals, their white and parched lips with the blood of the panting goat, which was itself expiring for want of moisture. Every glazed eye scrutinised, with horrible precision, the accuracy of the measured allowance, apparently numbering the red drops, as doled out by the officer in scanty portions. The animal was then cut up, and its interior, which still contained jellied blood and some moisture, was balanced and divided with the care and exactitude with which a miser weighs his gold. The mate said he merely extracted the fluid, chewing, but not swallowing the substance, and endeavoured to impress on his comrades the advantage of following his example. A few did, but the greater part could not control the fierceness of famine raging in their vitals. 'At this,' the mate added, 'from the torture I experienced, I did not wonder; but the event proved I was in the right. For, by not eating, I endured thirst better; and, after a few days, I had no inclination to eat, feeling a relief by keeping some substance in my mouth, no matter what, to chew; —tobacco, of which there was a little, was the best. We all watched with painful and intense anxiety the formation and changes of the clouds. Every speck in the heavens was commented on and scrutinized, its form, density, and altitude. At last, after successive hopes and disappointments, our eyes dim and our hearts sick, we beheld a dark and heavy cloud, evidently surcharged with rain, coming towards us. Those who have seen, or can conceive, the exhausted pilgrim, parched and perishing on a desert, wading through shifting mounds of scorching sands, with feeble gait, and maddening brain, when his wistful and eager eyes catch a first glimpse of the distant well, may faintly imagine what were our sensations. When the first drops touched our shrivelled lips, and fell on our throbbing temples, every gasping mouth was distended wide to heaven for the falling manna; our parched throats heaved and swelled like the waves. Fervent prayers were muttered by men, who would have died in battle blaspheming;—but they availed not; the watery cloud, on which their lives were suspended, mockingly displayed its riches, niggardly sprinkled them with a few scanty drops, as a sample of the inestimable treasure it contained, and fleeted onwards, till they beheld it mingle its waters in waste,—in the briny ocean! They covered, in despair, their inflamed eyes with their cracked and spongy hands, and groaned in agony!'

But who can go on describing tortures such as these men endured, every instant augmenting, comprising an eternity of immitigable suffering, though marked in the calendar but as seven days and seven hours?—a space so fleeting, to the free and happy, that it passes by and is scarcely noted, while on these forlorn seamen seven days did the work of seventy years. With rheumed, glassy, blood-shot eyes, haggard, wrinkled, and hollow cheeks, sunken mouth, swollen, slaty, and cracked lips, contracted nostrils, thinned and whitened hair, collapsed muscles, feeble and tottering gait, sepulchral and inarticulate voices, gabbling more like brutes than men; can the extremest age to which human existence has yet been stretched, with all its withering palsy and impotency, do more? In seven days and a few hours, youth, intellect, strength, were thus blasted! Let me be scorched to death in a volcano, blown into the air from a cannon, buried alive in the earth, drowned in water, but let me not die by wanting it!

Two, in their frenzy, threw themselves in the sea, slaked their thirst in its briny waters, and died under its cool canopy. One, after lying in idiotic insensibility, burst into fierce, yelling madness, tore the living flesh from his limbs, sucked his own blood, lay down, slept, and awoke no more. Four, besides the officer, remained on the seventh day. The sky, the ocean, the boat, every

EE

thing looked burning red and fiery. They had no hope when, on the morning of the eighth day, we rescued them from their shattered boat. What a crazed, wild, and ghastly band were they!— more like corpses uncharnelled, than living men. The weakest of the party, the mate, seemed alone to have retained his senses. After he was hoisted on the deck, and had collectedly looked around, he said, 'We are dying the death of the damned!—Give my men water!' Then, as if his last duty was performed, he pointed to his frothy lip, but could not speak; and the spirit, which had borne him up whilst contending with danger, now released from its post of duty, seemed to flee away, and his body sunk down lifeless. Certainly he would have died, calm and unshaken as he had lived, but for the skill of De Ruyter and Van Scolpvelt, who arrested the flight of life while hovering on his lips. After long struggles, lying convulsed with pain, his strength slowly returned, when the first intelligible and connected words he uttered were, 'Who are you? the devil?'—(this was to Van the doctor)—'where am I?' Another long interval elapsed, during which his intellect was besieging its abandoned citadel, when consciousness was restored, and he said, 'Where are my men? Have they got water? Let me see them,—poor fellows!' On reiterated assurances that all their wants were supplied, he asked for water for himself. A small portion was put to his lips. Like all the fluids which had been administered to him and his men, a very small quantity was swallowed; the larger portion came up again tinctured with blood, the swollen and inflamed glands having nearly stopped up the windpipe. His breast and temples were kept continually moistened with vinegar and water, which diminished his pain. He constantly repeated, 'This is not hell, for in hell there is no water.' Bleeding and bathing proved to be the most efficacious remedies; but for these De Ruyter thought they could not have been saved. Yet, after all, and with the whole skill of Van, we were only successful in preserving the mate and two of the men. One died raving mad; and it may be observed that he had drunk of sea-water, and partaken of the blood of the man who had died mad in the boat. The other had secretly and voraciously seized on the old hen, which he had appropriated to himself. The inflammation in his throat completely closed up the passage, and, bursting a blood-vessel, he too died. The remaining three were long subject to violent retchings and convulsive fits, to which, it was believed, they would be always subject.

The mate's recovery was the most decisive and rapid. This young man, whose name was Darvell, remained long on board with us, and I commenced a friendship with him, in the off-hand way of sailors. We liked each other, and, without saying a word on the subject, became friends for life. His was a short one; as it has been with all those to whom I have linked myself, and they are many,—or rather, they were many. At the age of thirty not one was left me. Friendship is dead to me; nothing is left but its memory. Never more will friendship's balm refresh my withered heart. Meaner things have had their mausoleums, their columns, and their pyramids; on me devolves the task to write the epitaphs of my departed friends, and it shall be done by narrating their deeds. I have said Darvell's life was short; his restless and daring spirit forced him on from danger to danger, ever the leader of that devoted band, called the forlorn hope, but no longer of the pre-torian phalanxes of kings. His riper judgment shook off, with dis-dain, the fetters which had manacled him in boyhood. Darvell, on his return to Europe, became a leader of the forlorn hope of the heroic few, who are to be found in the van of those fighting for liberty. No sooner was the flag of freedom unfurled in the New World by spirits like his own, than he hastened to join their ranks. His bleached bones may still glitter on the yellow sands of Peru; where the small vessel he commanded was driven on shore and wrecked, in a chivalrous action he fought with a Spanish force ten times his superior.

CHAPTER XXXV

This Paphian army took its march
Into the outer courts of Neptune's state.

KEATS

Whence came ye, merry damsels! whence came ye?
So many, and so many, and such glee?

Ibid.

THE gale, having for some days abated, was followed by a calm, in which we lay pitching and tossing, owing to the heavy swell, without advancing, like a rocked cradle, or the beating time of soldiers with their feet. The elements, like those who live in them, rest after toil; and, in tranquil waters and balmy breezes, we regained the lee-way we had lost, keeping a north-east course, till we soon found ourselves amongst the Sunda islands, which spangle the eastern ocean, thick, bright, and countless as the fleecy clouds of a mackerel-back sky in summer, defying the patient and indefatigable toil of successive navigators to designate or number. They were of all forms and sizes, beginning from the embryo coral reef, over which swept the yet unwrinkled wave, where nature's minutest architect was at work, carrying on her mightiest designs; that little dark artificer laying its foundations under the ocean, where mariner's plummet-line could never sound, and uprearing islands and uniting them into vast continents. Those already completed were fair and beautiful, with mountain, stream, and valley; lawns, and deep dells, covered with forests, fruits, and flowers; Edens where nature spontaneously yielded all that man should want. The listless islanders, as we approached them in our boats, seemed to gaze on us with wonder at the folly of the strange people, who could wander restless about on the desert waste of waters, in barks built of trees, under groves of which they dosingly lay, pampered by their fruits, never thinned to form even a canoe. By signs we made known our want of water and fruit, they pointed to the stream and the trees. They neither aided nor opposed our landing, and procuring what we wanted.

Many lovely islands were uninhabited; others might be considered as civilized, for they had commerce, vessels, and arms, with their never-failing attendants, war, vice, and robbery. At some distance from the large island of Cumbava we fell in with two large fleets of proas, engaged in desperate conflict. There being scarcely any wind stirring at the time, the night was closing in ere we approached them near enough to interrupt their naval contention. When I observed to De Ruyter that I supposed the navies of these islanders were contending for supremacy over the sea, he replied, 'Or fighting for a cocoa-nut!'—for he perceived they were our friends, the warlike Malays, whose proas were attacking the cocoa-nut-trading proas of Cumbava, and the Celebes, whose merchant-fleets had combined against the men-of-war of the former. He added, 'The Malays have met their match; for both these islanders are heroically addicted to fighting, and will perhaps unite together and attack us—so clear your decks.'

During the night it was calm, and at day-break the Malay fleet paddled towards us: the traders, keeping an opposite course, were soon out of sight. The Malays evidently were deceived by our appearance, and mistook us for traders, as a few shots from our heavy guns changed their war-whoops to shrieking cries, and they fled in disorder. Shortly after, we brought-to on the easternmost side of the island of Cumbava, continuing to seize every opportunity of supplying our vessels with fresh provisions, and most of the islands furnishing us with an abundance of bananas, shadock, cocoa-nuts, cabbage-palm, yams, and sweet potatoes, and many with wild hogs, fowls, and fish; so that we lived well, and had little sickness.

While we lay at Cumbava bartering for what we wanted at a small village, we had all supped on board the grab. I was returning to the schooner with Zela, the night being, as was usual, exceedingly clear and calm, when I heard a blowing and splashing in the water near the shore, as from a shoal of walrusses, and its calm surface was broken and glittering with sparks of light, bright as fire-flies. Zela said—

'Hasten on board! the natives are swimming off from the shore; and I have heard my father say they often attack vessels by this mode of quietly surprising them.'

I hailed the grab, which was just ahead of me, gave them warning, hastened on board, and roused up the men to arm themselves. Then, standing on the gangway, I clearly distinguished a multitude of dark heads, with long black hair floating on the water, rapidly nearing us. We hailed them in half a dozen languages, but received no other answer than a loud flapping in the water, and a shrill chirping sound, more like a flock of those sea birds, by sailors called Mother Carey's Chickens, getting on the wing, than the approach of warriors. Some of my men wanted to fire on them; but I, observing that, whatever they were, they were unarmed, forbad it. Zela and her little Adoo cried out—

'Why, they are all women!—what do they want?' And so they were.

A loud and simultaneous laugh burst from the grab, and my quarter-master, holding a night-glass, exclaimed—

'Look, captain, there be a shoal of mermaids a-boarding the grab!'

Still not knowing what to make of it, I ordered our fierce and armed sailors to stand back, and waved my hand, making signs

for the floating visitors to come on board. This was quickly understood, and, in a few minutes, we were boarded in all directions by
these aquatic ladies, who clambered up by the chains, the gangway,
the bow, and the stern, till our deck was covered. There was no
doubt as to the sex of these our unexpected assailants; and our
men, with their pistols, cutlasses, and boarding-pikes, cut a
ridiculous figure enough as they confronted women, who, so far
from having arms of offence, or being scaled in armour of defence,
had no other weapons than what nature had furnished them with,
and no other covering than an immensity of jetty long hair. Their
love of perfect freedom was too unbounded to be compromised
by the affected propriety of a fig leaf; and they stood before us
unblushingly as Mother Eve is said to have done before the fall.

De Ruyter hailed me with—'Darvell has served out to each of
my men two of the water nymphs; yet still there is a lot on deck,
cooing like turtle doves for mates. How are you supplied? Can
you dispose of our superfluity?'

'Let Darvell,' I answered, 'come on board here and see; they
are as thick as cockroches.'

Darvell, although he had not recovered his strength, was convalescent, and his spirit, like De Ruyter's, was too buoyant and
mercurial to be long depressed by any suffering, and his company
was an antidote to melancholy. He came on board and said,—
'The ladies, who have paid us this unceremonious, but friendly
visit, inhabit a village near at hand. Their lords left them a few
days ago, and went to sea to revenge some wrong they had received
from the Malay proas, belonging to one of the neighbouring islands.
So the women have come on board to revenge themselves on their
husbands for loving fighting better than them. It is the fate of
warriors to be cornuted, and they deserve it. Give me your muster
roll, and let me go round and see that every man taketh unto himself two women, and the officers three or four, according to their
rank. Poligamy, in such cases, is not only lawful but meritorious.'

Away went Darvell laughing and hallooing the men. Meanwhile
the absurd womankind had lost no time in selecting their mates.
Some of the sailors, too scrupulously virtuous, had betaken themselves for safety to the rigging, and thought to escape by going
into the tops and on the yards, but they were followed by the
nymphs, who ran up the shrouds like monkeys. Two of the darkest,
ugliest, and oldest, with pieces of fish bone stuck through the

cartiledge of their noses and ears, with necklaces, bracelets, and anklets of sharks' and human teeth, begrimed with paint, and frightfully tattooed, had fixed their fangs on the old, sedate, quarter master, hauling him to the starboard and port, and contending which should have him. He shook them off as the bated bull does the dogs which fasten on him, while they, for a time, with the tenacity of the true breed, magnanimously maintained their hold. The sturdy seaman pathetically exclaimed 'Whew! these sea cows beat the Gosport sharks all to nothing! I'd rather founder in such another hurricane as we had off Borneo, than under such water spouts as these. Paws off!—bitch savages!—or I'll heave you overboard. Belike you be fish, for you smell damnably of blubber oil. I'd rather splice myself to a bit of rotten junk!'

The matrons, for such they assuredly were, separately believed the quarter master's reluctance was not directed to both, and therefore proceeded to decide the right of possession by the laws of duello. They sounded to the charge with a yell so shrilly loud that it would have deafened the sound of the war trumpets of an army, each fixing one claw in the other's hair, and the other on the dewlap. They tore and shook one another with the ferocity of wild hogs, and had not their hides been as thick and tough as hogs', they would have been flayed alive. During this clapper-clawing the quarter master, after having sluiced a bucket of water over them without effect, applied a rope's end so lustily to their backs and sides that they shriekingly fled; but Darvell insisting on it that the quarter master alone could govern such shrewish squaws, allotted them to him.

Never was such a hubbub heard as was kept up on board the vessel during the night. Yet, in justice to the ladies, I must say that many of them, if not fair, were young, sleek-skinned, and of pretty Moorish features; but I was so entirely devoted to Zela, that my thoughts never veered for an instant to any other. True it was, I had been boyishly indiscreet enough to give into the joke of bantering and playing pranks on the widow of Yug. I had better have played them on the stealthy and malignant panther; for what is so relentless and dastardly cruel as a vicious and disappointed woman? But, vanish, accursed retrospection! Keep aloof from me, memory, thou subtle and intruding devil!

With the dawn of day the amphibious females assembled, like a flock of teal, on the deck, having gleaned the sailors' offerings of buttons, nails, beads, old shirts, waistcoats, jackets, and other discarded clothing, with which they had ridiculously bedizened themselves. The vanity of the sex was now in high play; for I observed, as they strutted about in their motley-coloured attire, partially covering their persons, one in a check shirt, another with a white jacket, some with only a solitary stocking or shoe, and others with gaudy handkerchiefs instinctively applied to their heads, that they scanned with watchful eyes, which among them had got what they considered the most valuable present. At length they all became fixed in astonishment and jealousy, at beholding the frightful squaw, the triumphant heroine, who had successfully insinuated herself into the good graces of the quarter-master, whom she had so bewitched, that he, with princely prodigality, bestowed on her a robe of honour, an ancient scarlet waist-coat! This was the identical vest that, sparkling on his broad chest, had caused such devastation in the hearts of the fair damsels at Plymouth, and to which he confessedly owed much of his good fortune, having won the heart and hand of a celebrated west-country belle from a host of suitors. All the water-nymphs, at the sight of this brilliant squaw proudly stalking among them, like a queen pre-eminent, clapped their hands with a divided feeling of envy and delight; then shrieked, and, eager to avoid comparison, hastened to hide their inferior decorations by plumping headlong into the water, chattering and clattering like sea-mews till they reached the land.

CHAPTER XXXVI

> The earth, whose mine was on its face, unsold,
> The glowing sun and produce all its gold;
> The freedom which can call each grot a home;
> The general garden where all steps may roam;
> Where nature owns a nation as her child,
> Exulting in the enjoyments of the wild;
> Their shells, their fruits, the only wealth they know,
> Their unexploring navy the canoe;
> Their sport the dashing breakers and the chase;
> Their strangest sight an European face.
>
> BYRON

To avoid a repetition of these nocturnal orgies, we got under weigh, threading cautiously, and with difficulty, the groups of islands; many of which were unknown, or unmarked on any chart. At some we landed, while our vessels lay off and on, awaiting us; and, in calm weather, we anchored at others, where we generally found fruits and water. Although De Ruyter, besides his being an able nagivator, had the advantage of much personal knowledge of the Indian archipelago, yet we had much to contend with; for the multitude of local currents, in the space of a few leagues, ran to every point in the compass; and often were so impetuous that our vessels, even with favourable breezes, were hurried along in contrary directions to each other, and to the courses we were steering. Sometimes we were driven through channels of coral reefs, embayed by shoals, out of which we had infinite difficulty in groping our way with the lead. Many times we thus parted company, and, more than once, jostled together. Besides the momentary fear of being wrecked, the toil and hardship we endured is not to be described; although our vessels were admirably adapted for the intricacy of the navigation.

At sea, scudding fast in a fine vessel, or, on the desert, gallopping on a fleet horse, I have felt my blood, hurrying through its channels, tingling with pleasure; but, like all pleasures of strong excitement, they are short-lived, and dearly purchased by the painful lassitude which follows such enjoyment. On the other hand, I have felt my soul thrilled with rapture, unalloyed by retrospection or deadened by satiety, in wandering over and exploring unknown, or at least unmarked, and uninhabited islands, in the Indian archipelago, accompanied by my Zela. Gazing in mute astonishment at every fruit, herb, tree, and flower, our very ignorance of their names and properties enhanced our admiration. Even those we were familiar with seemed of a more exquisite description. The formation and hues of the rocks, sands, shells, and weeds, to our enthusiastic and untaught eyes, resembled nothing we had previously seen. The very sea around, the noise of the surf, the sky, the clouds above, the untainted atmosphere we breathed, the birds, the lizards, the insects, and larger animals, appeared new and strange. In that awful solemnity of nature, undisturbed by human innovation, carrying on her works in beautiful grandeur, Zela scrutinized, with girlish delight, some little unknown floweret, whilst I stood entranced, gazing on a titanic tree, on whose wide-spreading branches monkeys and parrots had formed their kingdoms, and under whose broad shade an army might have stood sheltered. We often thought ourselves, and perhaps were, the first intruders on these hallowed solitudes. The birds and beasts viewed us with wonder, but fled not. They thought, or rather I thought for them, 'What, is man at last come here? Not satisfied with, what he calls, usurping the four portions of the globe, must his dominion spread over the fifth, some space of which is yet untenanted by him? Has providence, like a step-father abandoned his first children, robbing us of our birth-right, leaving us no place where we may rest our weary wings? Why is life given us to be taken away for man's pastime, to be tortured to pamper his insatiable appetites? He is a monster, endowed with sovereignty over nature's works, only to mar and destroy them!'

As I am not writing a history of discovery, I leave to be de-scribed, by more systematic circumnavigators, with all the honour and profit thereunto accruing, every one of these islands, now comprehended in the fifth division of the world; limiting myself, as at starting, to simply the history of my own life, and that which is immediately connected with it.

After a long and circuitous navigation we made the Aroo islands, one of which none that has seen can ever forget. It lies in the centre of the group, and far surpasses all that the most imaginative of eastern poets has conceived. The birds of the sun (or, as they are usually called, birds of Paradise) are natives of this paradise; as is the lory, whose varied and distinctly marked colours exceed in brightness the rarest tulips. Then there are the mina, of deeper blue than the sky, with crest, beak, and legs out-glittering gold, the wild peacock, and an infinity of little scarlet humming-birds, dazzling the sight with their extreme beauty; while the spices on which they live fill the air with sweet smells. Zela screamed with joy, and wept to go on shore; but the wild islanders forbad it.

Getting a distant view of Papua, or New Guinea, we kept a northerly course for a few days; but our salt provisions becoming scanty, we changed our course to the westward, and returned by a parallel line, till we arrived at the Dutch spice-island of Amboyna. Here we found them in all the bustle of an expected attack by the English, to which, however, the governor did not give credit; and De Ruyter was too politic to give him his real opinion on the subject, least efforts might have been made to detain us, in order to assist in their defence, or, at least, our supplies would not have been attainable. We therefore hastily purchased what was necessary, or rather what we could get, took our departure, and soon after captured a small vessel, being the third prize we had made on this cruise. She was freighted—or as the quarter-master, who prided himself on correct orthoëpy, persisted in saying, *frighted*— with cloves, mace, and nutmegs. We transhipped the spicery, and let the vessel go.

Our next destination was the island of Celebes, which we made without encountering any event worth recording, and anchored off Fort Rotterdam, at Maccassar, a Dutch settlement, as the name of the fort indicates. This island lies between Java and Borneo; it is shaped like a huge tarantula, a small body with four disproportionately long legs, which stretch into the sea in narrow and lengthened peninsulas.

CHAPTER XXXVII

But feast to-night! to-morrow we depart!
Strike up the dance, the festal bowl fill high,
Drain every drop! to-morrow we may die.
                                        BYRON

WE were all delighted, after our long, fatiguing, and anxious navigation among the islands, to find ourselves securely moored in a beautiful harbour near to a very pretty European town, which supplied all our wants. For some days the discipline on board was relaxed, and we revelled in the enjoyment of abundance, and the luxury of undisturbed rest; which can only be duly appreciated by those who have hungered and toiled. Several Dutch vessels were lying here, bound to the spice-islands; from these we replenished our stores of European articles, such as wine, cheese, biscuits, and an ample supply of genuine skedam, which poor Louis used to say was indispensable as the rudder and compass.

As a neutral vessel lay in the port, we shipped Darvell, and the men we had rescued, on board her. Both De Ruyter and myself parted from that gallant young officer with deep regret. In those days of my youth my heart was glowing with feeling, and, as has been seen, readily formed alliances with noble minds like Darvell's. Such men as he, (though I cannot believe there are many,) may still live; and perhaps, occasionally, I may come unknowingly in contact with them; but my heart is chilled, and my affections almost extinguished. I no longer feel myself moved to claim kindred with them; my soul is absorbed in selfish and vain regret for those I have loved and lost, and shrinks from new ties, if not with loathing, yet with cold indifference. I am become ascetic and morbid; so I will not slander human nature by contrasting Darvell and the friends of my youth, such as they were to me, with the worldlings among whom I now associate, and whom, with sneering mockery, I designate as 'dear,' on every scrap of paper which necessity compels me to address to them, either for the purpose of an invitation to dinner, or an appointment for a duel. Let me, however, although no verbal critic, protest against the profanation of the word friend. In this my history I must be honest, make a distinction between the oriental diamond and its worthless imitation of paste, and separate the grain from the chaff—gossamer words, that weigh nothing, from substantial realities heavier than gold. With heartfelt reluctance I parted with Darvell, and it is painful for me now to dismiss him with so faint an outline as I have traced on this paper.

De Ruyter having discovered the grab's bowsprit to be sprung, and both vessels being in want of spars, we got under weigh, and went round to the bay of Bonny on the southern coast. In this most spacious and magnificent of bays we anchored close to the shore; and, after De Ruyter had communicated with the Rajah, who issued orders to his subjects, the Bonnians, not to molest nor interfere with us, we sent the carpenter and a party of men to select the timber. While De Ruyter was employed in striking his masts and unshipping his bowsprit, we overhauled the schooner's rigging, and set about destroying the rats and other vermin; which, by the by, (I mean the rats,) in some measure compensated for the damage they had done to the ship and provisions, by furnishing, in their own persons, to hungry mariners, a not unpalatable relish, besides many an hour's excellent sport, in which we used to hunt and spear them. At one period, I remember, we had run so short of provisions, and what we had was so salt, hard, and unsavoury, that the price of a brace of rats on board of us rose to a quarter dollar; while the Borneo breed, long bodied, short legged, round quartered, sleek skinned, and fine eared, were readily disposed of at a fraction more. When skinned, split open, sprinkled with pepper and salt, and nicely broiled, they furnished a salubrious and piquante relish for breakfast. The hind quarters were then as exquisite to my palate, as the thighs of wood-cocks, and the tainted haunches of venison, are to shore-going grand gourmands. But the daintiest viands soonest pall on the palate; I had been surfeited with turtle, and, revelling on the bountiful supplies we got from the shore, rat-diet became nauseous, and we cleared out the schooner to be rid of them—centipedes, scorpions, cockroches, and other intruders. Doctor Van Scolpvelt provided a villanous composition, the smoking fumes of which, he averred, would smother all the devils in hell, if he could hermetically seal its gates. We distributed this kill-devil hell-paste in several parts of the vessel, ignited it, and battened down the hatchways, destroying, 'at one fell swoop,' all the reptiles which infested and annoyed us. This, and cleaning and restoring the schooner's hull and rigging to that nice order on which sailors pride themselves—for no eye is so fastidious and critical as a sailor's—stowing the holds, cutting wood, getting water, sending the sick on shore, repairing the sails, and casks, setting up the standing rigging, and other matters, kept all hands at work for a considerable time.

While this was going on I made frequent excursions on shore, and maintained a friendly intercourse with the Bonnians, who, next to the warlike Malays, were the people I best liked; they were friendly, frank, hospitable, honest, enterprising, and brave. The Dutch policy here was the same as that employed by the English on the continent of India—the exciting and fomenting intestine wars among the native princes, in order to secure and augment their own possessions; besides, on the part of the Dutch, reaping the collateral, and indeed principal advantage of being furnished with the prisoners of war for slaves, whom they exported to Java and the spice-islands. In other respects their settlement on this island was convenient, as maintaining open a line of communication with their other residencies in the east. In the great bay of Bonny there was a fine river, leading to a large lake in the interior, which the Rajah wisely forbad the Europeans from surveying, well knowing the covetousness of their eyes, as he said, was only to be exceeded by the rapacity of their hands.

In one of my excursions around the great bay, I had provided myself with a sean for fishing, and weapons for the chase. As we were pulling along the shore of the southernmost point, we opened, through a somewhat narrow entrance, to a smaller bay. It was perfectly calm, but the ground-swell rolled in heavily, and we heard the surf breaking on the shelving-beach at its extremity or bottom; above which arose a small, but rocky and rugged hill, bare on the sides, but crowned with majestic timber and patches of underwood. On each side of the bay the land was high, broken, and shelving, with jagged and rent rocks, whose sharp points continued in successive lines, bearing a most forbidding and inhospitable aspect. The prolific and rife vegetation of the east appeared vainly struggling for existence on its arid surface. Only those low and creeping plants thrived well, with wiry roots to insinuate themselves into the fissures of the hardest stone, till, swelling into wedges they break through them, and enter the hard crust of the earth. Around the entire margin of this bay, formed like a horse-shoe, was laid, I suppose by the waves, a carpet of the finest and smoothest sand; its yellow surface here and there stained with glittering shells, and bones bleached by the salt-water and the sun, but without a single pebble. The general transparent blueness of the water, indicative of its depth, and the absence of rocks and shoals, was the more remarkable as contrasted with the peculiar abruptness and ruggedness of its shores, on which there did not appear enough of level surface for the foundation of a fisherman's cot, nor were there any signs of human habitation.

Impressed with the idea that this bay must be an excellent place to haul the sean in, I determined to try it; and putting the helm up, impelled by the swell, we ran the boat directly in. I luffed to, about midway down, and, running the boat, on the weather or sea-side, slap on the beach, the sides of which were nearly as steep as a washing-basin, we landed our tackle, and a small tent I always carried with me for Zela. We again launched the boat with the sean, the men pulling deeper into the bay for a shallower and more favourable place for hauling it. Zela and myself strolled along the beach, collecting specimens of the finest shells I had seen. On the first cast of the sean, near the bottom of the bay, where the water was shallow, and the tide just turned, coming in, we had the heaviest haul of fish I ever saw or heard of, and of the most varied and finest kind. We literally heaped them up on the beach like hay-cocks; and continued, in sheer wantonness, to cast and draw, so highly were the men excited, till our eyes became satiated. In spite of the truism that the eye is a thousand times more insatiable than the mouth, for we had no more than seven mouths to fill, we toiled on, robbing the ocean of enough to cram the maws of a famished fleet. At last the greediest imagination was surfeited; and every man selecting what he thought it possible to carry, not eat, each bearing more than would have sufficed the party, we retraced our steps to where we first landed, lighted fires, and then man might truly have been designated a cooking animal, for all were cooks. The sportsman's brag that he don't toil to fill the pot was here belied; for we devoured the produce of our sport with a greediness that begot a general surfeit.

CHAPTER XXXVIII

And under the caves,
Where the shadowy waves
Are as green as the forest night;
Outspeeding the shark,
And the sword-fish dark,
Under the ocean foam.

SHELLEY

I LEFT Zela with her Malay handmaidens, and, aided by a boar-spear, ascended, with one of the men, an Arab, the rough rocks to overlook the bay. In my youth I loved climbing and scrambling up rocks and mountains; now I seldom intrude on the dweller of a second story, and my greatest enemy or friend may avoid me altogether on the third; so humbled is the aspiring spirit of my youth particularly after dinner. We wound our way along the precipitous sides of the rude barrier, which encompassed us, towards the bite, or bottom of the bay; and, rather wearied, gained a rude and jutting ledge of rocks, forming a small platform, nearly half-way to the summit. There I seated myself, lighted my pipe, and looked down on the entire bay, which lay under my feet; and further onwards, the bay of Bonny, which, banked in by islands on the sea-side, appeared an extensive lake. Looking down on the water, its aspect was flat and unruffled; many of the pictur-esque proas of the natives were scudding in with the last of the sea-breeze. On the narrow strip of bright sand, which lay round the water like a golden frame to a dark, oval Venetian picture, lay our little boat, the fishing-net drawn over, and its ends spreading along the beach, like a black spider veiled in its grey web.

My hawk-eyed Arab now pointed out to me a line of dark spots, moving rapidly in the water, rounding the arm of the sea, and entering the great bay. At first I thought they were canoes capsized, coming in keel uppermost; but the Arab declared they were sharks, and said, 'The bay is called Shark's Bay; and their coming in from the sea is an infallible sign of bad weather.' A small pocket-telescope convinced me they were large blue sharks. I counted eight; their fins and sharp backs were out of the water. After sailing majestically up the great bay till they came opposite the mouth of our smaller one, they turned towards it in a regular line; one, the largest I had seen any where, taking the lead, like an admiral. He had attained the entrance, with the other seven following, when some monster arose from the bottom, near the shore, where he had been lurking, opposed his further progress, and a conflict instantly ensued. The daring assailant I distinguished to be a sword-fish, or sea-unicorn, the knight-errant of the sea, attacking every thing in its domain; his head is as hard and as rough as a rock, out of the centre of which grows horizontally an ivory spear, longer and far tougher than any warrior's lance; with this weapon he fights. The shark, with a jaw larger and stronger than a crocodile's, with a mouth deep and capacious, strikes also with his tail, in tremendous force and rapidity, enabling him to repel any sudden attack by confusing or stunning his foe, till he can turn on his back, which he is obliged to do ere he can use his mouth. This wily and ex-perienced shark, not daring to turn and expose his more vulner-able parts to the formidable sword of his enemy, lashed at him with his heavy tail, as a man uses a flail, working the water into a sylla-bub. Meanwhile, in honour, I suppose, or in the love of fair play, his seven compatriot sharks stood aloof, lying to with their fins, in no degree interfering in the fray. Frequently I could observe, by the water's eddying in concentric ripples, that the great shark had sunk to the bottom, to seek refuge there, or elude his enemy by beating up the sand; or, what is more probable, by this man-œuvre to lure the sword-fish downwards, which, when enraged, will blindly plunge its armed head against a rock, in which case its horn is broken; or, if the bottom is soft, it becomes transfixed, and then would fall an easy prey. De Ruyter, while in a country vessel, had her struck by one of these fish, (perhaps mistaking her for a whale, which, though of the same species, it often attacks,) with such velocity and force, that its sword passed completely through the bow of the vessel; and, having been broken by the shock, it was with great difficulty extracted. It measured seven feet; about one foot of it, the part attached to the head, was hollow, and the size of my wrist; the remainder was solid, and very heavy, being indeed the exquisite ivory of which the eastern people manu-facture their beautiful chess-men. But to return to our sea-combat, which continued a long time, the shark evidently getting worsted. Possibly the bottom, which was clear, was favourable for his enemy; whose blow, if he succeeds in striking while the shark is

Ff

descending, is fatal. I think he had struck him, for the blue shark is seldom seen in shoal or discoloured water; yet now he floundered on towards the bottom of the bay, madly lashing the water into foam, and rolling and pitching like a vessel dismasted. For a few minutes his conqueror pursued him, then wheeled round and disappeared; while the shark grounded himself on the sand, where he lay writhing and lashing the shore feebly with his tail. His six companions, with seeming unconcern, wore round, and, slowly moving down the bay, returned by the outlet at which they had entered. Hastening down to the scene of action, I saw no more of them. My boat's crew were assembled at the bottom of the bay, firing muskets at the huge monster as he lay aground; before I could join them, he was despatched, and his dead carcase laid on the beach like a stranded vessel. Leaving him and them, I ran along the beach for half a mile to regain Zela's tent.

CHAPTER XXXIX

And all my knowledge is that joy is gone,
And this thing woe crept in among our hearts,
There to remain for ever, as I fear.

KEATS

WHEN close upon the tent, I caught the sounds of moaning and wailing within. Stooping down at the low entrance, I saw the sand spotted with blood. I burst through the canvas screen, and stood motionless as marble; and my heart felt as heavy and cold. My eyes dizzy, my senses bewildered, I gazed on what I thought the lifeless remains of Zela, stretched out like a corpse. Her black and dripping hair, in bloody and tangled masses, over her pallid bosom, looked like a dark shroud. Her eyes and mouth were half closed; she was unconscious, insensible. The Malay girls knelt by her on each side in despair, sobbing, tearing their hair, and rending their garments. They made signs to me as I entered, but Zela absorbed every faculty. I made an effort to approach; I tried to speak, but, heart-struck, I staggered, and should have fallen, had I not grasped the stancheon which supported the tent. With my eyes fast riveted on Zela, I thought I saw her eyelids move; then the sound of her voice thrilled through my frame, and re-called my fleeting faculties, though her words were inarticulate.

Kneeling by her side, I loosened her vest, put my hand on her heart, and felt it moving. I pressed my lips to hers; they were white, but still warm with life. I raised her head, and rubbed her hands; the blue veins on her beautiful eyelids, forehead, and neck swelled out, and a slight flush of crimson spread over her. She opened wildly her large dark eyes, reminding me forcibly of the first time I had encountered their magic fascination. 'Dearest Zela,' I stammered out, 'what is the matter?'

She gazed on me, as if with an effort to collect her powers of mind, and, in her low musical voice, answered slowly and distinctly,—'Nothing, love, if you are here. I am well,—very well. But you are ill,—you appear very ill.'

She then made an effort to turn on her side, but groaned with pain, and fell back powerless. After closing her eyes for a minute, she again opened them, and said, 'Oh, yes! I remember I have had a fall, and hurt myself a little,—nothing more. Oh! where is Adoo?—she fell too,—do, dear, see to her! I shall soon be well.'

I looked at the Malayan girl, who was supporting her on the opposite side. Her face and hands were streaming with blood; but without wasting a thought on herself, she was watching Zela as eagerly as I had done. She dried her eyes with her hair, and her dark features brightened as her mistress gave her a look of recognition. I interrogated her as to Zela's hurts; she pointed to her head, and several parts of her body. Angry at my folly in having, for an instant, neglected that on which so much depended, and, inspired by the overwhelming reaction of hope, with a hand, that had never trembled till then, I examined her wounds. After having persuaded her to drink some wine and water, she in vain besought me, (never till then in vain,) to first attend to Adoo. Even had I consented, the true-hearted little barbarian, although bleeding to death, would have died uncomplainingly, ere she would have permitted me to stanch her blood while her mistress's was flowing. The wounds on Zela's body, head, legs, and arms were many; yet, (and I had some skill in surgery,) they did not appear to me dangerous. Her insensibility had been occasioned by the blows on her head, and by loss of blood. There were severe bruises on her side and back, which gave her the greatest pain; and their consequences filled me with dread. But now that animation was restored, and with it her presence of mind, she contrived to lull my fears, and strengthen my hopes.

My attention was then directed to Adoo, at whom Zela shriekingly pointed. The poor little girl, whom I had hardly noticed, the
instant her fears for her mistress had in some degree subsided, fell
senseless on the sand. Her legs and one of her hands were almost
cut through, and the sand, where she had been seated, was in a
puddle from the quantity of blood she had lost. I tore the remainder
of my shirt into bandages, stanched and bound up her wounds;
but, with every care, it was long ere she gave indications of returning life.

The sailors had been for some time assembled round the tent,
anxious to ascertain the fate of those within: they were ignorant of
the circumstance, having been drawn down the bay watching the
sharks. I went out, and ordered them instantly to prepare the boat
for returning on board. The cockswain pointed to the sea, and
said—

'The boat can't live, Sir, in such weather.'

'Weather!—why it is a calm!'

I looked at the great bay, and beheld with dismay that one of
those squalls, so frequent in tropical climates, had suddenly come
on. Savage at this new evil, and the dreadful consequences of
delay, which might be fatal to Zela, I ran to the point, and, ascending the rocks, the first blast of the gale, which caught me, would
have borne me over them, had I not held on with my hands. It
was blowing a complete hurricane—the sun had disappeared in
the gloom—night prematurely was setting in—the sky was black
and lowering, and the sea was an entire sheet of foam.

It did not require an instant's thought as to the total impossibility of venturing out in such weather. The clouds too seemed
surcharged with thunder and water; I therefore hastened back
with the men, and we all turned to, hauling the boat up high and
dry, and securing the tent by every possible means. The boat-
sails and tackle were added—the sand was channelled all round—
rocks were placed on the tent-pegs, and dry wood collected for
firing. Luckily, we had a keg of water and bread in the boat, with
some other necessaries I never left the ship without, and, what
was of the utmost importance, a lantern. With the darkness the
storm increased, and in eddying gusts roared up the bay with a
force that seemed to rock the hills.

During the night we were all kept on the alert, first to prevent
the tent from being blown away, and then from being washed into

the sea by the floods or rain which followed. So loud and continued was the thunder, reverberating among the hills, that it was like the deafening explosions when rocks are blasted in a tunnel, or in a deep mine. As I walked to and fro on the beach, in melancholy forebodings, I wished the lightning would rend the rocks on each side, till, crumbling down, they filled up the bay beneath, and buried us all together. The invocation I made then, I have never revoked—would that it had been accomplished!

CHAPTER XL[1]

Thy cheek is pale
For one whose cheek is pale: thou dost bewail
His tears who weeps for thee.   *   *   *
*   *   *   *   'Tis she, but lo!
How changed, how full of ache, how gone in woe!

KEATS

The rain having lulled the wind, to keep Zela as much as possible from the wet sand, I sat down, leaning against the tent-pole, and supported her in my arms. On the morning I learnt the following particulars. She said—

'Two hours after your departure—Oh, would you had never left me! for I feel it is not your fate that hangs on me, as you have often told me, but mine on yours! Why, then, did you not let me go with you to the mountain? You have seen me climb, and have said nothing but the lizard could follow me.'

I answered, 'Yes, but remember you were then as light as a bird; now your weight is increased by the burthen you have within you. Our first child prematurely lost its life by your rash exertions in saving its father.'

'Could I hesitate to sacrifice my child to rescue its father? A child's life, weighed in the balance by a wife's hand, is but a feather against the heavy loss of a husband. Besides, who, that is an orphan, would willingly bring into this cruel world a being so helpless and wretched as itself?'

After giving vent to her feelings, she proceeded to satisfy my first inquiries regarding her present situation, and said, 'I strolled along the beach to the point of rocks at the entrance of the bay, and, coming to a sheltered and shady place, I determined to bathe with Adoo; the water looked so smooth and cool. The other little girl was posted to prevent intrusion. Then, knowing you admire the coral trees, which grow under the water, and seeing some very beautiful ones, I told Adoo to dive and bring me up a branch. It was of the deep crimson, which you said was the best. Owing to its brittleness, it was a long time before we could get an entire one. While we were still looking about, we heard a great noise in the water near us; and Adoo, who you know, has good eyes, saw something coming in from the sea, and told me there were benetas jumping about in play, a sign of bad weather at hand. She then told me she saw you coming along the beach, and added, "I can swim better than you, and will be the first on shore to welcome him."

'She swam faster than a fish, and I scolded her for her ill-natured exertions to shame her mistress, for I had vowed to be the first on land. She continued to jeer and mock me, until she landed on a rock, difficult to ascend, high out of the water, and slippery with weeds and moss. At that instant I heard the other girl, whom I had left as sentinel, shriek out,—"Sharks!—sharks!" I thought she was bantering, and was still hesitating, when I knew by her face she spoke the truth, and endeavoured to get up as Adoo had done. She stood on the verge of a ledge of rocks. The loud flapping of the sharks was behind me, and I heard the seamen shouting. Adoo stooped down, and gave me her hand; hastily I caught hold of it, and tried, with all my strength to climb up. Adoo held my right hand; with my left I seized on some sea-weed. My alarm added to my weight, already too heavy to be supported by such helps, and the sea-weeds gave way. Adoo would not let me go, nor could her feet cling to the slimy sea-grass, so that we both fell. Yet she did not fall upon me, or I must have then died;— poor girl! she threw herself headlong on the low rocks, and I fell on my side. The coral rocks are sharp, and I must have lain there, had not Adoo and her companion got me out of the water,— I know not how. I knew nothing more till I awoke, and found myself here in great pain. Then you came; and since that I have been better, much better!'

Continuing to repeat, 'much better!' Zela sunk into a restless sleep, exhausted by loss of blood and intense pain. I knew, by experience, that such unquiet slumbers is not refreshment; it is but depriving us of the consciousness of where and how we are afflicted. The brain is then crowded with horrid shapes, and imagined tortures, far worse than realities, such as the most cunning of human tyrants could never devise. I sponged the dewy drops from her throbbing temples; her groans smote my heart. It was evident that the internal injuries she had received were worse than I had apprehended; exterior wounds could not so convulse her. Gloomy forebodings filled my mind, and almost tempted me to antedate, what I dared not contemplate, her loss, by ending my fears at once, and our lives together. My pistols lay by my side, and my eyes were fixed on them, when one of the seamen came to the door of the tent, and told me the squall had blown over, and the weather was clearing.

We waited another hour for the swell to be moderate, during which time we made the boat as commodious as possible. The tent was struck, and every thing being in readiness, I carried Zela on board; and afterwards Adoo, who would allow no one to touch her but myself. The men, to shew they felt for one who never spoke but in kindness, and never appeared amongst them but to confer some favour, exerted their utmost strength at the oars to expedite our passage. Still the waves were rolling in heavily from the sea; but that was in our favour; and the boat, constructed for whale-fishing, floated lightly, and moved almost as rapidly as a sea-swallow; though, at that time, I did not think so. I relieved the men alternately at the oars; and my intense anxiety and impatience was assuaged by physical labour. We pulled the distance, which was little less than three leagues, within two hours. The grab's deck was crowded as we flew past her; the men perceived by our rapidity that something had happened, and De Ruyter inquired what was the matter. Without replying to his question, I begged he would lose no time in coming on board the schooner with the doctor. In the schooner also I saw the men ranged along the gangway; and, in another instant, we shot up along-side of her. A chair was soon slung, lowered from the main-yard into the boat, and Zela was hoisted on the deck. Without speaking a word, indeed I could hardly distinguish the features of the crowd of familiar faces gazing on us, I bore her directly into the cabin.

The doctor and De Ruyter were quickly on board. When they entered the cabin, and beheld the change which four and twenty hours had made in Zela's beautiful face and form, De Ruyter involuntarily shuddering, closed his eyes, and pressed his hands over his face; while the hitherto imperturbable doctor, who, except on hearing of Louis' death, had never shewn the least sympathy with human woe, now took the glasses from his eyes, and wiped them. Then, with a tenderness foreign to his usual practice, he proceeded to unbind and examine the wounds of his gentle patient. Not a question was asked by either of them; and, during the whole process, no other words were spoken than the brief account I was compelled to give for the instruction and guidance of the doctor.

The most learned in human physiognomy might have gazed for ever on Van's unchanging features without a chance of reading his thoughts. After dressing her wounds, he carefully examined the bruises on her body, and, giving her a preparation of opium, left her. I followed, and warmly essayed to fathom his thoughts. He was struck by the alteration in my bearing towards him; for, when suffering in my own person from wounds or sickness, I had still maintained my bantering and jeering manner, and often vexed him beyond endurance. But now my pride was humbled; for I had faith in Van's skill, on which all my hopes depended, and was meek and obedient as the most abject slave to the most imperious and powerful of masters. It is almost needless to say that the poor faithful attendant, Adoo, lacked little of the care that was bestowed on her mistress. She was laid on the opposite couch; and it was evident her strength was greater, or her sufferings infinitely less acute; for her features had undergone but a slight and nearly imperceptible change, whilst Zela's were so contracted by spasms, that she was scarcely to be recognized.

CHAPTER XLI

Thy voice was a sweet tremble in mine ear,
Made tuneable by every sweetest vow,
And those sad eyes were spiritual and clear:
How changed thou art! how pallid, chill, and drear!

KEATS

Save thine, 'incomparable oil,' Macassar!

BYRON

AFTER watching Zela till she slept, I went on deck where I found De Ruyter waiting for me. I gave him a detailed account of all that had led to this fatal calamity; for I could not divest myself of a conviction that it would terminate fatally. His arguments to the contrary, although they were rational and wise, could not shake my belief. Firmly fixed was the presentiment that the spring-tide, which had borne me on triumphantly to the attainment of perfect happiness, was turned, ebbing back to the sea, and that mine and my happiness would be left a stranded wreck. To relax the tense chords, strainingly drawn from heart to brain, De Ruyter endeavoured to divert my thoughts to the discussion of other topics. He told me he had, on the previous evening, received intelligence, coming through an infallible channel, that the Governor General of India had, at length, determined on fitting out an expedition, (with the details of which he was in possession,) for the wresting of the Isle of France out of the hands of the French.

'It has been made known to me,' said De Ruyter, 'through my correspondent, an Armenian merchant, who resides at the seat of government, and has found means of diving to the very bottom of every council held there. This enterprise has been long, very long in contemplation; but now they have resolved to carry it into execution. This will materially alter my plans. We have no time to lose; we must exert ourselves to the utmost in expediting the refitment and equipment of our vessels.'

At another time this would have aroused me, had I been bed-ridden with a jungle-fever; but now, in the most animating part of his discourse, while detailing the naval and military force to be employed, and the names of their respective commanders, a death-like torpor, which had stolen up my limbs, and weighed on my body like lead, at length ascended to my eye-lids, which it sealed, and I fell into the profoundest sleep I can remember. De Ruyter, as I afterwards discovered, had carefully covered me with flags, and placed a sentinel over me to prevent my being disturbed. Since Zela's accident, I had not taken food; and De Ruyter had artfully induced me to drink a cup of strong coffee, under the plea of keeping me awake. This he had drugged with opium, to enforce that rest, without which he foresaw my strength of body and mind would be prostrated. I did not awake till the evening, and wondered how I could have enjoyed such a long and undisturbed sleep at such a time.

I hastily descended to the cabin, and found the doctor examining his patients. They were both sitting up, supported by cushions. The Malay girl was considerably better; but Zela's mind only seemed to have benefited: her bodily sufferings had undergone no change. Her face, which before was rosy, bright, and pure as the first tints of morning, was now shaded with the dim hue of sickness: her eyes were dull, and her lips without colour. De Ruyter and the doctor remained on board us during the wearisome night, the greater part of which I passed in the cabin, supporting Zela in my arms, where alone she seemed to find relief.

The next day, in compliance with De Ruyter's wish to prepare for sea, I returned to my duties. He kindly offered to relieve me from them; but I mechanically resumed my business, as formerly, and active employment was of the utmost service in preserving the strength of my body, which otherwise would have sunk under the weight of my tortured mind. No longer, as before, was I above fate and circumstance, therefore happy—but full of evil forebodings. My heart was swollen by painful emotions, rendered still more preying by the necessity of repressing them. On the third day, when her sufferings became so gnawingly acute as to threaten a speedy termination, scarcely was I sensible; I possessed only a half kind of feeling that death was a most desirable end; and when those violent throes and writhings ceased to convulse her frame, when she sunk into a helpless, senseless torpor, when she lay so motionless that I thought she was dead, I stood over her with a fierce firmness, startling the iron-nerved doctor, and exclaimed, 'She is then dead!'

Van was then holding her tiny wrist between his gaunt finger and thumb, and answered, 'You are ignorant. She lives. The crisis of her danger is past. She is no more dead than I am;—she is asleep.'

His words were as balsamic oil. The stern, the painful rigidity of fortitude, to which I had worked myself, relaxed into softness, with the same feeling of composure, as when our fibres are released from the grasp of a spasm, and are lulled into repose; and such was the relief Zela then experienced. Satisfied with the truth of this, I went on deck as one revived, and beheld the scene shining beautifully under that magic light, in which it is the privilege of joy to clothe the world. My spirits became, as it were, embalmed in bliss. I hastened on board the grab to communicate my happiness to De Ruyter and the old Rais. Every man participated in my joy for the restoration of her, whose kindness, courage, and gentleness had penetrated the breasts of the roughest, and impressed their stubborn hearts with admiration.

Once more was I alert in my duty, no longer an indifferent spectator. The news De Ruyter had heard he now retold me; and, having completed our repairs, we weighed our anchors and put to sea. The Rajah, with whom De Ruyter was on a friendly footing, gave him, at taking leave, a large quantity of different oils and balsams, for which this island is as celebrated as Java for its poisons. Among the rest was a large proportion of kiapootee and colalava oil, and the oleaginous extract from a fruit-tree, since that period become so notorious in Europe, (by name I mean,)—Macassar oil. I may mention here that it was some of this very oil, given by the Rajah to medicine Zela's hurts, that, on my return to England, through the means of a servant, found its way into the hands of a perfumer; it was a quart bottle, and must have possessed the miraculous properties of the widow's cruise of oil. Certainly the pure vegetable, gelatinous oils, of this island and the Moluccas, are beneficial both to the skin and hair; for the natives, in the two essential articles of beauty, surpass all the world, and retain them even in extreme age. Indeed I never remember to have there seen grey hair or bald heads; and even the aged retain their suppleness of limb and softness of skin. This I should have attributed to their fine climate, simplicity of diet, and abstinence from ardent spirits, were it not that many other nations participate in these advantages, without enjoying the same results; therefore I think their balsamic oils must possess a rare virtue. The bald head of Socrates may have added dignity to his appearance; but the bald cocoa-nut shaped skulls of modern mortals are disgusting, and to them I commend the liberal use of the oil of Macassar,—if they can get it.

In this voyage De Ruyter's object being exclusively to return, as speedily as possible, to the Isle of France, it was determined not to run out of our course, nor be diverted from our main design, either by putting into any one of the islands, near which we might pass, or by giving chase to any vessel, except such as were steering in the same direction. In passing the straits of Sunda, De Ruyter run in near enough to communicate with the shore by a boat, but did not anchor. He had an interview with the governor, General Jansens, at Batavia, and received a confirmation of the news he had heard at the Celebes. Taking in a few boatloads of fresh provisions, we forthwith proceeded on our voyage. De Ruyter's wish was, in our long run across the Indian ocean, from the straits of Sunda to the Isle of France, that we should make the best of our way, without the detention of keeping together. Besides, as accidents might happen to one of us, either by falling in with English men-of-war, (for intelligence had reached us that a squadron of frigates was in those seas, bound, it was conjectured, for the Isle of France,) or by squalls, or calms, or by one of the thousand disasters attendant on a long voyage, the risk would be lessened by our holding different courses, as then one of us might be calculated to reach his destination, on which the fate of the French settlement seemed to hang. For this purpose I had been furnished with duplicates of the despatches, with full power to act in De Ruyter's name in his own particular affairs. But all these prudent and wise considerations were overruled by my anxiety, indeed by the urgent necessity for Doctor Van Scolpvelt's attendance on Zela, who continued in such a state of debility, that it was still doubtful if she would not sink under it. Van's skill had triumphed at a moment of the utmost peril; in saving her life he had bound me to him for ever; his medical knowledge, that had been heretofore so lightly thought of by me, I now reverenced as a superhuman attribute, belonging to him alone. It was therefore fixed that we should, running all chances, keep together; except in the event of our being pursued by an enemy of superior force, when it would be indispensable for us to separate and make our escape.

CHAPTER XLII

O, vulture witch, hast thou never heard of mercy?
Could not thy harshest vengeance be content,
But thou must nip this tender innocent
Because I loved her?

KEATS

So, at last,
This nail is in my temple!

KEATS' MS.

ORDINARY events during a voyage do not bear relating. A man might as well seek to be amused by perusing a merchant's ledger as a sea common-place journal. Yet had it been otherwise, I must confess, such was my weakness, that I was no longer capable of attending to, much less of recording the scenes, which indeed passed before my eyes, but left no impression on my mind, bright and vivid at the moment perhaps, as the line of light shot by a star through the heavens at night, yet as fading and transitory; or like the sparkling furrow left by our vessel's deep keel in the dark waters, expunged as soon as made. The wings of my spirit would no longer bear me up; my imagination remained hovering over the sick couch of Zela; my mind was dyed in the same melancholy hue of the drooping object I contemplated. Ours were no common ties; she had been as a bird driven by the tempest from the land, that sought refuge in my bosom; and like a darling bird, too delicate to be entrusted in others' hands, I alone fostered and cherished her. Still the doctor, dividing his time between the two vessels, continued to predict her ultimate restoration to health; but he confessed the shock her delicate frame had received required time and care.

We had been nearly a month at sea, and a certain change for the better had taken place in her constitution. After sitting up with her, as usual, all night, I lay slumbering uneasily on the deck under the awning, my mind haunted by the horrible dream of the poisonous hag of Java, when I was awakened by Adoo, who had nearly recovered from her wounds. By the agitation depicted on her strongly marked features, I saw that something disastrous had taken place. Before she could utter a connected sentence, I was by Zela's couch. She was writhing in extreme pain, and said that her stomach was burning. I called to the mate on deck to make a signal to the grab for the doctor, but she, unfortunately, was nearly out of sight a-head, and it was almost a calm. Questioning Adoo as to the cause of Zela's present state, she pointed to a jar on the table, and told me that, her mistress not having eaten anything for a long time, she, with the other girl, had hunted in the store-room for something that would tempt her to eat. They found that jar of preserved fruit; when her mistress, fond of sweetmeats, ate a great deal, and gave some to the other little girl, who was seized with the same pain after eating it. 'Seeing my mistress liked it,' said Adoo, 'I did but taste one of the fruit, and it has made me sick. I am sure there is poison in that jar.'

The word *poison* pierced my brain like a barbed arrow. Looking at the newly-opened jar, which had been closed with more than ordinary care by a resinous gum, I emptied out a portion of the fruit. They were a very fine sort of the wild green and yellow nutmegs, preserved in white sugar-candy. Had the small green snake, a native of Java, whose venom is the deadliest of all its tribe, erected its crest from out the jar, it would not so have shaken my nerves. For I remembered I had, at the widow's, eaten many preserved nutmegs from a jar, the counterpart of the one before me, and that they had made me sick; when an old woman—a confidential slave of the widow, whose heart I had won by giving her a small silver box to fasten round the arm, containing a scrap of papyrus with a hieroglyphic charm, brought from Mecca, telling her it was a passport to admit her, alone of all the sex, into paradise; then she looked at me, long and steadily, and said, 'Have you angered my mistress already?' I laughed at the question. At that moment the widow came into the room in high spirits, patted my cheeks, and ran away to make me some coffee. As soon as she was gone, the old woman again addressed me with, 'I was going to say, if my mistress is angry, and if you have eaten nutmegs prepared by her hands, you had better keep to yourself the talisman, which is to unlock the gates of paradise. You are too young and too happy to go there. I once told a husband of my mistress the same. He was a good man, and gave my son his freedom. I told him not to eat nutmegs, when,—ah!—when—'

'And why not?' I inquired.

'He asked me the same question,' replied the old woman. 'But you men are all infidels; you believe nothing that women say if they are old, and, what is worse, everything if they are young. My mistress saw another man she liked better; and I heard her one day say bitter things of my master. The next day I saw her give him those sweet things to eat, and he became sick; when he was carried out of the house, and another man came in, and put on his slippers and turban. But I can read my mistress's thoughts; as yet she loves you, and will do you no harm. So I shall keep the charm, for I shall want it soon; but mind you do not make my mistress angry, for then she is deadly as the poison of the cheetic-tree, which grows in the jungle, on which the sun never shines.'

Our conversation was again interrupted by the widow, and half a dozen slaves bringing coffee and cold water. This warning made some impression at the time, for I desisted from eating the most delicious sweetmeats in the world; and it had been strengthened, before I left the island, by many corroborating stories from others. Often had I afterwards congratulated myself on escaping from her fangs, when sweltering with venom. Now the frightful belief flashed on my mind, that the cunning strumpet, aided by the devil himself, had, as it were, stretched her arm across the Indian ocean to ship the poisoned jar; for by no investigation could I ascertain how or when it came on board.

While I stood pondering over the accursed fruit, half uncon-scious where I was, I thought I could hear the fiendish laugh of the widow mocking me. I thought I could see her, as she stood in the stern of the boat, threatening and cursing me as I left the harbour of Batavia, and began to repay her with loud and savage imprecations, till Zela, alarmed at my looks and gestures, believing me mad, forgot for a moment her own agony, took hold of my hand, pulled me on the bed, and soothed me with the softest accents, assuring me she was getting better. She bade me lay my head on her bosom, and she would rub it, for she saw the veins were distended on it. She said, almost playfully, 'I can bear any pain but that of seeing you suffer. Your looks, my love, affright me. Take this fruit,' (giving me a pomegranate,) 'which the poet Hafiz calls the pearl of fruits; and thus I imitate the example of the shell of the ocean, to fill with pearls the hand which wounds it.'

The calmness with which she talked deceived me for a moment; but this effort of her mind almost destroyed her frail body: for then she talked wildly and incoherently, the subversion of her intellect foretelling the fatal issue that was at hand. Every muscle and nerve was writhing, as with a separate agony; her features were distorted; and in vain I tried every method I could think of to alleviate her pain. The poison was working on her vitals, and her mental derangement was a relief.

When at last the doctor came and saw her, it was evident that even his science could not avail. He examined the jar, compared the symptoms of his patients, and confessed that my suspicions were well grounded. But I am totally unequal to the task of narrating, step by step, the ravages that the venom worked on her. She wasted, day by day, till she became almost a shadow. I never left her; and in her lucid intervals, which were few, she clung to me with more than her wonted fondness; and we mingled our tears, renewing our vows never to part. The truest words of the poet are, 'The love which is born of sorrow, like it, is true.' Sorrow was the parent of our attachment. I remembered she once said to me, when reveling in health and happiness at our hut in Borneo, 'I saw you enter the tent where I was a prisoner. All others fled. It was the house of death. You came, like an angel, to save. Though you could not save my father, you avenged and consoled him when dying. How then could I but admire you? When afterwards you attached yourself to me (by what charm influenced I am yet to learn), my admiration was, on the instant, love. For you approached me, and offered those sympathies which are the smaller links of that invisible chain love delights to wear for ever; because our senses, says Hafiz, wait upon our imagination like the most submissive slaves.'

My God! how shall I find words to tell the death of her who had felt and spoken thus? If all were concentrated into one word, that could express my feelings, to give it utterance would destroy my reason!

Picking the seeds from a pomegranate, and making ruby-coloured letters on the bed, such as, in our happy days, had been the means of conveying our ideas when ignorant of each other's language, and singing fragments of Arabian songs, was now her constant habit. One night she was startled, in the midst of her wild notes, by a voice from the deck calling out that the Isle of France was in sight. She screamed out, 'I am glad of it, very glad, dearest husband. Only, love, take me in your arms to carry me on shore; I am too weak to walk.' Then throwing herself, with her last collected strength, in my arms, as I knelt by her low couch, she clasped me round the neck with her thin hands, and saying,— 'Now I am well and happy! I live in his heart!'—with her lips pressed to mine, she yielded up her mortality!

CHAPTER XLIII

> Upon those pallid lips
> So sweet even in their silence; on those eyes
> That image sleep in death; upon that form
> Yet safe from the worm's outrage, let no tear
> Be shed—not even in thought.
>
> SHELLEY

> Now let me borrow
> For moments few, a temperament as stern
> As Pluto's sceptre, that my words not burn
> These uttering lips, while I in calm speech tell
> How specious heaven was changed to real hell.
>
> KEATS

To attempt to portray what I felt then, or even now feel, when time and sorrow (though nothing like to this) have almost dried up my heart, would be indeed walking in a vain shadow, and disquieting myself in vain by it. The followers of Mahomet are tutored, from their youth, to suppress from the scrutiny of others all outward tokens of the secret counsels of the heart. In the east this is imperative as the law of self-preservation. In the west it is done far more effectually, if not so generally, by those who a philosopher would suppose were in derision misnamed noble, whose feelings, if they are impregnated with any at their birth (which is doubtful, considering the seed they spring from), are eradicated with as much care as is bestowed in Persia on the shoots and branches of the cherry-tree, designed for pipe-sticks, every bud that threatens to burst through the rind being instantly rubbed off, to preserve the smoothness and polish of the exterior. Whether I had lavished on Zela the last tear of sorrow, or from the benumbing effects which follow grief, or intense excitement, I do not know; but a torpor came over my mind, encouraged by the liberal use of opium, which I then first learned to use, like the Chinese, by smoking it through a reed, and I rapidly acquired a stoical apathy

Gg

of look, that the gravest Turk, sitting in divan, or the most stick-like lords,

> 'Fellows of no merit,
> Slight and puff'd souls, that walk like shadows by,
> Leaving no print of what they are,'

would have envied, and despaired of imitating. De Ruyter, with all his knowledge of human nature, was perplexed to account for so new and strange a transition of character. To judge by my deportment, my years seemed trebled in a day. He would have thought me mad, or fast verging on that malady, but that all my actions demonstrated a methodical regularity and precision, which I had shewn no signs of in my days of happiness. I appeared not to mourn; and I never wept, nor uttered a single complaint. My habits, which had before been sufficiently abstemious, occasion-ally dashed by extremes of the contrary, were now undeviatingly such as the wisest would have applauded. The driest and most monotonous duties, which I had hitherto neglected, were now ful-filled with a scrupulous exactitude. What was most strange this change took place the instant Zela's spirit left me. Her body was still on board.

But let me return to my story. Having informed De Ruyter of my intentions regarding the remains of Zela, I drafted the greater portion of my men on board the grab; and we then parted company. She went directly into Port St. Louis, and I round to Port Bourbon, on the south-east side of the island, where we had anchored on my first visit to it. De Ruyter, after delivering des-patches, which he had brought from Java, and conferring with the Governor, was to ride over to me, accompanied by the doctor and the old Rais. I had retained on board the schooner merely sufficient men to work her, principally natives of the east, the faithful tribe of a now chieftainless house. On the same night I anchored in Port Bourbon.

During the short interval that, in such a climate, intervenes between death and decomposition, I had pondered intensely on the least repulsive mode by which it was practicable to dispose of her remains. Death's common receptacle, the earth, naturally first engaged my thoughts; and the arbour, made by our united hands, in De Ruyter's garden, fragrant with flowers, seemed a fitting spot. But as I remembered, when digging in the soil, the myriads of disgusting worms and beetles, I shudderingly banished that idea. The clear deep vault of the beautiful element which I loved, and, floating on whose surface, both of us had spent our lives, what could molest her there?—but my imagination reverted to the horrid scene that had taken place after Louis' interment. Then I thought I would have the body embalmed, and treasure it with me through life; but there was so many insurmountable obstacles in the way, I was compelled to deny myself that consolation. At last I thought on the heathen ceremony of destroying the body by fire,[1] or rather not destroying, but restoring it into its primitive state, by remingling it with the elements of which it is an atom. The funeral-pile, the purification by fire, the simple, yet touching rites, the examples of the god-like heathen philosophers, whose bodies had been thus immolated, all conspired to work on my mind, and fix my determination to this point. De Ruyter approved of it, and the doctor readily undertook to provide every thing necessary, and give his assistance in the execution of what he was perfectly acquainted with by theory. For this purpose I had anchored in Port Bourbon, as the most secluded part of the island. There was no commerce there, and no other habitations in or near it than three or four paltry huts. The Dutch had, at some period, commenced the foundation of a town there, but it had long been totally abandoned, and its ruins were choked up with reeds and rushes.

At the earliest dawn of day I pointed out a spot, deep in the bottom of the harbour, and sent a party of my Arab crew to pitch a tent, and collect a large quantity of dry fuel. Then, secluding myself in the cabin, I spent the entire day—the last in which I could contemplate her who had been to me what the sun is to the earth.

The little Malayan girl, who had partaken of the poisoned fruit, was still suffering from its effects. She was removed to another part of the vessel. Either through the strength of her constitution, unbroken by previous sickness, or from the smaller quantity she had eaten, together with the antidotes the doctor used, she not only lived, but hopes, though faint, were entertained of her recovery;—I had no feeling left for her. Adoo had wept and moaned herself into a stupid insensibility; and it was only by force she could be induced to take nourishment:—yet I even gazed on her with apathy, and her sighs and groans made no more impression on me, than the wind howling amidst the shrouds in a gale.

It was past midnight when my lonely contemplations were interrupted, by a man on deck telling me there was a signal from the shore.

This was the signal, concerted with De Ruyter, to apprize me of his approach. The boats were in readiness; one I sent for him and his party, and manned the long-boat of the grab, which he had lent me for the occasion. I had robed Zela in the richest costume of her country: her yellow vest was spangled with little rubies, and her chemise and flowing drawers, of sea-green Indian crape, were edged with gold; her outer garments were of the finest muslin of India; her slippers and the embroidered kerchiefs which bound up her hair, and concealed her bosom and the lower part of her face, were beaded and embossed with pearls. I preserved but one braid of her long, dark, silken hair, and, placing that in my breast, I kissed her eyelids, cheeks, and lips. Carefully folding her in a large Arab barican, or cloak of white camel's hair, I conveyed her into the boat. I was a mere machine. The blood in my veins was stagnant. I remember only that when De Ruyter came to me, the efforts I made to speak with composure had nearly stifled me. When he told me they were all ready on shore, I feared I could not walk along the boat, yet I sternly refused to be assisted. I got over the boat's quarter into the sea; and, pressing my precious burthen closely to my breast, and warily preventing the water from touching her, I walked through the surf to the shore. Its coolness strengthened me, and I was enabled to stagger on to the spot, where stood the funeral pile. I could recognise no other object. The figures that flitted about, and those who stopped to speak to me, looked like spectres gliding in a dance of death. A black iron furnace, like a coffin, was placed on the pile. After standing for some time entranced at its side, my senses, by some means, were sufficiently restored to make me aware of the necessity of going through what I had undertaken. I placed the body within the iron shell as delicately as a mother lays her sleeping child in its cradle. Then De Ruyter, the old Rais, and others withdrew me a short distance away, and held me there. Oils, spices, musk, camphor, and ambergris, I was afterwards told, were thrown in by baskets full. Dry bamboos and damped reeds thickly covered all; so that, when ignited, I could see nothing but a dark, impenetrable pyramid of smoke. I tried to speak; then entreated by signs, for my throat was dry as death, that they would unhand me; but they held me fast, and my strength had totally fled. Owing to some confusion, the cause of which I did not then ascertain,— (it was the rescuing of Adoo, who had thrown herself into the flames,) I found myself unfettered; and, with the intention of doing the same thing, I sprung forward, but, stumbling from weakness, or over some object in my way, I fell on the sand, so near the fire that my outstretched hands were severely burnt. What followed I know not, for I remained insensible. When restored to reason, I was swinging in a cot on the deck of the schooner.

The utmost human nature can endure and survive, I suffered. I cursed the strength of my body, harder and stronger than steel, that retained, in despite of my ardent longing for death, the spirit of life within me. De Ruyter's urgent affairs kept him at the town of Port St. Louis; but he frequently came over to me in the night. A small case, containing Zela's ashes, was given me; it was ever near me. I had been strongly urged to accompany De Ruyter to the town, or to his country-house, but I would not leave the schooner.

CHAPTER XLIV

Am I to leave this haven of my rest,
This cradle of my glory, this soft clime,
This calm luxuriance of blissful light.

KEATS

But custom maketh blind and obdurate
The loftiest hearts;—he had beheld the woe
In which mankind was bound, but deemed that fate,
Which made them abject, would preserve them so

SHELLEY

NEARLY a month had elapsed, when De Ruyter, coming on board one night, found me calmer and more attentive to his discourse than usual. He then told me he had been strongly urged, nay, importuned by the Governor of the island, to take despatches to Europe, conveying the information he had brought; and that information was now further corroborated by unquestionable authority from several quarters. The word *Europe* at first startled me; for I had learnt to loathe it, and consider the east as my country. But now the case was altered. I wished to bid adieu to the objects which surrounded me. I wished to remove myself to the opposite extremity of the world,—I cared not where or how, so that I could, by action and change, banish thoughts, and learn to forget the past. De Ruyter, comprehending the workings of my mind, gave me time for reflection. He then asked me what I thought on the subject. I answered that I was unable to think, and therefore could not advise; but I told him my wishes, and urged him implicitly to follow his own judgment. 'What judgment I have,' he said, 'floats on the surface. My mind is at all times ready to answer on the instant. It is plain the English will be paramount in India for a while, and that all other European nations will be driven from their settlements on the Indian islands. Our stay here cannot arrest the progress of events. A wise man, when he finds himself badly placed in one spot, will remove to another. The weak and timid, like silly birds, drop into the jaws of the rattlesnake. I only hesitated to hear your wishes; so you may prepare the schooner for sea; to do which you must run her round to Port St. Louis. As the grab is merely adapted for the Indian seas, I shall sell or leave her; and we will proceed together in the schooner. The business requires haste; so you had better turn the hands up, and get out with this land breeze.'

This I did, and externally resumed the stoical fortitude which had left me for a time. Early on the next day I was at Port St. Louis, and all the busy preparations of going to sea for a long voyage commenced. The government stores, artificers, and seamen were severally put in requisition, by command of the Governor-General, to expedite the equipment of the schooner. As I had lost all relish for eating and sleeping, and never left the schooner for an instant, at the expiration of a few days every thing was completed, and we lay ready to put to sea at an hour's notice.

Nor did my grief make me so selfish as to forget or neglect those dependent on me. I consulted with De Ruyter on the best means of providing for Adoo, and Zela's other little girl, who was still emaciated and wasting, and the remaining Arabs of her house, now reduced to twelve. He first talked with the old Rais on the subject; and, with his boundless liberality, gave him the choice of an entire plantation on his estate on the island, as a free gift to him and his, without stipulation; or money to purchase a vessel, in which he might trade as a merchant, or return to his country, and spend the remainder of his life at ease, amidst his kindred and countrymen. It would be a tedious recital to detail all that passed on the occasion. The old Arab seaman, although of the desert, had a heart and head that neither years nor hardships could render insensible. Long debating on the matter with him, De Ruyter ascertained that his wish was to return to the land of his fathers. It was therefore decided that Zela's Arabs and her two attendants should return with him. The Arabs were, by their own election, to become the followers of the Rais; and the Malayan girls were to be formally adopted by him.

It is scarcely necessary to say that every individual was amply rewarded, nor were their deserts so much considered as their fidelity to their mistress. Had their avarice been as great as that of priests, my prodigal gifts must have satisfied them; if indeed the insatiable maws of priests can ever be glutted, while aught remains to be extorted. But with these simple-hearted people, whatever other vices they may have had, avarice, the worst of all, though it had entered their dark bosoms, had not usurped the first place there. For the loss of the last blood of their race, the utter extinction of one of the purest Arabian tribes, whose pedigree went back to thousands of years, to the fathers of the human race, they gave vent to their grief in loud and clamorous yells; whilst I, 'a cannibal of my own heart,' nourished mine in silence.

I well know it would be in vain to reason with Adoo on the necessity of her leaving me; and it required all the influence De Ruyter had over me to induce me to be separated from this last link connecting me with the past. But his reasons were so many and unanswerable, that at length I was compelled to submit, and he undertook to effect our separation by stratagem. Although I continued to protest strongly and urgently against this, to my sorrow it took place; and its sad result filled my cup of misery to overflowing, and, like a poisonous oil, it floats on the surface.

The eastern portion of our crew was discharged, the grab was sold, and the Europeans on board of her were transhipped to the schooner. We had no difficulty in completing our number of hands, as so many seamen were anxious to return to their country. De Ruyter provided for his oldest followers in various modes; some were rewarded by gifts of land on his estate, a portion of which he disposed of, including the house; and he took care to register the freedom of those whom he had emancipated.

At any other time the metamorphosis my body was compelled to undergo, not from the caterpillar to the winged butterfly, but from the butterfly to the caterpillar, would have mortified me. In short I laid aside the free, graceful, and pleasant garb of the east for the detestable and ludicrous fashion of the west. I would rather my legs were in the stocks, than my throat. The chains of a galley-slave do not cramp a man's limbs more than buckram, starch, and the modern tightness of dress. My first transition to a sailor's jacket and trowsers I could have borne uncomplainingly, had it ended there.

CHAPTER XLV

A little shallow, floating near the shore,
Caught the impatient wandering of his gaze;
It had been long abandoned, for its sides
Gaped wide with many a rift, and its frail joints
Swayed with the undulations of the tide.

SHELLEY

IT was a year afterwards that I received the afflicting news of Adoo. When she discovered that the schooner, bearing the ashes of her mistress, had left the port, contrary to her usual habits, but with the cunning and inflexible determination of her nature, she listened to all the kind-hearted Rais could say to soothe her, and appearing, if not satisfied, yet resigned to circumstances, she succeeded in lulling her adopted father's suspicions. Then stealing out at night, she swam to a country vessel; and, casting off the painter, by which her boat was secured, with the rope held between her teeth, she floated out of the harbour with the land-wind. When she believed herself safe from discovery, she got on board the boat and paddled directly out to sea, her mind bent on the single object of escape, evidently in the vain hope of overtaking the schooner. She had never perhaps reflected on its folly; as to the danger, where her affections were, thither was she impelled, and no impediment could arrest her steps.

The Rais, aware of her flight in the morning, with great sagacity traced her to having taken the boat of the Arab vessel, and, without a moment's delay, engaged a large boat, manned her with his Arabs, proceeded a long way to sea in our track, and cruised about for two days, in hopes of falling in with her. But not succeeding, he carefully marked the setting of the swell and currents since the night of her escape, ran back to the island, and coasted along its east side, questioning the people in the fishing-boats and those on shore, but without avail. There are two small islands at the eastern extremity of the Isle of France, called Round Islands, when, going on towards one of these, he discovered a small boat, which proved to be the one taken from the Arab vessel. She was bilged, filled with water, and lying on the rocks, on which the swell of the breakers had washed and left her. The island was without fresh water or inhabitants; every spot, rock, and hollow crevice in it were examined, without discovering the slightest vestige of Adoo. The neighbouring island, and the coast immediately adjoining was also searched. Her death seemed certain; but the manner of it was, and is, involved in mystery.

This news I felt as a sword thrust through my body, or as a probe forced into a newly cicatriced wound. It shewed at least that a portion of the sensibility of my heart was restored. This event, of which I could not help thinking De Ruyter was the origin, formed the only instance where I ever had to repent the having yielded up my strong impulses to his sound judgment. Henceforth I determined that whatever manacles might bind my limbs, no fetters should incarcerate my mind.

> 'I have lived thus many years,
> And run through all these follies men call fortunes,
> Yet never fixed on any good and constant
> But what I made myself: why should I grieve then
> At what I may mould any way?'

I cannot recal an event worth recording previously to our departure from the Isle of France, nor during our passage to Europe. More than once we were chased; but few vessels that ever floated could keep way with the schooner in any weather. In the English channel the British cruisers lay around us like the coral islands in the Sooloo archipelago; we had escaped the peril of the one, so we managed to elude the pursuit of the other. After an unprecedented quick passage we anchored in the port of St. Malo in France, then full of French privateers and ships of war.

Ere we had been an hour at anchor De Ruyter was posting on his road to Paris, to deliver his despatches to the government, whilst I remained in charge of the schooner.

We had a small cargo of the finest tea, coffee, spices, and, by some accident or other, a few tons of white crystal sugar. This last I mention, as, at that period, the price of sugar was so high in France that it was sold at an enormous profit, nearly clearing the expenses of the voyage. Our other East Indian produce was sold at almost an equally high rate; and I saw that trade, not war, was the most direct and only certain road leading to wealth, though I was utterly indifferent to its accumulation. My sentiments, changed in many things, have remained, to the present hour, unaltered on this head.

The voyage, and more particularly the extreme hardships we endured, with the privations attending so long a run in so small a craft and many hands, all conspired, bracing my collapsed muscles, to keep me alive. Yet I was still very weak and emaciated; my body was so thin that the skin seemed stretched to bursting over my gaunt and bony form; my face was haggard and care-worn to a degree unexampled in one so young;—for I had hardly yet attained the age at which the law, as if in mockery, tells us we are free agents, while it heaps responsibility on us, and thrusts us forth to earn our bitter bread by the sweat of our brows, like Cain, with every man's hand against us,—though Cain had, literally, the world for his garden, while we find every spot pre-occupied. In this struggle for existence, each is compelled to turn his hand against every man.

CHAPTER XLVI

Sylla was first of victors; but our own,
The sagest of usurpers, Cromwell, he
Too swept off senates, while he hew'd the throne
Down to a block.

BYRON

Look to the east, where Ganges' swarthy race
Shall shake its usurpation to its base;
Lo! there rebellion rears her ghastly head,
And glares the Nemesis of native dead,
Till Indus rolls a deep purpureal flood,
And claims his long arrears of northern blood.
So may ye perish!

Ibid.

SEVEN or eight days had passed when De Ruyter returned to St. Malo. Several long conferences had passed between him and the French Emperor. De Ruyter represented him as so wrapt up in schemes for aggrandizing himself in Europe, that he afforded little attention to things out of it; and he asserted that if he could mono-polize the East Indian trade, as the English had done, he would not permit it; for it could merely tend to enrich a few individuals, whilst it must ultimately ruin the nation at large. 'And so,' he added, 'the English will find it, if they continue it on the same footing.'

De Ruyter answered him that he was of the same opinion; but as the foundation of the political power of England was her com-merce, that was the vulnerable side to be assailed; and as the Isle of France, having two excellent ports, St. Louis and Bourbon, besides one at the isle of Bourbon——'

'What!' exclaimed Napoleon, 'are the wealth and blood of France to be expended to maintain islands in the Indian ocean, which are but idle pyramids to commemorate the name of an accursed dynasty, that should be blotted from the page of history altogether, and for ever?'

De Ruyter, with his usual fearless frankness, observed,

'What signifies a name? It can be——'

'A name!' interrupted Napoleon, hurriedly,—'a name!—why it is every thing! The puny rocks, so designated, are worthless—

let the English have them!—they will value them for the legitimacy
of their appellations. Tell me, for I am referred to you on the
present state of India, can any thing be done there? What is your
opinion? We have heard of you, and your *name* is a great one; it
has long slept; but, by report, its spirit lives revived in you. I will
be your pioneer, and put you in a way to add to its greatness. You
have an example,' he continued, after a pause, 'you have an example in your country, Holland, that a commercial nation may
rapidly become great; yet that is transitory, it never has endured,
it never can endure. A nation, to be lasting, must build on the
foundation of its own soil. We have no difficulty in finding leaders
for our soldiers; look at those men (pointing to a regiment of his
guards, drawn up outside the Tuilleries), there is not among them
but could, and many of them assuredly will, be able generals. Yet
I have searched in vain, throughout the nation, for a single De
Witt, De Ruyter, or Van Tromp; else would I hasten the down-
fall of a nation, whose vaunted wooden ramparts are formidable
only as the wall of China, while neighbouring nations are less
powerful. Our Gallic nation are all bilious; this is a spur to them on
shore; but on the water they are sea-sick. I had been a sailor, if
my liver would have allowed me. I never entered a boat but the
heaving of the sea made me feel helpless as a puling baby. Our
admirals are worse. I remember two of the oldest, with me at
Boulogne, looked qualmish at merely seeing the vessels pitch and
roll in the port. An Englishman, a twelvemonth at sea, is sick of
the shore after a week's absence. But our empire is on the land;
and thirty millions of men in the very heart of Europe, will and
must endure firm as the centre of the earth itself.'

Napoleon then questioned De Ruyter, in detail and minutely,
concerning the native princes of India, their strength, the population of their countries, their divisions among themselves, their
religions, their revenues, and their characters, and more particularly concerning their courage and abilities. As De Ruyter went on,
he made hasty remarks, in a low tone, as if indifferent to what he
said being heard or not.

He concluded with, 'It is strange that the Turks and Chinese
are the only people who, whether conquerors or conquered, have
attained the only useful end of conquest, a real augmentation of
their national strength. If intolerance and bigotry enabled them
to do this, the English ought also to have succeeded; for they are

more intolerant and bigoted than either. They cannot mingle nor unite themselves with any other people, not even with their nearest neighbours, the Scotch and the Irish. They go forth with a bayonet in one hand, and a halter in the other; never, for a moment will they lay them aside; after a lapse of centuries they have not advanced a single step in men's minds or hearts. Therefore the end must be that the natives of India, from the Himmalehan mountains to the sea, with one voice giving vent to their long pent-up execrations, will arise, exterminating their haughty oppressors, and every record of their ignominious slavery.'

In long and repeated audiences which De Ruyter had with Napoleon, the Emperor, when alone with him, spoke, openly and unhesitatingly, his opinions; and he was pleased with the equal frankness of De Ruyter, his discriminating knowledge of men teaching him that he had a man to deal with as strong-minded as himself, not to be dazzled or daunted by the idle parade of a court, or the insignia of arbitrary sovereignty. Napoleon was the only monarch that De Ruyter did not thoroughly despise, and him he hated for his selfish and insatiable ambition.

'He has, indeed,' said De Ruyter, 'shaken some of the palsied, old legitimate dotards from their mouldering, worm-eaten thrones; and, doffing their purple robes, held them up to the derision of mankind. Yet, doing this, he vainly thought to perpetuate tyranny by substituting military despots, by whom he hopes to secure himself, and bind the ambitious by gratitude or interest, as if the ambitious could feel for anything but themselves. Much good, on the whole, may and will ensue; but we owe him nothing, for he designed nothing but evil. A rusty bolt is the most difficult to withdraw; but once removed, though replaced, it will never hold securely. What a master's hand teaches his workmen for his own benefit, will be, some day, turned to their own advantage. Napoleon has taught our children to play the game of hocus-pocus with popes, priests, kings, and other straw-stuffed scarecrows; they, (for we, their fathers, still cling to the rocking-horse and rattle,) despising the toys of our times, will cast them aside for ever, and play a manlier game.'

De Ruyter moreover added, that the Emperor had requested to see him again, hinting he should employ him, and, as bounty-money, tendered him less than the value of a shilling—the ribbon of the legion of honour.

'They would have disgraced me,' he said, 'by creating me a chevalier—I'd rather be a Chevalier d'Industrie. Let us dispose of our cargo, and conclude the business which brought us here. I never *served* but one man—Washington! I was then a boy. In France, during a part of the revolution, I sought to complete my apprenticeship to liberty: although, in France, I found many men professing to teach, when I had learnt enough from my first master to discover they were empirics.

'Politics apart, my dear fellow, will you act wisely,—will you return to your own country? See what changes have taken place in your family. They are numerous and wealthy. Surely some among them must be worthy of your love. It is foolish to wantonly estrange yourself from human ties; and your health and strength are woefully shattered. A winter's voyage to America will destroy you. Try a few months in your own climate. At the expiration of that time I will return; or, if prevented by events not to be foreseen, you can rejoin me in America, or elsewhere.'

I had a great deal of difficulty in bringing my mind to this point, yet at last I determined on it; but not till De Ruyter was leaving St. Malo. The period soon arrived; most of his crew were now Americans, picked up in exchange for French and other foreigners. Americans, which is not to be wondered at, dislike being detained in any country but their own.

CHAPTER XLVII

'God save the king!' and kings,
For if he don't, I doubt if men will longer;
I think I hear a little bird who sings,
The people by and by will be the stronger:
The veriest jade will wince whose harness wrings
So much into the raw as quite to wrong her
Beyond the rules of posting; and the mob
At last fall sick of imitating Job.

BYRON

For I will teach, if possible, the stones
To rise against earth's tyrants. Never let it
Be said, that we still truckle unto thrones;
But ye, our children's children! think how we
Shew'd *what things were* before the world was free!

Ibid.

As England and France were then at war, De Ruyter inquired into the best means of my crossing the channel; and, at St. Malo, this was no insurmountable difficulty. The islands of Jersey and Guernsey, belonging to England, are inhabited, almost exclusively, by the French or their descendants; and, as they lie nearly in mid-channel of the broadest part of the English and French coast, the people are perfectly neutral in their politics. When ordinary communications are shut up by war, these islanders always contrive to keep theirs open. During the last war they were notorious; both governments were believed to have used them as channels by which they acquired information of each other's movements. The boatman, with whom I engaged to run me across, had certainly been employed by the agents of France and England; who had, on those occasions, given him a sealed pass, which he was directed to shew if stopped by any of the king's officers, and which he was always obliged to return before he was paid.

I am totally unable to write what I felt when the moment arrived which was to separate me from the man I loved better, a thousand times, than ever before one man could love another. The sun was setting, and the night wind must have been cold, for my limbs shook, and I could hardly support myself. I was obliged to hold on the iron rail of the stone steps, leading from the quay to the

boat in which I was to embark. When we had descended, to be in
a line with the boat, I was insensible to the water, which worked
up to my knees. Exhausted as if I had run a race, yet my movements were solemn as the chief mourner at a funeral. De Ruyter
also was touched; his bronzed face was of a leaden hue; though
I believe he talked calmly and distinctly, I could not afterwards
remember a word he had said, but, 'Farewell, my dear boy!'
Then, with an effort to speak more cheerfully, he added the consolatory words, 'In six months we meet again!'

His hand waved a last farewell! My heart—I thought nothing
more could move it—swelled to bursting; and my eyelids which,
since Zela's death, had been dry and hot, became moist. The
heart is the organ of true wisdom, gifted with prophetic power;
it looks into futurity. Though De Ruyter's words were, 'We shall
meet again,' a prediction so rational to the judgment that mine
could not gainsay it; yet my heart, never before doubting that
what he averred must be, now refused to register what he said—
it added to his words, 'Farewell, for ever!'

What could I but cling to De Ruyter? Like one suspended over
a cliff by a single rope, I held to him; and the feelings that over-
came me at parting were as seeing that rope giving way, or as,
with more appalling agony, a sailor fallen into the sea at midnight, catching the last glimpse of his ship, his limbs paralysed,
his swelling heart bursts. I am one whose faith is, that love and
friendship, with ardent natures, are like those trees of the torrid
zone which yield fruit but once, and then die.

On the night of our separation, De Ruyter returned to Paris.
Not only the minds of men, but often their associations, are visibly
charactered on their outside. It is a mystical book, which all stare
on, and many pretend to expound, but few are the number who
comprehend it. Cromwell and Napoleon, in the west, were of the
gifted few: by those means they ascended thrones. In the east,
the only 'study of mankind is man.' They have no Miss Edgeworth,[1] nor any of those millinering cutters-out of human nature
into certain patterns of given rules in education. They do not
measure men by one common standard; but those gifted with
strong sight pry into the individual characters of others, often
with the precision and truth with which a chemist investigates
matter.

Napoleon, whose mind and conceptions took a wide range,

although his actions were guided by self-interest, reminds us of Bacon's words—'Wisdom for a man's self is a depraved thing; it is the wisdom of rats, that will be sure to leave a house before it falls: it is the wisdom of the fox, that thrusts out the badger: and whereas they have all their time sacrificed to themselves, they have often, in the end, sacrificed themselves to the inconstancy of fortune, whose wings they thought, by their self-wisdom, to have pinioned.' Surely this is applicable to Napoleon.

But to return to De Ruyter. The Emperor, struck with his noble mien and extensive information, determined to employ him. He made him many offers—promotion in his navy, the command of the coast, and the marine department bordering the English Channel—a Residency in a West Indian island, or a return to the East. Napoleon, unlike legitimate kingly blockheads, not bound down in Holy Alliances to act as neighbours act—(by the by, where is the Holy Alliance[1] of God's anointed? I was told it was to last for ever!)—Napoleon thought and acted for himself. All his proposals to De Ruyter were made in the first person; and the rejection, unenvenomed by ministers, was not offensive. By these conferences the Emperor learnt that De Ruyter had a spirit to be moved, but not to be blindly hurried on by glory and ambition. He therefore gave him scope to act in his own way, bending his actions to bear on the designs then in hand. De Ruyter was at length induced to send the schooner to America under the charge of his mate, taking the precaution to change her French papers for those of America, through the American chargé d'affaires in Paris.

De Ruyter's first undertaking in the Emperor's service was a secret mission to Italy. I only know its main design—against him profanely denominated God's Vicar, and the blaspheming crew who say they are moved by the spirit of the deity. Had Napoleon been sincere in his detestation of these vermin, and fearless in act as De Ruyter, he would not have clipped their wide-spreading branches, merely altering their form, but have uprooted the huge upas extending its baneful influence far and wide, and destroyed it to its root for ever. Whilst, for the good of all mankind, De Ruyter was investigating into the means of this uprooting, he was struck in the back with a stiletto, at the dark angle of a narrow street formed by the palace of a cardinal. This and other circumstances were enough to fix the treachery on the cowardly and

Hh

atrocious priests, whose red stockings are emblematic of their sanguinary nature. His presence of mind was seconded by promptitude of hand rapid as lightning, and the assassin's dagger was turned against his own heart with an aim that seldom erred. De Ruyter escaped with a slight wound, completed his mission with increased zeal, and returned to Paris.

I could then merely ascertain that soon afterwards he embarked at Toulon in a French corvette, went to Corsica and Sardinia, and thence to the coast of Barbary, in the Gulf of Cabes. Beating up for Tunis, they fell in with an English frigate. The officer of the corvette, which was placed under De Ruyter's control, not under his command, was brave as he was inflexibly headstrong. He had persisted, till the last moment, too late to correct his error, in maintaining that the English vessel was a corvette, and not, as De Ruyter averred, a frigate; besides stinging De Ruyter by boasting allusions to his country, his duty, his reputation, and the unsullied honours of the grand and invincible nation.

De Ruyter was standing in the most exposed situation, on the taffrail, sinking his despatches over the stern, when the halliards of the French ensign were shot away. He and the French captain were in the act of re-hoisting it, when they were both pierced by a hundred balls from a broadside of cannister shot, from the frigate's carronades, which swept along the corvette's deck, almost clearing it.

His body was found enveloped in the folds of the tri-coloured flag, under which he had fought so long victoriously;—it was then his winding-sheet. Let me borrow the words of a Russian poet[1] for his eulogy and epitaph; they are worthy of him, and far better than I can find in my own mind:—

> 'He lived, he fought
> For truth and wisdom; foremost of the brave,
> Him glory's idle glances dazzled not;
> 'Twas his ambition, generous and great,
> A life to life's great end to consecrate!'

CHAPTER XLVIII

A fisherman he had been in his youth,
And still a sort of fisherman was he;
But other speculations were, in sooth,
Added to his connection with the sea.

BYRON

Be still the unimaginable lodge
For solitary thinkings; such as dodge
Conception to the very bourn of heaven,
Then leave the naked brain.

KEATS

The world is full of orphans.

MS.—BYRON

'In six months we meet again!' rung in my ears as the boat was pulled round the pier, and beside the walls of the town to windward. I lost sight of the harbour; and the voices of the men on board the schooner, cheering me as I passed, died away. I was compelled to arouse myself to steer the boat, which was indeed of the smallest description, a mere punt, of fifteen feet long, and five feet beam; a man and a boy were my crew. During the night we made little way. There was a light but steady breeze blowing from the north-west, directly in our teeth. We hugged the shore, pulling up to the southward, towards Cherbourg, making little way with our two oars. After seven hours tugging against the breeze, we let go the grapnel, and the man and his boy went to sleep. I kept a look-out, and saw the fishing boats and a privateer lugger creeping out to sea, and crawling along the coast; but they could not see an object so low in the water and insignificant as our boat. A thorough seaman never sleeps more than four hours at a spell; at the expiration of that time it was broad day-light, and the old seaman arose, pulling off a water-proof, shaggy, pea-green jacket, and shaking himself like an old mastiff. The young sea-whelp, coiled up under the bow, in a space where a spaniel would have turned and twisted for a long time ere he could have stowed himself in comfort, endured many curses and some kicks before he turned out of his kennel. The seaman then, dipping a couple of his fingers in the water, rubbed his eyes, which is called a privateer's wash; and lifting a small ten-gallon keg, he placed it on his lap, and supported it like a baby. At this, the boy handed him a wooden scoop, used for baling the water out of the boat, when he drew the spigot till it was about a third part full of brandy, first asked me if I would take a sup of the doctor, then drank it off like new milk, handed the boy a drop, and replaced the keg. Thus refreshed, he fished out of his pocket a small telescope, took a survey all round the compass, declared the coast was clear, and ordered the boy to weigh the grapnel, whilst he shipped the boat's mast. Under a small sprit-sail and jib we made a stretch over. We did not lay our course, but the tide was running up Channel, and carried us to windward.

Associated with men of many different nations, I had acquired a habit of studying their dissimilarities of character; and the man in the boat being unlike any thing I had hitherto seen, I, by degrees, turned the tide of my thoughts from brooding on the past, to the fellow who was continually before my eyes. Like all old seamen, he was remarkably taciturn. Whether he was French or English it was impossible to tell either by his looks or language; for he used both languages indiscriminately, and pronounced both equally badly. His visage was hard and bluff as a rock, of which it seemed a fragment; his hair, never sophisticated by a comb, and matted together with salt-water, resembled dark sea-weed, speckled with incrustations of salt; his chin and throat were covered with a week's growth of gristled stubble; his figure was short, particularly square, and, with his red cap, shaggy pea-green jacket down to his knees, and tarpaulin trowsers, had he been seated on a rock in India, I think I should have had a shot at him, mistaking him for an ugly specimen of the walrus. By degrees, I gathered from him that he was a native of Guernsey, but had, for some reason or other, migrated to Jersey, where he had married the widow of a drowned smuggler. She inherited from her deceased husband a snug cabin, built in the bite of a sandy bay; and he was prouder than a lord of the rights and privileges of this manor, although it consisted entirely of barren sand; for on that the sea, at every spring-tide, sported, and thence arose his wealth. On the overflowing of the sea depended his livelihood, like the Egyptians on the overflowing of the Nile, and the people of India on that of the Ganges; for the high tides in the Channel are frequently preludes to gales, and gales are followed by wrecks, when, favoured by the tides, which swept directly into the said bite, formed into a narrow bay by reefs, casks and other buoyant articles were borne thither, of which his hawk-eyed wife, always on the watch, made lawful prize. A few days before, he had thus picked up two pipes of Lisbon wine, which he called a god-send, and promised me as many gallons as I chose, seeing I did not seem to like the other genuine stuff he drank. He said, he sometimes, on shore, drank a tub or two of wine, if it was strong; but it didn't do to take to sea, took up too much room, and didn't make a man's inside water-proof, which good Nantz[1] would. Besides smuggling in a retail sort of way, he sometimes aided and abetted the wholesale smug-glers, by acting as their pilot; for he had been five-and-twenty years constantly at sea in the Channel, and knew every bay, creek, and landmark. Nor was he very particular in his services; as he often piloted the ships of war of France as well as of England, being equally acquainted and friendly with both coasts.

We turned to windward during the day, occasionally using the oars, for the wind was light, the hardy boatman taking advantage of the tides and currents, without which we should have done nothing. Towards nightfall he said, 'We must now make those *rochers* to windward, before the tide shall turn;—moor boat under their lee till three in the morning, *demain matin*, when it shall again turn in our favour. To-morrow, at night, you shall, *sans être apperçu*, run in my cove, and you stay there as long as— *comme il vous plaira.*'

Accordingly we struck the mast of the boat, and pulled her up to the rocks; they were four or five, about as big, above water, as the mud barges used in the Thames. I climbed up the largest, while the old pilot said, 'I generally touches at these *rochers*, to pick up a few red coats,' (lobsters,) '*parceque ma chere femme* has deucedly *gout* for them; and there be plenty *ici*.'

He then began spinning me a long yarn about the habits of eels and lobsters, which abounded among the rocks, and that the eels went there purposely to eat lobsters. The way they got them was by blockading the holes wherein the lobsters took refuge, when casting off their old coats; if they ventured forth ere the new shells were hardened, the eels attacked and devoured them. He then went to work with a sort of harpoon, and succeeded in striking and bringing up both eels and lobsters; while the boy, with a knife, dislodged oysters, muscles, limpets and periwinkles. After a fishy supper, the pilot, having unlocked his jaw by repeated applications to the brandy keg, told me long and curious stories concerning his sea-adventures with French and English, including the Flying Dutchman, which marvel he plentifully vouched with oaths, about as true as a common affidavit. At last, giving me the boat's sail for a bed, he stretched himself out on the jagged rocks, and slept soundly as the unsanctified in a comfortable pew of a church; —I wish the benches were softer, and the cushions higher, as then more people might be tempted to take a nap; it is my only reason for never going.

It was not then the hardness of my couch, nor did it disturb me that I was placed, like a bird, on a solitary rock in the sea. It was a fit resting-place for an outcast and isolated being like myself. Ere I entered on the new era of life before me, my thoughts naturally reverted to the past. I sat pondering on a destiny so strange as mine, wondering how it would end.

There are more helpless beings in the world than orphans, whose young affections sleep like frozen waterfalls, till love, from some being, like the sun in spring, rises and awakens their peaceful slumbers; or rather their affections are created in that moment, and the vacancy in their hearts is filled up in the most harmonious manner. Far more cruel is the lot of those, (and the world is full of them,) who have hard-hearted and unfeeling parents; or, still worse, those who are selfish and indifferent, exacting from their helpless and dependent offspring duty and obedience, without giving, in return, a single glance of kindness, chilling by frowns the spontaneous love which flows from children in torrents. I was of this forlorn tribe. My parents' hard usage and abandonment had long gnawed at my heart, till years of absence, in which both body and mind had expanded, taught me that it was the worst of slavery to submit the freedom of either to those whom we cannot esteem nor love. The pride of my nature impelled me to shake off the bondage. I did so. I could not endure the weight of slavery; but I cheerfully put on the heaviest chains the foes of liberty have to impose,—and they are heavy. I walked with an elevated front. Alone I withstood a fate that would have over-powered thousands, often defeated, it is true, but ever, in losing, I have still won. In this hard struggle I had little refreshment but from the fountains of my own soul. Had I not clung to myself, the atrocity of others had made me a demon. In the very onset of my freedom I gained, what neither wealth nor rank can purchase, the friendship of the really noble; and the far dearer love of one, the gentlest child of nature, a being on whom I might securely repose. My spirit basked in the brightness of her presence. I could neither then, nor now, conceive our love to be a childish passion, nor that it would not cling to me throughout my life. For the union of two hearts, formed to meet, nature had strung our souls with the same chord; and, whether together or apart, it vibrated the same sound, the same aspiration, a sympathy so perfect that it was a balsam poured on our hearts, leaving nothing on earth or in heaven to desire. We had loved with an excess of affection, which can alone justify excess. It happened to us as to a child, who, seizing upon a branch and bending the whole tree over him, becomes embowered amidst clusters of golden fruit. Alas! I imagined not that her sepulchre was placed by destiny so near her cradle. The light, which love lent me for a moment, was extinguished never more to be rekindled. Misfortune threw her huge shadow across my path, and I was doomed to walk benighted beneath the mid-day sun, never more to know peace nor rest till my dust is mingled with Zela's, atom to atom. What joy in this world for one who has drank misanthropy out of the fulness of love? My being was an aching void. My heart refused to give forth any fruit. The fulness of sorrow is great, but how much greater is its emptiness? I thought, in the sea around me, I could behold the fragments of my ship-wrecked life floating. I stood up and, speaking aloud, said, 'When will the swell and storm die away, and the dead calm of this great ocean come? When shall I be given up by its depths, and be borne unresistingly upon its bosom to the distant, still shores of eternity?'

CONCLUSION

So on our heels a fresh protection treads,
A power more strong in beauty, born of us
And fated to excel us, as we pass
In glory that old darkness.

KEATS

I AM continuing this history of my life.[1] I have not been a passive instrument of arbitrary despotism, nor shall I be found consorting with worldly slaves who crouch round the wealthy and powerful. On my return to Europe, I found that earth's despots had gathered together all their gladiators to restore the accursed dynasty of the Bourbons. The war-cry in Europe was, the inviolability and omnipotency of legitimate tyrants, while helots, bigots, and fools, were let loose to exterminate liberty. I found every where a price set upon the heads of patriots; they were robbed, prosecuted, judicially murdered, or scoffed at, and driven from the herd of society like the pariahs of India; to associate with them was to lose caste. From my soul, I, who had suffered so much from tyranny, abhorred oppression. I sided with the weak against the strong; and swore to dedicate myself, hand and heart, to war, even to the knife, against the triple alliance of hoary-headed impostors, their ministers, and priests. When tyranny had triumphed, I followed the fortunes of those invincible spirits who wandered, exiled outcasts, over the world, and lent my feeble aid to unveil the frauds contained in worn-out legends which have so long deluded mankind.

Alas! those noble beings are no more! They have fallen martyrs to the noble cause they so ably advocated. But they have left enduring monuments, and their names will live for ever. Would they had lived to see the tree they had helped to plant put forth its blossoms! Had they survived to the present year 1830,[2] how would they have rejoiced at beholding the leagued conspiracy of tyrants broken, their blood-hound priests muzzled, and the confederacy of nobles to domineer over the people paralysed by a blow, the precursor of their overthrow! The world has a right to expect that France, from her position and general information, will take the lead and keep it. Liberal and enlightened opinions have progressively manifested themselves in every part of Europe. 'There is a reflux in the tide of human things which bears the shipwrecked hopes of men into a secure haven, after the storms are past.'

> 'The very darkness shook, as with a blast
> Of subterranean thunder at the cry;
> The hollow shore its thousand echoes cast
> Into the night, as if the sea, the sky,
> The earth, rejoiced with new-born liberty!'
>
> SHELLEY

Yes, the sun of freedom is dawning on the pallid slaves of Europe, awakening them from their long and death-like torpor. The spirit of liberty, like an eagle, is hovering over the earth, and the minds of men are tinged with its golden hues. Let France, like the eagle it once assumed in mockery for its emblem, now, in reality, teach her new-born offspring to soar aloft, undazzled by the bright luminary, when it shall have ascended to its meridian glory. Every eye and every hope of the good and wise are fixed on France; and with her every bosom containing a single generous impulse, is vibrating in sympathy. 'Methinks those who now live have survived an age of despair:'

> 'For freedom's battle once begun,
> Bequeathed from bleeding sire to son,
> Though baffled oft, is ever won.'
>
> BYRON

THE END

GLOSSARY OF STRANGE WORDS
MOSTLY ANGLO-INDIAN

━━━━━━

Abbah: a primitive Moslem woollen garment consisting of a square of
  cloth with a hole for the head.
Acheenian: the North West of Sumatra was known as Acheen.
Arekee: chewing nut from an areca tree, a type of palm tree.
Argola: perhaps a *nargela* or hubble-bubble pipe.
Arrack: strong spirits made usually from coconut or rice.
Arrican: old name for the islands at the mouth of the Ganges.
Atta: otto or essence of roses.

Baboo: native (disparaging).
Bahr: tiger.
Barakan or *barican*: blanket.
Barb: a variety of pigeon.
Beneta: perhaps the bennet, a fish about three feet long, purple and gold
  with red tail and yellow fins.
Betel box: box for holding betal leaf which was chewed with chinam.
Bheestie: water carrier.
Buffaloe-hackerie: two-wheeled covered carriage drawn by bullocks.
Bumbalo: dried fish.
Bunyan: Hindu trader.

Callians: hubble-bubble pipes.
Calliopash and Calliopee: the edible parts of a turtle, next to the upper and
  lower shells respectively.
Ceiba: the God-tree or silk cotton tree of the West Indies.
Chichta: cobra-di-capella or hooded snake.
Chillam: the bowl of a pipe which holds the tobacco and charcoal.
Chinam: plaster made usually from shell lime, sometimes chewed with
  tobacco.
Chokey: watchman's house or police station.
Cobra-di-capella: hooded snake.
Coir: coconut fibre.
Congee: water in which rice has been cooked.
Couries: small white shells used as a medium of exchange instead of coins.

Creese: dagger.
Cudgeree-pot: cooking pot. Kedgeree is a dish of re-cooked rice often eaten with fish.

Dow: dhow, Arab vessel of about 150 to 250 tons, sometimes armed.
Dustoory: commission payment or bribe.
Dutch dogger: type of fishing vessel.

Faoo: a kind of bird, unidentified.

Gaowalaman: man in charge of a food store.
Ghee: butter made from buffalo's milk boiled so as to resemble oil in consistency.
Grab: large Indian coasting vessel with two masts.

Henna: red dye.
Houdah: seat fitted on an elephant's back.

Jageree: coarse sugar made from a jaggery tree, a type of palm.
Jeel: stagnant lagoon.

Kantak: apparently a tree which grows in Mauritius; unidentified.
Kattie: a measure of weight equal to about 1⅓ lb.
Kiapootee: cajuput oil.
Kiar: made from the wood of the Khair tree which grows in India.
Kladi: an edible root vegetable, usually called keladi or calladium.

Loorie or *lory*: lorikeet, small, brightly-coloured parrot.

Mahout: elephant driver.
Malik: master.
Masuli: masulah boats, boats used at Madras whose planks were sewn with coir yarn and which were thus able to ride the high surf. They were rowed by twelve men double-banked.
Mohr: mhorr, a kind of gazelle.
More: mohur, a gold coin.
Muckarunga: a multi-coloured Indian bird.

Nâch girls: professional dancing girls.
Neem tree: a tree which grows all over India and has a reputation for medicinal properties.

Padama: patamar, type of vessel which was used in Indian waters, because of its speed, to sail in front of a fleet or to carry dispatches.
Paddy: rice in the husk.
Palanquin: covered litter or conveyance.

Peeta: perhaps the type of cloth worn by a rich man.
Peons: orderlies.
Pepul tree: Indian species of fig tree.
Pice: small copper coin.
Plantain: banana.
Proa: prahu, type of war vessel used in Malaya. They had about 80 rowers and 40 to 60 fighting men.
Punka: large swinging fan.

Rackee: strong spirits.
Rais: the captain of a vessel.
Rattan: type of climbing palm tree.

Sangaree: cold spiced wine.
Santon: hermit or holy man.
Sepoy: native soldier of the East India Company.
Serang: boatswain.
Shadock: fruit resembling a large orange.
Shallop: type of boat.
Simoon: hot, dry, suffocating wind that blows in the deserts of Africa and Asia.
Skedam: Schiedam, strongly flavoured Dutch gin from the town of that name, also known as Hollands and Schnapps.
Snow: type of vessel similar to a brig with two masts, square rigged.

Toddy: the sap obtained from various species of palm used as a drink, sometimes fermented. Presumably sugared whisky and hot water has some resemblance to the taste.
Toon: an Indian timber resembling mahogany.
Tope: plantation.
Turmeric: a spice, the chief ingredient of curry.

Upas: a poisonous tree from Java which, according to legend, destroyed all living things within a wide radius.

Yakoonoo: tree with yellow berries and foetid smell that grows in Mauritius; unidentified.

Zennanah: women's quarters.

EXPLANATORY NOTES

Page 1. (1) *My grandfather was a general*: Lieutenant-General Harry Tre-lawny who took part in the American War of Independence.

(2) *my father*: Lieutenant-Colonel Charles Trelawny, later altered to Trelawny-Brereton, who married Maria, sister of Sir Christopher Hawkins of Trewithen, Cornwall. The records tend to confirm Trelawny's description of his father's character.

Page 3. *Every succeeding year*: two sons and four daughters. The elder son, Harry, served for a while in the Army and inherited the family estates on the death of his father in 1821.

Page 4. *a raven*: The story of the raven was one of Trelawny's favourites. E. E. Williams, while with Byron and the Shelleys at Pisa in 1822, noted in his journal for 18 February: 'Trelawny called and told us excellent story of his having attacked (when young) a clip winged raven that was suffered to run about his [father's garden.]'.

Page 8. *Mr. Sayers*: Trelawny attended the Royal Fort Boarding School at St. Michael's Hill, Bristol, whose Headmaster from 1790 to 1813 was the Reverend Samuel Seyer.

Page 17. *the Superb*: Trelawny joined H.M.S. *Superb* under the command of Captain Keats on 15 October 1805 'for a passage to join the *Colossus*' as the muster records. She anchored off Plymouth for a few days for stores and to take on board Admiral Duckworth, but it is doubtful whether the *Superb* could have reached Trafalgar in time for the battle even without this diversion. The encounter with H.M.S. *Pickle* took place on 3 November.

Page 18. (1) *the Colossus, Captain Morris*: These words were omitted from the first edition presumably to make identification of the author more difficult. The other reference to Captain Morris on p. 25 was, however, overlooked.

(2) *Dr. Burney's Navigation School*: The account books of the school record that in December 1805 Mr. Trelawny paid £7. 11s. 6d.

Page 20. *merry-andrew*: clown.

Page 21. *marines*: empty bottles.

Page 22. *shrub*: a drink of lemon or orange juice and rum.

Page 24. (1) *Bruce*: James Bruce the African explorer, who visited Abyssinia in 1770, probably the first European in modern times to do so. He describes in his *Travels* (1790, iii. 266) how the Abyssinian king sat at the council table shut up in a kind of box.

(2) *blue ruin*: gin.

Page 25. *hunkses*: crusty, miserly old people.

Page 27. *We went to sea*: Trelawny refers here to his time in H.M.S. *Resistance* under the command of Captain Charles Adam in 1808. The voyage described in Chapter X occurred before this and Trelawny has misremembered the chronology of his naval career.

Page 32. *I was drafted*: first to the *Puissant* guardship at Spithead, and then, a few days later, to the frigate H.M.S. *Woolwich* under the command of the famous naval surveyor, Captain Francis Beaufort.

Page 34. *I should be re-drafted*: The records show that Trelawny spent some further time in the guardship at Spithead and then joined H.M.S. *Cornelia*, a frigate under the command of Captain Edgell.

Page 35. *Captain A——*: Captain Charles Adam (see pp. 27 ff.).

Page 37. *Aston*: called in the first manuscript version 'Reginald de Aston'.

Page 44. *the celebrated author*: Charles Dibdin, who wrote numerous naval and patriotic songs, was given a gratuity of £200 a year by the Government when he retired from the stage in 1803.

Page 47. *with secret instructions*: Trelawny's ship, the *Cornelia*, was sent to explore the uninhabited island of Diego Garcia to see whether it might provide a suitable anchorage for the fleet being assembled to invade Mauritius.

Page 51. *De Ruyter*: To the end of his life Trelawny maintained that the *Adventures* was a true story. Talking to William Michael Rossetti in 1872, he is reported as having said that 'the person there named de Ruyter really existed. He was of Dutch extraction named Senouf (as I understood the name) and had a commission from Napoleon as a privateer.' No trace can be found in the records of any privateer of the time called Senouf (or of de Ruyter or de Witt). It seems likely, however, that Rossetti misheard the name—his parenthesis seems to acknowledge uncertainty that he has got it right—and that what Trelawny said was Surcouf. Robert Surcouf (1773-1827) was one of the most successful French privateers of the Napoleonic period. From his base in Mauritius he made numerous forays into the Indian Ocean, doing immense damage to British trade. His captures of the East Indiamen *Triton* and *Kent* in particular were astonishing feats of daring accomplished with a handful of men against greatly superior forces and earned him a place in the naval history of the war. Surcouf could not have been known personally to Trelawny. He had left Mauritius for France before the victorious British invasion forces arrived in the island in 1810. However, Trelawny must have heard a good deal about him, both truth and legend. At the time of his first voyage to India in 1807 in H.M.S. *Woolwich*, the news that Surcouf's ship, the *Revenant*, was in the Bay of Bengal caused a panic in the British settlements. The Governor-General demanded reinforcements, marine insurance rates soared, the East India Company strengthened the armament of their ships and fitted anti-boarding devices, and a reward was offered for Surcouf dead or alive. For months on end, at the time of Trelawny's naval service, the talk in the Eastern fleets was all of Surcouf. Trelawny himself served for a time in H.M.S. *Piedmontaise*—a prize vessel enrolled in the Royal Navy but which before her capture in 1808 had been part of a squadron under Surcouf's command. The correspondences between the fictional de Ruyter and the real Surcouf are far from exact. Like de Ruyter, Surcouf knew the Indian Ocean as well as any man and combined trade with privateering. He too had a fine house in Mauritius. Like de Ruyter (cf. pp. 89f.) Surcouf ran into trouble with the colonial authorities in Mauritius for attacking British ships without proper authority, and he did have several audiences with Napoleon in which he advised him to concentrate on attacking British trade (cf. p. 451). But Surcouf was not—as de Ruyter is said to have been—a naturalized American, nor was he of Dutch extraction. He did not fight alongside George Washington or Tippoo Sultan nor was he killed in a naval battle near Tunis. The various battles in the *Adventures* do not appear to be based on Surcouf's real exploits. Some of de Ruyter's exploits can be shown to be derived from the experiences of Trelawny's friend, Edward Ellerker Williams (see note to p. 312), and no doubt there were other influences. Nevertheless the conjecture that de Ruyter is mainly based on the character of Surcouf seems a likely one. To many of his British enemies, Surcouf was a hero, a brave and chivalrous opponent, skilful and resourceful, liable to appear over the horizon anywhere in the Eastern seas, and fight against the odds. It would have been an easy step to attribute to him the political views and to hang on to his imagined personality the other qualities which Trelawny most admired.

Page 63. Cobbett's book on the subject: William Cobbett advocated, in for example his *Political Register* for 1825, that workers should refuse to accept payment in paper money or, if they did accept, should oblige the banks to change it into coin at once. This, he believed, would force down prices.

Page 77. Volney's 'Ruins of Empires and Laws of Nature!': The Count de Volney's famous book first appeared in French in 1791. It is a mixture of romantic melancholy about the past and visions of a future when reason and liberty would triumph over tyrants and priests. Trelawny's own attitudes were remarkably similar and he may well have been influenced by the book.

Page 87. *blues*: bluestockings.

Page 90. *Tippoo Sahib*: Tippoo, Sultan of Mysore, fought a long campaign against the British in India until he was killed in the storming of Seringapatam in 1799.

Page 103. *French letter of marque*: a commission from the French Government appointing an armed merchant ship to be a privateer with the privileges of a French warship.

Page 106. This incident has some resemblance to one described in chapter XLVI of *The King's Own* by Captain Marryat. *The King's Own* was first published in 1830, the year Trelawny completed the *Adventures* and it is possible that he had read it. However, there is no strong reason for supposing that the similarities in the two stories are other than accidental, based perhaps on similar experiences in the Navy.

Page 130. *Boerhaave*: Hermann Boerhaave (1668–1738), the famous Dutch physician of Leyden who attracted students from all over Europe, and from whom derive modern methods of medical instruction. Winschotan appears to be an invention: he is not known to the Wellcome Institute.

Page 132. *Your fleet once mutinied*: a reference to the Spithead mutiny of 1797.

Page 159. (1) *Owen of Lanark*: Robert Owen of New Lanark, one of the first mill-owners of the industrial revolution to acknowledge a paternal responsibility for his workers and to work for their welfare both by propaganda and by providing facilities for his own employees and their families.

(2) *Hannah More*: authoress and founder of the Religious Tract Society. Her novel *Coelebs in search of a Wife*, published in 1809, was one of the best-sellers of its day.

Page 172. *Voltaire: Lettre aux Welches*: Voltaire's *Discours aux Velches* which he published under the name of Antoine Vade is a satirical piece on the French claim to be first nation of the universe.

Page 174. *Alnaschar*: In the *Arabian Nights*, Alnaschar dreams of being wealthy. He is about to achieve his ambition, having invested all his money in glassware, when he kicks the glass and destroys his dream.

Page 175. *her name was Zela*: Trelawny said that the name should be pronounced with the accent on the second syllable. In describing his marriage to Zela, he was probably drawing on his own experience in marrying Tersitsa, the young sister of Odysseus, the Greek chieftain, with whom initially he had no language in common. Like Zela in the *Adventures*, Tersitsa was aged about twelve or thirteen at the time. Trelawny had a daughter by Tersitsa called Zella who died in England in 1906.

Page 201. *recent, learned, and unprejudiced traveller*: From the manuscript and references in his notebook it appears that Trelawny intended to refer to Reginald Heber, whose *Narrative of a Journey through the Upper Provinces of India* appeared in 1828.

Page 215. *Spallanzani*: the Italian Abbé Spallanzani who conducted experiments by mutilating animals in various ways, and seeing how their performance was affected. An English translation of his book, *Dissertations Relative to the Natural History of Animals and Vegetables*, appeared in 1797.

Page 224. *Greenwich Hospital*: the refuge for old sailors near London.

Page 225. *Morin*: Jean Morin (1591–1659), Bible scholar and theological controversialist.

Page 243. *Shrewsbury*: The editors of the first edition altered this to 'New York', partly no doubt because Strong is said to be an American but perhaps also to prevent identification. Strong may be a real character.

Page 260. *inexpressibles*: trousers.

Page 264. *his Britannic Majesty's ship*, *Victory*: There is no mention of any such incident in the Captain's Log of the *Victory* for the voyage home after Trafalgar.

Page 268. *Nory*: J. W. Norie's *Epitome of Navigation*, first published in 1803.

Page 281. *Hong*: merchants in the Chinese ports who had a monopoly of foreign trade.

Page 302. *Buffon*: Georges Louis Leclerc, Comte de Buffon (1707–88). His famous *Histoire Naturelle, Générale et Particulière*, contained the first systematic description of animals and plants. This whole passage about the orang outang contains a good deal of fantasy. Trelawny's notebook contains a drawing of a jungle admee sitting in his house complete with cooking pot.

Page 312. *Rhotuk*: The chapters on the tiger hunt, although set in Borneo, are drawn from the actual experiences in India of Edward Ellerker Williams. Williams, who was nearly the same age as Trelawny, spent a short time in the navy before joining the army in India in 1811. A few years later he returned to England with Jane, the wife of another officer, and in 1821 after various travels they moved to Italy and settled in Pisa as Mr. and Mrs. Williams. They became close friends of the Shelleys. Jane was the subject of many of Shelley's poems and Williams's journal is one of the most important sources for the last year of the poet's life.

Williams was drowned with Shelley in 1822, and some of his papers came into the possession of Trelawny. Among them was a long account of a lion and tiger hunt in March 1814 in the area of Rhotuk, 80 miles north-west of Delhi, which Williams wrote, presumably with a view to publication, under the title of 'Sporting Sketches during a Short Stay in Hindustane'. The chapters on the hunting expedition in the *Adventures* clearly owe much to Williams, but Trelawny transformed a dull recital of animal slaughter into a highly imaginative adventure story. Needless to say there is far more bloodshed both of men and of animals in Trelawny than in Williams, and the whole episode is made far more romantic. It is unlikely that Trelawny himself ever took part in a lion or tiger hunt.

Page 335. *All nature teaches us*: it appears from the manuscript that Trelawny originally included several direct insults of his own mother in this passage, but unfortunately the wording cannot be recovered in full.

Page 336. *Michael Cassio*: the Lieutenant in *Othello*.

Page 351. *Tchibookdgee*: the Pipe-bearer to the Sultan, an official of the Ottoman Court.

Page 362. *The ball had entered*: A letter from Trelawny's mother of 16 October 1813, shortly after his return to England from the East Indies, records that 'his health has been much affected by that climate and the expedition to Java. He has a pistol ball in his knee which is troublesome.'

Page 396. *General Jansens*: There was a General Janssens who was Governor of Java for several months in 1811, but he appears not to have arrived until a few days after Trelawny's ship sailed.

Page 429. This chapter and the next have been amended in the manuscript and much of the first version is irrecoverable.

Page 443. *destroying the body by fire*: Trelawny may be drawing here on his experience in burning Shelley's body on the beach at Viareggio in 1822.

Page 456. *Miss Edgeworth*: Maria Edgeworth's novels of fashionable life, beginning with *Castle Rackrent* in 1810, enjoyed great vogue at the time.

Page 457. *Holy Alliance*: In the period after Waterloo the absolutist monarchs of Europe bound themselves to assist one another in putting down revolution. Trelawny gives some further opinions on this triple alliance on p. 464.

Page 458. *Russian poet*: Gabriel Derzhavin, 'the greatest and wildest of the Russian Poets' according to Trelawny.

Page 461. *Nantz*: brandy from Nantes.

Page 464. (1) The editors of the first edition, with an eye to the future, inserted before the second sentence of this chapter 'The sequel will prove that . . .'

(2) *the present year 1830*: This passage celebrates the July Revolution of 1830 in France which liberals regarded, at the time, as a triumph for their cause. The editors of the first edition added a reference to 'its glorious successor 1831', no doubt intending to celebrate the passage of the Reform Bill.

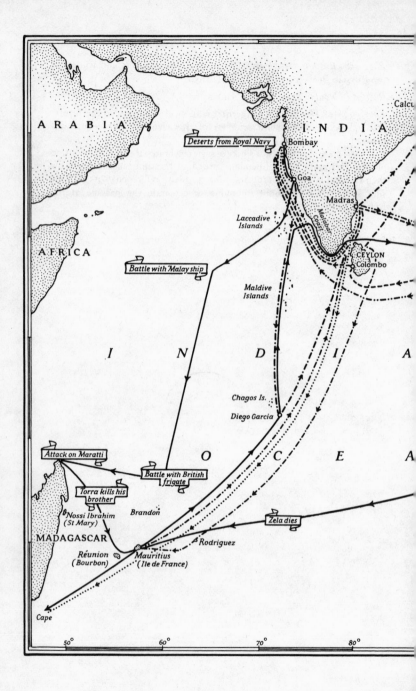

ARABIA

INDIA

Calcu

Deserts from Royal Navy Bombay

Goa

Madras

Laccadive
Islands

CEYLON
Colombo

AFRICA

Battle with Malay ship

Maldive
Islands

I   N   D   I   A

Chagos Is.

Diego Garcia

Attack on Maratti

O   C   E   A

Battle with British
frigate

Torra kills his
brother

Nossi Ibrahim
(St Mary)

Brandon

Zela dies

MADAGASCAR

Réunion
(Bourbon)

Rodriguez

Mauritius
(Ile de France)

Cape

50°   60°   70°   80°